THE TRAVELERS

What Readers Are Saying About THE TRAVELERS

"Through two time lines, serenity and peace must be found. The Travelers tells the story of a modern film maker and a family of World War II who through their link are set to remedy a supernatural mystery that persists through time. A novel with plenty of intriguing concepts, The Travelers is a solidly recommended read which should not be overlooked"—*Midwest Book Review*

Tragedy wrestles hope in this philosophically rich hybrid of genres. Time travel and alien visitation tropes are refreshed by empathetic characters fighting internal ghosts as well as confronting otherworldly visitors. Love, both strong and faltering, resonates through this complex speculative tragedy of loss and redemption, which is strengthened by complex plotting and rich dialogue, though the rushed conclusion dilutes the emotional payoff. This mystical paean to parental love is sure to appeal to fans of both romance and science fiction.—*Publisher's Weekly*

… an involving tale of personal redemption set against a backdrop of supernatural events. Meditations on introspection and bravery prove thoughtful in this mysterious, eloquent novel. A fast, often provocative read whose turns are both surprising and engaging.—*ForeWord*

Engrossing. Once I started this book I could not stop reading. It's an amazing story written by a writer who knows his craft.—*Booklover, Amazon reader review*

Every once in a while I come across a book I fall in love with. This is one of them. The descriptions of the ship are historically accurate, as are the recollections of the war. I was impressed with the concise writing, the fluidity of the story line, the perfect pacing, the memorable lines and the wisdom in the dialogue.—*C. Stephan, reader*

...goes beyond fantasy to portray the life journeys of the characters to the limits of anxiety, despair, grief, and joy. A great read that not only entertains but challenges the reader to put him or herself in the shoes of the characters and perhaps examine his/her own priorities in life.—*Marie S. reader*

The Travelers is an excellent choice for anyone who loves time travel in their science fiction. Be prepared to read it more than once though. I know I will!—*Long And Short Reviews*

What an awesome journey! I couldn't put it down. I love a story that sucks me in and holds my attention ; while I'm dying to know what will happen next .—*Cindy Marek, reader*

"I'm working on a documentary about the career of the liner *Queen Mary* and I came across a radio signal that was first transmitted from her in 1947 but was just received a few days ago. Repeatedly. Why don't you tell me the government's take on it?"

There was a long moment of silence, but Guy heard volumes in it.

She knew.

"What information could the Pentagon have that CNN hasn't already reported? They've been running the story all morning, very tongue-in-cheek, I might add. There's a very good possibility that there is a hoaxer in southern California." Her words were defensive yet dismissive. She let a few moments pass, waiting for a counter response. "The general consensus is it's just a fluke, a message that somehow became space-bound through some freak atmospheric anomaly and has now re-entered the earth's atmosphere through the very same anomaly. The Pentagon's official stand is that if it's not a hoax, then it is simply a signal that has been bouncing around through space all these years."

"Perhaps, but CNN and the rest of the world don't know about the seventy times that the message was received by the *Leviathan*, now do they? And what an obscure message to use as a hoax, particularly in the middle of the North Atlantic, don't you agree?"

Silence, then, "Someone from *Leviathan* has contacted you?"

"Julie, let's not play cloak and dagger. I know firsthand this is much more than an atmospheric anomaly, and so do you. That message has not been random. It's been concentrated in specific locations."

"Guy, I could lose my job." Her voice lost all cordiality. "How do I know what I tell you won't show up thinly disguised in your documentary?"

"You know me better than that, Julie. This is not research for the documentary. There is much more involved than an old radio signal, believe me. Just tell me what old man Van Cleve knows, and do I *ever* have a story to tell you."

Guy heard a sigh of concession, and she asked, "Are you on a secure phone?"

BURST Presents

The Travelers

By

Keith Wayne McCoy

BURST
www.burstbooks.ca
A Division of Champagne Books

ISBN 978-1-77155-168-7
February 2014
Cover Art by Trisha FitzGerald
Produced in Canada

Champagne Book Group
19-3 Avenue SE
High River, AB T1V 1G3
Canada

Dedication

For My Mother and Father.

Prelude

Somewhere in the Pegasus Constellation
Five decades earlier

Long ago and oh, so far away, a skeletal, long-haired young woman walked through the desolation of her collapsed civilization with a toddling, equally skeletal boy on one side and a girl, a bit older but even thinner, on the other. They were naked, along with all their fellow inhabitants as if the shame of body had not permeated their planet.

She looked up at the three moons beginning their splendid glow in the late summer dusk. The heavens were her hope and consolation, and she searched the budding stars for a movement of light that would indicate the arrival of escape from a fallen world for her children. She made her way up into the hills where other mothers with children were migrating. The stench of decay assailed her, and she turned to see an uneaten dog devouring one of its hunters.

Hunger weighed heavily upon her, and she instantly thought of her children. Love was no longer gentle and nurturing, merely a bitter fight for survival. She ached with a maternal instinct she resented and despised. War had taken her lover and the father of her children. Chaos and despair reigned. The inner music of her mind had segued into a dissonant rhythm of adversity.

They trudged through the high, green grass, near to attaining the summit some hundred yards higher, when they stopped, hand-in-hand. Snow-capped mountains in the distance washed pink in the light. She looked up the hill to see the hopeful ones swinging lanterns above their heads to attract their prospective saviors. Like them, she hoped for transportation to a distant world where her beloved children would have no need to fight and cry for sustenance, and the opportunity to grow up in a civilized society.

She still had parents and younger brothers and sisters to care for. She would return after finding sustenance for her own, no matter the heartbreak. She had responsibilities here to those she loved nearly as much as her own. She would not and could not abandon the clan. This was their way.

Suddenly a yelp arose, and the woman looked up to the sky to see a moving point of light, brighter and bigger than the stars far behind it, grow in size as it approached the hilltop. A strong rush of very warm air swept the grass flat, and she felt the pores in her face open. The cheers continued despite the fact that only a handful would gain access to the portal that would appear randomly on the hill.

Miraculously, the shimmering, undulating portal opened less than twenty feet below her. Since she had not climbed the summit, she had an advantage over the multitudes who had. She made straight away for the glowing, rippling opening, dragging her children in tow.

First, the returning mothers emerged, destitute and alone, some weeping, some dazed, all spent, solemn, and heartbroken. They placed their feet back on the land of their birth and proceeded childless to face the ungodly realities waiting below.

The woman and her children watched the procession from a corner of the portal where they could easily slip through. The woman was elated with her luck until another woman, older, with a single child in her arms, broke through the waiting crowd and pushed toward the corner. She shoved the young woman backward just as the embarkation began. All civility evaporated and mothers and offspring trampled each other to reach the portal. The vertical surface rolled and splashed.

The children, knocked from the woman's grasp, lay crying. In a moment of instinct, she jerked them up into her arms and leaned far over, opened her mouth wide, and bit down hard on the arm of the older mother. There was a scream of pain as she fell backward. The woman dived into the portal with her children, her big toe barely passing through as the rippling ceased. The portal abruptly closed.

High above on the vessel, winded but triumphant, she meandered through the milling mothers and children to a luminous, clear bulkhead and looked down. This would be the last glimpse of her world until her god deemed she should return alone. A single tear fell as she watched the crowd below disperse in heavy despair and trek back down the hill to a living nightmare.

One

Long Beach, California, 2004

The corpse of the *Queen Mary* lay mammoth and reposed at her berth, while the California sun blazed lazily on her superstructure. No smoke issued from her towering stacks. In another time, the water surrounding her would have churned with heaving tugs and curious pleasure craft, the hustle and bustle of departure or arrival full upon her.

Today, she was too perfect. No encrustations of brine at her shining waterline or streaks of rust trailing from her anchors. She was waxen and immaculate, like a loved one in a casket. In life, the bridge windows high above were her eyes, ever wary of the North Atlantic. Still, the ghost of alertness hung about them though they stared dead ahead at waterfront hotels.

The cliff-like rise of her bow from placid waters gave no hint of the monstrous waves that thundered past her stem when she charged across the Atlantic in a frantic fury. Once a living entity on the high seas, now permanently tethered to land, long since disemboweled of her engines and power plants.

Inside, stillness stalked the aging corridors, pressing hard against the gloss of paneling and columns, whispering down the staircases, rippling over the empty pool. Even the occasional sound of a footstep or snatch of conversation seemed more memory than reality.

To the casual observer, the older woman who stepped from the taxi seemed inconspicuous from the legions of former passengers and crew who often came to revisit a chapter in their rapidly closing personal histories. Jessica Bennett stood tall, elegantly dressed in a navy blue suit and pearls. Still an attractive woman in her seventies, she did not defy her years. Eddies of wrinkles pooled under her eyes and at the corners of her mouth. Silver glistened through her faded sandy hair and her back surely was not as straight as it had once been.

She stood with a suitcase in one hand, shielded her eyes with the other and lifted her head in a long moment of communion with the ship. The *Queen Mary's* old, unmistakable profile loomed against the brilliant blue sky. It was utterly unlike Jess's first glimpse of destiny when the fog and drizzle of an overcast Southampton obliterated all but the sharp prow and a bridge wing.

Another taxi broke her reverie, and she moved toward the entrance, where a man directed her to a wide gangway of enclosed glass, not at all like the narrow, open one from decades past.

When she stepped aboard the promenade deck, fifty-seven years rushed around her. The same teak decking lay underfoot. The confident march of windows paraded down the portside overlooking a parking lot rather than the restless Atlantic. The ship's plaza was still the busiest place aboard, buzzing with visitors, their suitcases and trams scattered haphazardly.

The girl at the purser's desk was impossibly sweet and comfortable with older visitors. She spoke a bit too loudly and explained things in a deliberate cadence some visitors must have found patronizing. "Mrs. Bennett, after you've settled in your cabin, Mr. Turner and the production crew are expecting you in the Grand Salon. That's the former first class dining room, as you may recall, on R deck." she smiled and pointed toward the elevators. "Will you need any assistance? A wheelchair or walking aid?"

Mrs. Bennett turned without answering.

Disappointment awaited her in the cabin. Although original in paneling and décor, a television and modern telephone sang in disharmony with the art deco surroundings. The throb of the engines, once as palpable as a heartbeat, no longer lived in the slight chatter of paneling. There was no sense of thrill or immediacy since departure was not imminent.

After unpacking, Jess didn't go to meet the production crew as instructed. Instead, she followed a tour group that filed past a T in the corridor outside her cabin. Children in shorts popped their gum and gawked at displays, then pulled at their parents with cries of hunger and impatience.

She wandered from the group when they moved to an escalator going below deck and went slowly through first class corridors that were largely unchanged from sailing days. She remembered the precise location of the lounge and found it closed; the large formal doors locked. But she saw a smaller door farther down that was evidently a service entrance. It was unlocked and she stepped into the hushed gloom of a room that possessed far, unseen reaches.

Muffled light hovered from large circular windows near the ceiling, and the massive veneered columns rose in silent majesty before her, suggesting an Egyptian palace. She had the vivid feeling that the room reared from slumber to wakefulness with her entrance, aware of her presence after so many years. Perhaps surprised and ready to meditate over the past with her. Not wishing to break the spell, she walked slowly and soundlessly to a chair in a recessed part of the room and sat in the shadows.

~ * ~

"You're forty years old." Lynn eyed him as a mother would a child she was scolding.

Guy scooped vegetables into the wok but didn't turn to face her.

"We can't forever be 'the kids living in sin on the fourth floor.' There comes a time in life when you just have to be decisive. I don't feel alive anymore, Guy. I feel as if we've somehow stalled."

He hadn't expected the argument. Lynn had been restless for a few months, he knew, but he hadn't known how deeply, nor the nature of her unease.

"Where in hell is this coming from?" He didn't look up as he seasoned the stir-fry. "Society expects every woman in her thirties to wrestle with this, and now you think it's your turn. You're just playing the stereotyped part. Why?"

"Playing the part? Do you think I saw this coming?" Lynn's voice sounded dry, irritated.

He sensed her trying to engage his eyes, but he would not raise his head.

"This is new to me, but it may be as natural as a first period. Do you know I wake up in the night, every night, scared to death of lost time? That ticking clock is real."

"A ticking clock? For God's sake," he said, shaking his head. "A ticking clock. Well, since we're arguing in clichés, here's mine.

It's a shitty, rotten world, and I'm not selfish enough to bring another life into it. How's that?"

She slammed a cabinet door and triumphantly captured his stare. "Do you think you're the only one to have been called 'nigger?' The only one who had an unhappy childhood? Don't you think everyone looks back with some amount of resentment? You're not hiding behind those lies, Guy. I won't let you. You *are* selfish, pure and simple."

The room grew quiet as both gathered their wits, then Lynn asked softly, "What is it about children? It is so selfish I want to have your children?"

He tried appeasement. "We'll marry, if that's what you want. You know that's what I want. How can you not know that?"

"Of course I want that. But only if it's a precursor to becoming parents."

"What?"

"Marriage isn't as essential to me as being a mother." Her tone carried an unmistakable note of finality, and the ugly head of stalemate rose between them. The hum of the refrigerator insulted the sudden quiet.

"Essential," he repeated dully.

"At this time, yes." Her eyes were moist, but her expression remained steadfast.

"How essential?"

She didn't reply.

He lay in bed that night and worried just how essential, which had perhaps been her intention. The next morning he rose while she slept with her naked, brown back turned to him. In the bathroom, he found the round, pink container for birth control pills. He opened what seemed an exotic pocket watch with tiny pills at odd time marks and no hands. He was searching for some sort of schedule in the archaic design when he became aware of her watching him in the mirror. Having vilified himself, he calmly replaced the container and brushed his teeth.

Now aboard the *Queen Mary*, Guy pushed away the memory of his argument with Lynn. His fingers half-gripped, half-caressed the camera, the lens that protected him from the world, allowed him to watch, to see, without participating. This professional voyeurism gave him the authority to capture moments in time, freeze them, replay them. Gave him power to control life around him.

"Push for the emotional," he said to Rebecca, his young intern. "Don't discourage tears or anger. A historical documentary should be more like a living zoo, rather than a musty library. If the final result seems sentimental, so be it. It's their story. We're just along for the ride." He smiled and added, "Of course, if it's too cornball, we can always leave it on the editing floor."

Again his fight with Lynn surfaced. *Leave it on the editing floor.*

Rebecca laughed and nodded, her smooth low ponytail bobbing over her shoulder, but Guy noticed her gaze lingering over his facial features as he flipped through a list of interviewees. Her admiring stares didn't elicit self-esteem in him, but rather despair. Unfortunately, his good looks and perceived curse of skin color intertwined inextricably. *You are one good-looking nigger.* The words of his high school basketball coach came back to him, as clearly as if the man stood beside him now, his slow, guttural voice frighteningly animal-like in Guy's ear.

The coach had walked to Guy and softly stroked his jaw line with a thick index finger and said "Damn," as if incredulous.

Guy stood stiff with indecision and shock, breathing heavily. Fight or flight. No adult males in Guy's life, no one ever to show affection, however inappropriate. He had forever distanced himself from the world of men. The implication his good looks were extraordinary for a black person, undeserved even, never left him.

When he met Lynn while freelance-filming her grandfather's eightieth birthday, she didn't admire his physical presence. She'd dismissed him as a shallow pretty boy until she spoke with him. Her economic judgment of people attracted Guy immediately.

Rebecca's bright chatter brought Guy back to the present, and he looked up to see the flash of her too-white smile as she delicately touched an elderly man's elbow, pointing him toward a reception table.

The aged and eccentric congregated for coffee and pastries in the Grand Salon, once called the First Class Dining Room. Their babble and raucous laughter drifted against the exotic paneling and elaborate bronze doors, designed to complement diners in dress and tuxedo and echo the soft chime of silver and crystal. A great floor-to-ceiling tapestry-style painting titled *Merry England*, and a massive black and gold map of the North Atlantic depicting the *Queen's* northern and southern routes faced each other from opposite ends of the room. Aesthetically superior, they were aloof and imperious to the din below. The room no longer held dining tables draped in crisp white tended by anxious waiters; instead, collapsible tables and metal chairs sprawled throughout the room in a pattern of afterthought.

Since Guy had so little in common with men, he relied upon his military background for conversation. They had scheduled former waiters, bellboys, stewards, officers, and chefs for interviews, but most of the men who gathered today were World War II vets transported to the European theatre aboard the *Queen Mary* in her troop colors. In those days, they called her the *Grey Ghost*. When he questioned the men on their exploits, he took honest interest in their replies.

The war brides, young girls native to Europe who met and fell, perhaps wantonly, in love with GIs, were his favorite interviews. The United States government brought them to the New World by the thousands aboard *Queen Mary*. At war's end, they suddenly realized they were leaving home, and their reactions of sorrow, bewilderment, and adventure created great fodder for film.

Guy and Rebecca acquainted themselves with the first interviewees scheduled for filming in alphabetical order. "This is James and Jessica Bennett," Rebecca said brightly, introducing Guy to a tall, dark-skinned man with bright white hair and a small, auburn-haired woman. Rebecca's words clearly startled the older couple in front of them.

"Jess?" Jim said.

Rebecca read from the list. "James Bennett, a GI transported on the *Queen Mary* in 1943, and Jessica, his war bride from England, who came to the States aboard her in September of 1947."

When Guy looked at the woman, she politely explained, "I'm the *second* Mrs. Bennett." Her response sounded forlorn, as if she had resigned herself to the refrain long ago.

"Is Jess here?" Jim asked.

Rebecca flipped through the pages. "I'm sorry for the confusion, but, yes, she arrived this morning. I was using the archive list of GIs and war brides rather than the address list. You live in Hermosa Beach, California and your ex-wife lives in Herald, Illinois?"

Jim nodded, mystified. "I haven't seen her in almost forty years."

"I've never even met her," Mrs. Bennett told them.

"I've been interviewing couples together," Guy said. "Will she have an objection?"

"Jess is, or *was*, I should say, an unpredictable woman. I really have no idea."

"She registered several hours ago," Rebecca said, searching the crowd. "She should be here by now."

"And she still has a fine carriage," Jim whispered, looking intently beyond them with a gaze that instantly told of longing and loss, a whole history of two lives torn apart by love.

They all turned to see the tall woman in navy blue and pearls emerging from the crowd. Jim moved forward with all the formality of meeting a foreign dignitary. Like looking into a cruel mirror, a moment of unmistakable shock crossed both of their faces when they surveyed the handiwork of the years on each other's faces.

"Hello, Jim," Jess said evenly. Decades hung in the air.

"Jess, it is so good to see you, I must say." Jim's voice carried the sweet residue of affection reserved for the long-loved. They didn't touch; this hesitance the only evidence of some ancient unpleasantness.

"Jess, this is my wife, Barbara. We've been together thirty-two years."

Jess extended her hand. "It's a pleasure. You are a very fortunate woman."

The pleasure on James Bennett's face was as pure as a child's.

"I know," Barbara said, apparently wholly downcast by it all.

Guy took the woman's hand. "Mrs. Bennett, I'm Guy Turner. Thank you so much for accepting our invitation and flying out here for this production. I want this to be the definitive documentary on our grand lady and, hopefully, you good folks will help me to that end."

Jess looked back at Jim. "I needed to come once more before I died. You understand?"

He nodded gravely, leaving the others out of the drama. "I looked for B27, but the cabin numbers have changed since 1947. I couldn't be sure which one was ours."

Jess's face sagged. "I'm sorry to hear that. I wanted so to see it again."

"Do you have any objections to being interviewed together?" Guy asked.

"I'm comfortable with that," Jess said.

"Good. You're scheduled for eleven thirty." He looked at Rebecca for confirmation, then pointed. "Yes, eleven thirty, in that private dining room. I'm honored to have met all of you, and I look forward to working with you." He spoke in his most unctuous voice, the voice reserved for his professional persona. "Enjoy your breakfast, and I'll see you in a few hours."

As Guy and Rebecca moved to another couple, Guy noticed that Jim pulled the chair for Jess but, in his nervous haste, completely forgot his wife who seated herself.

Two

"Bing Crosby, Charles Laughton, Katherine Hepburn..." recited a one-time headwaiter.

"A cruise ship is emphatically *not* the same thing as a luxury liner," a former steward explained haughtily. "A giant ship like this was built for the express purpose of mass transportation at magnificent speed, not a leisurely bob in the sea. Cruise ships have no purpose but holiday. And no class, I might add."

"The Duke and Duchess of Windsor were aboard with forty-seven pieces of luggage," recalled a bellboy. "They had a favorite suite and once, the Duchess decided she wanted the color scheme changed to electric blue in mid-ocean. And we did it."

"Winston Churchill, Elizabeth Taylor, Ambassador Kennedy..."

"There were over ten thousand troops aboard when we approached the coast of Scotland on a zigzag course," said a GI, waving his hand like a fish. "So that the Nazis couldn't get a torpedo fix on her, you see. *Curacoa* was an anti-aircraft cruiser sent out to escort us into port and when I saw her come alongside, I knew she was too close."

"Eleanor Roosevelt, the Von Trapps, Marlene Dietrich..."

"A group of us aboard *Curacoa* went up on deck to watch the *Queen* and take pictures," said a British sailor. "We got closer and closer and soon enough, her shadow fell on us and I suddenly knew we couldn't get out of her way. I don't know which ship missed which zigzag but I remember one of the chaps called out, 'Snap her now, you'll not get a better angle' when all hell broke loose."

"The Queen Mother, Alfred Hitchcock, the Marx Brothers..."

An elderly man wiped his eyes. "I saw the broken stern

floating down our side and all the men thrown into the ocean. The captain was under Admiralty orders never to stop lest we be torpedoed and all we could do was throw our life vests overboard."

"This one was born en route to New York in August of 1936," an elderly mother told with feigned disgust as she nodded toward her daughter. "A month early, naturally. My husband and I were strolling sun deck when I thought to myself, 'Now that must have been a large wave to hit me way up here,' then realized my water had just broke." The daughter laughed and her mother added, "But we made out very well. The steward collected nearly two hundred pounds for us!"

"Spencer Tracey, Queen Wilhelmina of the Netherlands, Bob Hope..."

"She was moving entire divisions in single crossings," said a GI who had somehow managed to fit into his original uniform. "Hitler offered a quarter of a million dollars and the Iron Cross to any submarine commander who could sink her. We all scanned the horizon nervously, believe me, and when planes flew overhead, there was near panic until they were identified as one of our own."

"The most beautiful thing I've ever seen was this dining room decked out at dinner with women in formal gowns and jewels with their men in smart black and white, all the crystal, china, and silver glistening like a feast in a fairytale castle. In your lifetime, you will *never* see the glory of this room as in those days, I guarantee you."

"Henry Ford, Jackie Bouvier, King Faisal II..."

"She still has the world's record for the most passengers on a single ship, sixteen thousand six hundred and thirty-eight GIs and crew in August, 1943," a one-time mess boy told proudly. "I know. I was aboard."

"I started out as a dishwasher on the *Aquitania*," said another. "I worked *Caronia*, *Berengaria*, and *Queen Elizabeth* but not one of them had a soul. She was a trooper, and her profile was so world-famous you couldn't possibly mistake her for any other ship. And once, when we arrived at the Rock of Gibraltar, someone had the gall to radio, 'What ship? What ship?' and we responded, 'What rock? What rock?'"

"We prayed and prayed for the end of the war," recounted a war bride beside her husband of sixty-one years. "But when it finally did, I realized I wasn't ready to leave England. Daddy was dying, and I was very much a mama's girl and I... I..." She began weeping and her husband wrapped an arm around her. "I can never forget my mama standing at dockside looking up at this colossus, scared by the thought of my leaving on her, probably knowing I would never see her again."

"Listen," said a steward intensely as he leaned forward as though preparing to tell a secret. "Some of us stewards did so well off the tips that we made more money than the captain. There's a story of the captain who stepped off the *Mary* and rode the train home while a steward had his own car waiting at the dockside. That's the gospel truth."

Guy sometimes took a trembling hand in his or even offered a hug after a particularly emotional interview, the old thrill of empowerment swelling from somewhere deep within him. This was his first production with complete creative control. What initially seemed a staggering responsibility had transformed into a sweet promise of success judging from the quality of this morning's interviews. Of course, there were the inevitable guffaws destined for the cutting room floor that Guy good-naturedly endured, but stunned his intern.

"My sister and I came to America in tourist class," a woman said with a slight Hungarian accent. She smiled at her husband beside her and continued, "Sammy saw us at a dance the first night out and I knew he was watching me. He didn't notice my sister as she was a few pounds overweight."

"A few pounds overweight?" exclaimed her husband. "Why, one of her titties was as big as my head!"

Another couple was arguing before their interview even began. "I tell you we are in room B475," said a woman with heavily lacquered hair, stiff as a football helmet.

"No," countered her husband. "It's B457. Tell you what, if you're right, I'll give you a bump. If I'm right, you give me a bump."

"Then I lose either way," she complained bitterly.

One woman asked, "Isn't Elizabeth Taylor supposed to be interviewed for this?"

"Well, yes, later in the week," Guy replied.

"Just call me when she's here. I'd rather wait and be interviewed beside her." With a smile, she rose, gathered her purse and promptly left them both open-mouthed.

Guy wondered what awaited when he saw Jim and Jess Bennett sitting together. The old man's eagerness was nakedly apparent in his quick glances and nervous hands. Guy felt sorry for

Jim, a novelty. She sat with an obvious remoteness about her, not of aloofness or superiority, but of a removal from the present, as though she were reluctant to be a physical presence anywhere. She was an enigma to Guy from their first meeting with a cloying sense of mystery his voyeuristic sensibilities couldn't resist. Yet, he had a vague dislike for her, perhaps because of the infectious hurt and regret that emanated from Jim the moment he knew she was aboard.

Jim began. "I was a nineteen-year-old boy from southern Illinois who had never seen the ocean, let alone an ocean liner. Even in battleship gray and stripped of her luxury, she was a beautiful sight. She was like a lovely woman caught without makeup and jewelry. We were all scared boys heading into the unknown, wishing for our mothers, to tell you the truth. I vowed that if I survived the war, I would travel home on the *Queen* in her peacetime guise. And I did." He smiled. "With a British wife."

Jess pulled from her purse a yellowed card with a stylized version of the *Queen Mary* under the American and British flags. She read, "'I wish you success and good fortune as you begin a new life in the great country of your adoption,' signed by Captain Cyril Illingworth. All the war brides received these when we embarked at Southampton. President Truman passed the act to bring all of us over beginning in 1945, but Jim wanted to wait until this ship was a luxury liner again. And so, we came over in September of 1947. First class, he insisted."

Jim smiled. "I didn't care how much it cost. I wanted her to be as impressed as I was."

"Were you impressed?" Guy asked.

"Back then our days consisted of rations, bombing raids and not much money. It was a very bleak time. No one had anything then, so coming on this ship after the hardships of war and seeing such beauty was quite overwhelming, especially on this scale. I was very much out of my element. It was an emotional time as I was leaving home and my mother. I had no brothers or sisters, so she had nothing when I left. Tremendous guilt, let me tell you. But, I guess there was a certain amount of excitement about starting a new life with a husband in a country I had always dreamed of." She turned knowingly to Jim and said in a frank voice not intended for the camera, "My life really began on that voyage."

"*How* did your life begin on that voyage?" Guy asked.

Neither responded immediately. They looked blankly at him

as though they couldn't believe he had the audacity to ask such an intensely personal question.

"I thought you only needed two to three minutes of memories," Jess said. "Haven't we given that?"

"I always like to have as many memories as possible to choose from," Guy explained. "There may be hidden jewels that will never be found if we stop too soon."

"Words can't describe it," Jess finally said in a precise tone. "Memories of a lifetime. All I can say to you."

Guy instantly knew she was closing the door on the subject.

"Memorable but uneventful," Jim added and looked down at his feet.

Guy looked to Jess, preparing to coax her, but her eyes reproved him as effectively as her mouth. She would say no more. He knew then she had come only to see the ship again. The documentary was simply a pretext for a final visit. As with all enigmas, the unspoken was a secret room with a shut door, forbidden and alluring. She had locked the door, and he underwent the frustration of denial. When did love end? And if it did not end, as Guy suspected in Jim's case at least, what could have eclipsed it to the point of living apart without contact for decades?

"Well," Guy sighed, dejected, and hoped she could hear his disappointment. "Evidently our session is over." Neither responded. "I hope you'll join us this evening for dinner and dancing. We plan to film impromptu reunions with other passengers and crew. If you need..."

A sudden expression of happy surprise lit Jess's face as she looked beyond Guy's shoulder and past the cameraman. Both men followed her gaze out the door to an older gentleman waiting with a young woman and a small child, perhaps his daughter and grandson.

"Excuse me," Jess said and both men watched her rise and walk to the child. She knelt before the boy, and they could barely hear her cooing, "Aren't you a darling?"

The mother beamed at the flattery, and Jess gently brushed her fingers through his brown curls. The child leaned against his mother, smiling shyly, yet serene in the adulation. Jess said something to his mother, who nodded a response and Jess opened her arms in hopeful invitation. He stood solemn for a moment, then timidly stepped forward. She scooped him up on her hip as she stood and resumed her sweet chatter. He took an intense interest in her pearl necklace and lifted it to his mouth with chubby fingers. Embarrassed, the mother moved to scold him but Jess waved her away, laughing, and caressed his cheek.

Guy thought he perceived a sad, faraway look in Jim's face, almost apprehension, as they watched Jess's transformation. Guy looked back to the woman and child who were mutually delighted in each other's company, and for the first time that day, he thought of Lynn.

~ * ~

Big Band and Swing music reverberated throughout that old room, but the intended sensation of an echo from the past was simply too sentimental. The period clothes and hairstyles sported by the band members only reinforced the sad sense of a lost age. Yet Guy marveled at the genuine camaraderie that existed between strangers as they gathered in small groups of easy conversation and recollections. Guy remembered Lynn's ticking clock. He'd found it trite and cliché a few nights ago, but now it ticked in his own ears as he looked about at the age-afflicted. And not merely a physical affliction but mental. What regrets and haunted memories must accompany the daily specter of mortality? Lynn's nightly panic attacks seemed understandable in the spectacle of this room.

Guy dutifully danced with several older widowed women who greeted his invitation with wrinkled blushes. He shied away from younger women whose acceptance might prove problematic to their fathers or grandfathers. There were only a handful of black guests in the crowd. All were former passengers, not officers or World War II vets, a commentary on society's view of his race in the middle of the last century.

He had just begun to dance with Rebecca when he heard the slightest commotion behind him and turned to see Jim Bennett walking hastily to the door, his face flushed with humiliation and his wife scrambling to keep up. Others had turned as well, and their expressions were of shock and dismay. Jess Bennett glared after her ex-husband, her eyes wide and her mouth thin with anger. She reminded Guy of a cat with its ears laid back after a strike.

"Would you care to walk over there for me and find out what just happened?" Guy asked Rebecca. She was obviously reluctant to leave his arms and contemplated his request with a crooked smile. "Please," he mouthed softly and she pulled away with a playful pout on her lips.

When she returned she said, “Evidently, he indicated to the waiter not to refill his ex-wife’s drink. She caught him shaking his head and thought it heavy-handed, so she slapped him a good one.”

“Good God. Nothing classier than a lush.”

The girl raised her eyebrows at him, and he responded, “My mother.”

~ * ~

Jess Bennett became very drunk. She was attempting to dance the Charleston to the band’s rendition of *Jeepers Creepers* when Guy noticed her. She fell to her knees, laughing, then lifted herself with the easy bounce of the intoxicated. She didn’t stagger so much as tiptoe with involuntary quick steps as if a heavy wind were at her back. When she stopped, she bobbed so lightly on her toes she appeared to have invisible balloons attached to her shoulders. She climbed a chair and stood, much to the gasps of her audience, and was just negotiating the tabletop when Guy grabbed her at the waist.

She smiled down at him and said, “Oh, is it finally my turn for a dance?” She threw both arms around him and hung from his neck. “We old dames still have quite a bit of life left in us, good-looking. Just let me show you.”

“Mrs. Bennett, what is your cabin number?” he asked.

A slab of hair hung across her face. “Where’s my purse? Someone took my purse, the thieving bastards.”

Rebecca rushed beyond her, picked the purse up from the floor and searched it for her key. “A135,” she said to Guy.

“When I find out who kept the bottle pouring...” he growled.

Guy stumbled with Jess who sadly said, “It’s been so long. So long.”

He knew the eyes of the room were on him as he struggled and finally lifted her in his arms and marched for the door.

She outstretched her arm as if they were figure-skaters, laughing, “Twirl me!” In the corridor, she looked up into his face, smiling. Her eyes were mere slits, nearly overcome by the heavy rolls in her eyelids.

“I think I’ll have a chocolate ear,” she said, and before he understood her, she reached up and licked his left ear. In a reflex, he lifted his shoulder and tipped his head to wipe the wetness, and she kissed him hard on the lips. He shifted her when she made another pass, cocking his head away from her.

“And everything old is new again!” she sang as they stepped

into the elevator. Shortly after the doors closed, she fell asleep against him with such suddenness Guy feared she may have expired in his arms until she began taking deep, even breaths.

"Your lip is bleeding," Rebecca told him. As soon as the doors opened, she ran ahead to Jess' cabin and unlocked the door.

"I'll feel sorry for her tomorrow morning," she said in the doorway as Guy stepped past her.

"She won't remember a thing. They never do."

He laid Jess gently on the bed, and she awoke with a start, clutching his wrist. He pulled from her, anticipating another lunge, but she held tight. Her eyes were despondent with an intensity beyond intoxication, and she said, "I have seen beyond the pale."

"Mrs. Bennett, if you'll just relax," he told her, but she rose from the mattress until she was inches from his face.

"I have seen beyond the pale," she whispered. Her wild eyes held his for a long moment as though her words should solicit a specific response from him. When she didn't receive it, she fell back, threw an arm across her face and began weeping.

The girl looked at him, uncomprehending.

"Don't worry, she'll be fine," he said distastefully and wiped his lip with the back of his hand. "That's just the sob of a lush. Believe me."

~ * ~

As soon as he unlocked the apartment door, the pool of darkness and silence enveloped him, and he knew. He flipped the light switch, and there were empty spaces on the wall and in the CD cabinet. The sofa table was as desolate as a recently timbered forest with only two framed photographs remaining and the hutch was completely empty of her grandmother's china. In the kitchen, all of her sweet, feminine knick-knacks were gone, and the bathroom vanity was equally barren.

He was in the apartment of a bachelor.

There was no letter on the bed or table. No explanation needed. The newly open spaces in the bookshelves spoke succinctly of her absence.

"There comes a time in life when you just have to be decisive," she had said. She watched him in the mirror that morning and became decisive herself.

He pulled his coat and tie off and dropped them onto a chair in a defiant way, then went to the balcony. He couldn't stand the ringing silence of the apartment. He lit a cigarette and lay on the lounger for the long night ahead.

Three

Three months later, the North Atlantic

The USS *Leviathan* ran cool and deep, gliding, stealthy among the sea creatures. A predator to mankind alone. On this night, Grisham, the Systems Officer-in-Charge, stood before a monitoring panel, executing yet another endless round of checks and tests. When asked by friends or even complete strangers how he coped with the monotony of a submariner's life, his standard response was, "Just as routine as a bowel movement," much to his wife's consternation.

Leviathan had been at sea nearly a month, but only two days after leaving Norfolk, despair had steadily crept amid Grisham's relentless duties and rooted. Despair so marked that he considered swallowing his pride and asking his doctor for anti-depressants. And this was accompanied by a sexual tension that he had never experienced in his fourteen years at sea. Only three days remained before they docked in Norfolk, but like the perpetually erect missiles frustrated with eagerness for their single unthinkable objective, he was frustrated by the weight of exile that seemed as oppressive as the sea bearing against the titanium steel.

But tonight his melancholy was broken by a curious event.

As his finger edged toward a lighted key in the panel, a tiny bolt of static electricity struck him. An electrical short, he thought, then the overhead lights dimmed and brightened sporadically accompanied by a low hum. The steel deck throbbed beneath his feet while the flimsy, utilitarian light brackets tittered above. Only a few seconds had passed when he heard not quite a scream but rather a shocked squeal of pain.

"Who in the hell is that?" asked a head poking from the

control room.

As Grisham followed the cries, they reminded him of the moans accompanying orgasm. Inside the radio room, they found Atkins, the specialist, down on his knees, slumped against a chair with his index fingers massaging ears. A single tear hung from his chin. His headphones drummed the top of the console beside him in eerie sympathy with the surging lights and quivering metal.

"Atkins, what happened?" Grisham asked as he rushed to him and knelt.

Atkins shook his head and pointed to his ears. "I can't hear you," he shouted, unaware of his pitch. He obviously couldn't hear himself. "The signal came in and I—"

"Somebody get the doctor," Grisham yelled over his shoulder, then turned back to Atkins. "A signal?"

Others had gathered outside the door in the narrow corridor, talking in excited voices and looking up and down at the pulsing phenomena around them. Bursts of static electricity shot from the metal corners and panels when inadvertently touched, or even at the suggested approach of a finger or elbow. Clothing crackled with every movement.

"Navy Reconnaissance Satellites indicate the mother of all electrical storms on the surface," someone called out from the control room. "We may be encountering a freak atmospheric condition."

"An electrical storm doesn't penetrate the depths, dildo," said Borders from the navigation room.

"Did I *say* it was penetrating the ocean depths, smart ass?" came the response. "It may be affecting incoming communication."

Borders had a commanding though heavy-handed voice, Grisham had always thought, and now he stood in the center of the gathered men, easily drowning their prattle. "Seven years ago off the coast of Florida, we were at six hundred feet when a cruise ship went right over the top of us. Sonar had miscalculated our interception. There was never any possibility of collision at that depth. But when she went over us, her screws sounded like fucking Armageddon. That's what is happening here, I'm sure of it."

Grisham shook his head. "Nah, this is too rhythmical. Atkins said it was a signal."

"A *signal*?" Borders asked incredulously. "How?"

"By God, it's Morse!" a young ensign said. Despite the angry bite of static electricity, he wrapped his hand around an overhead pipe. With blank eyes, he looked as though he were reading Braille.

Stillman, the commander, was a man of little words, or more often than not, none at all. He was not particularly tall, with thinning red hair and small, delicate features. His mouth, cast in a perpetual straight line of sternness, and his fixed glare was unable, or perhaps unwilling, to bestow kindness or compassion. Together, his eyes and mouth gave him a countenance so disarming that many were reluctant to look directly into his face. He glanced into the radio room to note the doctor treat Atkins, then walked purposefully past the gathered men. Barefoot and clad only in boxers, he headed straight to the navigation room. Everyone quieted, and Grisham could hear him asking sonar what else was in the vicinity. Negative was the reply.

"What's that?" he asked, and must have been pointing.

"A fishing trawler, sir. Fifty-seven miles northwest, just off the Grand Banks."

"Grisham, systems?" he asked sparingly.

"Negative, sir."

The commander stepped into the cramped radio room where the doctor was exploring Atkin's ear canals with a light. "Remarkably, his eardrums aren't busted," the doctor said as he regarded the gently bouncing headphones. "He'll be tender for quite a few days."

The commander had opened his mouth to question Atkins when the erratic lighting and vibration abruptly ceased. The headphones lay dead.

"It was Morse code, sir," Atkins yelled.

The doctor shook his head with a "Sssh!"

"Morse?" Stillman asked in an almost accusatory tone. "What type of transmitter could do this?"

"I don't know," Atkins yelled then caught himself. "I don't know, but it was a standard modulated carrier wave coming through on more than one frequency."

Stillman looked at him skeptically. "More than one frequency? How is that possible, son?"

He shook his head and brought his fingers to his ears again. Moments later, with a furious hiss of static electricity, the episode began again. Commander Stillman seemed angered by the resumption and snapped his fingers at Grisham. "You know Morse?"

Grisham nodded.

"Get him paper and pen," he ordered no one in particular.

Grisham obediently went to the headphones with the blind intention of putting them on, but then he realized the danger of mindless routine and sat at the console, holding the headphones several inches from his ear. "It's addressed to DCVA from GBTT," he said as he listened and wrote.

Stillman snapped his fingers at the young ensign and pointed to a monitor. "Find those call letters."

He jumped to the keyboard and began typing through a snapping underbrush of electric blue. "I have no listing for Delta Charlie Victor Alpha." A moment later he said, "Golf Bravo Tango Tango is *Queen Elizabeth 2*."

"Dammit," Stillman muttered through his teeth. "Sonar," he yelled through the door, "Check your traffic report again!"

There was an adroit pause to indicate a double-check, then, "Negative, sir. Only the trawler."

"Where in hell is *QE2*?"

"Sir, I don't believe she's even on the transatlantic route now."

Stillman huffed irritably then turned back to Grisham, his eyes narrowed, waiting.

"It seems to be a weather report and greeting from their captain, sir."

Atkins sat in a chair now, the doctor stuffing cotton in his ears, and said, "GBTT is the call sign of the *QE2*, but it *was* the call sign of the *Queen Mary* before she was retired. Cunard transferred it before *QE2*'s maiden voyage."

The commander stared at him.

"That's just an interesting footnote to students of radio call signs, sir."

"And what does that 'interesting footnote' have to do with this situation, Atkins?"

"That would explain the absence of the recipient's call signs in our database," he replied, and his voice rose again. "It must no longer exist."

Commander Stillman walked angrily to Atkins and stood with his hands at his hips, head bent forward. "Are you suggesting that your ears were nearly blown off by a message sent from a retired luxury liner in the middle of the last century?"

Atkins swallowed. "I'm not suggesting anything, sir. I have no idea."

Suddenly, the lights were constant again, the headphones silent, and the steel of *Leviathan* seemed as imperturbable as ever.

Grisham began, "Message DCVA from GBTT. 1700 Zulu, position 41 46 North, 50 14 West. Speed 29.8 knots. Wind northeast at 12, barometer 98.1. Cloudy but clear. Encountered a moderate gale this morning, gave passengers fits. Following winds today, confused swell. Best regards and long live the king. Illingworth."

There was absolute quiet and Grisham had the chilling sensation that he had just transcribed a message from the dead. He caught the slightest flicker of uneasiness in Stillman's eyes before he looked to the ceiling as though he were searching beyond the steel, through the depths of the sea to the very heavens. Seconds later he gave no notice when the message began coursing through *Leviathan* once more.

"Sir," Atkins said timidly, "there hasn't been a king in England for more than fifty years."

Everyone within hearing distance simply stared at him and each other. There was certainly nothing to say.

~ * ~

Guy phoned Lynn's mother at work again. When she came on the line, she said singsong, "Guy Turner, whatever am I going to do with you?" but he detected the first tone of impatience.

"Mrs. Thorne, I'm driving up to Seattle this weekend and would appreciate your help in convincing Lynn that..."

"Guy, I've told you, you can't come here." She had the same earnest finality in her voice as her daughter. "Lynn will not see you, and I absolutely cannot be your ally against my daughter. I'm sorry, but I can't help you."

Guy leaned his head against the wall with a soft thump and closed his eyes. Tears of anger formed, but he fought them furiously. "How long is she going to punish me? Three months are enough already! She's made her point, and now it's time to talk."

"Hon, she's not punishing you. What would that accomplish? She has simply washed her hands of you, I'm sorry to say. I know how cruel that sounds, but she has always seen things in black and white, never gray. Even as a child she recognized the time to cut and run, whether it was clarinet lessons or relationships. And isn't that a philosophy we should all have? I envy her, to tell you the truth. It may hurt initially, but what's the point in prolonging the pain in a relationship that isn't going anywhere?"

"But I *want* to marry. I'm not dragging my feet. I've always wanted that."

Mrs. Thorne dropped her voice. "Guy, I love you, always have, and my sincerest wish has been that you two marry. You're sensitive, intelligent and would make a choice son-in-law. But marriage necessarily includes children for Lynn. And that means grandchildren for me, so I can't help but be biased."

"I've explained to her that I can't bring a black…"

She cut him off in a flash and spoke very sternly: "Don't play the race card, Guy! I can't believe you would use that as an excuse. You insult my ancestors and your own when you pull a stunt like that. After the long road our people have traveled, you should be ashamed of yourself to say you deny giving life because of your skin color. And if you're *not* ashamed of yourself, you should be pitied for being so damned ignorant!"

Guy was unable to respond, or rather feared his voice may break if he did.

She sighed and said softly, "I'm sorry for that, but it's true. I don't know what your real reasons are but life marches on, baby, so you better find someone with the same outlook on life as you or you'll never be happy. I'm sure there are women out there who could care less about motherhood, but Lynn isn't one of them."

There was an uneasy silence on both ends, then she said, "Guy, please remember this. If you're not honest with yourself, you certainly can't be honest with those who love you."

"What's that supposed to mean?" he asked.

"Well, you need to think about that. Goodbye, Guy."

~ * ~

A magnificent electrical storm split the billowing, black skies above Long Beach with supernatural pale-violet streaks. For a moment or two the buildings, streets, and smooth sea were illuminated in uncanny daylight, then plunged into appalling darkness somehow blacker than the night. The *Queen Mary*'s flood-lit stacks fought valiantly to maintain their stark superiority against the antagonistic skies, then repeatedly and completely washed in a great scorn of purple-white.

A few days earlier Guy had been on the forecastle when the ship's whistle blew as it did every morning at ten. He and the other day-trippers unfortunate enough to be on deck hunkered down and covered their ears against the angry roar of a great, captured animal in unfamiliar surroundings. “Dear God,” someone had said as car alarms sounded in the parking lot in a cacophony of whoops. But the silence that followed was like an explosion to Guy, the startled sound of bare existence. Guy likewise simply existed. He had always known loneliness but never as such an intimate companion. He was infinitely depressed and imagined that he and the ship shared the same wish, to cease existence. Not with a spectacular end but rather a quiet slip into oblivion.

But today, Guy had intended to spend only the early afternoon at *Queen Mary* exploring the archives for that extra minutia of memorabilia before settling into the editing room, but day turned to night after Mr. Vaughn, the ship’s CEO, visited with ’suggestions.’ Guy had immersed himself into the documentary since Lynn left him, and the great liner quickly became his mistress. There was a moribund loneliness about her that Guy now identified with, an inexplicable sense of hopelessness and helplessness. Her captains were long dead, her passengers nonexistent, and she would never again hasten into a turnabout voyage. She was an enormous monument to the fragility of time; a fact Guy pondered often.

“This is the very suite Winston Churchill stayed in en route to the Quebec Conference to meet with President Roosevelt,” Mr. Vaughn said, as he tried to unlock the door. “You know he traveled to North America three times on the *Queen Mary* during the war, not to mention the countless times during peace.”

“Yes,” Guy replied in a weary tone. “It will be part of the narration.” He wanted nothing more than to be at home, sitting in the dark with a cigarette as he did most nights, emptying his mind of everything but the loss of Lynn.

“But couldn’t you at least film the tub where he planned D-Day?” Mr. Vaughn asked. “He sat in it with toy boats and harbors while his aides surrounded him. How many people do you suppose know that?”

The lights flickered, and Guy said, “Mr. Vaughn, we have over two hundred hours of film to edit for a two-hour documentary. I assure you we have more than enough images to choose from.”

The little man examined the keys closely and chose another while Guy waited impatiently. “But to actually see the very tub in which that piece of history was planned is quite extraordinary, I promise you.” Again, the knob would not turn. Mr. Vaughn glanced down the corridor and said, "Now surely you got a shot of that never-ending hallway?"

"Yes, we have it."

"Do you know what 'sheer' is?" Mr. Vaughn asked as the lights dimmed and brightened.

"Yes, that's the convex curving of the deck," Guy said obligingly. "The deck is so long you can't see the end."

"A hallway over seven hundred feet long," Mr. Vaughn said, and shook his head in awe.

Indeed, the corridor dipped lightly far ahead of them. The paneling glowed in warm tones from the softly lit fixtures in the ceiling corners while the lines of handrails on either side led the eye even further. The cabin doors were like silent, regal sentries standing guard over a hallowed pathway that stretched into the past, measured by years rather than feet. The deck began to rise imperceptibly into the distance. Then there was the golden blur of door, panel, and handrail as they melded mysteriously into one with the final illusion of a pin-prick of darkness reaching infinitely upward.

When Guy raised a hand to rub his eyes, static electricity jumped from his fingertips to his eyelashes. Mr. Vaughn jerked his hand back when the key shocked him with a blue snap upon contact with the doorknob. "For heaven's sake," he said, and Guy watched as he began examining the keys again with infuriating slowness.

Guy had decided to lie regarding a previous engagement and make a hasty exit when he heard an unusual sound down the corridor. A soft, rippling sound like water running over rocks in a shallow creek. He turned, and a figure appeared in the distance, walking toward them through the slashes of golden light given off by the light fixtures. Guy turned back to the CEO.

"Mr. Vaughn, I really need to run," he said. "I'm sorry, but I still have quite a bit to do at the studio tonight."

Mr. Vaughn half twisted with what Guy assumed would be an appeal to stay. Instead the keys fell to the carpeting with a metallic whimper, and he whispered, "Good heavens." Guy followed his gaze. With pure and absolute astonishment he watched as the figure grew clear. An old, long-haired woman, completely naked, approaching with small, tentative steps.

Out of the corner of his eye, Guy saw Mr. Vaughn shakily lift a cell phone to his ear. "Security to Main Deck," he said in a low tone. "The Churchill Suite."

She was a deeply lined, dark-skinned woman with feet horribly misshapen by arthritis. Her gray hair swung behind her waist as she walked, her shoulders raised and rounded. Her hips drooped ponderously, more from age than extra weight, and her breasts hung like pears against her chest with dark, olive-colored nipples. The return of Eve after five hundred generations.

Then she stood before them like a timid deer, her eyes pensive as she looked from one man to the other, perhaps in the hope of detecting compassion. She settled her dark eyes on Guy and moved closer. Her eyes did not reflect the depths of madness or dementia but rather an incessant plea. She swallowed before speaking as though choosing her words carefully in fear of misunderstanding. When she opened her mouth, the voice that fell from her lips was deep and strong though she spoke slowly in a language Guy did not recognize. It sounded faintly Latin with many l's and t's. When she finished, she was silent, waiting, and begging him for an answer with her eyes.

Guy could only return a stare of incomprehension. She brought a shaky hand to her face in anguish. Then she looked down and mumbled softly to herself, and when he saw her lids were brimming, he, too, shared in her frustration. Suddenly her facial features became resolute, and she met his eyes again with more determination than before. Another approach had obviously occurred to her. Raising her hand without moving her eyes from his, she held before him a plastic nametag upside down in her fingers, the recessed letters yellow with age. Then, with pronunciation as clear and resonant as the peal of a bell on a cold, crisp morning, she uttered the name on the tag, "Bennett."

The effect on Guy was a needling tingle in the small of his back that whirled up his spine to the base of his skull and down again.

"I don't understand," Guy replied and could hardly hear his own voice but she evidently understood him from his blinking expression.

She looked to Mr. Vaughn, who could only regard her with his mouth agape. She turned back to Guy. She repeated, even slower but with greater urgency, emphasizing each syllable, "Ben-nett. Ben-nett." She looked up to him imploringly, but when she recognized the futility of communication, her arm fell limp and heavy and she began weeping.

The two men stood helplessly dumbstruck as she stood before them for a moment, a portrait of despair; then she turned and began walking back down the corridor, sobbing softly.

Though shocked, Guy had no impression of the supernatural. She was a mortal who spoke in a foreign tongue. But time as he had always known it stalled when she began her retreat. Halfway down the corridor her feet did not seem to fall on the carpeting, as though she were walking up an invisible incline that did not match the true rise of the deck. There was the rippling sound again; then she shimmered like a heat wave rising from the pavement and quite simply disappeared.

Now there was no movement of time, just a dislocating sense that the current of life was pulling him into deeper waters of reality than he was ever meant to encounter. An undertow of fear dragged him along, his stream of consciousness flowing faster and deeper until he thought he must surely pass out. The utter reality of the experience crashed in waves upon him until there was nothing in his existence but her pathetic eyes holding his, those dark, helpless, searching eyes that overwhelmed everything, past and present. The empty corridor already haunted him, or rather the memory of her departure from it haunted him, playing over and over in his mind. Then, far away, he heard his heartbeat beckoning him, louder and louder, marking the seconds of a world changed forever. Time abruptly tumbled into its proper march with his heart and mind racing wildly to keep up.

Mr. Vaughn had collapsed against the door with a dazed, uncomprehending expression when Guy returned to the present. The bewildered man reached for Guy's arm as he sank and brought a hand to his chest, gasping for breath. Two security guards rounded the corner from the opposite end of the corridor and broke into a run with guns drawn when they saw Guy standing over the fallen man.

"He's having a heart attack!" Guy shouted irritably, and some semblance of normality returned. As one guard knelt beside Mr. Vaughn, the other called for an ambulance. Ozone hung heavily in the air.

It required his greatest act of courage to look back down the corridor. It was quiet and undisturbed as though years had passed since those bare feet had padded down the carpeting and, for a moment, he wondered if it had really happened. He noticed something on the carpeting where she had stood before them, and when he squatted to retrieve it, his knees trembled so violently he had to balance himself with a hand on the wall.

He stood and looked down at the nametag in his palm, contemplating his own newly found Rosetta stone and the long journey he was about to embark upon.

Four

The windshields on the freeway glinted like wet stones in the morning sun. The sky was a vacuum of clear blue and the few clouds scuttled by at a hushed pace. In the predictable light of day, Guy had difficulty believing anything extraordinary had occurred, yet the truth prevailed by the tangible press of the nametag in his shirt pocket as he drove to the hospital. Each time the traffic lulled, he pulled it out and studied it with childlike fascination.

Too shaken to go by ambulance with Mr. Vaughn, he had rushed home the night before, almost in tears to share the evening's event with warm, attentive Lynn. He had paced through the night with every light in the apartment on. But by dawn, his heart which had raced with fear was leaping with excitement. Though still shaken, the voyeur in him was awakened at the unimaginable secret conferred to him. As he navigated traffic, he hummed the Allegretto from Beethoven's Seventh Symphony, a theme that always suggested the majestic mystery of life to him.

Twice before in his life, the flames of the unknown had kindled his soul, hinting at hidden truths he'd never been able to divine fully, perhaps wasn't meant to. He could only bask in the warm, enigmatic glory they evoked. At age eleven, he had attended a church revival with neighborhood kids out of sheer boredom. After sniggering at the speaker and debating whether to crawl under the pew and sneak out, he finally listened. The words seemed to stir something within him that had slumbered since birth. Then there was a call to the altar. He inexplicably rose, pulled as if by magnet to the front of the church. To his horror, he began to cry uncontrollably and experienced a sorrow that was strangely sweet, self-pity somehow without moroseness, and accepted Christ as his savior. In later years, he wondered if he hadn't simply succumbed to a psychological power of suggestion rather than anything of a spiritual nature, but he preferred the latter, smug beyond of the scope of science and reason.

Then, with Lynn, he attended a Beethoven symphony sponsored by the cable network he worked for. Although emphatically uncomfortable with the heavily affected people in gowns, jewels, and tuxedos, he went in deference to Lynn who looked forward to 'dressing up'.

The first movement seemed as pretentious as the patrons listening to it. He leaned over and said, "Kinda sags in comparison to my Marvin Gaye collection, don't you think?"

She gave him a charged look while he pretended to doze. But the second movement began with a deeply somber opening chord that immediately plucked a symbiotic string deep within him. A dark, marching rhythm followed that sounded eerily familiar, like music he had heard all of his life but never outside himself. It grew and grew until he was enraptured.

Moved to the edge of his seat, he underwent a profound nakedness as if the strings and woodwinds were emanating from his very soul. The sound soared within and without him, the harmony and rhythm of life, alive with trial and triumph, dissonant but beautiful, the deep mystery of existence. Lynn watched the music's influence on him, pleased, and whispered "Allegretto."

It rose, driving hard but delicate, exhausting him as it bloomed with higher and higher octaves until the tremendous climax finally pounded through his rib cage. His melancholy view of life now had a theme.

Both events, although unnerving and unexpected, were transient passages that ennobled him to the possibility, even the certainty, of something unknown yet infinitely greater than his daily, discontented self. Now the desperate eyes of a foreign woman held him with heavy power, prompting yet another journey of self, one of deliverance he hoped. That ancient music now resurrected, was as vital and ever-present as his pulse. His heart surged in anticipation of the coming crescendo.

~ * ~

Mr. Vaughn was sitting up in his bed, staring out the window when Guy opened the door. That immaculate man was an incongruous sight in a nondescript hospital gown, the heart monitor blipping beside him, and an IV line trailing from a pole to the top of his hand. Their eyes met, and they exchanged a silent acknowledgement of their shared experience, something that belonged uniquely to them. They were intimate strangers. Guy didn't even know his first name.

Bill Somers, the ship's historian with whom Guy had worked closely for nearly six months, sat near the door. Obviously apprised of the previous nights' events, he rose formally, as though Guy should be accorded respect.

"She was real?" Mr. Vaughn asked simply, more a plea for reassurance than a question.

Guy opened his palm, revealing the nametag. Mr. Vaughn turned his head and closed his eyes as though the physical evidence weighed too heavily on him.

"What have the doctors said?"

Mr. Vaughn turned to Guy and smiled weakly. "A massive shock attack. But only a light heart attack." He resumed his stare out the window. "I dismissed a young housekeeper two days ago after she ran screaming from the Lounge. She saw that woman, but I thought she was just a silly girl making a play for attention in front of tourists. I didn't have a choice."

"May I look at that?" the historian asked.

Guy inexplicably hesitated a moment, then allowed him to take the nametag from his palm.

"Bennett", he said, handling the plastic as though it were a sacred relic. "Just as Mr. Vaughn described. This definitely looks to be from a military uniform, probably World War II." He had a manner of voice and posture that suggested he would be quite comfortable lecturing before a chalkboard.

Guy, unable to resist, instantly took the nametag from him and dropped it protectively into his shirt pocket. "She has...*visited* before?"

"Yes," Bill answered in a confident voice. "I have something that should be of great interest to you." He pulled a sheet of paper from a folder lying on the table next to the chair and handed it to Guy. "A few days ago, I received an anonymous phone call from a Norfolk man who serves on the navy sub *Leviathan*. After asking several questions about *Queen Mary*'s call sign, he finally revealed that the *Leviathan* received this message more than seventy times in a forty-eight-hour period while on maneuvers in the North Atlantic. Initially, they thought it was from *QE2*, which has the same call sign, but the references clearly prove it to be from *Queen Mary*."

"Illingworth," Guy read aloud. "He was captain when she ran over the *Curacoa*."

"He was also captain in the years immediately after the war when she carried the war brides. That can't be a wartime message. Otherwise, it would have been coded and most certainly would not have included her coordinates. So we have a post-war greeting with a reference to the king that dates it prior to his death in 1953. And the fact Illingworth was captain firmly places it in 1947."

"In 1947? How can you be sure?"

"Illingworth retired within a year after her return to peacetime in July, 1947, which significantly narrows the time frame."

"What's the correlation between this message and last night?" Guy asked.

"Static electricity and an electrical storm," he replied grandly, confident in his hypothesis. "There have been several electrical storms over Long Beach the past two days and Mr. Vaughn tells me you both encountered static electricity before the...visit."

Guy glanced at Mr. Vaughn, but he still stared out the window. "I don't follow."

"The *Leviathan* also encountered electrical storms and an outbreak of static electricity while receiving the message. Whatever we're dealing with evidently disrupts the natural electrical balance in the atmosphere. And ham radio operators all over southern California picked up that same message."

"How do you know?"

"After hearing of your experience last night, I called the Search for Extraterrestrial Intelligence, or SETI, this morning to ask about the significance of the message. I was surprised to learn that they already knew of it. Evidently, they'd been swamped by calls every time there was an electrical storm, but the person I spoke with was entirely dismissive about it. I did not reveal the *Leviathan* incident to him. He indicated that man-made signals are not considered a contact regardless of their uniqueness. Their dishes received the same signals, but they were not incoming from space. They all originated in our atmosphere."

"That's because whatever or whoever sent it was already in our atmosphere before they began transmitting," Guy said with faint irritation. "How did she find the ship?"

"The *Queen Mary* is the only three-stacker in the world. And her profile has always been unmistakable, especially, I should think, when viewed from above."

A bubble of laughter escaped Guy, but it was not genuine. Neither Mr. Vaughn nor Bill, the historian, laughed with him. He brought a hand to his forehead and said, "I can't believe we're having this conversation. Listen to what you're suggesting. We are all insane!"

Mr. Vaughn looked up at him gloomily. "You saw what I saw." His tone made laughter seem very inappropriate, and Guy considered himself reproved.

"I have no doubt that the military is investigating," Bill Somers continued. "Not only did a navy sub pick up the signals, but I received a suspicious phone call the day before I spoke with the *Leviathan* man, ostensibly from a high school student doing a report on radio communications. I thought it odd that his only questions concerned Illingworth, the history of *Queen Mary*'s call sign and the radio frequency she used in peacetime." He arched an eyebrow and lowered his tone. "That was no high school student."

"I can't imagine why the military is interested in her radio frequency. What can that tell them?"

He shrugged. "I'm curious as to what government satellites and NORAD have picked up. You worked in the Pentagon for several years. Do you have any open military channels?"

"I was assigned to General Walter Van Cleve for six years," Guy answered.

"Now the President's National Security Advisor?" Bill asked, impressed.

Guy nodded. "But Julie Austin, a girl I dated while I was at the Pentagon, is now a defense analyst under him. I'll start with her. I don't want to raise any unnecessary flags." Guy began pacing. "In 1947, the original message was somehow intercepted and after that interception, it was retransmitted as an only means of communication. It served as a beacon to that woman, guiding her to the ship. For whatever reason, she's trying desperately to find 'Bennett' again."

He stopped to absorb his words, looking vacantly at the sunshine spilling over the windowsill. "She held the name tag upside down. She obviously couldn't read it. She simply repeated to me what someone told her it said. She was beyond hope. Frantic, actually." A thrill of the memory raced down his spine.

"The Cunard Line did not retain passenger manifests," the historian noted, "although occasionally you find passenger lists on internet auction sites. We do, however, have our archive lists of former passengers, crew and servicemen that we have been piecing together ourselves over the years. You utilized those lists for your interviews."

"Any Bennetts?" Guy asked.

"The actress Joan Bennett traveled eastbound in August of 1947 but your best bet is a returning GI and his war bride who came to the states in September. James and Jessica. You interviewed both of them, do you remember?"

Guy shook his head. "I interviewed hundreds. I forgot most of them as soon as they stood."

"They were the only Bennetts in that time frame. You should certainly remember the woman. I'll not forget her. She had a bit much to drink and you carried her—"

"Ah, son of a bitch!" Guy exploded when the memory of a wet ear and busted lip rushed over him. He groaned with the realization. "That's Murphy's Law for you." The thought of Jess Bennett deflated him, and he sat heavily in the chair and leaned forward placing his head in his hands. He stayed in that position for several moments then said, "I'll need their phone number and address."

"They're divorced. But I have his. He lives in Hermosa Beach, but I'm not certain about hers."

"Thank God, he's closest. I don't care to see her again." He thought a moment. "I can't place him. Of course that should come as no surprise. Any man would be diminished next to her."

Mr. Vaughn leaned forward and increased the volume on the television as a female news anchor told the story of an old radio signal echoing from the skies above Long Beach, California with a smug smile that suggested that no one take her words too seriously. They listened and exchanged glances.

"Mr. Turner," Mr. Vaughn said as Guy stood. He looked steadily at him. "I would appreciate it if you didn't use my name if you discuss our experience with anyone. I need time to resolve myself to exactly what we saw. Please."

Guy nodded and replied in a thoughtful voice, "I believe we have just seen beyond the pale."

~ * ~

"Well, well," Julie said in a relaxed, homey way. "Tell me,

have you been taken off the market yet?" She sounded as though she were settling back in her chair with the phone, ready to visit.

"No, but I came very close."

"Listen here, I am not interested in a long-distance romance if that's what you're up to," she feigned offense.

"This isn't a social call, I'm sorry to say."

"Have you turned gay?" she asked quite deadpan.

Guy laughed. "That might certainly make things easier. Actually, I'm on a fact-gathering mission, and I'm sure you can help."

"Oh, really? Should I be flattered?"

"Baby, you are my source in the United States government."

"And what, pray tell, could I possibly offer you in the way of facts?"

"I'm working on a documentary about the career of the liner *Queen Mary* and I came across a radio signal that was first transmitted from her in 1947 but was just received a few days ago. Repeatedly. Why don't you tell me the government's take on it?"

There was a long moment of silence, but Guy heard volumes in it.

She knew.

"What information could the Pentagon have that CNN hasn't already reported? They've been running the story all morning, very tongue-in-cheek, I might add. There's a very good possibility that there is a hoaxer in southern California." Her words were defensive yet dismissive. She let a few moments pass, waiting for a counter response. "The general consensus is it's just a fluke, a message that somehow became space-bound through some freak atmospheric anomaly and has now re-entered the earth's atmosphere through the very same anomaly. The Pentagon's official stand is that if it's not a hoax, then it is simply a signal that has been bouncing around through space all these years."

"Perhaps, but CNN and the rest of the world don't know about the seventy times that the message was received by the *Leviathan*, now do they? And what an obscure message to use as as a hoax, particularly in the middle of the North Atlantic, don't you agree?"

Silence, then, "Someone from *Leviathan* has contacted you?"

"Julie, let's not play cloak and dagger. I know firsthand this is much more than an atmospheric anomaly, and so do you. That message has not been random. It's been concentrated in specific locations."

"Guy, I could lose my job." Her voice lost all cordiality. "How do I know what I tell you won't show up thinly disguised in your documentary?"

"You know me better than that, Julie. This is not research for the documentary. There is much more involved than an old radio signal, believe me. Just tell me what old man Van Cleve knows, and do I *ever* have a story to tell you."

Guy heard a sigh of concession, and she asked, "Are you on a secure phone?"

"Yes."

Julie assumed an authoritative voice, as though she were giving a briefing. "A NATO satellite was destroyed by the strength of the signal and two private telecommunication satellites were knocked out of orbit. Defense Department satellites have picked it up in every frequency wave known to mankind. Russian intelligence reveals that their hydrophones on the continental shelf also picked up every signal, as did our Navy's. A fishing boat off Newfoundland reported electrical storms and loss of navigational systems during the duration of each signal." She paused and said, "Is that confirmation enough for you?"

"Did NORAD track anything incoming from deep space?" The implication of his question sounded foolish.

"Nothing from NORAD or Hubble. Whatever it is has no detectable mass and defies the laws of physics as we know it. But our best detection of the anomaly in our atmosphere came from, of all places, the National Oceanographic and Atmospheric Administration. Their weather radar and satellites tracked the exact entry of the electrical disturbance into our atmosphere four days ago then followed it from mid-Atlantic to the coastlines of the entire Northern Hemisphere until it stopped over southern California."

"Because the search ended in Long Beach," Guy said.

"Not so fast, sweetheart. The signals and storms resumed over that same spot in the North Atlantic this morning, about four hundred zulu."

Guy's pulse quickened, remembering the woman's desperation. "Then we only have another day or two before she finally gives up."

"Gives up? Who?"

"Why is the military so interested in the *Queen Mary*'s

original radio frequency?" There was absolute quiet on the other end. "Julie, what is the military going to do with that radio frequency?"

"This is *the* contact, Guy," she said softly in a purely rational tone. "That message is our only form of communication. Quite simply, the Navy plans to respond by transmitting the message exactly as the original and, hopefully, it will be recognized as an invitation, so to speak. The aircraft carrier *Thomas Jefferson* is altering course from the Azores and making all possible speed to that spot in the North Atlantic even as we speak."

Shock froze Guy's mind. "My God. Why not somewhere in the continental United States or even aboard the *Queen Mary*?"

"Obviously, we don't know what to expect. The President himself directed the attempt occur as far from the civilian population as possible. What more secluded location than the middle of the North Atlantic?"

"Listen to me, Julie," he said, the urgency in the foreign woman's eyes now transposed to his voice. "There is an older civilian man who I believe holds the key to all this. Don't let them transmit until I get him up there. Please help me. We've *got* to get him there Julie, that's why she's here. *Convince Van Cleve to hold off!*"

"Who is 'she' Guy? What is wrong with you?"

"Let me tell you my story, then repeat it to Van Cleve and I'll call you in a few hours. I have to pay a visit to that senior citizen first."

"Guy, why would—"

"There's no logical explanation for what I'm about to tell you," he began with haste.

~ * ~

I am absolutely spellbound. The road to Hermosa Beach unrolled before Guy. Wouldn't Lynn love to share this enchantment? Wouldn't the subject of motherhood seem suddenly insignificant in the wake of this miracle-mystery? Moments of absolute awe washed over him like a wave at the seashore each time he pondered the intense reality of the previous evening. He wondered if up until this time in his life, he had simply been treading water, hopelessly adrift in the rising and receding tides of Lynn. Now a new wave of reality plunged him under, overwhelming as it bore down, gathering strength to carry him to some distant, unknown shore.

He passed tanned seniors on bicycles as he pulled into a cul-de-sac populated by single-level ranch houses. The overall face of the neighborhood was one of relaxation and simplicity. The Bennett's home, situated among thick ornamentals, lent an unmistakable air of secrecy to the place. Or perhaps it was simply Guy's anticipation of the revelation that waited beyond them.

Barbara Bennett answered the door smiling, her improbably-auburn hair neatly coiffed. "Jim is so flattered you called," she whispered conspiratorially. "Not many young people want to listen to World War II stories, you know. Thank you for giving a boost to his old ego."

Jim Bennett appeared in the hall behind her and Guy immediately remembered him, particularly his thinly veiled hurt. "Come in, come in," he said as though insulted Guy was still outside. He shook his hand in a hearty man's grip and before shutting the door, he looked past him expectantly to the car. "Where's the cameraman?"

Guy suffered a pang of guilt, a momentary regret for having lied to them over the phone. "I thought I might just ask some questions if that's all right with you."

"Fine, fine," he said without disappointment. "I think it's important the spoiled young people of today hear of their grandparent's war hardships. If it weren't for us…," he said, wagging a finger.

Jim led Guy down the hall to a large family room dominated by a wide bay window overlooking the back lawn. This unpretentious room, intended entirely for retirement and leisure, contained overstuffed sofas and recliners on a plain, oval carpet. Its only concession to formality was one elegant table, obviously an heirloom, covered with books and magazines. Guy walked to a wall hung entirely with pictures and absently looked at school photos, sepia-tones, and family portraits. He had not considered the exchange of pleasantries and was now unsure how to embark upon his questions. He caressed the nametag in his pants pocket, debating whether to simply thrust it at the man or calmly place it on the table. He stood undecided before a wedding photo with a redheaded groom who could only be Barbara's son.

"Do you have children?" Barbara asked cheerfully.

Like an automaton, Guy responded quickly from some obscure imperative to use the same refrain each time the subject of children arose. "Oh, I would *never* bring a child of color into this damned world."

Barbara drew back at his response. "I'm sorry. I hope I didn't touch upon something unpleasant."

Jim stared at him curiously.

Guy had to rectify the situation. "Please forgive me. It's just I am eternally explaining to my aunts and uncles why I'm not a father." There was an awkward moment, then "Won't you lead me through your family?"

She smiled all forgiving, a sweet, simple woman who was the very antithesis of Jess Bennett. "This is my son, Allen, and his wife, Connie," she went on and Guy was grateful for the outlet, for the time to think.

They moved down the wall, through the decades, when, suddenly, the now familiar rush of thrill caught him as he stared once again into the eyes that haunted him, this time a pair of them. "And this is Jim's son, Zachary, and daughter, Kathleen."

Guy edged closer, his heart beating wildly as he recognized the olive skin and dark eyes of a little boy and girl. They smiled back at him, gap-toothed, from school pictures that looked to be from the fifties.

Stunned, his voice wavered for a moment then he swiveled round and faced Jim. "*Who* are they?"

Five

The couple regarded him warily, undoubtedly wondering if they had permitted a mad man into their home. "But I told you," Barbara said, perplexed. "They are Jim's children, Zach and Kathleen."

Guy reached into his pants pocket, pulled the tag out and held it before him in much the same manner the old woman presented it to him. He allowed it to guide him forward like a golden scepter. Guy had never witnessed such a subtle blending of expressions, ranging from uncertainty to astonishment, as he saw on Jim's face as the piece of plastic drew closer and more distinct. A great, long-locked door was swinging open and Guy could feel the blood pounding in his ears. Finally, Guy stood before him while the old man examined the object in his hand with incredulity.

Barbara, unsure whether to be concerned or not, said plaintively, "Jim? Jim, what is it?"

Jim sought Guy's eyes. "How?" he whispered.

"Last night. In a corridor aboard the *Queen Mary*."

"You saw her?" he asked and the affirming pronoun was a thrilling relief to Guy.

Guy nodded. "She is desperate to find you. Incredibly frantic."

Jim raised a hand to his temple as though he had the slightest of headaches and walked slowly to the bay window. "She's reached her hour of reckoning." He sounded softly bemused, thoughtful. "The doors are closing."

"Jim?" Barbara said again, completely lost.

"She knows she's reached her final years and certain aspects of her life are not in order." Jim spoke lightly and without inflection as though the suddenness of this manifestation had drained all the strength from his body. “They never are for any one of us.” He raised his other hand and brought both together in a prayerful manner before his chin. “Good God.” He remained in this posture for perhaps a minute, looking unseeing over the back lawn, then turned to Guy. “How does she look?”

“She hasn’t aged as well as you.”

Jim grunted. “She was young and beautiful when I last saw her.”

“Who is she?”

Guy perceived an aura of concession from Jim, some sort of relief the secret was finally in the light, ready for an exorcism into absolution. “The only other living person who knows all of this, spoken of this, and shared it with me is Jess. You’ll have to let my old mind fathom all of this for a moment.”

Guy glanced at Barbara, but she was staring fixedly at her husband, the mention of the other wife very apparent on her face.

Jim sat in a recliner and hunched forward with his trembling hands between his knees. He seemed suddenly out of place here, transient, as though he were in a waiting room. He looked up at Guy. “Jess and I left Southampton with only each other. We arrived in New York with two children.”

“*Her* children.”

“Yes, her children.”

Barbara, now truly alarmed, walked to Jim’s side and said, “I don’t understand, darling.”

Guy sat down opposite him, leaned forward and offered the nametag to Jim.

Jim tenderly took it from him and held it reverently in his palm. Guy saw tears forming.

To deter them, he spoke gently as if to a child. “There was a message sent during your voyage in 1947 which is how she found you to begin with. That same message has repeated over and over from that spot in the North Atlantic and Long Beach for the past four days. CNN has been reporting those in Long Beach, but they don’t know about the ones received by a submarine in the North Atlantic. And when I saw her, she said your name quite clearly.” Guy gave a mystified look and said, “Her eyes,” as if he had just remembered them.

Jim smiled with wet eyes full of understanding. “She wants to know what has become of her babies.”

"Jim, who are you talking about?" Barbara asked.

Guy was intent upon Jim's responses and paid no heed to Barbara. "Do her children know?"

Jim shook his head mournfully. "They are sleeping in a cemetery, in southern Illinois. They never knew. They were very small when they…when they arrived, you see."

"Jim," Barbara said.

"How did they die?" Guy asked. "How old?" He experienced a terrible need to know.

"Kathleen was a very asthmatic child but normal in every way. She developed a rare lung disease in her late teens, and it took her life when she was twenty-one. We had years to prepare for her death, knew it was coming. Jess and I had never been closer. Grief sometimes does that. But Zach's death was completely unexpected. He was all boy, very wild, and one afternoon less than nine months after Kathleen's death, he was in a car accident. He was home from college and had been speeding down our country roads when he swung to avoid a deer and hit a tree. He was pinned behind the steering wheel. I got there just before the paramedics released the seat. He was completely conscious, even telling jokes after he learned the other three boys weren't injured. I thought he was fine and stood there scolding him through the window. But the steering wheel had been acting as a compression to his internal organs and as soon as the seat released, the blood surged into his chest. He died before my eyes." Jim looked carefully away. "Jess never recovered from it."

"Jim," Barbara tried again, louder and more determined. "What are you saying? Kathleen and Zach weren't yours?"

Jim offered her his hand. "Please sit and I'll tell you everything. I've kept things from you."

His words had an adulterous ring to them and Barbara looked so downtrodden at that moment that Guy considered apologizing to her for inflicting this pain upon her.

"Mr. Bennett," Guy said. "I need you to tell me, quickly—"

"I'm Jim," he interrupted. "I think we've gone beyond formalities, don't you?"

"Jim, I need you to quickly tell me about that woman and her children. We haven't much time. The carrier *Thomas Jefferson* is racing to that spot in the North Atlantic with the express purpose of making contact with that woman. I have some pull at the Pentagon, and I am sure I can get you up there but we must move fast. You are the key to all of this, but they won't wait for long. You can surely imagine the significance of this moment to human history."

"I've had fifty-seven years to ponder that significance. But Jess is your so-called 'key', not me. Human history means nothing to Jess, but she's still a grieving mother. She may not have given birth to them, but they belonged to her and she will need to...to *express* to that poor woman that her children were loved and taken care of. And are now gone."

Guy's heart sank. "Jim, there simply isn't the time to let her be a part of this. I am going to call my contact in the Pentagon in an hour or so to see what arrangements she's procured. We can't involve your ex-wife. I, frankly, think it would be too great a trial for us to take her."

Jim gave Guy an angry look giving the distinct impression of a shoving match. "I will not under any circumstances go without Jess. That woman will want to see Jess, not me. Motherhood is a mystery to you and me, but they share a language we can never hope to understand. Especially grieving mothers. Jess will want to go. She deserves to go!"

Battle flags had unexpectedly risen, but Guy was prepared to counter any participation of Jess Bennett. "I am not being unfair when I say that Mrs. Bennett is a very difficult person. And an alcoholic. I have firsthand experience with that. We can't contend with her and all her excess baggage at a time like this."

Jim eased back in the recliner, in full appraisal of Guy. "Who in the hell are you to make this kind of decision? Who are you to judge her? This concerns her immeasurably more than it does you. That woman has been in our waking thoughts all our adult lives, not yours." He leaned forward again and looked directly into Guy's eyes so there could be no mistaking his resolve. "Jess goes before I go."

Until now, the drama had seemingly belonged wholly to Guy, with himself cast as the mighty hero. But in a bolt of lightning from a lovelorn old man, he was recast as nothing more than a bit player, a mere catalyst to the two true leads. Yet an inevitable fondness had grown for this sad man, a first for Guy, and he regretted appearing diminished in his eyes.

"You are right, of course," Guy said, humbled, but very unhappy about the prospect of involving Jess Bennett. "I suppose I have no right to keep her from this."

"I make no apologies for her. Jess is Jess. She has her share of flaws, to be sure. But so do you and me." Jim looked at his wife and indicated the sofa beside him. "Please." She sat, and he gave Guy a deeply somber look but there was anxiousness in his eyes, a readiness to share. "We have an hour before you call your friend?"

Guy nodded.

"Then let me tell you our story, young man."

~ * ~

"My journey to adulthood began in New York harbor. The sight of the city was shocking enough, but I can't begin to describe to you what the sight of the *Queen Mary* towering at her dock was like to a nineteen-year-old boy about to embark. She was so long, like a skyscraper laid on its side. I remember awe and fear simultaneously. Awe at her sheer presence and fear at what she represented. The war. The war had always seemed far away and almost imaginary when it came to us out of the radio in our parlor where we sat with the breeze blowing gently through the window and the smell of my mother's cooking drifting from the kitchen. Even the tearful goodbyes as I boarded the train for boot camp didn't have as great an effect on me. But this giant, beautiful gray monster demanded fear and I knew she was about to deliver me from childhood to manhood whether I wanted it or not.

"Over twelve thousand of us embarked on that voyage. It was dangerous. The rumor swept the ship Hitler had put out a contract on her, and I remember scanning the swells for a periscope. With our brave masks on, we cursed the Nazis and played poker all the way over but fear hung heavy in the air and made liars of every one of us. Death is the great leveler, and I had prepared myself to jump overboard when the torpedoes struck and simply gulp in the water and be done with it. But we zigzagged into Gourock, Scotland, and a new fear swept over me when I saw land. I had never known an enemy, or at least one that hated me enough to take my life. I wondered if I wouldn't have been better off to have died at sea.

"As it turned out, my company was immediately ordered to London to aid with the daily aftermath of the blitz. My only sight and sound of the enemy was when they flew over in the night. The sirens would wail, and there was a mad dash for cover, then the sound of twentieth century anger all around us. The resilience of the British amazed me. No sooner had the danger passed than they were out sifting through the destruction, determined to hold their heads high. That's how I met Jess. I saw a girl with almond-shaped blue eyes and a white band in her honey hair helping an elderly couple search for their shoes in the rubble. I offered to help and was infatuated immediately. During the next bombing, I had the pleasure of holding her tight against me. I hadn't expected to encounter girls, let alone fall in love with one, but that's just how it happened.

"We spent as much time together as my duties permitted. She lived in a tiny flat with her mother. Her father was dead, and she had no brothers or sisters. A very bleak existence, I thought. Of course, I had two brothers and a sister, so our home was never quiet. Jess and her mother taught me the sweet tradition of tea-time, and there in the middle of a war, we established our very own comfortable routine. But it didn't last. After the German surrender, my company received orders to go into Germany for 'clean-up'; a confusing term at the time but, as I was to discover, really meant burying the dead."

Jim sighed heavily and looked out the window, deep in memories. "Jess knew something was wrong as soon as I walked in the door. I don't know how, since the power was out that evening, and the flat was full of shadows. She couldn't see my face yet she asked immediately, 'What is it?' I told her. Her mother gasped then sobbed softly. I'll never forget the way the candle lit Jess's face when she turned her profile in front of the window and made not a sound. Untouchable, so far away. This was the first time I had encountered that peculiar aspect of her. I walked to her and grasped her at the waist but she pulled away as though in anger. She rushed out into the street and when I caught up with her, she wouldn't look at me. I felt guilty yet had done nothing to deserve it. We walked silently in the warm dusk until we came to a small bench in a little wooded area between streets, what the British call 'the commons.' Hardly romantic, but there we sat."

Jim paused for a time and looked lovingly again at the nametag in his palm. "I took off this nametag and folded it in her hands. I didn't have the money to buy a ring so I asked her to keep this and marry me if and when I returned. This little piece of plastic was an implicit promise and only then did she begin to cry, hard and angry. I held her, and she knotted her fists against my back. Her tears soaked my shoulder. Seeing Jess cry is like witnessing a historic event.

"Afterward, she calmly placed the nametag like a brooch on her shawl collar and we held each other and kissed very passionately for a time with both of us in tears all the while. My love for her suddenly overwhelmed me and leaving her was more traumatic than the voyage over or the relentless bombings.

"She was as cool as the overcast skies the next morning, but I had come to understand that as one of the undercurrents of her personality, the deepest love masquerading as resentment, a haven for her where it was safer to be bitter than honest. She allowed only a small peck to her cheek, but she was caressing the nametag as she watched me board the bus. I was heavy-hearted to leave that wounded face, let me tell you.

"My first day on the continent was an initiation to horror. Three or four of us stood smoking in the street of a small German village. I can't remember its name. The sound of gunfire split the air. The boy next to me had been telling a dirty joke. The smile was still on his face even after his brains misted over me. We dropped like sacks of potatoes, and I had the misfortune of lying face to face to that poor boy. He lay completely still except for the fingers of his left hand dancing in the cobble. He was a dead boy grinning with the sunlight in his eyes. The sniper turned out to be an old woman sympathetic to the Nazis. That was the most horrific thing I'd ever seen, and it was several nights before I could close my eyes without seeing that death grin. But more horror awaited.

"I had seen the destruction the Germans were capable of in London but I had only heard of their atrocities against the Jews. One rainy afternoon a few days later, I watched a train arrive with concentration camp survivors, and it's a sight I will carry to my grave. Little did I know it would repeat itself in the middle of the North Atlantic."

Guy and Barbara exchanged glances.

"A band of living skeletons staggered from the train as in a nightmare and several of us were physically sick, not only from the sight but the smell of rot, as well. I believe starvation is the most haunting sight of human afflictions and never have I had such raw pity and hatred for the human race as I did that afternoon." Jim closed his eyes and gave a slight shake of the head. "There's no need to recount the details of what we found at the concentration camps.

"I was discharged in January of 1946 very much a full-grown, world-weary man and it seemed I had been away from Jess for years. Jess was quite a looker in her day, and she would certainly have had no problem finding a suitor, believe me. But she ran to me like a child, squealing, and jumped in my arms. The first thing I looked for and noticed was the nametag on her shawl. She covered me with hungry kisses and her mother finally had to scold her for making a scene. My God, were we in love!"

Guy looked at Barbara, but she absently traced a pattern on the arm of the sofa.

"Their church had been destroyed, so Jess and I married in her tiny flat with only her mother, the vicar, and the vicar's wife in attendance. There was some discussion of bringing her mother to the states with us but, in the end, she decided to stay so that she could be buried next to her husband. The three of us lived together until September of 1947 when I was finally firm with Jess and told her it was time to start our new life. My family was anxious to see me and my new wife. I didn't meet her cool resistance as I had expected because I believe she was excited about starting that new life, despite leaving her mother. I could see that excitement in the smiles she gave, in spite of herself, when I described home in southern Illinois with baseball in the back field, jumping from the tree tire at the creek, hide-and-seek in the cemetery at night, or how my mother became a tyrant during canning time. She especially liked to hear about Halloween and hayrides. And so, I had my father wire over nearly all of my savings so Mr. and Mrs. James Bennett could cross the pond in first class.

"We arrived at the Southampton docks on a dark, foggy morning and Jess and her mother were both quite subdued, understandably. The fog drifted in thick blankets around us, but an endless black wall of portholes, and those famous stacks peeked through. This was the first time Jess had ever seen her and the first time I'd seen her in peacetime colors so when the occasional ray of sunshine melted through the fog and we saw her clearly in all her glory, our breath was taken away, literally. We had no choice but be staggered by her, like being in the presence of royalty."

Guy was familiar with that lifelike facet of the *Queen Mary* and could easily imagine her asserting her dominance over the entire harbor.

"Jess embraced her mother fiercely for a very long time but never broke. Her mother sobbed, as you can imagine, but Jess held her tight and silently hid her face in her mother's hair. Her mother understood her much better than I and undoubtedly knew her daughter was screaming inside. After they parted, we walked up a narrow canvas gangway with *Queen Mary* emblazoned on its sides. Jess never looked back. She didn't want to wave to her mother from the railing as we pulled away from the dock. Safer that way, I suspect.

"We found ourselves in another world. *Queen Mary* was not at all what I remembered as a troopship. Looking back, I can see how young we were with only one suitcase between us, standing so completely overwhelmed by those glistening wood interiors. We really were backward kids, barely out of our teens, and we wandered for hours taking everything in. How simple we must have appeared. She lingered in the first class swimming pool with its elaborate staircase and balcony, richly tiled all the way to the ceiling that was mother of pearl. It was empty but not quiet with the water splashing against the sides with the movement of the ship. The first class lounge was the most beautiful room on the ship and in light of what we would encounter there in a few days, I will grant you Jess recalls every mirror, chair, and column just as I do. I remember how hesitant she was when we opened the door to our stateroom, B27, starboard forward. At first, she wouldn't step over the threshold but peered in as if she were afraid her shoes would soil the carpeting.

"The dining room was as soaring and majestic as any cathedral I had seen. We were both embarrassed to be so under-dressed. Good God, we were out of place with those tuxedoes and gowns all around us. I wore my uniform, which had some formality, but poor Jess had only a yellow chiffon dress she'd bought for Easter services a few years before. 'Memories of a lifetime,' I kept whispering to her. When a waiter came to our table and began to flambe a dish, all diners turned excitedly toward us. Jess was mortified. When the flames burst upward, she screamed and brought a ripple of laughter. Our unease must have been glaringly obvious because an older couple watched us from a nearby table for some time, smiling at us, and we were certainly the topic of their conversation. Before dessert, they came over and introduced themselves as Frank and Emily Schofield from upstate New York. They placed us under their wing for the rest of the voyage.

"Now, Guy, sometimes older people take a vicarious interest in young people in love because that is a part of their lives that has become history. As you age, you'll understand the fascination, mark my words. Well, Mr. and Mrs. Schofield had been married for so long they were able to complete each other's sentences. Or, Mrs.

Schofield completed his sentences. She always carried their conversation. I have never met another human being who could talk like her. Her husband rarely finished a sentence, and he simply nodded when she asked, 'Isn't that right, Frank?' I told Jess we needed to open a porthole after she left to let all the words out.

"They owned three restaurants in Manhattan and were expert people-watchers. Mrs. Schofield proudly told us she knew from first sight we were not newlyweds but were just beginning our marriage, we had never been aboard a luxury liner, and we weren't traveling for pleasure. She also informed us she would be happy to read our tea leaves.

"The Schofields were early risers and knocked on our cabin door each morning at five for a 'constitutional' walk on the promenade deck. Jess was queasy this particular morning after an incredibly rough gale the day before and almost didn't get out of bed."

Guy interrupted with some wonder, "The message indicated there had been rough weather and, in fact, Illingworth commented it 'gave passengers fits'."

Jim nodded. "Yes, it was quite rough but September 6 dawned with a much smoother sea. At the last moment, Jess decided to go with us. It was bitterly cold, but the first rays of sunlight reached out over the ocean casting the *Queen Mary* in bronze. We walked and waited for the sun to peek over the horizon, listening to Mrs. Schofield talk all the while."

"Do you remember an electrical storm?" Guy asked.

"Yes. Lightning streaked from the dark clouds across the western sky. Yet there was no thunder."

"What about static electricity?"

Jim nodded gravely. "But that was overshadowed by our concern when the deck lights went out and then, within seconds, the engines stopped."

Guy's pulse quickened as that inner music drove onward in tempo and timbre, a marching progression toward the crescendo of revelation. "That was the electrical interference again but much closer. Close enough to trip every breaker," he ventured. "And with the electrical systems gone, the engines must have shut down completely. I'll bet the navigational systems were gone as well."

"I have no idea," Jim said. "The decks were deserted at that hour except for some officers on their rounds. We saw two of them racing toward the bridge, no doubt to inquire about the sudden stopping. We hadn't felt anything to indicate a collision, and I remember wondering if she hadn't thrown a propeller. But that didn't explain the loss of power. The *Queen Mary* was absolutely dead in the water. It was a strange feeling to drift after being at a full gallop for three days. The sunshine slowly faded as those dark clouds from the west overcame us. The humidity changed, as well. Our coats and shawls became unbearably warm, and condensation was forming on the promenade windows. Streaks of lightning began striking all around the ship, and we decided to wait in the lounge until a steward or bellboy appeared for us to question."

Jim took a deep breath and looked sideways at Guy. "And then began the most extraordinary event in our lives."

Six

Guy leaned closer to Jim, hanging on every word. Jim stammered a moment or two, deeply moved by recalling the event aloud for the first time. The man swallowed and interlaced his fingers, then stared up into Guy's eyes and spoke in a deepened voice. "Have you ever had an event so possess you that you judge all others by it? An event so much larger than life that you feel belittled but still in awe?"

Guy nodded. "I believe I experienced the ultimate one last night."

"Well, yes, you did. But let me go back a bit. When I was in Germany, I walked past a convent very early one drab morning, and the voices that reached my ears transformed me. Despite the horror that had taken place there, this exquisite chorus rose up and baptized that place with a peace beyond my understanding. One voice sang out... anguished but beautiful, and it was answered by many. I stood stunned by its splendid nobility, even though I didn't understand a word."

Jim looked upward, toward the ceiling, his face bright with the memory. "The voices held the awesomeness of a countryside in full sunshine, or a field of unbroken snow, the sound of pure humanity and existence. I wish I could tell you what the hymn was, but I had certainly never heard anything like it before or since."

"*Dixit dominus*?" Guy offered.

Jim lifted a shoulder, let it fall. "I'm afraid I don't know what that is. But I felt privileged to hear it, felt I was *meant* to hear it. For whatever reason, it spoke very clearly to me. Can you understand?"

"Yes," Guy whispered, astounded that he actually had something in common with another man, particularly something so intimate. “Mine was ‘Allegretto,’ from Beethoven’s Seventh Symphony.”

“This event had that same affect, but on a much deeper level. The sensation of being in the presence of something so far beyond human experience it couldn’t be grasped. Something spiritual, I guess, like the voices from that convent.” Jim closed his eyes as he continued speaking. “Anyway, with the power gone, the lounge was cast in twilight. A perpetual overcast making everything darkly vibrant. I stood beside Mrs. Schofield, who sat talking. We faced Jess and Mr. Schofield, who also sat. I heard something over Mrs. Schofield’s voice that I can only describe as the soft rustling of leaves.”

“Or water running over rocks? A rippling sound?”

Jim’s eyes opened wide. “Yes!” Exuberant, he raised a finger. “That is exactly what it sounded like! Exactly. I looked over Jess’s head and saw three figures descending slowly from behind the columns, as though they were walking down invisible steps. Mrs. Schofield was so shocked into silence that she drew a deep breath and held it with her eyes wide and bulging. Jess and Mr. Schofield twisted around, their dropped jaws simultaneously. The figures seemed to float as they came closer, passing behind another column, then gained substance. Jess whimpered in fear and leaped up from the sofa and looked as though she might flee.”

Jim spread his arms to each side, his palms open. “We saw quite clearly then, a young, exotic, long-haired woman, naked, with a child in each hand, a boy and girl, and they were naked, as well. That young woman was beautiful...olive skin...dark hair hanging past her waist. She gazed wide-eyed about the room. The girl was about two years old, and the boy was no more than a year. He tottered along, and it was obvious he hadn’t been walking too long. They looked Mediterranean, but their faces were emaciated, their eye sockets hollowed out. She was also afraid, and she hesitated before she approached us.”

Jim grew quiet a moment, staring off into memory then he again turned his eyes toward Guy. “She looked across our faces and decided upon Jess, I guess, because she appeared about the same age. And she was a female. She began speaking, but of course, we couldn’t understand what she said.” Jim stopped and closed his eyes, lost in another time. “I can hear that broken voice, still. So sad and filled with desperation.

"Jess brought a hand to her mouth, her eyes were wide as the woman beseeched her in that unknown language." He leaned forward, his eyes bright and wet. "Then, she spoke a language we all understood. She lifted the girl's arm and pointed to the girl's ribs and pelvis. Poor little thing, her bones protruded like a skeleton's. The woman looked back at Jess, a haunted look about her...their eyes locked." Jim nodded. "Jess understood immediately why the woman was there and what she wanted. The woman wept, showed Jess the boy's ribs.

"I had seen that same scene when the concentration camp survivors stepped from the train. I hoped I would never see anything like that again. Wherever they came from, whatever predicament they were forced to endure, we could not know. But anyone could see they were in dire straits. That woman's face was wild with desperation. I could hardly bear to hear her cry. It was a moment both incredible and heartbreaking."

Barbara sniffed, and Guy turned. So lost in the story, he forgot she sat with them. Jim looked at his wife, blinked, then looked toward the window.

"Jess gently reached out and took that pitiful creature's hands," he said. "Her show of compassion brought more tears. Jess did not cry, but she somehow commiserated with that woman, and they shared a language beyond words in the twilight of that vast room." He stared at his hands, now lying in his lap like old sheets of parchment.

He took a deep breath and resumed his story. "Jess pulled the stranger close and she dropped her head to Jess's shoulder, sobbing for a long moment. Then she straightened, wiped her tears, and knelt to the children. She spoke softly to them in that strange language. They listened to her intently, and both looked up at Jess at the same time."

Jim rubbed his arms. "It gives me chills just remembering their uncertain stare. The woman embraced and kissed each of them, then stood and was turning to walk the way she had come, when Jess reached for her again and took her hand. Jess took the nametag from her shawl and placed it in the woman's hand. 'Bennett,' Jess said, pointing at herself with her free hand. 'Bennett.' The woman looked at the tag in her palm then at Jess. 'Bennett,' Jess said, inviting her to repeat the word.

"The woman timidly opened her mouth." Jim looked at Guy,

his eyes wide. “My name fell from the lips of a woman who visited from God only knows where. ‘Bennett,’ she said. She repeated it three more times.” He shook his head and stared at the nametag in his hand, still amazed at what had transpired those many years ago. “I had given Jess this nametag as a promise of my love for her. She in turn gave it to that woman as a promise to love her babies.” He pushed his forearm toward Guy so he might see the goose bumps. “My God, young man, can you even begin to imagine that scene? Can you?”

“No, I can’t imagine,” Guy said. “I truly cannot.” He stared at the little piece of plastic, a trinket imbued with history even richer than he could have anticipated. He still had a sense it belonged to him in some way and barely resisted the urge to take it from Jim.

Barbara wept quietly and cast a furtive glance over her shoulder to the children’s school pictures as though seeing them for the first time.

“The woman folded the nametag in her palm and turned to walk the way she had come,” said Jim. “Her shoulders were wracked and she hurried away, sobbing loudly now. The little girl ran after her, but the woman seemed to ascend again just a foot or so off the carpeting and just…just…” Jim stared beyond Guy with a faraway look. “Lightning flashed, and the woman shimmered for a moment, then she was simply no longer there, as if she had stepped through a doorway.”

Jim sat quiet for a moment and the pause after such a recollection reverberated like a piano key sounding in a deserted room.

“The little girl fell to the carpeting and called out an unknown word, then lay there crying,” Jim continued. “Jess was right there to pick her up and comfort her. The boy remained oblivious. He sat happily on the carpeting, picking at its designs. After that, everything happened so quickly I can hardly recall what we did next. It was like the suspension you feel at the top of the teeter-totter before the sudden downward rush.” Jim moved his hands up and down opposite one another as he spoke.

“The next thing I remember, I was trotting down a corridor with the boy in my arms, following Jess, carrying the sobbing girl. The lights flickered on, and I looked behind me for the Schofields. Mrs. Schofield looked very feeble as Mr. Schofield led her by the arm. Steward bells rang madly and the poor stewards were falling over themselves to answer their curious passengers. We passed a bellhop who glanced at the naked children, then shot a hard look at Jess and I. By the time we were in the cabin, the engines were throbbing far below. The *Queen Mary* was underway.

"Jess paced with the girl, cooing, but the boy had fallen asleep, and I laid him on the bed. Mrs. Schofield sat very quiet and pale, in a state of shock. 'Has she spoken yet?' I asked Mr. Schofield. He shook his head. He looked very white himself, and I worried for them both.

"The girl still whimpered and called out in an unknown language for several minutes, but eventually she cried herself to sleep. Jess laid her beside her brother. None of us spoke for the longest time. Jess and I just stood at the bed staring down at the miraculous mystery thrust upon us from this mid-ocean encounter with a fellow traveler.

"Golden rays flooded through the portholes and I was surprised the sun had not yet fully risen. I had lost all track of time. It seemed as though hours had passed since the children had arrived when, in reality, it could only have been minutes.

"After a time, Mr. Schofield stood and joined us at the bed. 'Never in all my wildest dreams,' he said over and over. I remember how he nervously folded and unfolded his arms. Then he said, 'They come from a place that never had to pay for Adam and Eve's sin.'

"I didn't understand, and the look I gave him must have told him so. 'They're not ashamed of their bodies,' he explained.

"'They've suffered,' Mrs. Schofield said in a spent voice, and we all looked at her. She staggered upright, dazed and very subdued. She slowly motioned to Jess. 'Come, dear,' she said. 'We must shop for clothes.' Jess looked reluctant to leave them and said, 'The shops won't be open at this hour.' Mrs. Schofield said very confidently, 'A steward *will* open for me. We must get back before they wake up.' Jess took a shuddering breath and finally pulled herself away, then followed Mrs. Schofield out the door.

"No sooner had the door closed behind them than the girl awoke. She leaped from the bed and looked wildly about the room, shifting from one leg to the other. I thought by her manner that she was having a sleepwalking nightmare, but Mr. Schofield said excitedly, 'Get her to the bathroom!' I grabbed her and ran to the toilet and sat her on it. She peed and had the most confused expression as she looked down at the toilet. I wiped her, picked her up, and paced as I had seen Jess do. I was certain she would cry again, but she wearily laid her head on my shoulder and wrapped her little arms around me. It was an oddly comforting feeling. All my nervousness left with that warm, bony bundle in my arms.

"'We should order something for her to eat,' Mr. Schofield said. I agreed, and he picked up the white telephone and ordered cabin service. When I tried to put down the girl, she threw a fit and gripped me tightly. So, when the food arrived, I sat her on my lap and held the plate for her. She obviously didn't recognize the utensils, but picked up the toast and scrambled eggs with her fingers with a delicacy beyond her years. When she was finished, she simply sucked the tips of her thumb and forefinger clean," said Jim, holding up his fingers in memory.

"It was very elegant and mannered, almost humorous. I don't have to tell you how fascinated we were watching her, and I'm sure Mr. Schofield's mind traveled down the same pathways of imagination as mine.

"When Jess and Mrs. Schofield came back, she reached for Jess right away, the bond already secured. Mrs. Schofield had bought several dresses, suits for the boy, stockings, underwear, and slippers. She held up two pairs of slippers to Mr. Schofield and me, a pink pair and a blue pair. 'We couldn't find childrens' shoes so they'll have to wear these until we get to New York.'"

"What a thoughtful woman," said Barbara, and again Guy turned, startled by her presence.

Jim nodded, smiled, and patted his wife's hand. Then he turned back to Guy. "Jess sat with the girl and tenderly pulled stockings onto her feet. The girl didn't fight, but watched with great interest. Pulling the dress over her head, however...that proved much more problematic." Jim chuckled. "She cried and called out in that strange language, for her mother, I suppose, but Jess cooed and rocked her until the child was finally pliant in her hands.

"Meanwhile, the boy woke, sat bolt upright and looked round with sheer terror on his face. When he spotted his sister, he immediately ran to her and reached up. Jess knelt so he could touch her, then he climbed onto Jess's other hip. Jess rose with both of them hanging onto her, and I thought how the three of them looked so natural together, picture perfect, but for the boy's nakedness. Jess looked at me and said, 'Her name is Kathleen, after my grandmother. His name is Zachary, after your grandfather.'

"It struck me then that Jess and I were now different people than we had been just an hour earlier, and nothing would ever be the same again. She wasn't exactly a stranger, but she was now more than a wife."

Jim again looked out the window, staring into the past. "Jess had splintered before my eyes, had been completely redefined, to both herself and to me. I am ashamed to say her sudden empowerment disturbed me. From that morning on, she would never belong solely to me again. Not to say that I ever knew anything less than pure love for those children, but they were harbingers of change. The path I envisioned for our lives suddenly forked. I followed Jess down the path we were clearly meant to take." He looked at Guy and shrugged then a smile crept across his papery lips.

"Those children ate everything placed before them in the same delicate manner, and they napped most of the day. There was more whimpering, sure, especially when it grew dark. At one point, the boy ran to a chair and stood on it to look out the porthole to the night sky, and he cried the same word the girl used when her mother left her. The stars and moon were brighter at sea than on land, much more dominant, and many times that first night, I caught Jess at the porthole, also staring up to the sky.

"Jess and I didn't sleep or eat, but we stood and sat by turns, always looking down on the sleeping children with the same sense of awe, weak-kneed from the reality of the unreality. Time didn't exist that first night, and before we knew it, the first ray of sunshine reached through the portholes.

"Mrs. Schofield sat through the night in silent meditation, but at dawn she stood and walked unsteadily to the bed and abruptly began crying. 'Dear God, that poor woman! That poor, poor woman!' She buried her face in her hands and, between tears and gasps for air, we heard broken fragments of sentences. She was a wreck. Jess, of course, didn't break. She's amazingly strong, but her face filled with tender compassion as she watched Mr. Schofield take his wife by the arm and gently coax her from the cabin. Mrs. Schofield was actually the bravest of the four of us. She did what we all were on the verge of doing—let loose our emotions."

Jim held open his hands. "I guess you could call me a male chauvinist, but I wasn't about to show how frayed my nerves were in front of Jess, who was an expert at hiding hers. I could only hope she wouldn't see my hands trembling.

"The children had slept through the night, hardly changing positions, and I wondered what they and their mother endured that made them so weary. When the boy opened his eyes, mine was the first face he saw, and the sweetest grin spread across his face." Jim smiled at the memory. "I already had simple love for those children, as if we had journeyed together a long way for a very long time. We were made inseparable by the experience.

"We ordered cabin service for our meals. We couldn't even consider eating in the dining room with them, which suited Jess fine. They were livelier that day because of their full bellies, plus they had a day and night of sleep, so after breakfast, we decided to venture outside of the cabin.

"They watched each other being dressed and groomed with great interest, paying particular attention to the hairbrush. The clothes hung on them. The slippers, oh, they hated the slippers. We diligently put them back on each time they removed them. When I rapped on the Schofields' door, Mr. Schofield answered and whispered that Mrs. Schofield was exhausted and had just fallen to sleep. He told me they would visit us in the evening. He looked like a hundred-year-old man.

"We roamed the rich corridors and lounges hand-in-hand. In one gallery, Kathleen was entranced by a silver vase full of red carnations. She tiptoed up and gently ruffled them with her finger. Imagine the steward's surprise to find not a single carnation in any of the vases, because Jess pulled every one of them for Kathleen!" Jim chuckled.

"Jess was afraid the children would catch colds easily, being so underweight, so we walked the enclosed promenade deck, rather than the sun deck. I hoisted both of them up to the window to see the great bow plowing through the ocean, but evidently they had seen an ocean before. They were much more interested in the ship herself. They rattled doorknobs, picked up the receiver of the white telephones and listened to the operator's voice come through. They examined sofas, tables, light switches, silverware, china, vases, handrails, and especially the toilets. Oh, they enjoyed flushing the toilets." He grinned. "Anything but everything, I tell you, invited their curiosity. The elevators startled them the first time we used them, but after that they were infatuated. Jess and I indulged them all the while.

"Jess wanted to show them the swimming pool. She had never

seen one herself, before we boarded the *Queen Mary,* and her fascination had not waned. There were a handful of splashing swimmers, and Jess watched with something approaching envy. If she'd had a bathing suit, I believe I could have coaxed her to take a plunge.

"Zachary needed no coaxing. He took a flying jump and plunged in fully clothed. Scared me half to death. I immediately jumped in after him, but he was in no danger. He swam like a fish. Each time he was within my grasp, he dove and swam away."

Guy laughed, imagining the scene, and Jim grinned at him and nodded. "It must have been comical to see a fully clothed man struggling to catch a small boy, because the laughter echoed crazily against that vaulted ceiling," Jim said. "I finally grabbed Zachary, and he giggled for the first time. No one laughed harder than Jess. It was the first time I had heard her laugh since before I left for Germany. It was a very good sound to hear.

"That evening, we bathed the children together, and they had a grand time. Jess and I were soaked and exhausted by the time we finished. The Schofields came over as we were drying them. Mrs. Schofield had collected herself dramatically since the day before, but her eyes remained puffy. She took over drying Zach from me in a very methodical manner. She looked to Jess. 'We insist upon being part of their lives. You don't expect us to simply say goodbye after...after all that's happened, do you?'

"Jess shook her head and said, 'Of course not.' Mrs. Schofield arched an eyebrow. 'Frank and I plan to visit you in Illinois. We want to be a part of their lives, and yours.' Then she stopped drying and looked at Jess with a most sincere expression. 'A part of you will always be with us now. Don't you know that?' Jess nodded, and Mr. Schofield still folded and unfolded his arms each time he looked at the children.

"We were due to dock in New York late the next morning. After breakfast, the officers passed us at a brisker pace. The passengers hustled in and out of their cabins preparing to disembark and trying to flag bellboys. The corridors were full of luggage and trunks. We only had our one suitcase and a bag of clothing for the children, so we escaped that nightmare.

"'We'll meet you on the pier,' Mrs. Schofield called to us in the corridor then she disappeared back into their cabin.

"'I want to see everything again,' Jess said to me with childlike enthusiasm. 'I want to memorize everything, so I can treasure it in my heart for as long as I live.' I wished I had bought a camera before we left England, but I had pretty well depleted my savings to get first class tickets. We set out for the dining room and stood below that huge black and gold map of the North Atlantic. It had a crystal *Queen Mary* that had moved along the route as the ship herself had, and now stopped at the glistening skyscrapers representing New York. We viewed the pool from the overhanging balcony one deck above, in case Zachary decided to take another plunge. Jess stayed very quiet, and she moved about in solemn reverence. She knew as well as I that we would never have such an adventure again.

"Turns out, visiting the lounge was a mistake. Kathleen remembered very well and ran behind the columns, frantically calling for her mother. Zach followed his sister. They raced around each column expectantly, and Jess and I stood heartbroken as we watched them. Kathleen began crying and ran to Jess, burying her face in Jess's thigh. I picked up Zach, and we left hastily for the sun deck.

"Crowds were already gathering at the rails in anticipation of landfall. The city throbbed just over the horizon—we could feel it. It was a gloriously bright morning, and Kathleen's tear-stained face dissipated into a broad smile when she saw the towering stacks above us. Her eyes were like saucers as she leant back in Jess's arms to take them in fully. Jess made a broad, sweeping motion with her arm, trying to encompass the ship, and said, '*Queen Mary*.' She repeated it slowly several times, and Kathleen studied her lips. 'Keen Mawi,' the girl managed gleefully, and we clapped and made over her so much that she said it again and again."

Even now, Jim's face beamed with pride, and he smiled at Barbara, whose own smile registered certain sadness.

"New York was just a speck off the starboard bow," Jim continued. "But then the city burst upon us and kept growing. Passengers lined the rails as we passed the Statue of Liberty, and the cameras clicked like locusts on a summer night. Jess absolutely beamed, and I could have sworn she even had tears in her eyes.

"I lifted Kathleen to my shoulders, and she posed her arm in imitation of Lady Liberty, which attracted the attention of a photographer. 'Splendid,' he said and snapped a picture. Zach squatted and pressed his face against the lower bars of the railing and watched the tugs far below us with rapt attention.

"Jess lingered on board as long as she could, until finally the chaos of housekeepers and stewards preparing for a turnabout voyage gave us reason to leave. As when we had boarded her, Jess kept her head down, fearful to look back, I suppose, lest she cry.

"Mr. and Mrs. Schofield were waiting on the pier for us. Mrs. Schofield placed one white-gloved hand to my face and kissed my cheek, then she moved on to the children. She stooped and kissed both of them and said words that made Jess and I lift our heads sharply. 'Take care of Mommy and Daddy, my dears.'"

Jim held out his palms. "This was the first time we had been referred to as parents. I was shocked, but Jess had a quizzical look on her face at first, then she shined with pure pride. Mr. Schofield took my hand and said not a word, but gave me the most intent look I've ever received. It was as though he imparted silent strength to me. He pulled out his wallet, took out four one-hundred-dollar bills and handed them to me. I objected, of course. Mrs. Schofield said, 'Please let us do this much. You'll have to buy them more clothes, and don't forget shoes. Buy them just a pinky-finger too big, so they might grow into them,' she instructed us.

"Jess was saved for last. Mr. Schofield simply took her by the shoulders and kissed her on both cheeks in the European manner. Mrs. Schofield gazed intently at Jess and was preparing to say something, but they suddenly embraced fiercely as women do when emotions run too deep for expression. She turned and hurried away, crying. Jess watched her with the deepest compassion. But we saw them again...for a week every summer, until their deaths.

"The four of us, our new family, lingered on the pier, waiting for the crowds to thin before we hailed a taxi." Jim smiled crookedly. "The truth is, we were very sad to leave the *Queen Mary*. We stared at that majestic bulk towering above us for over an hour. Kathleen said 'Keen Mawi' with a smile, and we sadly made our way to the street. That ship marked the beginning of our golden age, a piece of personal history that we wished we could repeat endlessly like a never-ending circle."

Jim leaned forward. "As a matter of fact, Guy, the *Queen Mary* has come full circle. She carried me toward manhood on my first voyage, then our life-changing encounter on the return voyage. Now, over fifty years later, your experience aboard her has brought Jess and I together with you, and hopefully, with that woman. She was meant to be a miraculous, pivotal point in all our lives." He shook his head in naked awe. "There is definitely a divine hand at work, don't you agree?"

Guy took a long, deep breath before answering. "I'm not sure." He considered the providential nature of his relationship with these strangers. Was divine clockwork of fate responsible for bringing them to this moment, this situation? Predestination negated free will, so Guy rejected it. He actually preferred the notion, however illusory, of eternal choice. The idea of a divine clock, set into irrevocable motion for each individual, made all of life seem irrelevant.

"Why bother with agonizing over life's decisions if they've already been decided for us?" he asked Jim.

"They haven't. But God knows before you do what your decision will be." Jim inclined his head and raised his brows. "Surely you've heard the saying, 'Our time is not God's time.' He sees the past and future as present. He knows which decision will bring about His will and which will not."

Guy frowned. "Then why are so many wrong decisions made?"

"Who are we to say they are wrong, in regards to His will? Judas made a terrible decision, but it was the one God intended. If he hadn't, there would have been no crucifixion and no resurrection." Jim leaned back and regarded Guy as a teacher does a student. "What if Mrs. Schofield did not decide to take us along on her early morning constitutional at the precise time the children and their mother arrived? What if Jess had decided to stay in bed, and there was no mother-figure for that woman to leave her children with?" He paused, and locked eyes with Guy. "What if that radio message you told me about was not sent and intercepted?"

Guy gave a doubtful smile. "It could have all been chance. Simple choices."

Jim shook his head adamantly. "I believe Jess and I were meant to meet each other in the rubble that morning in London. I believe we were meant to encounter that woman and children. We were meant to raise them as our own."

Barbara shifted uncomfortably on her chair, then stood and cleared her throat. "I'll make tea." She padded softly toward the kitchen, leaving the two men alone.

Guy leaned forward, his elbows on his knees, and he spoke softly. "Were the children both meant to die so young? What was the reason for their existence, let alone their arrival, if they barely reached adulthood? God's will?" Guy sat back again. "I'm not sure I'm prepared to accept that."

Jim took a deep breath, exhaled slowly. "Neither was Jess," he said resignedly. He looked about the room and sighed as if in deep contemplation of raising an unpleasant subject. Then he turned back to Guy. "I'd like to talk about Jess, now."

Seven

"Homecoming belonged to Jess. My parents were waiting at the train depot for us and as soon as we stepped off the train with a child each, my mother let out a shocked gasp and brought a hand to her mouth. Fortunately, my dark skin, hair, and eyes were a good match to the children. 'You can't deny them, boy,' my father said. He was thrilled but Mama did the math. She knew our wedding date. Nine-month-old Zachary could be the product of our eighteen-month marriage but there was no way Kathleen was conceived lawfully. Bastard children were a disgrace in those days and Mama looked at Jess as though she were a tramp. I immediately coaxed Mama to walk down the train depot with me. I wrapped an arm around her and poured on my best 'your baby boy' charm and convinced her Jess was the love of my life and we had consummated that love only after I told Jess I may not come back. The shame of premarital sex explained why I hadn't written of them in my letters. Mama didn't seem to remember I had gone into Germany only *after* the surrender.

"Everything worked for us, including the war. If they didn't have their shots, it was because of the shortages of war. If they didn't have birth certificates, it was because they were destroyed during the blitz. If they had unusual accents and speech, it was because of an American father and a British mother. If they were too thin, it was because of food rationing. If Kathleen was born out of wedlock, it was because of my imminent orders to Germany and possible, if not certain, death.

"We made up birthdays for them and Jess was embarrassed that she would have to pretend to be less than 'pure' but such was our situation. 'Why must I be made a tart?' she agonized to me in private.

"Tart or not, Jess fell in love at first sight of our farm house. My grandfather had built it. It was, and still is, I suppose, a great Victorian mass of porches and gabled dormers. To her, it was a mansion and I will never forget how her mouth dropped as she edged closer to the dash when we pulled up the drive. The London flat's entire sitting room and kitchen would have fit comfortably in our front parlor. My sister and younger brothers were waiting on the porch for us and they ran to greet me with a flurry of bear hugs and kisses. After an awkward few minutes of appraisal, one of my brothers took Jess's hand to show her the house while my sister and other brother rushed to take the children. My sister accepted Jess as her sister and my brothers had their crushes on her, stammering and laughing nervously in her presence. I had never seen my father try to impress anyone but he was very intrigued by my young wife and was very much a charmer anytime she was near. Mama had an air of disapproval for several days but she couldn't resist her own grandchildren, bastards or not.

"The memory of our encounter in mid-Atlantic still sent chills up our backs so we naturally thought explaining the children would be our ultimate test. But Jess was of much more interest to my family and community than the children. Don't get me wrong. Kathleen and Zachary received their fair share of adulation but Jess was everyone's darling. Her British accent was exotic to Herald, Illinois and Mama soon became proud of the attention her first daughter-in-law attracted in church and at the store. Shortly after our arrival, Jess had a 'tea' for all the neighbors and church women and they showed up in all their finery and sat in mama's parlor like genteel belles, erect and proper, sipping from their cups and eating something called crumpets with their plump pinky fingers extended. It was like a little girl's dress-up party but with adults. Mama glowed in glory and she and Jess began their own daily tradition of tea for two at tea-time, a welcome break from their chores. One young girl I graduated from high school with even curtsied gravely when introduced to Jess! 'Like meeting the Queen,' she said. I didn't have the heart to tell her of Jess's humble origins in a London flat.

"Except for the awkwardness of being 'tarted up', a phrase Jess always used, she absolutely never believed herself an outsider. She told me a few weeks after our homecoming she had never been happier in her life and seemed surprised considering she was unaccustomed to constant noise and activity. I also think she figured she was in some way insulting her mother by being so adjusted and content. When I mentioned finding our own place, she bowed her head and asked that I let her revel in being part of a family for just a little longer. She never showed interest in leaving so I never raised the subject again.

"The children cried less and less every night and recognized Jess and I as 'Mommy' and 'Daddy.' The first time Zach called my father 'Pa-Pa,' he wept. The children explored their new world with the same curiosity they had shown on the *Queen Mary*. Everyone commented on their curiosity. It was fascinating to see them so awestruck by things we took for granted, the staircase and banister, the radio, and especially food. My mother, disturbed by their thinness, spoiled them in the kitchen. They mastered spoons and forks quickly and soon their little bellies became round and their energy resonated within the walls of our old house. Outside, they ran joyfully barefoot over the lawn and their giggles and squeals carried on the country breezes well into the evenings. They were content and Jess was content. Blessedly so. I tell you, whenever Jess smiled or laughed out loud I believed God was blessing me." Jim smiled bashfully at Guy, a bit sadly. "I guess I'm just a sentimental old man."

Guy shook his head. "Not at all," he said, and wondered when the last time was he had seen Lynn smile. The answer was unwelcome.

"I didn't work in the fields with Dad but got a job as an insurance salesman. It was rough going in the beginning but eventually, I made a very good living for my family. As long as I had Jess and the kids at home at the end of the day, I was happy. I know I must sound like an incredible simpleton to you but all I wanted out of life was my wife and kids in rural southern Illinois. Those were truly our golden years. My brothers and sister married and moved off to the cities, Mama and Dad grew old as the children grew up. Jess's accent faded and she assumed our Midwestern twang although she still used 'bloody' and 'bum' quite a bit. Our love grew stronger during those years. Our arguments always ended with tender apologies and lovemaking in the night."

"What about the children?" Guy asked. "Was there ever a time during childhood that indicated they were...different?"

"They were absolutely no different from other children. Kathleen had a speech impediment early on, I think because she had already begun a language with her real mother when she arrived, but it disappeared once she started school. Zach had appendicitis when he was seven and there was a flickering moment of worry the surgeon may discover he was not anatomically correct." Jim laughed and looked at the ceiling. "When Kathleen began her period, she ran to me and told me she must have hurt herself on the bicycle seat. Jess's mother was very prudish and had never discussed such things, so naturally Jess didn't either. Together, we endured the growing pains of acne, training bras, and first loves."

Jim paused and looked out over the lawn. "All the while, the memory, the irrevocable truth of that woman haunted us like a ghost flitting about at every momentous event in their lives. There were times I would find Jess's solitary figure leaning against a porch column, contemplating the night sky. We would lie in bed at night while the crickets cheeped and the wind breathed through the curtains, staring at the ceiling, knowing each other awake and in deep thought. That was the time of our most intimate conversations with whispered promises of love and, of course, musings about our children. That was the only time we discussed the nature of their arrival and wondered at that poor woman's heart-wrenching decision."

"You must have driven yourself mad wondering where they came from, why they left," Guy said.

"Many times in the night. Many, many times. It was apparently a world very much like ours because they were unfazed by the natural world. Oceans, trees, grass, animals, clouds, snow, and rain held no unusual fascination for them. Our man-made world, however, was a different story."

"You must know the fact of their existence has a disturbing impact on the theory of evolution," Guy said.

"How is that?"

Guy looked him squarely in the eye and said in a deeply profound voice, "If they were physically just like us, it means evolution is a predestined path."

Jim thought a moment then gave a little shrug. "I am not a deep thinker and have never pretended to be one. As far as I am concerned, they were gifts from God who chose us to save them. End of speculation."

Jim's sincere belief in fate seemed a stubborn refusal to see beyond the bounds of the private domain of his own mind. Guy wondered if Jim was unable to ponder such deep thoughts. He didn't know whether to admire him for his devotion or to pity him for it.

"When the Schofields visited, they carried on the charade that the children were ours, even in private. They would silently watch the children from their lawn chairs with looks of privileged knowledge but they never spoke of our encounter on the *Queen Mary*. And each time they visited, she insisted upon buying the children shoes and leaving money on the dresser. The depth of our kindred relationship was obvious, particularly at leave-taking with such long embraces and Mrs. Schofield's tears. This was the only time my mother ever skirted an uncomfortable question, 'How could you possibly have such close ties with people you only met at dinner for a few days at sea?'

"Jess became the pillar of our family, more from her stubbornness not to reveal herself than true strength, I believe. I was out of town the day Dad died. He had a heart attack in the fields early that morning, and one of the hands came running to the house, bypassed my mother and went straight to Jess whom he knew would take over while Mama fell apart. Jess called the ambulance then outran Mama into the fields. It was clearly too late to save him so they both dropped in the ruts on either side of him, and each took a hand. You can imagine my mother's agony as he spoke his goodbyes to her, and then he looked to Jess and told her, 'Thank you for bringing so much life to our house. I sure would like to see my babies one more time. Take care of them now. Take care of Mama. Take care of Jimmy. You are just what he has always needed.' Then he turned his eyes back to Mama and took his last breath.

"Jess picked out his casket and the clothes he would wear while Mama lay on the sofa shattered. Jess waited on the porch swing for the children to get off the school bus and gently broke the news to them then embraced their racking bodies. In those days, the dead lay in state in their own homes and Jess prepared the front parlor for his casket and the onslaught of flowers. She took care of every detail. She offered her shoulder to my brothers and sister when they arrived. And she was there for me. We were all in shock and grief and depended on Jess for comfort, and to make decisions. Truth be told, she was burdened with more than she deserved but, knowing Jess, would she have permitted anything less?

"After Dad died, Mama was never the same and had seemingly grown old overnight. She deferred to Jess on everything.

Jess was the disciplinarian and only used me as the ultimate threat of punishment to the children. But I can't remember ever striking either of them. They were good children, and I say that not as a proud parent but as a matter of fact. Oh, Zach had a wild streak, make no doubt of that, but he was simply all boy. A good boy. And Kathleen had some friction with Jess as she grew into a young woman, but most girls are that way. Jess was a threat to her independence, but their spats never lasted long. Jess always had the final say."

Jim sighed and looked down at his clasped hands. "Kathleen suddenly had a bad cough and trouble catching her breath the summer she turned seventeen. She had always been asthmatic, and we assumed it was allergies. But it persisted, and our family doctor couldn't find anything, so he referred us to a specialist in St. Louis. He diagnosed a rare lung disease much like cystic fibrosis, which usually strikes children. There was no cure. I've always wondered if it wasn't a common disease from wherever she came that had lain dormant. We were devastated but Jess steeled herself. She was the one who told Kathleen she would not get better. Jess asked to be held in the nights and her goodbye kisses lingered every morning but she never wept.

"Perhaps Kathleen learned some of Jess's resolve because she was never morose or angry. She continued to fuss with her brother, kept up with her classmate's escapades, and even maintained a relationship with a boyfriend until the daily gruel of clearing her lungs became too much for him.

"Mama always seemed to be wringing a handkerchief and drying her eyes, in a perpetual state of grief in the ten years since losing Daddy. Comforting Mama became as much a part of Jess's daily routine as taking care of Kathleen. Then one morning, Mama simply didn't wake up. The coroner told us she was ate up with cancer. The shock of death descended over the house once again, and Jess took over. Kathleen sat at the burial service with an oxygen tank at her side, and I could see the horror in Jess's eyes as she realized the family plot was also waiting for her daughter.

"Kathleen was hospitalized the last three months of her life and when the time came, Jess, Zach, and I gathered around her bed as she said her goodbyes. Her breathing became labored, and it hurt me like hell to see my girl suffer. She pulled the oxygen tubes from her nostrils and motioned us closer. She was too weak to hug us but kissed each of us on the mouth and stared at us with limpid eyes, trying to calm her breathing, or perhaps, to stop it altogether and put herself out of misery. She rested her eyes on Jess a moment then they glazed over. 'Oh, Mommy,' she said and was gone."

Jim swallowed but did not look up. His rheumy eyes seemed lost in the past. "Jess broke down and I was allowed to hold her as the tears fell. She trembled against me like so many years before when I gave her this nametag and left for Germany. Bitterness and sorrow were sisters and, strange as it may sound. I felt like a great man by exorcising them for her. I was allowed to be the strong one for that little time.

"As I told you, we were prepared for Kathleen's death. Jess and I commiserated together, were actually drawn closer through our grief. She hardly let me out of her sight, which thrilled me beyond measure. She leaned on me literally and metaphorically, and I relished the role. She didn't let go of my hand throughout the visitation or burial service. Mrs. Schofield flew in and stayed for a week after the funeral, ostensibly for emotional support, but Jess only wanted me. She was really there, I think, to say her goodbyes to us as she had grown terribly feeble since her husband's death the spring before. Thank God, she wasn't alive nine months later to see what Jess became."

They sat in silence for a minute and Jim's melancholy tainted the air. "I was in town when someone ran to me, telling of the wreck on the blacktop. I'd heard the sirens and seen the ambulance and police car race through the square. I got there just as the other three boys were pulled out through the back door. Zach began apologizing as soon as he saw me. 'It was the deer's fault,' he said with a sly smile. I reached in and jabbed the air in front of his face with my finger, scolding him for speeding. He rolled his eyes and maintained his innocence. But when the seat was released, he looked up to me with a quizzical look, the lines on his brow suddenly ridged as if he had a headache. Then a bubble of bright blood rose from his lips, and he was gone."

Jim made a deep sighing "whew" and slowly shook his head. "I pushed away one of the paramedics and reached in for my boy but they fought me and tried to save him. He was a big boy but I lifted him like I had that morning on the *Queen Mary* then sat on the grass and rocked him. Blood ran from his mouth down my shirt and tie. It was so sudden. As startling and unexpected as gunfire. I held him until the coroner came and took him away.

"Mrs. Dagley came out of the house as soon as I pulled up the drive. She was crying but as I was soon to discover, not simply for Zach. 'She's in a bad way, Jim. A *bad* way.' The front parlor was in shambles. Pictures knocked from the wall, the fireplace mantel viciously swiped of clock, candles, and pictures now lay shattered on the floor. The coffee table was overturned, the television had a gaping, jagged hole in it, and Dad's heavy console radio lay toppled. She was sitting in the wing chair with her back to me. 'Jess,' I said softly as I tramped through the debris. She did not turn. I came to the side of her and her profile exactly as it had been that evening in London when I broke the news of my orders for Germany. She was still breathing deeply from her exertions. I knelt and took her hand, but she stared fixedly at some point on the floor. 'Jess, he's gone. Our baby is gone.' I began weeping, but she had absolutely no response. I got down on my knees and placed my head on her lap. 'Our baby, Jess, our baby.' But she was as cold as the winter wind. I lifted my head from her lap and said, 'For God's sake, Jess, I have his blood all over me!' But there was nothing. Nothing at all.

"The pastor came and after he offered his condolences to me, I took him to the parlor. He got down on a knee before her and took her hand. He just said something to the effect it was not ours to question God and offered her pious platitudes. She slowly turned her head as if suddenly aware of his presence and spat in his eye. 'Jess!' I shouted, aghast. The pastor stood and wiped the spittle and suggested I call the doctor. I called old Dr. Mitchell to come to the house. As he prepared a syringe, he said, 'Jess, this is a sedative. I'm going to put it directly into the muscle. You'll feel much more comfortable in just a minute.' She brushed the syringe away with an upswing of her arm and said in a hateful voice, 'Just let me alone.' When I walked him to the door, he said in a confidential tone, 'In my professional opinion, you'll need to take her to a psychiatrist in Evansville if she doesn't snap out of it. Call me if she wants the sedative.'

"Neighbors and family traipsed in and out, each trying unsuccessfully to rouse Jess. She simply nodded with the haunted look of the day on her face. Several women cleaned the parlor with Jess just sitting there consumed in flames of bitterness. Word got out she was hostile to the living and wasn't responding to visitors, so the phone rang non-stop with just as many inquiries about her as condolences for Zach.

"I felt very alone in the world. I had never picked out a casket before nor the clothes a corpse would wear. Mrs. Dagley helped me. Instead of the classy black dress she'd worn to Mama and Kathleen's funerals, she threw on a red dress and flat-heeled shoes, no makeup. Her hair was a mess. During visitation, she stood before the casket and stared at our boy for four hours, memorizing his features. She didn't acknowledge a single mourner. 'She'll be fine,' I assured them. At the cemetery, she lifted her eyes to the perfectly clear blue sky and stared fixedly. I've wondered ever since if she was contemplating God or that foreign woman.

"Jess took to drinking heavily in the evenings. I came home from work and cooked, but she rarely ate. Often she just had a bowl of cereal. I did the washing, cleaning, lawn work, and errands while she slept. In the evenings, she awoke fully and sat drinking and smoking until the early hours of the morning. I kept nursing a hope, a desire she would finally snap out of it and come back to me. When I touched her intimately in bed, she lay stiff as a mannequin, taking no pleasure and returning no affection. I tried to talk to her, at the time and place of our most intimate conversations in the past. But she was always drunk by then and passed out soon after her head hit the pillow.

"About a week after the funeral, as she trudged up the stairs, I said to her, 'Can't we please talk, Jess? Please? We'll both feel so much better.' She stopped and looked down at me with a solid stare of helplessness and said in a dead tone, 'I'm sorry, Jim, but I have nothing left. Nothing. I can't help it. I'm sorry.' She turned wearily and continued on up.

"No one could reach her. She ignored me when I asked her to go to a grief counselor with me. One morning I was on my way out the door for work, when she rose from the chair after a night of drinking and smoking. A blind fury caught me, and I couldn't control myself. I had never laid a hand on her in anger but I slapped her hard across the face and grabbed her by the shoulders and shook her just as hard as I could, trying to jar the depression out of her. 'This has gone on long enough! Snap out of it, Jess! Now!'

"She was not shocked into submission but gave a malevolent look and said, 'Life sure as bloody hell goes on, doesn't it, Jim?' I replied in a shout, 'We have no choice in the matter! Accept what you've been given and move on!' Derisive, she shook her head and said, 'It must be a blessing to be so simple.' The insult calmed me superficially, and I said softly, 'Jess, you've gone over the edge. That's all. We'll go and see a doctor and get better. Okay?' She turned from me and headed for the staircase. 'God has pushed me over the edge. No doctor can fix that.'

"We existed like this for six months, the darkest time of my life. Finally, I got up one night, determined to give her an ultimatum. I had been planning it for weeks, summoning up enough courage to do it, and feel confident in its outcome. I went down to the parlor early enough to catch her while she was still coherent. She sat in the dark, the tip of her cigarette glowing orange and the ice cubes softly ringing against the glass. 'Jess,' I said, 'please let's talk. I can't take much more. We can't go on like this. I can't. I don't want to leave, but I will unless we talk. I'll leave Jess, I will. Things have to get better between us. Isn't our love still alive? Isn't it?'

"There was a gulf of blackness between us and I waited for her voice to float across it, frightened and begging. 'Go back to bed,' she said in a disinterested voice, as the orange tip of her cigarette arced slowly upward and burned brighter for a moment. It was over. I knew just as surely as I had when Zach died before my eyes our marriage was dead.

"I'd been in southern California on business conferences and had always liked the beach communities, so I decided in a horrified instant to go there. I had nowhere else to go. The next morning, I packed a suitcase and left in cold silence. I longed to hear her voice, still held out that flickering hope she would stop me but she watched from an upstairs window and made not a move."

The tears began running down Jim's face and his voice quivered with the effort to contain himself. "Kathleen and Zach were unwillingly dead. But my loss of Jess was worse than theirs because she was dead by choice." He looked to Guy with a face full of sheer agony and cried in despair, "*How could she*?" He immediately buried his face in his hands and sobbed with a great, rocking force that rattled the springs of the chair.

Guy drew back from him, uncomfortable with the depth of such emotion. Distracted, he thought, *I should go to him, put my arm around him*. Instead, he jumped from the chair and backed away.

He looked at Barbara and said, "I need to make that phone call."

She stared at him with something that may have been disdain. He walked toward the phone on the antique table and left a wife with the unenviable task of comforting her husband for the atrocities committed by an ex-wife.

Eight

Guy knew he was cowardly to walk away from the stricken couple but couldn't help himself. Men are not equipped for such situations, he told himself without the least sense of self-justification, though it surprised him that he was distressed to see Jim in such anguish. Guy dialed Julie's Pentagon extension and a woman came on the line and transferred the call. Julie picked up on the first ring and said breathlessly, "Guy?"

"What did the old man think of our story?"

There was a moment's hesitation then Guy heard the unmistakable echo of her voice when she said, "Guy, you're on a speaker phone in his office."

Before Guy had a chance to apologize, the deeply authoritative voice of General Walter Van Cleve boomed through the phone. "Turner, you will depart southern California via a commercial aircraft to Norfolk, Virginia. I can't authorize a cross-country military flight, as it would arouse suspicion. At the Naval Air Station, Oceana, you and your civilian complement will board a Lear jet for the flight to the *Thomas Jefferson* in the North Atlantic. Everything is contingent upon her arrival early tomorrow evening. She is expected to arrive at nineteen hundred Zulu so plan on that as your rendezvous time. You have a day and a half. Questions?"

"Sir, there is another civilian involved, a woman in Illinois. I don't believe we have time to involve her, do we?"

"If you leave LAX immediately, you can accommodate her by leaving Illinois in the early morning. Is O'Hare close to her?"

"What is the closest airport to Herald, Jim?" Guy called across the room.

"That would be Evansville, Indiana or St. Louis, Missouri,"

Jim answered.

"Evansville or St. Louis," Guy repeated into the phone.

"A small airport like Evansville will undoubtedly have a layover. I suggest a non-stop flight out of St. Louis into Dulles. At any rate, you can't leave Oceana Naval Air Station until the *Thomas Jefferson* is nearing position tomorrow evening. You're left to your own devices to make sure you are at the base by fourteen hundred tomorrow. You should have plenty of time."

"Yes, sir," Guy said, accepting the fact they would be taking Jess Bennett along with them.

"Remember, mum is the word. This comes straight from the White House, Turner. I'll see you tomorrow evening." The general paused and added cryptically, "The message will be transmitted regardless of your presence." There was a curt click on the other end, and Guy turned to the expectant faces across the room. Jim had stood, and Barbara still worried over him, looking very small and overwhelmed.

"We'll have to take a non-stop flight out of St. Louis into Dulles. We have to be at the Naval Air Station, Oceana, in Virginia Beach by two o'clock tomorrow afternoon, and then we'll take a Lear jet out to the *Thomas Jefferson*."

Jim wiped his eyes and cleared his throat. "Why don't we fly into Evansville this afternoon and rent a car? It's less than an hour drive to Herald then we can leave for St. Louis early in the morning. It's about a three-hour drive from Herald, but, like you said, it would be a non-stop flight."

Guy nodded, and Jim walked toward the table. "I guess it's time to call Jess." He self-consciously smoothed his hair and straightened his collar then lifted the receiver and dialed without consulting an address book. Guy experienced an inexplicable sadness for the man who had never forgotten the number.

Barbara looked at Guy and said, "I'll go pack some things for him."

As she walked quickly for the hall, Guy stopped her. "Mrs. Bennett, I'm very sorry to have put you through this. I hadn't thought how awkward it would be for you."

She looked up to him with eyes suddenly moist. "That's just the lament of the second wife. We are forever second choice, no matter how much our husbands say they love us."

"Well, again, I'm sorry to have put you through so much. I

didn't consider asking you to go with us. He may need you. Would you like to accompany him?"

She gave a polite smile. "Two wives? Now that *would* be awkward. No, this is a journey for the three of you. I trust that you'll be there if he needs you. Like you said, this is a lot to go through—"

Jim speaking into the phone interrupted their conversation. "Jess, this is Jim." There was a slight pause as both evidently gathered their wits. "Something unexpected has come up. We have to talk. I...no, I can't discuss it over the phone. I just wanted to let you know I was coming. I should be in Herald sometime this afternoon." Another pause. "Jess, please, I can't discuss this over the phone. I'll see you in a few hours. Goodbye."

~ * ~

Gravity fought but finally surrendered to the climbing plane with one last punishing jolt. There had been absolute quiet on the ascent but once they attained cruising altitude, the incessant chatter began. Guy looked about at his fellow travelers and wondered about their separate journeys. He noticed a teenage girl sneaking peaks at him while the young couple across the aisle held hands and spoke tenderly to each other. Newlyweds, perhaps, on their way to a honeymoon. He recognized a certain superiority to them, infinite privilege, as if he had been granted exclusive entrance to a destination they could never envision.

He was troubled as he hurtled toward that destination. The voyeuristic suspense of revelation, the excitement of trespassing into someone's private territory slowly dissipated by a growing personal involvement he hadn't anticipated. He felt drawn to Jim as if the old man had some sort of unexplainable hold on him. The emotional recollection of a few hours before stirred something deep within the well of his heart, something unknown he instinctively knew he did not want to draw up. A subtle shift was taking place within him, fraught with anxiety and an impending sense of time ticking away. The begging eyes of the foreign woman hung before him each time he closed his eyes and the prospect of failure weighed heavy on him. His stomach churned, and he noticed that his fingers fumbled when he released his seatbelt after the safety light went off.

Jim turned toward him in the seat beside him and said, "I don't think I'm out of line in asking to know a little about you. You know a hell of a lot about me. After all, we've become a significant part of each other's lives now."

Guy smiled. "What would you like to know?"

Jim nodded toward the teenage girl. "You're a good-looking man, obviously. I don't see a wedding ring. A man can't look like you and not have someone in his life, male or female."

Guy sighed and leaned his head back. "Her name is Lynn. She isn't speaking to me right now. She's with her mother in Seattle." He was quiet a moment, hoping that just enough information would satisfy him, but Jim waited. "She forced a stalemate on me," Guy said.

"It takes two to have a stalemate," Jim said with a steady, inquisitive look.

"We had a row over kids, of all things."

"Kids?"

"She wants them, I don't. And the icing on the cake was when she caught me counting her birth control pills."

Jim closed his eyes and winced as if pained by Guy's foolishness.

"I know, I know, but I had to find out how determined she was. I can't understand her wanting to bring a black child into this world."

Jim regarded Guy with a sardonic smile that made him feel as if caught in a lie. "I don't believe that. Didn't believe it when you said it to Barb. Too obvious, too easy. A man of your intelligence and success has come too far to be that pessimistic about his skin color. I think it's pure bullshit."

A sudden flush of heat rushed through Guy's body, and he was unsure how to respond.

"What's the truth of the matter, friend?" Jim asked soothingly. "Give it to me straight."

The old man's curious eyes settled upon him, gently coaxing, with an honest sympathy and compassion in them that made Guy want to confide all to him. From somewhere deep within, the truth rose until it was just below the surface of secrecy and Guy was startled to feel it bubbling through, sputtering on his tongue.

"I...I never had a father," he said, and a tremendous shock immediately hung between them.

"Well, now," Jim said and settled back in his seat, seeming to summon the necessary strength to address such an admission.

Guy looked at him in disbelief, feeling suddenly naked and lonelier than he could ever remember. The truth, never spoken, released at last, now made honest and real. "I can't be a father," he said lightly in a perplexed tone. "I never had a father."

"Fatherhood isn't taught. It's innate. Natural."

"You don't understand," Guy said. He leaned forward, cradled his head in his hands and looked down at his feet, angry with himself for his complete, unexpected frankness. "I would fail a child miserably. The world is cruel enough, let alone to enter it without having been reasonably prepared."

Guy's subconscious blamed his absent father, a phantom black man blamed for every tribulation of childhood. Guy had suffered rage for the awkwardness he experienced in sports or the painful shyness when roughhoused by friends' fathers. He had not known until this moment how deeply that absence impinged upon his adult relationships.

Jim turned in his seat so he could survey Guy fully during this remarkable conversation. "Let me tell you something. I'm not bragging, but I considered myself a fine father. I can't say my father taught me to be a good father. I don't believe I, in turn, taught Zach. Dad was an affectionate man, but I never once remember him giving me fatherly advice. He was not an enlightened man, but he taught me through example without even knowing it. I will tell you the simple secret to parenthood is unconditional love. The kind of love you cannot control. There is no more peaceful feeling in the world than when a child crawls up in your lap then falls asleep against you. Nothing finer. You are helpless to love them, especially when they are your own. I can promise you have nothing to dread or be fearful about. It is one of the richest experiences in life."

Guy shook his head uneasily. "I have a lot of demons to exorcise before I can look at parenthood as you do. You see, I'm not a very good prospect to any woman who wants a family."

"Nonsense. You are a man searching for self, a man already embarked on the journey toward what Lynn prizes most. She would be heartened to know of this conversation." He smiled. "Now tell me about this girl. What kind of love do you have for her?"

Still in shock over his admission, Guy knew Jim could not be satiated now. "I don't understand what you're asking."

Jim settled back and rested his head comfortably. "Well, there's love and then there's good old-fashioned fucking. There is a difference between the two."

Guy sensed another flush. This was definitely a conversation for men, and he believed himself inadequate to participate. He looked around to see if anyone was eavesdropping. “Everyone is familiar with the latter but the first is a trickier proposition.”

“Exactly. Who is the first person you think of when you swing out of bed in the morning? Whose approval do you value above all others? Who do you want to hold your hand when you’re dying?”

Guy nodded. “I ache for her, I miss her so much.”

“That’s the truest love, young one, the love God intended. And, unfortunately, the most painful. Wouldn’t be love if it didn’t hurt.”

“I don’t know how to live without her.”

“Then *run* to her. Just as fast as your legs will take you.”

“I’m afraid it may be too late for that.”

“Not necessarily. Stalemates can be broken. Be honest with her as you have been with me. It’s our nature to be introverted when it comes to honesty about emotions, and when we painfully expose them for women to see, they lap it up. You can never go wrong with a display of emotional honesty in front of a woman. Women swoon at honesty from men.”

“You make it sound easy.”

“Your solution *is* easy. Be honest and make the first move. But maintaining that relationship won’t be easy as long as you shut yourself off emotionally each time you have a disagreement. Women are the stronger of the species and don’t you forget it. They can use their mastery of emotion as a weapon against us because they know we are weak in that respect. When a man learns to acknowledge and accept this, he saves himself a lot of heartache and headache.”

“I must be listening to the voice of experience.”

“Listen, I’ve had a woman at the center of my life for nearly sixty years plus a daughter for twenty-one of those. I’ve encountered all the valleys and the peaks. Everything I know about the many moods of womankind I learned during menstrual cycles.”

Guy laughed helplessly. “That sounds like a book title.”

Jim nodded and arched an eyebrow. “In that case, the sequel would be *And Then Some*.” He turned serious again and lifted a finger. “Don’t ever underestimate the power of a woman. We both know how men are empowered by crude language about women when they are alone with other men, but I would rather have a root canal than be a lone man entering a room full of women. Every woman has the ability to belittle a man and put him in his place.

Respect them for it." He patted Guy's leg heartily. "Talk to her."

A little silence followed, and then Guy asked, "Who do you want to hold your hand when you're dying?" The question seemed to catch Jim's vulnerability and he looked vacantly past Guy out the window. Perhaps he had violated an unspoken agreement, overstepped the bounds of their honesty with each other. Certain that he was not going to answer, he said, "I'm sorry, I should not have asked that."

Jim continued to stare out the window. "Barb is a wonderful, sweet-tempered woman. She takes very good care of me, and she is the very definition of a loyal, doting wife." Then he turned and found Guy's eyes and said, "But she isn't Jess."

~ * ~

Guy discerned a distinct departure from civilization after landing in Evansville. The city seemed a forgotten, sleepy outpost after the bustle of LAX and the mad connecting flights in Denver and Chicago. The interstate lent the only familiar ring of LA. Within minutes, it too disappeared, merging into a two-lane highway that unrolled through a small town with quaint shops and an old courthouse on the square that was Christmas card perfect. Jim drove and slowed at each site he recalled with interest. The landscape fascinated Guy with rolling hills and a bridge over a tree-lined river. He had never seen pure nature stretching in every direction. He wanted to drowse in the sunlight pouring through the window and remembered he had not slept the night before. But energy constituted of sheer nervousness buoyed him. A sign just beyond the Illinois state line welcomed them to the 'Land of Lincoln.'

The road turned and dipped through curving corridors of overhanging trees where they encountered sparse and leisurely traffic. When they passed a tract of new homes with saplings and newly sodded lawns, Jim groaned. "That used to be a forest I hunted in as a boy."

They turned onto a blacktop road and Guy saw a church spire on a distant hill glistening above the treetops. Guy's arrival in the country offered him another new reality. There were no walls of steel and glass here but somehow the farmhouses were just as imposing with their wrap-around porches, old-fashioned roof angles and a magical sense of suspended time.

"Where are the sidewalks and taxis?" Guy asked facetiously.

Jim laughed. "Are you in cultural shock?"

Guy shook his head. "It's absolutely beautiful."

Jim shined with pride. "This is God's country."

Deep woods rose on either side then receded dreamlike behind them. The church was a spectacle of bright white built on the highest point of land in clear command of the cornfields and wide belts of trees below. The car climbed the sweep of hill covered with gravestones under tall, somber cedars. As they mounted the hilltop, Jim pulled onto a narrow paved road beside the church.

"You don't mind if I visit the kids, do you?"

"Not at all."

The white gravestones nearest the church were quite old and many looked like salt blocks slowly dissolving away. Jim drove into a newer section of granite markers and stopped. The sweet sound of birds singing bedazzled Guy as soon as he got out of the car. A tractor droned in a nearby field. The vista of countryside from this point was breathtaking and Guy had the sensation of stepping into a lush landscape painting. He held back a step or two as Jim meandered through the cemetery and stopped before two identical markers. Kathleen's had a floral saddle of red carnations and Guy instantly recalled the story of the girl's fascination with the flowers aboard *Queen Mary*. Jim knelt on one knee and pulled at tufts of grass growing against the base of Zach's marker. He stayed in that position a moment as if praying then stood and stared down. Guy wondered if he was contemplating his own mortality or that of his children. He was a man standing at the edge of eternity and a sudden love and sympathy for him swept over Guy.

They walked back to the car together in silence and Guy was acutely aware of his unwitting presence in what seemed such a private matter. They followed the downward slope at a funereal pace, until they turned back onto the blacktop, then crossed a small creek and drove parallel to another belt of trees. Less than a quarter of a mile from the cemetery, Jim pulled onto a gravel drive that tunneled through a wood. Sunlight flashed through the canopy of tree limbs and softly dappled against the windows. Along the heavily overgrown drive, branches clawed down the sides of the car.

The woods thinned and the sunlight brightened. Then, abruptly, the woods were behind them and Guy beheld the Bennett homestead. He understood immediately Jess's first awestruck view of the house. It rose grandly above the oak-lined drive with a turret standing at attention on the east side of the wrap-around porch and two gables flanking a central section with fish scale siding in the upper reaches. The roof was not a single roof at all but a mountainous mass of lines and angles leaving the beholder with no clear impression of a beginning or end. The quintessential Victorian farmhouse.

As they drove closer, however, they saw that several of the oaks were dead and the lawn was waist-high in weeds, rippling like waves in the breeze. The teardrop shaped roof tiles were faded to a gritty gray, with many of them missing. The white clapboard siding was peeling away to reveal dry, blackened wood beneath. One of the broken stain-glass windows beneath a dormer in the roof appeared backed by cardboard tacked onto it from the inside.

"My God," Jim whispered and Guy could feel the heartbreak of his homecoming.

They pulled up a circular drive and stopped below six wide steps leading up to the porch. They got out and surveyed the ruin. The house, in a battle of reclamation with nature, appeared to withdraw from reality, forgotten and left to brood over the past. In a word, lifeless. Guy could see what once was in full glory but now towered above them decrepit, bitter, and withering away through the years. He could not escape the sense of passing time.

Jim cupped a shaky hand to his forehead and looked sadly up at the house his grandfather had built. "Love and memory are the only things that endure," he said.

The central steps creaked ominously beneath their feet but the porch itself was still sound though in dire need of a sweeping. Jim lifted the brass knocker, green with age, and rapped three times. A voice called out from the opposite side of the porch, near the turret. "Jim, I'm out here."

Guy followed Jim down the porch and lingered behind a column when he saw Jess Bennett standing in a small garden wearing old jeans, gloves, and an immense straw hat. There were roses and red carnations growing in a tenderly nurtured plot surrounded by weeds and overgrown box hedges. The smallest hope nearly choked by despair.

The unease was palpable in the humid summer air and Guy watched Jess bring her hands to her hips and lift her chin. "Are you dying?" she asked archly.

Jim shook his head. "No. Can we go inside, please? You may want to sit down."

Guy thought he detected a certain relief in her. She stared up at Jim a long moment without changing position then pulled her gloves off and dropped them to the ground, before climbing the porch steps.

Before she stepped into the shadows of the porch, Guy noticed she wore makeup, a touch of lipstick, and a hint of eyeliner. She flashed a startled look at him and Jim said, "You remember Guy Turner from the *Queen Mary*, don't you?"

"Of course," she said and nodded in puzzled acknowledgement. "What is the meaning of this, Jim?"

"Inside, please?"

She gave him a skeptical look before leading the men down the cool shade of the porch to the main entrance. The three stepped inside a great hall with a dark staircase and banister beyond and a tarnished brass chandelier above. Guy could almost hear the ancient sound of children's shoes clattering up and down the risers. Newspapers and magazines were stacked against the walls, and a foyer table before the staircase was so thick with dust that he couldn't see the wood grain.

"Would you like a cup of tea?" she asked as she dropped her straw hat onto a bow-back chair.

"No, thank you," Jim said.

"I'm fine," Guy said.

She cocked her head at them and said, affronted, "My house may be cluttered but my dishes are clean, I assure you."

"I'm fine, really," Guy replied.

"Let's go into the parlor, Jess," Jim said with some urgency.

The parlor was large with formal woodwork, a hardwood floor, and turn-of-the century furniture including a dusty desk and coffee table, a faded empire sofa, two threadbare wing chairs and a bulky console radio occupying a full corner. The wallpaper was water-stained and peeling and he could not discern the original color or pattern. Guy realized, in the dead silence, this was the room Jess violently decimated so many years before,

Jim and Jess stood before the wing chairs but did not sit down.

"Jess, listen carefully," Jim began. "Have you heard on the television a news report about the radio signal from the *Queen Mary*?"

She shook her head. "I don't have a television."

"Well, a few days ago, a submarine in the North Atlantic..."

I don't belong here. His voyeuristic tendencies were strangely absent. He walked into the dining room and stood before the fireplace. He pretended to admire the dusty knick-knacks and photos but carefully watched the couple through a mirror above the mantelpiece. He heard Jim's low tones drifting through the suffocating quiet and saw the precise punctuations of his hands.

Jess looked at him intently. Jim stopped and pointed a finger at Guy. When he pulled the nametag from his pocket and held it before her, she slowly sagged onto the edge of the chair and lightly brought a hand to her chest. She turned her head sharply toward Guy as Jim spoke much more animatedly.

She arose without moving her eyes from Guy's back and walked slowly into the dining room until she stood behind him. His heart leaped wildly in his chest as he awkwardly turned to face her, feeling more an outsider now than ever. She brought a hand up and rested it on his arm. Her eyes appealed mutely, the mouth half open with shock and she looked somehow smaller.

For several interminable seconds, she simply studied him, apparently at a loss for words. Finally, she found her voice and slowly pleaded, "All I want in this world, all I *need* in this world, is to see that woman."

Nine

The only phone in the house was a rotary dial mounted on a kitchen wall. As he phoned St. Louis' Lambert airport, Guy watched Jess contemplating the nametag in her cupped hands. Her absorbed expression spoke in the silent vocabulary of the spellbound.

The earliest flight into Dulles left St. Louis at ten a.m. central standard time. "Is Illinois central standard or eastern?" he asked her, wondering where Jim had gone.

Without averting her eyes from the nametag, Jess said vacantly, "We're central standard. Washington is an hour ahead of us."

The loss of an hour left little leeway for delays of any kind. Nausea and nerves nearly overcame him once again. What they were attempting loomed larger and larger with two helpless women now pleading for his intercession. It had been less than twenty-four hours since his encounter with the foreign woman but it seemed like days. Reality blurred, threatening to become as indistinct as a dream. He could hear that inner music progressing onward, louder and more intimidating as it rose with a panic-inducing sense of urgency.

The repeated sound of a door closing then creaking open echoed down the hall. Finally, Jess loudly said, "Jim, that bathroom door has been sprung for years. I don't have any use for privacy but if you do, use the one upstairs." Then she added tartly, "But I don't believe you have anything I haven't seen before." Guy looked to her and she gave him a small, knowing grin then turned back to the nametag.

Guy understood his newfound intimacy with these strangers knew no bounds from the sound of Jim urinating sounded down the hall.

He booked three seats for the flight, hung up, and immediately found Jess Bennett's eyes fixed on him. "This is so enormous, I can hardly grasp it," she said in a voice barely above a whisper. "I never considered I might see her again. In my mind's eye she is eternally youthful, forever a young girl."

Jim stood in the doorway and the three of them stared awkwardly at each other. Guy sensed that the house had not contained human interaction for so many years that every glance and utterance in the heavy emptiness met with a grim contempt.

"I have a pot roast in the freezer," Jess finally said. "Do you cook?" she asked Guy.

"I know my way around a kitchen."

"Good." She slapped her knees and stood. "You can peel the potatoes and carrots and dice the celery. Jim, there are some ears of corn on the back porch that need to be shucked."

Jim looked very pleased. "Why, I haven't shucked an ear of corn in years."

"I'll defrost the roast and make some rolls. Come, come."

The kitchen was large with cabinets to the ceiling and an old-fashioned gooseneck water faucet. An oak sideboard with a beveled mirror and a matching pedestal table with claw feet would most certainly be the delight of an antique collector. The thick dust layered on everything made the deathly state of the room's disuse tangible. This was clearly a kitchen intended for a family, not a solitary person.

Jess quickly pulled the roast out of the freezer and vegetables out of the fridge. She let the vegetables fall to the counter, and then placed the roast in a microwave that looked obtrusively modern in this kitchen. She pulled a knife from a drawer and held it out to Guy. "Don't just stand there, good-looking, hop to it. I'll get those potatoes for you."

Guy gingerly took the knife and looked up to see Jim smiling at him from the back porch as he ripped husks from the corn and dropped them into a bushel basket at his feet.

Jess stood at a butcher block, measuring flour into a large bowl. "Your sister and brother-in-law were here in June," she said to Jim.

"School reunion?"

She nodded. "They brought their granddaughter, Whitney, with them. I tell you, she looks so much like your father it hurt to look at her."

"Is that right? Well, Tom and Helen were in California just last month and they stayed with us a few days and drove up the coast. He had open heart surgery a year ago, you know."

"How old is he?"

Jim looked to the ceiling as he mentally tabulated. "Let's see, he has to be seventy-two or seventy-three."

"Your father was sixty-seven when he died. I assume your doctor watches your heart?"

"No problem with the ticker so far," Jim said and quickly knocked on the doorframe.

The heavy air seemed cleansed by the easy conversation and Guy went about his task in the warming glow of cordiality. He perceived relief for Jim and that relief extended to himself. Only during the pauses in conversation did the silence drift back down upon them.

During one of those pauses, Jess visibly slowed her kneading and finally stopped altogether. She looked over at Guy. Her voice changed to a mixture of gravity and child-like curiosity when she asked, "What does she look like now, that poor woman?"

Unintentionally flippant, he shook his head and carelessly said, "She's ancient." Realizing too late the harshness of his words, he apologized.

"Don't apologize," Jess said, holding up a floured hand. "Old age happens to the best of us."

Guy wondered if her question was one all older people had regarding their contemporaries, when memories of their past outnumbered their hopes for the future, curious as to whether the worn path to old age is rockier for some than others.

"Say, whatever happened to Brother Watkins?" Jim asked.

Jess smiled crookedly and raised her brows. "His wife died and two years later he married Sandra Shoemaker."

There was a sharp intake of air from Jim and he stood in shocked motionlessness. "The old slut?" Jess and Guy looked at each other and burst into laughter. Jim's eyes desperately searched the floor as though for some explanation. "I can't believe it. A pastor and an older woman who had been with so many men? Why?"

"Maybe he preached about the sins of the flesh for so many years he became curious and decided to marry the expert. Pastors are humans too."

Guy idly wondered if he was the same pastor Jess had spit on. Jim shook his head in disbelief and resumed shucking the corn. When Guy finished preparing the vegetables, he suddenly remembered he hadn't bathed since the previous morning. "Mrs. Bennett, would you care if I showered while we wait to eat? So much has happened I haven't taken the time."

"Call me Jess and yes, you may. Did you pack fresh clothes?"

"No. Everything has been so rushed..."

"Put your clothes outside the door, and I'll wash them for you. You can wear one of Jim's old robes while they dry."

Guy remembered the sprung door and asked, "Can I use the bathroom upstairs?"

"There's only a bathtub up there, a giant, claw-footed thing that takes forever to fill. Don't worry, I promise not to look in." She bowed her head to him and murmured, "Although I have always been curious about that particular rumor, I'll resist seeing for myself." She winked at him as she turned to place the rolls in the oven. Jim laughed in a low tone.

In the bathroom, Guy leaned against the door as he undressed and after he dropped his clothes outside, he quickly wedged a hamper under the doorknob.

~ * ~

The robe smelled unpleasantly of mothballs, the odor of stagnation and long, lost time. The Bennetts were setting the table when Guy entered the dining room. The table had been cleared of clutter and wiped to a gleam. A silver candelabra now adorned the center. Jess had changed into a cream pantsuit, two gold chains hung about her neck with two matching bracelets at her right wrist. Her precise placement of the silverware suggested to Guy she was actually eager for company and wished nothing less than perfect formality to celebrate this chance gathering.

"Your clothes will be dry in a while, then I'll iron them later," she said.

"Oh no, please, I don't expect you to..."

"Nonsense," she said nonchalantly. "It will be nice to iron a man's clothing again. So many years."

Jim looked to her with what Guy perceived as annoyance at her words but she did not seem to notice.

"I would offer you both a cocktail before we eat but if I start, I won't be able to stop and I couldn't possibly bear to watch you drink without having one myself." She said this with evident acceptance of her frailty, her curse, and for the first time, Guy experienced a tinge of sympathy for her.

Each of them carried a dish to the dining room table but the crowning achievement of their toils that afternoon was the steaming pot roast Jess proudly held high. She and Jim sat at opposite ends of the table, evidently out of a never-forgotten habit from years gone by and Guy took a side chair close to Jim.

"I hope the rolls aren't too done on the bottom," Jess said happily and passed the pan to Guy.

"Shouldn't we say grace?" asked Jim.

Jess looked blankly at him a moment, and then lowered the pan and bowed her head with obvious inconvenience. He thanked God for good health, good food, and His presence in their daily lives. He asked blessings for the souls of his children and parents, and lastly, he asked that His gracious hand bring them together with "that remarkable woman" surely yet safely.

Guy noticed Jess did not say "amen." To his embarrassment, he found he was famished. Every flavor seemed intensified in much the same manner reality had been intensified since the encounter. "Those rolls are delicious," he said, reaching for another. "I'm sorry to make a pig of myself but I haven't eaten since yesterday. The food on the plane doesn't count."

Jess smiled. "It's flattering to have a man enjoy my cooking again. Good food, good company, and good conversation. It brings life back to the old place."

Guy caught another angry glance from Jim and easily guessed at its roots.

Jess carefully placed the nametag above her plate, gazing tenderly.

"How did this country life suit you after growing up in London, Mrs. Bennett...Jess?" Guy asked when the silence made him uneasy.

"Oh, I loved it the moment we disembarked from the train. For me, it was like stepping into a fairy tale. Everyone knew each other and cared about each other. Everyone visited and went to church together. The fields, hills, and woods were heavenly. For the first time in my life, I didn't feel lonely. Remember the ice cream social at the church, Jim? Right after we came home?"

Jim nodded without a word, leaving Jess to recount the

memory without any input from him.

Jess, perhaps noticing Jim's increasing withdrawal and alert for conflict, turned her attention to Guy. "The children ran and played with other children on the church grounds, Jim showed me off and I had never been hugged by so many people in my life. Mind you, they were all strangers, but it was very much a homecoming to me."

Jim continued eating without even raising his head. The unresolved nature of their relationship once again hung in the air like static electricity.

"Do you know what a 'party line' is?" Jess asked Guy.

"No, I can't say that I do," Guy responded with too much enthusiasm. It seemed they were simply going through the motions, pretending conviviality.

"Well, years ago you shared your telephone number with several neighbors. Everyone was on the same circuit, you see, and could eavesdrop on all conversations. During the Korean War, Tommy Blair was stationed overseas and once when he called his wife, Marion, she could hardly hear him. 'Marion, it sure is good to hear your voice,' he told her but she said, 'What did you say?' He repeated, 'Marion, it sure is good to hear you.' Again, she said, 'What did you say?' Louder, Tommy said, 'Marion, I am sure glad to hear you.' When she once again said, 'What?' an irritated voice blurted out over the line, 'For God's sake, Marion, he says it sure is good to hear you! Damn!"

Guy laughed aloud heartily and hoped Jim would join him but the old man persisted in eating his corn on the cob as though nothing at all had been said.

"Marion died of emphysema seven years ago, Jim," Jess said, obviously trying to engage him. "But Tommy didn't grieve for long. He became more involved in the church, joined some local historical chapters, babysat for his great grandchild, and just lived more robustly than he ever had."

Jim narrowed his eyes toward Jess and said, "Well at least he didn't stop living. Didn't *die* himself because someone he loved was dead. He taught a damn good lesson, don't you think?"

A moment of deadly silence crept between the three, the calm before the storm. Guy wanted to leave the table quietly. He ventured a sideways glance at Jess. For a fraction of a moment, he saw her wilt like a tender-petalled flower in the summer sun then she clenched the arms of her chair and he thought dismally, "She will not let it pass. She will not."

Incredibly, she shifted her stare from Jim, settled her eyes on Guy and very brightly began another conversation. "Guy, have you noticed how very simple my ex-husband is? Isn't that a blessing for him? Wouldn't it be wonderful if we could all live in Jim's world?" She smiled and tipped her head with overt happiness. "Death and grief are just trifling things to be endured. Nothing more." She raised her arms upward and lifted her head toward the ceiling, still smiling in pretend ecstasy. "Let's just be happy to be alive. Praise God, *alleluia*!" she said jubilantly.

Jim quickly stood and leaned over the table, jabbing the air with his finger. "That is unfair, Jess! I loved those children just as much as you and I grieved, let me tell you, I grieved. Just as much for you as I did for them!"

"Life is so lovely," she continued with joyful scorn. "Let's enjoy the rest of our lives as though nothing happened. The past is in the past." Suddenly her mouth twisted and she turned back to Guy and spoke in a sharper tone. "Our children were sleeping in the God-damned ground, but life must go on!" She swung her head furiously with each word. "Sing no sad songs for the dead, life goes on, life goes on!"

"But I wasn't sleeping in the God-damned ground," Jim shouted. "I wasn't dead!"

Guy bowed his head and looked down at his plate, heartbroken for Jim and full of spleen toward Jess.

"You are seventy-eight years old," Jim said accusingly. "Seventy-eight but you've only lived half that many years. What do you have to show for yourself? You threw two lives away because two were taken from you. You just wouldn't try to get over it. Your grief and bitterness just went on and on and on."

She stood and looked directly at Jim, tight-jawed and thin-lipped. "That's because you left me to grieve for both of us, you complacent son of a bitch!"

Guy wanted to reach out and slap that vile mouth, stop the flow of hatefulness, but instead he stood so quickly his chair fell backward with a slam that befitted the atmosphere of the room and he left hastily for the back porch.

~ * ~

He placed a cigarette in his mouth and stood at the porch

railing looking out upon the great back lawn. The lighter trembled in his hand. A collapsing barn stood in the distance, its doors yawning with loneliness and emptiness, the metal roof streaked with rust. It had been dead a long time. The sun was setting in an exquisite display of purple and orange while the insects and the birds had already begun their somnolent songs.

Inevitably, he considered the absence of Lynn. He imagined her standing next to him, her hand in his, the warm comfort of her existence in his life, the two of them forever facing forward. Then his heart became heavier than he could ever remember as he realized that he had probably lost her forever. Theirs was a dead relationship like the Bennett's.

He heard the screen door open behind him and stiffened to the sound of light footsteps drifting toward him. "Those will kill you," Jess Bennett said. He did not turn. She came to stand beside him and looked out into the warm dusk. "Can I have one?"

Without turning to face her, he offered her the pack and lighter. She took one and lit it herself. They stood in silence, neither venturing a glance at the other. Jess finally said, "I'm sorry for what happened in there. It was unfair of me to do that to you." She said it perfunctorily, under duress.

"I'm not the one you owe an apology," he said and drew deeply.

"I can't help how I am. He knows that."

"Sounds like self-justification to me."

"Don't be so quick to judge me," she snapped. "I've loved Jim Bennett longer than you've been alive."

Guy couldn't help but look at her when she said this, staggered by the duplicities of the old woman.

"That's right. There has never been another man. He's the only man I've ever been with or loved. I remember how he feels, he smells, he tastes." She spoke the words as though they were delicious morsels on her tongue. "No other man could possibly measure up to my memory of him."

"So you punished him," Guy said dryly.

"I *freed* him," she said vehemently and if she were taller, her face would have been inches from his. "I made the only choice I could, the right choice. Something died inside me. I knew I would never be the same, and he deserved better than I would ever be able to give him. Understand this, young man, it was the bravest choice I ever had to make. Bravery is a difficult thing, perhaps the hardest thing of all. I did it because I loved him and didn't want him to have a false hope I could change. I'm glad he found Barbara, but I hate her. I absolutely hate her because she has my man. And I have no one to blame but myself."

They both looked out at the wavering shadows of the trees as the sun made one last reaching ray of orange across the land. "The first time I came up the drive I had the sensation I was expected, something had been waiting here all my life. The house, the family, the kids, this country life. I grew up a melancholy girl in London and never hoped for such happiness. Didn't know it existed. Then along came James Bennett, the most beautiful human being I had ever seen, and I felt like a peasant girl singled out by a prince. Then, of course, there were those five minutes on the *Queen Mary* when that woman gave me her all. The most momentous minutes of my life, of *anyone's life*, I daresay. My life with Jim and the children was heaven on earth. I should have known it couldn't last. I've carried the memories of those years with me all of my life. They're the only things that have kept me going."

Guy didn't offer a nod of understanding, didn't believe she deserved a hint of cordiality.

She seemed to accept his bleakness toward her, perhaps felt she had earned it, and continued, "Even as a child, I always pictured my life as a path through the woods. It's always night and the moonlit path unrolls so far into the distance I can't see the end. The woods on either side are alive with the people and events I encountered in good times and bad. My mother is in the shadows, Jim and the Schofields, the children, and, of course, that pitiful young woman. I followed the path unfailingly until Zach died. I could have suffered through the void of losing just one of them, but both was simply too much for me. Void is a kind word. It was like a double amputation and I fell off the path and lost my way. I simply existed." She blew smoke and was quiet a moment. "I considered killing myself and joining them, but I knew God would not forgive me and I couldn't risk never seeing them again."

"I assumed from your treatment of the pastor the day Zach died that your faith was strained beyond forbearance and you'd become an atheist."

"Hardly. Only an egotistical fool can look up into the night sky and say there is no God. No, I'm convinced of God's existence.

After the children died, I decided God was cruelly indifferent. I had to be angry with someone. Who better than God?"

"And Jim."

She sighed and nodded. "Yes, and Jim, God love him. You always hurt the one you love the most." She suddenly lifted her hands to his face and turned him toward her. "But you have given me this miracle, this one last chance to find my way before I die. I can see the end of the path. *Please help me*."

Guy pulled from her and stared away. He became aware of her eyes on him, followed by the wave of self-consciousness he always experienced when he caught someone admiring him. But Jess Bennett seemed to be peering past his features, through skin and bone, probing his very soul, feeling his woundedness.

"You're a melancholy person too, aren't you?" she asked, more comment than question.

He did not answer. He felt like a specimen under a microscope to which she devoted her full attention.

"Jim told me everything he knew about you while you showered. An unhappy childhood, insecure adulthood, a lost love. You know unhappiness. I could tell the first time I met you on the *Queen Mary*. Such a sad young man. A handsome, but sad young man. You have a quality under that veneer of self-confidence. You know what I think? You're just as frightened and bitter about your path as I am mine."

She twisted around completely until she was leaning back against the porch railing and staring straight up into his face. "Listen to this old woman. You're too young to know this, but some day your youth will be gone. In its place will come an awful wisdom. And a horrid moment it can be when you realize it has come too late to change anything." She flicked her cigarette away and stood upright. "When you feel you've finally learned enough to live, you're old enough to die." As she proceeded to go inside, she lightly grasped his wrist. "Don't tarry."

The silence that followed accentuated her words and the solitude of the country seemed to mock him, to show just how sinister a calm peace could be, a silence in which the mind festered. Night had settled over the countryside and fireflies winked lazily over the lawn.

He believed this haunted couple had tricked him into revealing painful truths. They would not permit him to be a voyeur but insisted he be a reluctant participant. The evening before he'd considered himself an archeologist uncovering an ancient coffin only to find it his own Pandora's Box. He'd never had plans for tomorrow once he had escaped his past. Life was a linear path, as Jess Bennett noted. He held fast to a prolonged present where he could take shelter from the specters of the past and the future, through the vicarious thrill of watching other people engaged in the pressing occupation of living.

The Bennetts had pushed him to the brink and exposed him to the future. He knew the truth had always been lying inside, incontrovertible and frightening but hidden beneath veils of secrecy. A dull, fading ember had suddenly sparked to life and glowed hotter and brighter, burning through.

He condemned himself an immoral liar and coward. "You're the only person that makes me happy," he often told Lynn. "Without you, I don't exist." He made her feel essential and, so, gave her a sense of responsibility toward him. She would smile tenderly at him, unaware he blackmailed her while he silently celebrated his twisted triumph. He kept both of them steadfastly immobile, many miles from yesterday, never reaching toward tomorrow. All of his life he had exploited his skin color without conscience, using it as a weapon to bleed every last drop of sympathy.

He and Jim both grieved for living women, but there the similarities ended. To his chagrin, he realized he had much more in common with Jess than Jim. She was not a delicate woman, and she wore her self-possession as armor. Her years of despair had resolved her into a sadly bitter but completely self-sufficient woman who frightened Guy for his own future. He resented Jess for her wicked mercy and Jim for forcing him into admissions that had been safely unspoken. For the first time, he felt distinctly uncharitable toward the foreign woman for her pleading, urgent eyes. They had at once sent him fleeing away from the past and hurtling toward the future. He had the sense of being taken apart on a workbench, violated and broken for all to see.

Defeated, he went into the house.

~ * ~

They were sitting on the floor of the parlor, going through photographs spread haphazardly on the floor and coffee table. Jim was weeping. Jess, lost in the long, cool shadows of memory, lifted her eyes to watch him, unruffled, as though his tears were simply an indignity that must pass.

"How else can I tell that poor creature about our children's lives?" Jess asked Guy as if she had found the only solution to a difficult dilemma. She was sorting the photos into separate stacks.

"I have a feeling," Guy began carefully. They looked up at him. "I have a feeling that you need to make this trip by yourselves. I'll get you to the airport and make sure you are safely on your way, but then you'll be on your own. I don't really feel that this is my journey."

They looked at him blankly for a moment. "Whatever are you talking about?" Jess demanded.

Guy looked down at his feet. "Doors have opened I am not prepared to enter. It's difficult to explain."

Jess lifted her chin high. "You're going," she said sharply. She spoke as if he was foolish for having even considered not going. "You're as much a part of this as we are."

Jim was not condescending but gentle and beseeching. "You have a responsibility to that woman to see this through. She pleaded with you, just as she did with Jess and I. Like you said, *her eyes*. You'll see them in your dreams the rest of your life. Imagine if you don't help her."

After a moment of silence, Jess repeated, "You're going." The finality and sternness in her voice settled the debate. She considered it the end of the discussion, so both men remained quiet.

Guy sat on the sofa and Jess solicitously passed a photograph to him and waited for his reaction. A young Jim in uniform, standing very erect with hands at his hips. A tall, broad-shouldered man with thick arms. His teeth were square, and his dark skin made him look very healthy. A beautiful human being, indeed. He looked to Jess and nodded. She covertly arched an eyebrow seeming to say, "Didn't I tell you so." She gathered some photographs from the floor. "Go through these and separate any that strike you as authentic and real. No school pictures but those that catch them truly alive. I want her to know they were happy."

The first photo he picked up was one of the four of them sitting on a porch swing. Jim took up half the swing, his dark hair and eyes making his teeth look almost too brightly white. Long-haired Kathleen leaned her head against Jim's arm while a tiny Zach gleefully clapped his hands together, smiling toothlessly from Jess's lap. But the most remarkable person in the photo was Jess. She was very young with what Guy regarded as handsome features. Her jaw was firm and strong, her cheekbones high and pronounced, her blonde hair lifting across her face in the breeze. Her smile, indeed her entire body language, spoke of pure contentment that reached out to him through the decades.

Such happiness, Guy thought, and immediately envied them and pitied them.

The next was a snapshot of a Christmas tree in this very room with the children standing solemnly on either side of a severe, school-marmish woman whom he assumed to be Jim's mother. Another, in color, showed a view of the front lawn with the children, obviously older, riding bicycles down the drive. The house shone breathtakingly white behind them. Guy could imagine the glory of summers past in this house.

A gentle breeze hinting of rain drifted through the screen windows. Outside, the crickets cheeped loudly. Inside, the house dozed around them. Guy's eyes were heavy, and he had never been so tired. The photos blurred before him, and he thought, I will just lay my head back and rest my eyes for a moment. *Just a moment.*

He tucked the robe securely between his thighs lest Jess's curious eyes roved over him and slowly lifted his legs and laid his head on the armrest. But the current of sleep carried him gently down, down through the shafted depths, darker and warmer, until reality completely receded, and he sank into a serene oblivion.

Ten

At first, there was a disjointed cascade of images. A soft, red carnation against smooth granite. The nametag silently somersaulted through the weightless black firmament. Then came a magnificent vision of the giant *Queen Mary* underway through a celestial sea, her portholes as brightly lit as the backdrop of constellations. Sprays of nebulous light burst at her bow and starlight churned in her wake, all intent upon the irresistible luminosity of the earth.

Suddenly he found himself walking down a path with deep woods on either side, heavy with night. The path itself remained washed in diffused, blue beams of moonlight stretching through the canopy of branches. He walked forward, neither fleeing nor seeking, but with some murky imperative to firmly place one foot in front of the other, moving deliberately down a predestined path with only darkness at the end.

He sensed the coolness of earth beneath his feet and realized he was barefoot. When he looked down, he was completely naked, his penis hanging limp. He looked over his shoulder. With each step, the woods silently gathered and closed behind him. Moving relentlessly forward was the only option afforded him. The woods were deeply warm and still with no sound of slumbering insects or birds, not even a rustling breeze.

Yet the woods were alive.

Voices fell on his ears from somewhere far within. A mysterious, grave, and beautiful aria sung in an unknown tongue drifted crisply through the branches and lingered about the leaves. He saw dim figures ahead, hardly more than shadows, standing at the edges of the path on either side, waiting. A shadow materialized into a small black boy looking up at him with innocent eyes, a cherished playmate from childhood, long dead of leukemia. He stood solemnly watching as Guy passed.

Kathleen and Zach stood together, holding hands. They were young children with their mother's eyes, eyes that begged him on behalf of both mothers.

His mother stepped forward, young and drunken but with a penitential manner, trembling with tears. "I'm sorry," she slurred. "I did my best. Forgive me. Oh, *please* forgive me!" She covered her face with her hands, racked with sobs, as he moved away from her.

Somewhere, the steady march of the Allegretto began drifting in its sacred timbre, blending with the hallowed voices to become a darkly majestic fugue of his life.

A sudden rustle of underbrush erupted from the woods beside him, and Jess Bennett emerged wild-eyed and bedraggled. "I can't find my way," she cried to him in a panic. "You must help me before it's too late. *I can see the end*!" She flung herself back into the woods and still Guy moved forward, urged along by some blind and unwanted compulsion toward the black void at the end of the unrolling path.

In an instant, the woods and path ahead began disfiguring. The sides of the tree trunks facing the path became radiant with an amber cast and then began resolving themselves into solid walls of paneling down a softly lit corridor. The earth beneath his feet became free of pebbles and dampness, and he noticed the unmistakable soft crush of carpeting. The overhanging branches lowered themselves into a ceiling. Cabin doors rose from the vines and thickets and began swinging open of their own accord as he approached. In the doorways stood harbingers of Guy's past: lovers and the unloved; the accursed and the willfully forgotten, each long since banished to the dark principalities of memory.

The divulging doors swung slowly and silently, seeming to revel in each recollection. Jim stood shaking his head in one doorway. "He never had a father." His sad countenance made Guy feel doubly naked.

A figure appeared at the end of the corridor, barely a step out of the blackness. Guy hurried along with dogged instinct, the distance between them closing. The figure materialized into the naked, old foreign woman ambling toward him with the same resolute determination as he. Her fixed, unblinking gaze reaching him in their pleading, yearning way. Anxiety surged through him to meet her quickly and comfort her, to assure her that he could and would help her. He began to lope down the corridor and instantly saw her features shift into youthfulness while her dark eyes remained unchanged.

When he reached her, he recognized her with shock as Lynn.

She held his shocked stare for a moment, speaking to him without words, somehow a displeased comment. Woefully, she lowered her brimming eyes and turned to walk away. He stretched his hand out for her, but he was just out of the reach of her naked, brown back. He stumbled and fell, calling her name but could not hear himself. The only sound in his ears was the drumming of his heart, the melancholy cluster of voices, and the low, marching music. He struggled to his feet and ran for her but she had arrived at the attendant darkness and turned to look at him one last time, with a sad disregard, then joined the dark annihilation.

The empty corridor unrolled before him, and he was borne reluctantly backward and held steadfast, denied progress despite his exhausting charge. He had lost her, but he desperately struggled to reach her. A soft creak of woodwork sounded from somewhere above. As he ran, a clock ticked off seconds, louder and more distinct, drowning the voices and dirge, an intonation of rapidly passing time. He experienced a pang of longing and loss, despair and fear; then the soft creak of woodwork once again settled down upon him. Almost immediately, the corridor evaporated before him, and he lost his footing. He rose lazily through the warm depths of sleep until he broke the surface of wakefulness.

The parlor lifted itself around him. The gray, half-light of dawn had stolen into the room, and he heard the drowsy sound of rain showering the lawn and dripping from the eaves. A fresh, green scent filled the room. The pendulum of the grandfather clock in the foyer swung slowly as if time was apathetic to the frenzied chase of his dream.

A crocheted quilt covered him. His ironed pants and shirt lay crisply draped across a wing chair. The sound of running water wafted down the hall from the bathroom or kitchen.

Something had awakened him. He was about to lift his head and swing upright when the sound of creaking wood once again settled upon him. Someone was on the staircase. He held his eyes open in slits and watched the last few steps that were visible to him in the foyer.

The creaking softly continued until a hand gently gripped the newel post and he saw Jess slowly descend, landing softly like an autumn leaf from a tree. She pulled a red satin robe tight around her and remained still, staring at him, evidently to ascertain he still slept. He inhaled deeply and exhaled slowly, insuring the illusion. Satisfied, she began treading lightly down the hall toward the sound of running water.

He waited until he heard the sprung door of the bathroom whine ever so slightly. In an instant, he was up, tiptoeing across the parlor and peering cautiously around the corner. The light from the bathroom cast an elongated rectangle of yellow across the hall floor. His excited heart thumped in his chest as he covertly rounded the corner and pressed his head and back to the wall, his arms and hands flat. He slid his feet without lifting them as though he was on a narrow ledge. The water stopped running. For a dreadful moment, his heart beat even harder and he was certain they'd catch him. But the awakened voyeur in him coaxed him on. He slowly approached the well of silence and finally reached the doorjamb. As slowly as he could persuade his neck muscles to strain, he looked past the partially open door.

Jim was standing before the sink with a towel wrapped around his waist, his face lathered with shaving cream. He held a razor in his right hand. Steam rolled upward from the pedestal sink, undulating wetly against the mirror. Jess traced his spine then shrugged the robe from her shoulders. It fell to her feet.

Jess Bennett had a surprisingly lithe figure with rounded buttocks and still shapely calves. Only her raised back and veined hands betrayed her. She took the razor from Jim and softly, slowly, sensually began shaving him. Guy could not see Jim's expression through the constant rise and fall of steam on the mirror but it must certainly have been one of whirling shock and, hopefully, elation as well.

Even the gentle dipping of the razor into the hot water seemed choreographed for this blessed moment. When she finished his throat and right cheek, she bent and tenderly kissed his shoulder, a pendant breast brushing his upper arm. As she moved to his other side, she kissed the back of his neck and left shoulder then cocked his head and resumed shaving. Her eyes roamed the details of his face.

There was something intensely satisfying about what Guy saw and he found himself aroused. She took Jim's hand and led him to the shower. She opened the door without releasing his hand and reached in to turn on the water. She calmly pulled the towel from his waist and he followed her obediently inside.

Guy breathlessly watched their revival through the textured glass door, a refracting, living mosaic of entwined figures celebrating an ancient passion. She was loving him, telling him the truth through the rhythm of flesh. Their marriage came alive to Guy then, no longer lost to the musing decades of sorrow but a genuine, physical expression of an everlasting adoration.

Guy watched their rippling endearment behind the glass for a long moment, entranced, and then turned away to quietly slink back down the hall to the parlor, marveling at the warm cloak of tranquility that suddenly enveloped him.

~ * ~

In addition to a shoulder bag filled with photos, Guy looked down at a small heap of luggage Jess had placed before the entrance. He wondered what type of trip she could possibly be anticipating. A woman's prerogative he supposed and anxiously looked at his watch.

Jim sat on the bottom step tying his shoes while Jess primped before a mirror over an ancient, long-unused console. "Are you sure you don't want me to fry some bacon and eggs? I can do it in a jiffy."

Guy shook his head and said, "No, no. We must get on the road. We'll pick up something on the way." He sounded harsher than he had intended but an internal clock ticked insistently in his ears.

Jess threw him a disinterested glance and turned back to the mirror. Jim stood ready with her trench coat and an umbrella. As she smoothed the jacket of her purple suit, she said, "I guess we really should go nude. She would feel so much more comfortable, don't you agree?"

The sincerity of her remarks disoriented Guy for a moment and he looked at her in abject disbelief. Jim laughed and Guy abruptly remembered her peculiar sense of humor. He rolled his eyes and began gathering the luggage. "Let's go, let's go."

"Just a moment, good-looking." Jess lifted the nametag from the console and now, so many years later, she once again delicately pinned it as a brooch on her jacket. She caressed it thoughtfully, and then took a deep breath. She said in a lightly quivering voice that couldn't quite conceal her excitement or her exultation. "I'm ready."

Eleven

They began their journey in pouring rain. As Guy packed the peeling, battered luggage into the trunk of the car, he saw Jim and Jess emerge from the porch under the umbrella Jim held. Jess stepped delicately down the steps, cool elegance and mystery, as Jim held her by the elbow. Her confessions of the night before and her private revelation to Jim at daybreak had not dispelled the enigmatic aura that hung about her. He perceived something still hidden beneath her stony mask. She was like a statue that would take millennia to wear and erode away.

"Please put the snaps in the car with us," she said to Guy. "We can sort them further on the way."

He snatched the shoulder bag out of the trunk and slammed it shut. As he pitched the shoulder bag into the back seat, Jim and Jess stood undecided on the other side of the car.

"I'll be fine in the back," Jess told Jim. "The men should ride in the front."

"On no, no," he countered. "I insist. I couldn't possibly—"

"Just get in the car," Guy said impatiently. "There's no time for talk."

They looked across the car roof at his reproach for a stunned moment, and then Jim opened the front door for Jess, closed the umbrella and sat heavily in the back seat. His door had hardly closed before Guy pressed the accelerator and they rounded the circular drive. The driveway through the woods was so dark that Guy had to turn on the lights to navigate. When they emerged, the hills and fields were misty landscapes, dreary and uninviting, yet the distant belts of trees stood nobly in the downpour. The ditches overflowed and the weeds, so tall and spiked the day before, now flowed beneath the current like stippling schools of fish.

"You'll need to get on Route 45 North," Jim said. "Then hit Interstate 64."

Guy nodded and glanced at his watch.

"Would you like me to drive part of the way? I've driven it many times."

"No. By God, I'm going to get you there, hell or high water." Did they hear the determination in his voice? Or just the viciousness? *They can't hear that internal clock.* Their journey, *their journey.* Then the pleading face of the foreign woman floated before him and he involuntarily ground his teeth.

The church and cemetery appeared through the gloom with their proud sense of generations but they seemed to have receded before nature this morning, as remote from civilization as the moon. Somewhere beyond the mists, beneath the rain-soaked ground, the two reasons for this fantastic journey slept on.

When they reached the highway, Guy pulled out with a shriek of thrown gravel. Jess fastened her seat belt and Jim leaned over the seat and placed his hand upon Guy's shoulder. "It's barely past daybreak. We have plenty of time."

Guy did not answer and the hand slowly slipped away.

The drab countryside rolled past them, yesterday's magical splendor of far-reaching land lost behind slashing sheets of rain. The farmhouses were equally unimpressive, desolate and lonely under dark, churning clouds. He considered their simple occupants, probably sleeping to the drum of rain, blissfully ignorant of three travelers traversing an unbelievable realm just a few hundred feet from their front porches. The absence of even a hint of stirring humanity disturbed him, depressed him, and he was angry that the solitary nature of this mission pressed squarely upon his shoulders.

"Hand me some of those snaps, Jim," Jess said. He passed a handful over the seat and she began studying them. "This one of Zach with his first catfish I'm unsure about. Do you think she would understand?"

"He's grinning from ear to ear, isn't he? That should tell her everything she needs to know."

They passed photos back and forth and it seemed to Guy they were reminiscing rather than sorting the best from the ordinary. When they occasionally chuckled over one, anger rose within his throat, threatening to flare past his lips. *No appreciation whatsoever for my plight*. His rancor grew. He sensed himself teetering between vindictive violence and tears.

Once, Jess asked Jim lightly about Barbara, like the dipping of a toe into cool water. It may have seemed a casual question to Jim but Guy knew her terrible desire to justify her hatred for his wife. He spoke of children, grandchildren, and great-grandchildren, and Guy experienced a momentary sadness for Jess as she sat listening and occasionally lying with a pleasant comment.

Guy remained quiet, eyes focused on the highway but trembling inside. He had never experienced so many contrasting emotions brewing at once and wondered how much the human spirit could withstand before being utterly crushed.

"This is the last town before the interstate," Jim said. "We better get our breakfasts now."

Guy pulled into the first fast-food restaurant he saw. Without consultation, he wheeled into the drive-through and instructed the attendant at the speaker-box to "give us three coffees and three breakfast sandwiches." When she politely began to recite the various sandwiches available, he interrupted her curtly and said, "Whatever you have ready now."

When he pulled forward and handed her a bill, she turned to the cash drawer and he said quickly, "We don't have time for change. Just give me the food."

She stared blankly at him, seemingly hurt by his shortness, and handed him the coffees and sandwiches. Her eyes were still on the car as it squealed onto the highway.

When he caught Jim and Jess exchanging glances, he said, "Am I the only one who appreciates the time factor here? If we don't make the airport, I can't get you to Oceana. Pure and simple."

"We're going to make it," Jess said firmly and grasped his shoulder. "You're going to bring me and that woman together this very day. I know it."

For a fleeting moment, Guy thanked God for her confidence even as the oppressive knot in his stomach tightened.

The interstate was all cloaked headlights and taillights in the deluge. Plumes of water rose behind each vehicle like sails unfurling. Guy stayed in the left lane, speeding past those drivers who were obviously unsure of their safety and driving the speed limit. On two occasions, a car pulled out in front of him and stayed infuriatingly even with the overtaken car while Guy fumed wildly behind. "God-dammit! What's wrong with these people?"

The third time a car leisurely pulled to the left, his temper seized him and he tailgated the car before him and laid on the horn until it swung back into the right lane. He violently pounded the dash with his fist and looked past Jess to the driver, now opposite him, gave the finger, and shouted, "Fuck you!"

Jess brought a hand to her chest, startled, and said, "Honey, Jim will drive for a while. Let's pull over and switch."

Guy ignored her and offered no apology. Jim and Jess Bennett insisted he be architect of this impossible drama and they were definitely going to understand what exactly they were asking of him. The release liberated him in some inappropriate way and he no longer felt the need for civility. After all, weren't they intimate strangers now?

The rain fell harder, striking the windshield with a fury that made the whip of wipers pointless. Water surged against the fenders and underbody, pulled the steering wheel and veering the sides of the car toward the shoulders as though the rain's sole purpose was to impede him.

"Oh my," Jess said. "I can't even see the center line. Hadn't we better stop until it blows over?"

Guy gave no response and she passed a worried look to Jim. Guy saw him in the rearview mirror raise his eyebrows to her.

Guy swung from right to left as he navigated the slower drivers. The only sound inside the car was the rustle of photographs and an occasional short conversation between Jim and Jess. Guy caught her eyes drifting over him while she spoke and knew instinctively she was alarmed, masking her concern with meaningless chatter.

Failure snapped at his heels, or rather his bumper. He had the unnerving feeling his past, his adult years, his every deficiency was keeping astride of the car, taunting him, condemning him, forecasting failure. In the rearview mirror, he saw Jim staring out the window in placid stillness. Instantly, he knew the old man's journey had ended with the gray break of dawn in the steaming bathroom where he received his long-awaited reward, the promise, the assurance of an unbroken love. He was simply along for the ride now.

Shortly, he saw flashing lights ahead and the bright red glare of taillights as the vehicles before him slowed tentatively before stopping completely.

"Son of a bitch," Guy moaned wearily. "Now what?"

Someone was swinging a flashlight while walking to each vehicle. Guy rolled down the window for a police officer in yellow slicks and was temporarily stunned by the cool smite of rain against his face.

"A tanker truck jackknifed about an hour ago and overturned," he recited, punctuating his words with weary hands. He had obviously conveyed this information many times already. "It's full of compressed hydrogen. We're waiting for technicians to examine for leaks before turning it upright. Might have to evacuate a square mile."

Guy stared straight ahead, anger tightening every muscle in his body. His white knuckles clenched the steering wheel.

"How long do we have to wait?" Jess asked troubled. "We must catch a plane at ten." For the first time, Guy heard true fright in her voice.

"I have no idea, lady," the officer replied and moved on at a reluctant pace.

"Thought we should have left earlier," Guy said and maliciously shoved the gear lever to park.

~ * ~

For an hour, he did not speak as they sat anxiously. Consumed by a useless rage, he vented his entire life's misfortune through a deadly silence, a quiet time for the mind to fester. This rage was familiar to him. A memory of childhood played in his mind. A time when the hot misery of summer never seemed to end. He had begged a quarter from his mother for the ice cream truck and ended up standing behind a father with his small son perched upon his shoulders.

"Cherry or grape snow cone?" he asked. When the boy asked for both, the father laughed and reached up to grab his son's belly. *I would like to beat him about the knees with a baseball bat.* Guy remembered the searing anger that shot through him as father and son walked away happily.

Unexpectedly, another memory born of the same rage and hatred took hold of him. A much earlier memory of his young, innocent self when he awoke to moans from his mother's bedroom. He stood before her open door and watched her, barely conscious, regard him with half open eyes. A broad, white back made an awful movement between her legs as she arched to have him deeper. The stranger looked over his shoulder at him without missing a thrust and slammed the door in his face.

Fearing any conversation might fire the gun of his temper, Guy's passengers looked forlornly out the rain-slashed windows in silence. When the car lights before them began moving slowly forward, Jess perked up and Jim leaned over the seat. They moved past an officer waving them onto the shoulder and around the wreck. The tanker's tires hung askew like the legs of an animal being devoured by lions. Debris littered both sides of the pavement and Guy did not recognize anything even slightly resembling the truck's cab. The ambulance was probably unnecessary.

As they reached the outskirts of St. Louis, the traffic thickened and the drivers became more aggressive. The lanes multiplied, overpasses and underpasses swelled with vehicles, and giant green signs commanded all below with haughty intimidation.

Guy engrossed himself in a race of time against faceless opponents. He changed lanes, overtook other drivers maniacally, and was almost amused when Jess placed her hands against the dash to brace herself. Several times her right foot pressed an invisible brake on the floorboard.

The turn lane for the airport was finally upon them and Guy experienced simultaneous floods of relief that they had arrived and fear that they may very well be too late.

"It's 9:52," he said. Then all three saw the traffic clearly bottlenecked behind a car sideswiped by an SUV with crumpled hood and grill. The police had not yet arrived and the drivers were between the wrecks arguing. They came to another complete stop and Guy threw up his arms and laughed bitterly. "Man, it wasn't meant to be. Wasn't meant! But I tried, God-dammit. Can't say I didn't try."

Jess Bennett looked fearfully through the windshield as she edged forward to see. "No," she said in a disconnected voice. Then her car door was opening and she vanished into the rain.

Guy stared at the open door thunderstruck a moment, then sharply turned the steering wheel and jumped the curb with something scraping ominously beneath. He parked on the narrow median between lanes and turned the car off. He had no sooner popped the trunk open than Jim was out of the car with the bag of photos flung over his shoulder and trying to gather their luggage.

"I'll get those," Guy said. Jim turned to him, handed over two bags, shoved one under his arm and took off.

At that moment, the driver in the car that had been behind them lowered his window and shouted through the rain, "What in hell do you think you're doing, you dumb nigger?"

Before Guy had a chance to respond, Jim reached into the car and punched the man in the face. His head was thrown backward violently against the headrest then bounced forward to hit the steering wheel. He was out cold and the horn blared abashedly for him.

The men zigzagged between cars and saw Jess running as fast as a seventy-eight-year-old woman could through a grassy area adjacent to the main terminal. The onslaught of rain was blinding and the notion of a titanic struggle between himself and nature returned to him, scared him. He passed Jim who slopped heavily onward, often stopping to pull his shoe from the mud. Guy had almost come astride of Jess when his right foot slipped sideways and he slid completely down onto his left side. Mud and water saturated his pant leg and as he attempted to stand, he fell to his knees before finally regaining his balance.

Jim stopped to offer a hand but Guy waved him on. "Go! Go! Go!"

Jess entered the terminal first without looking back. When the men reached her, she stood pitifully still, looking very small, searching fruitlessly in every direction, completely lost in the bureaucracy of the huge terminal. Did she want to cry but was too stubborn, Guy wondered.

"Concourse C," Guy shouted and waved them frantically on. "I'll get the tickets." At the counter, he looked up at the precise moment to see their flight indicated "Boarding" had begun to flash with urgency.

With tickets in one hand, one piece of luggage in his other, and the other tucked under his arm, he caught up with the Bennetts. The distinctly feminine clack of Jess's low heels echoed softly as she ran with her hair swinging, her coat tails flapping, and her belt buckle swinging in broken circles behind her. Jim reared backward as he ran, quite erect, which pushed his abdomen forward and made him look comically corpulent. The luggage bounced against Guy's side and the hip he had fallen on began to reprove him viciously. The crowds stopped, turned with shock, and stared dumbfounded at their stampede.

Guy stumbled over a pet taxi and heard a startled yelp from inside just as they reached a security checkpoint. Jim and Guy threw the luggage and shoulder bag onto a conveyor belt and urged the security attendant to hurry.

Nonplussed when Jess tried to enter the metal detector, the attendant said sedately, "You'll have to wait a moment, ma'am. Everyone else does." She glared at him with tightened lips and Guy absently thought what a shame it was that there was no time for the stranger to experience the full grit of Jess Bennett.

After an unnecessary display of thoroughness, he allowed Jess through and she ran.

Suddenly an alarm sounded. The attendant demanded they open the suspect piece of luggage. Jim popped the snaps and the attendant reached in and pulled out a rusted toy police car. Guy glanced in and saw a pair of bronzed baby shoes on a plaque, a large top with yellowing string still attached, and sheets of crayon-scribbled paper lining the bottom. The attendant replaced the car, pulled up a small glass jar and held it to the light.

When Guy looked questioningly at him, he replied simply, "teeth."

Beyond security, a gate agent was clipping a red velvet rope in place and Jess cried, "Wait! Wait! Oh, please wait!"

The attendant asked Guy to remove his shoes for examination. Guy's hand tightened into a fist but when he saw the agent oblige Jess and pull the rope back, his thumb and fingers relaxed and regained blood. He slipped out of his shoes quickly and threw them, wet and muddy, as hard as he could onto the conveyor belt. The attendant's crisp, white shirt was splashed with a spray of brown and he stiffened and closed his eyes. He carefully lifted a shoe and examined it inside and out. "Thank you, sir," he said, clearly annoyed. Guy grabbed his shoes and ran.

Jim and Jess waited for him with the gate agent, begging her to wait just a moment longer. Guy handed the young woman their tickets and she waved them on and ran along with them down a narrow corridor.

Inside the plane, claustrophobia gripped Guy. After the run through the vast, open space of the terminal, the tightly enclosed, airless interior was like the eyes transitioning from bright sunlight to pitch blackness.

Somehow in the mayhem, Guy was the first to walk down the aisle. Passengers glanced at his mud-slicked pants leg, then at the harried couple behind him. He wondered what their impressions were of their breathless arrival, of the sight of a young black man with an older white man and woman. He sat by the window and tied his shoes, with Jess beside him and Jim next on the aisle. He stood to store the luggage in the overhead compartment but when he reached for the shoulder bag of photos, Jess took it out of his reach and clutched it. "I'll hold these."

The plane began wobbling backward and the stewardess instructed him to please sit down and fasten his belt. The plane was still for a moment. Then the sonorous voice of the captain welcomed them and promised better weather in Washington.

Jim's breathing was still labored. Guy remembered the heart ailments of his father and brother and leaned past Jess to ask how he felt. He dismissed him with a wave of the hand and continued to catch his breath while rubbing his knuckles. "I haven't clocked anyone since I was a teenager."

Suddenly, there was a shriek of engines and the plane rocked wildly and rumbled beneath them at great speed. Guy noticed a pressure on his knee and looked down to see Jess's frail hand gripping him, oblivious to the mud. A show of affection or, an attempt at reassurance? A glance at her face immediately told the story of faded beauty. The skin was very loose this morning, translucent as tissue paper hanging from her jaws and draped around her neck. Her head lay back, eyes closed, and the hair she had so carefully styled that morning now hung about her face like damp moss. As the plane lifted off, she stiffened straight in her seat and tightened her grip.

The realization struck Guy at once, as certain as death. The poor woman had never flown.

Twelve

The most intense journeys are never geographical.

Guy Turner assumed as he stopped the rental car before the gate at Oceana his responsibilities were about to be relieved. The military could complete the journey and he could peacefully vanish into his old, safe role of voyeur. He had trod dangerously close to a chasm, narrow and easily traversable but deep, possibly bottomless, with a swirling darkness so great he chose not to risk slipping.

The sun was shining and a breeze blew hot and heavy into the car as he rolled down the window for a sergeant stepping from a gatehouse. “General Walter Van Cleve has arranged for air transportation for me and two other civilians.”

“Your permit, please,” the young man said.

The request jarred Guy. “Permit? I told you, General Van Cleve is expecting us.”

The sergeant repeated himself. “Your permit, please, sir.”

Anger once again took dominion of Guy and he jumped out of the car and stared down at the young man. In a fury, he said, “I don’t have a permit. General Van Cleve is expecting us. Open this gate at once!”

The sergeant breathed deeply and said evenly, “You cannot have access to the hardstand without a permit.”

Guy spoke in a menacingly slow cadence through clenched teeth: “Get on the horn and talk to someone, *anyone*, who is in communication with the general and tell them Guy Turner has arrived. Now!”

Guy was clearly exceeding the authority of the man, bullying him, and the resentment showed. The sergeant matched Guy’s stare a long moment, perhaps waiting long enough so the decision to phone a superior appeared to be his own. He went into the glass-enclosed gatehouse and picked up the phone.

An airstrip was within sight, so tantalizingly close the impulse of violence bloomed within Guy. The demon of impediment jeered at him anew after a rainstorm, slow drivers, two wrecks, and a mad flight through a crowded airport terminal.

Inside the gatehouse, the sergeant hung up, looked Guy in the eyes and shook his head doubtfully.

Guy closed his eyes and slowly said, "Dial the Pentagon, extension 4212, and let me talk to whoever answers."

The sergeant grew weary. "You are a visitor without a permit. I suggest you contact the Pentagon on your own to obtain a permit. You will not be granted access without one."

Two MPs approached from behind the gate. "Is there a problem, Sergeant?" one asked.

Without warning, the seething temper that Guy had barely harnessed throughout the day finally escaped him and without his conscious knowledge or consent, his fist drew back and he watched the young man behind the glass reflexively cower and cover his face.

For a flashing moment, Guy Turner did not exist. He was absorbed into the dark eternity from which he had been born, senseless and blameless. He did not hear the explosion of shattering glass or feel the shards embed in his knuckles. He did not see the petrified face of the sergeant as Guy lifted him and dragged forward by the throat.

Then, like a spell broken, he jerked into cognizance. He heard Jess screaming and the MPs shouting with their weapons drawn and felt the strong tug of Jim's hands on his wrist. Incredulously, he looked into the red, gasping face of the sergeant and easily detected the man's neck throb in his grip with each heartbeat.

They'd reached an impasse.

Whatever had swollen and crested within began to course fiercely out of him. He released the sergeant as his legs simultaneously gave way beneath him. He fell to his knees and abandoned himself completely to despair. He cupped his face into his hands and burst out crying like a child, hard and bitterly. The flow was swift and honest, carrying him along in monstrous waves that crashed down upon all he had rigidly suppressed his entire life, washing away the dams of his soul.

Jess's hand slipped under his armpit and pulled. "Get up," she said crossly. "I won't let you do this. Not now."

He choked on a sob. Aware of Jim's hand on his back and his kind voice, "Come now, friend, come now," he collapsed further, bowing his head nearly to the concrete. He cried for an absent father, a drunken mother, severe Jess, gentle Jim, and lost Lynn. But mostly he cried for himself and his sad lot in life.

"I can't take anymore," he barely managed. "I don't have anything left. Everything's gone from me. Nothing at all left."

A staff car arrived and an Air Force major got out and approached them. "Mr. and Mrs. Bennett?" he asked. "Mr. Turner?"

The Bennetts released him as they stood and both answered, "Yes."

"I'm sorry for the delay," he said, and stared in amazement at Guy crumpled on the concrete amid shattered glass and the sergeant heaving for breath.

"Thank God someone has finally come," Jess said shortly. "That young man has been nothing but rude and inept. A complete inconvenience."

"Dignitaries have been flying in all day and in the chaos we overlooked the fact you would arrive by car. I am under strict orders from very high up to involve as few personnel as possible. So, if you'll come with me please. We've been expecting you."

Jess laid her hands on his shoulders and spoke against his ear, gentler this time, "Let's go, good-looking. Didn't you hear? They've been expecting us. We're on our way."

Guy lost all hope of controlling himself. He watched the watery mixture of blood and tears drip to the concrete and whimpered, "Go on without me. I'm finished. I told you I don't have anything left. Just go on."

Jim's thick hands reached around him and pulled. Guy stood shakily, hiding his face, as the blood ran from his hand, down his wrist to saturate his shirtsleeve. Jim took his hand, pulled out a white handkerchief, and wrapped it tenderly around Guy's knuckles and tied it. The act of kindness brought fresh tears but he no longer fought them. He was beyond shame or embarrassment. The surrender was powerful and unstoppable with an inexplicable sense of euphoria as grief rapidly drained from him.

Behind them, the officer ordered the rental car parked within the gate, and emphatically advised the sergeant and MPs that they did *not* see three civilians arrive at that gate that day.

"Could one of those young men carry our luggage?" Jess asked humbly, even helplessly, and Guy was once more in awe of her considerable chameleon skills.

The Bennetts flanked Guy and led him through the gate and to the car, handling him quite carefully as he was suddenly a very fragile human being. He sat in the middle with the couple cosseting him on either side. The major drove and one MP sat in the front seat. They were driven past a barracks section and out onto an airstrip. A Lear jet glistened brightly white on the tarmac, looking like a remote-controlled toy in comparison to the 747 they had just disembarked. A hatch opened and steps folded down as they left the car. Jess held Guy's hand behind her as she boarded and Jim kept a hand on his back. The major and MP loaded the luggage.

I am being coddled. He could never remember a time in his life when human beings had shown him such compassion. Reduced, defenseless against his emotions, his eyes brimmed again. He could not escape a feeling this was a necessary leg of his journey, that the horrendous morning had been a predestined ordeal to finally break him and lay something essential on his human heart to endure. Through the tears and trembling of his chest, his soul soared with an incredible freedom, a sense of having been challenged by an old adversary and that he'd not only survived but won.

"I'll not sit by the window," Jess announced. She motioned for Jim to take the seat and he obliged. She sat in the middle and Guy sat beside her at the aisle. She placed her hand atop his.

Two generals sat forward, stately men in blue and gold with ribbons and braided cords. They turned to stare with interest as Guy wept. A civilian woman with bird-like features and small, round glasses turned from conferring with them and smiled. She closed a briefcase and prepared to stand when a stewardess dressed in an Air Force uniform asked everyone to fasten their belts.

The white bird lightly swayed into a turn then straightened, and hesitated a moment as though catching its breath before gathering speed and shrieking down the runway. Jess stiffened and her hand pressed down hard against Guy's until they were airborne.

The stewardess wordlessly knelt beside Guy and took his wrapped hand. She removed the bloody handkerchief, opened a first-aid kit, and began plucking glass fragments from his knuckles with tweezers, dropping them into a paper cup. Guy watched tranquilly through wet, swollen eyes, comforted like a child who had fallen in the park, pampered by his mother. Next, she applied the antiseptic and wrapped his hand tight and thick with gauze. Jim thanked her on Guy's behalf.

The forty year-old man had become a child and the role reversal moved him in some basic, human way toward a more acquiescent existence. He thought of Jim's simplicity, his deferential attitude toward life, and no longer pitied him but rather admired him and better understood him.

The woman with the briefcase walked back to them and introduced herself as Professor Geneva Thomas, a linguistics expert at Georgetown University. "I represent the White House," she said grandly. "The President sent me to brief you on the protocol the government has devised for communication with an alien intelligence."

"She's a woman," Jess corrected her dryly.

Professor Thomas was taken aback a moment then lifted her briefcase to the headrest of the seat before them. "These are the tools we have deemed necessary to begin a dialogue. This is an assortment of picture cards depicting different aspects of life on earth. Also, we have created a special CD and player much like that on the *Voyager* spacecraft which she may take with her to further her and her kind's understanding of us."

"I should move," Guy said as she struggled to access the contents of the briefcase while standing.

"Thank you," she said and moved to take his seat.

Before he rose, Jess gripped his hand and said simply, "No."

Guy remained seated.

Professor Thomas eyed Jess with what may have been irritation but her voice remained pleasant. "Mrs. Bennett, you are the person she is most likely to seek out. It is necessary for you to understand the dynamics of beginning a dialogue. It will be very complicated without these tools."

"We began a dialogue fifty-seven years ago and we understood each other quite well, thank you."

Professor Thomas twisted her mouth and spoke in a steady stream as if to deter further non-cooperation. "This is one of the most monumental events in human history, Mrs. Bennett, and we simply cannot allow you to ignore the importance of greeting her properly. You are representing the entire population of this planet."

"She's not here to greet the entire population of this planet,"

Jess said testily. "She's here to find out what became of the two children she was forced to orphan."

"They were extraterrestrials."

"They were my children."

There was complete silence as the woman must have realized she could not tame Jess Bennett. "You are a *guest* of the United States government," she began less than cordially, "so I suggest—"

"I don't like you," Jess concluded in her frankest voice. "Please go away."

The professor took the sudden truth with an expression that was at once shocked, dumbfounded, and disdainful. With an indignant sweep of her briefcase, she tramped forward, sat by herself and shook her head negatively at one of the generals.

Guy heard a slight chuckle from Jim then there was absolute quiet as they roared east, arcing through the blue stratosphere of the present toward the enchanted hope of a rendezvous with the distant past.

~ * ~

"I'm a liar," Guy said in a voice as vacant as his stare at an invisible but absorbing object on his pants leg.

Jim snored loudly but Jess had not napped at all as far as Guy knew. She cocked her head and brushed her fingers over his cheek.

"How are you a liar, good-looking?"

He did not lift his head. "Running from the truth is the same thing as lying, and I've been running all my life."

"You said back at the house doors had opened, doors you didn't want to enter. They were doors opening on the truth weren't they?"

He nodded slowly.

"Do you know why those doors opened?"

"No. I thought I would be a heroic spectator to all of this. Not a participant. I'm overwhelmed."

"Let me tell you why. You've witnessed the pain and suffering that comes from love, and it struck a chord in your own life and scared the hell out of you. This journey opened that locked door of truth we all live with but pretend isn't there. That's it, isn't it?"

Guy closed his eyes and nodded. "There's something about Jim, something about the way he told me your story. He made it mine by somehow forcing me to look at my own story. He has a quality. His...his..."

Guy searched.

"His goodness," Jess said and smiled wanly. "He's full of goodness."

Guy looked directly at her then. "Yes. His goodness."

She sighed. "I used to resent him for his simplicity, his ability to suffer and then move on. Perhaps I was jealous. Whatever. He was prepared to continue living, but I was too enraged to accept the cross I was expected to bear. It was easier to blame God and resent Jim than face the truth I was not as strong and resilient as I let on. Do you understand?"

"Yes," Guy said with conviction. He gave her an earnest, insistent look. "I'm a liar and a coward." She shook her head but he continued, "I've never been ashamed of my color. Life hasn't been easy as a black person, I'll grant you, but I can't honestly say all the sadness I've suffered was a result of it. It was always easier to blame my flesh than confront the true demons within."

"Jim's not intimidated by the truth. He doesn't hide from it or seek it. I once asked him how he rationalized the suffering of the holocaust victims he witnessed in Germany. He rarely discussed what he saw there. I told him the prayers of those six million Jews *must* have reached God. Why, oh, why, I beseeched him. He looked me in the eye and said he didn't know why and, furthermore, we weren't to question why because we wouldn't understand even if God sat down on the porch swing with us and told us all. That's how he has lived his life. Take the knocks, don't ask questions, and get on with it."

Guy remembered how Jim dismissed him after he mentioned the ramifications his children raised in regards to evolution.

Jess shifted so she was facing him and took his hand. "It's important to me that you like me or at least understand me. I can't bear the thought of your thinking I'm some bombastic, evil woman. I can see your fondness for Jim and I understand your aversion toward me for hurting him. All I ask is that you accept me for who I am, a flawed, bitter, old woman. But also a human being who suffers just like you."

"I... I *recognize* you," Guy said.

She lifted her chin righteously. "I thought you might."

The plane struck turbulence, dropped into an air pocket, and rocked. Jess squeezed his hand and held her breath until the plane settled. Her fear made her warm and human to Guy. Jim stirred, repositioned himself, and continued to snore.

She looked over her shoulder at Jim. Then she turned back to Guy. “You and I pale in comparison. You and I spend our lives wondering why. Jim has lived his life wondering how. That’s his greatest lesson, isn’t it? It’s not *why* you live but *how* you live.”

Guy pondered a moment as her words registered then he agreed. “Yes. That’s true. I’ve really only know him for a day and a half, but I believe he’s the only man I’ve ever loved. He’s a better man than me.”

“He’s the best,” she said, and the magical note of passion in her voice floated in the air like motes in a sunlit window.

Thirteen

As the last, soft orange rays of sunlight waned through the cabin windows, the twilight of unreality deepened. It had been a day of running panic but now as the three hurtled passively into nightfall, it seemed that the tightly woven fabric of reality had diminished to a single thread drawn taut and finally snapped. Time dropped away, leaving their minds standing still in an introspection of past and future.

Jess sat absently stroking the nametag at her throat deep in thought. Jim had awakened and gently tapped his foot as he gazed through the window. Guy brooded over his journey that began two nights before in a haunted corridor on the *Queen Mary* when the unreal became real. The journey was too extreme to embrace as a series of seconds ticking off in real time. The notion was numbing. A human being from another world, an unknown civilization somewhere beyond the stars.

The music of the Allegretto rose strongly from deep within and played in Guy's mind, rising and building in an elaborate progression of mystery and anticipation that he believed the Bennetts would hear emanating from his head if they listened closely. He wanted to believe in that ancient, melancholy symphony of human existence, the darkly persistent sound of the soul being uplifted.

The lights in the cabin became more apparent when the sun died completely and the black windows reflected the interior. Shortly, they perceived the slightest dulling of engine thrust as the plane banked to starboard. As the wing dipped, they peered through the window to see the USS *Thomas Jefferson* below, a brilliant diamond on the ocean with smaller vessels surrounding her like the lesser accents of a ring. A circle of light shone on the deck beside the tall, steel island of superstructure, brighter than the runway, impossible to regard as anything less than a yearning appeal of invitation.

Excitement returned to Guy as the plane prepared for the final approach. What waited in the dim, unfathomable hours ahead? Disappointment or the suspension of belief? The plane straightened and the stewardess asked them to fasten their belts. The plane fell beneath them into a steep descent, the stewardess staggered to a seat, and Jess clutched the men's hands on either side of her. Guy, startled by the rapid plunge, pushed back against his seat, swallowed, and held his head erect as his internal organs rose inside him.

"Dear God, be with us," Jess murmured, tightening her grip as they dropped to the screeching protest of engines.

Down, down, until they leveled for a moment before a ghastly bounce of a landing jostled them forward to the limits of their belts and the plane thundered and shuddered ahead.

"We're going to go over!" Jess screamed with her eyes tightly closed.

At the last possible moment, there came a sharp tug to their stomachs as they sprung backward and the craft was instantly still. Outside light filled the windows as they began to slowly taxi. The three trembled as they released their belts. The generals stood and indicated for them to exit first. Professor Thomas stared sourly away from Jess with tightly pursed lips.

"Our luggage," Jess said, and Guy and Jim gathered it obediently. She still held the shoulder bag of photos.

The hatch opened, the steps folded down and Jess shielded her eyes as the glare of light poured through the opening. Guy looked out onto the deck, heard a "ten-shun!" and saw the glistening sabers of a double line of honor guard. Cameras flashed.

As his eyes adjusted, he saw on the runway servicemen in dress uniforms from each branch of the service in addition to the Royal Navy, the French Republican Guard, and a pair of Middle Eastern representatives he did not recognize. They drilled on in anticipation of formally greeting a party of dignitaries from beyond the stars. Guy and the Bennetts were oblivious to them in the carpet of light tossed on the deck from a dozen or more floodlights banked on steel tiers in a circular formation. A dais lay in the center with floral wreaths on all sides. Crisp bunting lifted and waved in the sea air. Flags from many nations flapped on their poles. Around the plane, knotted groups of people of all sizes edged closer, dim in the brightness save for the occasional reflection of light frozen on spectacles.

Guy knew instinctively he and the Bennetts were attracting the attention of all who watched. Two officers lifted their hands to Jess, but she stepped down with Jim's help. There was excited conversation and whispers, along with the rhythmical fall of boots from the drilling teams.

Guy was certain unseen eyes pinned their scrutiny on the regal, descending woman with her low heels, nylons, and skirt spattered with mud dried to the color of a brown paper bag. They saw the disheveled hair and mussed makeup. Yet when she turned her head to look behind, to look for her men, Guy saw that her face was purely ethereal, ageless, aglow with expectation. Not only had fifty-seven years melted from her in the harsh glare of light but something still deeper. Her very soul seemed exposed. She was resplendent in a glowing aura of dignity and revelation. She looked above the crowd, up to the ugly, gray island standing like a fortress in the middle of the North Atlantic.

"Not exactly the *Queen Mary*," he heard her say.

Guy was conscious of his throbbing, mud-caked leg as he stepped down behind the Bennetts but stifled the feeling when he saw Julie and General Van Cleve waiting at the bottom.

Julie kissed him on the cheek. "We began transmitting an hour and a half ago," she said tersely.

General Van Cleve took his wrapped hand, a gloomy but austere man who said, "Turner" in barest acknowledgement. He weighed the Bennetts briefly and took their hands when Guy introduced them.

Standing beside the general was a man who struck astonishment in Guy and Jim.

"Mr. Vice President," Guy stammered, and Jim stood with his mouth open.

"A pleasure, I'm sure," he said, and took each man's hand. He looked to Jess and was prepared to receive her hand, but she still looked at Julie, unimpressed by his presence.

"An hour and a half?" she asked and the disheartened tone in her voice was unmistakable.

Julie nodded and Jess turned away, wandered past the watching crowd toward a section of the deck in deepest shadow. Jim followed, but a vaguely familiar man stopped Guy, someone of academic or political significance.

"You saw this creature?" the man asked in an interrogative manner.

"Yes, I saw her two nights ago."

A translator stood between them and spoke in rapid Russian to a tall, medal-bedecked man looming behind.

"She simply appeared and disappeared before your eyes?"

"She did."

"Incredible," he said, shaking his head. "A technology so advanced we can't even contemplate it, able to travel the stars, yet she came out of desperation from that same civilization because she and her children were allowed to starve. Absolutely fantastic."

The tall Russian looked to his translator like a hungry vulture, eager for every scrap of conversation.

Guy saw the dark figures of the Bennetts standing at the railing. Jim's hands were atop Jess's shoulders. She looked up at the black sky pierced by starlight that reached out to her from a billion years before. Orion hunted in all his exquisite vitality. The heavens now held a strange presence for Guy, no longer a cold void with knifepoints of light but a glittering ocean of shining black, alive with the supernatural certainty of existence. A fifty-seven-year-old radio signal sent forth into that miraculous firmament, humanity's invitation for a convergence of love, longing, and loss with space, the past, and future.

He walked to the Bennetts and heard the sea lapping against the hull far below, the loneliest sound in the world. The deck swayed beneath them, rose, and then dropped indifferently.

They were crushed. The day made them intimate companions and, as such, they now shared the misery of disappointment. He remembered Jim's recollection of a young Jess standing in profile in a candlelit window when he told her he was going to Germany. Like that night, her expression was invisible, but her despair seeped into the darkness like a sinister mist.

Guy heard the heavy tread of boots on the deck, a shouted order, then the steady rise and fall began again. A camera flashed in their direction and Guy caught a flickering sight of Jess's solemn repose. Her bitterness was contagious. He saw her defeat and grief, experienced the years of spreading agony reserved for those who suffer the utmost cruelty. No one could help her. That helplessness pressed on his heart. "*Dear God, hasn't she suffered enough? Haven't the three of us been punished beyond human endurance?*" He despised God for the will He was imposing on them and allowed Jess Bennett's dark silence to swallow him up. Anger seemed more fitting than disappointment and he wallowed in it.

Finally, he felt obligated to speak and said, "I'm sorry. I tried, but I was a lousy prospect from the beginning. You see, luck has never been my friend. I'm afraid I doomed you."

Jim reared back sharply and irritably growled, "Stop that!"

Guy and Jess jerked their heads toward the unexpected admonishment.

"Stop feeling sorry for yourself, dammit!" Jim stood at the edge of night, halfway in a beam of light and Guy saw him scowl with his teeth set, eyes narrowed, and nostrils flared. "Nobody expects more from you than you're able to give. Who said you were responsible for anything that happened today?" Jim turned and looked out over the invisible ocean. "Everybody has a reason to pity themselves, not just you. Who in the hell do you think you are that fate would choose you and you alone to torment?"

The paternal scolding shocked Guy, but he loved Jim for it, knew he had waited years for those pointed words to be aimed and fired at him. Jess's dark silhouette looked up at Jim in stark relief. Guy knew she was regarding him anew, in either astonishment or admiration, possibly both.

Then Guy thought another camera was flashing on them but this light was all encompassing, shivering as it split the night. Lightning from the east. He looked up to rolling, boiling black clouds tinged with a glowing gold on the outer fringes. Jagged streaks of angry purple spiked the ocean around them as a gust of concentrated heat bore down and tempered the cold, salty air. In the moments that followed, he would always remember the stabbing shock of excitement when Jess's jacket crackled blue with static electricity.

There was hardly time for a sharp intake of stunned breath when a voice shouted excitedly, "She's in the ready rooms!"

The three ran out of the darkness and followed a phalanx of people crowding into the base of the island. The honor guards stood looking furtively at each other. No one had told them what to do in this unexpected instance. The heavily illuminated dais, obviously designated as a formal greeting point, stood abandoned as military and civilian alike fled inside. The moment was hectic and hysterical.

Inside, the lights flickered off, on, off, and the emergency lights glowed ineffectively down a steel corridor and stairwell. Guy was aware of running feet and jostling shoulders and elbows. In the chaos, the Allegretto accumulated all around him in a tremendous climax, building and booming in haunting splendor.

At a human knot, they were blocked and Guy shouted, "Let her through!"

The ranks broke and Jess led her men through a tight path. A requiem of faces turned to look at the woman pushing purposefully through them.

"The galley! In the galley!" they heard echoing down the packed corridor.

People squeezed together in a doorway, standing tiptoe, and peering over shoulders as if admiring an infant in a baby buggy. The luggage hampered Guy and Jim as they struck against the haunches of the crowd. They heard awed whispers ahead and sensed a collective sense of held breath. Jess squirmed between a last set of shoulders and stood still. Guy looked over her head.

In the dim orange glow of emergency lights, the naked old woman stood beneath hanging pots and pans, fearfully looking back at the strangers gathered against the walls and behind the counters.

The bag of photos slipped from Jess's shoulder and plopped to the floor, but she seemed not to notice. She edged forward with an expression of amazed rapture and fascination. She lifted both hands and offered them to the woman without taking her eyes off her. The equally exhilarated foreign woman looked to the nametag at Jess's throat and said "Bennett" in a weary, relieved voice.

They touched. They took each other's hands and whole civilizations rose and fell in their reunion.

Suddenly, a camera flashed, exploding the galley with swift shock waves of intense light. The woman backed away, startled, and frightfully glanced over the faces.

Jess turned her full grit toward the perpetrator. "Let us alone," she hissed.

The photographer, in navy uniform, was disarmed and lowered the camera. "But I must, ma'am," he lightly protested. "For history's sake."

Jess exhaled her words hatefully to the entire crowd: "Get. Out. *Now*!" She glared at one and all.

A moment of stunned silence hung in the air then men of rank and circumstance began filing out, passing disgruntled eyes over to Jess Bennett like wayward boys reproved by their mothers.

Guy set the suitcases down and started to follow the exodus.

Jess said, "Not you. You belong with us."

The foreign woman looked at him. At the moment of recognition, that sweet, feeble woman smiled at him. Then she assumed a most somber expression and lifted her chin majestically high toward him, a grave salutation from another world. Guy nodded in acknowledgement.

The lights flickered on, and the women studied each other closely and again clasped hands, joyful with each other's presence. The naked woman spoke a short sentence, a definite inquiry, and she looked beyond Jess. She looked at the two men and back to Jess. She repeated herself, looking about.

The dreaded moment had arrived. The melancholy music of his life had thundered to its climax and segued into the faintly hallowed voices of his dream, sustaining a long, steady note as though any variation of tone might mar the sacredness of the scene. Guy's heart broke for her and his eyes filled until he heard a whimper escape Jess. He lodged the rising cry in his own throat so he might witness the great unveiling of Jess Bennett. His heart beat faster at the prospect of seeing her true, hidden self than it had at his first encounter with the foreign woman.

Jim looked exceedingly grim, and he closed his eyes and turned his head down. However, the unfolding drama was too great to resist and Guy watched him swallow and lift his eyes back to his stricken wife.

Jess's shoulders hunched uncontrollably and, suddenly, her sobs split the silence. She gave up the grief she had ferociously concealed and lived with for so long. Guy realized an instant solidarity between himself and her. He was seeing through all her harsh pretenses to her naked self, as she had been in body that morning.

The woman frowned. She stooped to look into Jess's face, searching. Jess trembled violently as she matched the woman's stare, speaking with her eyes, answering the innocent, awful question.

The woman understood.

She straightened and her face twisted into an approximation of agony and fresh regret and she instantly looked upward and cried out to some deity. The sobs of both women rent the air. With nothing left for either of them, they clung to each other and wept.

A camera flashed from the doorway, stealing the moment forever. An officer crouched in front of the photographer with a video camera on his shoulder. A crowd clambered closely behind them with heads stretching up from behind shoulders.

Tears fell, drops of despair, until unexpectedly, the foreign woman pulled from Jess and began coughing, almost choking, doubling over with the effort. It was a sickening, phlegmy, necrotic sound rising from very deep within. She looked up to Jess with her weary eyes and all who heard must have recognized the rattle and understood the urgent nature of her visit.

Guy said a silent prayer for her soul that it would find whatever safe harbor dead travelers seek.

Jess gazed on in sympathy, delicately took the woman's hand and led her to a row of metal and vinyl chairs against a drab bulkhead. The woman looked down at a chair a moment then sat awkwardly, following Jess's example.

"Guy," Jess called. "Please bring me the photos."

Her face was wet but serene and content as she watched him walk to her. She smiled as a fulfilled human being, transparent to him now. With her transformation came the certain knowledge he was a different person himself. He had crossed a treacherous void and now stood looking back, intent and ready for the rest of the journey.

The foreign woman reached out and took his hand as he passed the shoulder bag to Jess. She held him with haunted, plaintive eyes that spoke of an emptiness greater than he had ever known. Her fate showed in her worn face, and Guy pitied her.

Jess lifted a photograph and offered it to the woman who took it and dangled it out between two fingers and curiously studied it. Jess pointed emphatically to the image. The woman saw and cupped the photograph in her hands and examined it with a mixture of bliss and amazement. She anxiously smiled as Jess presented another and another. She wiped her eyes and laughed lightly and opened her mouth in an 'o' when joy bubbled in her throat.

Jim brought the small suitcases over and sat beside the woman. She looked at a photograph then glanced at him. She dabbed a finger at the image. He smiled an affirmation to her. He lifted a scuffed, porcelain doll to her and she caressed the ruffles. She seemed to understand the significance of toys and handled each with extreme interest.

Guy watched as the three diverted sorrow from themselves with the contents of the cases and photos. He himself had passed through several states of wonder at the woman's presence and the spellbinding unfolding of Jess Bennett. The total effect was like having taken a powerful drug, an elixir of life. Standing there, something returned to him, or perhaps something that had never been present at all. He was living now rather than merely existing. Life came to him with an unknown vigor. He realized an unmistakable deliverance from his past and had traveled farther in two days than all his forty years combined. He had come a long way to this defining moment and a bold thought crossed his mind. He found himself equal to Lynn, ready to match her dream, to grasp and share it.

Suddenly, Jess bent her head into a boy's tiny sailor suit and began to weep cruelly. Her muffled sobs prompted the foreign woman to reach her arm around Jess and pull her head under her own. Tears streamed down her face but she did not utter a word. None was necessary, as they were both fluent in the language of grief.

For what seemed several minutes but may have only been seconds, Jess allowed herself to be comforted, to be a suffering human being reveling in the compassion of another. Guy cherished her then and a voyeuristic part of him wished the night would go on forever.

Then the rippling sound he had heard two nights before drifted gently from a far corner. A hulking, stainless steel oven wavered behind the disturbance as though seen through a heat wave. Guy watched as the two cameramen scampered into the room on their hands and knees and headed for the corner. One of them picked up a fork from a table and flung it into the undulating portal and it disappeared for a moment, and then was thrown back, the tines crackling blue with static electricity. The camera flashed, flashed and flashed.

Jess gathered a handful of photos, hastily chose some clothes and toys, and packed them into one of the suitcases. The three stood and Jess offered the suitcase to the woman. She gripped it and hesitantly looked back at the waiting wave. She was clearly not ready to leave. Jess quickly embraced the woman, and the tears began once more. The woman reached her arm around Jim's neck and leaned up to his shoulder. He awkwardly placed his big hands on her bare, bulging back. She looked at Guy and gave a brittle smile, a goodbye and a thank you that would remain distinct in his mind until his death.

The suitcase seemed cumbersome for her weathered frame, and she walked pitifully away from them, sobbing. Jess brought a hand to her mouth and reached out with her other hand as if to magically still the woman's despair. She leaned on Jim and cried against his chest. Jim stood tall and stoic, a solid man relishing his role.

Guy wiped his eyes and watched the woman step fragilely toward the shimmering opening, and simply disappear. The waves faded behind her and the enchanted moment was complete. Nothing was left unspoken and the beautifully desired reunion had come and gone without misery or a lingering wretchedness, but left in its wake an absolute healing that descended like a peaceful veil. All who had watched the scene would date their lives with this night, this shining moment of a lifetime. Then, with a perceptible reluctance, breath returned and time once again resumed its relentless march down the path of eternity.

Fourteen

Jess smiled at him over her cup of coffee. They had busied themselves in the kitchen that morning, preparing an elaborate breakfast, subconsciously forestalling the dreaded goodbyes with something commonplace. Jim did not raise his head from his plate lest he make eye contact. Guy cast lingering glances at each of them, trying to memorize them. Their minutes together were numbered.

After breakfast, without comment, they left the kitchen, stood in the foyer and finally, valiantly, faced the inevitable. Jess spoke first.

"You are all Jim and I have," she said flatly. "The government won't release what just happened to us in our lifetimes and probably not in yours. All the players will be gone." She took his hand, placed the nametag on his palm and folded his fingers around it. "We have no one else to leave this to. Tell our story to someone you love. Tell your children and grandchildren and keep our memories alive. You can make us and our story immortal." She took his clasped hand and kissed it, and then her dusky eyes took hold of him and steadied him. "Thank you for giving me peace," she whispered, her voice breaking lightly. Then, in a stronger cadence, she told him, "Remember, good-looking, it's not *why* you live but *how* you live." The eyes held him a moment longer, burning the words into him and she released him.

She took both of Jim's hands and laced her tiny fingers in his. She swallowed as she looked up into his face. "There are things I want you to know and never forget." Her voice sounded unnatural, the words a visible effort.

The sad, dreamy sound bit into Guy, and he discovered his voyeuristic inclination completely gone. The moment did not belong to him so he turned and left the foyer, closing the door behind him.

The sun shone brightly, promising him something despite his sickness of heart. The insects and birds wildly celebrated nature as he stepped off the porch. He stopped at the bottom step and slowly drank the view. The treetops in the distance shimmered in the light and the green fields rolled on under the slow-moving shadows of clouds. The barest breeze breathed across his face. The church steeple peeked from its hill, locating him, and seemed to beckon from afar.

Behind him, the Bennetts were closing doors forever. The future stretched portentously before him and he thought of the pioneers from centuries past who had traveled to this piece of land and shared the same meditation of tomorrow as he. They must have been daunted by the wilderness looming in front of them yet understood that they were servants to destiny. Like all travelers who finally settle and clear the way for the birth of civilization, they contented themselves with a complicity to become immemorial to succeeding generations so they, too, might live, love, and die in the same sacrosanct contemplation of existence since time began.

Standing there, Guy's past overlapped his future and he perceived he had always been expected here for this one fleeting moment of frozen present. In a sunburst of awareness, he knew exactly where he had been and where he was going. The Bennetts and the foreign woman had been waiting for him all their lives. The time had come and they receded behind him. Now he would tread forward with the buoyant hope that Lynn was somewhere ahead, wanting and waiting.

The door opened behind him and Jim walked purposefully off the porch and down the steps, passing him in a hurry to get to the car, expressionless, his head held high. He opened the driver's door, sat heavily, and started the engine.

Guy looked behind at Jess who had come to stand beside a peeling column. She folded her arms and watched uneasy but resolute. He remembered Jim's description of a similar scene many years ago when he boarded a bus in England, leaving her. She had stood stone-faced that day, too. The deepest love masquerading as resentment.

Guy walked to the car and opened the passenger door. Before sitting, he looked up to Jess and said a doleful, hollow goodbye. The house was watchful, listening, behind her. She was unmoved, impermeable, so he sat and closed the door.

The gravel softly popped under the tires as Jim rounded the circular drive with a set jaw, clearly determined not to talk. As the drive straightened, Guy saw Jim venture a glance in the rearview mirror. Guy knew with a sudden, inhuman certainty he would never see her again and, unable to resist, twisted completely around in his seat and looked back. She was still standing exactly as they had left her, no longer pleading or bitter but a forlorn figure at the end of her path, reckoning the journey. She must have seen him turn as she waved sullenly once. A single tear dashed down his cheek just as they entered the woods, and she disappeared behind the summer foliage.

Epilogue

The café was crowded and loud. Absorbed by a magazine, she absently nibbled a bagel. He waited for her to lift her head. Wearing a yellow turtleneck with her hair shorn close to her head and her caramel skin shining, she looked like a college student.

Four unruly boys rose from the table that separated them, and she was diagonal to him. Perhaps feeling eyes on her, she looked over and instantly appeared trapped, shocked, like a deer caught in the headlights. Eager to flee, she searched for an escape. She stood to leave, dropping the bagel to the floor, but he rushed to her.

"Please, please," he said. He wanted to touch her but wasn't sure he had a real right to. "Just a minute is all I ask, and then I'll disappear forever if that's what you want."

Her mouth was set petulantly, and she would not look at him. After a dreadful few moments of indecision, he was ebullient when she sat, her gaze downcast to the checkered floor. Her chin quivered and she folded her trembling hands primly in her lap. She was very near tears.

"I want what you want, Lynn," Guy said softly, bending his head to look into her face. "Not because I know that's what you want to hear but because I want it for myself."

She closed her eyes as if impatiently waiting for his words to cease.

He reached into his pocket, pulled out the nametag and held it out in his open hand for her to see. She gave a curious glance at it then lifted her dark, puzzled eyes to his.

"You see," he began in the most honest voice he had ever dared. "I have seen beyond the pale."

Author's Note:

The characters and events depicted in this novel are obviously fictitious; however, the errant radio signal from the *Queen Mary* has some merit of truth.

The *Queen Elizabeth* 2 did indeed inherit the call sign GBTT from her legendary predecessor and in February of 1978, the radio man on duty received a message addressed to that call sign and assumed it was intended for his ship. The message was, in fact, a World War II coded instruction for the *Queen Mary* serving as a troopship. Decades after it was sent, it arrived to baffle the captain and crew of a different *Queen* sailing in a different era.

Was the signal an elaborate, obscure hoax perpetrated in the middle of the North Atlantic? Or had it originally become space-bound through some freak atmospheric condition and "bounced" through the cosmos for nearly forty years to be intercepted and sent by intelligence yet to be identified? These questions are matters of contention that will likely never be resolved.

An Exciting New Gothic Suspense Story From Keith Wayne McCoy

READ THE PREVIEW

CASTLES BURNING

My dead father sits at night with no lights on. The outdoor floodlights sparkle in his eyes. The house is still, save for the grandfather clock ticking in the vestibule. I enter the parlor quietly, careful not to wake my mother upstairs. I tiptoe in front of him and settle cross-legged at his feet.

I cannot touch him yet. Crazed, despairing pirouettes fill my soul just looking at him, let alone touching him. Would I run screaming through the hallways of Lockwood, falling and crawling about in lunatic distress? Or, perhaps, pass out once again when upon reaching out and taking his hand, if I do not feel the warmth I long for? Is his soul still there, inside, patiently waiting for the morning of eternity? Or is it disturbed it has been denied the peace in death all souls deserve?

"I'm so sorry, Daddy," I say, breaking the silence. He is imperious as he listens. "But she is ill. And worst of all, doesn't even realize it. In her mind, she is justified in what she did to you. We should have seen the signs years ago." I bring a hand to my face in fresh horror of what sits before me. "Tell me how to make it right," I plead. "Let me know what to do and I'll do it for you. I don't want anybody to see what she's done."

I begin to cry. From far memory, I hear my father's gentle voice. *Now, now. None of that.* I try to remember the place and time. I cry harder.

Now, now. None of that.

Through the corridor of time, I am transported back to a boat rowing to the shore where my mother waited. His great, thick arms pulled us closer to her. All of the dread and resentment of childhood was full upon me as I watched her emerge, clearer and clearer. I urged ignorance of her presence, just that once. I longed for the opposite way, another shore.

With the recollection, an idea stirs within me. A small thought at first that explodes into soaring fireworks of certainty. I am uplifted as a plan arouses me from the slumber of depression into a manic awakening. The masterful plot excites me. I feel ennobled with the knowledge we will not be forsaken to satisfy her will this time.

My resolve is undeniable. I smile in the darkness.

An Exciting New Fantasy From KM Tolan

READ THE PREVIEW

TRACKS

Electronic ISBN: 9781771550901
Paperback ISBN: 9781771551007

One

Vincent swept back a lock of greasy black hair and watched two punks having their nighttime fun with one of the back alley's denizens. Same idiots he'd noticed hanging around the corner bar earlier. One hood was a shaggy tough with a scalp like rat hide. His smaller blond buddy wore a leather jacket even the bum they were rolling would pass up. The object of their affections might be mistaken for another sack of garbage left beside the dumpster, save for the groans and pleas while they beat him.

He glanced around the building's corner. Streetlamps cast yellow reflections across the otherwise empty pavement at the alley's mouth. Help wouldn't be coming. Chicago's finest didn't give a shit about this place, and why should they? Flop houses, hookers, and drunks. Welcome to West Madison. Shrugging his long brown coat over a nondescript dark T-shirt, he buttoned the duster against the evening's damp and stepped from beneath the bar's flashing sign. The crumpled bills in his pocket, earned from replacing a jukebox's blown amplifier, should ensure at least one day's worth of warm meals.

The old Indian motorcycle still leaned against the grimy brick wall where he left it. The cracked and peeling seat looked a lot like the one thug's jacket. Vincent swung onto the machine with an inner smile. Sure, his ride looked like crap, but only until you heard the engine rumble to life. He was good at fixing things. Most things. His eye caught the glint of metal in the flash of the bar's red neon. A sickening thud followed. Jesus, did they have to use a pipe on the poor bastard?

Sighing, he slid off the seat. That drunk would be him one day if the best he managed were odd jobs at dead-end bars. He fished a pair of brass knuckles from the duster's pocket, the coat being the only good thing his father left behind before running away years back. Not much for words, Vincent charged the two, their backs bent to the business of kicking the fallen vagrant. Rat-hair spun around in time to lose a few front teeth. Shifting his weight, he slammed a boot into the other's gut, bouncing him against the rusted bin like a ragdoll.

Rat-hair took to his heels clutching what was left of his mouth. Blondie bolted after him, pausing only to puke up an offering to the gutter gods. Yeah. Punks. They came with the territory, along with drifters like him and the bum lying at his feet. Damn if those two hadn't worked the tramp over good. He pocketed the knuckles and pivoted on a worn heel. *Not my problem.*

"Please…stay a moment." The words bubbled up from behind him.

He paused, took a breath, and then turned once more to consider the bloody heap. Most bums smelled of booze and piss, but this one looked more like an executive gone bad on his luck, yet still trying to hold the threads together. The victim's gray coat looked frayed only at the edges, though the wool was blotched by what those punks did to him. He even had himself a fancy-looking cane, not that it had helped the old man fend off West Madison's brand of vermin. Maybe the fellow simply took a wrong turn. He knew about wrong turns.

The man's busted-up jaw worked with effort, its gray bristles caked with blood. "A moment…just till the Westbound comes. Don't wanna meet it alone."

The plaintive entreaty tugged at him. Usually, he walked away from these things. Usually, however, didn't include a deep gash across the head right down to the bone. Vincent glanced back at the bar. Fat chance he'd get an ambulance out here. Poor guy's only crime was in being out of money, and finally out of luck. Just another of life's little blessings showered down by a loving God.

"I'll call you a doctor, old timer."

A rasping laugh squeezed out from surprisingly even teeth. "Too late for that, son. Number 9's done pulled out of Asheville. Heading to that big ol' Rock Candy Mountain." The man shuddered and coughed up red spittle.

Damn, you're going to die right here. He sat down beside the man, not having heard such lingo in the ten long years since Katy and Dad performed their vanishing acts. Hobo talk—stuff his father brought home from the rail yard where he worked. Vincent eased his arms around the man's bony shoulders, ignoring the sticky wetness seeping through the seat of his jeans. Poor bastard looked to have hopped his last boxcar. Nobody deserved to go like this—propped up like sack of refuse.

"I'll stay with you until your train comes, old timer." His throat constricted. "I had a sister who liked trains."

"Find her." The words struggled to whisper their way past bruised lips. Gnarled fingers scrapped at the pocket of patchwork pants that would have done a banker proud in their prime. The tramp pulled out a worn nickel.

Surprised at the chillingly appropriate request from a dying man's crumbling consciousness, he reached out and caught the coin before it rolled from relaxed fingers. A cold hand loosely grasped his wrist, and then slipped off after one long final exhale. Vincent stared into glassy eyes, wondering if the other's blank stare would punch a hole in someone's world once they found out about this wretch's ugly fate. Even hobos had family somewhere, didn't they?

He eased the body down and rose. "Hope you caught your train, old man."

He turned the nickel around in his fingers. The coin's front and back had been altered. A hobo nickel. Looked like a girl's face on one side, though he couldn't be sure in the dim light. He slid the nickel into his duster next to the brass knuckles. Yeah. Find his sister. Katy's anniversary was coming up again, and he'd spend another pointless hour staring down at weeds just like the year before. That and listening to Mom's accusations. If anyone needed disappearing, she did. The family he once called his own had long since buried themselves in Katy's field, himself included. Just too stubborn to admit it. Well, maybe Dad had figured things out. He'd taken off fast enough.

A bright beam dazzled Vincent's eyes, swept down to the

body, and returned to his face.

Now you assholes show up. Vincent ran for his bike, knowing damn well what those cops inside the patrol car were thinking, especially with his record. He stomped down on the Indian's starter and wheeled the bike around while the cops were still making up their minds about whether or not he was worth the trouble. The motor woke with a spattering snarl, sending the rear tire spinning on wet cobblestones before finding purchase. He shot toward the police car before it finished backing into a turn.

The cop was one of the few smart ones. The driver-side door swung open in an attempt to block him from leaving the alley. Swearing, Vincent jumped the shallow curb, sending the bike along the sidewalk. This would be a bad time for somebody to stagger out of the bar. Lady Luck resurfaced. Maybe she enjoyed a good chase. Fine. He'd give her and the cops all the entertainment they could stomach. The Indian responded with a throaty roar gaining him West Madison. A siren howled its frustration behind him. Traffic was light at this hour. If he made Columbus Park, they'd never find him. In addition to fixing things, he also knew how to run.

A warren of tenements and back streets surrounded his goal, and Vincent made use of them all. The pack chasing him picked up more hounds as he led them into a rat's nest of dead ends and sharp turns. Silently coast the Indian up one street. Cut through a gap in a sagging fence somewhere else. Double back in the shadows. Soon it sounded like half of Chicago was after him. Hell of a send-off. Too bad. He still had a couple weeks rent left on his room.

His T-shirt clung to him because of either sweat or the old man's blood. He leaned hard into the turns, the old brown duster flapping like a cape. The long coat offered some protection against the night's chill. An inviting dark patch grew beyond a string of streetlights. The park. The neighborhood behind him looked like Christmas with all those flashing lights. He idled the bike's engine, killed the headlight, and endured the jolt and rattle while coasting across the intervening avenue and over the curb.

Time to play pinball with the trees. Branches clawed at him, near misses with dark trunks adding to the hammering in his chest. The surrounding streets offered only so much illumination, but he knew these paths and ponds. Ahead waited a black sea of wide fields under whose concealment he would slip away from those screaming banshees.

Vincent's first steady breath came after staring across the night toward distant lines of blinking red lights. His triumph disintegrated into a grimace. Those bastards got a good look at him, and this time it wasn't about stealing a quick meal. What little life he'd managed to scrape together up here was gone, courtesy of a moment's misplaced pity. God only knew where he was headed now, other than it wouldn't be anywhere near Chicago. He patted the bike's gas tank, grateful he'd just filled it. He needed somewhere to collect his thoughts and figure out how to deal with this latest serving of shit. His shoulders slumped. Like there was a choice, right?

Home. Bad memories or not, he could walk away from there a lot easier than some Chicago jail. He turned the handlebars south for the distant farmlands of his torn adolescence.

He eased out of the park and kept to side streets, skirting the Cisco rail yards and chancing one of the canal bridges. Caution dictated detours and a slow drive, turning a two-hour trip into a nervous exodus costing twice the time. The state of Indiana begrudgingly surrendered stores and residential areas to more rural surroundings until settling on the dark silhouettes of cornfields beneath a May moon.

He pulled over onto a gravel swath and gave himself a chance to catch up. The only thing to worry about out here was bugs in his teeth. The sky was cool and clear, allowing an audience of stars to applaud his latest screw-up in silent derision. His shoulders sagged under the realization of how two years of shit jobs hadn't improved his worth in anyone's eyes. Go to the big city. Carve out a new beginning. *Now look at me.* Mom would have herself a good laugh before spitting Katy in his face again.

Cursing, he revved up the Indian and kept speeding southward until he crossed the Will County line in the pre-dawn's pearly glow. Even his duster couldn't keep the teeth-clenching chill at bay. Never mind. Wind was good. It kept him awake and cast an illusion of freedom around a future caged by his past. Sure, keep traveling and maybe find himself some obscure yellow-dog town. Sink into anonymity by becoming someone's field hand. Amounting to nothing was easy, but even being a nobody came with a cost. He didn't have enough money to get out of state. Heading home didn't mean he was walking up to Mom like a beggar, he reasoned. This was honest pay for giving her a little extra satisfaction.

Roosters heralded a wan sun as the Indian's tires negotiated ruts along the old gravel road where he grew up. His neighborhood was a slight rise of sandy clay overlooking a brushy field. Another year wrought only slight improvements along the irregular row of small houses. Some folks got around to replacing drab asphalt sheets with new siding. Such wasn't the case with the gray three-bedroom home capped by a non-descript brown roof. Vincent pulled into the yard, frowning down at what once had been a flowerbed until crabgrass overwhelmed it. The small barn in back looked more like a decayed deck of collapsed cards, the sagging roof having given way. Dad would've hated seeing how rundown things had gotten here.

His key probably still worked, but he decided instead to rap his knuckles on the screen door's peeling brown paint. He glanced at his watch. Just past seven. She should be up.

The inner door squeaked open. For a moment, Vincent looked upon the woman's graying hair and hard lines without attaching any meaning to them. The faded green-and-blue patterned dress hanging off her slight frame reached out and wrapped him in heavy memories. "Mom."

Her brown eyes sank into wrinkled slits. For a moment she looked about to slam the door in his face. Her voice was a thin drawl of country life dipped in bitterness. "What do *you* want?"

"Something to eat and a little gas money. I'll be out of your hair after that."

She peered around his shoulder. "Police after you again?"

"They're always after me," he threw back, following her into a small kitchen. The yellow cabinets looked freshly washed, and judging from the delicious smell, she was baking bread. Yeah, there was a loaf already cooling on a long wooden table. He helped himself to a thick slice, the crust still hot.

"You get yourself a new table?" he ventured, hoping to steer conversation into warmer climes.

"You'd know that if you'd come around other than when you're asking for a handout. It's Katy's anniversary. Go out and pay her respect."

He drew in a long breath. "It's not for a couple months, Mom."

Vincent jumped as his mother slammed an iron pan down on the counter. "It's Katy's anniversary, damn you!" She twisted to face him, her venomous expression no less potent now than during those tortuous years after his father had run out on them. "You go out there and tell her you're sorry. You promised your father you'd take care of her when you took her, so get out there."

"Yeah, I promised," Vincent muttered, trying to keep his temper in check. As if a twelve-year-old kid was going to deliver on such an oath. Didn't matter. Apparently, every damn day was Katy's anniversary these days, so he'd best play along. He needed the shuteye, not to mention money and breakfast. He'd get nothing if he kept pissing her off.

"I hope the police find you. God knows you deserve prison."

God knows why I keep coming back here. Disgusted with himself for thinking this visit would be an improvement over the last; Vincent grabbed an apple from a bowl on the counter and turned for the door. He glanced outside at his bike, tempted to— Do what? Start walking somewhere near the state line when his tank ran dry? Stuffing the fruit in a coat pocket, he shouldered open the screen door.

"Is that blood on your backside?"

The sound of genuine concern made him pause. Even a precious moment's glimpse at the mother she used to be was worth stopping for. "It's not mine, Mom, and no, I didn't kill anyone. There was an accident. I helped all I could."

"Accident," she snorted. "I bet you helped. That was your father's good work coat."

"I'll get it cleaned." Shaking his head, he walked down the dirt drive, thankful she didn't blame him for Dad's disappearance on top of everything else. Or maybe she did. One day Dad was there. The next…

Vincent hated him for leaving, but Dad had stuck up for him the day Katy vanished. Said it wasn't his fault. How in hell wasn't it his fault? Obviously, Dad went looking for Katy. Why couldn't his father have taken him along?

How little the field across from the house had changed, though these days it looked a lot smaller than he remembered. Same half-hearted attempt at trees. Same Medusa's hair of grass, burrs, and brambles. Same churn in his guts while tromping toward a line of undergrowth along a creek that should've dried up by now. Ages ago, the stream had been an adventure to reach, something to plan an afternoon around. It was easy to think the creek was a world away back then. Now, he needed a few minutes to reach the same area, with only old nightmares to lengthen the walk.

Vincent stared down at the brief bank along a muddy bend, watching tiny shapes dart and wiggle beneath filmy water. A small frog plopped into the stream, chasing after a dragon fly. Sighing, he closed his eyes, his fingers closing around the coin in the pocket of his father's coat. A gift from a dying bum to a stranger's sister who was probably dead already. That was the worst of it. Not knowing if he had a sister. Or a father. He pulled out the nickel. It belonged here more than he did. His hand paused in mid-toss, catching something odd about the coin's face. Ah yes—a hobo nickel.

He studied the feminine features replacing Thomas Jefferson's head. Carved into the gleaming coin with exquisite detail was a woman-child's bemused face, her hair a swirling cloud beneath a fanciful top hat. The eyes were wide with an excited sort of innocence expertly captured in the silvery metal. The old man must've worked on the nickel for years. He wondered if the hobo also sought to leave a piece of his soul behind—a grasp at immortality, perhaps.

He flipped the coin around. The image of Monticello was gone, polished down to a mirror finish. In its place was a bas-relief of two circles touching. A hobo sign like those his father taught him when Mom wasn't around. This one meant something about not giving up if he remembered right.

He stuffed the nickel back in his pocket. Bad enough to see the artist ending up thrown away with the trash. His art deserved a kinder fate. Don't give up. A good piece of advice for any man, let alone a bum. He looked up into clouded skies. "You'll get this when I find you, Katy."

He turned back toward the house, a quick meal, and if he was lucky, enough cash to get him as far away from Chicago as the old bike could manage. He pushed his way through a tangle of saplings and wild flowers, and then broke out into an open stretch of field divided by white ballast and gleaming rails. His heart did a belly flop into his stomach. He lurched toward the tracks with drunken footsteps, praying the vision would hold long enough for him to once again feel the crunch of stones beneath his soles.

The iron rail with its bright surface felt substantial enough to his tentative kick. Damn if the track wasn't humming to him like the purr of a backstreet cat looking for scraps. Swallowing, he stepped between the rails and stomped hard on a tie. The metal beneath his feet was real. Actually real. He glanced over his shoulder, expecting another oncoming light. Not this time. There was only the line wavering into a distant shimmer. No matter. Facing west in the direction Katy's train had disappeared into, he leaned into a steady trot.

"About damn time," Vincent muttered.

About The Author

Keith Wayne McCoy majored in Creative Writing at the University of Southern Indiana. *The Travelers* was a quarter-finalist in the 2011 Amazon Breakthrough Novel Award. In addition to writing, Mr. McCoy is a world-class collector of furniture and memorabilia from the 1930s luxury liner *Queen Mary*. He lives in southern Illinois.

Visit our website for our growing catalogue of quality books.
www.burstbooks.ca

CPSIA information can be obtained at www.ICGtesting.com
Printed in the USA
LVOW10s1448220415

435654LV00021B/1170/P

Abide in My Word

Mass Readings at Your Fingertips®

2019

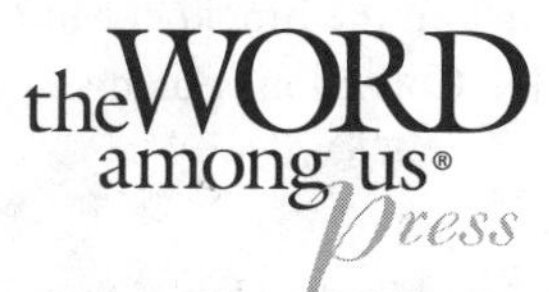

The Word Among Us Press
7115 Guilford Drive
Frederick, MD 21704
www.wau.org

ISBN: 978-1-59325-338-7
ISSN: 1546-0231

Published with the approval of the Committee on Divine Worship, United States Conference of Catholic Bishops

Scripture readings are from the Roman Catholic liturgical calendar for use in the United States. Celebration of solemnities, feasts, memorials, or other observances particular to your country, diocese, or parish may result in some variation.

Cover design by Suzanne Earl

Cover image: *The Lord's Prayer (Le Pater Noster)*
Watercolor by James Tissot
Located in the Brooklyn Museum
Photo: ART Collection / Alamy Stock Photo
© Alamy

Made and printed in the United States of America

Table of Contents

Introduction

When Jesus saw the crowds, he went up the mountain, and after he had sat down, his disciples came to him. He began to teach them, saying . . . "This is how you are to pray: Our Father in heaven, hallowed be your name, your kingdom come, your will be done, on earth as in heaven. Give us today our daily bread; and forgive us our debts, as we forgive our debtors; and do not subject us to the final test, but deliver us from the evil one."

—Matthew 5:1-2; 6:9-13

Dear Friends in Christ,

God is a loving Father. He is not far off. He is not impersonal. He is Jesus' Father, and he is ours, too, and we can turn to him for all our needs. Jesus wants his disciples to know this loving Father, and so he teaches them the Our Father when they approach him.

Reflecting on the Our Father, Pope Francis observed that "the Father who is in heaven knows what you need before you ask him" (Morning Meditation, June 20, 2013). Relating to God as a Father who knows and loves us personally, Pope Francis noted, is "the key to prayer."

Featured on the cover of *Abide in My Word 2019* is the painting entitled *The Lord's Prayer* by James Tissot. In it we see Jesus introducing the concept of God as their Father to his disciples. Those sitting at Jesus' feet are enthralled: their hands are open and their eyes are fixed on him as he teaches. They are hungry for what Jesus is sharing with them and enraptured by his words and his very person.

This year, Jesus is inviting you, too, to encounter him personally and grow deeper in your prayer life. He desires to teach you more about his Father and prayer. Meditating on the Scripture readings contained in *Abide in My Word 2019* can certainly help you. The Scripture readings contained in this book have been chosen by the Church as the Mass readings for each day of the year, as designated in the official *Lectionary for Mass for Use in the Dioceses of the United States of America,* which uses the *New American Bible* translation. During this liturgical year, the Church is following the Gospel of Luke (Year C) on Sundays and Cycle I for the weekday readings. (Year A focuses on the Gospel of Matthew and Year B on the Gospel of Mark.)

On Sundays, the first reading at Mass offers us selections from the historical books of the Old Testament as well as from the prophets and the wisdom books. The responsorial psalms or canticles complement and expand on these readings, and provide for us a means to voice our prayerful response to God. The second reading generally presents selections from the Acts of the Apostles and the letters written by Paul and others to the early Christians. On weekdays, usually only one reading—from either the Old or New Testament—precedes the psalm.

In the Gospel readings—the climax of the Liturgy of the Word of each Sunday and weekday Mass throughout the liturgical year—we have an opportunity to encounter Jesus, just as the first disciples did. Through the Gospel writers, we see Jesus' actions unfold before our eyes and hear his words to us.

We rejoice that many thousands of Catholics continue to find that *Abide* provides a helpful focus for their daily prayer and meditation. We pray that you will experience being drawn closer to Jesus and his Father as you read the word of God in the Scripture readings for this year.

The Word Among Us Press

JANUARY

Tuesday, January 1

Solemnity of Mary, the Holy Mother of God
The Octave Day of the Nativity of the Lord

First Reading
NUMBERS 6:22-27

The LORD said to Moses: "Speak to Aaron and his sons and tell them: This is how you shall bless the Israelites. Say to them:

The LORD bless you and keep you!
The LORD let his face shine upon you, and be gracious to you!
The LORD look upon you kindly and give you peace!

So shall they invoke my name upon the Israelites, and I will bless them."

Responsorial Psalm
PSALM 67:2-3, 5, 6, 8
R. May God bless us in his mercy.

May God have pity on us and bless us;
may he let his face shine upon us.
So may your way be known upon earth;
among all nations, your salvation. **R.**
May the nations be glad and exult
because you rule the peoples in equity;
the nations on the earth you guide. **R.**
May the peoples praise you, O God;
may all the peoples praise you!
May God bless us,
and may all the ends of the earth fear him! **R.**

Second Reading
GALATIANS 4:4-7

Brothers and sisters: When the fullness of time had come, God sent his Son, born of a woman, born under the law, to ransom those under the law, so that we might receive adoption as sons. As proof that you are sons, God sent the Spirit of his Son into our hearts, crying out, "Abba, Father!" So you are no longer a slave but a son, and if a son then also an heir, through God.

Gospel
LUKE 2:16-21

The shepherds went in haste to Bethlehem and found Mary and Joseph, and the infant lying in the manger. When they saw this, they made known the message that had been told them about this child. All who heard it were amazed by what had been told them by the shepherds. And Mary kept all these things, reflecting on them in her heart. Then the shepherds returned, glorifying and praising God for all they had heard and seen, just as it had been told to them.

When eight days were completed for his circumcision, he was named Jesus, the name given him by the angel before he was conceived in the womb.

Wednesday, January 2

First Reading
1 JOHN 2:22-28

Beloved: Who is the liar? Whoever denies that Jesus is the Christ. Whoever denies the Father and the Son, this is the antichrist. Anyone who denies the Son does not have the Father, but whoever confesses the Son has the Father as well.

Let what you heard from the beginning remain in you. If what you heard from the beginning remains in you, then you will remain in the Son and in the Father. And this is the promise that he made us: eternal life. I write you these things about those who would deceive you. As for you, the anointing that you received from him remains in you, so that you do not need anyone to teach you. But his anointing teaches you about everything and is true and not false; just as it taught you, remain in him.

And now, children, remain in him, so that when he appears we may have confidence and not be put to shame by him at his coming.

Responsorial Psalm
PSALM 98:1, 2-3ab, 3cd-4
R. All the ends of the earth have seen the saving power of God.

Sing to the LORD a new song,
  for he has done wondrous deeds;
His right hand has won victory for him,
  his holy arm. **R.**
The LORD has made his salvation known:
  in the sight of the nations he has revealed his justice.
He has remembered his kindness and his faithfulness
  toward the house of Israel. **R.**

All the ends of the earth have seen
    the salvation by our God.
Sing joyfully to the LORD, all you lands;
    break into song; sing praise. **R.**

Gospel
JOHN 1:19-28

This is the testimony of John. When the Jews from Jerusalem sent priests and Levites to him to ask him, "Who are you?" He admitted and did not deny it, but admitted, "I am not the Christ." So they asked him, "What are you then? Are you Elijah?" And he said, "I am not." "Are you the Prophet?" He answered, "No." So they said to him, "Who are you, so we can give an answer to those who sent us? What do you have to say for yourself?" He said:

"I am *the voice of one crying out in the desert,*
'Make straight the way of the Lord,'

as Isaiah the prophet said." Some Pharisees were also sent. They asked him, "Why then do you baptize if you are not the Christ or Elijah or the Prophet?" John answered them, "I baptize with water; but there is one among you whom you do not recognize, the one who is coming after me, whose sandal strap I am not worthy to untie." This happened in Bethany across the Jordan, where John was baptizing.

Thursday, January 3

First Reading
1 JOHN 2:29–3:6

If you consider that God is righteous, you also know that everyone who acts in righteousness is begotten by him.

See what love the Father has bestowed on us that we may be called the children of God. Yet so we are. The reason the world does not know us is that it did not know him. Beloved, we are God's children now; what we shall be has not yet been revealed. We do know that when it is revealed we shall be like him, for we shall see him as he is. Everyone who has this hope based on him makes himself pure, as he is pure.

Everyone who commits sin commits lawlessness, for sin is lawlessness. You know that he was revealed to take away sins, and in him there is no sin. No one who remains in him sins; no one who sins has seen him or known him.

Responsorial Psalm

PSALM 98:1, 3cd-4, 5-6

R. All the ends of the earth have seen the saving power of God.

Sing to the LORD a new song,
for he has done wondrous deeds;
His right hand has won victory for him,
his holy arm. **R.**
All the ends of the earth have seen
the salvation by our God.
Sing joyfully to the LORD, all you lands;
break into song; sing praise. **R.**
Sing praise to the LORD with the harp,
with the harp and melodious song.
With trumpets and the sound of the horn
sing joyfully before the King, the LORD. **R.**

Gospel

JOHN 1:29-34

John the Baptist saw Jesus coming toward him and said, "Behold, the Lamb of God, who takes away the sin of the world. He is the one of whom I said, 'A man is coming after me who ranks ahead of me because he existed before me.' I did not know him, but the reason why I came baptizing with water was that he might be made known to Israel." John testified further, saying, "I saw the Spirit come down like a dove from the sky and remain upon him. I did not know him, but the one who sent me to baptize with water told me, 'On whomever you see the Spirit come down and remain, he is the one who will baptize with the Holy Spirit.' Now I have seen and testified that he is the Son of God."

Friday, January 4

First Reading

1 JOHN 3:7-10

Children, let no one deceive you. The person who acts in righteousness is righteous, just as he is righteous. Whoever sins belongs to the Devil, because the Devil has sinned from the beginning. Indeed, the Son of God was revealed to destroy the works of the Devil. No one who is begotten by God commits sin, because God's seed remains in him; he cannot sin because he is begotten by God. In this way, the children of God and the children of the Devil are made plain; no one who fails to act in righteousness belongs to God, nor anyone who does not love his brother.

Responsorial Psalm
PSALM 98:1, 7-8, 9
R. All the ends of the earth have seen the saving power of God.
Sing to the LORD a new song,
for he has done wondrous deeds;
His right hand has won victory for him,
his holy arm. **R.**
Let the sea and what fills it resound,
the world and those who dwell in it;
Let the rivers clap their hands,
the mountains shout with them for joy before the LORD. **R.**
The LORD comes;
he comes to rule the earth;
He will rule the world with justice
and the peoples with equity. **R.**

Gospel
JOHN 1:35-42
John was standing with two of his disciples, and as he watched Jesus walk by, he said, "Behold, the Lamb of God." The two disciples heard what he said and followed Jesus. Jesus turned and saw them following him and said to them, "What are you looking for?" They said to him, "Rabbi" (which translated means Teacher), "where are you staying?" He said to them, "Come, and you will see." So they went and saw where he was staying, and they stayed with him that day. It was about four in the afternoon. Andrew, the brother of Simon Peter, was one of the two who heard John and followed Jesus. He first found his own brother Simon and told him, "We have found the Messiah," which is translated Christ. Then he brought him to Jesus. Jesus looked at him and said, "You are Simon the son of John; you will be called Cephas," which is translated Peter.

Saturday, January 5

First Reading
1 JOHN 3:11-21
Beloved: This is the message you have heard from the beginning: we should love one another, unlike Cain who belonged to the Evil One and slaughtered his brother. Why did he slaughter him? Because his own works were evil, and those of his brother righteous. Do not be amazed, then, brothers and sisters, if the world hates you. We know that we have passed from death to life because we love our brothers. Whoever does not love remains in death. Everyone who hates his brother is a

murderer, and you know that no murderer has eternal life remaining in him. The way we came to know love was that he laid down his life for us; so we ought to lay down our lives for our brothers. If someone who has worldly means sees a brother in need and refuses him compassion, how can the love of God remain in him? Children, let us love not in word or speech but in deed and truth.

Now this is how we shall know that we belong to the truth and reassure our hearts before him in whatever our hearts condemn, for God is greater than our hearts and knows everything. Beloved, if our hearts do not condemn us, we have confidence in God.

Responsorial Psalm
PSALM 100:1b-2, 3, 4, 5

R. Let all the earth cry out to God with joy.

Sing joyfully to the LORD, all you lands;
serve the LORD with gladness;
come before him with joyful song. **R.**
Know that the LORD is God;
he made us, his we are;
his people, the flock he tends. **R.**
Enter his gates with thanksgiving,
his courts with praise;
Give thanks to him; bless his name. **R.**
The LORD is good:
the LORD, whose kindness endures forever,
and his faithfulness, to all generations. **R.**

Gospel
JOHN 1:43-51

Jesus decided to go to Galilee, and he found Philip. And Jesus said to him, "Follow me." Now Philip was from Bethsaida, the town of Andrew and Peter. Philip found Nathanael and told him, "We have found the one about whom Moses wrote in the law, and also the prophets, Jesus, son of Joseph, from Nazareth." But Nathanael said to him, "Can anything good come from Nazareth?" Philip said to him, "Come and see." Jesus saw Nathanael coming toward him and said of him, "Here is a true child of Israel. There is no duplicity in him." Nathanael said to him, "How do you know me?" Jesus answered and said to him, "Before Philip called you, I saw you under the fig tree." Nathanael answered him, "Rabbi, you are the Son of God; you are the King of Israel." Jesus answered and said to him, "Do you believe because I told you that I saw you under the fig tree? You will see greater things than this." And he said to him, "Amen, amen, I say to you, you will see the sky opened and the angels of God ascending and descending on the Son of Man."

Sunday, January 6

The Epiphany of the Lord

First Reading
ISAIAH 60:1-6

Rise up in splendor, Jerusalem! Your light has come,
the glory of the Lord shines upon you.
See, darkness covers the earth,
and thick clouds cover the peoples;
but upon you the LORD shines,
and over you appears his glory.
Nations shall walk by your light,
and kings by your shining radiance.
Raise your eyes and look about;
they all gather and come to you:
your sons come from afar,
and your daughters in the arms of their nurses.

Then you shall be radiant at what you see,
your heart shall throb and overflow,
for the riches of the sea shall be emptied out before you,
the wealth of nations shall be brought to you.
Caravans of camels shall fill you,
dromedaries from Midian and Ephah;
all from Sheba shall come
bearing gold and frankincense,
and proclaiming the praises of the LORD.

Responsorial Psalm
PSALM 72:1-2, 7-8, 10-11, 12-13
R. Lord, every nation on earth will adore you.
O God, with your judgment endow the king,
and with your justice, the king's son;
he shall govern your people with justice
and your afflicted ones with judgment. **R.**
Justice shall flower in his days,
and profound peace, till the moon be no more.
May he rule from sea to sea,
and from the River to the ends of the earth. **R.**
The kings of Tarshish and the Isles shall offer gifts;
the kings of Arabia and Seba shall bring tribute.
All kings shall pay him homage,
all nations shall serve him. **R.**

For he shall rescue the poor when he cries out,
    and the afflicted when he has no one to help him.
He shall have pity for the lowly and the poor;
    the lives of the poor he shall save. **R.**

Second Reading
EPHESIANS 3:2-3a, 5-6

Brothers and sisters: You have heard of the stewardship of God's grace that was given to me for your benefit, namely, that the mystery was made known to me by revelation. It was not made known to people in other generations as it has now been revealed to his holy apostles and prophets by the Spirit: that the Gentiles are coheirs, members of the same body, and copartners in the promise in Christ Jesus through the gospel.

Gospel
MATTHEW 2:1-12

When Jesus was born in Bethlehem of Judea, in the days of King Herod, behold, magi from the east arrived in Jerusalem, saying, "Where is the newborn king of the Jews? We saw his star at its rising and have come to do him homage." When King Herod heard this, he was greatly troubled, and all Jerusalem with him. Assembling all the chief priests and the scribes of the people, he inquired of them where the Christ was to be born. They said to him, "In Bethlehem of Judea, for thus it has been written through the prophet:

And you, Bethlehem, land of Judah,
    are by no means least among the rulers of Judah;
since from you shall come a ruler,
    who is to shepherd my people Israel."

Then Herod called the magi secretly and ascertained from them the time of the star's appearance. He sent them to Bethlehem and said, "Go and search diligently for the child. When you have found him, bring me word, that I too may go and do him homage." After their audience with the king they set out. And behold, the star that they had seen at its rising preceded them, until it came and stopped over the place where the child was. They were overjoyed at seeing the star, and on entering the house they saw the child with Mary his mother. They prostrated themselves and did him homage. Then they opened their treasures and offered him gifts of gold, frankincense, and myrrh. And having been warned in a dream not to return to Herod, they departed for their country by another way.

Monday, January 7

First Reading

1 JOHN 3:22–4:6

Beloved: We receive from him whatever we ask, because we keep his commandments and do what pleases him. And his commandment is this: we should believe in the name of his Son, Jesus Christ, and love one another just as he commanded us. Those who keep his commandments remain in him, and he in them, and the way we know that he remains in us is from the Spirit whom he gave us.

Beloved, do not trust every spirit but test the spirits to see whether they belong to God, because many false prophets have gone out into the world. This is how you can know the Spirit of God: every spirit that acknowledges Jesus Christ come in the flesh belongs to God, and every spirit that does not acknowledge Jesus does not belong to God. This is the spirit of the antichrist who, as you heard, is to come, but in fact is already in the world. You belong to God, children, and you have conquered them, for the one who is in you is greater than the one who is in the world. They belong to the world; accordingly, their teaching belongs to the world, and the world listens to them. We belong to God, and anyone who knows God listens to us, while anyone who does not belong to God refuses to hear us. This is how we know the spirit of truth and the spirit of deceit.

Responsorial Psalm

PSALM 2:7bc-8, 10-12a

R. I will give you all the nations for an inheritance.

The LORD said to me, "You are my Son;
 this day I have begotten you.
Ask of me and I will give you
 the nations for an inheritance
 and the ends of the earth for your possession." **R.**
And now, O kings, give heed;
 take warning, you rulers of the earth.
Serve the LORD with fear, and rejoice before him;
 with trembling rejoice. **R.**

Gospel

MATTHEW 4:12-17, 23-25

When Jesus heard that John had been arrested, he withdrew to Galilee. He left Nazareth and went to live in Capernaum by the sea, in the region of Zebulun and Naphtali, that what had been said through Isaiah the prophet might be fulfilled:

Land of Zebulun and land of Naphtali,
the way to the sea, beyond the Jordan,
Galilee of the Gentiles,
the people who sit in darkness
have seen a great light,
on those dwelling in a land overshadowed by death
light has arisen.

From that time on, Jesus began to preach and say, "Repent, for the Kingdom of heaven is at hand."

He went around all of Galilee, teaching in their synagogues, proclaiming the Gospel of the Kingdom, and curing every disease and illness among the people. His fame spread to all of Syria, and they brought to him all who were sick with various diseases and racked with pain, those who were possessed, lunatics, and paralytics, and he cured them. And great crowds from Galilee, the Decapolis, Jerusalem, and Judea, and from beyond the Jordan followed him.

Tuesday, January 8

First Reading

1 JOHN 4:7-10

Beloved, let us love one another, because love is of God; everyone who loves is begotten by God and knows God. Whoever is without love does not know God, for God is love. In this way the love of God was revealed to us: God sent his only-begotten Son into the world so that we might have life through him. In this is love: not that we have loved God, but that he loved us and sent his Son as expiation for our sins.

Responsorial Psalm

PSALM 72:1-2, 3-4, 7-8

R. Lord, every nation on earth will adore you.

O God, with your judgment endow the king,
and with your justice, the king's son;
He shall govern your people with justice
and your afflicted ones with judgment. **R.**
The mountains shall yield peace for the people,
and the hills justice.
He shall defend the afflicted among the people,
save the children of the poor. **R.**
Justice shall flower in his days,
and profound peace, till the moon be no more.

May he rule from sea to sea,
and from the River to the ends of the earth. **R.**

Gospel
MARK 6:34-44

When Jesus saw the vast crowd, his heart was moved with pity for them, for they were like sheep without a shepherd; and he began to teach them many things. By now it was already late and his disciples approached him and said, "This is a deserted place and it is already very late. Dismiss them so that they can go to the surrounding farms and villages and buy themselves something to eat." He said to them in reply, "Give them some food yourselves." But they said to him, "Are we to buy two hundred days' wages worth of food and give it to them to eat?" He asked them, "How many loaves do you have? Go and see." And when they had found out they said, "Five loaves and two fish." So he gave orders to have them sit down in groups on the green grass. The people took their places in rows by hundreds and by fifties. Then, taking the five loaves and the two fish and looking up to heaven, he said the blessing, broke the loaves, and gave them to his disciples to set before the people; he also divided the two fish among them all. They all ate and were satisfied. And they picked up twelve wicker baskets full of fragments and what was left of the fish. Those who ate of the loaves were five thousand men.

Wednesday, January 9

First Reading
1 JOHN 4:11-18

Beloved, if God so loved us, we also must love one another. No one has ever seen God. Yet, if we love one another, God remains in us, and his love is brought to perfection in us.

This is how we know that we remain in him and he in us, that he has given us of his Spirit. Moreover, we have seen and testify that the Father sent his Son as savior of the world. Whoever acknowledges that Jesus is the Son of God, God remains in him and he in God. We have come to know and to believe in the love God has for us.

God is love, and whoever remains in love remains in God and God in him. In this is love brought to perfection among us, that we have confidence on the day of judgment because as he is, so are we in this world. There is no fear in love, but perfect love drives out fear because fear has to do with punishment, and so one who fears is not yet perfect in love.

Responsorial Psalm

PSALM 72:1-2, 10, 12-13

R. Lord, every nation on earth will adore you.

O God, with your judgment endow the king,
  and with your justice, the king's son;
He shall govern your people with justice
  and your afflicted ones with judgment. **R.**
The kings of Tarshish and the Isles shall offer gifts;
  the kings of Arabia and Seba shall bring tribute. **R.**
For he shall rescue the poor when he cries out,
  and the afflicted when he has no one to help him.
He shall have pity for the lowly and the poor;
  the lives of the poor he shall save. **R.**

Gospel

MARK 6:45-52

After the five thousand had eaten and were satisfied, Jesus made his disciples get into the boat and precede him to the other side toward Bethsaida, while he dismissed the crowd. And when he had taken leave of them, he went off to the mountain to pray. When it was evening, the boat was far out on the sea and he was alone on shore. Then he saw that they were tossed about while rowing, for the wind was against them. About the fourth watch of the night, he came toward them walking on the sea. He meant to pass by them. But when they saw him walking on the sea, they thought it was a ghost and cried out. They had all seen him and were terrified. But at once he spoke with them, "Take courage, it is I, do not be afraid!" He got into the boat with them and the wind died down. They were completely astounded. They had not understood the incident of the loaves. On the contrary, their hearts were hardened.

Thursday, January 10

First Reading

1 JOHN 4:19–5:4

Beloved, we love God because he first loved us. If anyone says, "I love God," but hates his brother, he is a liar; for whoever does not love a brother whom he has seen cannot love God whom he has not seen. This is the commandment we have from him: Whoever loves God must also love his brother.

Everyone who believes that Jesus is the Christ is begotten by God, and everyone who loves the Father loves also the one begotten by him. In this way we know that we love the children of God when we love God and obey his commandments. For the love of God is this, that we keep his commandments. And his commandments are not burdensome, for whoever is begotten by God conquers the world. And the victory that conquers the world is our faith.

Responsorial Psalm

PSALM 72:1-2, 14 and 15bc, 17

R. Lord, every nation on earth will adore you.

O God, with your judgment endow the king,
  and with your justice, the king's son;
He shall govern your people with justice
  and your afflicted ones with judgment. **R.**
From fraud and violence he shall redeem them,
  and precious shall their blood be in his sight.
May they be prayed for continually;
  day by day shall they bless him. **R.**
May his name be blessed forever;
  as long as the sun his name shall remain.
In him shall all the tribes of the earth be blessed;
  all the nations shall proclaim his happiness. **R.**

Gospel

LUKE 4:14-22a

Jesus returned to Galilee in the power of the Spirit, and news of him spread throughout the whole region. He taught in their synagogues and was praised by all.

He came to Nazareth, where he had grown up, and went according to his custom into the synagogue on the sabbath day. He stood up to read and was handed a scroll of the prophet Isaiah. He unrolled the scroll and found the passage where it was written:

The Spirit of the Lord is upon me,
  because he has anointed me
    to bring glad tidings to the poor.
He has sent me to proclaim liberty to captives
  and recovery of sight to the blind,
    to let the oppressed go free,
and to proclaim a year acceptable to the Lord.

Rolling up the scroll, he handed it back to the attendant and sat down, and the eyes of all in the synagogue looked intently at him. He said to them, "Today this Scripture passage is fulfilled in your hearing." And all spoke highly of him and were amazed at the gracious words that came from his mouth.

Friday, January 11

First Reading

1 JOHN 5:5-13

Beloved: Who indeed is the victor over the world but the one who believes that Jesus is the Son of God?

This is the one who came through water and Blood, Jesus Christ, not by water alone, but by water and Blood. The Spirit is the one who testifies, and the Spirit is truth. So there are three who testify, the Spirit, the water, and the Blood, and the three are of one accord. If we accept human testimony, the testimony of God is surely greater. Now the testimony of God is this, that he has testified on behalf of his Son. Whoever believes in the Son of God has this testimony within himself. Whoever does not believe God has made him a liar by not believing the testimony God has given about his Son. And this is the testimony: God gave us eternal life, and this life is in his Son. Whoever possesses the Son has life; whoever does not possess the Son of God does not have life.

I write these things to you so that you may know that you have eternal life, you who believe in the name of the Son of God.

Responsorial Psalm

PSALM 147:12-13, 14-15, 19-20

R. Praise the Lord, Jerusalem. (or R. Alleluia.)

Glorify the LORD, O Jerusalem;
 praise your God, O Zion.
For he has strengthened the bars of your gates;
 he has blessed your children within you. **R.**
He has granted peace in your borders;
 with the best of wheat he fills you.
He sends forth his command to the earth;
 swiftly runs his word! **R.**
He has proclaimed his word to Jacob,
 his statutes and his ordinances to Israel.
He has not done thus for any other nation;
 his ordinances he has not made known to them. Alleluia. **R.**

Gospel

LUKE 5:12-16

It happened that there was a man full of leprosy in one of the towns where Jesus was; and when he saw Jesus, he fell prostrate, pleaded with him, and said, "Lord, if you wish, you can make me clean." Jesus stretched out his hand, touched him, and said, "I do will it. Be made clean." And the leprosy left him immediately. Then he ordered him not to tell anyone, but "Go, show yourself to the priest and offer for your cleansing what Moses prescribed; that will be proof for them." The report about him spread all the more, and great crowds assembled to listen to him and to be cured of their ailments, but he would withdraw to deserted places to pray.

Saturday, January 12

First Reading

1 JOHN 5:14-21

Beloved: We have this confidence in him that if we ask anything according to his will, he hears us. And if we know that he hears us in regard to whatever we ask, we know that what we have asked him for is ours. If anyone sees his brother sinning, if the sin is not deadly, he should pray to God and he will give him life. This is only for those whose sin is not deadly. There is such a thing as deadly sin, about which I do not say that you should pray. All wrongdoing is sin, but there is sin that is not deadly.

We know that anyone begotten by God does not sin; but the one begotten by God he protects, and the Evil One cannot touch him. We know that we belong to God, and the whole world is under the power of the Evil One. We also know that the Son of God has come and has given us discernment to know the one who is true. And we are in the one who is true, in his Son Jesus Christ. He is the true God and eternal life. Children, be on your guard against idols.

Responsorial Psalm

PSALM 149:1-2, 3-4, 5-6a and 9b

R. The Lord takes delight in his people. (or R. Alleluia.)

Sing to the LORD a new song
  of praise in the assembly of the faithful.
Let Israel be glad in their maker,
  let the children of Zion rejoice in their king. **R.**
Let them praise his name in the festive dance,
  let them sing praise to him with timbrel and harp.
For the LORD loves his people,
  and he adorns the lowly with victory. **R.**
Let the faithful exult in glory;
  let them sing for joy upon their couches;
Let the high praises of God be in their throats.
  This is the glory of all his faithful. Alleluia. **R.**

Gospel
JOHN 3:22-30

Jesus and his disciples went into the region of Judea, where he spent some time with them baptizing. John was also baptizing in Aenon near Salim, because there was an abundance of water there, and people came to be baptized, for John had not yet been imprisoned. Now a dispute arose between the disciples of John and a Jew about ceremonial washings. So they came to John and said to him, "Rabbi, the one who was with you across the Jordan, to whom you testified, here he is baptizing and everyone is coming to him." John answered and said, "No one can receive anything except what has been given from heaven. You yourselves can testify that I said that I am not the Christ, but that I was sent before him. The one who has the bride is the bridegroom; the best man, who stands and listens for him, rejoices greatly at the bridegroom's voice. So this joy of mine has been made complete. He must increase; I must decrease."

Sunday, January 13

The Baptism of the Lord

First Reading
ISAIAH 42:1-4, 6-7 (or ISAIAH 40:1-5, 9-11)

Thus says the LORD:
Here is my servant whom I uphold,
  my chosen one with whom I am pleased,
upon whom I have put my spirit;
  he shall bring forth justice to the nations,
not crying out, not shouting,
  not making his voice heard in the street.
A bruised reed he shall not break,
  and a smoldering wick he shall not quench,
until he establishes justice on the earth;
  the coastlands will wait for his teaching.

I, the LORD, have called you for the victory of justice,
  I have grasped you by the hand;
I formed you, and set you
  as a covenant of the people,
  a light for the nations,
to open the eyes of the blind,
  to bring out prisoners from confinement,
  and from the dungeon, those who live in darkness.

Responsorial Psalm

PSALM 29:1-2, 3-4, 3, 9-10
(or PSALM 104:1b-2, 3-4, 24-25, 27-28, 29-30)
R. The Lord will bless his people with peace.

Give to the LORD, you sons of God,
give to the LORD glory and praise,
give to the LORD the glory due his name;
adore the LORD in holy attire. **R.**
The voice of the LORD is over the waters,
the LORD, over vast waters.
The voice of the LORD is mighty;
the voice of the LORD is majestic. **R.**
The God of glory thunders,
and in his temple all say, "Glory!"
The LORD is enthroned above the flood;
the LORD is enthroned as king forever. **R.**

Second Reading

ACTS 10:34-38 (or TITUS 2:11-14; 3:4-7)

Peter proceeded to speak to those gathered in the house of Cornelius, saying: "In truth, I see that God shows no partiality. Rather, in every nation whoever fears him and acts uprightly is acceptable to him. You know the word that he sent to the Israelites as he proclaimed peace through Jesus Christ, who is Lord of all, what has happened all over Judea, beginning in Galilee after the baptism that John preached, how God anointed Jesus of Nazareth with the Holy Spirit and power. He went about doing good and healing all those oppressed by the devil, for God was with him."

Gospel

LUKE 3:15-16, 21-22

The people were filled with expectation, and all were asking in their hearts whether John might be the Christ. John answered them all, saying, "I am baptizing you with water, but one mightier than I is coming. I am not worthy to loosen the thongs of his sandals. He will baptize you with the Holy Spirit and fire."

After all the people had been baptized and Jesus also had been baptized and was praying, heaven was opened and the Holy Spirit descended upon him in bodily form like a dove. And a voice came from heaven, "You are my beloved Son; with you I am well pleased."

Monday, January 14

(First Week in Ordinary Time)

First Reading
HEBREWS 1:1-6

Brothers and sisters: In times past, God spoke in partial and various ways to our ancestors through the prophets; in these last days, he spoke to us through the Son, whom he made heir of all things and through whom he created the universe,

who is the refulgence of his glory,
the very imprint of his being,
and who sustains all things by his mighty word.
When he had accomplished purification from sins,
he took his seat at the right hand
of the Majesty on high,
as far superior to the angels
as the name he has inherited is more excellent than theirs.

For to which of the angels did God ever say:

You are my Son; this day I have begotten you?

Or again:

I will be a father to him, and he shall be a Son to me?

And again, when he leads the first born into the world, he says:

Let all the angels of God worship him.

Responsorial Psalm
PSALM 97:1 and 2b, 6 and 7c, 9
R. Let all his angels worship him.

The LORD is king; let the earth rejoice;
let the many isles be glad.
Justice and judgment are the foundation of his throne. **R.**
The heavens proclaim his justice,
and all peoples see his glory.
Let all his angels worship him. **R.**
Because you, O LORD, are the Most High over all the earth,
exalted far above all gods. **R.**

Gospel
MARK 1:14-20

After John had been arrested, Jesus came to Galilee proclaiming the Gospel of God: "This is the time of fulfillment. The Kingdom of God is at hand. Repent, and believe in the Gospel."

As he passed by the Sea of Galilee, he saw Simon and his brother Andrew casting their nets into the sea; they were fishermen. Jesus said to them, "Come after me, and I will make you fishers of men." Then they left their nets and followed him. He walked along a little farther and saw James, the son of Zebedee, and his brother John. They too were in a boat mending their nets. Then he called them. So they left their father Zebedee in the boat along with the hired men and followed him.

Tuesday, January 15

First Reading
HEBREWS 2:5-12

It was not to angels that God subjected the world to come, of which we are speaking.

Instead, someone has testified somewhere:

What is man that you are mindful of him,
or the son of man that you care for him?
You made him for a little while lower than the angels;
you crowned him with glory and honor,
subjecting all things under his feet.

In "subjecting" all things to him, he left nothing not "subject to him." Yet at present we do not see "all things subject to him," but we do see Jesus "crowned with glory and honor" because he suffered death, he who "for a little while" was made "lower than the angels," that by the grace of God he might taste death for everyone.

For it was fitting that he, for whom and through whom all things exist, in bringing many children to glory, should make the leader to their salvation perfect through suffering. He who consecrates and those who are being consecrated all have one origin. Therefore, he is not ashamed to call them "brothers" saying:

I will proclaim your name to my brethren,
in the midst of the assembly I will praise you.

Responsorial Psalm
PSALM 8:2ab and 5, 6-7, 8-9
R. You have given your Son rule over the works of your hands.
O LORD, our Lord,
how glorious is your name over all the earth!
What is man that you should be mindful of him,
or the son of man that you should care for him? **R.**
You have made him little less than the angels,
and crowned him with glory and honor.
You have given him rule over the works of your hands,
putting all things under his feet. **R.**
All sheep and oxen,
yes, and the beasts of the field,
The birds of the air, the fishes of the sea,
and whatever swims the paths of the seas. **R.**

Gospel
MARK 1:21-28
Jesus came to Capernaum with his followers, and on the sabbath he entered the synagogue and taught. The people were astonished at his teaching, for he taught them as one having authority and not as the scribes. In their synagogue was a man with an unclean spirit; he cried out, "What have you to do with us, Jesus of Nazareth? Have you come to destroy us? I know who you are—the Holy One of God!" Jesus rebuked him and said, "Quiet! Come out of him!" The unclean spirit convulsed him and with a loud cry came out of him. All were amazed and asked one another, "What is this? A new teaching with authority. He commands even the unclean spirits and they obey him." His fame spread everywhere throughout the whole region of Galilee.

Wednesday, January 16

First Reading
HEBREWS 2:14-18
Since the children share in blood and Flesh, Jesus likewise shared in them, that through death he might destroy the one who has the power of death, that is, the Devil, and free those who through fear of death had been subject to slavery all their life. Surely he did not help angels but rather the descendants of Abraham; therefore, he had to become like his brothers and sisters in every way, that he might be a merciful and faithful high priest before God to expiate the sins of the people. Because he himself was tested through what he suffered, he is able to help those who are being tested.

Responsorial Psalm

PSALM 105:1-2, 3-4, 6-7, 8-9

R. The Lord remembers his covenant for ever. (or R. Alleluia.)

Give thanks to the LORD, invoke his name;
make known among the nations his deeds.
Sing to him, sing his praise,
proclaim all his wondrous deeds. **R.**
Glory in his holy name;
rejoice, O hearts that seek the LORD!
Look to the LORD in his strength;
seek to serve him constantly. **R.**
You descendants of Abraham, his servants,
sons of Jacob, his chosen ones!
He, the LORD, is our God;
throughout the earth his judgments prevail. **R.**
He remembers forever his covenant
which he made binding for a thousand generations—
Which he entered into with Abraham
and by his oath to Isaac. **R.**

Gospel

MARK 1:29-39

On leaving the synagogue Jesus entered the house of Simon and Andrew with James and John. Simon's mother-in-law lay sick with a fever. They immediately told him about her. He approached, grasped her hand, and helped her up. Then the fever left her and she waited on them.

When it was evening, after sunset, they brought to him all who were ill or possessed by demons. The whole town was gathered at the door. He cured many who were sick with various diseases, and he drove out many demons, not permitting them to speak because they knew him.

Rising very early before dawn, he left and went off to a deserted place, where he prayed. Simon and those who were with him pursued him and on finding him said, "Everyone is looking for you." He told them, "Let us go on to the nearby villages that I may preach there also. For this purpose have I come." So he went into their synagogues, preaching and driving out demons throughout the whole of Galilee.

Thursday, January 17

First Reading

HEBREWS 3:7-14

The Holy Spirit says:

Oh, that today you would hear his voice,
"Harden not your hearts as at the rebellion
in the day of testing in the desert,
where your ancestors tested and tried me
and saw my works for forty years.
Because of this I was provoked with that generation
and I said, 'They have always been of erring heart,
and they do not know my ways.'
As I swore in my wrath,
'They shall not enter into my rest.'"

Take care, brothers and sisters, that none of you may have an evil and unfaithful heart, so as to forsake the living God. Encourage yourselves daily while it is still "today," so that none of you may grow hardened by the deceit of sin. We have become partners of Christ if only we hold the beginning of the reality firm until the end.

Responsorial Psalm
PSALM 95:6-7c, 8-9, 10-11
R. If today you hear his voice, harden not your hearts.
Come, let us bow down in worship;
let us kneel before the LORD who made us.
For he is our God,
and we are the people he shepherds, the flock he guides. **R.**
Oh, that today you would hear his voice:
"Harden not your hearts as at Meribah,
as in the day of Massah in the desert,
Where your fathers tempted me;
they tested me though they had seen my works." **R.**
Forty years I was wearied of that generation;
I said: "This people's heart goes astray,
they do not know my ways."
Therefore I swore in my anger:
"They shall never enter my rest." **R.**

Gospel
MARK 1:40-45
A leper came to him and kneeling down begged him and said, "If you wish, you can make me clean." Moved with pity, he stretched out his hand, touched the leper, and said to him, "I do will it. Be made clean." The leprosy left him immediately, and he was made clean. Then, warning him sternly, he dismissed him at once. Then he said to him, "See that you tell no one anything, but go, show yourself to the priest and offer for your cleansing what Moses prescribed; that will be proof for

them." The man went away and began to publicize the whole matter. He spread the report abroad so that it was impossible for Jesus to enter a town openly. He remained outside in deserted places, and people kept coming to him from everywhere.

Friday, January 18

First Reading
HEBREWS 4:1-5, 11

Let us be on our guard while the promise of entering into his rest remains, that none of you seem to have failed. For in fact we have received the Good News just as our ancestors did. But the word that they heard did not profit them, for they were not united in faith with those who listened. For we who believed enter into that rest, just as he has said:

As I swore in my wrath,
"They shall not enter into my rest,"

and yet his works were accomplished at the foundation of the world. For he has spoken somewhere about the seventh day in this manner, *And God rested on the seventh day from all his works*; and again, in the previously mentioned place, *They shall not enter into my rest.*

Therefore, let us strive to enter into that rest, so that no one may fall after the same example of disobedience.

Responsorial Psalm
PSALM 78:3 and 4bc, 6c-7, 8
R. Do not forget the works of the Lord!
What we have heard and know,
  and what our fathers have declared to us,
  we will declare to the generation to come
The glorious deeds of the LORD and his strength. **R.**
That they too may rise and declare to their sons
  that they should put their hope in God,
And not forget the deeds of God
  but keep his commands. **R.**
And not be like their fathers,
  a generation wayward and rebellious,
A generation that kept not its heart steadfast
  nor its spirit faithful toward God. **R.**

Gospel

MARK 2:1-12

When Jesus returned to Capernaum after some days, it became known that he was at home. Many gathered together so that there was no longer room for them, not even around the door, and he preached the word to them. They came bringing to him a paralytic carried by four men. Unable to get near Jesus because of the crowd, they opened up the roof above him. After they had broken through, they let down the mat on which the paralytic was lying. When Jesus saw their faith, he said to him, "Child, your sins are forgiven." Now some of the scribes were sitting there asking themselves, "Why does this man speak that way? He is blaspheming. Who but God alone can forgive sins?" Jesus immediately knew in his mind what they were thinking to themselves, so he said, "Why are you thinking such things in your hearts? Which is easier, to say to the paralytic, 'Your sins are forgiven,' or to say, 'Rise, pick up your mat and walk'? But that you may know that the Son of Man has authority to forgive sins on earth"—he said to the paralytic, "I say to you, rise, pick up your mat, and go home." He rose, picked up his mat at once, and went away in the sight of everyone. They were all astounded and glorified God, saying, "We have never seen anything like this."

Saturday, January 19

First Reading

HEBREWS 4:12-16

The word of God is living and effective, sharper than any two-edged sword, penetrating even between soul and spirit, joints and marrow, and able to discern reflections and thoughts of the heart. No creature is concealed from him, but everything is naked and exposed to the eyes of him to whom we must render an account.

Since we have a great high priest who has passed through the heavens, Jesus, the Son of God, let us hold fast to our confession. For we do not have a high priest who is unable to sympathize with our weaknesses, but one who has similarly been tested in every way, yet without sin. So let us confidently approach the throne of grace to receive mercy and to find grace for timely help.

Responsorial Psalm

PSALM 19:8, 9, 10, 15

R. Your words, Lord, are Spirit and life.

The law of the LORD is perfect,
refreshing the soul;

The decree of the LORD is trustworthy,
giving wisdom to the simple. **R.**
The precepts of the LORD are right,
rejoicing the heart;
The command of the LORD is clear,
enlightening the eye. **R.**
The fear of the LORD is pure,
enduring forever;
The ordinances of the LORD are true,
all of them just. **R.**
Let the words of my mouth and the thought of my heart
find favor before you,
O LORD, my rock and my redeemer. **R.**

Gospel
MARK 2:13-17

Jesus went out along the sea. All the crowd came to him and he taught them. As he passed by, he saw Levi, son of Alphaeus, sitting at the customs post. Jesus said to him, "Follow me." And he got up and followed Jesus. While he was at table in his house, many tax collectors and sinners sat with Jesus and his disciples; for there were many who followed him. Some scribes who were Pharisees saw that Jesus was eating with sinners and tax collectors and said to his disciples, "Why does he eat with tax collectors and sinners?" Jesus heard this and said to them, "Those who are well do not need a physician, but the sick do. I did not come to call the righteous but sinners."

Sunday, January 20

Second Sunday in Ordinary Time

First Reading
ISAIAH 62:1-5

For Zion's sake I will not be silent,
for Jerusalem's sake I will not be quiet,
until her vindication shines forth like the dawn
and her victory like a burning torch.

Nations shall behold your vindication,
and all the kings your glory;
you shall be called by a new name
pronounced by the mouth of the LORD.

You shall be a glorious crown in the hand of the LORD,
a royal diadem held by your God.
No more shall people call you "Forsaken,"
or your land "Desolate,"
but you shall be called "My Delight,"
and your land "Espoused."
For the LORD delights in you
and makes your land his spouse.
As a young man marries a virgin,
your Builder shall marry you;
and as a bridegroom rejoices in his bride
so shall your God rejoice in you.

Responsorial Psalm

PSALM 96:1-2, 2-3, 7-8, 9-10

R. Proclaim his marvelous deeds to all the nations.

Sing to the LORD a new song;
sing to the LORD, all you lands.
Sing to the LORD; bless his name. **R.**
Announce his salvation, day after day.
Tell his glory among the nations;
among all peoples, his wondrous deeds. **R.**
Give to the LORD, you families of nations,
give to the LORD glory and praise;
give to the LORD the glory due his name! **R.**
Worship the LORD in holy attire.
Tremble before him, all the earth;
say among the nations: The LORD is king.
He governs the peoples with equity. **R.**

Second Reading

1 CORINTHIANS 12:4-11

Brothers and sisters: There are different kinds of spiritual gifts but the same Spirit; there are different forms of service but the same Lord; there are different workings but the same God who produces all of them in everyone. To each individual the manifestation of the Spirit is given for some benefit. To one is given through the Spirit the expression of wisdom; to another, the expression of knowledge according to the same Spirit; to another, faith by the same Spirit; to another, gifts of healing by the one Spirit; to another, mighty deeds; to another, prophecy; to another, discernment of spirits; to another, varieties of tongues; to another, interpretation of tongues. But one and the same Spirit produces all of these, distributing them individually to each person as he wishes.

Gospel
JOHN 2:1-11

There was a wedding at Cana in Galilee, and the mother of Jesus was there. Jesus and his disciples were also invited to the wedding. When the wine ran short, the mother of Jesus said to him, "They have no wine." And Jesus said to her, "Woman, how does your concern affect me? My hour has not yet come." His mother said to the servers, "Do whatever he tells you." Now there were six stone water jars there for Jewish ceremonial washings, each holding twenty to thirty gallons. Jesus told the them, "Fill the jars with water." So they filled them to the brim. Then he told them, "Draw some out now and take it to the headwaiter." So they took it. And when the headwaiter tasted the water that had become wine, without knowing where it came from—although the servers who had drawn the water knew—, the headwaiter called the bridegroom and said to him, "Everyone serves good wine first, and then when people have drunk freely, an inferior one; but you have kept the good wine until now." Jesus did this as the beginning of his signs at Cana in Galilee and so revealed his glory, and his disciples began to believe in him.

Monday, January 21

First Reading
HEBREWS 5:1-10

Brothers and sisters: Every high priest is taken from among men and made their representative before God, to offer gifts and sacrifices for sins. He is able to deal patiently with the ignorant and erring, for he himself is beset by weakness and so, for this reason, must make sin offerings for himself as well as for the people. No one takes this honor upon himself but only when called by God, just as Aaron was. In the same way, it was not Christ who glorified himself in becoming high priest, but rather the one who said to him:

You are my Son:
this day I have begotten you;

just as he says in another place,

You are a priest forever
according to the order of Melchizedek.

In the days when he was in the Flesh, he offered prayers and supplications with loud cries and tears to the one who was able to save him from death, and he was heard because of his reverence. Son though he was, he learned obedience from what he suffered; and when he was made perfect, he became the source of eternal salvation for all who obey him.

Responsorial Psalm
PSALM 110:1, 2, 3, 4
R. You are a priest for ever, in the line of Melchizedek.

The LORD said to my Lord: "Sit at my right hand
till I make your enemies your footstool." **R.**
The scepter of your power the LORD will stretch forth from Zion:
"Rule in the midst of your enemies." **R.**
"Yours is princely power in the day of your birth, in holy splendor;
before the daystar, like the dew, I have begotten you." **R.**
The LORD has sworn, and he will not repent:
"You are a priest forever, according to the order of Melchizedek." **R.**

Gospel
MARK 2:18-22

The disciples of John and of the Pharisees were accustomed to fast. People came to Jesus and objected, "Why do the disciples of John and the disciples of the Pharisees fast, but your disciples do not fast?" Jesus answered them, "Can the wedding guests fast while the bridegroom is with them? As long as they have the bridegroom with them they cannot fast. But the days will come when the bridegroom is taken away from them, and then they will fast on that day. No one sews a piece of unshrunken cloth on an old cloak. If he does, its fullness pulls away, the new from the old, and the tear gets worse. Likewise, no one pours new wine into old wineskins. Otherwise, the wine will burst the skins, and both the wine and the skins are ruined. Rather, new wine is poured into fresh wineskins."

Tuesday, January 22

[Day of Prayer for the Legal Protection of Unborn Children. Readings from the *Lectionary for Mass,* vol. IV, the Mass "For Peace and Justice," nos. 887–891, may be substituted for those listed here.]

First Reading
HEBREWS 6:10-20

Brothers and sisters: God is not unjust so as to overlook your work and the love you have demonstrated for his name by having served and continuing to serve the holy ones. We earnestly desire each of you to demonstrate the same eagerness for the fulfillment of hope until the end, so that you may not become sluggish, but imitators of those who, through faith and patience, are inheriting the promises.

When God made the promise to Abraham, since he had no one greater by whom to swear, *he swore by himself,* and said, *I will indeed bless you and multiply you.* And so, after patient waiting, Abraham obtained the promise. Now, men swear by someone greater than themselves; for them an oath serves as a guarantee and puts an end to all argument. So when God wanted to give the heirs of his promise an even clearer demonstration of the immutability of his purpose, he intervened with an oath, so that by two immutable things, in which it was impossible for God to lie, we who have taken refuge might be strongly encouraged to hold fast to the hope that lies before us. This we have as an anchor of the soul, sure and firm, which reaches into the interior behind the veil, where Jesus has entered on our behalf as forerunner, becoming high priest forever according to the order of Melchizedek.

Responsorial Psalm
PSALM 111:1-2, 4-5, 9 and 10c
R. The Lord will remember his covenant for ever.
(or R. Alleluia.)

I will give thanks to the LORD with all my heart
in the company and assembly of the just.
Great are the works of the LORD,
exquisite in all their delights. **R.**
He has won renown for his wondrous deeds;
gracious and merciful is the LORD.
He has given food to those who fear him;
he will forever be mindful of his covenant. **R.**
He has sent deliverance to his people;
he has ratified his covenant forever;
holy and awesome is his name.
His praise endures forever. **R.**

Gospel
MARK 2:23-28

As Jesus was passing through a field of grain on the sabbath, his disciples began to make a path while picking the heads of grain. At this the Pharisees said to him, "Look, why are they doing what is unlawful on the sabbath?" He said to them, "Have you never read what David did when he was in need and he and his companions were hungry? How he went into the house of God when Abiathar was high priest and ate the bread of offering that only the priests could lawfully eat, and shared it with his companions?" Then he said to them, "The sabbath was made for man, not man for the sabbath. That is why the Son of Man is lord even of the sabbath."

Wednesday, January 23

First Reading

HEBREWS 7:1-3, 15-17

Melchizedek, king of Salem and priest of God Most High, met Abraham as he returned from his defeat of the kings and *blessed him.* And Abraham apportioned to him *a tenth of everything.* His name first means righteous king, and he was also "king of Salem," that is, king of peace. Without father, mother, or ancestry, without beginning of days or end of life, thus made to resemble the Son of God, he remains a priest forever.

It is even more obvious if another priest is raised up after the likeness of Melchizedek, who has become so, not by a law expressed in a commandment concerning physical descent but by the power of a life that cannot be destroyed. For it is testified:

You are a priest forever according to the order of Melchizedek.

Responsorial Psalm

PSALM 110:1, 2, 3, 4

R. You are a priest for ever, in the line of Melchizedek.

The LORD said to my Lord: "Sit at my right hand
till I make your enemies your footstool." **R.**
The scepter of your power the LORD will stretch forth from Zion:
"Rule in the midst of your enemies." **R.**
"Yours is princely power in the day of your birth, in holy splendor;
before the daystar, like the dew, I have begotten you." **R.**
The LORD has sworn, and he will not repent:
"You are a priest forever, according to the order of Melchizedek." **R.**

Gospel

MARK 3:1-6

Jesus entered the synagogue. There was a man there who had a withered hand. They watched Jesus closely to see if he would cure him on the sabbath so that they might accuse him. He said to the man with the withered hand, "Come up here before us." Then he said to the Pharisees, "Is it lawful to do good on the sabbath rather than to do evil, to save life rather than to destroy it?" But they remained silent. Looking around at them with anger and grieved at their hardness of heart, Jesus said to the man, "Stretch out your hand." He stretched it out and his hand was restored. The Pharisees went out and immediately took counsel with the Herodians against him to put him to death.

Thursday, January 24

First Reading

HEBREWS 7:25–8:6

Jesus is always able to save those who approach God through him, since he lives forever to make intercession for them.

It was fitting that we should have such a high priest: holy, innocent, undefiled, separated from sinners, higher than the heavens. He has no need, as did the high priests, to offer sacrifice day after day, first for his own sins and then for those of the people; he did that once for all when he offered himself. For the law appoints men subject to weakness to be high priests, but the word of the oath, which was taken after the law, appoints a son, who has been made perfect forever.

The main point of what has been said is this: we have such a high priest, who has taken his seat at the right hand of the throne of the Majesty in heaven, a minister of the sanctuary and of the true tabernacle that the Lord, not man, set up. Now every high priest is appointed to offer gifts and sacrifices; thus the necessity for this one also to have something to offer. If then he were on earth, he would not be a priest, since there are those who offer gifts according to the law. They worship in a copy and shadow of the heavenly sanctuary, as Moses was warned when he was about to erect the tabernacle. For God says, "See that you make everything according to the pattern shown you on the mountain." Now he has obtained so much more excellent a ministry as he is mediator of a better covenant, enacted on better promises.

Responsorial Psalm

PSALM 40:7-8a, 8b-9, 10, 17

R. Here am I, Lord; I come to do your will.

Sacrifice or oblation you wished not,
  but ears open to obedience you gave me.
Burnt offerings or sin-offerings you sought not;
  then said I, "Behold I come." **R.**
"In the written scroll it is prescribed for me,
To do your will, O my God, is my delight,
  and your law is within my heart!" **R.**
I announced your justice in the vast assembly;
  I did not restrain my lips, as you, O LORD, know. **R.**
May all who seek you
  exult and be glad in you,

And may those who love your salvation
say ever, "The LORD be glorified." **R.**

Gospel
MARK 3:7-12

Jesus withdrew toward the sea with his disciples. A large number of people followed from Galilee and from Judea. Hearing what he was doing, a large number of people came to him also from Jerusalem, from Idumea, from beyond the Jordan, and from the neighborhood of Tyre and Sidon. He told his disciples to have a boat ready for him because of the crowd, so that they would not crush him. He had cured many and, as a result, those who had diseases were pressing upon him to touch him. And whenever unclean spirits saw him they would fall down before him and shout, "You are the Son of God." He warned them sternly not to make him known.

Friday, January 25

The Conversion of Saint Paul the Apostle

First Reading
ACTS 22:3-16 (or ACTS 9:1-22)

Paul addressed the people in these words: "I am a Jew, born in Tarsus in Cilicia, but brought up in this city. At the feet of Gamaliel I was educated strictly in our ancestral law and was zealous for God, just as all of you are today. I persecuted this Way to death, binding both men and women and delivering them to prison. Even the high priest and the whole council of elders can testify on my behalf. For from them I even received letters to the brothers and set out for Damascus to bring back to Jerusalem in chains for punishment those there as well.

"On that journey as I drew near to Damascus, about noon a great light from the sky suddenly shone around me. I fell to the ground and heard a voice saying to me, 'Saul, Saul, why are you persecuting me?' I replied, 'Who are you, sir?' And he said to me, 'I am Jesus the Nazorean whom you are persecuting.' My companions saw the light but did not hear the voice of the one who spoke to me. I asked, 'What shall I do, sir?' The Lord answered me, 'Get up and go into Damascus, and there you will be told about everything appointed for you to do.' Since I could see nothing because of the brightness of that light, I was led by hand by my companions and entered Damascus.

"A certain Ananias, a devout observer of the law, and highly spoken of by all the Jews who lived there, came to me and stood there and said, 'Saul, my brother, regain your sight.' And at that very moment I regained my sight and saw him. Then he said, 'The God of our ancestors designated you to know his will, to see the Righteous One, and to hear the sound of his voice; for you will be his witness before all to what you have seen and heard. Now, why delay? Get up and have yourself baptized and your sins washed away, calling upon his name.'"

Responsorial Psalm
PSALM 117:1bc, 2
R. Go out to all the world and tell the Good News.
(or R. Alleluia, alleluia.)
Praise the LORD, all you nations;
glorify him, all you peoples! **R.**
For steadfast is his kindness toward us,
and the fidelity of the LORD endures forever. **R.**

Gospel
MARK 16:15-18
Jesus appeared to the Eleven and said to them: "Go into the whole world and proclaim the Gospel to every creature. Whoever believes and is baptized will be saved; whoever does not believe will be condemned. These signs will accompany those who believe: in my name they will drive out demons, they will speak new languages. They will pick up serpents with their hands, and if they drink any deadly thing, it will not harm them. They will lay hands on the sick, and they will recover."

Saturday, January 26

Saints Timothy and Titus, Bishops

First Reading
2 TIMOTHY 1:1-8 (or TITUS 1:1-5)
Paul, an Apostle of Christ Jesus by the will of God for the promise of life in Christ Jesus, to Timothy, my dear child: grace, mercy, and peace from God the Father and Christ Jesus our Lord.

I am grateful to God, whom I worship with a clear conscience as my ancestors did, as I remember you constantly in my prayers, night and day. I yearn to see you again, recalling your tears, so that I may be filled with joy, as I recall your sincere faith that first lived in your grandmother Lois and in your mother Eunice and that I am confident lives also in you.

For this reason, I remind you to stir into flame the gift of God that you have through the imposition of my hands. For God did not give us a spirit of cowardice but rather of power and love and self-control. So do not be ashamed of your testimony to our Lord, nor of me, a prisoner for his sake; but bear your share of hardship for the Gospel with the strength that comes from God.

Responsorial Psalm
PSALM 96:1-2a, 2b-3, 7-8a, 10
R. Proclaim God's marvelous deeds to all the nations.

Sing to the LORD a new song;
  sing to the LORD, all you lands.
Sing to the LORD; bless his name. **R.**
Announce his salvation, day after day.
Tell his glory among the nations;
  among all peoples, his wondrous deeds. **R.**
Give to the LORD, you families of nations,
  give to the LORD glory and praise;
  give to the LORD the glory due his name! **R.**
Say among the nations: The LORD is king.
He has made the world firm, not to be moved;
  he governs the peoples with equity. **R.**

Gospel
MARK 3:20-21

Jesus came with his disciples into the house. Again the crowd gathered, making it impossible for them even to eat. When his relatives heard of this they set out to seize him, for they said, "He is out of his mind."

Sunday, January 27

Third Sunday in Ordinary Time

First Reading
NEHEMIAH 8:2-4a, 5-6, 8-10

Ezra the priest brought the law before the assembly, which consisted of men, women, and those children old enough to understand. Standing at one end of the open place that was before the Water Gate, he read out of the book from daybreak till midday, in the presence of the men, the women, and those children old enough to understand; and all the people listened attentively to the book of the law. Ezra the scribe stood on a wooden platform that had been made for the occasion. He opened the scroll so that all the people might see it—for he was standing higher up than any of the people—; and, as he opened it, all the people rose. Ezra blessed the LORD, the great God, and all the people, their hands raised high, answered, "Amen, amen!" Then they bowed down and prostrated themselves before the LORD, their faces to the ground. Ezra read plainly from the book of the law of God, interpreting it so that all could understand what was read. Then Nehemiah, that is, His Excellency, and Ezra the priest-scribe and the Levites who were instructing the people said to all the people: "Today is holy to the LORD your God. Do not be sad, and do not weep"—for all the people were weeping as they heard the words of the law. He said further: "Go, eat rich foods and drink sweet drinks, and allot portions to those who had nothing prepared; for today is holy to our LORD. Do not be saddened this day, for rejoicing in the LORD must be your strength!"

Responsorial Psalm
PSALM 19:8, 9, 10, 15
R. Your words, Lord, are Spirit and life.

The law of the LORD is perfect,
  refreshing the soul;
the decree of the LORD is trustworthy,
  giving wisdom to the simple. **R.**
The precepts of the LORD are right,
  rejoicing the heart;
the command of the LORD is clear,
  enlightening the eye. **R.**
The fear of the LORD is pure,
  enduring forever;
the ordinances of the LORD are true,
  all of them just. **R.**
Let the words of my mouth and the thought of my heart
  find favor before you,
O LORD, my rock and my redeemer. **R.**

Second Reading
1 CORINTHIANS 12:12-30 (or 1 CORINTHIANS 12:12-14, 27)

Brothers and sisters: As a body is one though it has many parts, and all the parts of the body, though many, are one body, so also Christ. For in one Spirit we were all baptized into one body, whether Jews or Greeks, slaves or free persons, and we were all given to drink of one Spirit.

Now the body is not a single part, but many. If a foot should say, "Because I am not a hand I do not belong to the body," it does not for this reason belong any less to the body. Or if an ear should say, "Because I am not an eye I do not belong to the body," it does not for this reason belong any less to the body. If the whole body were an eye, where would the hearing be? If the whole body were hearing, where would the sense of smell be? But as it is, God placed the parts, each one of them, in the body as he intended. If they were all one part, where would the body be? But as it is, there are many parts, yet one body. The eye cannot say to the hand, "I do not need you," nor again the head to the feet, "I do not need you." Indeed, the parts of the body that seem to be weaker are all the more necessary, and those parts of the body that we consider less honorable we surround with greater honor, and our less presentable parts are treated with greater propriety, whereas our more presentable parts do not need this. But God has so constructed the body as to give greater honor to a part that is without it, so that there may be no division in the body, but that the parts may have the same concern for one another. If one part suffers, all the parts suffer with it; if one part is honored, all the parts share its joy.

Now you are Christ's body, and individually parts of it. Some people God has designated in the church to be, first, apostles; second, prophets; third, teachers; then, mighty deeds; then gifts of healing, assistance, administration, and varieties of tongues. Are all apostles? Are all prophets? Are all teachers? Do all work mighty deeds? Do all have gifts of healing? Do all speak in tongues? Do all interpret?

Gospel

LUKE 1:1-4; 4:14-21

Since many have undertaken to compile a narrative of the events that have been fulfilled among us, just as those who were eyewitnesses from the beginning and ministers of the word have handed them down to us, I too have decided, after investigating everything accurately anew, to write it down in an orderly sequence for you, most excellent Theophilus, so that you may realize the certainty of the teachings you have received.

Jesus returned to Galilee in the power of the Spirit, and news of him spread throughout the whole region. He taught in their synagogues and was praised by all.

He came to Nazareth, where he had grown up, and went according to his custom into the synagogue on the sabbath day. He stood up to read and was handed a scroll of the prophet Isaiah. He unrolled the scroll and found the passage where it was written:

The Spirit of the Lord is upon me,
because he has anointed me
to bring glad tidings to the poor.
He has sent me to proclaim liberty to captives
and recovery of sight to the blind,
to let the oppressed go free,
and to proclaim a year acceptable to the Lord.

Rolling up the scroll, he handed it back to the attendant and sat down, and the eyes of all in the synagogue looked intently at him. He said to them, "Today this Scripture passage is fulfilled in your hearing."

Monday, January 28

First Reading

HEBREWS 9:15, 24-28

Christ is mediator of a new covenant: since a death has taken place for deliverance from transgressions under the first covenant, those who are called may receive the promised eternal inheritance.

For Christ did not enter into a sanctuary made by hands, a copy of the true one, but heaven itself, that he might now appear before God on our behalf. Not that he might offer himself repeatedly, as the high priest enters each year into the sanctuary with blood that is not his own; if that were so, he would have had to suffer repeatedly from the foundation of the world. But now once for all he has appeared at the end of the ages to take away sin by his sacrifice. Just as it is appointed that human beings die once, and after this the judgment, so also Christ, offered once to take away the sins of many, will appear a second time, not to take away sin but to bring salvation to those who eagerly await him.

Responsorial Psalm

PSALM 98:1, 2-3ab, 3cd-4, 5-6

R. Sing to the Lord a new song, for he has done marvelous deeds.

Sing to the LORD a new song,
for he has done wondrous deeds;
His right hand has won victory for him,
his holy arm. **R.**
The LORD has made his salvation known:
in the sight of the nations he has revealed his justice.
He has remembered his kindness and his faithfulness
toward the house of Israel. **R.**
All the ends of the earth have seen
the salvation by our God.
Sing joyfully to the LORD, all you lands;
break into song; sing praise. **R.**
Sing praise to the LORD with the harp,
with the harp and melodious song.
With trumpets and the sound of the horn
sing joyfully before the King, the LORD. **R.**

Gospel
MARK 3:22-30

The scribes who had come from Jerusalem said of Jesus, "He is possessed by Beelzebul," and "By the prince of demons he drives out demons."

Summoning them, he began to speak to them in parables, "How can Satan drive out Satan? If a kingdom is divided against itself, that kingdom cannot stand. And if a house is divided against itself, that house will not be able to stand. And if Satan has risen up against himself and is divided, he cannot stand; that is the end of him. But no one can enter a strong man's house to plunder his property unless he first ties up the strong man. Then he can plunder his house. Amen, I say to you, all sins and all blasphemies that people utter will be forgiven them. But whoever blasphemes against the Holy Spirit will never have forgiveness, but is guilty of an everlasting sin." For they had said, "He has an unclean spirit."

Tuesday, January 29

First Reading
HEBREWS 10:1-10

Brothers and sisters: Since the law has only a shadow of the good things to come, and not the very image of them, it can never make perfect those who come to worship by the same sacrifices that they offer continually each year. Otherwise, would not the sacrifices have ceased to be offered, since the worshipers, once cleansed, would no longer have had any consciousness of sins? But in those sacrifices there is only a yearly remembrance of sins, for it is impossible that the blood of bulls and goats take away sins. For this reason, when he came into the world, he said:

Sacrifice and offering you did not desire,
but a body you prepared for me;
in burnt offerings and sin offerings you took no delight.
Then I said, As is written of me in the scroll,
Behold, I come to do your will, O God.

First he says, *Sacrifices and offerings, burnt offerings and sin offerings, you neither desired nor delighted in.* These are offered according to the law. Then he says, *Behold, I come to do your will.* He takes away the first to establish the second. By this "will," we have been consecrated through the offering of the Body of Jesus Christ once for all.

Responsorial Psalm
PSALM 40:2 and 4ab, 7-8a, 10, 11
R. Here am I Lord; I come to do your will.

I have waited, waited for the LORD,
and he stooped toward me.
And he put a new song into my mouth,
a hymn to our God. **R.**
Sacrifice or oblation you wished not,
but ears open to obedience you gave me.
Burnt offerings or sin-offerings you sought not;
then said I, "Behold I come." **R.**
I announced your justice in the vast assembly;
I did not restrain my lips, as you, O LORD, know. **R.**
Your justice I kept not hid within my heart;
your faithfulness and your salvation I have spoken of;
I have made no secret of your kindness and your truth
in the vast assembly. **R.**

Gospel
MARK 3:31-35

The mother of Jesus and his brothers arrived at the house. Standing outside, they sent word to Jesus and called him. A crowd seated around him told him, "Your mother and your brothers and your sisters are outside asking for you." But he said to them in reply, "Who are my mother and my brothers?" And looking around at those seated in the circle he said, "Here are my mother and my brothers. For whoever does the will of God is my brother and sister and mother."

Wednesday, January 30

First Reading
HEBREWS 10:11-18

Every priest stands daily at his ministry, offering frequently those same sacrifices that can never take away sins. But this one offered one sacrifice for sins, and took his seat forever at the right hand of God; now he waits until his enemies are made his footstool. For by one offering he has made perfect forever those who are being consecrated. The Holy Spirit also testifies to us, for after saying:

This is the covenant I will establish with them
after those days, says the Lord:
"I will put my laws in their hearts,
and I will write them upon their minds,"

he also says:

Their sins and their evildoing
I will remember no more.

Where there is forgiveness of these, there is no longer offering for sin.

Responsorial Psalm
PSALM 110:1, 2, 3, 4
R. You are a priest for ever, in the line of Melchizedek.
The LORD said to my Lord: "Sit at my right hand
till I make your enemies your footstool." **R.**
The scepter of your power the LORD will stretch forth from Zion:
"Rule in the midst of your enemies." **R.**
"Yours is princely power in the day of your birth, in holy splendor;
before the daystar, like the dew, I have begotten you." **R.**
The LORD has sworn, and he will not repent:
"You are a priest forever, according to the order of Melchizedek." **R.**

Gospel
MARK 4:1-20
On another occasion, Jesus began to teach by the sea. A very large crowd gathered around him so that he got into a boat on the sea and sat down. And the whole crowd was beside the sea on land. And he taught them at length in parables, and in the course of his instruction he said to them, "Hear this! A sower went out to sow. And as he sowed, some seed fell on the path, and the birds came and ate it up. Other seed fell on rocky ground where it had little soil. It sprang up at once because the soil was not deep. And when the sun rose, it was scorched and it withered for lack of roots. Some seed fell among thorns, and the thorns grew up and choked it and it produced no grain. And some seed fell on rich soil and produced fruit. It came up and grew and yielded thirty, sixty, and a hundredfold." He added, "Whoever has ears to hear ought to hear."

And when he was alone, those present along with the Twelve questioned him about the parables. He answered them, "The mystery of the Kingdom of God has been granted to you. But to those outside everything comes in parables, so that

they may look and see but not perceive,
and hear and listen but not understand,
in order that they may not be converted and be forgiven."

Jesus said to them, "Do you not understand this parable? Then how will you understand any of the parables? The sower sows the word. These are the ones on the path where the word is sown. As soon as they hear, Satan comes at once and takes away the word sown in them. And these are the ones sown on rocky ground who, when they hear the word, receive it at once with joy. But they have no roots; they last only for a time. Then when tribulation or persecution comes because of the word, they quickly fall away. Those sown among thorns are another sort. They are the people who hear the word, but worldly anxiety, the lure of riches, and the craving for other things intrude and choke the word, and it bears no fruit. But those sown on rich soil are the ones who hear the word and accept it and bear fruit thirty and sixty and a hundredfold."

Thursday, January 31

First Reading

HEBREWS 10:19-25

Brothers and sisters: Since through the Blood of Jesus we have confidence of entrance into the sanctuary by the new and living way he opened for us through the veil, that is, his flesh, and since we have "a great priest over the house of God," let us approach with a sincere heart and in absolute trust, with our hearts sprinkled clean from an evil conscience and our bodies washed in pure water. Let us hold unwaveringly to our confession that gives us hope, for he who made the promise is trustworthy. We must consider how to rouse one another to love and good works. We should not stay away from our assembly, as is the custom of some, but encourage one another, and this all the more as you see the day drawing near.

Responsorial Psalm

PSALM 24:1-2, 3-4ab, 5-6

R. Lord, this is the people that longs to see your face.

The LORD's are the earth and its fullness;
  the world and those who dwell in it.
For he founded it upon the seas
  and established it upon the rivers. **R.**
Who can ascend the mountain of the LORD?
  or who may stand in his holy place?
He whose hands are sinless, whose heart is clean,
  who desires not what is vain. **R.**
He shall receive a blessing from the LORD,
  a reward from God his savior.

Such is the race that seeks for him,
  that seeks the face of the God of Jacob. **R.**

Gospel
MARK 4:21-25

Jesus said to his disciples, "Is a lamp brought in to be placed under a bushel basket or under a bed, and not to be placed on a lampstand? For there is nothing hidden except to be made visible; nothing is secret except to come to light. Anyone who has ears to hear ought to hear." He also told them, "Take care what you hear. The measure with which you measure will be measured out to you, and still more will be given to you. To the one who has, more will be given; from the one who has not, even what he has will be taken away."

FEBRUARY

Friday, February 1

First Reading
HEBREWS 10:32-39

Remember the days past when, after you had been enlightened, you endured a great contest of suffering. At times you were publicly exposed to abuse and affliction; at other times you associated yourselves with those so treated. You even joined in the sufferings of those in prison and joyfully accepted the confiscation of your property, knowing that you had a better and lasting possession. Therefore, do not throw away your confidence; it will have great recompense. You need endurance to do the will of God and receive what he has promised.

For, after just a brief moment,
he who is to come shall come;
he shall not delay.
But my just one shall live by faith,
and if he draws back I take no pleasure in him.

We are not among those who draw back and perish, but among those who have faith and will possess life.

Responsorial Psalm
PSALM 37:3-4, 5-6, 23-24, 39-40
R. The salvation of the just comes from the Lord.
Trust in the LORD and do good,
that you may dwell in the land and be fed in security.
Take delight in the LORD,
and he will grant you your heart's requests. **R.**
Commit to the LORD your way;
trust in him, and he will act.
He will make justice dawn for you like the light;
bright as the noonday shall be your vindication. **R.**
By the LORD are the steps of a man made firm,
and he approves his way.
Though he fall, he does not lie prostrate,
for the hand of the LORD sustains him. **R.**
The salvation of the just is from the LORD;
he is their refuge in time of distress.

And the LORD helps them and delivers them;
he delivers them from the wicked and saves them,
because they take refuge in him. **R.**

Gospel

MARK 4:26-34

Jesus said to the crowds: "This is how it is with the Kingdom of God; it is as if a man were to scatter seed on the land and would sleep and rise night and day and the seed would sprout and grow, he knows not how. Of its own accord the land yields fruit, first the blade, then the ear, then the full grain in the ear. And when the grain is ripe, he wields the sickle at once, for the harvest has come."

He said, "To what shall we compare the Kingdom of God, or what parable can we use for it? It is like a mustard seed that, when it is sown in the ground, is the smallest of all the seeds on the earth. But once it is sown, it springs up and becomes the largest of plants and puts forth large branches, so that the birds of the sky can dwell in its shade." With many such parables he spoke the word to them as they were able to understand it. Without parables he did not speak to them, but to his own disciples he explained everything in private.

Saturday, February 2

The Presentation of the Lord

First Reading

MALACHI 3:1-4

Thus says the Lord GOD:
Lo, I am sending my messenger
to prepare the way before me;
And suddenly there will come to the temple
the LORD whom you seek,
And the messenger of the covenant whom you desire.
Yes, he is coming, says the LORD of hosts.
But who will endure the day of his coming?
And who can stand when he appears?
For he is like the refiner's fire,
or like the fuller's lye.
He will sit refining and purifying silver,
and he will purify the sons of Levi,
Refining them like gold or like silver
that they may offer due sacrifice to the LORD.

Then the sacrifice of Judah and Jerusalem
will please the LORD,
as in the days of old, as in years gone by.

Responsorial Psalm
PSALM 24:7, 8, 9, 10
R. Who is this king of glory? It is the Lord!
Lift up, O gates, your lintels;
reach up, you ancient portals,
that the king of glory may come in! **R.**
Who is this king of glory?
The LORD, strong and mighty,
the LORD, mighty in battle. **R.**
Lift up, O gates, your lintels;
reach up, you ancient portals,
that the king of glory may come in! **R.**
Who is this king of glory?
The LORD of hosts; he is the king of glory. **R.**

Second Reading
HEBREWS 2:14-18
Since the children share in blood and flesh, Jesus likewise shared in them, that through death he might destroy the one who has the power of death, that is, the Devil, and free those who through fear of death had been subject to slavery all their life. Surely he did not help angels but rather the descendants of Abraham; therefore, he had to become like his brothers and sisters in every way, that he might be a merciful and faithful high priest before God to expiate the sins of the people. Because he himself was tested through what he suffered, he is able to help those who are being tested.

Gospel
LUKE 2:22-40 (or LUKE 2:22-32)
When the days were completed for their purification according to the law of Moses, Mary and Joseph took Jesus up to Jerusalem to present him to the Lord, just as it is written in the law of the Lord, *Every male that opens the womb shall be consecrated to the Lord*, and to offer the sacrifice of *a pair of turtledoves or two young pigeons*, in accordance with the dictate in the law of the Lord.

Now there was a man in Jerusalem whose name was Simeon. This man was righteous and devout, awaiting the consolation of Israel, and the Holy Spirit was upon him. It had been revealed to him by the Holy Spirit that he should not see death before he had seen the Christ of the Lord. He came in the Spirit into the temple; and when the parents brought in the child Jesus to perform the custom of the law in regard to him, he took him into his arms and blessed God, saying:

"Now, Master, you may let your servant go
in peace, according to your word,
for my eyes have seen your salvation,
which you prepared in the sight of all the peoples:
a light for revelation to the Gentiles,
and glory for your people Israel."

The child's father and mother were amazed at what was said about him; and Simeon blessed them and said to Mary his mother, "Behold, this child is destined for the fall and rise of many in Israel, and to be a sign that will be contradicted—and you yourself a sword will pierce—so that the thoughts of many hearts may be revealed." There was also a prophetess, Anna, the daughter of Phanuel, of the tribe of Asher. She was advanced in years, having lived seven years with her husband after her marriage, and then as a widow until she was eighty-four. She never left the temple, but worshiped night and day with fasting and prayer. And coming forward at that very time, she gave thanks to God and spoke about the child to all who were awaiting the redemption of Jerusalem.

When they had fulfilled all the prescriptions of the law of the Lord, they returned to Galilee, to their own town of Nazareth. The child grew and became strong, filled with wisdom; and the favor of God was upon him.

Sunday, February 3

Fourth Sunday in Ordinary Time

First Reading

JEREMIAH 1:4-5, 17-19

The word of the LORD came to me, saying:

Before I formed you in the womb I knew you,
before you were born I dedicated you,
a prophet to the nations I appointed you.

But do you gird your loins;
stand up and tell them
all that I command you.
Be not crushed on their account,
as though I would leave you crushed before them;

for it is I this day
who have made you a fortified city,
a pillar of iron, a wall of brass,
against the whole land:
against Judah's kings and princes,
against its priests and people.
They will fight against you but not prevail over you,
for I am with you to deliver you, says the LORD.

Responsorial Psalm
PSALM 71:1-2, 3-4, 5-6, 15-17
R. I will sing of your salvation.

In you, O LORD, I take refuge;
let me never be put to shame.
In your justice rescue me, and deliver me;
incline your ear to me, and save me. **R.**
Be my rock of refuge,
a stronghold to give me safety,
for you are my rock and my fortress.
O my God, rescue me from the hand of the wicked. **R.**
For you are my hope, O Lord;
my trust, O God, from my youth.
On you I depend from birth;
from my mother's womb you are my strength. **R.**
My mouth shall declare your justice,
day by day your salvation.
O God, you have taught me from my youth,
and till the present I proclaim your wondrous deeds. **R.**

Second Reading
1 CORINTHIANS 12:31–13:13 (or 1 CORINTHIANS 13:4-13)

Brothers and sisters: Strive eagerly for the greatest spiritual gifts. But I shall show you a still more excellent way.

If I speak in human and angelic tongues, but do not have love, I am a resounding gong or a clashing cymbal. And if I have the gift of prophecy, and comprehend all mysteries and all knowledge; if I have all faith so as to move mountains, but do not have love, I am nothing. If I give away everything I own, and if I hand my body over so that I may boast, but do not have love, I gain nothing.

Love is patient, love is kind. It is not jealous, it is not pompous, it is not inflated, it is not rude, it does not seek its own interests, it is not quick-tempered, it does not brood over injury, it does not rejoice over wrongdoing but rejoices with the truth. It bears all things, believes all things, hopes all things, endures all things.

Love never fails. If there are prophecies, they will be brought to nothing; if tongues, they will cease; if knowledge, it will be brought to nothing. For we know partially and we prophesy partially, but when the perfect comes, the partial will pass away. When I was a child, I used to talk as a child, think as a child, reason as a child; when I became a man, I put aside childish things. At present we see indistinctly, as in a mirror, but then face to face. At present I know partially; then I shall know fully, as I am fully known. So faith, hope, love remain, these three; but the greatest of these is love.

Gospel

LUKE 4:21-30

Jesus began speaking in the synagogue, saying: "Today this Scripture passage is fulfilled in your hearing." And all spoke highly of him and were amazed at the gracious words that came from his mouth. They also asked, "Isn't this the son of Joseph?" He said to them, "Surely you will quote me this proverb, 'Physician, cure yourself,' and say, 'Do here in your native place the things that we heard were done in Capernaum.'" And he said, "Amen, I say to you, no prophet is accepted in his own native place. Indeed, I tell you, there were many widows in Israel in the days of Elijah when the sky was closed for three and a half years and a severe famine spread over the entire land. It was to none of these that Elijah was sent, but only to a widow in Zarephath in the land of Sidon. Again, there were many lepers in Israel during the time of Elisha the prophet; yet not one of them was cleansed, but only Naaman the Syrian." When the people in the synagogue heard this, they were all filled with fury. They rose up, drove him out of the town, and led him to the brow of the hill on which their town had been built, to hurl him down headlong. But Jesus passed through the midst of them and went away.

Monday, February 4

First Reading

HEBREWS 11:32-40

Brothers and sisters: What more shall I say? I have not time to tell of Gideon, Barak, Samson, Jephthah, of David and Samuel and the prophets, who by faith conquered kingdoms, did what was righteous, obtained the promises; they closed the mouths of lions, put out raging fires, escaped the devouring sword; out of weakness they were made powerful, became strong in battle, and turned back foreign invaders. Women received back their dead through resurrection. Some were tortured and would not accept deliverance, in order to obtain a better resurrection. Others endured mockery, scourging, even chains and imprisonment.

They were stoned, sawed in two, put to death at sword's point; they went about in skins of sheep or goats, needy, afflicted, tormented. The world was not worthy of them. They wandered about in deserts and on mountains, in caves and in crevices in the earth.

Yet all these, though approved because of their faith, did not receive what had been promised. God had foreseen something better for us, so that without us they should not be made perfect.

Responsorial Psalm
PSALM 31:20, 21, 22, 23, 24
R. Let your hearts take comfort, all who hope in the Lord.

How great is the goodness, O LORD,
which you have in store for those who fear you,
And which, toward those who take refuge in you,
you show in the sight of the children of men. **R.**
You hide them in the shelter of your presence
from the plottings of men;
You screen them within your abode
from the strife of tongues. **R.**
Blessed be the LORD whose wondrous mercy
he has shown me in a fortified city. **R.**
Once I said in my anguish,
"I am cut off from your sight";
Yet you heard the sound of my pleading
when I cried out to you. **R.**
Love the LORD, all you his faithful ones!
The LORD keeps those who are constant,
but more than requites those who act proudly. **R.**

Gospel
MARK 5:1-20

Jesus and his disciples came to the other side of the sea, to the territory of the Gerasenes. When he got out of the boat, at once a man from the tombs who had an unclean spirit met him. The man had been dwelling among the tombs, and no one could restrain him any longer, even with a chain. In fact, he had frequently been bound with shackles and chains, but the chains had been pulled apart by him and the shackles smashed, and no one was strong enough to subdue him. Night and day among the tombs and on the hillsides he was always crying out and bruising himself with stones. Catching sight of Jesus from a distance, he ran up and prostrated himself before him, crying out in a loud voice, "What have you to do with me, Jesus, Son of the Most High God? I adjure you by God, do not torment me!" (He had been saying to him, "Unclean spirit, come out of the man!") He asked him, "What is your name?" He replied, "Legion is my name. There are many of us." And he pleaded earnestly with him not to drive them away from that territory.

Now a large herd of swine was feeding there on the hillside. And they pleaded with him, "Send us into the swine. Let us enter them." And he let them, and the unclean spirits came out and entered the swine. The herd of about two thousand rushed down a steep bank into the sea, where they were drowned. The swineherds ran away and reported the incident in the town and throughout the countryside. And people came out to see what had happened. As they approached Jesus, they caught sight of the man who had been possessed by Legion, sitting there clothed and in his right mind. And they were seized with fear. Those who witnessed the incident explained to them what had happened to the possessed man and to the swine. Then they began to beg him to leave their district. As he was getting into the boat, the man who had been possessed pleaded to remain with him. But Jesus would not permit him but told him instead, "Go home to your family and announce to them all that the Lord in his pity has done for you." Then the man went off and began to proclaim in the Decapolis what Jesus had done for him; and all were amazed.

Tuesday, February 5

First Reading

HEBREWS 12:1-4

Brothers and sisters: Since we are surrounded by so great a cloud of witnesses, let us rid ourselves of every burden and sin that clings to us and persevere in running the race that lies before us while keeping our eyes fixed on Jesus, the leader and perfecter of faith. For the sake of the joy that lay before him Jesus endured the cross, despising its shame, and has taken his seat at the right of the throne of God. Consider how he endured such opposition from sinners, in order that you may not grow weary and lose heart. In your struggle against sin you have not yet resisted to the point of shedding blood.

Responsorial Psalm

PSALM 22:26b-27, 28 and 30, 31-32

R. They will praise you, Lord, who long for you.

I will fulfill my vows before those who fear him.
The lowly shall eat their fill;
  they who seek the LORD shall praise him:
  "May your hearts be ever merry!" **R.**
All the ends of the earth
  shall remember and turn to the LORD;

All the families of the nations
shall bow down before him.
To him alone shall bow down
all who sleep in the earth;
Before him shall bend
all who go down into the dust. **R.**
And to him my soul shall live;
my descendants shall serve him.
Let the coming generation be told of the LORD
that they may proclaim to a people yet to be born
the justice he has shown. **R.**

Gospel
MARK 5:21-43

When Jesus had crossed again in the boat to the other side, a large crowd gathered around him, and he stayed close to the sea. One of the synagogue officials, named Jairus, came forward. Seeing him he fell at his feet and pleaded earnestly with him, saying, "My daughter is at the point of death. Please, come lay your hands on her that she may get well and live." He went off with him and a large crowd followed him.

There was a woman afflicted with hemorrhages for twelve years. She had suffered greatly at the hands of many doctors and had spent all that she had. Yet she was not helped but only grew worse. She had heard about Jesus and came up behind him in the crowd and touched his cloak. She said, "If I but touch his clothes, I shall be cured." Immediately her flow of blood dried up. She felt in her body that she was healed of her affliction. Jesus, aware at once that power had gone out from him, turned around in the crowd and asked, "Who has touched my clothes?" But his disciples said to him, "You see how the crowd is pressing upon you, and yet you ask, Who touched me?" And he looked around to see who had done it. The woman, realizing what had happened to her, approached in fear and trembling. She fell down before Jesus and told him the whole truth. He said to her, "Daughter, your faith has saved you. Go in peace and be cured of your affliction."

While he was still speaking, people from the synagogue official's house arrived and said, "Your daughter has died; why trouble the teacher any longer?" Disregarding the message that was reported, Jesus said to the synagogue official, "Do not be afraid; just have faith." He did not allow anyone to accompany him inside except Peter, James, and John, the brother of James. When they arrived at the house of the synagogue official, he caught sight of a commotion, people weeping and wailing loudly. So he went in and said to them, "Why this commotion and weeping? The child is not dead but asleep." And they ridiculed him. Then he put them all out. He took along the child's father and mother and those who were with him and entered the room where the child was. He took the child by the hand and said to her, "*Talitha koum*," which means, "Little girl, I say to you, arise!" The girl, a child of twelve, arose immediately and walked around. At that they were utterly astounded. He gave strict orders that no one should know this and said that she should be given something to eat.

Wednesday, February 6

First Reading

HEBREWS 12:4-7, 11-15

Brothers and sisters: In your struggle against sin you have not yet resisted to the point of shedding blood. You have also forgotten the exhortation addressed to you as children:

My son, do not disdain the discipline of the Lord
or lose heart when reproved by him;
for whom the Lord loves, he disciplines;
he scourges every son he acknowledges.

Endure your trials as "discipline"; God treats you as his sons. For what "son" is there whom his father does not discipline? At the time, all discipline seems a cause not for joy but for pain, yet later it brings the peaceful fruit of righteousness to those who are trained by it.

So strengthen your drooping hands and your weak knees. Make straight paths for your feet, that what is lame may not be dislocated but healed.

Strive for peace with everyone, and for that holiness without which no one will see the Lord. See to it that no one be deprived of the grace of God, that no bitter root spring up and cause trouble, through which many may become defiled.

Responsorial Psalm

PSALM 103:1-2, 13-14, 17-18a

R. The Lord's kindness is everlasting to those who fear him.

Bless the LORD, O my soul;
and all my being, bless his holy name.
Bless the LORD, O my soul,
and forget not all his benefits. **R.**
As a father has compassion on his children,
so the LORD has compassion on those who fear him,
For he knows how we are formed;
he remembers that we are dust. **R.**

But the kindness of the LORD is from eternity
to eternity toward those who fear him,
And his justice toward children's children
among those who keep his covenant. **R.**

Gospel
MARK 6:1-6

Jesus departed from there and came to his native place, accompanied by his disciples. When the sabbath came he began to teach in the synagogue, and many who heard him were astonished. They said, "Where did this man get all this? What kind of wisdom has been given him? What mighty deeds are wrought by his hands! Is he not the carpenter, the son of Mary, and the brother of James and Joseph and Judas and Simon? And are not his sisters here with us?" And they took offense at him. Jesus said to them, "A prophet is not without honor except in his native place and among his own kin and in his own house." So he was not able to perform any mighty deed there, apart from curing a few sick people by laying his hands on them. He was amazed at their lack of faith.

Thursday, February 7

First Reading
HEBREWS 12:18-19, 21-24

Brothers and sisters: You have not approached that which could be touched and a blazing fire and gloomy darkness and storm and a trumpet blast and a voice speaking words such that those who heard begged that no message be further addressed to them. Indeed, so fearful was the spectacle that Moses said, "I am terrified and trembling." No, you have approached Mount Zion and the city of the living God, the heavenly Jerusalem, and countless angels in festal gathering, and the assembly of the firstborn enrolled in heaven, and God the judge of all, and the spirits of the just made perfect, and Jesus, the mediator of a new covenant, and the sprinkled Blood that speaks more eloquently than that of Abel.

Responsorial Psalm
PSALM 48:2-3ab, 3cd-4, 9, 10-11
R. O God, we ponder your mercy within your temple.
Great is the LORD and wholly to be praised
in the city of our God.
His holy mountain, fairest of heights,
is the joy of all the earth. **R.**

Mount Zion, "the recesses of the North,"
 the city of the great King.
God is with her castles;
 renowned is he as a stronghold. **R.**
As we had heard, so have we seen
 in the city of the LORD of hosts,
In the city of our God;
 God makes it firm forever. **R.**
O God, we ponder your mercy
 within your temple.
As your name, O God, so also your praise
 reaches to the ends of the earth.
Of justice your right hand is full. **R.**

Gospel
MARK 6:7-13

Jesus summoned the Twelve and began to send them out two by two and gave them authority over unclean spirits. He instructed them to take nothing for the journey but a walking stick—no food, no sack, no money in their belts. They were, however, to wear sandals but not a second tunic. He said to them, "Wherever you enter a house, stay there until you leave from there. Whatever place does not welcome you or listen to you, leave there and shake the dust off your feet in testimony against them." So they went off and preached repentance. The Twelve drove out many demons, and they anointed with oil many who were sick and cured them.

Friday, February 8

First Reading
HEBREWS 13:1-8

Let brotherly love continue. Do not neglect hospitality, for through it some have unknowingly entertained angels. Be mindful of prisoners as if sharing their imprisonment, and of the ill-treated as of yourselves, for you also are in the body. Let marriage be honored among all and the marriage bed be kept undefiled, for God will judge the immoral and adulterers. Let your life be free from love of money but be content with what you have, for he has said, *I will never forsake you or abandon you*. Thus we may say with confidence:

The Lord is my helper,
and I will not be afraid.
What can anyone do to me?

Remember your leaders who spoke the word of God to you. Consider the outcome of their way of life and imitate their faith. Jesus Christ is the same yesterday, today, and forever.

Responsorial Psalm
PSALM 27:1, 3, 5, 8b-9abc

R. The Lord is my light and my salvation.

The LORD is my light and my salvation;
  whom should I fear?
The LORD is my life's refuge;
  of whom should I be afraid? **R.**
Though an army encamp against me,
  my heart will not fear;
Though war be waged upon me,
  even then will I trust. **R.**
For he will hide me in his abode
  in the day of trouble;
He will conceal me in the shelter of his tent,
  he will set me high upon a rock. **R.**
Your presence, O LORD, I seek.
  Hide not your face from me;
do not in anger repel your servant.
  You are my helper: cast me not off. **R.**

Gospel
MARK 6:14-29

King Herod heard about Jesus, for his fame had become widespread, and people were saying, "John the Baptist has been raised from the dead; that is why mighty powers are at work in him." Others were saying, "He is Elijah"; still others, "He is a prophet like any of the prophets." But when Herod learned of it, he said, "It is John whom I beheaded. He has been raised up."

Herod was the one who had John arrested and bound in prison on account of Herodias, the wife of his brother Philip, whom he had married. John had said to Herod, "It is not lawful for you to have your brother's wife." Herodias harbored a grudge against him and wanted to kill him but was unable to do so. Herod feared John, knowing him to be a righteous and holy man, and kept him in custody. When he heard him speak he was very much perplexed, yet he liked to listen to him. Herodias had an opportunity one day when Herod, on his birthday, gave a banquet for his courtiers, his military officers, and the leading men of Galilee. His own daughter came in and performed a dance that delighted Herod and his guests. The king said to the girl, "Ask of me whatever you wish and I will grant it to you." He even swore many things to her,

"I will grant you whatever you ask of me, even to half of my kingdom." She went out and said to her mother, "What shall I ask for?" Her mother replied, "The head of John the Baptist." The girl hurried back to the king's presence and made her request, "I want you to give me at once on a platter the head of John the Baptist." The king was deeply distressed, but because of his oaths and the guests he did not wish to break his word to her. So he promptly dispatched an executioner with orders to bring back his head. He went off and beheaded him in the prison. He brought in the head on a platter and gave it to the girl. The girl in turn gave it to her mother. When his disciples heard about it, they came and took his body and laid it in a tomb.

Saturday, February 9

First Reading

HEBREWS 13:15-17, 20-21

Brothers and sisters: Through Jesus, let us continually offer God a sacrifice of praise, that is, the fruit of lips that confess his name. Do not neglect to do good and to share what you have; God is pleased by sacrifices of that kind.

Obey your leaders and defer to them, for they keep watch over you and will have to give an account, that they may fulfill their task with joy and not with sorrow, for that would be of no advantage to you.

May the God of peace, who brought up from the dead the great shepherd of the sheep by the Blood of the eternal covenant, furnish you with all that is good, that you may do his will. May he carry out in you what is pleasing to him through Jesus Christ, to whom be glory forever and ever. Amen.

Responsorial Psalm

PSALM 23:1-3a, 3b-4, 5, 6

R. The Lord is my shepherd; there is nothing I shall want.

The LORD is my shepherd; I shall not want.
    In verdant pastures he gives me repose.
Beside restful waters he leads me;
    he refreshes my soul. **R.**
He guides me in right paths
    for his name's sake.
Even though I walk in the dark valley
    I fear no evil; for you are at my side
With your rod and your staff
    that give me courage. **R.**

You spread the table before me
in the sight of my foes;
You anoint my head with oil;
my cup overflows. **R.**
Only goodness and kindness follow me
all the days of my life;
And I shall dwell in the house of the LORD
for years to come. **R.**

Gospel
MARK 6:30-34

The Apostles gathered together with Jesus and reported all they had done and taught. He said to them, "Come away by yourselves to a deserted place and rest a while." People were coming and going in great numbers, and they had no opportunity even to eat. So they went off in the boat by themselves to a deserted place. People saw them leaving and many came to know about it. They hastened there on foot from all the towns and arrived at the place before them.

When Jesus disembarked and saw the vast crowd, his heart was moved with pity for them, for they were like sheep without a shepherd; and he began to teach them many things.

Sunday, February 10

Fifth Sunday in Ordinary Time

First Reading
ISAIAH 6:1-2a, 3-8

In the year King Uzziah died, I saw the Lord seated on a high and lofty throne, with the train of his garment filling the temple. Seraphim were stationed above.

They cried one to the other, "Holy, holy, holy is the LORD of hosts! All the earth is filled with his glory!" At the sound of that cry, the frame of the door shook and the house was filled with smoke.

Then I said, "Woe is me, I am doomed! For I am a man of unclean lips, living among a people of unclean lips; yet my eyes have seen the King, the LORD of hosts!" Then one of the seraphim flew to me, holding an ember that he had taken with tongs from the altar.

He touched my mouth with it, and said, "See, now that this has touched your lips, your wickedness is removed, your sin purged."

Then I heard the voice of the Lord saying, "Whom shall I send? Who will go for us?" "Here I am," I said; "send me!"

Responsorial Psalm

PSALM 138:1-2, 2-3, 4-5, 7-8

R. In the sight of the angels I will sing your praises, Lord.

I will give thanks to you, O LORD, with all my heart,
  for you have heard the words of my mouth;
  in the presence of the angels I will sing your praise;
I will worship at your holy temple
  and give thanks to your name. **R.**
Because of your kindness and your truth;
  for you have made great above all things
  your name and your promise.
When I called, you answered me;
  you built up strength within me. **R.**
All the kings of the earth shall give thanks to you, O LORD,
  when they hear the words of your mouth;
and they shall sing of the ways of the LORD:
  "Great is the glory of the LORD." **R.**
Your right hand saves me.
  The LORD will complete what he has done for me;
your kindness, O LORD, endures forever;
  forsake not the work of your hands. **R.**

Second Reading

1 CORINTHIANS 15:1-11 (or 1 CORINTHIANS 15:3-8, 11)

I am reminding you, brothers and sisters, of the gospel I preached to you, which you indeed received and in which you also stand. Through it you are also being saved, if you hold fast to the word I preached to you, unless you believed in vain. For I handed on to you as of first importance what I also received: that Christ died for our sins in accordance with the Scriptures; that he was buried; that he was raised on the third day in accordance with the Scriptures; that he appeared to Cephas, then to the Twelve. After that, Christ appeared to more than five hundred brothers at once, most of whom are still living, though some have fallen asleep. After that he appeared to James, then to all the apostles. Last of all, as to one born abnormally, he appeared to me. For I am the least of the apostles, not fit to be called an apostle, because I persecuted the church of God. But by the grace of God I am what I am, and his grace to me has not been ineffective. Indeed, I have toiled harder than all of them; not I, however, but the grace of God that is with me. Therefore, whether it be I or they, so we preach and so you believed.

Gospel
LUKE 5:1-11

While the crowd was pressing in on Jesus and listening to the word of God, he was standing by the Lake of Gennesaret. He saw two boats there alongside the lake; the fishermen had disembarked and were washing their nets. Getting into one of the boats, the one belonging to Simon, he asked him to put out a short distance from the shore. Then he sat down and taught the crowds from the boat. After he had finished speaking, he said to Simon, "Put out into deep water and lower your nets for a catch." Simon said in reply, "Master, we have worked hard all night and have caught nothing, but at your command I will lower the nets." When they had done this, they caught a great number of fish and their nets were tearing. They signaled to their partners in the other boat to come to help them. They came and filled both boats so that the boats were in danger of sinking. When Simon Peter saw this, he fell at the knees of Jesus and said, "Depart from me, Lord, for I am a sinful man." For astonishment at the catch of fish they had made seized him and all those with him, and likewise James and John, the sons of Zebedee, who were partners of Simon. Jesus said to Simon, "Do not be afraid; from now on you will be catching men." When they brought their boats to the shore, they left everything and followed him.

Monday, February 11

First Reading
GENESIS 1:1-19

In the beginning, when God created the heavens and the earth, the earth was a formless wasteland, and darkness covered the abyss, while a mighty wind swept over the waters.

Then God said, "Let there be light," and there was light. God saw how good the light was. God then separated the light from the darkness. God called the light "day," and the darkness he called "night." Thus evening came, and morning followed—the first day.

Then God said, "Let there be a dome in the middle of the waters, to separate one body of water from the other." And so it happened: God made the dome, and it separated the water above the dome from the water below it. God called the dome "the sky." Evening came, and morning followed—the second day.

Then God said, "Let the water under the sky be gathered into a single basin, so that the dry land may appear." And so it happened: the water under the sky was gathered into its basin, and the dry land appeared. God called the dry land "the earth," and the basin of the water he called "the sea." God saw how good it was. Then God said, "Let the earth bring forth vegetation: every kind of plant that bears seed and every kind of fruit tree on earth that bears fruit with its seed in it." And so it happened: the earth brought forth every kind of plant that bears seed and every kind of fruit tree on earth that bears fruit with its seed in it. God saw how good it was. Evening came, and morning followed—the third day.

Then God said: "Let there be lights in the dome of the sky, to separate day from night. Let them mark the fixed times, the days and the years, and serve as luminaries in the dome of the sky, to shed light upon the earth." And so it happened: God made the two great lights, the greater one to govern the day, and the lesser one to govern the night; and he made the stars. God set them in the dome of the sky, to shed light upon the earth, to govern the day and the night, and to separate the light from the darkness. God saw how good it was. Evening came, and morning followed—the fourth day.

Responsorial Psalm

PSALM 104:1-2a, 5-6, 10 and 12, 24 and 35c

R. May the Lord be glad in his works.

Bless the LORD, O my soul!
O LORD, my God, you are great indeed!
You are clothed with majesty and glory,
robed in light as with a cloak. **R.**
You fixed the earth upon its foundation,
not to be moved forever;
With the ocean, as with a garment, you covered it;
above the mountains the waters stood. **R.**
You send forth springs into the watercourses
that wind among the mountains.
Beside them the birds of heaven dwell;
from among the branches they send forth their song. **R.**
How manifold are your works, O LORD!
In wisdom you have wrought them all—
the earth is full of your creatures;
Bless the LORD, O my soul! Alleluia. **R.**

Gospel

MARK 6:53-56

After making the crossing to the other side of the sea, Jesus and his disciples came to land at Gennesaret and tied up there. As they were leaving the boat, people immediately recognized him. They scurried about the surrounding country and began to bring in the sick on mats to wherever they heard he was. Whatever villages or towns or countryside he entered, they laid the sick in the marketplaces and begged him that they might touch only the tassel on his cloak; and as many as touched it were healed.

Tuesday, February 12

First Reading

GENESIS 1:20–2:4a

God said, "Let the water teem with an abundance of living creatures, and on the earth let birds fly beneath the dome of the sky." And so it happened: God created the great sea monsters and all kinds of swimming creatures with which the water teems, and all kinds of winged birds. God saw how good it was, and God blessed them, saying, "Be fertile, multiply, and fill the water of the seas; and let the birds multiply on the earth." Evening came, and morning followed—the fifth day.

Then God said, "Let the earth bring forth all kinds of living creatures: cattle, creeping things, and wild animals of all kinds." And so it happened: God made all kinds of wild animals, all kinds of cattle, and all kinds of creeping things of the earth. God saw how good it was. Then God said: "Let us make man in our image, after our likeness. Let them have dominion over the fish of the sea, the birds of the air, and the cattle, and over all the wild animals and all the creatures that crawl on the ground."

God created man in his image;
  in the divine image he created him;
  male and female he created them.

God blessed them, saying: "Be fertile and multiply; fill the earth and subdue it. Have dominion over the fish of the sea, the birds of the air, and all the living things that move on the earth." God also said: "See, I give you every seed-bearing plant all over the earth and every tree that has seed-bearing fruit on it to be your food; and to all the animals of the land, all the birds of the air, and all the living creatures that crawl on the ground, I give all the green plants for food." And so it happened. God looked at everything he had made, and he found it very good. Evening came, and morning followed—the sixth day.

Thus the heavens and the earth and all their array were completed. Since on the seventh day God was finished with the work he had been doing, he rested on the seventh day from all the work he had undertaken. So God blessed the seventh day and made it holy, because on it he rested from all the work he had done in creation.

Such is the story of the heavens and the earth at their creation.

Responsorial Psalm
PSALM 8:4-5, 6-7, 8-9
R. O Lord, our God, how wonderful your name in all the earth!

When I behold your heavens, the work of your fingers,
 the moon and the stars which you set in place—
What is man that you should be mindful of him,
 or the son of man that you should care for him? **R.**
You have made him little less than the angels,
 and crowned him with glory and honor.
You have given him rule over the works of your hands,
 putting all things under his feet. **R.**
All sheep and oxen,
 yes, and the beasts of the field,
The birds of the air, the fishes of the sea,
 and whatever swims the paths of the seas. **R.**

Gospel
MARK 7:1-13

When the Pharisees with some scribes who had come from Jerusalem gathered around Jesus, they observed that some of his disciples ate their meals with unclean, that is, unwashed, hands. (For the Pharisees and, in fact, all Jews, do not eat without carefully washing their hands, keeping the tradition of the elders. And on coming from the marketplace they do not eat without purifying themselves. And there are many other things that they have traditionally observed, the purification of cups and jugs and kettles and beds.) So the Pharisees and scribes questioned him, "Why do your disciples not follow the tradition of the elders but instead eat a meal with unclean hands?" He responded, "Well did Isaiah prophesy about you hypocrites, as it is written:

This people honors me with their lips,
 but their hearts are far from me;
in vain do they worship me,
 teaching as doctrines human precepts.

You disregard God's commandment but cling to human tradition." He went on to say, "How well you have set aside the commandment of God in order to uphold your tradition! For Moses said, *Honor your father and your mother*, and *Whoever curses father or mother shall die*. Yet you say, 'If someone says to father or mother, "Any support you might have had from me is *qorban*"' (meaning, dedicated to God), you allow him to do nothing more for his father or mother. You nullify the word of

God in favor of your tradition that you have handed on. And you do many such things."

Wednesday, February 13

First Reading

GENESIS 2:4b-9, 15-17

At the time when the LORD God made the earth and the heavens—while as yet there was no field shrub on earth and no grass of the field had sprouted, for the LORD God had sent no rain upon the earth and there was no man to till the soil, but a stream was welling up out of the earth and was watering all the surface of the ground—the LORD God formed man out of the clay of the ground and blew into his nostrils the breath of life, and so man became a living being.

Then the LORD God planted a garden in Eden, in the east, and he placed there the man whom he had formed. Out of the ground the LORD God made various trees grow that were delightful to look at and good for food, with the tree of life in the middle of the garden and the tree of the knowledge of good and evil.

The LORD God then took the man and settled him in the garden of Eden, to cultivate and care for it. The LORD God gave man this order: "You are free to eat from any of the trees of the garden except the tree of knowledge of good and evil. From that tree you shall not eat; the moment you eat from it you are surely doomed to die."

Responsorial Psalm

PSALM 104:1-2a, 27-28, 29bc-30

R. O bless the Lord, my soul!

Bless the LORD, O my soul!
O LORD, my God, you are great indeed!
You are clothed with majesty and glory,
robed in light as with a cloak. **R.**
All creatures look to you
to give them food in due time.
When you give it to them, they gather it;
when you open your hand, they are filled with good things. **R.**
If you take away their breath, they perish
and return to their dust.
When you send forth your spirit, they are created,
and you renew the face of the earth. **R.**

Gospel
MARK 7:14-23

Jesus summoned the crowd again and said to them, "Hear me, all of you, and understand. Nothing that enters one from outside can defile that person; but the things that come out from within are what defile."

When he got home away from the crowd his disciples questioned him about the parable. He said to them, "Are even you likewise without understanding? Do you not realize that everything that goes into a person from outside cannot defile, since it enters not the heart but the stomach and passes out into the latrine?" (Thus he declared all foods clean.) "But what comes out of the man, that is what defiles him. From within the man, from his heart, come evil thoughts, unchastity, theft, murder, adultery, greed, malice, deceit, licentiousness, envy, blasphemy, arrogance, folly. All these evils come from within and they defile."

Thursday, February 14

First Reading
GENESIS 2:18-25

The LORD God said: "It is not good for the man to be alone. I will make a suitable partner for him." So the LORD God formed out of the ground various wild animals and various birds of the air, and he brought them to the man to see what he would call them; whatever the man called each of them would be its name. The man gave names to all the cattle, all the birds of the air, and all the wild animals; but none proved to be the suitable partner for the man.

So the LORD God cast a deep sleep on the man, and while he was asleep, he took out one of his ribs and closed up its place with flesh. The LORD God then built up into a woman the rib that he had taken from the man. When he brought her to the man, the man said:

"This one, at last, is bone of my bones
    and flesh of my flesh;
this one shall be called 'woman,'
    for out of 'her man' this one has been taken."

That is why a man leaves his father and mother and clings to his wife, and the two of them become one flesh.

The man and his wife were both naked, yet they felt no shame.

Responsorial Psalm

PSALM 128:1-2, 3, 4-5

R. Blessed are those who fear the Lord.

Blessed are you who fear the LORD,
who walk in his ways!
For you shall eat the fruit of your handiwork;
blessed shall you be, and favored. **R.**
Your wife shall be like a fruitful vine
in the recesses of your home;
Your children like olive plants
around your table. **R.**
Behold, thus is the man blessed
who fears the LORD.
The LORD bless you from Zion:
may you see the prosperity of Jerusalem
all the days of your life. **R.**

Gospel

MARK 7:24-30

Jesus went to the district of Tyre. He entered a house and wanted no one to know about it, but he could not escape notice. Soon a woman whose daughter had an unclean spirit heard about him. She came and fell at his feet. The woman was a Greek, a Syrophoenician by birth, and she begged him to drive the demon out of her daughter. He said to her, "Let the children be fed first. For it is not right to take the food of the children and throw it to the dogs." She replied and said to him, "Lord, even the dogs under the table eat the children's scraps." Then he said to her, "For saying this, you may go. The demon has gone out of your daughter." When the woman went home, she found the child lying in bed and the demon gone.

Friday, February 15

First Reading

GENESIS 3:1-8

Now the serpent was the most cunning of all the animals that the LORD God had made. The serpent asked the woman, "Did God really tell you not to eat from any of the trees in the garden?" The woman answered the serpent: "We may eat of the fruit of the trees in the garden; it is only about the fruit of the tree in the middle of the garden that God said, 'You shall not eat it or even touch it, lest you die.'" But the serpent said to the woman: "You certainly will not die! No, God knows well that the moment you eat of it your eyes will be opened and you will be like gods who know what is good and what is evil." The woman saw that the tree was good for food, pleasing to the eyes, and desirable for gaining wisdom. So she took some of its fruit and ate it; and she also gave some to her husband, who was with her, and he ate it. Then the eyes of both of them were opened, and they realized that they were naked; so they sewed fig leaves together and made loincloths for themselves.

When they heard the sound of the LORD God moving about in the garden at the breezy time of the day, the man and his wife hid themselves from the LORD God among the trees of the garden.

Responsorial Psalm

PSALM 32:1-2, 5, 6, 7

R. Blessed are those whose sins are forgiven.

Blessed is he whose fault is taken away,
 whose sin is covered.
Blessed the man to whom the LORD imputes not guilt,
 in whose spirit there is no guile. **R.**
Then I acknowledged my sin to you,
 my guilt I covered not.
I said, "I confess my faults to the LORD,"
 and you took away the guilt of my sin. **R.**
For this shall every faithful man pray to you
 in time of stress.
Though deep waters overflow,
 they shall not reach him. **R.**
You are my shelter; from distress you will preserve me;
 with glad cries of freedom you will ring me round. **R.**

Gospel

MARK 7:31-37

Jesus left the district of Tyre and went by way of Sidon to the Sea of Galilee, into the district of the Decapolis. And people brought to him a deaf man who had a speech impediment and begged him to lay his hand on him. He took him off by himself away from the crowd. He put his finger into the man's ears and, spitting, touched his tongue; then he looked up to heaven and groaned, and said to him, "*Ephphatha*!" (that is, "Be opened!") And immediately the man's ears were opened, his speech impediment was removed, and he spoke plainly. He ordered them not to tell anyone. But the more he ordered them not to, the more they proclaimed it. They were exceedingly astonished and they said, "He has done all things well. He makes the deaf hear and the mute speak."

Saturday, February 16

First Reading

GENESIS 3:9-24

The LORD God called to Adam and asked him, "Where are you?" He answered, "I heard you in the garden; but I was afraid, because I was naked, so I hid myself." Then he asked, "Who told you that you were naked? You have eaten, then, from the tree of which I had forbidden you to eat!" The man replied, "The woman whom you put here with me—she gave me fruit from the tree, and so I ate it." The LORD God then asked the woman, "Why did you do such a thing?" The woman answered, "The serpent tricked me into it, so I ate it."

Then the LORD God said to the serpent:

"Because you have done this, you shall be banned
from all the animals
and from all the wild creatures;
On your belly shall you crawl,
and dirt shall you eat
all the days of your life.
I will put enmity between you and the woman,
and between your offspring and hers;
He will strike at your head,
while you strike at his heel."

To the woman he said:

"I will intensify the pangs of your childbearing;
in pain shall you bring forth children.
Yet your urge shall be for your husband,
and he shall be your master."

To the man he said: "Because you listened to your wife and ate from the tree of which I had forbidden you to eat,

"Cursed be the ground because of you!
In toil shall you eat its yield
all the days of your life.
Thorns and thistles shall it bring forth to you,
as you eat of the plants of the field.
By the sweat of your face
shall you get bread to eat,
Until you return to the ground,
from which you were taken;

For you are dirt,
    and to dirt you shall return."

The man called his wife Eve, because she became the mother of all the living.

For the man and his wife the LORD God made leather garments, with which he clothed them. Then the LORD God said: "See! The man has become like one of us, knowing what is good and what is evil! Therefore, he must not be allowed to put out his hand to take fruit from the tree of life also, and thus eat of it and live forever." The LORD God therefore banished him from the garden of Eden, to till the ground from which he had been taken. When he expelled the man, he settled him east of the garden of Eden; and he stationed the cherubim and the fiery revolving sword, to guard the way to the tree of life.

Responsorial Psalm
PSALM 90:2, 3-4abc, 5-6, 12-13
R. In every age, O Lord, you have been our refuge.
Before the mountains were begotten
    and the earth and the world were brought forth,
    from everlasting to everlasting you are God. **R.**
You turn man back to dust,
    saying, "Return, O children of men."
For a thousand years in your sight
    are as yesterday, now that it is past,
    or as a watch of the night. **R.**
You make an end of them in their sleep;
    the next morning they are like the changing grass,
Which at dawn springs up anew,
    but by evening wilts and fades. **R.**
Teach us to number our days aright,
    that we may gain wisdom of heart.
Return, O LORD! How long?
    Have pity on your servants! **R.**

Gospel
MARK 8:1-10

In those days when there again was a great crowd without anything to eat, Jesus summoned the disciples and said, "My heart is moved with pity for the crowd, because they have been with me now for three days and have nothing to eat. If I send them away hungry to their homes, they will collapse on the way, and some of them have come a great distance." His disciples answered him, "Where can anyone get enough bread to satisfy them here in this deserted place?" Still he asked them,

"How many loaves do you have?" They replied, "Seven." He ordered the crowd to sit down on the ground. Then, taking the seven loaves he gave thanks, broke them, and gave them to his disciples to distribute, and they distributed them to the crowd. They also had a few fish. He said the blessing over them and ordered them distributed also. They ate and were satisfied. They picked up the fragments left over—seven baskets. There were about four thousand people.

He dismissed the crowd and got into the boat with his disciples and came to the region of Dalmanutha.

Sunday, February 17

Sixth Sunday in Ordinary Time

First Reading
JEREMIAH 17:5-8

Thus says the LORD:
Cursed is the one who trusts in human beings,
  who seeks his strength in flesh,
  whose heart turns away from the LORD.
He is like a barren bush in the desert
  that enjoys no change of season,
but stands in a lava waste,
  a salt and empty earth.
Blessed is the one who trusts in the LORD,
  whose hope is the LORD.
He is like a tree planted beside the waters
  that stretches out its roots to the stream:
it fears not the heat when it comes;
  its leaves stay green;
in the year of drought it shows no distress,
  but still bears fruit.

Responsorial Psalm
PSALM 1:1-2, 3, 4 and 6
R. Blessed are they who hope in the Lord.

Blessed the man who follows not
  the counsel of the wicked,
nor walks in the way of sinners,
  nor sits in the company of the insolent,
but delights in the law of the LORD
  and meditates on his law day and night. **R.**

He is like a tree
 planted near running water,
that yields its fruit in due season,
 and whose leaves never fade.
Whatever he does, prospers. **R.**
Not so the wicked, not so;
 they are like chaff which the wind drives away.
For the LORD watches over the way of the just,
 but the way of the wicked vanishes. **R.**

Second Reading
1 CORINTHIANS 15:12, 16-20

Brothers and sisters: If Christ is preached as raised from the dead, how can some among you say there is no resurrection of the dead? If the dead are not raised, neither has Christ been raised, and if Christ has not been raised, your faith is vain; you are still in your sins. Then those who have fallen asleep in Christ have perished. If for this life only we have hoped in Christ, we are the most pitiable people of all.

But now Christ has been raised from the dead, the first fruits of those who have fallen asleep.

Gospel
LUKE 6:17, 20-26

Jesus came down with the Twelve and stood on a stretch of level ground with a great crowd of his disciples and a large number of the people from all Judea and Jerusalem and the coastal region of Tyre and Sidon. And raising his eyes toward his disciples he said:

"Blessed are you who are poor,
 for the kingdom of God is yours.
Blessed are you who are now hungry,
 for you will be satisfied.
Blessed are you who are now weeping,
 for you will laugh.
Blessed are you when people hate you,
 and when they exclude and insult you,
 and denounce your name as evil
 on account of the Son of Man.
Rejoice and leap for joy on that day!
Behold, your reward will be great in heaven.
For their ancestors treated the prophets in the same way.
But woe to you who are rich,
 for you have received your consolation.

Woe to you who are filled now,
  for you will be hungry.
Woe to you who laugh now,
  for you will grieve and weep.
Woe to you when all speak well of you,
  for their ancestors treated the false
    prophets in this way."

Monday, February 18

First Reading

GENESIS 4:1-15, 25

The man had relations with his wife Eve, and she conceived and bore Cain, saying, "I have produced a man with the help of the LORD." Next she bore his brother Abel. Abel became a keeper of flocks, and Cain a tiller of the soil. In the course of time Cain brought an offering to the LORD from the fruit of the soil, while Abel, for his part, brought one of the best firstlings of his flock. The LORD looked with favor on Abel and his offering, but on Cain and his offering he did not. Cain greatly resented this and was crestfallen. So the LORD said to Cain: "Why are you so resentful and crestfallen? If you do well, you can hold up your head; but if not, sin is a demon lurking at the door: his urge is toward you, yet you can be his master."

Cain said to his brother Abel, "Let us go out in the field." When they were in the field, Cain attacked his brother Abel and killed him. Then the LORD asked Cain, "Where is your brother Abel?" He answered, "I do not know. Am I my brother's keeper?" The LORD then said: "What have you done! Listen: your brother's blood cries out to me from the soil! Therefore you shall be banned from the soil that opened its mouth to receive your brother's blood from your hand. If you till the soil, it shall no longer give you its produce. You shall become a restless wanderer on the earth." Cain said to the LORD: "My punishment is too great to bear. Since you have now banished me from the soil, and I must avoid your presence and become a restless wanderer on the earth, anyone may kill me at sight." "Not so!" the LORD said to him. "If anyone kills Cain, Cain shall be avenged sevenfold." So the LORD put a mark on Cain, lest anyone should kill him at sight.

Adam again had relations with his wife, and she gave birth to a son whom she called Seth. "God has granted me more offspring in place of Abel," she said, "because Cain slew him."

Responsorial Psalm

PSALM 50:1 and 8, 16bc-17, 20-21

R. Offer to God a sacrifice of praise.

God the LORD has spoken and summoned the earth,
from the rising of the sun to its setting.
"Not for your sacrifices do I rebuke you,
for your burnt offerings are before me always." **R.**
"Why do you recite my statutes,
and profess my covenant with your mouth
Though you hate discipline
and cast my words behind you?" **R.**
"You sit speaking against your brother;
against your mother's son you spread rumors.
When you do these things, shall I be deaf to it?
Or do you think that I am like yourself?
I will correct you by drawing them up before your eyes." **R.**

Gospel

MARK 8:11-13

The Pharisees came forward and began to argue with Jesus, seeking from him a sign from heaven to test him. He sighed from the depth of his spirit and said, "Why does this generation seek a sign? Amen, I say to you, no sign will be given to this generation." Then he left them, got into the boat again, and went off to the other shore.

Tuesday, February 19

First Reading

GENESIS 6:5-8; 7:1-5, 10

When the LORD saw how great was man's wickedness on earth, and how no desire that his heart conceived was ever anything but evil, he regretted that he had made man on the earth, and his heart was grieved.

So the LORD said: "I will wipe out from the earth the men whom I have created, and not only the men, but also the beasts and the creeping things and the birds of the air, for I am sorry that I made them." But Noah found favor with the LORD.

Then the LORD said to Noah: "Go into the ark, you and all your household, for you alone in this age have I found to be truly just. Of every clean animal, take with you seven pairs, a male and its mate; and of the unclean animals, one pair, a male and its mate; likewise, of every clean bird of the air, seven pairs, a male and a female, and of all the unclean birds, one pair, a male and a female. Thus you will keep their issue alive over all the earth. Seven days from now I will bring rain down on the earth for forty days and forty nights, and so I will wipe out from the surface of the earth every moving creature that I have made." Noah did just as the LORD had commanded him.

As soon as the seven days were over, the waters of the flood came upon the earth.

Responsorial Psalm

PSALM 29:1a and 2, 3ac-4, 3b and 9c-10

R. The Lord will bless his people with peace.

Give to the LORD, you sons of God,
give to the LORD glory and praise,
Give to the LORD the glory due his name;
adore the LORD in holy attire. **R.**
The voice of the LORD is over the waters,
the LORD, over vast waters.
The voice of the LORD is mighty;
the voice of the LORD is majestic. **R.**
The God of glory thunders,
and in his temple all say, "Glory!"
The LORD is enthroned above the flood;
the LORD is enthroned as king forever. **R.**

Gospel

MARK 8:14-21

The disciples had forgotten to bring bread, and they had only one loaf with them in the boat. Jesus enjoined them, "Watch out, guard against the leaven of the Pharisees and the leaven of Herod." They concluded among themselves that it was because they had no bread. When he became aware of this he said to them, "Why do you conclude that it is because you have no bread? Do you not yet understand or comprehend? Are your hearts hardened? Do you have eyes and not see, ears and not hear? And do you not remember, when I broke the five loaves for the five thousand, how many wicker baskets full of fragments you picked up?" They answered him, "Twelve." "When I broke the seven loaves for the four thousand, how many full baskets of fragments did you pick up?" They answered him, "Seven." He said to them, "Do you still not understand?"

Wednesday, February 20

First Reading

GENESIS 8:6-13, 20-22

At the end of forty days Noah opened the hatch he had made in the ark, and he sent out a raven, to see if the waters had lessened on the earth. It flew back and forth until the waters dried off from the earth. Then he sent out a dove, to see if the waters had lessened on the earth. But the dove could find no place to alight and perch, and it returned to him in the ark, for there was water all over the earth. Putting out his hand, he caught the dove and drew it back to him inside the ark. He waited seven days more and again sent the dove out from the ark. In the evening the dove came back to him, and there in its bill was a plucked-off olive leaf! So Noah knew that the waters had lessened on the earth. He waited still another seven days and then released the dove once more; and this time it did not come back.

In the six hundred and first year of Noah's life, in the first month, on the first day of the month, the water began to dry up on the earth. Noah then removed the covering of the ark and saw that the surface of the ground was drying up.

Noah built an altar to the LORD, and choosing from every clean animal and every clean bird, he offered burnt offerings on the altar. When the LORD smelled the sweet odor, he said to himself: "Never again will I doom the earth because of man since the desires of man's heart are evil from the start; nor will I ever again strike down all living beings, as I have done.

As long as the earth lasts,
seedtime and harvest,
cold and heat,
Summer and winter,
and day and night
shall not cease."

Responsorial Psalm
PSALM 116:12-13, 14-15, 18-19
R. To you, Lord, I will offer a sacrifice of praise.
(or R. Alleluia.)
How shall I make a return to the LORD
for all the good he has done for me?
The cup of salvation I will take up,
and I will call upon the name of the LORD. **R.**
My vows to the LORD I will pay
in the presence of all his people.
Precious in the eyes of the LORD
is the death of his faithful ones. **R.**
My vows to the LORD I will pay
in the presence of all his people,
In the courts of the house of the LORD,
in your midst, O Jerusalem. **R.**

Gospel
MARK 8:22-26

When Jesus and his disciples arrived at Bethsaida, people brought to him a blind man and begged Jesus to touch him. He took the blind man by the hand and led him outside the village. Putting spittle on his eyes he laid his hands on the man and asked, "Do you see anything?" Looking up the man replied, "I see people looking like trees and walking." Then he laid hands on the man's eyes a second time and he saw clearly; his sight was restored and he could see everything distinctly. Then he sent him home and said, "Do not even go into the village."

Thursday, February 21

First Reading
GENESIS 9:1-13

God blessed Noah and his sons and said to them: "Be fertile and multiply and fill the earth. Dread fear of you shall come upon all the animals of the earth and all the birds of the air, upon all the creatures that move about on the ground and all the fishes of the sea; into your power they are delivered. Every creature that is alive shall be yours to eat; I give them all to you as I did the green plants. Only flesh with its lifeblood still in it you shall not eat. For your own lifeblood, too, I will demand an accounting: from every animal I will demand it, and from one man in regard to his fellow man I will demand an accounting for human life.

If anyone sheds the blood of man,
  by man shall his blood be shed;
For in the image of God
  has man been made.

Be fertile, then, and multiply; abound on earth and subdue it."

God said to Noah and to his sons with him: "See, I am now establishing my covenant with you and your descendants after you and with every living creature that was with you: all the birds, and the various tame and wild animals that were with you and came out of the ark. I will establish my covenant with you, that never again shall all bodily creatures be destroyed by the waters of a flood; there shall not be another flood to devastate the earth." God added: "This is the sign that I am giving for all ages to come, of the covenant between me and you and every living creature with you: I set my bow in the clouds to serve as a sign of the covenant between me and the earth."

Responsorial Psalm

PSALM 102:16-18, 19-21, 29 and 22-23

R. From heaven the Lord looks down on the earth.

The nations shall revere your name, O LORD,
  and all the kings of the earth your glory,
When the LORD has rebuilt Zion
  and appeared in his glory;
When he has regarded the prayer of the destitute,
  and not despised their prayer. **R.**

Let this be written for the generation to come,
  and let his future creatures praise the LORD:
"The LORD looked down from his holy height,
  from heaven he beheld the earth,
To hear the groaning of the prisoners,
  to release those doomed to die." **R.**

The children of your servants shall abide,
  and their posterity shall continue in your presence,
That the name of the LORD may be declared in Zion,
  and his praise, in Jerusalem,
When the peoples gather together,
  and the kingdoms, to serve the LORD. **R.**

Gospel

MARK 8:27-33

Jesus and his disciples set out for the villages of Caesarea Philippi. Along the way he asked his disciples, "Who do people say that I am?" They said in reply, "John the Baptist, others Elijah, still others one of the prophets." And he asked them, "But who do you say that I am?" Peter said to him in reply, "You are the Christ." Then he warned them not to tell anyone about him.

He began to teach them that the Son of Man must suffer greatly and be rejected by the elders, the chief priests, and the scribes, and be killed, and rise after three days. He spoke this openly. Then Peter took him aside and began to rebuke him. At this he turned around and, looking at his disciples, rebuked Peter and said, "Get behind me, Satan. You are thinking not as God does, but as human beings do."

Friday, February 22

The Chair of Saint Peter the Apostle

First Reading

1 PETER 5:1-4

Beloved: I exhort the presbyters among you, as a fellow presbyter and witness to the sufferings of Christ and one who has a share in the glory to be revealed. Tend the flock of God in your midst, overseeing not by constraint but willingly, as God would have it, not for shameful profit but eagerly. Do not lord it over those assigned to you, but be examples to the flock. And when the chief Shepherd is revealed, you will receive the unfading crown of glory.

Responsorial Psalm

PSALM 23:1-3a, 4, 5, 6

R. The Lord is my shepherd; there is nothing I shall want.

The LORD is my shepherd; I shall not want.
In verdant pastures he gives me repose;
Beside restful waters he leads me;
he refreshes my soul. **R.**
Even though I walk in the dark valley
I fear no evil; for you are at my side
With your rod and your staff
that give me courage. **R.**
You spread the table before me
in the sight of my foes;
You anoint my head with oil;
my cup overflows. **R.**
Only goodness and kindness follow me
all the days of my life;
And I shall dwell in the house of the LORD
for years to come. **R.**

Gospel

MATTHEW 16:13-19

When Jesus went into the region of Caesarea Philippi he asked his disciples, "Who do people say that the Son of Man is?" They replied, "Some say John the Baptist, others Elijah, still others Jeremiah or one of the prophets." He said to them, "But who do you say that I am?" Simon Peter said in reply, "You are the Christ, the Son of the living God." Jesus said to him in reply, "Blessed are you, Simon son of Jonah. For flesh and blood has not revealed this to you, but my heavenly Father. And so I say to you, you are Peter, and upon this rock I will build my

Church, and the gates of the netherworld shall not prevail against it. I will give you the keys to the Kingdom of heaven. Whatever you bind on earth shall be bound in heaven; and whatever you loose on earth shall be loosed in heaven."

Saturday, February 23

First Reading

HEBREWS 11:1-7

Brothers and sisters: Faith is the realization of what is hoped for and evidence of things not seen. Because of it the ancients were well attested. By faith we understand that the universe was ordered by the word of God, so that what is visible came into being through the invisible. By faith Abel offered to God a sacrifice greater than Cain's. Through this, he was attested to be righteous, God bearing witness to his gifts, and through this, though dead, he still speaks. By faith Enoch was taken up so that he should not see death, and *he was found no more because God had taken him*. Before he was taken up, he was attested to have pleased God. But without faith it is impossible to please him, for anyone who approaches God must believe that he exists and that he rewards those who seek him. By faith Noah, warned about what was not yet seen, with reverence built an ark for the salvation of his household. Through this, he condemned the world and inherited the righteousness that comes through faith.

Responsorial Psalm

PSALM 145:2-3, 4-5, 10-11

R. I will praise your name for ever, Lord.

Every day will I bless you,
  and I will praise your name forever and ever.
Great is the LORD and highly to be praised;
  his greatness is unsearchable. **R.**
Generation after generation praises your works
  and proclaims your might.
They speak of the splendor of your glorious majesty
  and tell of your wondrous works. **R.**
Let all your works give you thanks, O LORD,
  and let your faithful ones bless you.
Let them discourse of the glory of your Kingdom
  and speak of your might. **R.**

Gospel
MARK 9:2-13

Jesus took Peter, James, and John and led them up a high mountain apart by themselves. And he was transfigured before them, and his clothes became dazzling white, such as no fuller on earth could bleach them. Then Elijah appeared to them along with Moses, and they were conversing with Jesus. Then Peter said to Jesus in reply, "Rabbi, it is good that we are here! Let us make three tents: one for you, one for Moses, and one for Elijah." He hardly knew what to say, they were so terrified. Then a cloud came, casting a shadow over them; then from the cloud came a voice, "This is my beloved Son. Listen to him." Suddenly, looking around, the disciples no longer saw anyone but Jesus alone with them.

As they were coming down from the mountain, he charged them not to relate what they had seen to anyone, except when the Son of Man had risen from the dead. So they kept the matter to themselves, questioning what rising from the dead meant. Then they asked him, "Why do the scribes say that Elijah must come first?" He told them, "Elijah will indeed come first and restore all things, yet how is it written regarding the Son of Man that he must suffer greatly and be treated with contempt? But I tell you that Elijah has come and they did to him whatever they pleased, as it is written of him."

Sunday, February 24

Seventh Sunday in Ordinary Time

First Reading
1 SAMUEL 26:2, 7-9, 12-13, 22-23

In those days, Saul went down to the desert of Ziph with three thousand picked men of Israel, to search for David in the desert of Ziph. So David and Abishai went among Saul's soldiers by night and found Saul lying asleep within the barricade, with his spear thrust into the ground at his head and Abner and his men sleeping around him.

Abishai whispered to David: "God has delivered your enemy into your grasp this day. Let me nail him to the ground with one thrust of the spear; I will not need a second thrust!" But David said to Abishai, "Do not harm him, for who can lay hands on the LORD'S anointed and remain unpunished?" So David took the spear and the water jug from their place at Saul's head, and they got away without anyone's seeing or knowing or awakening. All remained asleep, because the LORD had put them into a deep slumber.

Going across to an opposite slope, David stood on a remote hilltop at a great distance from Abner, son of Ner, and the troops.

He said: "Here is the king's spear. Let an attendant come over to get it. The LORD will reward each man for his justice and faithfulness. Today, though the LORD delivered you into my grasp, I would not harm the LORD'S anointed."

Responsorial Psalm
PSALM 103:1-2, 3-4, 8, 10, 12-13
R. The Lord is kind and merciful.

Bless the LORD, O my soul;
and all my being, bless his holy name.
Bless the LORD, O my soul,
and forget not all his benefits. **R.**
He pardons all your iniquities,
heals all your ills.
He redeems your life from destruction,
crowns you with kindness and compassion. **R.**
Merciful and gracious is the LORD,
slow to anger and abounding in kindness.
Not according to our sins does he deal with us,
nor does he requite us according to our crimes. **R.**
As far as the east is from the west,
so far has he put our transgressions from us.
As a father has compassion on his children,
so the LORD has compassion on those who fear him. **R.**

Second Reading
1 CORINTHIANS 15:45-49

Brothers and sisters: It is written, *The first man, Adam, became a living being,* the last Adam a life-giving spirit. But the spiritual was not first; rather the natural and then the spiritual. The first man was from the earth, earthly; the second man, from heaven. As was the earthly one, so also are the earthly, and as is the heavenly one, so also are the heavenly. Just as we have borne the image of the earthly one, we shall also bear the image of the heavenly one.

Gospel
LUKE 6:27-38

Jesus said to his disciples: "To you who hear I say, love your enemies, do good to those who hate you, bless those who curse you, pray for those who mistreat you. To the person who strikes you on one cheek, offer the other one as well, and from the person who takes your cloak, do not withhold even your tunic. Give to everyone who asks of you, and from the one who takes what is yours do not demand it back. Do to others as you would have them do to you. For if you love those who love you, what credit is that to you? Even sinners love those who love them. And if you do good to those who do good to you, what credit is that to you? Even sinners do the same. If you lend money to those from whom you expect repayment, what credit is that to you? Even sinners lend to sinners, and get back the same amount. But rather, love your enemies and do good to them, and lend expecting nothing back; then your reward will be great and you will be children of the Most High, for he himself is kind to the ungrateful and the wicked. Be merciful, just as your Father is merciful.

"Stop judging and you will not be judged. Stop condemning and you will not be condemned. Forgive and you will be forgiven. Give, and gifts will be given to you; a good measure, packed together, shaken down, and overflowing, will be poured into your lap. For the measure with which you measure will in return be measured out to you."

Monday, February 25

First Reading

SIRACH 1:1-10

All wisdom comes from the LORD
  and with him it remains forever, and is before all time.
The sand of the seashore, the drops of rain,
  the days of eternity: who can number these?
Heaven's height, earth's breadth,
  the depths of the abyss: who can explore these?
Before all things else wisdom was created;
  and prudent understanding, from eternity.
The word of God on high is the fountain of wisdom
  and her ways are everlasting.
To whom has wisdom's root been revealed?
  Who knows her subtleties?
To whom has the discipline of wisdom been revealed?
  And who has understood the multiplicity of her ways?
There is but one, wise and truly awe-inspiring,
  seated upon his throne:
There is but one, Most High
  all-powerful creator-king and truly awe-inspiring one,
  seated upon his throne and he is the God of dominion.
It is the LORD; he created her through the Holy Spirit,
  has seen her and taken note of her.
He has poured her forth upon all his works,
  upon every living thing according to his bounty;
  he has lavished her upon his friends.

Responsorial Psalm

PSALM 93:1ab, 1cd-2, 5

R. The Lord is king; he is robed in majesty.

The LORD is king, in splendor robed;
robed is the LORD and girt about with strength. **R.**
And he has made the world firm,
not to be moved.
Your throne stands firm from of old;
from everlasting you are, O LORD. **R.**
Your decrees are worthy of trust indeed:
holiness befits your house,
O LORD, for length of days. **R.**

Gospel

MARK 9:14-29

As Jesus came down from the mountain with Peter, James, and John and approached the other disciples, they saw a large crowd around them and scribes arguing with them. Immediately on seeing him, the whole crowd was utterly amazed. They ran up to him and greeted him. He asked them, "What are you arguing about with them?" Someone from the crowd answered him, "Teacher, I have brought to you my son possessed by a mute spirit. Wherever it seizes him, it throws him down; he foams at the mouth, grinds his teeth, and becomes rigid. I asked your disciples to drive it out, but they were unable to do so." He said to them in reply, "O faithless generation, how long will I be with you? How long will I endure you? Bring him to me." They brought the boy to him. And when he saw him, the spirit immediately threw the boy into convulsions. As he fell to the ground, he began to roll around and foam at the mouth. Then he questioned his father, "How long has this been happening to him?" He replied, "Since childhood. It has often thrown him into fire and into water to kill him. But if you can do anything, have compassion on us and help us." Jesus said to him, "'If you can!' Everything is possible to one who has faith." Then the boy's father cried out, "I do believe, help my unbelief!" Jesus, on seeing a crowd rapidly gathering, rebuked the unclean spirit and said to it, "Mute and deaf spirit, I command you: come out of him and never enter him again!" Shouting and throwing the boy into convulsions, it came out. He became like a corpse, which caused many to say, "He is dead!" But Jesus took him by the hand, raised him, and he stood up. When he entered the house, his disciples asked him in private, "Why could we not drive the spirit out?" He said to them, "This kind can only come out through prayer."

Tuesday, February 26

First Reading

SIRACH 2:1-11

My son, when you come to serve the LORD,
stand in justice and fear,
prepare yourself for trials.
Be sincere of heart and steadfast,
incline your ear and receive the word of understanding,
undisturbed in time of adversity.
Wait on God, with patience, cling to him, forsake him not;
thus will you be wise in all your ways.
Accept whatever befalls you,
when sorrowful, be steadfast,
and in crushing misfortune be patient;
For in fire gold and silver are tested,
and worthy people in the crucible of humiliation.
Trust God and God will help you;
trust in him, and he will direct your way;
keep his fear and grow old therein.

You who fear the LORD, wait for his mercy,
turn not away lest you fall.
You who fear the LORD, trust him,
and your reward will not be lost.
You who fear the LORD, hope for good things,
for lasting joy and mercy.
You who fear the LORD, love him,
and your hearts will be enlightened.
Study the generations long past and understand;
has anyone hoped in the LORD and been disappointed?
Has anyone persevered in his commandments and been forsaken?
has anyone called upon him and been rebuffed?
Compassionate and merciful is the LORD;
he forgives sins, he saves in time of trouble
and he is a protector to all who seek him in truth.

Responsorial Psalm

PSALM 37:3-4, 18-19, 27-28, 39-40

R. Commit your life to the Lord, and he will help you.

Trust in the LORD and do good,
that you may dwell in the land and be fed in security.
Take delight in the LORD,
and he will grant you your heart's requests. **R.**

The LORD watches over the lives of the wholehearted;
 their inheritance lasts forever.
They are not put to shame in an evil time;
 in days of famine they have plenty. **R.**
Turn from evil and do good,
 that you may abide forever;
For the LORD loves what is right,
 and forsakes not his faithful ones. **R.**
The salvation of the just is from the LORD;
 he is their refuge in time of distress.
And the LORD helps them and delivers them;
 he delivers them from the wicked and saves them,
 because they take refuge in him. **R.**

Gospel
MARK 9:30-37

Jesus and his disciples left from there and began a journey through Galilee, but he did not wish anyone to know about it. He was teaching his disciples and telling them, "The Son of Man is to be handed over to men and they will kill him, and three days after his death the Son of Man will rise." But they did not understand the saying, and they were afraid to question him.

They came to Capernaum and, once inside the house, he began to ask them, "What were you arguing about on the way?" But they remained silent. For they had been discussing among themselves on the way who was the greatest. Then he sat down, called the Twelve, and said to them, "If anyone wishes to be first, he shall be the last of all and the servant of all." Taking a child, he placed it in their midst, and putting his arms around it, he said to them, "Whoever receives one child such as this in my name, receives me; and whoever receives me, receives not me but the One who sent me."

Wednesday, February 27

First Reading
SIRACH 4:11-19

Wisdom breathes life into her children
 and admonishes those who seek her.
He who loves her loves life;
 those who seek her will be embraced by the Lord.
He who holds her fast inherits glory;
 wherever he dwells, the LORD bestows blessings.

Those who serve her serve the Holy One;
  those who love her the LORD loves.
He who obeys her judges nations;
  he who hearkens to her dwells in her inmost chambers.
If one trusts her, he will possess her;
  his descendants too will inherit her.
She walks with him as a stranger
  and at first she puts him to the test;
Fear and dread she brings upon him
  and tries him with her discipline
  until she try him by her laws and trust his soul.
Then she comes back to bring him happiness
  and reveal her secrets to them
  and she will heap upon him
  treasures of knowledge and an understanding of justice.
But if he fails her, she will abandon him
  and deliver him into the hands of despoilers.

Responsorial Psalm

PSALM 119:165, 168, 171, 172, 174, 175

R. O Lord, great peace have they who love your law.

Those who love your law have great peace,
  and for them there is no stumbling block. **R.**
I keep your precepts and your decrees,
  for all my ways are before you. **R.**
My lips pour forth your praise,
  because you teach me your statutes. **R.**
May my tongue sing of your promise,
  for all your commands are just. **R.**
I long for your salvation, O LORD,
  and your law is my delight. **R.**
Let my soul live to praise you,
  and may your ordinances help me. **R.**

Gospel

MARK 9:38-40

John said to Jesus, "Teacher, we saw someone driving out demons in your name, and we tried to prevent him because he does not follow us." Jesus replied, "Do not prevent him. There is no one who performs a mighty deed in my name who can at the same time speak ill of me. For whoever is not against us is for us."

Thursday, February 28

First Reading
SIRACH 5:1-8

Rely not on your wealth;
say not: "I have the power."
Rely not on your strength
in following the desires of your heart.
Say not: "Who can prevail against me?"
or, "Who will subdue me for my deeds?"
for God will surely exact the punishment.
Say not: "I have sinned, yet what has befallen me?"
for the Most High bides his time.
Of forgiveness be not overconfident,
adding sin upon sin.
Say not: "Great is his mercy;
my many sins he will forgive."
For mercy and anger alike are with him;
upon the wicked alights his wrath.
Delay not your conversion to the LORD,
put it not off from day to day.
For suddenly his wrath flames forth;
at the time of vengeance you will be destroyed.
Rely not upon deceitful wealth,
for it will be no help on the day of wrath.

Responsorial Psalm
PSALM 1:1-2, 3, 4 and 6
R. Blessed are they who hope in the Lord.

Blessed the man who follows not
the counsel of the wicked
Nor walks in the way of sinners,
nor sits in the company of the insolent,
But delights in the law of the LORD
and meditates on his law day and night. **R.**
He is like a tree
planted near running water,
That yields its fruit in due season,
and whose leaves never fade.
Whatever he does, prospers. **R.**
Not so the wicked, not so;
they are like chaff which the wind drives away.
For the LORD watches over the way of the just,
but the way of the wicked vanishes. **R.**

Gospel
MARK 9:41-50

Jesus said to his disciples: "Anyone who gives you a cup of water to drink because you belong to Christ, amen, I say to you, will surely not lose his reward.

"Whoever causes one of these little ones who believe in me to sin, it would be better for him if a great millstone were put around his neck and he were thrown into the sea. If your hand causes you to sin, cut it off. It is better for you to enter into life maimed than with two hands to go into Gehenna, into the unquenchable fire. And if your foot causes you to sin, cut if off. It is better for you to enter into life crippled than with two feet to be thrown into Gehenna. And if your eye causes you to sin, pluck it out. Better for you to enter into the Kingdom of God with one eye than with two eyes to be thrown into Gehenna, where *their worm does not die, and the fire is not quenched*.

"Everyone will be salted with fire. Salt is good, but if salt becomes insipid, with what will you restore its flavor? Keep salt in yourselves and you will have peace with one another."

MARCH

Friday, March 1

First Reading
SIRACH 6:5-17

A kind mouth multiplies friends and appeases enemies,
and gracious lips prompt friendly greetings.
Let your acquaintances be many,
but one in a thousand your confidant.
When you gain a friend, first test him,
and be not too ready to trust him.
For one sort is a friend when it suits him,
but he will not be with you in time of distress.
Another is a friend who becomes an enemy,
and tells of the quarrel to your shame.
Another is a friend, a boon companion,
who will not be with you when sorrow comes.
When things go well, he is your other self,
and lords it over your servants;
But if you are brought low, he turns against you
and avoids meeting you.
Keep away from your enemies;
be on your guard with your friends.
A faithful friend is a sturdy shelter;
he who finds one finds a treasure.
A faithful friend is beyond price,
no sum can balance his worth.
A faithful friend is a life-saving remedy,
such as he who fears God finds;
For he who fears God behaves accordingly,
and his friend will be like himself.

Responsorial Psalm
PSALM 119:12, 16, 18, 27, 34, 35
R. Guide me, Lord, in the way of your commands.

Blessed are you, O LORD;
teach me your statutes. **R.**
In your statutes I will delight;
I will not forget your words. **R.**
Open my eyes, that I may consider
the wonders of your law. **R.**

Make me understand the way of your precepts,
and I will meditate on your wondrous deeds. **R.**
Give me discernment, that I may observe your law
and keep it with all my heart. **R.**
Lead me in the path of your commands,
for in it I delight. **R.**

Gospel
MARK 10:1-12

Jesus came into the district of Judea and across the Jordan. Again crowds gathered around him and, as was his custom, he again taught them. The Pharisees approached him and asked, "Is it lawful for a husband to divorce his wife?" They were testing him. He said to them in reply, "What did Moses command you?" They replied, "Moses permitted a husband to write a bill of divorce and dismiss her." But Jesus told them, "Because of the hardness of your hearts he wrote you this commandment. But from the beginning of creation, *God made them male and female. For this reason a man shall leave his father and mother and be joined to his wife, and the two shall become one flesh.* So they are no longer two but one flesh. Therefore what God has joined together, no human being must separate." In the house the disciples again questioned Jesus about this. He said to them, "Whoever divorces his wife and marries another commits adultery against her; and if she divorces her husband and marries another, she commits adultery."

Saturday, March 2

First Reading
SIRACH 17:1-15

God from the earth created man,
and in his own image he made him.
He makes man return to earth again,
and endows him with a strength of his own.
Limited days of life he gives him,
with power over all things else on earth.
He puts the fear of him in all flesh,
and gives him rule over beasts and birds.
He created for them counsel, and a tongue and eyes and ears,
and an inventive heart,
and filled them with the discipline of understanding.
He created in them knowledge of the spirit;
With wisdom he fills their heart;
good and evil he shows them.

He put the fear of himself upon their hearts,
and showed them his mighty works,
That they might glory in the wonder of his deeds
and praise his holy name.
He has set before them knowledge,
a law of life as their inheritance;
An everlasting covenant he has made with them,
his justice and his judgments he has revealed to them.
His majestic glory their eyes beheld,
his glorious voice their ears heard.
He says to them, "Avoid all evil";
each of them he gives precepts about his fellow men.
Their ways are ever known to him,
they cannot be hidden from his eyes.
Over every nation he places a ruler,
but God's own portion is Israel.
All their actions are clear as the sun to him,
his eyes are ever upon their ways.

Responsorial Psalm
PSALM 103:13-14, 15-16, 17-18
R. The Lord's kindness is everlasting to those who fear him.

As a father has compassion on his children,
so the LORD has compassion on those who fear him,
For he knows how we are formed;
he remembers that we are dust. **R.**
Man's days are like those of grass;
like a flower of the field he blooms;
The wind sweeps over him and he is gone,
and his place knows him no more. **R.**
But the kindness of the LORD is from eternity
to eternity toward those who fear him,
And his justice toward children's children
among those who keep his covenant. **R.**

Gospel
MARK 10:13-16

People were bringing children to Jesus that he might touch them, but the disciples rebuked them. When Jesus saw this he became indignant and said to them, "Let the children come to me; do not prevent them, for the Kingdom of God belongs to such as these. Amen, I say to you, whoever does not accept the Kingdom of God like a child will not enter it." Then he embraced the children and blessed them, placing his hands on them.

Sunday, March 3

Eighth Sunday in Ordinary Time

First Reading
SIRACH 27:4-7

When a sieve is shaken, the husks appear;
so do one's faults when one speaks.
As the test of what the potter molds is in the furnace,
so in tribulation is the test of the just.
The fruit of a tree shows the care it has had;
so too does one's speech disclose the bent of one's mind.
Praise no one before he speaks,
for it is then that people are tested.

Responsorial Psalm
PSALM 92:2-3, 13-14, 15-16
R. Lord, it is good to give thanks to you.

It is good to give thanks to the LORD,
to sing praise to your name, Most High,
to proclaim your kindness at dawn
and your faithfulness throughout the night. **R.**
The just one shall flourish like the palm tree,
like a cedar of Lebanon shall he grow.
They that are planted in the house of the LORD
shall flourish in the courts of our God. **R.**
They shall bear fruit even in old age;
vigorous and sturdy shall they be,
declaring how just is the LORD,
my rock, in whom there is no wrong. **R.**

Second Reading
1 CORINTHIANS 15:54-58

Brothers and sisters: When this which is corruptible clothes itself with incorruptibility and this which is mortal clothes itself with immortality, then the word that is written shall come about:

Death is swallowed up in victory.
Where, O death, is your victory?
Where, O death, is your sting?

The sting of death is sin, and the power of sin is the law. But thanks be to God who gives us the victory through our Lord Jesus Christ.

Therefore, my beloved brothers and sisters, be firm, steadfast, always fully devoted to the work of the Lord, knowing that in the Lord your labor is not in vain.

Gospel
LUKE 6:39-45
Jesus told his disciples a parable, "Can a blind person guide a blind person? Will not both fall into a pit? No disciple is superior to the teacher; but when fully trained, every disciple will be like his teacher. Why do you notice the splinter in your brother's eye, but do not perceive the wooden beam in your own? How can you say to your brother, 'Brother, let me remove that splinter in your eye,' when you do not even notice the wooden beam in your own eye? You hypocrite! Remove the wooden beam from your eye first; then you will see clearly to remove the splinter in your brother's eye.

"A good tree does not bear rotten fruit, nor does a rotten tree bear good fruit. For every tree is known by its own fruit. For people do not pick figs from thornbushes, nor do they gather grapes from brambles. A good person out of the store of goodness in his heart produces good, but an evil person out of a store of evil produces evil; for from the fullness of the heart the mouth speaks."

Monday, March 4

First Reading
SIRACH 17:20-24
To the penitent God provides a way back,
he encourages those who are losing hope
and has chosen for them the lot of truth.
Return to him and give up sin,
pray to the LORD and make your offenses few.
Turn again to the Most High and away from your sin,
hate intensely what he loathes,
and know the justice and judgments of God,
Stand firm in the way set before you,
in prayer to the Most High God.

Who in the nether world can glorify the Most High
in place of the living who offer their praise?
Dwell no longer in the error of the ungodly,
but offer your praise before death.

No more can the dead give praise
than those who have never lived;
You who are alive and well
shall praise and glorify God in his mercies.
How great the mercy of the LORD,
his forgiveness of those who return to him!

Responsorial Psalm
PSALM 32:1-2, 5, 6, 7
R. Let the just exult and rejoice in the Lord.
Blessed is he whose fault is taken away,
whose sin is covered.
Blessed the man to whom the LORD imputes not guilt,
in whose spirit there is no guile. **R.**
Then I acknowledged my sin to you,
my guilt I covered not.
I said, "I confess my faults to the LORD,"
and you took away the guilt of my sin. **R.**
For this shall every faithful man pray to you
in time of stress.
Though deep waters overflow,
they shall not reach him. **R.**
You are my shelter; from distress you will preserve me;
with glad cries of freedom you will ring me round. **R.**

Gospel
MARK 10:17-27

As Jesus was setting out on a journey, a man ran up, knelt down before him, and asked him, "Good teacher, what must I do to inherit eternal life?" Jesus answered him, "Why do you call me good? No one is good but God alone. You know the commandments: *You shall not kill; you shall not commit adultery; you shall not steal; you shall not bear false witness; you shall not defraud; honor your father and your mother.*" He replied and said to him, "Teacher, all of these I have observed from my youth." Jesus, looking at him, loved him and said to him, "You are lacking in one thing. Go, sell what you have, and give to the poor and you will have treasure in heaven; then come, follow me." At that statement, his face fell, and he went away sad, for he had many possessions.

Jesus looked around and said to his disciples, "How hard it is for those who have wealth to enter the Kingdom of God!" The disciples were amazed at his words. So Jesus again said to them in reply, "Children, how hard it is to enter the Kingdom of God! It is easier for a camel to pass through the eye of a needle than for one who is rich to enter the Kingdom of God." They were exceedingly astonished and said among themselves, "Then who can be saved?" Jesus looked at them and said, "For men it is impossible, but not for God. All things are possible for God."

Tuesday, March 5

First Reading

SIRACH 35:1-12

To keep the law is a great oblation,
and he who observes the
commandments sacrifices a peace offering.
In works of charity one offers fine flour,
and when he gives alms he presents his sacrifice of praise.
To refrain from evil pleases the LORD,
and to avoid injustice is an atonement.
Appear not before the LORD empty-handed,
for all that you offer is in fulfillment of the precepts.
The just one's offering enriches the altar
and rises as a sweet odor before the Most High.
The just one's sacrifice is most pleasing,
nor will it ever be forgotten.
In a generous spirit pay homage to the LORD,
be not sparing of freewill gifts.
With each contribution show a cheerful countenance,
and pay your tithes in a spirit of joy.
Give to the Most High as he has given to you,
generously, according to your means.

For the LORD is one who always repays,
and he will give back to you sevenfold.
But offer no bribes, these he does not accept!
Trust not in sacrifice of the fruits of extortion.
For he is a God of justice,
who knows no favorites.

Responsorial Psalm

PSALM 50:5-6, 7-8, 14 and 23

R. To the upright I will show the saving power of God.

"Gather my faithful ones before me,
those who have made a covenant with me by sacrifice."
And the heavens proclaim his justice;
for God himself is the judge. **R.**

“Hear, my people, and I will speak;
  Israel, I will testify against you;
  God, your God, am I.
Not for your sacrifices do I rebuke you,
  for your burnt offerings are before me always.” **R.**
“Offer to God praise as your sacrifice
  and fulfill your vows to the Most High.
He that offers praise as a sacrifice glorifies me;
  and to him that goes the right way I will show the salvation
    of God.” **R.**

Gospel

MARK 10:28-31

Peter began to say to Jesus, “We have given up everything and followed you.” Jesus said, “Amen, I say to you, there is no one who has given up house or brothers or sisters or mother or father or children or lands for my sake and for the sake of the Gospel who will not receive a hundred times more now in this present age: houses and brothers and sisters and mothers and children and lands, with persecutions, and eternal life in the age to come. But many that are first will be last, and the last will be first.”

Wednesday, March 6

Ash Wednesday

First Reading

JOEL 2:12-18

Even now, says the LORD,
  return to me with your whole heart,
  with fasting, and weeping, and mourning;
Rend your hearts, not your garments,
  and return to the LORD, your God.
For gracious and merciful is he,
  slow to anger, rich in kindness,
  and relenting in punishment.
Perhaps he will again relent
  and leave behind him a blessing,
Offerings and libations
  for the LORD, your God.

Blow the trumpet in Zion!
  proclaim a fast,

call an assembly;
Gather the people,
notify the congregation;
Assemble the elders,
gather the children
and the infants at the breast;
Let the bridegroom quit his room
and the bride her chamber.
Between the porch and the altar
let the priests, the ministers of the LORD, weep,
And say, "Spare, O LORD, your people,
and make not your heritage a reproach,
with the nations ruling over them!
Why should they say among the peoples,
'Where is their God?'"

Then the LORD was stirred to concern for his land
and took pity on his people.

Responsorial Psalm

PSALM 51:3-4, 5-6ab, 12-13, 14 and 17

R. Be merciful, O Lord, for we have sinned.

Have mercy on me, O God, in your goodness;
in the greatness of your compassion wipe out my offense.
Thoroughly wash me from my guilt
and of my sin cleanse me. **R.**
For I acknowledge my offense,
and my sin is before me always:
"Against you only have I sinned,
and done what is evil in your sight." **R.**
A clean heart create for me, O God,
and a steadfast spirit renew within me.
Cast me not out from your presence,
and your Holy Spirit take not from me. **R.**
Give me back the joy of your salvation,
and a willing spirit sustain in me.
O Lord, open my lips,
and my mouth shall proclaim your praise. **R.**

Second Reading

2 CORINTHIANS 5:20–6:2

Brothers and sisters: We are ambassadors for Christ, as if God were appealing through us. We implore you on behalf of Christ, be reconciled to God. For our sake he made him to be sin who did not know sin, so that we might become the righteousness of God in him.

Working together, then, we appeal to you not to receive the grace of God in vain. For he says:

In an acceptable time I heard you,
and on the day of salvation I helped you.

Behold, now is a very acceptable time; behold, now is the day of salvation.

Gospel
MATTHEW 6:1-6, 16-18

Jesus said to his disciples: "Take care not to perform righteous deeds in order that people may see them; otherwise, you will have no recompense from your heavenly Father. When you give alms, do not blow a trumpet before you, as the hypocrites do in the synagogues and in the streets to win the praise of others. Amen, I say to you, they have received their reward. But when you give alms, do not let your left hand know what your right is doing, so that your almsgiving may be secret. And your Father who sees in secret will repay you.

"When you pray, do not be like the hypocrites, who love to stand and pray in the synagogues and on street corners so that others may see them. Amen, I say to you, they have received their reward. But when you pray, go to your inner room, close the door, and pray to your Father in secret. And your Father who sees in secret will repay you.

"When you fast, do not look gloomy like the hypocrites. They neglect their appearance, so that they may appear to others to be fasting. Amen, I say to you, they have received their reward. But when you fast, anoint your head and wash your face, so that you may not appear to be fasting, except to your Father who is hidden. And your Father who sees what is hidden will repay you."

Thursday, March 7

First Reading
DEUTERONOMY 30:15-20

Moses said to the people: "Today I have set before you life and prosperity, death and doom. If you obey the commandments of the LORD, your God, which I enjoin on you today, loving him, and walking in his ways, and keeping his commandments, statutes and decrees, you will live and grow numerous, and the LORD, your God, will bless you in the land you are entering to occupy. If, however, you turn away your hearts and will not listen, but are led astray and adore and serve other gods, I tell you now that you will certainly perish; you will not have a long life on the land that you are crossing the Jordan to enter and occupy. I call heaven and earth today to witness against you: I have set before you life and death, the blessing and the curse. Choose life, then, that you and your descendants may live, by loving the LORD, your God, heeding his voice, and holding fast to him. For that will mean life for you, a long life for you to live on the land that the LORD swore he would give to your fathers Abraham, Isaac and Jacob."

Responsorial Psalm
PSALM 1:1-2, 3, 4 and 6
R. Blessed are they who hope in the Lord.

Blessed the man who follows not
the counsel of the wicked
Nor walks in the way of sinners,
nor sits in the company of the insolent,
But delights in the law of the LORD
and meditates on his law day and night. **R.**
He is like a tree
planted near running water,
That yields its fruit in due season,
and whose leaves never fade.
Whatever he does, prospers. **R.**
Not so the wicked, not so;
they are like chaff which the wind drives away.
For the LORD watches over the way of the just,
but the way of the wicked vanishes. **R.**

Gospel
LUKE 9:22-25

Jesus said to his disciples: "The Son of Man must suffer greatly and be rejected by the elders, the chief priests, and the scribes, and be killed and on the third day be raised."

Then he said to all, "If anyone wishes to come after me, he must deny himself and take up his cross daily and follow me. For whoever wishes to save his life will lose it, but whoever loses his life for my sake will save it. What profit is there for one to gain the whole world yet lose or forfeit himself?"

Friday, March 8

First Reading

ISAIAH 58:1-9a

Thus says the Lord GOD:
Cry out full-throated and unsparingly,
lift up your voice like a trumpet blast;
Tell my people their wickedness,
and the house of Jacob their sins.
They seek me day after day,
and desire to know my ways,
Like a nation that has done what is just
and not abandoned the law of their God;
They ask me to declare what is due them,
pleased to gain access to God.
"Why do we fast, and you do not see it?
afflict ourselves, and you take no note of it?"

Lo, on your fast day you carry out your own pursuits,
and drive all your laborers.
Yes, your fast ends in quarreling and fighting,
striking with wicked claw.
Would that today you might fast
so as to make your voice heard on high!
Is this the manner of fasting I wish,
of keeping a day of penance:
That a man bow his head like a reed
and lie in sackcloth and ashes?
Do you call this a fast,
a day acceptable to the LORD?
This, rather, is the fasting that I wish:
releasing those bound unjustly,
untying the thongs of the yoke;
Setting free the oppressed,
breaking every yoke;
Sharing your bread with the hungry,
sheltering the oppressed and the homeless;
Clothing the naked when you see them,
and not turning your back on your own.
Then your light shall break forth like the dawn,
and your wound shall quickly be healed;
Your vindication shall go before you,
and the glory of the LORD shall be your rear guard.

Then you shall call, and the LORD will answer,
you shall cry for help, and he will say: Here I am!

Responsorial Psalm
PSALM 51:3-4, 5-6ab, 18-19
R. A heart contrite and humbled, O God, you will not spurn.
Have mercy on me, O God, in your goodness;
in the greatness of your compassion wipe out my offense.
Thoroughly wash me from my guilt
and of my sin cleanse me. **R.**
For I acknowledge my offense,
and my sin is before me always:
"Against you only have I sinned,
and done what is evil in your sight." **R.**
For you are not pleased with sacrifices;
should I offer a burnt offering, you would not accept it.
My sacrifice, O God, is a contrite spirit;
a heart contrite and humbled, O God, you will not spurn. **R.**

Gospel
MATTHEW 9:14-15
The disciples of John approached Jesus and said, "Why do we and the Pharisees fast much, but your disciples do not fast?" Jesus answered them, "Can the wedding guests mourn as long as the bridegroom is with them? The days will come when the bridegroom is taken away from them, and then they will fast."

Saturday, March 9

First Reading
ISAIAH 58:9b-14
Thus says the LORD:
If you remove from your midst oppression,
false accusation and malicious speech;
If you bestow your bread on the hungry
and satisfy the afflicted;
Then light shall rise for you in the darkness,
and the gloom shall become for you like midday;
Then the LORD will guide you always
and give you plenty even on the parched land.
He will renew your strength,
and you shall be like a watered garden,
like a spring whose water never fails.

The ancient ruins shall be rebuilt for your sake,
and the foundations from ages past you shall raise up;
"Repairer of the breach," they shall call you,
"Restorer of ruined homesteads."

If you hold back your foot on the sabbath
from following your own pursuits on my holy day;
If you call the sabbath a delight,
and the LORD's holy day honorable;
If you honor it by not following your ways,
seeking your own interests, or speaking with malice—
Then you shall delight in the LORD,
and I will make you ride on the heights of the earth;
I will nourish you with the heritage of Jacob, your father,
for the mouth of the LORD has spoken.

Responsorial Psalm
PSALM 86:1-2, 3-4, 5-6
R. Teach me your way, O Lord, that I may walk in your truth.
Incline your ear, O LORD; answer me,
for I am afflicted and poor.
Keep my life, for I am devoted to you;
save your servant who trusts in you.
You are my God. **R.**
Have mercy on me, O Lord,
for to you I call all the day.
Gladden the soul of your servant,
for to you, O Lord, I lift up my soul. **R.**
For you, O Lord, are good and forgiving,
abounding in kindness to all who call upon you.
Hearken, O LORD, to my prayer
and attend to the sound of my pleading. **R.**

Gospel
LUKE 5:27-32

Jesus saw a tax collector named Levi sitting at the customs post. He said to him, "Follow me." And leaving everything behind, he got up and followed him. Then Levi gave a great banquet for him in his house, and a large crowd of tax collectors and others were at table with them. The Pharisees and their scribes complained to his disciples, saying, "Why do you eat and drink with tax collectors and sinners?" Jesus said to them in reply, "Those who are healthy do not need a physician, but the sick do. I have not come to call the righteous to repentance but sinners."

Sunday, March 10

First Sunday of Lent

First Reading
DEUTERONOMY 26:4-10

Moses spoke to the people, saying: "The priest shall receive the basket from you and shall set it in front of the altar of the LORD, your God. Then you shall declare before the LORD, your God, 'My father was a wandering Aramean who went down to Egypt with a small household and lived there as an alien. But there he became a nation great, strong, and numerous. When the Egyptians maltreated and oppressed us, imposing hard labor upon us, we cried to the LORD, the God of our fathers, and he heard our cry and saw our affliction, our toil, and our oppression. He brought us out of Egypt with his strong hand and outstretched arm, with terrifying power, with signs and wonders; and bringing us into this country, he gave us this land flowing with milk and honey. Therefore, I have now brought you the firstfruits of the products of the soil which you, O LORD, have given me.' And having set them before the LORD, your God, you shall bow down in his presence."

Responsorial Psalm
PSALM 91:1-2, 10-11, 12-13, 14-15
R. Be with me, Lord, when I am in trouble.

You who dwell in the shelter of the Most High,
who abide in the shadow of the Almighty,
say to the LORD, "My refuge and fortress,
my God in whom I trust." **R.**
No evil shall befall you,
nor shall affliction come near your tent,
for to his angels he has given command about you,
that they guard you in all your ways. **R.**
Upon their hands they shall bear you up,
lest you dash your foot against a stone.
You shall tread upon the asp and the viper;
you shall trample down the lion and the dragon. **R.**
Because he clings to me, I will deliver him;
I will set him on high because he acknowledges my name.
He shall call upon me, and I will answer him;
I will be with him in distress;
I will deliver him and glorify him. **R.**

Second Reading
ROMANS 10:8-13

Brothers and sisters: What does Scripture say?

The word is near you,
in your mouth and in your heart

—that is, the word of faith that we preach—, for, if you confess with your mouth that Jesus is Lord and believe in your heart that God raised him from the dead, you will be saved. For one believes with the heart and so is justified, and one confesses with the mouth and so is saved. For the Scripture says, *No one who believes in him will be put to shame.* For there is no distinction between Jew and Greek; the same Lord is Lord of all, enriching all who call upon him. For "everyone who calls on the name of the Lord will be saved."

Gospel
LUKE 4:1-13

Filled with the Holy Spirit, Jesus returned from the Jordan and was led by the Spirit into the desert for forty days, to be tempted by the devil. He ate nothing during those days, and when they were over he was hungry. The devil said to him, "If you are the Son of God, command this stone to become bread." Jesus answered him, "It is written, *One does not live on bread alone.*" Then he took him up and showed him all the kingdoms of the world in a single instant. The devil said to him, "I shall give to you all this power and glory; for it has been handed over to me, and I may give it to whomever I wish. All this will be yours, if you worship me." Jesus said to him in reply, "It is written:

You shall worship the Lord, your God,
and him alone shall you serve."

Then he led him to Jerusalem, made him stand on the parapet of the temple, and said to him, "If you are the Son of God, throw yourself down from here, for it is written:

He will command his angels concerning you, to guard you,

and:

With their hands they will support you,
lest you dash your foot against a stone."

Jesus said to him in reply, "It also says, *You shall not put the Lord, your God, to the test.*" When the devil had finished every temptation, he departed from him for a time.

Monday, March 11

First Reading

LEVITICUS 19:1-2, 11-18

The LORD said to Moses, "Speak to the whole assembly of the children of Israel and tell them: Be holy, for I, the LORD, your God, am holy.

"You shall not steal. You shall not lie or speak falsely to one another. You shall not swear falsely by my name, thus profaning the name of your God. I am the LORD.

"You shall not defraud or rob your neighbor. You shall not withhold overnight the wages of your day laborer. You shall not curse the deaf, or put a stumbling block in front of the blind, but you shall fear your God. I am the LORD.

"You shall not act dishonestly in rendering judgment. Show neither partiality to the weak nor deference to the mighty, but judge your fellow men justly. You shall not go about spreading slander among your kin; nor shall you stand by idly when your neighbor's life is at stake. I am the LORD.

"You shall not bear hatred for your brother in your heart. Though you may have to reprove him, do not incur sin because of him. Take no revenge and cherish no grudge against your fellow countrymen. You shall love your neighbor as yourself. I am the LORD."

Responsorial Psalm

PSALM 19:8, 9, 10, 15

R. Your words, Lord, are Spirit and life.

The law of the LORD is perfect,
refreshing the soul.
The decree of the LORD is trustworthy,
giving wisdom to the simple. **R.**
The precepts of the LORD are right,
rejoicing the heart.
The command of the LORD is clear,
enlightening the eye. **R.**
The fear of the LORD is pure,
enduring forever;
The ordinances of the LORD are true,
all of them just. **R.**

Let the words of my mouth and the thought of my heart
find favor before you,
O LORD, my rock and my redeemer. **R.**

Gospel
MATTHEW 25:31-46

Jesus said to his disciples: "When the Son of Man comes in his glory, and all the angels with him, he will sit upon his glorious throne, and all the nations will be assembled before him. And he will separate them one from another, as a shepherd separates the sheep from the goats. He will place the sheep on his right and the goats on his left. Then the king will say to those on his right, 'Come, you who are blessed by my Father. Inherit the kingdom prepared for you from the foundation of the world. For I was hungry and you gave me food, I was thirsty and you gave me drink, a stranger and you welcomed me, naked and you clothed me, ill and you cared for me, in prison and you visited me.' Then the righteous will answer him and say, 'Lord, when did we see you hungry and feed you, or thirsty and give you drink? When did we see you a stranger and welcome you, or naked and clothe you? When did we see you ill or in prison, and visit you?' And the king will say to them in reply, 'Amen, I say to you, whatever you did for one of these least brothers of mine, you did for me.' Then he will say to those on his left, 'Depart from me, you accursed, into the eternal fire prepared for the Devil and his angels. For I was hungry and you gave me no food, I was thirsty and you gave me no drink, a stranger and you gave me no welcome, naked and you gave me no clothing, ill and in prison, and you did not care for me.' Then they will answer and say, 'Lord, when did we see you hungry or thirsty or a stranger or naked or ill or in prison, and not minister to your needs?' He will answer them, 'Amen, I say to you, what you did not do for one of these least ones, you did not do for me.' And these will go off to eternal punishment, but the righteous to eternal life."

Tuesday, March 12

First Reading
ISAIAH 55:10-11

Thus says the LORD:
Just as from the heavens
the rain and snow come down
And do not return there
till they have watered the earth,
making it fertile and fruitful,

Giving seed to the one who sows
and bread to the one who eats,
So shall my word be
that goes forth from my mouth;

It shall not return to me void,
but shall do my will,
achieving the end for which I sent it.

Responsorial Psalm
PSALM 34:4-5, 6-7, 16-17, 18-19
R. From all their distress God rescues the just.
Glorify the LORD with me,
let us together extol his name.
I sought the LORD, and he answered me
and delivered me from all my fears. **R.**
Look to him that you may be radiant with joy,
and your faces may not blush with shame.
When the poor one called out, the LORD heard,
and from all his distress he saved him. **R.**
The LORD has eyes for the just,
and ears for their cry.
The LORD confronts the evildoers,
to destroy remembrance of them from the earth. **R.**
When the just cry out, the LORD hears them,
and from all their distress he rescues them.
The LORD is close to the brokenhearted;
and those who are crushed in spirit he saves. **R.**

Gospel
MATTHEW 6:7-15

Jesus said to his disciples: "In praying, do not babble like the pagans, who think that they will be heard because of their many words. Do not be like them. Your Father knows what you need before you ask him.

"This is how you are to pray:

Our Father who art in heaven,
hallowed be thy name,
thy Kingdom come,
thy will be done,
on earth as it is in heaven.
Give us this day our daily bread;
and forgive us our trespasses,
as we forgive those who trespass against us;

and lead us not into temptation,
    but deliver us from evil.

"If you forgive men their transgressions, your heavenly Father will forgive you. But if you do not forgive men, neither will your Father forgive your transgressions."

Wednesday, March 13

First Reading

JONAH 3:1-10

The word of the LORD came to Jonah a second time: "Set out for the great city of Nineveh, and announce to it the message that I will tell you." So Jonah made ready and went to Nineveh, according to the LORD's bidding. Now Nineveh was an enormously large city; it took three days to go through it. Jonah began his journey through the city, and had gone but a single day's walk announcing, "Forty days more and Nineveh shall be destroyed," when the people of Nineveh believed God; they proclaimed a fast and all of them, great and small, put on sackcloth.

When the news reached the king of Nineveh, he rose from his throne, laid aside his robe, covered himself with sackcloth, and sat in the ashes. Then he had this proclaimed throughout Nineveh, by decree of the king and his nobles: "Neither man nor beast, neither cattle nor sheep, shall taste anything; they shall not eat, nor shall they drink water. Man and beast shall be covered with sackcloth and call loudly to God; every man shall turn from his evil way and from the violence he has in hand. Who knows, God may relent and forgive, and withhold his blazing wrath, so that we shall not perish." When God saw by their actions how they turned from their evil way, he repented of the evil that he had threatened to do to them; he did not carry it out.

Responsorial Psalm

PSALM 51:3-4, 12-13, 18-19

R. A heart contrite and humbled, O God, you will not spurn.

Have mercy on me, O God, in your goodness;
    in the greatness of your compassion wipe out my offense.
Thoroughly wash me from my guilt
    and of my sin cleanse me. **R.**
A clean heart create for me, O God,
    and a steadfast spirit renew within me.
Cast me not out from your presence,
    and your Holy Spirit take not from me. **R.**

For you are not pleased with sacrifices;
should I offer a burnt offering, you would not accept it.
My sacrifice, O God, is a contrite spirit;
a heart contrite and humbled, O God, you will not spurn. **R.**

Gospel
LUKE 11:29-32

While still more people gathered in the crowd, Jesus said to them, "This generation is an evil generation; it seeks a sign, but no sign will be given it, except the sign of Jonah. Just as Jonah became a sign to the Ninevites, so will the Son of Man be to this generation. At the judgment the queen of the south will rise with the men of this generation and she will condemn them, because she came from the ends of the earth to hear the wisdom of Solomon, and there is something greater than Solomon here. At the judgment the men of Nineveh will arise with this generation and condemn it, because at the preaching of Jonah they repented, and there is something greater than Jonah here."

Thursday, March 14

First Reading
ESTHER C:12, 14-16, 23-25

Queen Esther, seized with mortal anguish, had recourse to the LORD. She lay prostrate upon the ground, together with her handmaids, from morning until evening, and said: "God of Abraham, God of Isaac, and God of Jacob, blessed are you. Help me, who am alone and have no help but you, for I am taking my life in my hand. As a child I used to hear from the books of my forefathers that you, O LORD, always free those who are pleasing to you. Now help me, who am alone and have no one but you, O LORD, my God.

"And now, come to help me, an orphan. Put in my mouth persuasive words in the presence of the lion and turn his heart to hatred for our enemy, so that he and those who are in league with him may perish. Save us from the hand of our enemies; turn our mourning into gladness and our sorrows into wholeness."

Responsorial Psalm
PSALM 138:1-2ab, 2cde-3, 7c-8
R. Lord, on the day I called for help, you answered me.
I will give thanks to you, O LORD, with all my heart,
for you have heard the words of my mouth;
in the presence of the angels I will sing your praise;

I will worship at your holy temple
 and give thanks to your name. **R.**
Because of your kindness and your truth;
 for you have made great above all things
 your name and your promise.
When I called, you answered me;
 you built up strength within me. **R.**
Your right hand saves me.
The LORD will complete what he has done for me;
 your kindness, O LORD, endures forever;
 forsake not the work of your hands. **R.**

Gospel
MATTHEW 7:7-12

Jesus said to his disciples: "Ask and it will be given to you; seek and you will find; knock and the door will be opened to you. For everyone who asks, receives; and the one who seeks, finds; and to the one who knocks, the door will be opened. Which one of you would hand his son a stone when he asked for a loaf of bread, or a snake when he asked for a fish? If you then, who are wicked, know how to give good gifts to your children, how much more will your heavenly Father give good things to those who ask him.

"Do to others whatever you would have them do to you. This is the law and the prophets."

Friday, March 15

First Reading
EZEKIEL 18:21-28

Thus says the Lord GOD: If the wicked man turns away from all the sins he committed, if he keeps all my statutes and does what is right and just, he shall surely live, he shall not die. None of the crimes he committed shall be remembered against him; he shall live because of the virtue he has practiced. Do I indeed derive any pleasure from the death of the wicked? says the Lord GOD. Do I not rather rejoice when he turns from his evil way that he may live?

And if the virtuous man turns from the path of virtue to do evil, the same kind of abominable things that the wicked man does, can he do this and still live? None of his virtuous deeds shall be remembered, because he has broken faith and committed sin; because of this, he shall die. You say, "The LORD's way is not fair!" Hear now, house of Israel: Is it my way that is unfair, or rather, are not your ways unfair? When someone virtuous turns away from virtue to commit iniquity, and dies, it is because of the iniquity he committed that he must die. But if the wicked, turning from the wickedness he has committed, does what is right and just, he shall preserve his life; since he has turned away from all the sins that he committed, he shall surely live, he shall not die.

Responsorial Psalm

PSALM 130:1-2, 3-4, 5-7a, 7bc-8

R. If you, O Lord, mark iniquities, who can stand?

Out of the depths I cry to you, O LORD;
 LORD, hear my voice!
Let your ears be attentive
 to my voice in supplication. **R.**
If you, O LORD, mark iniquities,
 LORD, who can stand?
But with you is forgiveness,
 that you may be revered. **R.**
I trust in the LORD;
 my soul trusts in his word.
My soul waits for the LORD
 more than sentinels wait for the dawn.
 Let Israel wait for the LORD. **R.**
For with the LORD is kindness
 and with him is plenteous redemption;
And he will redeem Israel
 from all their iniquities. **R.**

Gospel

MATTHEW 5:20-26

Jesus said to his disciples: "I tell you, unless your righteousness surpasses that of the scribes and Pharisees, you will not enter into the Kingdom of heaven.

"You have heard that it was said to your ancestors, *You shall not kill; and whoever kills will be liable to judgment.* But I say to you, whoever is angry with his brother will be liable to judgment, and whoever says to his brother, *Raqa,* will be answerable to the Sanhedrin, and whoever says, 'You fool,' will be liable to fiery Gehenna. Therefore, if you bring your gift to the altar, and there recall that your brother has anything against you, leave your gift there at the altar, go first and be reconciled with your brother, and then come and offer your gift. Settle with your opponent quickly while on the way to court. Otherwise your opponent will hand you over to the judge, and the judge will hand you over to the guard, and you will be thrown into prison. Amen, I say to you, you will not be released until you have paid the last penny."

Saturday, March 16

First Reading

DEUTERONOMY 26:16-19

Moses spoke to the people, saying: "This day the LORD, your God, commands you to observe these statutes and decrees. Be careful, then, to observe them with all your heart and with all your soul. Today you are making this agreement with the LORD: he is to be your God and you are to walk in his ways and observe his statutes, commandments and decrees, and to hearken to his voice. And today the LORD is making this agreement with you: you are to be a people peculiarly his own, as he promised you; and provided you keep all his commandments, he will then raise you high in praise and renown and glory above all other nations he has made, and you will be a people sacred to the LORD, your God, as he promised."

Responsorial Psalm

PSALM 119:1-2, 4-5, 7-8

R. Blessed are they who follow the law of the Lord!

Blessed are they whose way is blameless,
  who walk in the law of the LORD.
Blessed are they who observe his decrees,
  who seek him with all their heart. **R.**
You have commanded that your precepts
  be diligently kept.
Oh, that I might be firm in the ways
  of keeping your statutes! **R.**
I will give you thanks with an upright heart,
  when I have learned your just ordinances.
I will keep your statutes;
  do not utterly forsake me. **R.**

Gospel

MATTHEW 5:43-48

Jesus said to his disciples: "You have heard that it was said, *You shall love your neighbor and hate your enemy*. But I say to you, love your enemies, and pray for those who persecute you, that you may be children of your heavenly Father, for he makes his sun rise on the bad and the good, and causes rain to fall on the just and the unjust. For if you love those who love you, what recompense will you have? Do not the tax collectors do the same? And if you greet your brothers and sisters only, what is unusual about that? Do not the pagans do the same? So be perfect, just as your heavenly Father is perfect."

Sunday, March 17

Second Sunday of Lent

First Reading

GENESIS 15:5-12, 17-18

The Lord God took Abram outside and said, "Look up at the sky and count the stars, if you can. Just so," he added, "shall your descendants be." Abram put his faith in the LORD, who credited it to him as an act of righteousness.

He then said to him, "I am the LORD who brought you from Ur of the Chaldeans to give you this land as a possession." "O Lord GOD," he asked, "how am I to know that I shall possess it?" He answered him, "Bring me a three-year-old heifer, a three-year-old she-goat, a three-year-old ram, a turtledove, and a young pigeon." Abram brought him all these, split them in two, and placed each half opposite the other; but the birds he did not cut up. Birds of prey swooped down on the carcasses, but Abram stayed with them. As the sun was about to set, a trance fell upon Abram, and a deep, terrifying darkness enveloped him.

When the sun had set and it was dark, there appeared a smoking fire pot and a flaming torch, which passed between those pieces. It was on that occasion that the LORD made a covenant with Abram, saying: "To your descendants I give this land, from the Wadi of Egypt to the Great River, the Euphrates."

Responsorial Psalm

PSALM 27:1, 7-8, 8-9, 13-14

R. The Lord is my light and my salvation.

The LORD is my light and my salvation;
whom should I fear?
The LORD is my life's refuge;
of whom should I be afraid? **R.**
Hear, O LORD, the sound of my call;
have pity on me, and answer me.
Of you my heart speaks; you my glance seeks. **R.**
Your presence, O LORD, I seek.
Hide not your face from me;
do not in anger repel your servant.
You are my helper: cast me not off. **R.**
I believe that I shall see the bounty of the LORD
in the land of the living.
Wait for the LORD with courage;
be stouthearted, and wait for the LORD. **R.**

Second Reading

PHILIPPIANS 3:17–4:1 (or PHILIPPIANS 3:20–4:1)

Join with others in being imitators of me, brothers and sisters, and observe those who thus conduct themselves according to the model you have in us. For many, as I have often told you and now tell you even in tears, conduct themselves as enemies of the cross of Christ. Their end is destruction. Their God is their stomach; their glory is in their "shame." Their minds are occupied with earthly things. But our citizenship is in heaven, and from it we also await a savior, the Lord Jesus Christ. He will change our lowly body to conform with his glorified body by the power that enables him also to bring all things into subjection to himself.

Therefore, my brothers and sisters, whom I love and long for, my joy and crown, in this way stand firm in the Lord.

Gospel

LUKE 9:28b-36

Jesus took Peter, John, and James and went up the mountain to pray. While he was praying his face changed in appearance and his clothing became dazzling white. And behold, two men were conversing with him, Moses and Elijah, who appeared in glory and spoke of his exodus that he was going to accomplish in Jerusalem. Peter and his companions had been overcome by sleep, but becoming fully awake, they saw his glory and the two men standing with him. As they were about to part from him, Peter said to Jesus, "Master, it is good that we are here; let us make three tents, one for you, one for Moses, and one for Elijah." But he did not know what he was saying. While he was still speaking, a cloud came and cast a shadow over them, and they became frightened when they entered the cloud. Then from the cloud came a voice that said, "This is my chosen Son; listen to him." After the voice had spoken, Jesus was found alone. They fell silent and did not at that time tell anyone what they had seen.

Monday, March 18

First Reading

DANIEL 9:4b-10

"Lord, great and awesome God, you who keep your merciful covenant toward those who love you and observe your commandments! We have sinned, been wicked and done evil; we have rebelled and departed from your commandments and your laws. We have not obeyed your servants the prophets, who spoke in your name to our kings, our princes, our fathers, and all the people of the land. Justice, O Lord, is on your side; we are shamefaced even to this day: we, the men of Judah, the residents of Jerusalem, and all Israel, near and far, in all the countries to which you have scattered them because of their treachery toward you. O LORD, we are shamefaced, like our kings, our princes, and our fathers, for having sinned against you. But yours, O Lord, our God, are compassion and forgiveness! Yet we rebelled against you and paid no heed to your command, O LORD, our God, to live by the law you gave us through your servants the prophets."

Responsorial Psalm
PSALM 79:8, 9, 11 and 13
R. Lord, do not deal with us according to our sins.
Remember not against us the iniquities of the past;
 may your compassion quickly come to us,
 for we are brought very low. **R.**
Help us, O God our savior,
 because of the glory of your name;
Deliver us and pardon our sins
 for your name's sake. **R.**
Let the prisoners' sighing come before you;
 with your great power free those doomed to death.
Then we, your people and the sheep of your pasture,
 will give thanks to you forever;
 through all generations we will declare your praise. **R.**

Gospel
LUKE 6:36-38

Jesus said to his disciples: "Be merciful, just as your Father is merciful.

"Stop judging and you will not be judged. Stop condemning and you will not be condemned. Forgive and you will be forgiven. Give and gifts will be given to you; a good measure, packed together, shaken down, and overflowing, will be poured into your lap. For the measure with which you measure will in return be measured out to you."

Tuesday, March 19

Saint Joseph, Spouse of the Blessed Virgin Mary

First Reading
2 SAMUEL 7:4-5a, 12-14a, 16

The LORD spoke to Nathan and said: "Go, tell my servant David, 'When your time comes and you rest with your ancestors, I will raise up your heir after you, sprung from your loins, and I will make his kingdom firm. It is he who shall build a house for my name. And I will make his royal throne firm forever. I will be a father to him, and he shall be a son to me. Your house and your kingdom shall endure forever before me; your throne shall stand firm forever.'"

Responsorial Psalm
PSALM 89:2-3, 4-5, 27 and 29
R. The son of David will live for ever.

The promises of the LORD I will sing forever;
through all generations my mouth shall proclaim your faithfulness,
For you have said, "My kindness is established forever";
in heaven you have confirmed your faithfulness. **R.**
"I have made a covenant with my chosen one,
I have sworn to David my servant:
Forever will I confirm your posterity
and establish your throne for all generations." **R.**
"He shall say of me, 'You are my father,
my God, the Rock, my savior.'
Forever I will maintain my kindness toward him,
and my covenant with him stands firm." **R.**

Second Reading
ROMANS 4:13, 16-18, 22

Brothers and sisters: It was not through the law that the promise was made to Abraham and his descendants that he would inherit the world, but through the righteousness that comes from faith. For this reason, it depends on faith, so that it may be a gift, and the promise may be guaranteed to all his descendants, not to those who only adhere to the law but to those who follow the faith of Abraham, who is the father of all of us, as it is written, *I have made you father of many nations*. He is our father in the sight of God, in whom he believed, who gives life to the dead and calls into being what does not exist. He believed, hoping against hope, that he would become *the father of many nations*, according to what was said, *Thus shall your descendants be*. That is why *it was credited to him as righteousness*.

Gospel
MATTHEW 1:16, 18-21, 24a (or LUKE 2:41-51a)

Jacob was the father of Joseph, the husband of Mary. Of her was born Jesus who is called the Christ.

Now this is how the birth of Jesus Christ came about. When his mother Mary was betrothed to Joseph, but before they lived together, she was found with child through the Holy Spirit. Joseph her husband, since he was a righteous man, yet unwilling to expose her to shame, decided to divorce her quietly. Such was his intention when, behold, the angel of the Lord appeared to him in a dream and said, "Joseph, son of David, do not be afraid to take Mary your wife into your home. For it is through the Holy Spirit that this child has been conceived in her. She will bear a son and you are to name him Jesus, because he will save his people from their sins." When Joseph awoke, he did as the angel of the Lord had commanded him and took his wife into his home.

Wednesday, March 20

First Reading
JEREMIAH 18:18-20

The people of Judah and the citizens of Jerusalem said, "Come, let us contrive a plot against Jeremiah. It will not mean the loss of instruction from the priests, nor of counsel from the wise, nor of messages from the prophets. And so, let us destroy him by his own tongue; let us carefully note his every word."

Heed me, O LORD,
and listen to what my adversaries say.
Must good be repaid with evil
that they should dig a pit to take my life?
Remember that I stood before you
to speak in their behalf,
to turn away your wrath from them.

Responsorial Psalm
PSALM 31:5-6, 14, 15-16
R. Save me, O Lord, in your kindness.

You will free me from the snare they set for me,
for you are my refuge.
Into your hands I commend my spirit;
you will redeem me, O LORD, O faithful God. **R.**
I hear the whispers of the crowd, that frighten me from every side,
as they consult together against me, plotting to take my life. **R.**
But my trust is in you, O LORD;
I say, "You are my God."
In your hands is my destiny; rescue me
from the clutches of my enemies and my persecutors. **R.**

Gospel
MATTHEW 20:17-28

As Jesus was going up to Jerusalem, he took the Twelve disciples aside by themselves, and said to them on the way, "Behold, we are going up to Jerusalem, and the Son of Man will be handed over to the chief priests and the scribes, and they will condemn him to death, and hand him over to the Gentiles to be mocked and scourged and crucified, and he will be raised on the third day."

Then the mother of the sons of Zebedee approached Jesus with her sons and did him homage, wishing to ask him for something. He said to her, "What do you wish?" She answered him, "Command that these two sons of mine sit, one at your right and the other at your left, in your kingdom." Jesus said in reply, "You do not know what you are asking. Can you drink the chalice that I am going to drink?" They said to him, "We can." He replied, "My chalice you will indeed drink, but to sit at my right and at my left, this is not mine to give but is for those for whom it has been prepared by my Father." When the ten heard this, they became indignant at the two brothers. But Jesus summoned them and said, "You know that the rulers of the Gentiles lord it over them, and the great ones make their authority over them felt. But it shall not be so among you. Rather, whoever wishes to be great among you shall be your servant; whoever wishes to be first among you shall be your slave. Just so, the Son of Man did not come to be served but to serve and to give his life as a ransom for many."

Thursday, March 21

First Reading

JEREMIAH 17:5-10

Thus says the LORD:
Cursed is the man who trusts in human beings,
who seeks his strength in flesh,
whose heart turns away from the LORD.
He is like a barren bush in the desert
that enjoys no change of season,
But stands in a lava waste,
a salt and empty earth.
Blessed is the man who trusts in the LORD,
whose hope is the LORD.
He is like a tree planted beside the waters
that stretches out its roots to the stream:
It fears not the heat when it comes,
its leaves stay green;
In the year of drought it shows no distress,
but still bears fruit.
More tortuous than all else is the human heart,
beyond remedy; who can understand it?

I, the LORD, alone probe the mind
    and test the heart,
To reward everyone according to his ways,
    according to the merit of his deeds.

Responsorial Psalm

PSALM 1:1-2, 3, 4 and 6

R. Blessed are they who hope in the Lord.

Blessed the man who follows not
    the counsel of the wicked
Nor walks in the way of sinners,
    nor sits in the company of the insolent,
But delights in the law of the LORD
    and meditates on his law day and night. **R.**
He is like a tree
    planted near running water,
That yields its fruit in due season,
    and whose leaves never fade.
    Whatever he does, prospers. **R.**
Not so, the wicked, not so;
    they are like chaff which the wind drives away.
For the LORD watches over the way of the just,
    but the way of the wicked vanishes. **R.**

Gospel

LUKE 16:19-31

Jesus said to the Pharisees: "There was a rich man who dressed in purple garments and fine linen and dined sumptuously each day. And lying at his door was a poor man named Lazarus, covered with sores, who would gladly have eaten his fill of the scraps that fell from the rich man's table. Dogs even used to come and lick his sores. When the poor man died, he was carried away by angels to the bosom of Abraham. The rich man also died and was buried, and from the netherworld, where he was in torment, he raised his eyes and saw Abraham far off and Lazarus at his side. And he cried out, 'Father Abraham, have pity on me. Send Lazarus to dip the tip of his finger in water and cool my tongue, for I am suffering torment in these flames.' Abraham replied, 'My child, remember that you received what was good during your lifetime while Lazarus likewise received what was bad; but now he is comforted here, whereas you are tormented. Moreover, between us and you a great chasm is established to prevent anyone from crossing who might wish to go from our side to yours or from your side to ours.' He said, 'Then I beg you, father, send him to my father's house, for I have five brothers, so that he may warn them, lest they too come to this place of torment.' But Abraham replied, 'They have Moses and the prophets. Let them listen to them.' He said, 'Oh no, father Abraham, but if someone from the dead goes to them, they will repent.' Then Abraham said, 'If they will not listen to Moses and the prophets, neither will they be persuaded if someone should rise from the dead.'"

Friday, March 22

First Reading

GENESIS 37:3-4, 12-13a, 17b-28a

Israel loved Joseph best of all his sons, for he was the child of his old age; and he had made him a long tunic. When his brothers saw that their father loved him best of all his sons, they hated him so much that they would not even greet him.

One day, when his brothers had gone to pasture their father's flocks at Shechem, Israel said to Joseph, "Your brothers, you know, are tending our flocks at Shechem. Get ready; I will send you to them."

So Joseph went after his brothers and caught up with them in Dothan. They noticed him from a distance, and before he came up to them, they plotted to kill him. They said to one another: "Here comes that master dreamer! Come on, let us kill him and throw him into one of the cisterns here; we could say that a wild beast devoured him. We shall then see what comes of his dreams."

When Reuben heard this, he tried to save him from their hands, saying, "We must not take his life. Instead of shedding blood," he continued, "just throw him into that cistern there in the desert; but do not kill him outright." His purpose was to rescue him from their hands and return him to his father. So when Joseph came up to them, they stripped him of the long tunic he had on; then they took him and threw him into the cistern, which was empty and dry.

They then sat down to their meal. Looking up, they saw a caravan of Ishmaelites coming from Gilead, their camels laden with gum, balm and resin to be taken down to Egypt. Judah said to his brothers: "What is to be gained by killing our brother and concealing his blood? Rather, let us sell him to these Ishmaelites, instead of doing away with him ourselves. After all, he is our brother, our own flesh." His brothers agreed. They sold Joseph to the Ishmaelites for twenty pieces of silver.

Responsorial Psalm

PSALM 105:16-17, 18-19, 20-21

R. Remember the marvels the Lord has done.

When the LORD called down a famine on the land
 and ruined the crop that sustained them,

He sent a man before them,
  Joseph, sold as a slave. **R.**
They had weighed him down with fetters,
  and he was bound with chains,
Till his prediction came to pass
  and the word of the LORD proved him true. **R.**
The king sent and released him,
  the ruler of the peoples set him free.
He made him lord of his house
  and ruler of all his possessions. **R.**

Gospel
MATTHEW 21:33-43, 45-46

Jesus said to the chief priests and the elders of the people: "Hear another parable. There was a landowner who planted a vineyard, put a hedge around it, dug a wine press in it, and built a tower. Then he leased it to tenants and went on a journey. When vintage time drew near, he sent his servants to the tenants to obtain his produce. But the tenants seized the servants and one they beat, another they killed, and a third they stoned. Again he sent other servants, more numerous than the first ones, but they treated them in the same way. Finally, he sent his son to them, thinking, 'They will respect my son.' But when the tenants saw the son, they said to one another, 'This is the heir. Come, let us kill him and acquire his inheritance.' They seized him, threw him out of the vineyard, and killed him. What will the owner of the vineyard do to those tenants when he comes?" They answered him, "He will put those wretched men to a wretched death and lease his vineyard to other tenants who will give him the produce at the proper times." Jesus said to them, "Did you never read in the Scriptures:

The stone that the builders rejected
  has become the cornerstone;
by the Lord has this been done,
  and it is wonderful in our eyes?

Therefore, I say to you, the Kingdom of God will be taken away from you and given to a people that will produce its fruit." When the chief priests and the Pharisees heard his parables, they knew that he was speaking about them. And although they were attempting to arrest him, they feared the crowds, for they regarded him as a prophet.

Saturday, March 23

First Reading

MICAH 7:14-15, 18-20

Shepherd your people with your staff,
the flock of your inheritance,
That dwells apart in a woodland,
in the midst of Carmel.
Let them feed in Bashan and Gilead,
as in the days of old;
As in the days when you came from the land of Egypt,
show us wonderful signs.

Who is there like you, the God who removes guilt
and pardons sin for the remnant of his inheritance;
Who does not persist in anger forever,
but delights rather in clemency,
And will again have compassion on us,
treading underfoot our guilt?
You will cast into the depths of the sea all our sins;
You will show faithfulness to Jacob,
and grace to Abraham,
As you have sworn to our fathers
from days of old.

Responsorial Psalm

PSALM 103:1-2, 3-4, 9-10, 11-12

R. The Lord is kind and merciful.

Bless the LORD, O my soul;
and all my being, bless his holy name.
Bless the LORD, O my soul,
and forget not all his benefits. **R.**
He pardons all your iniquities,
he heals all your ills.
He redeems your life from destruction,
he crowns you with kindness and compassion. **R.**
He will not always chide,
nor does he keep his wrath forever.
Not according to our sins does he deal with us,
nor does he requite us according to our crimes. **R.**
For as the heavens are high above the earth,
so surpassing is his kindness toward those who fear him.
As far as the east is from the west,
so far has he put our transgressions from us. **R.**

Gospel
LUKE 15:1-3, 11-32

Tax collectors and sinners were all drawing near to listen to Jesus, but the Pharisees and scribes began to complain, saying, "This man welcomes sinners and eats with them." So to them Jesus addressed this parable. "A man had two sons, and the younger son said to his father, 'Father, give me the share of your estate that should come to me.' So the father divided the property between them. After a few days, the younger son collected all his belongings and set off to a distant country where he squandered his inheritance on a life of dissipation. When he had freely spent everything, a severe famine struck that country, and he found himself in dire need. So he hired himself out to one of the local citizens who sent him to his farm to tend the swine. And he longed to eat his fill of the pods on which the swine fed, but nobody gave him any. Coming to his senses he thought, 'How many of my father's hired workers have more than enough food to eat, but here am I, dying from hunger. I shall get up and go to my father and I shall say to him, "Father, I have sinned against heaven and against you. I no longer deserve to be called your son; treat me as you would treat one of your hired workers."' So he got up and went back to his father. While he was still a long way off, his father caught sight of him, and was filled with compassion. He ran to his son, embraced him and kissed him. His son said to him, 'Father, I have sinned against heaven and against you; I no longer deserve to be called your son.' But his father ordered his servants, 'Quickly, bring the finest robe and put it on him; put a ring on his finger and sandals on his feet. Take the fattened calf and slaughter it. Then let us celebrate with a feast, because this son of mine was dead, and has come to life again; he was lost, and has been found.' Then the celebration began. Now the older son had been out in the field and, on his way back, as he neared the house, he heard the sound of music and dancing. He called one of the servants and asked what this might mean. The servant said to him, 'Your brother has returned and your father has slaughtered the fattened calf because he has him back safe and sound.' He became angry, and when he refused to enter the house, his father came out and pleaded with him. He said to his father in reply, 'Look, all these years I served you and not once did I disobey your orders; yet you never gave me even a young goat to feast on with my friends. But when your son returns who swallowed up your property with prostitutes, for him you slaughter the fattened calf.' He said to him, 'My son, you are here with me always; everything I have is yours. But now we must celebrate and rejoice, because your brother was dead and has come to life again; he was lost and has been found.'"

Sunday, March 24

Third Sunday of Lent

First Reading

EXODUS 3:1-8a, 13-15 (for the First Scrutiny: EXODUS 17:3-7)

Moses was tending the flock of his father-in-law Jethro, the priest of Midian. Leading the flock across the desert, he came to Horeb, the mountain of God. There an angel of the LORD appeared to Moses in fire flaming out of a bush. As he looked on, he was surprised to see that the bush, though on fire, was not consumed. So Moses decided, "I must go over to look at this remarkable sight, and see why the bush is not burned."

When the LORD saw him coming over to look at it more closely, God called out to him from the bush, "Moses! Moses!" He answered, "Here I am." God said, "Come no nearer! Remove the sandals from your feet, for the place where you stand is holy ground. I am the God of your fathers," he continued, "the God of Abraham, the God of Isaac, the God of Jacob." Moses hid his face, for he was afraid to look at God. But the LORD said, "I have witnessed the affliction of my people in Egypt and have heard their cry of complaint against their slave drivers, so I know well what they are suffering. Therefore I have come down to rescue them from the hands of the Egyptians and lead them out of that land into a good and spacious land, a land flowing with milk and honey."

Moses said to God, "But when I go to the Israelites and say to them, 'The God of your fathers has sent me to you,' if they ask me, 'What is his name?' what am I to tell them?" God replied, "I am who am." Then he added, "This is what you shall tell the Israelites: I AM sent me to you."

God spoke further to Moses, "Thus shall you say to the Israelites: The LORD, the God of your fathers, the God of Abraham, the God of Isaac, the God of Jacob, has sent me to you.

"This is my name forever;
thus am I to be remembered through all generations."

Responsorial Psalm

PSALM 103:1-2, 3-4, 6-7, 8, 11 (for the First Scrutiny: PSALM 95:1-2, 6-7, 8-9)

R. The Lord is kind and merciful.

Bless the LORD, O my soul;
and all my being, bless his holy name.
Bless the LORD, O my soul,
and forget not all his benefits. **R.**

He pardons all your iniquities,
heals all your ills,
He redeems your life from destruction,
crowns you with kindness and compassion. **R.**
The LORD secures justice
and the rights of all the oppressed.
He has made known his ways to Moses,
and his deeds to the children of Israel. **R.**
Merciful and gracious is the LORD,
slow to anger and abounding in kindness.
For as the heavens are high above the earth,
so surpassing is his kindness toward those who fear him. **R.**

Second Reading
1 CORINTHIANS 10:1-6, 10-12 (for the First Scrutiny: ROMANS 5:1-2, 5-8)

I do not want you to be unaware, brothers and sisters, that our ancestors were all under the cloud and all passed through the sea, and all of them were baptized into Moses in the cloud and in the sea. All ate the same spiritual food, and all drank the same spiritual drink, for they drank from a spiritual rock that followed them, and the rock was the Christ. Yet God was not pleased with most of them, for they were struck down in the desert.

These things happened as examples for us, so that we might not desire evil things, as they did. Do not grumble as some of them did, and suffered death by the destroyer. These things happened to them as an example, and they have been written down as a warning to us, upon whom the end of the ages has come. Therefore, whoever thinks he is standing secure should take care not to fall.

Gospel
LUKE 13:1-9 (for the First Scrutiny: JOHN 4:5-42 or 4:5-15, 19b-26, 39a, 40-42)

Some people told Jesus about the Galileans whose blood Pilate had mingled with the blood of their sacrifices. Jesus said to them in reply, "Do you think that because these Galileans suffered in this way they were greater sinners than all other Galileans? By no means! But I tell you, if you do not repent, you will all perish as they did! Or those eighteen people who were killed when the tower at Siloam fell on them—do you think they were more guilty than everyone else who lived in Jerusalem? By no means! But I tell you, if you do not repent, you will all perish as they did!"

And he told them this parable: "There once was a person who had a fig tree planted in his orchard, and when he came in search of fruit on it but found none, he said to the gardener, 'For three years now I have come in search of fruit on this fig tree but have found none. So cut it down. Why should it exhaust the soil?' He said to him in reply, 'Sir, leave it for this year also, and I shall cultivate the ground around it and fertilize it; it may bear fruit in the future. If not you can cut it down.'"

Monday, March 25

The Annunciation of the Lord

First Reading

ISAIAH 7:10-14; 8:10

The LORD spoke to Ahaz, saying: Ask for a sign from the LORD, your God; let it be deep as the nether world, or high as the sky! But Ahaz answered, "I will not ask! I will not tempt the LORD!" Then Isaiah said: Listen, O house of David! Is it not enough for you to weary people, must you also weary my God? Therefore the Lord himself will give you this sign: the virgin shall be with child, and bear a son, and shall name him Emmanuel, which means "God is with us!"

Responsorial Psalm

PSALM 40:7-8a, 8b-9, 10, 11

R. Here I am, Lord; I come to do your will.

Sacrifice or oblation you wished not,
but ears open to obedience you gave me.
Holocausts or sin-offerings you sought not;
then said I, "Behold I come." **R.**
"In the written scroll it is prescribed for me,
To do your will, O my God, is my delight,
and your law is within my heart!" **R.**
I announced your justice in the vast assembly;
I did not restrain my lips, as you, O LORD, know. **R.**
Your justice I kept not hid within my heart;
your faithfulness and your salvation I have spoken of;
I have made no secret of your kindness and your truth
in the vast assembly. **R.**

Second Reading

HEBREWS 10:4-10

Brothers and sisters: It is impossible that the blood of bulls and goats takes away sins. For this reason, when Christ came into the world, he said:

"Sacrifice and offering you did not desire,
but a body you prepared for me;
in holocausts and sin offerings you took no delight.
Then I said, 'As is written of me in the scroll,
behold, I come to do your will, O God.'"

First he says, "Sacrifices and offerings, holocausts and sin offerings, you neither desired nor delighted in." These are offered according to the law. Then he says, "Behold, I come to do your will." He takes away the first to establish the second. By this "will," we have been consecrated through the offering of the Body of Jesus Christ once for all.

Gospel

LUKE 1:26-38

The angel Gabriel was sent from God to a town of Galilee called Nazareth, to a virgin betrothed to a man named Joseph, of the house of David, and the virgin's name was Mary. And coming to her, he said, "Hail, full of grace! The Lord is with you." But she was greatly troubled at what was said and pondered what sort of greeting this might be. Then the angel said to her, "Do not be afraid, Mary, for you have found favor with God. Behold, you will conceive in your womb and bear a son, and you shall name him Jesus. He will be great and will be called Son of the Most High, and the Lord God will give him the throne of David his father, and he will rule over the house of Jacob forever, and of his Kingdom there will be no end." But Mary said to the angel, "How can this be, since I have no relations with a man?" And the angel said to her in reply, "The Holy Spirit will come upon you, and the power of the Most High will overshadow you. Therefore the child to be born will be called holy, the Son of God. And behold, Elizabeth, your relative, has also conceived a son in her old age, and this is the sixth month for her who was called barren; for nothing will be impossible for God." Mary said, "Behold, I am the handmaid of the Lord. May it be done to me according to your word." Then the angel departed from her.

Tuesday, March 26

First Reading

DANIEL 3:25, 34-43 (or EXODUS 17:1-7)

Azariah stood up in the fire and prayed aloud:

"For your name's sake, O Lord, do not deliver us up forever,
or make void your covenant.

Do not take away your mercy from us,
  for the sake of Abraham, your beloved,
  Isaac your servant, and Israel your holy one,
To whom you promised to multiply their offspring
  like the stars of heaven,
  or the sand on the shore of the sea.
For we are reduced, O Lord, beyond any other nation,
  brought low everywhere in the world this day
  because of our sins.
We have in our day no prince, prophet, or leader,
  no burnt offering, sacrifice, oblation, or incense,
  no place to offer first fruits, to find favor with you.
But with contrite heart and humble spirit
  let us be received;
As though it were burnt offerings of rams and bullocks,
  or thousands of fat lambs,
So let our sacrifice be in your presence today
  as we follow you unreservedly;
  for those who trust in you cannot be put to shame.
And now we follow you with our whole heart,
  we fear you and we pray to you.
Do not let us be put to shame,
  but deal with us in your kindness and great mercy.
Deliver us by your wonders,
  and bring glory to your name, O Lord."

Responsorial Psalm
PSALM 25:4-5ab, 6 and 7bc, 8-9 (or PSALM 95:1-2, 6-7ab, 7c-9)
R. Remember your mercies, O Lord.
Your ways, O LORD, make known to me;
  teach me your paths,
Guide me in your truth and teach me,
  for you are God my savior. **R.**
Remember that your compassion, O LORD,
  and your kindness are from of old.
In your kindness remember me,
  because of your goodness, O LORD. **R.**
Good and upright is the LORD;
  thus he shows sinners the way.
He guides the humble to justice,
  he teaches the humble his way. **R.**

Gospel
MATTHEW 18:21-35 (or JOHN 4:5-42)

Peter approached Jesus and asked him, "Lord, if my brother sins against me, how often must I forgive him? As many as seven times?" Jesus answered, "I say to you, not seven times but seventy-seven times. That is why the Kingdom of heaven may be likened to a king who decided to settle accounts with his servants. When he began the accounting, a debtor was brought before him who owed him a huge amount. Since he had no way of paying it back, his master ordered him to be sold, along with his wife, his children, and all his property, in payment of the debt. At that, the servant fell down, did him homage, and said, 'Be patient with me, and I will pay you back in full.' Moved with compassion the master of that servant let him go and forgave him the loan. When that servant had left, he found one of his fellow servants who owed him a much smaller amount. He seized him and started to choke him, demanding, 'Pay back what you owe.' Falling to his knees, his fellow servant begged him, 'Be patient with me, and I will pay you back.' But he refused. Instead, he had him put in prison until he paid back the debt. Now when his fellow servants saw what had happened, they were deeply disturbed, and went to their master and reported the whole affair. His master summoned him and said to him, 'You wicked servant! I forgave you your entire debt because you begged me to. Should you not have had pity on your fellow servant, as I had pity on you?' Then in anger his master handed him over to the torturers until he should pay back the whole debt. So will my heavenly Father do to you, unless each of you forgives your brother from your heart."

Wednesday, March 27

First Reading
DEUTERONOMY 4:1, 5-9 (or EXODUS 17:1-7)

Moses spoke to the people and said: "Now, Israel, hear the statutes and decrees which I am teaching you to observe, that you may live, and may enter in and take possession of the land which the LORD, the God of your fathers, is giving you. Therefore, I teach you the statutes and decrees as the LORD, my God, has commanded me, that you may observe them in the land you are entering to occupy. Observe them carefully, for thus will you give evidence of your wisdom and intelligence to the nations, who will hear of all these statutes and say, 'This great nation is truly a wise and intelligent people.' For what great nation is there that has gods so close to it as the LORD, our God, is to us whenever we call upon him? Or what great nation has statutes and decrees that are as just as this whole law which I am setting before you today?

"However, take care and be earnestly on your guard not to forget the things which your own eyes have seen, nor let them slip from your memory as long as you live, but teach them to your children and to your children's children."

Responsorial Psalm

PSALM 147:12-13, 15-16, 19-20 (or PSALM 95:1-2, 6-7ab, 7c-9)

R. Praise the Lord, Jerusalem.

Glorify the LORD, O Jerusalem;
praise your God, O Zion.
For he has strengthened the bars of your gates;
he has blessed your children within you. **R.**
He sends forth his command to the earth;
swiftly runs his word!
He spreads snow like wool;
frost he strews like ashes. **R.**
He has proclaimed his word to Jacob,
his statutes and his ordinances to Israel.
He has not done thus for any other nation;
his ordinances he has not made known to them. **R.**

Gospel

MATTHEW 5:17-19 (or JOHN 4:5-42)

Jesus said to his disciples: "Do not think that I have come to abolish the law or the prophets. I have come not to abolish but to fulfill. Amen, I say to you, until heaven and earth pass away, not the smallest letter or the smallest part of a letter will pass from the law, until all things have taken place. Therefore, whoever breaks one of the least of these commandments and teaches others to do so will be called least in the Kingdom of heaven. But whoever obeys and teaches these commandments will be called greatest in the Kingdom of heaven."

Thursday, March 28

First Reading

JEREMIAH 7:23-28 (or EXODUS 17:1-7)

Thus says the LORD: This is what I commanded my people: Listen to my voice; then I will be your God and you shall be my people. Walk in all the ways that I command you, so that you may prosper.

But they obeyed not, nor did they pay heed. They walked in the hardness of their evil hearts and turned their backs, not their faces, to me. From the day that your fathers left the land of Egypt even to this day, I have sent you untiringly all my servants the prophets. Yet they have not obeyed me nor paid heed; they have stiffened their necks and done worse than their fathers. When you speak all these words to them, they will not listen to you either; when you call to them, they will not answer you. Say to them: This is the nation that does not listen to the voice of the LORD, its God, or take correction. Faithfulness has disappeared; the word itself is banished from their speech.

Responsorial Psalm

PSALM 95:1-2, 6-7, 8-9 (or PSALM 95:1-2, 6-7ab, 7c-9)

R. If today you hear his voice, harden not your hearts.

Come, let us sing joyfully to the LORD;
  let us acclaim the Rock of our salvation.
Let us come into his presence with thanksgiving;
  let us joyfully sing psalms to him. **R.**
Come, let us bow down in worship;
  let us kneel before the LORD who made us.
For he is our God,
  and we are the people he shepherds, the flock he guides. **R.**
Oh, that today you would hear his voice:
  "Harden not your hearts as at Meribah,
  as in the day of Massah in the desert,
Where your fathers tempted me;
  they tested me though they had seen my works." **R.**

Gospel

LUKE 11:14-23 (or JOHN 4:5-42)

Jesus was driving out a demon that was mute, and when the demon had gone out, the mute man spoke and the crowds were amazed. Some of them said, "By the power of Beelzebul, the prince of demons, he drives out demons." Others, to test him, asked him for a sign from heaven. But he knew their thoughts and said to them, "Every kingdom divided against itself will be laid waste and house will fall against house. And if Satan is divided against himself, how will his kingdom stand? For you say that it is by Beelzebul that I drive out demons. If I, then, drive out demons by Beelzebul, by whom do your own people drive them out? Therefore they will be your judges. But if it is by the finger of God that I drive out demons, then the Kingdom of God has come upon you. When a strong man fully armed guards his palace, his possessions are safe. But when one stronger than he attacks and overcomes him, he takes away the armor on which he relied and distributes the spoils. Whoever is not with me is against me, and whoever does not gather with me scatters."

Friday, March 29

First Reading

HOSEA 14:2-10 (or EXODUS 17:1-7)

Thus says the LORD:
Return, O Israel, to the LORD, your God;
you have collapsed through your guilt.
Take with you words,
and return to the LORD;
Say to him, "Forgive all iniquity,
and receive what is good, that we may render
as offerings the bullocks from our stalls.
Assyria will not save us,
nor shall we have horses to mount;
We shall say no more, 'Our god,'
to the work of our hands;
for in you the orphan finds compassion."

I will heal their defection, says the LORD,
I will love them freely;
for my wrath is turned away from them.
I will be like the dew for Israel:
he shall blossom like the lily;
He shall strike root like the Lebanon cedar,
and put forth his shoots.
His splendor shall be like the olive tree
and his fragrance like the Lebanon cedar.
Again they shall dwell in his shade
and raise grain;
They shall blossom like the vine,
and his fame shall be like the wine of Lebanon.

Ephraim! What more has he to do with idols?
I have humbled him, but I will prosper him.
"I am like a verdant cypress tree"—
Because of me you bear fruit!

Let him who is wise understand these things;
let him who is prudent know them.
Straight are the paths of the LORD,
in them the just walk,
but sinners stumble in them.

Responsorial Psalm

PSALM 81:6c-8a, 8bc-9, 10-11ab, 14 and 17 (or PSALM 95:1-2, 6-7ab, 7c-9)

R. I am the Lord your God: hear my voice.

An unfamiliar speech I hear:
"I relieved his shoulder of the burden;
his hands were freed from the basket.
In distress you called, and I rescued you." **R.**
"Unseen, I answered you in thunder;
I tested you at the waters of Meribah.
Hear, my people, and I will admonish you;
O Israel, will you not hear me?" **R.**
"There shall be no strange god among you
nor shall you worship any alien god.
I, the LORD, am your God
who led you forth from the land of Egypt." **R.**
"If only my people would hear me,
and Israel walk in my ways,
I would feed them with the best of wheat,
and with honey from the rock I would fill them." **R.**

Gospel

MARK 12:28-34 (or JOHN 4:5-42)

One of the scribes came to Jesus and asked him, "Which is the first of all the commandments?" Jesus replied, "The first is this: *Hear, O Israel! The Lord our God is Lord alone! You shall love the Lord your God with all your heart, with all your soul, with all your mind, and with all your strength.* The second is this: *You shall love your neighbor as yourself.* There is no other commandment greater than these." The scribe said to him, "Well said, teacher. You are right in saying, *He is One and there is no other than he.* And *to love him with all your heart, with all your understanding, with all your strength, and to love your neighbor as yourself* is worth more than all burnt offerings and sacrifices." And when Jesus saw that he answered with understanding, he said to him, "You are not far from the Kingdom of God." And no one dared to ask him any more questions.

Saturday, March 30

First Reading

HOSEA 6:1-6 (or EXODUS 17:1-7)

"Come, let us return to the LORD,
it is he who has rent, but he will heal us;

he has struck us, but he will bind our wounds.
He will revive us after two days;
on the third day he will raise us up,
to live in his presence.
Let us know, let us strive to know the LORD;
as certain as the dawn is his coming,
and his judgment shines forth like the light of day!
He will come to us like the rain,
like spring rain that waters the earth."

What can I do with you, Ephraim?
What can I do with you, Judah?
Your piety is like a morning cloud,
like the dew that early passes away.
For this reason I smote them through the prophets,
I slew them by the words of my mouth;
For it is love that I desire, not sacrifice,
and knowledge of God rather than burnt offerings.

Responsorial Psalm

PSALM 51:3-4, 18-19, 20-21ab (or PSALM 95:1-2, 6-7ab, 7c-9)

R. It is mercy I desire, and not sacrifice.

Have mercy on me, O God, in your goodness;
in the greatness of your compassion wipe out my offense.
Thoroughly wash me from my guilt
and of my sin cleanse me. **R.**
For you are not pleased with sacrifices;
should I offer a burnt offering, you would not accept it.
My sacrifice, O God, is a contrite spirit;
a heart contrite and humbled, O God, you will not spurn. **R.**
Be bountiful, O LORD, to Zion in your kindness
by rebuilding the walls of Jerusalem;
Then shall you be pleased with due sacrifices,
burnt offerings and holocausts. **R.**

Gospel

LUKE 18:9-14 (or JOHN 4:5-42)

Jesus addressed this parable to those who were convinced of their own righteousness and despised everyone else. "Two people went up to the temple area to pray; one was a Pharisee and the other was a tax collector. The Pharisee took up his position and spoke this prayer to himself, 'O God, I thank you that I am not like the rest of humanity—greedy, dishonest, adulterous—or even like this tax collector. I fast twice a week, and I pay tithes on my whole income.' But the tax collector stood off at a distance and would not even raise his eyes to heaven but beat his breast and prayed, 'O God, be merciful to me a sinner.' I tell you, the latter went home justified, not the former; for everyone who exalts himself will be humbled, and the one who humbles himself will be exalted."

Sunday, March 31

Fourth Sunday of Lent

First Reading

JOSHUA 5:9a, 10-12 (for the Second Scrutiny: 1 SAMUEL 16: 1b, 6-7, 10-13a)

The LORD said to Joshua, "Today I have removed the reproach of Egypt from you."

While the Israelites were encamped at Gilgal on the plains of Jericho, they celebrated the Passover on the evening of the fourteenth of the month. On the day after the Passover, they ate of the produce of the land in the form of unleavened cakes and parched grain. On that same day after the Passover, on which they ate of the produce of the land, the manna ceased. No longer was there manna for the Israelites, who that year ate of the yield of the land of Canaan.

Responsorial Psalm

PSALM 34:2-3, 4-5, 6-7 (for the Second Scrutiny: PSALM 23: 1-3a, 3b-4, 5, 6)

R. Taste and see the goodness of the Lord.

I will bless the LORD at all times;
his praise shall be ever in my mouth.
Let my soul glory in the LORD;
the lowly will hear me and be glad. **R.**
Glorify the LORD with me,
let us together extol his name.
I sought the LORD, and he answered me
and delivered me from all my fears. **R.**
Look to him that you may be radiant with joy,
and your faces may not blush with shame.
When the poor one called out, the LORD heard,
and from all his distress he saved him. **R.**

Second Reading

2 CORINTHIANS 5:17-21 (for the Second Scrutiny: EPHESIANS 5:8-14)

Brothers and sisters: Whoever is in Christ is a new creation: the old things have passed away; behold, new things have come. And all this is from God, who has reconciled us to himself through Christ and given us the ministry of reconciliation, namely, God was reconciling the world to himself in Christ, not counting their trespasses against them and entrusting to us the message of reconciliation. So we are ambassadors for Christ, as if God were appealing through us. We implore you on behalf of Christ, be reconciled to God. For our sake he made him to be sin who did not know sin, so that we might become the righteousness of God in him.

Gospel

LUKE 15:1-3, 11-32 (for the Second Scrutiny: JOHN 9:1-41 or 9:1, 6-9, 13-17, 34-38)

Tax collectors and sinners were all drawing near to listen to Jesus, but the Pharisees and scribes began to complain, saying, "This man welcomes sinners and eats with them." So to them Jesus addressed this parable: "A man had two sons, and the younger son said to his father, 'Father, give me the share of your estate that should come to me.' So the father divided the property between them. After a few days, the younger son collected all his belongings and set off to a distant country where he squandered his inheritance on a life of dissipation. When he had freely spent everything, a severe famine struck that country, and he found himself in dire need. So he hired himself out to one of the local citizens who sent him to his farm to tend the swine. And he longed to eat his fill of the pods on which the swine fed, but nobody gave him any. Coming to his senses he thought, 'How many of my father's hired workers have more than enough food to eat, but here am I, dying from hunger. I shall get up and go to my father and I shall say to him, "Father, I have sinned against heaven and against you. I no longer deserve to be called your son; treat me as you would treat one of your hired workers."' So he got up and went back to his father. While he was still a long way off, his father caught sight of him, and was filled with compassion. He ran to his son, embraced him and kissed him. His son said to him, 'Father, I have sinned against heaven and against you; I no longer deserve to be called your son.' But his father ordered his servants, 'Quickly bring the finest robe and put it on him; put a ring on his finger and sandals on his feet. Take the fattened calf and slaughter it. Then let us celebrate with a feast, because this son of mine was dead, and has come to life again; he was lost, and has been found.' Then the celebration began. Now the older son had been out in the field and, on his way back, as he neared the house, he heard the sound of music and dancing. He called one of the servants and asked what this might mean. The servant said to him, 'Your brother has returned and your father has slaughtered the fattened calf because he has him back safe and sound.' He became angry, and when he refused to enter the house, his father came out and pleaded with him. He said to his father in reply, 'Look, all these years I served you and not once did I disobey your orders; yet you never gave me even a young goat to feast on with my friends. But when your son returns who swallowed up your property with prostitutes, for him you slaughter the fattened calf.' He said to him, 'My son, you are here with me always; everything I have is yours. But now we must celebrate and rejoice, because your brother was dead and has come to life again; he was lost and has been found.'"

APRIL

Monday, April 1

First Reading

ISAIAH 65:17-21 (or MICAH 7:7-9)

Thus says the LORD:
Lo, I am about to create new heavens
and a new earth;
The things of the past shall not be remembered
or come to mind.
Instead, there shall always be rejoicing and happiness
in what I create;
For I create Jerusalem to be a joy
and its people to be a delight;
I will rejoice in Jerusalem
and exult in my people.
No longer shall the sound of weeping be heard there,
or the sound of crying;
No longer shall there be in it
an infant who lives but a few days,
or an old man who does not round out his full lifetime;
He dies a mere youth who reaches but a hundred years,
and he who fails of a hundred shall be thought accursed.
They shall live in the houses they build,
and eat the fruit of the vineyards they plant.

Responsorial Psalm

PSALM 30:2 and 4, 5-6, 11-12a and 13b (or PSALM 27:1, 7-8a, 8b-9abc, 13-14)

R. I will praise you, Lord, for you have rescued me.

I will extol you, O LORD, for you drew me clear
and did not let my enemies rejoice over me.
O LORD, you brought me up from the nether world;
you preserved me from among those going down into the pit. **R.**
Sing praise to the LORD, you his faithful ones,
and give thanks to his holy name.
For his anger lasts but a moment;
a lifetime, his good will.
At nightfall, weeping enters in,
but with the dawn, rejoicing. **R.**

"Hear, O LORD, and have pity on me;
O LORD, be my helper."
You changed my mourning into dancing;
O LORD, my God, forever will I give you thanks. **R.**

Gospel

JOHN 4:43-54 (or JOHN 9:1-41)

At that time Jesus left [Samaria] for Galilee. For Jesus himself testified that a prophet has no honor in his native place. When he came into Galilee, the Galileans welcomed him, since they had seen all he had done in Jerusalem at the feast; for they themselves had gone to the feast.

Then he returned to Cana in Galilee, where he had made the water wine. Now there was a royal official whose son was ill in Capernaum. When he heard that Jesus had arrived in Galilee from Judea, he went to him and asked him to come down and heal his son, who was near death. Jesus said to him, "Unless you people see signs and wonders, you will not believe." The royal official said to him, "Sir, come down before my child dies." Jesus said to him, "You may go; your son will live." The man believed what Jesus said to him and left. While the man was on his way back, his slaves met him and told him that his boy would live. He asked them when he began to recover. They told him, "The fever left him yesterday, about one in the afternoon." The father realized that just at that time Jesus had said to him, "Your son will live," and he and his whole household came to believe. Now this was the second sign Jesus did when he came to Galilee from Judea.

Tuesday, April 2

First Reading

EZEKIEL 47:1-9, 12 (or MICAH 7:7-9)

The angel brought me, Ezekiel, back to the entrance of the temple of the LORD, and I saw water flowing out from beneath the threshold of the temple toward the east, for the façade of the temple was toward the east; the water flowed down from the right side of the temple, south of the altar. He led me outside by the north gate, and around to the outer gate facing the east, where I saw water trickling from the right side. Then when he had walked off to the east with a measuring cord in his hand, he measured off a thousand cubits and had me wade through the water, which was ankle-deep. He measured off another thousand and once more had me wade through the water, which was now knee-deep. Again he measured off a thousand and had me wade; the water was up to my waist. Once more he measured off a thousand, but there was now a river through which I could not wade; for the water had risen so high it had become a river that could not be crossed except by swimming. He asked me, "Have you seen this, son of man?" Then he brought me to the bank of the river, where he had me sit. Along the bank of the river I saw very many trees on both sides. He said to me, "This water flows into the eastern district down upon the Arabah, and empties into the sea, the salt waters, which it makes fresh. Wherever the river flows, every sort of living creature that can multiply shall live, and there shall be abundant fish, for wherever this water comes the sea shall be made fresh. Along both banks of the river, fruit trees of every kind shall grow; their leaves shall not fade, nor their fruit fail. Every month they shall bear fresh fruit, for they shall be watered by the flow from the sanctuary. Their fruit shall serve for food, and their leaves for medicine."

Responsorial Psalm

PSALM 46:2-3, 5-6, 8-9 (or PSALM 27:1, 7-8a, 8b-9abc, 13-14)

R. The Lord of hosts is with us; our stronghold is the God of Jacob.

God is our refuge and our strength,
 an ever-present help in distress.
Therefore we fear not, though the earth be shaken
 and mountains plunge into the depths of the sea. **R.**
There is a stream whose runlets gladden the city of God,
 the holy dwelling of the Most High.
God is in its midst; it shall not be disturbed;
 God will help it at the break of dawn. **R.**
The LORD of hosts is with us;
 our stronghold is the God of Jacob.
Come! behold the deeds of the LORD,
 the astounding things he has wrought on earth. **R.**

Gospel

JOHN 5:1-16 (or JOHN 9:1-41)

There was a feast of the Jews, and Jesus went up to Jerusalem. Now there is in Jerusalem at the Sheep Gate a pool called in Hebrew Bethesda, with five porticoes. In these lay a large number of ill, blind, lame, and crippled. One man was there who had been ill for thirty-eight years. When Jesus saw him lying there and knew that he had been ill for a long time, he said to him, "Do you want to be well?" The sick man answered him, "Sir, I have no one to put me into the pool when the water is stirred up; while I am on my way, someone else gets down there before me." Jesus said to him, "Rise, take up your mat, and walk." Immediately the man became well, took up his mat, and walked.

Now that day was a sabbath. So the Jews said to the man who was cured, "It is the sabbath, and it is not lawful for you to carry your mat."

He answered them, "The man who made me well told me, 'Take up your mat and walk.'" They asked him, "Who is the man who told you, 'Take it up and walk'?" The man who was healed did not know who it was, for Jesus had slipped away, since there was a crowd there. After this Jesus found him in the temple area and said to him, "Look, you are well; do not sin any more, so that nothing worse may happen to you." The man went and told the Jews that Jesus was the one who had made him well. Therefore, the Jews began to persecute Jesus because he did this on a sabbath.

Wednesday, April 3

First Reading

ISAIAH 49:8-15 (or MICAH 7:7-9)

Thus says the LORD:
In a time of favor I answer you,
on the day of salvation I help you;
and I have kept you and given you as a covenant to the people,
To restore the land
and allot the desolate heritages,
Saying to the prisoners: Come out!
To those in darkness: Show yourselves!
Along the ways they shall find pasture,
on every bare height shall their pastures be.
They shall not hunger or thirst,
nor shall the scorching wind or the sun strike them;
For he who pities them leads them
and guides them beside springs of water.
I will cut a road through all my mountains,
and make my highways level.
See, some shall come from afar,
others from the north and the west,
and some from the land of Syene.
Sing out, O heavens, and rejoice, O earth,
break forth into song, you mountains.
For the LORD comforts his people
and shows mercy to his afflicted.

But Zion said, "The LORD has forsaken me;
my Lord has forgotten me."
Can a mother forget her infant,
be without tenderness for the child of her womb?
Even should she forget,
I will never forget you.

Responsorial Psalm

PSALM 145:8-9, 13cd-14, 17-18 (or PSALM 27:1, 7-8a, 8b-9abc, 13-14)

R. The Lord is gracious and merciful.

The LORD is gracious and merciful,
  slow to anger and of great kindness.
The LORD is good to all
  and compassionate toward all his works. **R.**
The LORD is faithful in all his words
  and holy in all his works.
The LORD lifts up all who are falling
  and raises up all who are bowed down. **R.**
The LORD is just in all his ways
  and holy in all his works.
The LORD is near to all who call upon him,
  to all who call upon him in truth. **R.**

Gospel

JOHN 5:17-30 (or JOHN 9:1-41)

Jesus answered the Jews: "My Father is at work until now, so I am at work." For this reason they tried all the more to kill him, because he not only broke the sabbath but he also called God his own father, making himself equal to God.

Jesus answered and said to them, "Amen, amen, I say to you, the Son cannot do anything on his own, but only what he sees the Father doing; for what he does, the Son will do also. For the Father loves the Son and shows him everything that he himself does, and he will show him greater works than these, so that you may be amazed. For just as the Father raises the dead and gives life, so also does the Son give life to whomever he wishes. Nor does the Father judge anyone, but he has given all judgment to the Son, so that all may honor the Son just as they honor the Father. Whoever does not honor the Son does not honor the Father who sent him. Amen, amen, I say to you, whoever hears my word and believes in the one who sent me has eternal life and will not come to condemnation, but has passed from death to life. Amen, amen, I say to you, the hour is coming and is now here when the dead will hear the voice of the Son of God, and those who hear will live. For just as the Father has life in himself, so also he gave to the Son the possession of life in himself. And he gave him power to exercise judgment, because he is the Son of Man. Do not be amazed at this, because the hour is coming in which all who are in the tombs will hear his voice and will come out, those who have done good deeds to the resurrection of life, but those who have done wicked deeds to the resurrection of condemnation.

"I cannot do anything on my own; I judge as I hear, and my judgment is just, because I do not seek my own will but the will of the one who sent me."

Thursday, April 4

First Reading

EXODUS 32:7-14 (or MICAH 7:7-9)

The LORD said to Moses, "Go down at once to your people whom you brought out of the land of Egypt, for they have become depraved. They have soon turned aside from the way I pointed out to them, making for themselves a molten calf and worshiping it, sacrificing to it and crying out, 'This is your God, O Israel, who brought you out of the land of Egypt!'" The LORD said to Moses, "I see how stiff-necked this people is. Let me alone, then, that my wrath may blaze up against them to consume them. Then I will make of you a great nation."

But Moses implored the LORD, his God, saying, "Why, O LORD, should your wrath blaze up against your own people, whom you brought out of the land of Egypt with such great power and with so strong a hand? Why should the Egyptians say, 'With evil intent he brought them out, that he might kill them in the mountains and exterminate them from the face of the earth'? Let your blazing wrath die down; relent in punishing your people. Remember your servants Abraham, Isaac and Israel, and how you swore to them by your own self, saying, 'I will make your descendants as numerous as the stars in the sky; and all this land that I promised, I will give your descendants as their perpetual heritage.'" So the LORD relented in the punishment he had threatened to inflict on his people.

Responsorial Psalm

PSALM 106:19-20, 21-22, 23 (or PSALM 27:1, 7-8a, 8b-9abc, 13-14)

R. Remember us, O Lord, as you favor your people.

Our fathers made a calf in Horeb
    and adored a molten image;
They exchanged their glory
    for the image of a grass-eating bullock. **R.**
They forgot the God who had saved them,
    who had done great deeds in Egypt,
Wondrous deeds in the land of Ham,
    terrible things at the Red Sea. **R.**
Then he spoke of exterminating them,
    but Moses, his chosen one,

Withstood him in the breach
to turn back his destructive wrath. **R.**

Gospel
JOHN 5:31-47 (or JOHN 9:1-41)

Jesus said to the Jews: "If I testify on my own behalf, my testimony is not true. But there is another who testifies on my behalf, and I know that the testimony he gives on my behalf is true. You sent emissaries to John, and he testified to the truth. I do not accept human testimony, but I say this so that you may be saved. He was a burning and shining lamp, and for a while you were content to rejoice in his light. But I have testimony greater than John's. The works that the Father gave me to accomplish, these works that I perform testify on my behalf that the Father has sent me. Moreover, the Father who sent me has testified on my behalf. But you have never heard his voice nor seen his form, and you do not have his word remaining in you, because you do not believe in the one whom he has sent. You search the Scriptures, because you think you have eternal life through them; even they testify on my behalf. But you do not want to come to me to have life.

"I do not accept human praise; moreover, I know that you do not have the love of God in you. I came in the name of my Father, but you do not accept me; yet if another comes in his own name, you will accept him. How can you believe, when you accept praise from one another and do not seek the praise that comes from the only God? Do not think that I will accuse you before the Father: the one who will accuse you is Moses, in whom you have placed your hope. For if you had believed Moses, you would have believed me, because he wrote about me. But if you do not believe his writings, how will you believe my words?"

Friday, April 5

First Reading
WISDOM 2:1a, 12-22 (or MICAH 7:7-9)

The wicked said among themselves,
thinking not aright:
"Let us beset the just one, because he is obnoxious to us;
he sets himself against our doings,
Reproaches us for transgressions of the law
and charges us with violations of our training.
He professes to have knowledge of God
and styles himself a child of the LORD.

To us he is the censure of our thoughts;
  merely to see him is a hardship for us,
Because his life is not like that of others,
  and different are his ways.
He judges us debased;
  he holds aloof from our paths as from things impure.
He calls blest the destiny of the just
  and boasts that God is his Father.
Let us see whether his words be true;
  let us find out what will happen to him.
For if the just one be the son of God, he will defend him
  and deliver him from the hand of his foes.
With revilement and torture let us put him to the test
  that we may have proof of his gentleness
  and try his patience.
Let us condemn him to a shameful death;
  for according to his own words, God will take care of him."
These were their thoughts, but they erred;
  for their wickedness blinded them,
and they knew not the hidden counsels of God;
  neither did they count on a recompense of holiness
  nor discern the innocent souls' reward.

Responsorial Psalm

PSALM 34:17-18, 19-20, 21 and 23 (or PSALM 27:1, 7-8a, 8b-9abc, 13-14)

R. The Lord is close to the brokenhearted.

The LORD confronts the evildoers,
  to destroy remembrance of them from the earth.
When the just cry out, the LORD hears them,
  and from all their distress he rescues them. **R.**
The LORD is close to the brokenhearted;
  and those who are crushed in spirit he saves.
Many are the troubles of the just man,
  but out of them all the LORD delivers him. **R.**
He watches over all his bones;
  not one of them shall be broken.
The LORD redeems the lives of his servants;
  no one incurs guilt who takes refuge in him. **R.**

Gospel
JOHN 7:1-2, 10, 25-30 (or JOHN 9:1-41)

Jesus moved about within Galilee; he did not wish to travel in Judea, because the Jews were trying to kill him. But the Jewish feast of Tabernacles was near.

But when his brothers had gone up to the feast, he himself also went up, not openly but as it were in secret.

Some of the inhabitants of Jerusalem said, "Is he not the one they are trying to kill? And look, he is speaking openly and they say nothing to him. Could the authorities have realized that he is the Christ? But we know where he is from. When the Christ comes, no one will know where he is from." So Jesus cried out in the temple area as he was teaching and said, "You know me and also know where I am from. Yet I did not come on my own, but the one who sent me, whom you do not know, is true. I know him, because I am from him, and he sent me." So they tried to arrest him, but no one laid a hand upon him, because his hour had not yet come.

Saturday, April 6

First Reading
JEREMIAH 11:18-20 (or MICAH 7:7-9)

I knew their plot because the LORD informed me;
at that time you, O LORD, showed me their doings.

Yet I, like a trusting lamb led to slaughter,
had not realized that they were hatching plots against me:
"Let us destroy the tree in its vigor;
let us cut him off from the land of the living,
so that his name will be spoken no more."

But, you, O LORD of hosts, O just Judge,
searcher of mind and heart,
Let me witness the vengeance you take on them,
for to you I have entrusted my cause!

Responsorial Psalm
PSALM 7:2-3, 9bc-10, 11-12 (or PSALM 27:1, 7-8a, 8b-9abc, 13-14)
R. O Lord, my God, in you I take refuge.

O LORD, my God, in you I take refuge;
save me from all my pursuers and rescue me,

Lest I become like the lion's prey,
to be torn to pieces, with no one to rescue me. **R.**
Do me justice, O LORD, because I am just,
and because of the innocence that is mine.
Let the malice of the wicked come to an end,
but sustain the just,
O searcher of heart and soul, O just God. **R.**
A shield before me is God,
who saves the upright of heart;
A just judge is God,
a God who punishes day by day. **R.**

Gospel
JOHN 7:40-53 (or JOHN 9:1-41)

Some in the crowd who heard these words of Jesus said, "This is truly the Prophet." Others said, "This is the Christ." But others said, "The Christ will not come from Galilee, will he? Does not Scripture say that the Christ will be of David's family and come from Bethlehem, the village where David lived?" So a division occurred in the crowd because of him. Some of them even wanted to arrest him, but no one laid hands on him.

So the guards went to the chief priests and Pharisees, who asked them, "Why did you not bring him?" The guards answered, "Never before has anyone spoken like this man." So the Pharisees answered them, "Have you also been deceived? Have any of the authorities or the Pharisees believed in him? But this crowd, which does not know the law, is accursed." Nicodemus, one of their members who had come to him earlier, said to them, "Does our law condemn a man before it first hears him and finds out what he is doing?" They answered and said to him, "You are not from Galilee also, are you? Look and see that no prophet arises from Galilee."

Then each went to his own house.

Sunday, April 7

Fifth Sunday of Lent

First Reading
ISAIAH 43:16-21 (for the Third Scrutiny: EZEKIEL 37: 12-14)

Thus says the LORD,
who opens a way in the sea
and a path in the mighty waters,

who leads out chariots and horsemen,
a powerful army,
till they lie prostrate together, never to rise,
snuffed out and quenched like a wick.
Remember not the events of the past,
the things of long ago consider not;
see, I am doing something new!
Now it springs forth, do you not perceive it?
In the desert I make a way,
in the wasteland, rivers.
Wild beasts honor me,
jackals and ostriches,
for I put water in the desert
and rivers in the wasteland
for my chosen people to drink,
the people whom I formed for myself,
that they might announce my praise.

Responsorial Psalm

PSALM 126:1-2, 2-3, 4-5, 6 (for the Third Scrutiny: PSALM 130:1-2, 3-4, 5-6, 7-8)

R. The Lord has done great things for us; we are filled with joy.

When the LORD brought back the captives of Zion,
we were like men dreaming.
Then our mouth was filled with laughter,
and our tongue with rejoicing. **R.**
Then they said among the nations,
"The LORD has done great things for them."
The LORD has done great things for us;
we are glad indeed. **R.**
Restore our fortunes, O LORD,
like the torrents in the southern desert.
Those that sow in tears
shall reap rejoicing. **R.**
Although they go forth weeping,
carrying the seed to be sown,
they shall come back rejoicing,
carrying their sheaves. **R.**

Second Reading

PHILIPPIANS 3:8-14 (for the Third Scrutiny: ROMANS 8:8-11)

Brothers and sisters: I consider everything as a loss because of the supreme good of knowing Christ Jesus my Lord. For his sake I have accepted the loss of all things and I consider them so much rubbish, that I may gain Christ and be found in him, not having any righteousness of my own based on the law but that which comes through faith in Christ, the righteousness from God, depending on faith to know him and the power of his resurrection and the sharing of his sufferings by being conformed to his death, if somehow I may attain the resurrection from the dead.

It is not that I have already taken hold of it or have already attained perfect maturity, but I continue my pursuit in hope that I may possess it, since I have indeed been taken possession of by Christ Jesus. Brothers and sisters, I for my part do not consider myself to have taken possession. Just one thing: forgetting what lies behind but straining forward to what lies ahead, I continue my pursuit toward the goal, the prize of God's upward calling, in Christ Jesus.

Gospel

JOHN 8:1-11 (for the Third Scrutiny: JOHN 11:1-45 or 11:3-7, 17, 20-27, 33b-45)

Jesus went to the Mount of Olives. But early in the morning he arrived again in the temple area, and all the people started coming to him, and he sat down and taught them. Then the scribes and the Pharisees brought a woman who had been caught in adultery and made her stand in the middle. They said to him, "Teacher, this woman was caught in the very act of committing adultery. Now in the law, Moses commanded us to stone such women. So what do you say?" They said this to test him, so that they could have some charge to bring against him. Jesus bent down and began to write on the ground with his finger. But when they continued asking him, he straightened up and said to them, "Let the one among you who is without sin be the first to throw a stone at her." Again he bent down and wrote on the ground. And in response, they went away one by one, beginning with the elders. So he was left alone with the woman before him. Then Jesus straightened up and said to her, "Woman, where are they? Has no one condemned you?" She replied, "No one, sir." Then Jesus said, "Neither do I condemn you. Go, and from now on do not sin any more."

Monday, April 8

First Reading

DANIEL 13:1-9, 15-17, 19-30, 33-62 (or DANIEL 13:41c-62 or 2 KINGS 4:18b-21, 32-37)

In Babylon there lived a man named Joakim, who married a very beautiful and God-fearing woman, Susanna, the daughter of Hilkiah; her pious parents had trained their daughter according to the law of Moses.

Joakim was very rich; he had a garden near his house, and the Jews had recourse to him often because he was the most respected of them all.

That year, two elders of the people were appointed judges, of whom the Lord said, "Wickedness has come out of Babylon: from the elders who were to govern the people as judges." These men, to whom all brought their cases, frequented the house of Joakim. When the people left at noon, Susanna used to enter her husband's garden for a walk. When the old men saw her enter every day for her walk, they began to lust for her. They suppressed their consciences; they would not allow their eyes to look to heaven, and did not keep in mind just judgments.

One day, while they were waiting for the right moment, she entered the garden as usual, with two maids only. She decided to bathe, for the weather was warm. Nobody else was there except the two elders, who had hidden themselves and were watching her. "Bring me oil and soap," she said to the maids, "and shut the garden doors while I bathe."

As soon as the maids had left, the two old men got up and hurried to her. "Look," they said, "the garden doors are shut, and no one can see us; give in to our desire, and lie with us. If you refuse, we will testify against you that you dismissed your maids because a young man was here with you."

"I am completely trapped," Susanna groaned. "If I yield, it will be my death; if I refuse, I cannot escape your power. Yet it is better for me to fall into your power without guilt than to sin before the Lord." Then Susanna shrieked, and the old men also shouted at her, as one of them ran to open the garden doors. When the people in the house heard the cries from the garden, they rushed in by the side gate to see what had happened to her. At the accusations by the old men, the servants felt very much ashamed, for never had any such thing been said about Susanna.

When the people came to her husband Joakim the next day, the two wicked elders also came, fully determined to put Susanna to death. Before all the people they ordered: "Send for Susanna, the daughter of Hilkiah, the wife of Joakim." When she was sent for, she came with her parents, children and all her relatives. All her relatives and the onlookers were weeping.

In the midst of the people the two elders rose up and laid their hands on her head. Through tears she looked up to heaven, for she trusted in the Lord wholeheartedly. The elders made this accusation: "As we were walking in the garden alone, this woman entered with two girls and shut the doors of the garden, dismissing the girls. A young man, who was hidden there, came and lay with her. When we, in a corner of the garden, saw this crime, we ran toward them. We saw them lying together, but the man we could not hold, because he was stronger than we; he opened the doors and ran off. Then we seized her and asked who the young man was, but she refused to tell us. We testify to this." The assembly believed them, since they were elders and judges of the people, and they condemned her to death.

But Susanna cried aloud: "O eternal God, you know what is hidden and are aware of all things before they come to be: you know that they have testified falsely against me. Here I am about to die, though I have done none of the things with which these wicked men have charged me."

The Lord heard her prayer. As she was being led to execution, God stirred up the holy spirit of a young boy named Daniel, and he cried aloud: "I will have no part in the death of this woman." All the people turned and asked him, "What is this you are saying?" He stood in their midst and continued, "Are you such fools, O children of Israel! To condemn a woman of Israel without examination and without clear evidence? Return to court, for they have testified falsely against her."

Then all the people returned in haste. To Daniel the elders said, "Come, sit with us and inform us, since God has given you the prestige of old age." But he replied, "Separate these two far from each other that I may examine them."

After they were separated one from the other, he called one of them and said: "How you have grown evil with age! Now have your past sins come to term: passing unjust sentences, condemning the innocent, and freeing the guilty, although the Lord says, 'The innocent and the just you shall not put to death.' Now, then, if you were a witness, tell me under what tree you saw them together." "Under a mastic tree," he answered. Daniel replied, "Your fine lie has cost you your head, for the angel of God shall receive the sentence from him and split you in two." Putting him to one side, he ordered the other one to be brought. Daniel said to him, "Offspring of Canaan, not of Judah, beauty has seduced you, lust has subverted your conscience. This is how you acted with the daughters of Israel, and in their fear they yielded to you; but a daughter of Judah did not tolerate your wickedness. Now, then, tell me under what tree you surprised them together." "Under an oak," he said. Daniel replied, "Your fine lie has cost you also your head, for the angel of God waits with a sword to cut you in two so as to make an end of you both."

The whole assembly cried aloud, blessing God who saves those who hope in him. They rose up against the two elders, for by their own words Daniel had convicted them of perjury. According to the law of Moses, they inflicted on them the penalty they had plotted to impose on their neighbor: they put them to death. Thus was innocent blood spared that day.

Responsorial Psalm

PSALM 23:1-3a, 3b-4, 5, 6 (or PSALM 17:1, 6-7, 8b and 15)

R. Even though I walk in the dark valley I fear no evil; for you are at my side.

The LORD is my shepherd; I shall not want.
In verdant pastures he gives me repose;
Beside restful waters he leads me;
he refreshes my soul. **R.**
He guides me in right paths
for his name's sake.
Even though I walk in the dark valley
I fear no evil; for you are at my side
With your rod and your staff
that give me courage. **R.**
You spread the table before me
in the sight of my foes;
You anoint my head with oil;
my cup overflows. **R.**
Only goodness and kindness follow me
all the days of my life;
And I shall dwell in the house of the LORD
for years to come. **R.**

Gospel

JOHN 8:12-20 (or JOHN 11:1-45)

Jesus spoke to them again, saying, "I am the light of the world. Whoever follows me will not walk in darkness, but will have the light of life." So the Pharisees said to him, "You testify on your own behalf, so your testimony cannot be verified." Jesus answered and said to them, "Even if I do testify on my own behalf, my testimony can be verified, because I know where I came from and where I am going. But you do not know where I come from or where I am going. You judge by appearances, but I do not judge anyone. And even if I should judge, my judgment is valid, because I am not alone, but it is I and the Father who sent me. Even in your law it is written that the testimony of two men can be verified. I testify on my behalf and so does the Father who sent me." So they said to him, "Where is your father?" Jesus answered, "You know neither me nor my Father. If you knew me, you would know my Father also." He spoke these words while teaching in the treasury in the temple area. But no one arrested him, because his hour had not yet come.

Tuesday, April 9

First Reading

NUMBERS 21:4-9 (or 2 KINGS 4:18b-21, 32-37)

From Mount Hor the children of Israel set out on the Red Sea road, to bypass the land of Edom. But with their patience worn out by the journey, the people complained against God and Moses, "Why have you brought us up from Egypt to die in this desert, where there is no food or water? We are disgusted with this wretched food!"

In punishment the LORD sent among the people saraph serpents, which bit the people so that many of them died. Then the people came to Moses and said, "We have sinned in complaining against the LORD and you. Pray the LORD to take the serpents away from us." So Moses prayed for the people, and the LORD said to Moses, "Make a saraph and mount it on a pole, and whoever looks at it after being bitten will live." Moses accordingly made a bronze serpent and mounted it on a pole, and whenever anyone who had been bitten by a serpent looked at the bronze serpent, he lived.

Responsorial Psalm

PSALM 102:2-3, 16-18, 19-21 (or PSALM 17:1, 6-7, 8b and 15)

R. O Lord, hear my prayer, and let my cry come to you.

O LORD, hear my prayer,
and let my cry come to you.
Hide not your face from me
in the day of my distress.
Incline your ear to me;
in the day when I call, answer me speedily. **R.**
The nations shall revere your name, O LORD,
and all the kings of the earth your glory,
When the LORD has rebuilt Zion
and appeared in his glory;
When he has regarded the prayer of the destitute,
and not despised their prayer. **R.**
Let this be written for the generation to come,
and let his future creatures praise the LORD:
"The LORD looked down from his holy height,
from heaven he beheld the earth,
To hear the groaning of the prisoners,
to release those doomed to die." **R.**

Gospel

JOHN 8:21-30 (or JOHN 11:1-45)

Jesus said to the Pharisees: "I am going away and you will look for me, but you will die in your sin. Where I am going you cannot come." So the Jews said, "He is not going to kill himself, is he, because he said, 'Where I am going you cannot come'?" He said to them, "You belong to what is below, I belong to what is above. You belong to this world, but I do not belong to this world. That is why I told you that you will die in your sins. For if you do not believe that I AM, you will die in your sins." So they said to him, "Who are you?" Jesus said to them, "What I told you from the beginning. I have much to say about you in condemnation. But the one who sent me is true, and what I heard from him I tell the world." They did not realize that he was speaking to them of the Father. So Jesus said to them, "When you lift up the Son of Man, then you will realize that I AM, and that I do nothing on my own, but I say only what the Father taught me. The one who sent me is with me. He has not left me alone, because I always do what is pleasing to him." Because he spoke this way, many came to believe in him.

Wednesday, April 10

First Reading

DANIEL 3:14-20, 91-92, 95 (or 2 KINGS 4:18b-21, 32-37)

King Nebuchadnezzar said: "Is it true, Shadrach, Meshach, and Abednego, that you will not serve my god, or worship the golden statue that I set up? Be ready now to fall down and worship the statue I had made, whenever you hear the sound of the trumpet, flute, lyre, harp, psaltery, bagpipe, and all the other musical instruments; otherwise, you shall be instantly cast into the white-hot furnace; and who is the God who can deliver you out of my hands?" Shadrach, Meshach, and Abednego answered King Nebuchadnezzar, "There is no need for us to defend ourselves before you in this matter. If our God, whom we serve, can save us from the white-hot furnace and from your hands, O king, may he save us! But even if he will not, know, O king, that we will not serve your god or worship the golden statue that you set up."

King Nebuchadnezzar's face became livid with utter rage against Shadrach, Meshach, and Abednego. He ordered the furnace to be heated seven times more than usual and had some of the strongest men in his army bind Shadrach, Meshach, and Abednego and cast them into the white-hot furnace.

Nebuchadnezzar rose in haste and asked his nobles, "Did we not cast three men bound into the fire?" "Assuredly, O king," they answered. "But," he replied, "I see four men unfettered and unhurt, walking in the fire, and the fourth looks like a son of God." Nebuchadnezzar exclaimed, "Blessed be the God of Shadrach, Meshach, and Abednego, who sent his angel to deliver the servants who trusted in him; they disobeyed the royal command and yielded their bodies rather than serve or worship any god except their own God."

Responsorial Psalm

DANIEL 3:52, 53, 54, 55, 56 (or PSALM 17:1, 6-7, 8b and 15)

R. Glory and praise for ever!

"Blessed are you, O Lord, the God of our fathers,
 praiseworthy and exalted above all forever;
And blessed is your holy and glorious name,
 praiseworthy and exalted above all for all ages." **R.**
"Blessed are you in the temple of your holy glory,
 praiseworthy and exalted above all forever." **R.**
"Blessed are you on the throne of your Kingdom,
 praiseworthy and exalted above all forever." **R.**
"Blessed are you who look into the depths
 from your throne upon the cherubim;
 praiseworthy and exalted above all forever." **R.**
"Blessed are you in the firmament of heaven,
 praiseworthy and glorious forever." **R.**

Gospel

JOHN 8:31-42 (or JOHN 11:1-45)

Jesus said to those Jews who believed in him, "If you remain in my word, you will truly be my disciples, and you will know the truth, and the truth will set you free." They answered him, "We are descendants of Abraham and have never been enslaved to anyone. How can you say, 'You will become free'?" Jesus answered them, "Amen, amen, I say to you, everyone who commits sin is a slave of sin. A slave does not remain in a household forever, but a son always remains. So if the Son frees you, then you will truly be free. I know that you are descendants of Abraham. But you are trying to kill me, because my word has no room among you. I tell you what I have seen in the Father's presence; then do what you have heard from the Father."

They answered and said to him, "Our father is Abraham." Jesus said to them, "If you were Abraham's children, you would be doing the works of Abraham. But now you are trying to kill me, a man who has told you the truth that I heard from God; Abraham did not do this. You are doing the works of your father!" So they said to him, "We were not born of fornication. We have one Father, God." Jesus said to them, "If God were your Father, you would love me, for I came from God and am here; I did not come on my own, but he sent me."

Thursday, April 11

First Reading

GENESIS 17:3-9 (or 2 KINGS 4:18b-21, 32-37)

When Abram prostrated himself, God spoke to him: "My covenant with you is this: you are to become the father of a host of nations. No longer shall you be called Abram; your name shall be Abraham, for I am making you the father of a host of nations. I will render you exceedingly fertile; I will make nations of you; kings shall stem from you. I will maintain my covenant with you and your descendants after you throughout the ages as an everlasting pact, to be your God and the God of your descendants after you. I will give to you and to your descendants after you the land in which you are now staying, the whole land of Canaan, as a permanent possession; and I will be their God."

God also said to Abraham: "On your part, you and your descendants after you must keep my covenant throughout the ages."

Responsorial Psalm

PSALM 105:4-5, 6-7, 8-9 (or PSALM 17:1, 6-7, 8b and 15)

R. The Lord remembers his covenant for ever.

Look to the LORD in his strength;
  seek to serve him constantly.
Recall the wondrous deeds that he has wrought,
  his portents, and the judgments he has uttered. **R.**
You descendants of Abraham, his servants,
  sons of Jacob, his chosen ones!
He, the LORD, is our God;
  throughout the earth his judgments prevail. **R.**
He remembers forever his covenant
  which he made binding for a thousand generations—
Which he entered into with Abraham
  and by his oath to Isaac. **R.**

Gospel

JOHN 8:51-59 (or JOHN 11:1-45)

Jesus said to the Jews: "Amen, amen, I say to you, whoever keeps my word will never see death." So the Jews said to him, "Now we are sure that you are possessed. Abraham died, as did the prophets, yet you say, 'Whoever keeps my word will never taste death.' Are you greater than our father Abraham, who died? Or the prophets, who died? Who do you make yourself out to be?" Jesus answered, "If I glorify myself, my glory is worth nothing; but it is my Father who glorifies me, of whom you say, 'He is our God.' You do not know him, but I know him. And if I should say that I do not know him, I would be like you a liar. But I do know him and I keep his word. Abraham your father rejoiced to see my day; he saw it and was glad." So the Jews said to him, "You are not yet fifty years old and you have seen Abraham?" Jesus said to them, "Amen, amen, I say to you, before Abraham came to be, I AM." So they picked up stones to throw at him; but Jesus hid and went out of the temple area.

Friday, April 12

First Reading

JEREMIAH 20:10-13 (or 2 KINGS 4:18b-21, 32-37)

I hear the whisperings of many:
"Terror on every side!
Denounce! let us denounce him!"
All those who were my friends
are on the watch for any misstep of mine.
"Perhaps he will be trapped; then we can prevail,
and take our vengeance on him."
But the LORD is with me, like a mighty champion:
my persecutors will stumble, they will not triumph.
In their failure they will be put to utter shame,
to lasting, unforgettable confusion.
O LORD of hosts, you who test the just,
who probe mind and heart,
Let me witness the vengeance you take on them,
for to you I have entrusted my cause.
Sing to the LORD,
praise the LORD,
For he has rescued the life of the poor
from the power of the wicked!

Responsorial Psalm

PSALM 18:2-3a, 3bc-4, 5-6, 7 (or PSALM 17:1, 6-7, 8b and 15)

R. In my distress I called upon the Lord, and he heard my voice.

I love you, O LORD, my strength,
O LORD, my rock, my fortress, my deliverer. **R.**
My God, my rock of refuge,
my shield, the horn of my salvation, my stronghold!
Praised be the LORD, I exclaim,
and I am safe from my enemies. **R.**
The breakers of death surged round about me,
the destroying floods overwhelmed me;

The cords of the nether world enmeshed me,
  the snares of death overtook me. **R.**
In my distress I called upon the LORD
  and cried out to my God;
From his temple he heard my voice,
  and my cry to him reached his ears. **R.**

Gospel

JOHN 10:31-42 (or JOHN 11:1-45)

The Jews picked up rocks to stone Jesus. Jesus answered them, "I have shown you many good works from my Father. For which of these are you trying to stone me?" The Jews answered him, "We are not stoning you for a good work but for blasphemy. You, a man, are making yourself God." Jesus answered them, "Is it not written in your law, 'I said, "You are gods"'? If it calls them gods to whom the word of God came, and Scripture cannot be set aside, can you say that the one whom the Father has consecrated and sent into the world blasphemes because I said, 'I am the Son of God'? If I do not perform my Father's works, do not believe me; but if I perform them, even if you do not believe me, believe the works, so that you may realize and understand that the Father is in me and I am in the Father." Then they tried again to arrest him; but he escaped from their power.

He went back across the Jordan to the place where John first baptized, and there he remained. Many came to him and said, "John performed no sign, but everything John said about this man was true." And many there began to believe in him.

Saturday, April 13

First Reading

EZEKIEL 37:21-28 (or 2 KINGS 4:18b-21, 32-37)

Thus says the Lord GOD: I will take the children of Israel from among the nations to which they have come, and gather them from all sides to bring them back to their land. I will make them one nation upon the land, in the mountains of Israel, and there shall be one prince for them all. Never again shall they be two nations, and never again shall they be divided into two kingdoms.

No longer shall they defile themselves with their idols, their abominations, and all their transgressions. I will deliver them from all their sins of apostasy, and cleanse them so that they may be my people and I may be their God. My servant David shall be prince over them, and there shall be one shepherd for them all; they shall live by my statutes and carefully observe my decrees. They shall live on the land that I gave to my servant Jacob, the land where their fathers lived; they shall live on it forever, they, and their children, and their children's children, with my servant David their prince forever. I will make with them a covenant of peace; it shall be an everlasting covenant with them, and I will multiply them, and put my sanctuary among them forever. My dwelling shall be with them; I will be their God, and they shall be my people. Thus the nations shall know that it is I, the LORD, who make Israel holy, when my sanctuary shall be set up among them forever.

Responsorial Psalm

JEREMIAH 31:10, 11-12abcd, 13 (or PSALM 17:1, 6-7, 8b and 15)

R. The Lord will guard us, as a shepherd guards his flock.

Hear the word of the LORD, O nations,
  proclaim it on distant isles, and say:
He who scattered Israel, now gathers them together,
  he guards them as a shepherd his flock. **R.**
The LORD shall ransom Jacob,
  he shall redeem him from the hand of his conqueror.
Shouting, they shall mount the heights of Zion,
  they shall come streaming to the LORD's blessings:
The grain, the wine, and the oil,
  the sheep and the oxen. **R.**
Then the virgins shall make merry and dance,
  and young men and old as well.
I will turn their mourning into joy,
  I will console and gladden them after their sorrows. **R.**

Gospel

JOHN 11:45-56 (or JOHN 11:1-45)

Many of the Jews who had come to Mary and seen what Jesus had done began to believe in him. But some of them went to the Pharisees and told them what Jesus had done. So the chief priests and the Pharisees convened the Sanhedrin and said, "What are we going to do? This man is performing many signs. If we leave him alone, all will believe in him, and the Romans will come and take away both our land and our nation." But one of them, Caiaphas, who was high priest that year, said to them, "You know nothing, nor do you consider that it is better for you that one man should die instead of the people, so that the whole nation may not perish." He did not say this on his own, but since he was high priest for that year, he prophesied that Jesus was going to die for the nation, and not only for the nation, but also to gather into one the dispersed children of God. So from that day on they planned to kill him.

So Jesus no longer walked about in public among the Jews, but he left for the region near the desert, to a town called Ephraim, and there he remained with his disciples.

Now the Passover of the Jews was near, and many went up from the country to Jerusalem before Passover to purify themselves. They looked for Jesus and said to one another as they were in the temple area, "What do you think? That he will not come to the feast?"

Sunday, April 14

Palm Sunday of the Passion of the Lord

***Gospel* (At the Procession of Palms)**
LUKE 19:28-40

Jesus proceeded on his journey up to Jerusalem. As he drew near to Bethphage and Bethany at the place called the Mount of Olives, he sent two of his disciples. He said, "Go into the village opposite you, and as you enter it you will find a colt tethered on which no one has ever sat. Untie it and bring it here. And if anyone should ask you, 'Why are you untying it?' you will answer, 'The Master has need of it.'" So those who had been sent went off and found everything just as he had told them. And as they were untying the colt, its owners said to them, "Why are you untying this colt?" They answered, "The Master has need of it." So they brought it to Jesus, threw their cloaks over the colt, and helped Jesus to mount. As he rode along, the people were spreading their cloaks on the road; and now as he was approaching the slope of the Mount of Olives, the whole multitude of his disciples began to praise God aloud with joy for all the mighty deeds they had seen. They proclaimed:

"Blessed is the king who comes
in the name of the Lord.
Peace in heaven
and glory in the highest."

Some of the Pharisees in the crowd said to him, "Teacher, rebuke your disciples." He said in reply, "I tell you, if they keep silent, the stones will cry out!"

First Reading
ISAIAH 50:4-7

The Lord GOD has given me
a well-trained tongue,

that I might know how to speak to the weary
a word that will rouse them.
Morning after morning
he opens my ear that I may hear;
and I have not rebelled,
have not turned back.
I gave my back to those who beat me,
my cheeks to those who plucked my beard;
my face I did not shield
from buffets and spitting.

The Lord GOD is my help,
therefore I am not disgraced;
I have set my face like flint,
knowing that I shall not be put to shame.

Responsorial Psalm
PSALM 22:8-9, 17-18, 19-20, 23-24
R. My God, my God, why have you abandoned me?
All who see me scoff at me;
they mock me with parted lips, they wag their heads:
"He relied on the LORD; let him deliver him,
let him rescue him, if he loves him." **R.**
Indeed, many dogs surround me,
a pack of evildoers closes in upon me;
they have pierced my hands and my feet;
I can count all my bones. **R.**
They divide my garments among them,
and for my vesture they cast lots.
But you, O LORD, be not far from me;
O my help, hasten to aid me. **R.**
I will proclaim your name to my brethren;
in the midst of the assembly I will praise you:
"You who fear the LORD, praise him;
all you descendants of Jacob, give glory to him;
revere him, all you descendants of Israel!" **R.**

Second Reading
PHILIPPIANS 2:6-11
Christ Jesus, though he was in the form of God,
did not regard equality with God
something to be grasped.
Rather, he emptied himself,
taking the form of a slave,

coming in human likeness;
and found human in appearance,
he humbled himself,
becoming obedient to the point of death,
even death on a cross.
Because of this, God greatly exalted him
and bestowed on him the name
which is above every name,
that at the name of Jesus
every knee should bend,
of those in heaven and on earth and under the earth,
and every tongue confess that
Jesus Christ is Lord,
to the glory of God the Father.

Gospel
LUKE 22:14–23:56 (or LUKE 23:1-49)

When the hour came, Jesus took his place at table with the apostles. He said to them, "I have eagerly desired to eat this Passover with you before I suffer, for, I tell you, I shall not eat it again until there is fulfillment in the kingdom of God." Then he took a cup, gave thanks, and said, "Take this and share it among yourselves; for I tell you that from this time on I shall not drink of the fruit of the vine until the kingdom of God comes." Then he took the bread, said the blessing, broke it, and gave it to them, saying, "This is my body, which will be given for you; do this in memory of me." And likewise the cup after they had eaten, saying, "This cup is the new covenant in my blood, which will be shed for you.

"And yet behold, the hand of the one who is to betray me is with me on the table; for the Son of Man indeed goes as it has been determined; but woe to that man by whom he is betrayed." And they began to debate among themselves who among them would do such a deed.

Then an argument broke out among them about which of them should be regarded as the greatest. He said to them, "The kings of the Gentiles lord it over them and those in authority over them are addressed as 'Benefactors'; but among you it shall not be so. Rather, let the greatest among you be as the youngest, and the leader as the servant. For who is greater: the one seated at table or the one who serves? Is it not the one seated at table? I am among you as the one who serves. It is you who have stood by me in my trials; and I confer a kingdom on you, just as my Father has conferred one on me, that you may eat and drink at my table in my kingdom; and you will sit on thrones judging the twelve tribes of Israel.

"Simon, Simon, behold Satan has demanded to sift all of you like wheat, but I have prayed that your own faith may not fail; and once you have turned back, you must strengthen your brothers." He said to him, "Lord, I am prepared to go to prison and to die with you." But he replied, "I tell you, Peter, before the cock crows this day, you will deny three times that you know me."

He said to them, "When I sent you forth without a money bag or a sack or sandals, were you in need of anything?" "No, nothing," they replied. He said to them, "But now one who has a money bag should take it, and likewise a sack, and one who does not have a sword should sell his cloak and buy one. For I tell you that this Scripture must be fulfilled in me, namely, *He was counted among the wicked;* and indeed what is written about me is coming to fulfillment." Then they said, "Lord, look, there are two swords here." But he replied, "It is enough!"

Then going out, he went, as was his custom, to the Mount of Olives, and the disciples followed him. When he arrived at the place he said to them, "Pray that you may not undergo the test." After withdrawing about a stone's throw from them and kneeling, he prayed, saying, "Father, if you are willing, take this cup away from me; still, not my will but yours be done." And to strengthen him an angel from heaven appeared to him. He was in such agony and he prayed so fervently that his sweat became like drops of blood falling on the ground. When he rose from prayer and returned to his disciples, he found them sleeping from grief. He said to them, "Why are you sleeping? Get up and pray that you may not undergo the test."

While he was still speaking, a crowd approached and in front was one of the Twelve, a man named Judas. He went up to Jesus to kiss him. Jesus said to him, "Judas, are you betraying the Son of Man with a kiss?" His disciples realized what was about to happen, and they asked, "Lord, shall we strike with a sword?" And one of them struck the high priest's servant and cut off his right ear. But Jesus said in reply, "Stop, no more of this!" Then he touched the servant's ear and healed him. And Jesus said to the chief priests and temple guards and elders who had come for him, "Have you come out as against a robber, with swords and clubs? Day after day I was with you in the temple area, and you did not seize me; but this is your hour, the time for the power of darkness."

After arresting him they led him away and took him into the house of the high priest; Peter was following at a distance. They lit a fire in the middle of the courtyard and sat around it, and Peter sat down with them. When a maid saw him seated in the light, she looked intently at him and said, "This man too was with him." But he denied it saying, "Woman, I do not know him." A short while later someone else saw him and said, "You too are one of them"; but Peter answered, "My friend, I am not." About an hour later, still another insisted, "Assuredly, this man too was with him, for he also is a Galilean." But Peter said, "My friend, I do not know what you are talking about." Just as he was saying this, the cock crowed, and the Lord turned and looked at Peter; and Peter remembered the word of the Lord, how he had said to him, "Before the cock crows today, you will deny me three times." He went out and began to weep bitterly. The men who held Jesus in custody were ridiculing and beating him. They blindfolded him and questioned him, saying, "Prophesy! Who is it that struck you?" And they reviled him in saying many other things against him.

When day came the council of elders of the people met, both chief priests and scribes, and they brought him before their Sanhedrin. They said, "If you are the Christ, tell us," but he replied to them, "If I tell you, you will not believe, and if I question, you will not respond. But from this time on the Son of Man will be seated at the right hand of the power of God." They all asked, "Are you then the Son of God?" He replied to them, "You say that I am." Then they said, "What further need have we for testimony? We have heard it from his own mouth."

Then the whole assembly of them arose and brought him before Pilate. They brought charges against him, saying, "We found this man misleading our people; he opposes the payment of taxes to Caesar and maintains that he is the Christ, a king." Pilate asked him, "Are you the king of the Jews?" He said to him in reply, "You say so." Pilate then addressed the chief priests and the crowds, "I find this man not guilty." But they were adamant and said, "He is inciting the people with his teaching throughout all Judea, from Galilee where he began even to here."

On hearing this Pilate asked if the man was a Galilean; and upon learning that he was under Herod's jurisdiction, he sent him to Herod who was in Jerusalem at that time. Herod was very glad to see Jesus; he had been wanting to see him for a long time, for he had heard about him and had been hoping to see him perform some sign. He questioned him at length, but he gave him no answer. The chief priests and scribes, meanwhile, stood by accusing him harshly. Herod and his soldiers treated him contemptuously and mocked him, and after clothing him in resplendent garb, he sent him back to Pilate. Herod and Pilate became friends that very day, even though they had been enemies formerly. Pilate then summoned the chief priests, the rulers, and the people and said to them, "You brought this man to me and accused him of inciting the people to revolt. I have conducted my investigation in your presence and have not found this man guilty of the charges you have brought against him, nor did Herod, for he sent him back to us. So no capital crime has been committed by him. Therefore I shall have him flogged and then release him."

But all together they shouted out, "Away with this man! Release Barabbas to us."—Now Barabbas had been imprisoned for a rebellion that had taken place in the city and for murder.—Again Pilate addressed them, still wishing to release Jesus, but they continued their shouting,

"Crucify him! Crucify him!" Pilate addressed them a third time, "What evil has this man done? I found him guilty of no capital crime. Therefore I shall have him flogged and then release him." With loud shouts, however, they persisted in calling for his crucifixion, and their voices prevailed. The verdict of Pilate was that their demand should be granted. So he released the man who had been imprisoned for rebellion and murder, for whom they asked, and he handed Jesus over to them to deal with as they wished.

As they led him away they took hold of a certain Simon, a Cyrenian, who was coming in from the country; and after laying the cross on him, they made him carry it behind Jesus. A large crowd of people followed Jesus, including many women who mourned and lamented him. Jesus turned to them and said, "Daughters of Jerusalem, do not weep for me; weep instead for yourselves and for your children for indeed, the days are coming when people will say, 'Blessed are the barren, the wombs that never bore and the breasts that never nursed.' At that time people will say to the mountains, 'Fall upon us!' and to the hills, 'Cover us!' for if these things are done when the wood is green what will happen when it is dry?" Now two others, both criminals, were led away with him to be executed.

When they came to the place called the Skull, they crucified him and the criminals there, one on his right, the other on his left. Then Jesus said, "Father, forgive them, they know not what they do." They divided his garments by casting lots. The people stood by and watched; the rulers, meanwhile, sneered at him and said, "He saved others, let him save himself if he is the chosen one, the Christ of God." Even the soldiers jeered at him. As they approached to offer him wine they called out, "If you are King of the Jews, save yourself." Above him there was an inscription that read, "This is the King of the Jews."

Now one of the criminals hanging there reviled Jesus, saying, "Are you not the Christ? Save yourself and us." The other, however, rebuking him, said in reply, "Have you no fear of God, for you are subject to the same condemnation? And indeed, we have been condemned justly, for the sentence we received corresponds to our crimes, but this man has done nothing criminal." Then he said, "Jesus, remember me when you come into your kingdom." He replied to him, "Amen, I say to you, today you will be with me in Paradise."

It was now about noon and darkness came over the whole land until three in the afternoon because of an eclipse of the sun. Then the veil of the temple was torn down the middle. Jesus cried out in a loud voice, "Father, into your hands I commend my spirit"; and when he had said this he breathed his last.

[Here all kneel and pause for a short time.]

The centurion who witnessed what had happened glorified God and said, "This man was innocent beyond doubt." When all the people who had gathered for this spectacle saw what had happened, they returned home beating their breasts; but all his acquaintances stood at a distance, including the women who had followed him from Galilee and saw these events.

Now there was a virtuous and righteous man named Joseph who, though he was a member of the council, had not consented to their plan of action. He came from the Jewish town of Arimathea and was awaiting the kingdom of God. He went to Pilate and asked for the body of Jesus. After he had taken the body down, he wrapped it in a linen cloth and laid him in a rock-hewn tomb in which no one had yet been buried. It was the day of preparation, and the sabbath was about to begin. The women who had come from Galilee with him followed behind, and when they had seen the tomb and the way in which his body was laid in it, they returned and prepared spices and perfumed oils. Then they rested on the sabbath according to the commandment.

Monday, April 15

Monday of Holy Week

First Reading

ISAIAH 42:1-7

Here is my servant whom I uphold,
  my chosen one with whom I am pleased,
Upon whom I have put my Spirit;
  he shall bring forth justice to the nations,
Not crying out, not shouting,
  not making his voice heard in the street.
A bruised reed he shall not break,
  and a smoldering wick he shall not quench,
Until he establishes justice on the earth;
  the coastlands will wait for his teaching.

Thus says God, the LORD,
  who created the heavens and stretched them out,
  who spreads out the earth with its crops,
Who gives breath to its people
  and spirit to those who walk on it:
I, the LORD, have called you for the victory of justice,
  I have grasped you by the hand;

I formed you, and set you
as a covenant of the people,
a light for the nations,
To open the eyes of the blind,
to bring out prisoners from confinement,
and from the dungeon, those who live in darkness.

Responsorial Psalm

PSALM 27:1, 2, 3, 13-14

R. The Lord is my light and my salvation.

The LORD is my light and my salvation;
whom should I fear?
The LORD is my life's refuge;
of whom should I be afraid? **R.**
When evildoers come at me
to devour my flesh,
My foes and my enemies
themselves stumble and fall. **R.**
Though an army encamp against me,
my heart will not fear;
Though war be waged upon me,
even then will I trust. **R.**
I believe that I shall see the bounty of the LORD
in the land of the living.
Wait for the LORD with courage;
be stouthearted, and wait for the LORD. **R.**

Gospel

JOHN 12:1-11

Six days before Passover Jesus came to Bethany, where Lazarus was, whom Jesus had raised from the dead. They gave a dinner for him there, and Martha served, while Lazarus was one of those reclining at table with him. Mary took a liter of costly perfumed oil made from genuine aromatic nard and anointed the feet of Jesus and dried them with her hair; the house was filled with the fragrance of the oil. Then Judas the Iscariot, one of his disciples, and the one who would betray him, said, "Why was this oil not sold for three hundred days' wages and given to the poor?" He said this not because he cared about the poor but because he was a thief and held the money bag and used to steal the contributions. So Jesus said, "Leave her alone. Let her keep this for the day of my burial. You always have the poor with you, but you do not always have me."

The large crowd of the Jews found out that he was there and came, not only because of him, but also to see Lazarus, whom he had raised from the dead. And the chief priests plotted to kill Lazarus too, because many of the Jews were turning away and believing in Jesus because of him.

Tuesday, April 16

Tuesday of Holy Week

First Reading

ISAIAH 49:1-6

Hear me, O islands,
listen, O distant peoples.
The LORD called me from birth,
from my mother's womb he gave me my name.
He made of me a sharp-edged sword
and concealed me in the shadow of his arm.
He made me a polished arrow,
in his quiver he hid me.
You are my servant, he said to me,
Israel, through whom I show my glory.

Though I thought I had toiled in vain,
and for nothing, uselessly, spent my strength,
Yet my reward is with the LORD,
my recompense is with my God.
For now the LORD has spoken
who formed me as his servant from the womb,
That Jacob may be brought back to him
and Israel gathered to him;
And I am made glorious in the sight of the LORD,
and my God is now my strength!
It is too little, he says, for you to be my servant,
to raise up the tribes of Jacob,
and restore the survivors of Israel;
I will make you a light to the nations,
that my salvation may reach to the ends of the earth.

Responsorial Psalm

PSALM 71:1-2, 3-4a, 5ab-6ab, 15 and 17

R. I will sing of your salvation.

In you, O LORD, I take refuge;
let me never be put to shame.
In your justice rescue me, and deliver me;
incline your ear to me, and save me. **R.**

Be my rock of refuge,
  a stronghold to give me safety,
  for you are my rock and my fortress.
O my God, rescue me from the hand of the wicked. **R.**
For you are my hope, O LORD;
  my trust, O God, from my youth.
On you I depend from birth;
  from my mother's womb you are my strength. **R.**
My mouth shall declare your justice,
  day by day your salvation.
O God, you have taught me from my youth,
  and till the present I proclaim your wondrous deeds. **R.**

Gospel
JOHN 13:21-33, 36-38

Reclining at table with his disciples, Jesus was deeply troubled and testified, "Amen, amen, I say to you, one of you will betray me." The disciples looked at one another, at a loss as to whom he meant. One of his disciples, the one whom Jesus loved, was reclining at Jesus' side. So Simon Peter nodded to him to find out whom he meant. He leaned back against Jesus' chest and said to him, "Master, who is it?" Jesus answered, "It is the one to whom I hand the morsel after I have dipped it." So he dipped the morsel and took it and handed it to Judas, son of Simon the Iscariot. After Judas took the morsel, Satan entered him. So Jesus said to him, "What you are going to do, do quickly." Now none of those reclining at table realized why he said this to him. Some thought that since Judas kept the money bag, Jesus had told him, "Buy what we need for the feast," or to give something to the poor. So Judas took the morsel and left at once. And it was night.

When he had left, Jesus said, "Now is the Son of Man glorified, and God is glorified in him. If God is glorified in him, God will also glorify him in himself, and he will glorify him at once. My children, I will be with you only a little while longer. You will look for me, and as I told the Jews, 'Where I go you cannot come,' so now I say it to you."

Simon Peter said to him, "Master, where are you going?" Jesus answered him, "Where I am going, you cannot follow me now, though you will follow later." Peter said to him, "Master, why can I not follow you now? I will lay down my life for you." Jesus answered, "Will you lay down your life for me? Amen, amen, I say to you, the cock will not crow before you deny me three times."

Wednesday, April 17

Wednesday of Holy Week

First Reading

ISAIAH 50:4-9a

The Lord GOD has given me
a well-trained tongue,
That I might know how to speak to the weary
a word that will rouse them.
Morning after morning
he opens my ear that I may hear;
And I have not rebelled,
have not turned back.
I gave my back to those who beat me,
my cheeks to those who plucked my beard;
My face I did not shield
from buffets and spitting.

The Lord GOD is my help,
therefore I am not disgraced;
I have set my face like flint,
knowing that I shall not be put to shame.
He is near who upholds my right;
if anyone wishes to oppose me,
let us appear together.
Who disputes my right?
Let him confront me.
See, the Lord GOD is my help;
who will prove me wrong?

Responsorial Psalm

PSALM 69:8-10, 21-22, 31 and 33-34

R. Lord, in your great love, answer me.

For your sake I bear insult,
and shame covers my face.
I have become an outcast to my brothers,
a stranger to my mother's sons,
because zeal for your house consumes me,
and the insults of those who blaspheme you fall upon me. **R.**
Insult has broken my heart, and I am weak,
I looked for sympathy, but there was none;
for consolers, not one could I find.

Rather they put gall in my food,
 and in my thirst they gave me vinegar to drink. **R.**
I will praise the name of God in song,
 and I will glorify him with thanksgiving:
"See, you lowly ones, and be glad;
 you who seek God, may your hearts revive!
For the LORD hears the poor,
 and his own who are in bonds he spurns not." **R.**

Gospel
MATTHEW 26:14-25

One of the Twelve, who was called Judas Iscariot, went to the chief priests and said, "What are you willing to give me if I hand him over to you?" They paid him thirty pieces of silver, and from that time on he looked for an opportunity to hand him over.

On the first day of the Feast of Unleavened Bread, the disciples approached Jesus and said, "Where do you want us to prepare for you to eat the Passover?" He said, "Go into the city to a certain man and tell him, 'The teacher says, "My appointed time draws near; in your house I shall celebrate the Passover with my disciples."'" The disciples then did as Jesus had ordered, and prepared the Passover.

When it was evening, he reclined at table with the Twelve. And while they were eating, he said, "Amen, I say to you, one of you will betray me." Deeply distressed at this, they began to say to him one after another, "Surely it is not I, Lord?" He said in reply, "He who has dipped his hand into the dish with me is the one who will betray me. The Son of Man indeed goes, as it is written of him, but woe to that man by whom the Son of Man is betrayed. It would be better for that man if he had never been born." Then Judas, his betrayer, said in reply, "Surely it is not I, Rabbi?" He answered, "You have said so."

Thursday, April 18

Holy Thursday: Evening Mass of the Lord's Supper

First Reading
EXODUS 12:1-8, 11-14 (Chrism Mass: ISAIAH 61:1-3a, 6a, 8b-9)

The LORD said to Moses and Aaron in the land of Egypt, "This month shall stand at the head of your calendar; you shall reckon it the first month of the year. Tell the whole community of Israel: On the tenth of this month every one of your families must procure for itself a lamb, one apiece for each household. If a family is too small for a whole lamb, it shall join the nearest household in procuring one and shall share in the lamb in proportion to the number of persons who partake of it. The lamb must be a year-old male and without blemish. You may take it from either the sheep or the goats. You shall keep it until the fourteenth day of this month, and then, with the whole assembly of Israel present, it shall be slaughtered during the evening twilight. They shall take some of its blood and apply it to the two doorposts and the lintel of every house in which they partake of the lamb. That same night they shall eat its roasted flesh with unleavened bread and bitter herbs.

"This is how you are to eat it: with your loins girt, sandals on your feet and your staff in hand, you shall eat like those who are in flight. It is the Passover of the LORD. For on this same night I will go through Egypt, striking down every firstborn of the land, both man and beast, and executing judgment on all the gods of Egypt—I, the LORD! But the blood will mark the houses where you are. Seeing the blood, I will pass over you; thus, when I strike the land of Egypt, no destructive blow will come upon you.

"This day shall be a memorial feast for you, which all your generations shall celebrate with pilgrimage to the LORD, as a perpetual institution."

Responsorial Psalm

PSALM 116:12-13, 15-16bc, 17-18 (Chrism Mass: PSALM 89:21-22, 25 and 27)

R. Our blessing-cup is a communion with the Blood of Christ.

How shall I make a return to the LORD
for all the good he has done for me?
The cup of salvation I will take up,
and I will call upon the name of the LORD. **R.**
Precious in the eyes of the LORD
is the death of his faithful ones.
I am your servant, the son of your handmaid;
you have loosed my bonds. **R.**
To you will I offer sacrifice of thanksgiving,
and I will call upon the name of the LORD.
My vows to the LORD I will pay
in the presence of all his people. **R.**

Second Reading

1 CORINTHIANS 11:23-26 (Chrism Mass: REVELATION 1:5-8)

Brothers and sisters: I received from the Lord what I also handed on to you, that the Lord Jesus, on the night he was handed over, took bread, and, after he had given thanks, broke it and said, "This is my body that is for you. Do this in remembrance of me." In the same way also the cup, after supper, saying, "This cup is the new covenant in my blood. Do this, as often as you drink it, in remembrance of me." For as often as you eat this bread and drink the cup, you proclaim the death of the Lord until he comes.

Gospel
JOHN 13:1-15 (Chrism Mass: LUKE 4:16-21)

Before the feast of Passover, Jesus knew that his hour had come to pass from this world to the Father. He loved his own in the world and he loved them to the end. The devil had already induced Judas, son of Simon the Iscariot, to hand him over. So, during supper, fully aware that the Father had put everything into his power and that he had come from God and was returning to God, he rose from supper and took off his outer garments. He took a towel and tied it around his waist. Then he poured water into a basin and began to wash the disciples' feet and dry them with the towel around his waist. He came to Simon Peter, who said to him, "Master, are you going to wash my feet?" Jesus answered and said to him, "What I am doing, you do not understand now, but you will understand later." Peter said to him, "You will never wash my feet." Jesus answered him, "Unless I wash you, you will have no inheritance with me." Simon Peter said to him, "Master, then not only my feet, but my hands and head as well." Jesus said to him, "Whoever has bathed has no need except to have his feet washed, for he is clean all over; so you are clean, but not all." For he knew who would betray him; for this reason, he said, "Not all of you are clean."

So when he had washed their feet and put his garments back on and reclined at table again, he said to them, "Do you realize what I have done for you? You call me 'teacher' and 'master,' and rightly so, for indeed I am. If I, therefore, the master and teacher, have washed your feet, you ought to wash one another's feet. I have given you a model to follow, so that as I have done for you, you should also do."

Friday, April 19

Friday of the Passion of the Lord (Good Friday)

First Reading
ISAIAH 52:13–53:12

See, my servant shall prosper,
  he shall be raised high and greatly exalted.
Even as many were amazed at him—
  so marred was his look beyond human semblance
  and his appearance beyond that of the sons of man—
so shall he startle many nations,
  because of him kings shall stand speechless;

for those who have not been told shall see,
 those who have not heard shall ponder it.

Who would believe what we have heard?
 To whom has the arm of the LORD been revealed?
He grew up like a sapling before him,
 like a shoot from the parched earth;
there was in him no stately bearing to make us look at him,
 nor appearance that would attract us to him.
He was spurned and avoided by people,
 a man of suffering, accustomed to infirmity,
one of those from whom people hide their faces,
 spurned, and we held him in no esteem.

Yet it was our infirmities that he bore,
 our sufferings that he endured,
while we thought of him as stricken,
 as one smitten by God and afflicted.
But he was pierced for our offenses,
 crushed for our sins;
upon him was the chastisement that makes us whole,
 by his stripes we were healed.
We had all gone astray like sheep,
 each following his own way;
but the LORD laid upon him
 the guilt of us all.

Though he was harshly treated, he submitted
 and opened not his mouth;
like a lamb led to the slaughter
 or a sheep before the shearers,
 he was silent and opened not his mouth.
Oppressed and condemned, he was taken away,
 and who would have thought any more of his destiny?
When he was cut off from the land of the living,
 and smitten for the sin of his people,
a grave was assigned him among the wicked
 and a burial place with evildoers,
though he had done no wrong
 nor spoken any falsehood.
But the LORD was pleased
 to crush him in infirmity.

If he gives his life as an offering for sin,
he shall see his descendants in a long life,
and the will of the LORD shall be accomplished through him.

Because of his affliction
he shall see the light in fullness of days;
through his suffering, my servant shall justify many,
and their guilt he shall bear.
Therefore I will give him his portion among the great,
and he shall divide the spoils with the mighty,
because he surrendered himself to death
and was counted among the wicked;
and he shall take away the sins of many,
and win pardon for their offenses.

Responsorial Psalm
PSALM 31:2, 6, 12-13, 15-16, 17, 25
R. Father, into your hands I commend my spirit.
In you, O LORD, I take refuge;
let me never be put to shame.
In your justice rescue me.
Into your hands I commend my spirit;
you will redeem me, O LORD, O faithful God. **R.**
For all my foes I am an object of reproach,
a laughingstock to my neighbors, and a dread to my friends;
they who see me abroad flee from me.
I am forgotten like the unremembered dead;
I am like a dish that is broken. **R.**
But my trust is in you, O LORD;
I say, "You are my God.
In your hands is my destiny; rescue me
from the clutches of my enemies and my persecutors." **R.**
Let your face shine upon your servant;
save me in your kindness.
Take courage and be stouthearted,
all you who hope in the LORD. **R.**

Second Reading
HEBREWS 4:14-16; 5:7-9
Brothers and sisters: Since we have a great high priest who has passed through the heavens, Jesus, the Son of God, let us hold fast to our confession. For we do not have a high priest who is unable to sympathize with our weaknesses, but one who has similarly been tested in

every way, yet without sin. So let us confidently approach the throne of grace to receive mercy and to find grace for timely help.

In the days when Christ was in the flesh, he offered prayers and supplications with loud cries and tears to the one who was able to save him from death, and he was heard because of his reverence. Son though he was, he learned obedience from what he suffered; and when he was made perfect, he became the source of eternal salvation for all who obey him.

Gospel
JOHN 18:1–19:42

Jesus went out with his disciples across the Kidron valley to where there was a garden, into which he and his disciples entered. Judas his betrayer also knew the place, because Jesus had often met there with his disciples. So Judas got a band of soldiers and guards from the chief priests and the Pharisees and went there with lanterns, torches, and weapons. Jesus, knowing everything that was going to happen to him, went out and said to them, "Whom are you looking for?" They answered him, "Jesus the Nazorean." He said to them, "I AM." Judas his betrayer was also with them. When he said to them, "I AM," they turned away and fell to the ground. So he again asked them, "Whom are you looking for?" They said, "Jesus the Nazorean." Jesus answered, "I told you that I AM. So if you are looking for me, let these men go." This was to fulfill what he had said, "I have not lost any of those you gave me." Then Simon Peter, who had a sword, drew it, struck the high priest's slave, and cut off his right ear. The slave's name was Malchus. Jesus said to Peter, "Put your sword into its scabbard. Shall I not drink the cup that the Father gave me?"

So the band of soldiers, the tribune, and the Jewish guards seized Jesus, bound him, and brought him to Annas first. He was the father-in-law of Caiaphas, who was high priest that year. It was Caiaphas who had counseled the Jews that it was better that one man should die rather than the people.

Simon Peter and another disciple followed Jesus. Now the other disciple was known to the high priest, and he entered the courtyard of the high priest with Jesus. But Peter stood at the gate outside. So the other disciple, the acquaintance of the high priest, went out and spoke to the gatekeeper and brought Peter in. Then the maid who was the gatekeeper said to Peter, "You are not one of this man's disciples, are you?" He said, "I am not." Now the slaves and the guards were standing around a charcoal fire that they had made, because it was cold, and were warming themselves. Peter was also standing there keeping warm.

The high priest questioned Jesus about his disciples and about his doctrine. Jesus answered him, "I have spoken publicly to the world. I have always taught in a synagogue or in the temple area where all the

Jews gather, and in secret I have said nothing. Why ask me? Ask those who heard me what I said to them. They know what I said." When he had said this, one of the temple guards standing there struck Jesus and said, "Is this the way you answer the high priest?" Jesus answered him, "If I have spoken wrongly, testify to the wrong; but if I have spoken rightly, why do you strike me?" Then Annas sent him bound to Caiaphas the high priest.

Now Simon Peter was standing there keeping warm. And they said to him, "You are not one of his disciples, are you?" He denied it and said, "I am not." One of the slaves of the high priest, a relative of the one whose ear Peter had cut off, said, "Didn't I see you in the garden with him?" Again Peter denied it. And immediately the cock crowed.

Then they brought Jesus from Caiaphas to the praetorium. It was morning. And they themselves did not enter the praetorium, in order not to be defiled so that they could eat the Passover. So Pilate came out to them and said, "What charge do you bring against this man?" They answered and said to him, "If he were not a criminal, we would not have handed him over to you." At this, Pilate said to them, "Take him yourselves, and judge him according to your law." The Jews answered him, "We do not have the right to execute anyone," in order that the word of Jesus might be fulfilled that he said indicating the kind of death he would die. So Pilate went back into the praetorium and summoned Jesus and said to him, "Are you the King of the Jews?" Jesus answered, "Do you say this on your own or have others told you about me?" Pilate answered, "I am not a Jew, am I? Your own nation and the chief priests handed you over to me. What have you done?" Jesus answered, "My kingdom does not belong to this world. If my kingdom did belong to this world, my attendants would be fighting to keep me from being handed over to the Jews. But as it is, my kingdom is not here." So Pilate said to him, "Then you are a king?" Jesus answered, "You say I am a king. For this I was born and for this I came into the world, to testify to the truth. Everyone who belongs to the truth listens to my voice." Pilate said to him, "What is truth?"

When he had said this, he again went out to the Jews and said to them, "I find no guilt in him. But you have a custom that I release one prisoner to you at Passover. Do you want me to release to you the King of the Jews?" They cried out again, "Not this one but Barabbas!" Now Barabbas was a revolutionary.

Then Pilate took Jesus and had him scourged. And the soldiers wove a crown out of thorns and placed it on his head, and clothed him in a purple cloak, and they came to him and said, "Hail, King of the Jews!" And they struck him repeatedly. Once more Pilate went out and said to them, "Look, I am bringing him out to you, so that you may know that I find no guilt in him." So Jesus came out, wearing the crown of thorns and the purple cloak. And he said to them, "Behold, the man!" When the chief priests and the guards saw him they cried out, "Crucify him, crucify him!" Pilate said to them, "Take him yourselves and crucify him. I find no guilt in him." The Jews answered, "We have a law, and according to that law he ought to die, because he made himself the Son of God." Now when Pilate heard this statement, he became even more afraid, and went back into the praetorium and said to Jesus, "Where are you from?" Jesus did not answer him. So Pilate said to him, "Do you not speak to me? Do you not know that I have power to release you and I have power to crucify you?" Jesus answered him, "You would have no power over me if it had not been given to you from above. For this reason the one who handed me over to you has the greater sin." Consequently, Pilate tried to release him; but the Jews cried out, "If you release him, you are not a Friend of Caesar. Everyone who makes himself a king opposes Caesar."

When Pilate heard these words he brought Jesus out and seated him on the judge's bench in the place called Stone Pavement, in Hebrew, Gabbatha. It was preparation day for Passover, and it was about noon. And he said to the Jews, "Behold, your king!" They cried out, "Take him away, take him away! Crucify him!" Pilate said to them, "Shall I crucify your king?" The chief priests answered, "We have no king but Caesar." Then he handed him over to them to be crucified.

So they took Jesus, and, carrying the cross himself, he went out to what is called the Place of the Skull, in Hebrew, Golgotha. There they crucified him, and with him two others, one on either side, with Jesus in the middle. Pilate also had an inscription written and put on the cross. It read, "Jesus the Nazorean, the King of the Jews." Now many of the Jews read this inscription, because the place where Jesus was crucified was near the city; and it was written in Hebrew, Latin, and Greek. So the chief priests of the Jews said to Pilate, "Do not write 'The King of the Jews,' but that he said, 'I am the King of the Jews.'" Pilate answered, "What I have written, I have written."

When the soldiers had crucified Jesus, they took his clothes and divided them into four shares, a share for each soldier. They also took his tunic, but the tunic was seamless, woven in one piece from the top down. So they said to one another, "Let's not tear it, but cast lots for it to see whose it will be," in order that the passage of Scripture might be fulfilled that says:

They divided my garments among them,
and for my vesture they cast lots.

This is what the soldiers did. Standing by the cross of Jesus were his mother and his mother's sister, Mary the wife of Clopas, and Mary of

Magdala. When Jesus saw his mother and the disciple there whom he loved he said to his mother, “Woman, behold, your son.” Then he said to the disciple, “Behold, your mother.” And from that hour the disciple took her into his home.

After this, aware that everything was now finished, in order that the Scripture might be fulfilled, Jesus said, “I thirst.” There was a vessel filled with common wine. So they put a sponge soaked in wine on a sprig of hyssop and put it up to his mouth. When Jesus had taken the wine, he said, “It is finished.” And bowing his head, he handed over the spirit.

[Here all kneel and pause for a short time.]

Now since it was preparation day, in order that the bodies might not remain on the cross on the sabbath, for the sabbath day of that week was a solemn one, the Jews asked Pilate that their legs be broken and that they be taken down. So the soldiers came and broke the legs of the first and then of the other one who was crucified with Jesus. But when they came to Jesus and saw that he was already dead, they did not break his legs, but one soldier thrust his lance into his side, and immediately blood and water flowed out. An eyewitness has testified, and his testimony is true; he knows that he is speaking the truth, so that you also may come to believe. For this happened so that the Scripture passage might be fulfilled:

Not a bone of it will be broken.

And again another passage says:

They will look upon him whom they have pierced.

After this, Joseph of Arimathea, secretly a disciple of Jesus for fear of the Jews, asked Pilate if he could remove the body of Jesus. And Pilate permitted it. So he came and took his body. Nicodemus, the one who had first come to him at night, also came bringing a mixture of myrrh and aloes weighing about one hundred pounds. They took the body of Jesus and bound it with burial cloths along with the spices, according to the Jewish burial custom. Now in the place where he had been crucified there was a garden, and in the garden a new tomb, in which no one had yet been buried. So they laid Jesus there because of the Jewish preparation day; for the tomb was close by.

Saturday, April 20

Holy Saturday / Easter Vigil

First Reading
GENESIS 1:1–2:2 (or GENESIS 1:1, 26-31a)

In the beginning, when God created the heavens and the earth, the earth was a formless wasteland, and darkness covered the abyss, while a mighty wind swept over the waters.

Then God said, "Let there be light," and there was light. God saw how good the light was. God then separated the light from the darkness. God called the light "day," and the darkness he called "night." Thus evening came, and morning followed—the first day.

Then God said, "Let there be a dome in the middle of the waters, to separate one body of water from the other." And so it happened: God made the dome, and it separated the water above the dome from the water below it. God called the dome "the sky." Evening came, and morning followed—the second day.

Then God said, "Let the water under the sky be gathered into a single basin, so that the dry land may appear." And so it happened: the water under the sky was gathered into its basin, and the dry land appeared. God called the dry land "the earth," and the basin of the water he called "the sea." God saw how good it was. Then God said, "Let the earth bring forth vegetation: every kind of plant that bears seed and every kind of fruit tree on earth that bears fruit with its seed in it." And so it happened: the earth brought forth every kind of plant that bears seed and every kind of fruit tree on earth that bears fruit with its seed in it. God saw how good it was. Evening came, and morning followed—the third day.

Then God said: "Let there be lights in the dome of the sky, to separate day from night. Let them mark the fixed times, the days and the years, and serve as luminaries in the dome of the sky, to shed light upon the earth." And so it happened: God made the two great lights, the greater one to govern the day, and the lesser one to govern the night; and he made the stars. God set them in the dome of the sky, to shed light upon the earth, to govern the day and the night, and to separate the light from the darkness. God saw how good it was. Evening came, and morning followed—the fourth day.

Then God said, "Let the water teem with an abundance of living creatures, and on the earth let birds fly beneath the dome of the sky." And so it happened: God created the great sea monsters and all kinds of swimming creatures with which the water teems, and all kinds of winged birds. God saw how good it was, and God blessed them, saying, "Be fertile, multiply, and fill the water of the seas; and let the birds multiply on the earth." Evening came, and morning followed—the fifth day.

Then God said, "Let the earth bring forth all kinds of living creatures: cattle, creeping things, and wild animals of all kinds." And so it happened: God made all kinds of wild animals, all kinds of cattle, and all kinds of creeping things of the earth. God saw how good it was.

Then God said: "Let us make man in our image, after our likeness. Let them have dominion over the fish of the sea, the birds of the air, and the cattle, and over all the wild animals and all the creatures that crawl on the ground."

God created man in his image;
in the image of God he created him;
male and female he created them.

God blessed them, saying: "Be fertile and multiply; fill the earth and subdue it. Have dominion over the fish of the sea, the birds of the air, and all the living things that move on the earth." God also said: "See, I give you every seed-bearing plant all over the earth and every tree that has seed-bearing fruit on it to be your food; and to all the animals of the land, all the birds of the air, and all the living creatures that crawl on the ground, I give all the green plants for food." And so it happened. God looked at everything he had made, and he found it very good. Evening came, and morning followed—the sixth day.

Thus the heavens and the earth and all their array were completed. Since on the seventh day God was finished with the work he had been doing, he rested on the seventh day from all the work he had undertaken.

Responsorial Psalm

PSALM 104:1-2, 5-6, 10, 12, 13-14, 24, 35 (or PSALM 33:4-5, 6-7, 12-13, 20 and 22)

R. Lord, send out your Spirit, and renew the face of the earth.

Bless the LORD, O my soul!
O LORD, my God, you are great indeed!
You are clothed with majesty and glory,
robed in light as with a cloak. **R.**

You fixed the earth upon its foundation,
not to be moved forever;
with the ocean, as with a garment, you covered it;
above the mountains the waters stood. **R.**

You send forth springs into the watercourses
that wind among the mountains.
Beside them the birds of heaven dwell;
from among the branches they send forth their song. **R.**

You water the mountains from your palace;
the earth is replete with the fruit of your works.
You raise grass for the cattle,
and vegetation for man's use,
producing bread from the earth. **R.**
How manifold are your works, O LORD!
In wisdom you have wrought them all—
the earth is full of your creatures.
Bless the LORD, O my soul! **R.**

Second Reading

GENESIS 22:1-18 (or GENESIS 22:1-2, 9a, 10-13, 15-18)

God put Abraham to the test. He called to him, "Abraham!" "Here I am," he replied. Then God said: "Take your son Isaac, your only one, whom you love, and go to the land of Moriah. There you shall offer him up as a holocaust on a height that I will point out to you." Early the next morning Abraham saddled his donkey, took with him his son Isaac and two of his servants as well, and with the wood that he had cut for the holocaust, set out for the place of which God had told him.

On the third day Abraham got sight of the place from afar. Then he said to his servants: "Both of you stay here with the donkey, while the boy and I go on over yonder. We will worship and then come back to you." Thereupon Abraham took the wood for the holocaust and laid it on his son Isaac's shoulders, while he himself carried the fire and the knife. As the two walked on together, Isaac spoke to his father Abraham: "Father!" Isaac said. "Yes, son," he replied. Isaac continued, "Here are the fire and the wood, but where is the sheep for the holocaust?" "Son," Abraham answered, "God himself will provide the sheep for the holocaust." Then the two continued going forward.

When they came to the place of which God had told him, Abraham built an altar there and arranged the wood on it. Next he tied up his son Isaac, and put him on top of the wood on the altar. Then he reached out and took the knife to slaughter his son. But the LORD's messenger called to him from heaven, "Abraham, Abraham!" "Here I am!" he answered. "Do not lay your hand on the boy," said the messenger. "Do not do the least thing to him. I know now how devoted you are to God, since you did not withhold from me your own beloved son." As Abraham looked about, he spied a ram caught by its horns in the thicket. So he went and took the ram and offered it up as a holocaust in place of his son. Abraham named the site Yahweh-yireh; hence people now say, "On the mountain the LORD will see."

Again the LORD's messenger called to Abraham from heaven and said: "I swear by myself, declares the LORD, that because you acted as you did in not withholding from me your beloved son, I will bless you abundantly and make your descendants as countless as the stars of the sky and the sands of the seashore; your descendants shall take possession of the gates of their enemies, and in your descendants all the nations of the earth shall find blessing—all this because you obeyed my command."

Responsorial Psalm
PSALM 16:5, 8, 9-10, 11
R. You are my inheritance, O Lord.

O LORD, my allotted portion and my cup,
 you it is who hold fast my lot.
I set the LORD ever before me;
 with him at my right hand I shall not be disturbed. **R.**
Therefore my heart is glad and my soul rejoices,
 my body, too, abides in confidence;
because you will not abandon my soul to the netherworld,
 nor will you suffer your faithful one to undergo corruption. **R.**
You will show me the path to life,
 fullness of joys in your presence,
 the delights at your right hand forever. **R.**

Third Reading
EXODUS 14:15–15:1

The LORD said to Moses, "Why are you crying out to me? Tell the Israelites to go forward. And you, lift up your staff and, with hand outstretched over the sea, split the sea in two, that the Israelites may pass through it on dry land. But I will make the Egyptians so obstinate that they will go in after them. Then I will receive glory through Pharaoh and all his army, his chariots and charioteers. The Egyptians shall know that I am the LORD, when I receive glory through Pharaoh and his chariots and charioteers."

The angel of God, who had been leading Israel's camp, now moved and went around behind them. The column of cloud also, leaving the front, took up its place behind them, so that it came between the camp of the Egyptians and that of Israel. But the cloud now became dark, and thus the night passed without the rival camps coming any closer together all night long. Then Moses stretched out his hand over the sea, and the LORD swept the sea with a strong east wind throughout the night and so turned it into dry land. When the water was thus divided, the Israelites marched into the midst of the sea on dry land, with the water like a wall to their right and to their left.

The Egyptians followed in pursuit; all Pharaoh's horses and chariots and charioteers went after them right into the midst of the sea. In the night watch just before dawn the LORD cast through the column of the fiery cloud upon the Egyptian force a glance that threw it into a panic; and he so clogged their chariot wheels that they could hardly drive. With that the Egyptians sounded the retreat before Israel, because the LORD was fighting for them against the Egyptians.

Then the LORD told Moses, "Stretch out your hand over the sea, that the water may flow back upon the Egyptians, upon their chariots and their charioteers." So Moses stretched out his hand over the sea, and at dawn the sea flowed back to its normal depth. The Egyptians were fleeing head on toward the sea, when the LORD hurled them into its midst. As the water flowed back, it covered the chariots and the charioteers of Pharaoh's whole army which had followed the Israelites into the sea. Not a single one of them escaped. But the Israelites had marched on dry land through the midst of the sea, with the water like a wall to their right and to their left. Thus the LORD saved Israel on that day from the power of the Egyptians. When Israel saw the Egyptians lying dead on the seashore and beheld the great power that the LORD had shown against the Egyptians, they feared the LORD and believed in him and in his servant Moses.

Then Moses and the Israelites sang this song to the LORD:

> I will sing to the LORD, for he is gloriously triumphant;
> horse and chariot he has cast into the sea.

Responsorial Psalm

EXODUS 15:1-2, 3-4, 5-6, 17-18

R. Let us sing to the Lord; he has covered himself in glory.

I will sing to the LORD, for he is gloriously triumphant;
  horse and chariot he has cast into the sea.
My strength and my courage is the LORD,
  and he has been my savior.
He is my God, I praise him;
  the God of my father, I extol him. **R.**
The LORD is a warrior,
  LORD is his name!
Pharaoh's chariots and army he hurled into the sea;
  the elite of his officers were submerged in the Red Sea. **R.**
The flood waters covered them,
  they sank into the depths like a stone.
Your right hand, O LORD, magnificent in power,
  your right hand, O LORD, has shattered the enemy. **R.**
You brought in the people you redeemed
  and planted them on the mountain of your inheritance—

the place where you made your seat, O LORD,
the sanctuary, LORD, which your hands established.
The LORD shall reign forever and ever. **R.**

Fourth Reading
ISAIAH 54:5-14

The One who has become your husband is your Maker;
his name is the LORD of hosts;
your redeemer is the Holy One of Israel,
called God of all the earth.
The LORD calls you back,
like a wife forsaken and grieved in spirit,
a wife married in youth and then cast off,
says your God.
For a brief moment I abandoned you,
but with great tenderness I will take you back.
In an outburst of wrath, for a moment
I hid my face from you;
but with enduring love I take pity on you,
says the LORD, your redeemer.
This is for me like the days of Noah,
when I swore that the waters of Noah
should never again deluge the earth;
so I have sworn not to be angry with you,
or to rebuke you.
Though the mountains leave their place
and the hills be shaken,
my love shall never leave you
nor my covenant of peace be shaken,
says the LORD, who has mercy on you.
O afflicted one, storm-battered and unconsoled,
I lay your pavements in carnelians,
and your foundations in sapphires;
I will make your battlements of rubies,
your gates of carbuncles,
and all your walls of precious stones.
All your children shall be taught by the LORD,
and great shall be the peace of your children.
In justice shall you be established,
far from the fear of oppression,
where destruction cannot come near you.

Responsorial Psalm

PSALM 30:2, 4, 5-6, 11-12, 13

R. I will praise you, Lord, for you have rescued me.

I will extol you, O LORD, for you drew me clear
and did not let my enemies rejoice over me.
O LORD, you brought me up from the netherworld;
you preserved me from among those going down into the pit. **R.**
Sing praise to the LORD, you his faithful ones,
and give thanks to his holy name.
For his anger lasts but a moment;
a lifetime, his good will.
At nightfall, weeping enters in,
but with the dawn, rejoicing. **R.**
Hear, O LORD, and have pity on me;
O LORD, be my helper.
You changed my mourning into dancing;
O LORD, my God, forever will I give you thanks. **R.**

Fifth Reading

ISAIAH 55:1-11

Thus says the LORD:
All you who are thirsty,
come to the water!
You who have no money,
come, receive grain and eat;
come, without paying and without cost,
drink wine and milk!
Why spend your money for what is not bread,
your wages for what fails to satisfy?
Heed me, and you shall eat well,
you shall delight in rich fare.
Come to me heedfully,
listen, that you may have life.
I will renew with you the everlasting covenant,
the benefits assured to David.
As I made him a witness to the peoples,
a leader and commander of nations,
so shall you summon a nation you knew not,
and nations that knew you not shall run to you,
because of the LORD, your God,
the Holy One of Israel, who has glorified you.

Seek the LORD while he may be found,
call him while he is near.

Let the scoundrel forsake his way,
and the wicked man his thoughts;
let him turn to the LORD for mercy;
to our God, who is generous in forgiving.
For my thoughts are not your thoughts,
nor are your ways my ways, says the LORD.
As high as the heavens are above the earth,
so high are my ways above your ways
and my thoughts above your thoughts.

For just as from the heavens
the rain and snow come down
and do not return there
till they have watered the earth,
making it fertile and fruitful,
giving seed to the one who sows
and bread to the one who eats,
so shall my word be
that goes forth from my mouth;
my word shall not return to me void,
but shall do my will,
achieving the end for which I sent it.

Responsorial Psalm

ISAIAH 12:2-3, 4, 5-6

R. You will draw water joyfully from the springs of salvation.

God indeed is my savior;
I am confident and unafraid.
My strength and my courage is the LORD,
and he has been my savior.
With joy you will draw water
at the fountain of salvation. **R.**
Give thanks to the LORD, acclaim his name;
among the nations make known his deeds,
proclaim how exalted is his name. **R.**
Sing praise to the LORD for his glorious achievement;
let this be known throughout all the earth.
Shout with exultation, O city of Zion,
for great in your midst
is the Holy One of Israel! **R.**

Sixth Reading
BARUCH 3:9-15, 32–4:4

Hear, O Israel, the commandments of life:
listen, and know prudence!
How is it, Israel,
that you are in the land of your foes,
grown old in a foreign land,
defiled with the dead,
accounted with those destined for the netherworld?
You have forsaken the fountain of wisdom!
Had you walked in the way of God,
you would have dwelt in enduring peace.
Learn where prudence is,
where strength, where understanding;
that you may know also
where are length of days, and life,
where light of the eyes, and peace.
Who has found the place of wisdom,
who has entered into her treasuries?

The One who knows all things knows her;
he has probed her by his knowledge—
the One who established the earth for all time,
and filled it with four-footed beasts;
he who dismisses the light, and it departs,
calls it, and it obeys him trembling;
before whom the stars at their posts
shine and rejoice;
when he calls them, they answer, "Here we are!"
shining with joy for their Maker.
Such is our God;
no other is to be compared to him:
he has traced out the whole way of understanding,
and has given her to Jacob, his servant,
to Israel, his beloved son.

Since then she has appeared on earth,
and moved among people.
She is the book of the precepts of God,
the law that endures forever;
all who cling to her will live,
but those will die who forsake her.
Turn, O Jacob, and receive her:
walk by her light toward splendor.

Give not your glory to another,
your privileges to an alien race.
Blessed are we, O Israel;
for what pleases God is known to us!

Responsorial Psalm
PSALM 19:8, 9, 10, 11
R. Lord, you have the words of everlasting life.
The law of the LORD is perfect,
refreshing the soul;
the decree of the LORD is trustworthy,
giving wisdom to the simple. **R.**
The precepts of the LORD are right,
rejoicing the heart;
the command of the LORD is clear,
enlightening the eye. **R.**
The fear of the LORD is pure,
enduring forever;
the ordinances of the LORD are true,
all of them just. **R.**
They are more precious than gold,
than a heap of purest gold;
sweeter also than syrup
or honey from the comb. **R.**

Seventh Reading
EZEKIEL 36:16-17a, 18-28
The word of the LORD came to me, saying: Son of man, when the house of Israel lived in their land, they defiled it by their conduct and deeds. Therefore I poured out my fury upon them because of the blood that they poured out on the ground, and because they defiled it with idols. I scattered them among the nations, dispersing them over foreign lands; according to their conduct and deeds I judged them. But when they came among the nations wherever they came, they served to profane my holy name, because it was said of them: "These are the people of the LORD, yet they had to leave their land." So I have relented because of my holy name which the house of Israel profaned among the nations where they came. Therefore say to the house of Israel: Thus says the Lord GOD: Not for your sakes do I act, house of Israel, but for the sake of my holy name, which you profaned among the nations to which you came. I will prove the holiness of my great name, profaned among the nations, in whose midst you have profaned it. Thus the nations shall know that I am the LORD, says the Lord GOD, when in their sight I prove my holiness through you. For I will take you away from among the na-

tions, gather you from all the foreign lands, and bring you back to your own land. I will sprinkle clean water upon you to cleanse you from all your impurities, and from all your idols I will cleanse you. I will give you a new heart and place a new spirit within you, taking from your bodies your stony hearts and giving you natural hearts. I will put my spirit within you and make you live by my statutes, careful to observe my decrees. You shall live in the land I gave your fathers; you shall be my people, and I will be your God.

Responsorial Psalm

PSALM 42:3, 5; 43:3, 4 (when baptism is not celebrated: ISAIAH 12:2-3, 4bcd, 5-6 or PSALM 51:12-13, 14-15, 18-19)

R. Like a deer that longs for running streams, my soul longs for you, my God.

Athirst is my soul for God, the living God.
    When shall I go and behold the face of God? **R.**
I went with the throng
    and led them in procession to the house of God,
amid loud cries of joy and thanksgiving,
    with the multitude keeping festival. **R.**
Send forth your light and your fidelity;
    they shall lead me on
and bring me to your holy mountain,
    to your dwelling-place. **R.**
Then will I go in to the altar of God,
    the God of my gladness and joy;
then will I give you thanks upon the harp,
    O God, my God! **R.**

Epistle

ROMANS 6:3-11

Brothers and sisters: Are you unaware that we who were baptized into Christ Jesus were baptized into his death? We were indeed buried with him through baptism into death, so that, just as Christ was raised from the dead by the glory of the Father, we too might live in newness of life.

For if we have grown into union with him through a death like his, we shall also be united with him in the resurrection. We know that our old self was crucified with him, so that our sinful body might be done away with, that we might no longer be in slavery to sin. For a dead person has been absolved from sin. If, then, we have died with Christ, we believe that we shall also live with him. We know that Christ, raised from the dead, dies no more; death no longer has power over him. As to his death, he died to sin once and for all; as to his life, he lives for God.

Consequently, you too must think of yourselves as being dead to sin and living for God in Christ Jesus.

Responsorial Psalm

PSALM 118:1-2, 16-17, 22-23

R. Alleluia, alleluia, alleluia.

Give thanks to the LORD, for he is good,
 for his mercy endures forever.
Let the house of Israel say,
 "His mercy endures forever." **R.**
The right hand of the LORD has struck with power;
 the right hand of the LORD is exalted.
I shall not die, but live,
 and declare the works of the LORD. **R.**
The stone the builders rejected
 has become the cornerstone.
By the LORD has this been done;
 it is wonderful in our eyes. **R.**

Gospel

LUKE 24:1-12

At daybreak on the first day of the week the women who had come from Galilee with Jesus took the spices they had prepared and went to the tomb. They found the stone rolled away from the tomb; but when they entered, they did not find the body of the Lord Jesus. While they were puzzling over this, behold, two men in dazzling garments appeared to them. They were terrified and bowed their faces to the ground. They said to them, "Why do you seek the living one among the dead? He is not here, but he has been raised. Remember what he said to you while he was still in Galilee, that the Son of Man must be handed over to sinners and be crucified, and rise on the third day." And they remembered his words. Then they returned from the tomb and announced all these things to the eleven and to all the others. The women were Mary Magdalene, Joanna, and Mary the mother of James; the others who accompanied them also told this to the apostles, but their story seemed like nonsense and they did not believe them. But Peter got up and ran to the tomb, bent down, and saw the burial cloths alone; then he went home amazed at what had happened.

Sunday, April 21

Easter Sunday of the Resurrection of the Lord

First Reading

ACTS 10:34a, 37-43

Peter proceeded to speak and said: "You know what has happened all over Judea, beginning in Galilee after the baptism that John preached, how God anointed Jesus of Nazareth with the Holy Spirit and power. He went about doing good and healing all those oppressed by the devil, for God was with him. We are witnesses of all that he did both in the country of the Jews and in Jerusalem. They put him to death by hanging him on a tree. This man God raised on the third day and granted that he be visible, not to all the people, but to us, the witnesses chosen by God in advance, who ate and drank with him after he rose from the dead. He commissioned us to preach to the people and testify that he is the one appointed by God as judge of the living and the dead. To him all the prophets bear witness, that everyone who believes in him will receive forgiveness of sins through his name."

Responsorial Psalm

PSALM 118:1-2, 16-17, 22-23

R. This is the day the Lord has made; let us rejoice and be glad. (or R. Alleluia.)

Give thanks to the LORD, for he is good,
for his mercy endures forever.
Let the house of Israel say,
"His mercy endures forever." **R.**
"The right hand of the LORD has struck with power;
the right hand of the LORD is exalted.
I shall not die, but live,
and declare the works of the LORD." **R.**
The stone which the builders rejected
has become the cornerstone.
By the LORD has this been done;
it is wonderful in our eyes. **R.**

Second Reading

COLOSSIANS 3:1-4 (or 1 CORINTHIANS 5:6b-8)

Brothers and sisters: If then you were raised with Christ, seek what is above, where Christ is seated at the right hand of God. Think of what is above, not of what is on earth. For you have died, and your life is hidden with Christ in God. When Christ your life appears, then you too will appear with him in glory.

Gospel
JOHN 20:1-9 (or LUKE 24:1-12 or at an afternoon or evening Mass: LUKE 24:13-35)

On the first day of the week, Mary of Magdala came to the tomb early in the morning, while it was still dark, and saw the stone removed from the tomb. So she ran and went to Simon Peter and to the other disciple whom Jesus loved, and told them, "They have taken the Lord from the tomb, and we don't know where they put him." So Peter and the other disciple went out and came to the tomb. They both ran, but the other disciple ran faster than Peter and arrived at the tomb first; he bent down and saw the burial cloths there, but did not go in. When Simon Peter arrived after him, he went into the tomb and saw the burial cloths there, and the cloth that had covered his head, not with the burial cloths but rolled up in a separate place. Then the other disciple also went in, the one who had arrived at the tomb first, and he saw and believed. For they did not yet understand the Scripture that he had to rise from the dead.

Monday, April 22

First Reading
ACTS 2:14, 22-33

On the day of Pentecost, Peter stood up with the Eleven, raised his voice, and proclaimed: "You who are Jews, indeed all of you staying in Jerusalem. Let this be known to you, and listen to my words.

"You who are children of Israel, hear these words. Jesus the Nazorean was a man commended to you by God with mighty deeds, wonders, and signs, which God worked through him in your midst, as you yourselves know. This man, delivered up by the set plan and foreknowledge of God, you killed, using lawless men to crucify him. But God raised him up, releasing him from the throes of death, because it was impossible for him to be held by it. For David says of him:

I saw the Lord ever before me,
with him at my right hand I shall not be disturbed.
Therefore my heart has been glad and my tongue has exulted;
my flesh, too, will dwell in hope,
because you will not abandon my soul to the nether world,
nor will you suffer your holy one to see corruption.
You have made known to me the paths of life;
you will fill me with joy in your presence.

My brothers, one can confidently say to you about the patriarch David that he died and was buried, and his tomb is in our midst to this day.

But since he was a prophet and knew that God had sworn an oath to him that he would set one of his descendants upon his throne, he foresaw and spoke of the resurrection of the Christ, that neither was he abandoned to the netherworld nor did his flesh see corruption. God raised this Jesus; of this we are all witnesses. Exalted at the right hand of God, he poured forth the promise of the Holy Spirit that he received from the Father, as you both see and hear."

Responsorial Psalm
PSALM 16:1-2a and 5, 7-8, 9-10, 11
R. Keep me safe, O God; you are my hope. (or R. Alleluia.)
Keep me, O God, for in you I take refuge;
  I say to the LORD, "My Lord are you."
O LORD, my allotted portion and my cup,
  you it is who hold fast my lot. **R.**
I bless the LORD who counsels me;
  even in the night my heart exhorts me.
I set the LORD ever before me;
  with him at my right hand I shall not be disturbed. **R.**
Therefore my heart is glad and my soul rejoices,
  my body, too, abides in confidence;
Because you will not abandon my soul to the nether world,
  nor will you suffer your faithful one to undergo corruption. **R.**
You will show me the path to life,
  fullness of joys in your presence,
  the delights at your right hand forever. **R.**

Gospel
MATTHEW 28:8-15
Mary Magdalene and the other Mary went away quickly from the tomb, fearful yet overjoyed, and ran to announce the news to his disciples. And behold, Jesus met them on their way and greeted them. They approached, embraced his feet, and did him homage. Then Jesus said to them, "Do not be afraid. Go tell my brothers to go to Galilee, and there they will see me."

While they were going, some of the guard went into the city and told the chief priests all that had happened. The chief priests assembled with the elders and took counsel; then they gave a large sum of money to the soldiers, telling them, "You are to say, 'His disciples came by night and stole him while we were asleep.' And if this gets to the ears of the governor, we will satisfy him and keep you out of trouble." The soldiers took the money and did as they were instructed. And this story has circulated among the Jews to the present day.

Tuesday, April 23

First Reading
ACTS 2:36-41

On the day of Pentecost, Peter said to the Jewish people, "Let the whole house of Israel know for certain that God has made him both Lord and Christ, this Jesus whom you crucified."

Now when they heard this, they were cut to the heart, and they asked Peter and the other Apostles, "What are we to do, my brothers?" Peter said to them, "Repent and be baptized, every one of you, in the name of Jesus Christ, for the forgiveness of your sins; and you will receive the gift of the Holy Spirit. For the promise is made to you and to your children and to all those far off, whomever the Lord our God will call." He testified with many other arguments, and was exhorting them, "Save yourselves from this corrupt generation." Those who accepted his message were baptized, and about three thousand persons were added that day.

Responsorial Psalm
PSALM 33:4-5, 18-19, 20 and 22
R. The earth is full of the goodness of the Lord.
(or R. Alleluia.)

Upright is the word of the LORD,
and all his works are trustworthy.
He loves justice and right;
of the kindness of the LORD the earth is full. **R.**
See, the eyes of the LORD are upon those who fear him,
upon those who hope for his kindness,
To deliver them from death
and preserve them in spite of famine. **R.**
Our soul waits for the LORD,
who is our help and our shield.
May your kindness, O LORD, be upon us
who have put our hope in you. **R.**

Gospel
JOHN 20:11-18

Mary Magdalene stayed outside the tomb weeping. And as she wept, she bent over into the tomb and saw two angels in white sitting there, one at the head and one at the feet where the Body of Jesus had been. And they said to her, "Woman, why are you weeping?" She said to them, "They have taken my Lord, and I don't know where they laid him." When she had said this, she turned around and saw Jesus there, but did not know it was Jesus. Jesus said to her, "Woman, why are you weeping? Whom are you looking for?" She thought it was the gardener and said to him, “Sir, if you carried him away, tell me where you laid him, and I will take him.” Jesus said to her, “Mary!” She turned and said to him in Hebrew, “Rabbouni,” which means Teacher. Jesus said to her, “Stop holding on to me, for I have not yet ascended to the Father. But go to my brothers and tell them, ‘I am going to my Father and your Father, to my God and your God.’” Mary went and announced to the disciples, “I have seen the Lord,” and then reported what he had told her.

Wednesday, April 24

First Reading

ACTS 3:1-10

Peter and John were going up to the temple area for the three o'clock hour of prayer. And a man crippled from birth was carried and placed at the gate of the temple called “the Beautiful Gate” every day to beg for alms from the people who entered the temple. When he saw Peter and John about to go into the temple, he asked for alms. But Peter looked intently at him, as did John, and said, “Look at us.” He paid attention to them, expecting to receive something from them. Peter said, “I have neither silver nor gold, but what I do have I give you: in the name of Jesus Christ the Nazorean, rise and walk.” Then Peter took him by the right hand and raised him up, and immediately his feet and ankles grew strong. He leaped up, stood, and walked around, and went into the temple with them, walking and jumping and praising God. When all the people saw him walking and praising God, they recognized him as the one who used to sit begging at the Beautiful Gate of the temple, and they were filled with amazement and astonishment at what had happened to him.

Responsorial Psalm

PSALM 105:1-2, 3-4, 6-7, 8-9

R. Rejoice, O hearts that seek the Lord. (or R. Alleluia.)

Give thanks to the LORD, invoke his name;
make known among the nations his deeds.
Sing to him, sing his praise,
proclaim all his wondrous deeds. **R.**
Glory in his holy name;
rejoice, O hearts that seek the LORD!
Look to the LORD in his strength;
seek to serve him constantly. **R.**
You descendants of Abraham, his servants,
sons of Jacob, his chosen ones!
He, the LORD, is our God;
throughout the earth his judgments prevail. **R.**

He remembers forever his covenant
which he made binding for a thousand generations—
Which he entered into with Abraham
and by his oath to Isaac. **R.**

Gospel

LUKE 24:13-35

That very day, the first day of the week, two of Jesus' disciples were going to a village seven miles from Jerusalem called Emmaus, and they were conversing about all the things that had occurred. And it happened that while they were conversing and debating, Jesus himself drew near and walked with them, but their eyes were prevented from recognizing him. He asked them, "What are you discussing as you walk along?" They stopped, looking downcast. One of them, named Cleopas, said to him in reply, "Are you the only visitor to Jerusalem who does not know of the things that have taken place there in these days?" And he replied to them, "What sort of things?" They said to him, "The things that happened to Jesus the Nazarene, who was a prophet mighty in deed and word before God and all the people, how our chief priests and rulers both handed him over to a sentence of death and crucified him. But we were hoping that he would be the one to redeem Israel; and besides all this, it is now the third day since this took place. Some women from our group, however, have astounded us: they were at the tomb early in the morning and did not find his Body; they came back and reported that they had indeed seen a vision of angels who announced that he was alive. Then some of those with us went to the tomb and found things just as the women had described, but him they did not see." And he said to them, "Oh, how foolish you are! How slow of heart to believe all that the prophets spoke! Was it not necessary that the Christ should suffer these things and enter into his glory?" Then beginning with Moses and all the prophets, he interpreted to them what referred to him in all the Scriptures. As they approached the village to which they were going, he gave the impression that he was going on farther. But they urged him, "Stay with us, for it is nearly evening and the day is almost over." So he went in to stay with them. And it happened that, while he was with them at table, he took bread, said the blessing, broke it, and gave it to them. With that their eyes were opened and they recognized him, but he vanished from their sight. Then they said to each other, "Were not our hearts burning within us while he spoke to us on the way and opened the Scriptures to us?" So they set out at once and returned to Jerusalem where they found gathered together the Eleven and those with them who were saying, "The Lord has truly been raised and has appeared to Simon!" Then the two recounted what had taken place on the way and how he was made known to them in the breaking of the bread.

Thursday, April 25

First Reading
ACTS 3:11-26

As the crippled man who had been cured clung to Peter and John, all the people hurried in amazement toward them in the portico called "Solomon's Portico." When Peter saw this, he addressed the people, "You children of Israel, why are you amazed at this, and why do you look so intently at us as if we had made him walk by our own power or piety? The God of Abraham, the God of Isaac, and the God of Jacob, the God of our fathers, has glorified his servant Jesus whom you handed over and denied in Pilate's presence, when he had decided to release him. You denied the Holy and Righteous One and asked that a murderer be released to you. The author of life you put to death, but God raised him from the dead; of this we are witnesses. And by faith in his name, this man, whom you see and know, his name has made strong, and the faith that comes through it has given him this perfect health, in the presence of all of you. Now I know, brothers and sisters, that you acted out of ignorance, just as your leaders did; but God has thus brought to fulfillment what he had announced beforehand through the mouth of all the prophets, that his Christ would suffer. Repent, therefore, and be converted, that your sins may be wiped away, and that the Lord may grant you times of refreshment and send you the Christ already appointed for you, Jesus, whom heaven must receive until the times of universal restoration of which God spoke through the mouth of his holy prophets from of old. For Moses said:

A prophet like me will the Lord, your God, raise up for you
from among your own kin;
to him you shall listen in all that he may say to you.
Everyone who does not listen to that prophet
will be cut off from the people.

"Moreover, all the prophets who spoke, from Samuel and those afterwards, also announced these days. You are the children of the prophets and of the covenant that God made with your ancestors when he said to Abraham, *In your offspring all the families of the earth shall be blessed.* For you first, God raised up his servant and sent him to bless you by turning each of you from your evil ways."

Responsorial Psalm

PSALM 8:2ab and 5, 6-7, 8-9

R. O Lord, our God, how wonderful your name in all the earth! (or R. Alleluia.)

O LORD, our Lord,
how glorious is your name over all the earth!
What is man that you should be mindful of him,
or the son of man that you should care for him? **R.**
You have made him little less than the angels,
and crowned him with glory and honor.
You have given him rule over the works of your hands,
putting all things under his feet. **R.**
All sheep and oxen,
yes, and the beasts of the field,
The birds of the air, the fishes of the sea,
and whatever swims the paths of the seas. **R.**

Gospel

LUKE 24:35-48

The disciples of Jesus recounted what had taken place along the way, and how they had come to recognize him in the breaking of bread.

While they were still speaking about this, he stood in their midst and said to them, "Peace be with you." But they were startled and terrified and thought that they were seeing a ghost. Then he said to them, "Why are you troubled? And why do questions arise in your hearts? Look at my hands and my feet, that it is I myself. Touch me and see, because a ghost does not have flesh and bones as you can see I have." And as he said this, he showed them his hands and his feet. While they were still incredulous for joy and were amazed, he asked them, "Have you anything here to eat?" They gave him a piece of baked fish; he took it and ate it in front of them.

He said to them, "These are my words that I spoke to you while I was still with you, that everything written about me in the law of Moses and in the prophets and psalms must be fulfilled." Then he opened their minds to understand the Scriptures. And he said to them, "Thus it is written that the Christ would suffer and rise from the dead on the third day and that repentance, for the forgiveness of sins, would be preached in his name to all the nations, beginning from Jerusalem. You are witnesses of these things."

Friday, April 26

First Reading

ACTS 4:1-12

After the crippled man had been cured, while Peter and John were still speaking to the people, the priests, the captain of the temple guard, and the Sadducees confronted them, disturbed that they were teaching the people and proclaiming in Jesus the resurrection of the dead. They laid hands on Peter and John and put them in custody until the next day, since it was already evening. But many of those who heard the word came to believe and the number of men grew to about five thousand.

On the next day, their leaders, elders, and scribes were assembled in Jerusalem, with Annas the high priest, Caiaphas, John, Alexander, and all who were of the high-priestly class. They brought them into their presence and questioned them, "By what power or by what name have you done this?" Then Peter, filled with the Holy Spirit, answered them, "Leaders of the people and elders: If we are being examined today about a good deed done to a cripple, namely, by what means he was saved, then all of you and all the people of Israel should know that it was in the name of Jesus Christ the Nazorean whom you crucified, whom God raised from the dead; in his name this man stands before you healed. He is *the stone rejected by you, the builders, which has become the cornerstone.* There is no salvation through anyone else, nor is there any other name under heaven given to the human race by which we are to be saved."

Responsorial Psalm

PSALM 118:1-2 and 4, 22-24, 25-27a

R. The stone rejected by the builders has become the cornerstone. (or R. Alleluia.)

Give thanks to the LORD, for he is good,
 for his mercy endures forever.
Let the house of Israel say,
 "His mercy endures forever."
Let those who fear the LORD say,
 "His mercy endures forever." **R.**
The stone which the builders rejected
 has become the cornerstone.
By the LORD has this been done;
 it is wonderful in our eyes.
This is the day the LORD has made;
 let us be glad and rejoice in it. **R.**

O LORD, grant salvation!
O LORD, grant prosperity!
Blessed is he who comes in the name of the LORD;
we bless you from the house of the LORD.
The LORD is God, and he has given us light. **R.**

Gospel
JOHN 21:1-14

Jesus revealed himself again to his disciples at the Sea of Tiberias. He revealed himself in this way. Together were Simon Peter, Thomas called Didymus, Nathanael from Cana in Galilee, Zebedee's sons, and two others of his disciples. Simon Peter said to them, "I am going fishing." They said to him, "We also will come with you." So they went out and got into the boat, but that night they caught nothing. When it was already dawn, Jesus was standing on the shore; but the disciples did not realize that it was Jesus. Jesus said to them, "Children, have you caught anything to eat?" They answered him, "No." So he said to them, "Cast the net over the right side of the boat and you will find something." So they cast it, and were not able to pull it in because of the number of fish. So the disciple whom Jesus loved said to Peter, "It is the Lord." When Simon Peter heard that it was the Lord, he tucked in his garment, for he was lightly clad, and jumped into the sea. The other disciples came in the boat, for they were not far from shore, only about a hundred yards, dragging the net with the fish. When they climbed out on shore, they saw a charcoal fire with fish on it and bread. Jesus said to them, "Bring some of the fish you just caught." So Simon Peter went over and dragged the net ashore full of one hundred fifty-three large fish. Even though there were so many, the net was not torn. Jesus said to them, "Come, have breakfast." And none of the disciples dared to ask him, "Who are you?" because they realized it was the Lord. Jesus came over and took the bread and gave it to them, and in like manner the fish. This was now the third time Jesus was revealed to his disciples after being raised from the dead.

Saturday, April 27

First Reading
ACTS 4:13-21

Observing the boldness of Peter and John and perceiving them to be uneducated, ordinary men, the leaders, elders, and scribes were amazed, and they recognized them as the companions of Jesus. Then when they saw the man who had been cured standing there with them, they could say nothing in reply. So they ordered them to leave the Sanhedrin, and conferred with one another, saying, "What are we to do with these men? Everyone living in Jerusalem knows that a remarkable sign was done through them, and we cannot deny it. But so that it may not be spread any further among the people, let us give them a stern warning never again to speak to anyone in this name."

So they called them back and ordered them not to speak or teach at all in the name of Jesus. Peter and John, however, said to them in reply, "Whether it is right in the sight of God for us to obey you rather than God, you be the judges. It is impossible for us not to speak about what we have seen and heard." After threatening them further, they released them, finding no way to punish them, on account of the people who were all praising God for what had happened.

Responsorial Psalm
PSALM 118:1 and 14-15ab, 16-18, 19-21
R. I will give thanks to you, for you have answered me.
(or R. Alleluia.)

Give thanks to the LORD, for he is good,
for his mercy endures forever.
My strength and my courage is the LORD,
and he has been my savior.
The joyful shout of victory
in the tents of the just. **R.**
"The right hand of the LORD is exalted;
the right hand of the LORD has struck with power."
I shall not die, but live,
and declare the works of the LORD.
Though the LORD has indeed chastised me,
yet he has not delivered me to death. **R.**
Open to me the gates of justice;
I will enter them and give thanks to the LORD.
This is the gate of the LORD;
the just shall enter it.
I will give thanks to you, for you have answered me
and have been my savior. **R.**

Gospel
MARK 16:9-15

When Jesus had risen, early on the first day of the week, he appeared first to Mary Magdalene, out of whom he had driven seven demons. She went and told his companions who were mourning and weeping. When they heard that he was alive and had been seen by her, they did not believe.

After this he appeared in another form to two of them walking along on their way to the country. They returned and told the others; but they did not believe them either.

But later, as the Eleven were at table, he appeared to them and rebuked them for their unbelief and hardness of heart because they had not believed those who saw him after he had been raised. He said to them, "Go into the whole world and proclaim the Gospel to every creature."

Sunday, April 28

Second Sunday of Easter or Sunday of Divine Mercy

First Reading

ACTS 5:12-16

Many signs and wonders were done among the people at the hands of the apostles. They were all together in Solomon's portico. None of the others dared to join them, but the people esteemed them. Yet more than ever, believers in the Lord, great numbers of men and women, were added to them. Thus they even carried the sick out into the streets and laid them on cots and mats so that when Peter came by, at least his shadow might fall on one or another of them. A large number of people from the towns in the vicinity of Jerusalem also gathered, bringing the sick and those disturbed by unclean spirits, and they were all cured.

Responsorial Psalm

PSALM 118:2-4, 13-15, 22-24

R. Give thanks to the Lord for he is good, his love is everlasting. (or R. Alleluia.)

Let the house of Israel say,
"His mercy endures forever."
Let the house of Aaron say,
"His mercy endures forever."
Let those who fear the LORD say,
"His mercy endures forever." **R.**
I was hard pressed and was falling,
but the LORD helped me.
My strength and my courage is the LORD,
and he has been my savior.
The joyful shout of victory
in the tents of the just: **R.**
The stone which the builders rejected
has become the cornerstone.

By the LORD has this been done;
 it is wonderful in our eyes.
This is the day the LORD has made;
 let us be glad and rejoice in it. **R.**

Second Reading
REVELATION 1:9-11a, 12-13, 17-19

I, John, your brother, who share with you the distress, the kingdom, and the endurance we have in Jesus, found myself on the island called Patmos because I proclaimed God's word and gave testimony to Jesus. I was caught up in spirit on the Lord's day and heard behind me a voice as loud as a trumpet, which said, "Write on a scroll what you see." Then I turned to see whose voice it was that spoke to me, and when I turned, I saw seven gold lampstands and in the midst of the lampstands one like a son of man, wearing an ankle-length robe, with a gold sash around his chest.

When I caught sight of him, I fell down at his feet as though dead. He touched me with his right hand and said, "Do not be afraid. I am the first and the last, the one who lives. Once I was dead, but now I am alive forever and ever. I hold the keys to death and the netherworld. Write down, therefore, what you have seen, and what is happening, and what will happen afterwards."

Gospel
JOHN 20:19-31

On the evening of that first day of the week, when the doors were locked, where the disciples were, for fear of the Jews, Jesus came and stood in their midst and said to them, "Peace be with you." When he had said this, he showed them his hands and his side. The disciples rejoiced when they saw the Lord. Jesus said to them again, "Peace be with you. As the Father has sent me, so I send you." And when he had said this, he breathed on them and said to them, "Receive the Holy Spirit. Whose sins you forgive are forgiven them, and whose sins you retain are retained."

Thomas, called Didymus, one of the Twelve, was not with them when Jesus came. So the other disciples said to him, "We have seen the Lord." But he said to them, "Unless I see the mark of the nails in his hands and put my finger into the nailmarks and put my hand into his side, I will not believe."

Now a week later his disciples were again inside and Thomas was with them. Jesus came, although the doors were locked, and stood in their midst and said, "Peace be with you." Then he said to Thomas, "Put your finger here and see my hands, and bring your hand and put it into my side, and do not be unbelieving, but believe." Thomas answered and said to him, "My Lord and my God!" Jesus said to him, "Have you come to believe because you have seen me? Blessed are those who have not seen and have believed."

Now Jesus did many other signs in the presence of his disciples that are not written in this book. But these are written that you may come to believe that Jesus is the Christ, the Son of God, and that through this belief you may have life in his name.

Monday, April 29

First Reading

ACTS 4:23-31

After their release Peter and John went back to their own people and reported what the chief priests and elders had told them. And when they heard it, they raised their voices to God with one accord and said, "Sovereign Lord, maker of heaven and earth and the sea and all that is in them, you said by the Holy Spirit through the mouth of our father David, your servant:

Why did the Gentiles rage
and the peoples entertain folly?
The kings of the earth took their stand
and the princes gathered together
against the Lord and against his anointed.

Indeed they gathered in this city against your holy servant Jesus whom you anointed, Herod and Pontius Pilate, together with the Gentiles and the peoples of Israel, to do what your hand and your will had long ago planned to take place. And now, Lord, take note of their threats, and enable your servants to speak your word with all boldness, as you stretch forth your hand to heal, and signs and wonders are done through the name of your holy servant Jesus." As they prayed, the place where they were gathered shook, and they were all filled with the Holy Spirit and continued to speak the word of God with boldness.

Responsorial Psalm

PSALM 2:1-3, 4-7a, 7b-9

R. Blessed are all who take refuge in the Lord. (or R. Alleluia.)

Why do the nations rage
and the peoples utter folly?
The kings of the earth rise up,
and the princes conspire together
against the LORD and against his anointed:

"Let us break their fetters
  and cast their bonds from us!" **R.**
He who is throned in heaven laughs;
  the LORD derides them.
Then in anger he speaks to them;
  he terrifies them in his wrath:
"I myself have set up my king
  on Zion, my holy mountain."
I will proclaim the decree of the LORD. **R.**
The LORD said to me, "You are my Son;
  this day I have begotten you.
Ask of me and I will give you
  the nations for an inheritance
  and the ends of the earth for your possession.
You shall rule them with an iron rod;
  you shall shatter them like an earthen dish." **R.**

Gospel
JOHN 3:1-8

There was a Pharisee named Nicodemus, a ruler of the Jews. He came to Jesus at night and said to him, "Rabbi, we know that you are a teacher who has come from God, for no one can do these signs that you are doing unless God is with him." Jesus answered and said to him, "Amen, amen, I say to you, unless one is born from above, he cannot see the Kingdom of God." Nicodemus said to him, "How can a man once grown old be born again? Surely he cannot reenter his mother's womb and be born again, can he?" Jesus answered, "Amen, amen, I say to you, unless one is born of water and Spirit he cannot enter the Kingdom of God. What is born of flesh is flesh and what is born of spirit is spirit. Do not be amazed that I told you, 'You must be born from above.' The wind blows where it wills, and you can hear the sound it makes, but you do not know where it comes from or where it goes; so it is with everyone who is born of the Spirit."

Tuesday, April 30

First Reading
ACTS 4:32-37

The community of believers was of one heart and mind, and no one claimed that any of his possessions was his own, but they had everything in common. With great power the Apostles bore witness to the resurrection of the Lord Jesus, and great favor was accorded them all. There was no needy person among them, for those who owned property or houses would sell them, bring the proceeds of the sale, and put them at the feet of the Apostles, and they were distributed to each according to need.

Thus Joseph, also named by the Apostles Barnabas (which is translated "son of encouragement"), a Levite, a Cypriot by birth, sold a piece of property that he owned, then brought the money and put it at the feet of the Apostles.

Responsorial Psalm
PSALM 93:1ab, 1cd-2, 5
R. The Lord is king; he is robed in majesty. (or R. Alleluia.)

The LORD is king, in splendor robed;
robed is the LORD and girt about with strength. **R.**
And he has made the world firm,
not to be moved.
Your throne stands firm from of old;
from everlasting you are, O LORD. **R.**
Your decrees are worthy of trust indeed:
holiness befits your house,
O LORD, for length of days. **R.**

Gospel
JOHN 3:7b-15

Jesus said to Nicodemus: "'You must be born from above.' The wind blows where it wills, and you can hear the sound it makes, but you do not know where it comes from or where it goes; so it is with everyone who is born of the Spirit." Nicodemus answered and said to him, "How can this happen?" Jesus answered and said to him, "You are the teacher of Israel and you do not understand this? Amen, amen, I say to you, we speak of what we know and we testify to what we have seen, but you people do not accept our testimony. If I tell you about earthly things and you do not believe, how will you believe if I tell you about heavenly things? No one has gone up to heaven except the one who has come down from heaven, the Son of Man. And just as Moses lifted up the serpent in the desert, so must the Son of Man be lifted up, so that everyone who believes in him may have eternal life."

MAY

Wednesday, May 1

First Reading

ACTS 5:17-26 (or for the Memorial of St. Joseph the Worker: GENESIS 1:26–2:3 or COLOSSIANS 3:14-15, 17, 23-24)

The high priest rose up and all his companions, that is, the party of the Sadducees, and, filled with jealousy, laid hands upon the Apostles and put them in the public jail. But during the night, the angel of the Lord opened the doors of the prison, led them out, and said, "Go and take your place in the temple area, and tell the people everything about this life." When they heard this, they went to the temple early in the morning and taught. When the high priest and his companions arrived, they convened the Sanhedrin, the full senate of the children of Israel, and sent to the jail to have them brought in. But the court officers who went did not find them in the prison, so they came back and reported, "We found the jail securely locked and the guards stationed outside the doors, but when we opened them, we found no one inside." When the captain of the temple guard and the chief priests heard this report, they were at a loss about them, as to what this would come to. Then someone came in and reported to them, "The men whom you put in prison are in the temple area and are teaching the people." Then the captain and the court officers went and brought them, but without force, because they were afraid of being stoned by the people.

Responsorial Psalm

PSALM 34:2-3, 4-5, 6-7, 8-9 (or PSALM 90:2, 3-4, 12-13, 14 and 16)

R. The Lord hears the cry of the poor. (or R. Alleluia.)

I will bless the LORD at all times;
  his praise shall be ever in my mouth.
Let my soul glory in the LORD;
  the lowly will hear me and be glad. **R.**
Glorify the LORD with me,
  let us together extol his name.
I sought the LORD, and he answered me
  and delivered me from all my fears. **R.**
Look to him that you may be radiant with joy,
  and your faces may not blush with shame.
When the poor one called out, the LORD heard,
  and from all his distress he saved him. **R.**

The angel of the LORD encamps
    around those who fear him, and delivers them.
Taste and see how good the LORD is;
    blessed the man who takes refuge in him. **R.**

Gospel
JOHN 3:16-21 (or MATTHEW 13:54-58)
God so loved the world that he gave his only-begotten Son, so that everyone who believes in him might not perish but might have eternal life. For God did not send his Son into the world to condemn the world, but that the world might be saved through him. Whoever believes in him will not be condemned, but whoever does not believe has already been condemned, because he has not believed in the name of the only-begotten Son of God. And this is the verdict, that the light came into the world, but people preferred darkness to light, because their works were evil. For everyone who does wicked things hates the light and does not come toward the light, so that his works might not be exposed. But whoever lives the truth comes to the light, so that his works may be clearly seen as done in God.

Thursday, May 2

First Reading
ACTS 5:27-33
When the court officers had brought the Apostles in and made them stand before the Sanhedrin, the high priest questioned them, "We gave you strict orders did we not, to stop teaching in that name. Yet you have filled Jerusalem with your teaching and want to bring this man's blood upon us." But Peter and the Apostles said in reply, "We must obey God rather than men. The God of our ancestors raised Jesus, though you had him killed by hanging him on a tree. God exalted him at his right hand as leader and savior to grant Israel repentance and forgiveness of sins. We are witnesses of these things, as is the Holy Spirit whom God has given to those who obey him."

When they heard this, they became infuriated and wanted to put them to death.

Responsorial Psalm
PSALM 34:2 and 9, 17-18, 19-20
R. The Lord hears the cry of the poor. (or R. Alleluia.)
I will bless the LORD at all times;
    his praise shall be ever in my mouth.

Taste and see how good the LORD is;
  blessed the man who takes refuge in him. **R.**
The LORD confronts the evildoers,
  to destroy remembrance of them from the earth.
When the just cry out, the LORD hears them,
  and from all their distress he rescues them. **R.**
The LORD is close to the brokenhearted;
  and those who are crushed in spirit he saves.
Many are the troubles of the just man,
  but out of them all the LORD delivers him. **R.**

Gospel
JOHN 3:31-36

The one who comes from above is above all. The one who is of the earth is earthly and speaks of earthly things. But the one who comes from heaven is above all. He testifies to what he has seen and heard, but no one accepts his testimony. Whoever does accept his testimony certifies that God is trustworthy. For the one whom God sent speaks the words of God. He does not ration his gift of the Spirit. The Father loves the Son and has given everything over to him. Whoever believes in the Son has eternal life, but whoever disobeys the Son will not see life, but the wrath of God remains upon him.

Friday, May 3

Saints Philip and James, Apostles

First Reading
1 CORINTHIANS 15:1-8

I am reminding you, brothers and sisters, of the Gospel I preached to you, which you indeed received and in which you also stand. Through it you are also being saved, if you hold fast to the word I preached to you, unless you believed in vain. For I handed on to you as of first importance what I also received: that Christ died for our sins in accordance with the Scriptures; that he was buried; that he was raised on the third day in accordance with the Scriptures; that he appeared to Cephas, then to the Twelve. After that, he appeared to more than five hundred brothers and sisters at once, most of whom are still living, though some have fallen asleep. After that he appeared to James, then to all the Apostles. Last of all, as to one born abnormally, he appeared to me.

Responsorial Psalm
PSALM 19:2-3, 4-5
R. Their message goes out through all the earth.
(or R. Alleluia.)

The heavens declare the glory of God;
and the firmament proclaims his handiwork.
Day pours out the word to day;
and night to night imparts knowledge. **R.**
Not a word nor a discourse
whose voice is not heard;
Through all the earth their voice resounds,
and to the ends of the world, their message. **R.**

Gospel
JOHN 14:6-14

Jesus said to Thomas, "I am the way and the truth and the life. No one comes to the Father except through me. If you know me, then you will also know my Father. From now on you do know him and have seen him." Philip said to him, "Master, show us the Father, and that will be enough for us." Jesus said to him, "Have I been with you for so long a time and you still do not know me, Philip? Whoever has seen me has seen the Father. How can you say, 'Show us the Father'? Do you not believe that I am in the Father and the Father is in me? The words that I speak to you I do not speak on my own. The Father who dwells in me is doing his works. Believe me that I am in the Father and the Father is in me, or else, believe because of the works themselves. Amen, amen, I say to you, whoever believes in me will do the works that I do, and will do greater ones than these, because I am going to the Father. And whatever you ask in my name, I will do, so that the Father may be glorified in the Son. If you ask anything of me in my name, I will do it."

Saturday, May 4

First Reading
ACTS 6:1-7

As the number of disciples continued to grow, the Hellenists complained against the Hebrews because their widows were being neglected in the daily distribution. So the Twelve called together the community of the disciples and said, "It is not right for us to neglect the word of God to serve at table. Brothers, select from among you seven reputable men, filled with the Spirit and wisdom, whom we shall appoint to this task, whereas we shall devote ourselves to prayer and to the ministry of the word." The proposal was acceptable to the whole community, so they chose Stephen, a man filled with faith and the Holy Spirit, also Philip, Prochorus, Nicanor, Timon, Parmenas, and Nicholas of Antioch, a convert to Judaism. They presented these men to the Apostles who prayed and laid hands on them. The word of God continued to spread, and the number of the disciples in Jerusalem increased greatly; even a large group of priests were becoming obedient to the faith.

Responsorial Psalm

PSALM 33:1-2, 4-5, 18-19

R. Lord, let your mercy be on us, as we place our trust in you. (or R. Alleluia.)

Exult, you just, in the LORD;
praise from the upright is fitting.
Give thanks to the LORD on the harp;
with the ten-stringed lyre chant his praises. **R.**
Upright is the word of the LORD,
and all his works are trustworthy.
He loves justice and right;
of the kindness of the LORD the earth is full. **R.**
See, the eyes of the LORD are upon those who fear him,
upon those who hope for his kindness,
To deliver them from death
and preserve them in spite of famine. **R.**

Gospel

JOHN 6:16-21

When it was evening, the disciples of Jesus went down to the sea, embarked in a boat, and went across the sea to Capernaum. It had already grown dark, and Jesus had not yet come to them. The sea was stirred up because a strong wind was blowing. When they had rowed about three or four miles, they saw Jesus walking on the sea and coming near the boat, and they began to be afraid. But he said to them, "It is I. Do not be afraid." They wanted to take him into the boat, but the boat immediately arrived at the shore to which they were heading.

Sunday, May 5

Third Sunday of Easter

First Reading

ACTS 5:27-32, 40b-41

When the captain and the court officers had brought the apostles in and made them stand before the Sanhedrin, the high priest questioned them, "We gave you strict orders, did we not, to stop teaching in that name? Yet you have filled Jerusalem with your teaching and want to bring this man's blood upon us." But Peter and the apostles said in reply, "We must obey God rather than men. The God of our ancestors raised Jesus, though you had him killed by hanging him on a tree. God exalted him at his right hand as leader and savior to grant Israel repentance and forgiveness of sins. We are witnesses of these things, as is the Holy Spirit whom God has given to those who obey him."

The Sanhedrin ordered the apostles to stop speaking in the name of Jesus, and dismissed them. So they left the presence of the Sanhedrin, rejoicing that they had been found worthy to suffer dishonor for the sake of the name.

Responsorial Psalm

PSALM 30:2, 4, 5-6, 11-12, 13

R. I will praise you, Lord, for you have rescued me. (or R. Alleluia.)

I will extol you, O LORD, for you drew me clear
  and did not let my enemies rejoice over me.
O LORD, you brought me up from the netherworld;
  you preserved me from among those going down into the pit. **R.**
Sing praise to the LORD, you his faithful ones,
  and give thanks to his holy name.
For his anger lasts but a moment;
  a lifetime, his good will.
At nightfall, weeping enters in,
  but with the dawn, rejoicing. **R.**
Hear, O LORD, and have pity on me;
  O LORD, be my helper.
You changed my mourning into dancing;
  O LORD, my God, forever will I give you thanks. **R.**

Second Reading

REVELATION 5:11-14

I, John, looked and heard the voices of many angels who surrounded the throne and the living creatures and the elders. They were countless in number, and they cried out in a loud voice:

"Worthy is the Lamb that was slain
  to receive power and riches, wisdom and strength,
  honor and glory and blessing."

Then I heard every creature in heaven and on earth and under the earth and in the sea, everything in the universe, cry out:

"To the one who sits on the throne and to the Lamb
be blessing and honor, glory and might,
forever and ever."

The four living creatures answered, "Amen," and the elders fell down and worshiped.

Gospel
JOHN 21:1-19 (or JOHN 21:1-14)

At that time, Jesus revealed himself again to his disciples at the Sea of Tiberias. He revealed himself in this way. Together were Simon Peter, Thomas called Didymus, Nathanael from Cana in Galilee, Zebedee's sons, and two others of his disciples. Simon Peter said to them, "I am going fishing." They said to him, "We also will come with you." So they went out and got into the boat, but that night they caught nothing. When it was already dawn, Jesus was standing on the shore; but the disciples did not realize that it was Jesus. Jesus said to them, "Children, have you caught anything to eat?" They answered him, "No." So he said to them, "Cast the net over the right side of the boat and you will find something." So they cast it, and were not able to pull it in because of the number of fish. So the disciple whom Jesus loved said to Peter, "It is the Lord." When Simon Peter heard that it was the Lord, he tucked in his garment, for he was lightly clad, and jumped into the sea. The other disciples came in the boat, for they were not far from shore, only about a hundred yards, dragging the net with the fish. When they climbed out on shore, they saw a charcoal fire with fish on it and bread. Jesus said to them, "Bring some of the fish you just caught." So Simon Peter went over and dragged the net ashore full of one hundred fifty-three large fish. Even though there were so many, the net was not torn. Jesus said to them, "Come, have breakfast." And none of the disciples dared to ask him, "Who are you?" because they realized it was the Lord. Jesus came over and took the bread and gave it to them, and in like manner the fish. This was now the third time Jesus was revealed to his disciples after being raised from the dead.

When they had finished breakfast, Jesus said to Simon Peter, "Simon, son of John, do you love me more than these?" Simon Peter answered him, "Yes, Lord, you know that I love you." Jesus said to him, "Feed my lambs." He then said to Simon Peter a second time, "Simon, son of John, do you love me?" Simon Peter answered him, "Yes, Lord, you know that I love you." Jesus said to him, "Tend my sheep." Jesus said to him the third time, "Simon, son of John, do you love me?" Peter was distressed that Jesus had said to him a third time, "Do you love me?" and he said to him, "Lord, you know everything; you know that I love you." Jesus said to him, "Feed my sheep. Amen, amen, I say to you, when you were younger, you used to dress yourself and go where you wanted; but when you grow old, you will stretch out your hands, and someone else will dress you and lead you where you do not want to go." He said this signifying by what kind of death he would glorify God. And when he had said this, he said to him, "Follow me."

Monday, May 6

First Reading

ACTS 6:8-15

Stephen, filled with grace and power, was working great wonders and signs among the people. Certain members of the so-called Synagogue of Freedmen, Cyreneans, and Alexandrians, and people from Cilicia and Asia, came forward and debated with Stephen, but they could not withstand the wisdom and the Spirit with which he spoke. Then they instigated some men to say, "We have heard him speaking blasphemous words against Moses and God." They stirred up the people, the elders, and the scribes, accosted him, seized him, and brought him before the Sanhedrin. They presented false witnesses who testified, "This man never stops saying things against this holy place and the law. For we have heard him claim that this Jesus the Nazorean will destroy this place and change the customs that Moses handed down to us." All those who sat in the Sanhedrin looked intently at him and saw that his face was like the face of an angel.

Responsorial Psalm

PSALM 119:23-24, 26-27, 29-30

R. Blessed are they who follow the law of the Lord!
(or R. Alleluia.)

Though princes meet and talk against me,
your servant meditates on your statutes.
Yes, your decrees are my delight;
they are my counselors. **R.**
I declared my ways, and you answered me;
teach me your statutes.
Make me understand the way of your precepts,
and I will meditate on your wondrous deeds. **R.**
Remove from me the way of falsehood,
and favor me with your law.
The way of truth I have chosen;
I have set your ordinances before me. **R.**

Gospel
JOHN 6:22-29

[After Jesus had fed the five thousand men, his disciples saw him walking on the sea.] The next day, the crowd that remained across the sea saw that there had been only one boat there, and that Jesus had not gone along with his disciples in the boat, but only his disciples had left. Other boats came from Tiberias near the place where they had eaten the bread when the Lord gave thanks. When the crowd saw that neither Jesus nor his disciples were there, they themselves got into boats and came to Capernaum looking for Jesus. And when they found him across the sea they said to him, "Rabbi, when did you get here?" Jesus answered them and said, "Amen, amen, I say to you, you are looking for me not because you saw signs but because you ate the loaves and were filled. Do not work for food that perishes but for the food that endures for eternal life, which the Son of Man will give you. For on him the Father, God, has set his seal." So they said to him, "What can we do to accomplish the works of God?" Jesus answered and said to them, "This is the work of God, that you believe in the one he sent."

Tuesday, May 7

First Reading
ACTS 7:51–8:1a

Stephen said to the people, the elders, and the scribes: "You stiff-necked people, uncircumcised in heart and ears, you always oppose the Holy Spirit; you are just like your ancestors. Which of the prophets did your ancestors not persecute? They put to death those who foretold the coming of the righteous one, whose betrayers and murderers you have now become. You received the law as transmitted by angels, but you did not observe it."

When they heard this, they were infuriated, and they ground their teeth at him. But Stephen, filled with the Holy Spirit, looked up intently to heaven and saw the glory of God and Jesus standing at the right hand of God, and Stephen said, "Behold, I see the heavens opened and the Son of Man standing at the right hand of God." But they cried out in a loud voice, covered their ears, and rushed upon him together. They threw him out of the city, and began to stone him. The witnesses laid down their cloaks at the feet of a young man named Saul. As they were stoning Stephen, he called out, "Lord Jesus, receive my spirit." Then he fell to his knees and cried out in a loud voice, "Lord, do not hold this sin against them"; and when he said this, he fell asleep.

Now Saul was consenting to his execution.

Responsorial Psalm
PSALM 31:3cd-4, 6 and 7b and 8a, 17 and 21ab
R. Into your hands, O Lord, I commend my spirit.
(or R. Alleluia.)

Be my rock of refuge,
 a stronghold to give me safety.
You are my rock and my fortress;
 for your name's sake you will lead and guide me. **R.**
Into your hands I commend my spirit;
 you will redeem me, O LORD, O faithful God.
My trust is in the LORD;
 I will rejoice and be glad of your mercy. **R.**
Let your face shine upon your servant;
 save me in your kindness.
You hide them in the shelter of your presence
 from the plottings of men. **R.**

Gospel
JOHN 6:30-35

The crowd said to Jesus: "What sign can you do, that we may see and believe in you? What can you do? Our ancestors ate manna in the desert, as it is written:

He gave them bread from heaven to eat."

So Jesus said to them, "Amen, amen, I say to you, it was not Moses who gave the bread from heaven; my Father gives you the true bread from heaven. For the bread of God is that which comes down from heaven and gives life to the world."

So they said to Jesus, "Sir, give us this bread always." Jesus said to them, "I am the bread of life; whoever comes to me will never hunger, and whoever believes in me will never thirst."

Wednesday, May 8

First Reading
ACTS 8:1b-8

There broke out a severe persecution of the Church in Jerusalem, and all were scattered throughout the countryside of Judea and Samaria, except the Apostles. Devout men buried Stephen and made a loud lament over him. Saul, meanwhile, was trying to destroy the Church; entering house after house and dragging out men and women, he handed them over for imprisonment.

Now those who had been scattered went about preaching the word. Thus Philip went down to the city of Samaria and proclaimed the Christ to them. With one accord, the crowds paid attention to what was said by Philip when they heard it and saw the signs he was doing. For unclean spirits, crying out in a loud voice, came out of many possessed people, and many paralyzed and crippled people were cured. There was great joy in that city.

Responsorial Psalm

PSALM 66:1-3a, 4-5, 6-7a

R. Let all the earth cry out to God with joy. (or R. Alleluia.)

Shout joyfully to God, all the earth,
 sing praise to the glory of his name;
 proclaim his glorious praise.
Say to God, "How tremendous are your deeds!" **R.**
"Let all on earth worship and sing praise to you,
 sing praise to your name!"
Come and see the works of God,
 his tremendous deeds among the children of Adam. **R.**
He has changed the sea into dry land;
 through the river they passed on foot;
 therefore let us rejoice in him.
He rules by his might forever. **R.**

Gospel

JOHN 6:35-40

Jesus said to the crowds, "I am the bread of life; whoever comes to me will never hunger, and whoever believes in me will never thirst. But I told you that although you have seen me, you do not believe. Everything that the Father gives me will come to me, and I will not reject anyone who comes to me, because I came down from heaven not to do my own will but the will of the one who sent me. And this is the will of the one who sent me, that I should not lose anything of what he gave me, but that I should raise it on the last day. For this is the will of my Father, that everyone who sees the Son and believes in him may have eternal life, and I shall raise him on the last day."

Thursday, May 9

First Reading

ACTS 8:26-40

The angel of the Lord spoke to Philip, "Get up and head south on the road that goes down from Jerusalem to Gaza, the desert route." So he got up and set out. Now there was an Ethiopian eunuch, a court official of the Candace, that is, the queen of the Ethiopians, in charge of her entire treasury, who had come to Jerusalem to worship, and was returning home. Seated in his chariot, he was reading the prophet Isaiah. The Spirit said to Philip, "Go and join up with that chariot." Philip ran up and heard him reading Isaiah the prophet and said, "Do you understand what you are reading?" He replied, "How can I, unless someone instructs me?" So he invited Philip to get in and sit with him. This was the Scripture passage he was reading:

Like a sheep he was led to the slaughter,
and as a lamb before its shearer is silent,
so he opened not his mouth.
In his humiliation justice was denied him.
Who will tell of his posterity?
For his life is taken from the earth.

Then the eunuch said to Philip in reply, "I beg you, about whom is the prophet saying this? About himself, or about someone else?" Then Philip opened his mouth and, beginning with this Scripture passage, he proclaimed Jesus to him. As they traveled along the road they came to some water, and the eunuch said, "Look, there is water. What is to prevent my being baptized?" Then he ordered the chariot to stop, and Philip and the eunuch both went down into the water, and he baptized him. When they came out of the water, the Spirit of the Lord snatched Philip away, and the eunuch saw him no more, but continued on his way rejoicing. Philip came to Azotus, and went about proclaiming the good news to all the towns until he reached Caesarea.

Responsorial Psalm
PSALM 66:8-9, 16-17, 20
R. Let all the earth cry out to God with joy. (or R. Alleluia.)

Bless our God, you peoples,
loudly sound his praise;
He has given life to our souls,
and has not let our feet slip. **R.**
Hear now, all you who fear God, while I declare
what he has done for me.
When I appealed to him in words,
praise was on the tip of my tongue. **R.**
Blessed be God who refused me not
my prayer or his kindness! **R.**

Gospel
JOHN 6:44-51

Jesus said to the crowds: "No one can come to me unless the Father who sent me draw him, and I will raise him on the last day. It is written in the prophets:

They shall all be taught by God.

Everyone who listens to my Father and learns from him comes to me. Not that anyone has seen the Father except the one who is from God; he has seen the Father. Amen, amen, I say to you, whoever believes has eternal life. I am the bread of life. Your ancestors ate the manna in the desert, but they died; this is the bread that comes down from heaven so that one may eat it and not die. I am the living bread that came down from heaven; whoever eats this bread will live forever; and the bread that I will give is my Flesh for the life of the world."

Friday, May 10

First Reading
ACTS 9:1-20

Saul, still breathing murderous threats against the disciples of the Lord, went to the high priest and asked him for letters to the synagogues in Damascus, that, if he should find any men or women who belonged to the Way, he might bring them back to Jerusalem in chains. On his journey, as he was nearing Damascus, a light from the sky suddenly flashed around him. He fell to the ground and heard a voice saying to him, "Saul, Saul, why are you persecuting me?" He said, "Who are you, sir?" The reply came, "I am Jesus, whom you are persecuting. Now get up and go into the city and you will be told what you must do." The men who were traveling with him stood speechless, for they heard the voice but could see no one. Saul got up from the ground, but when he opened his eyes he could see nothing; so they led him by the hand and brought him to Damascus. For three days he was unable to see, and he neither ate nor drank.

There was a disciple in Damascus named Ananias, and the Lord said to him in a vision, "Ananias." He answered, "Here I am, Lord." The Lord said to him, "Get up and go to the street called Straight and ask at the house of Judas for a man from Tarsus named Saul. He is there praying, and in a vision he has seen a man named Ananias come in and lay his hands on him, that he may regain his sight." But Ananias replied, "Lord, I have heard from many sources about this man, what evil things he has done to your holy ones in Jerusalem. And here he has authority from the chief priests to imprison all who call upon your name." But the Lord said to him, "Go, for this man is a chosen instrument of mine to carry my name before Gentiles, kings, and children of Israel, and I will show him what he will have to suffer for my name." So Ananias went and entered the house; laying his hands on him, he said, "Saul, my brother, the Lord has sent me, Jesus who appeared to you on the way by which you came, that you may regain your sight and be filled with the Holy Spirit." Immediately things like scales fell from his eyes and he regained his sight. He got up and was baptized, and when he had eaten, he recovered his strength.

He stayed some days with the disciples in Damascus, and he began at once to proclaim Jesus in the synagogues, that he is the Son of God.

Responsorial Psalm
PSALM 117:1bc, 2
R. Go out to all the world and tell the Good News.
(or R. Alleluia.)

Praise the LORD, all you nations;
glorify him, all you peoples! **R.**
For steadfast is his kindness toward us,
and the fidelity of the LORD endures forever. **R.**

Gospel
JOHN 6:52-59

The Jews quarreled among themselves, saying, "How can this man give us his Flesh to eat?" Jesus said to them, "Amen, amen, I say to you, unless you eat the Flesh of the Son of Man and drink his Blood, you do not have life within you. Whoever eats my Flesh and drinks my Blood has eternal life, and I will raise him on the last day. For my Flesh is true food, and my Blood is true drink. Whoever eats my Flesh and drinks my Blood remains in me and I in him. Just as the living Father sent me and I have life because of the Father, so also the one who feeds on me will have life because of me. This is the bread that came down from heaven. Unlike your ancestors who ate and still died, whoever eats this bread will live forever." These things he said while teaching in the synagogue in Capernaum.

Saturday, May 11

First Reading
ACTS 9:31-42

The Church throughout all Judea, Galilee, and Samaria was at peace. She was being built up and walked in the fear of the Lord, and with the consolation of the Holy Spirit she grew in numbers.

As Peter was passing through every region, he went down to the holy ones living in Lydda. There he found a man named Aeneas, who had been confined to bed for eight years, for he was paralyzed. Peter said to him, "Aeneas, Jesus Christ heals you. Get up and make your bed." He got up at once. And all the inhabitants of Lydda and Sharon saw him, and they turned to the Lord.

Now in Joppa there was a disciple named Tabitha (which translated is Dorcas). She was completely occupied with good deeds and almsgiving. Now during those days she fell sick and died, so after washing her, they laid her out in a room upstairs. Since Lydda was near Joppa, the disciples, hearing that Peter was there, sent two men to him with the request, "Please come to us without delay." So Peter got up and went with them. When he arrived, they took him to the room upstairs where all the widows came to him weeping and showing him the tunics and cloaks that Dorcas had made while she was with them. Peter sent them all out and knelt down and prayed. Then he turned to her body and said, "Tabitha, rise up." She opened her eyes, saw Peter, and sat up. He gave her his hand and raised her up, and when he had called the holy ones and the widows, he presented her alive. This became known all over Joppa, and many came to believe in the Lord.

Responsorial Psalm
PSALM 116:12-13, 14-15, 16-17
R. How shall I make a return to the Lord for all the good he has done for me? (or R. Alleluia.)

How shall I make a return to the LORD
for all the good he has done for me?
The cup of salvation I will take up,
and I will call upon the name of the LORD. **R.**
My vows to the LORD I will pay
in the presence of all his people.
Precious in the eyes of the LORD
is the death of his faithful ones. **R.**
O LORD, I am your servant;
I am your servant, the son of your handmaid;
you have loosed my bonds.
To you will I offer sacrifice of thanksgiving,
and I will call upon the name of the LORD. **R.**

Gospel
JOHN 6:60-69

Many of the disciples of Jesus who were listening said, "This saying is hard; who can accept it?" Since Jesus knew that his disciples were murmuring about this, he said to them, "Does this shock you? What if you were to see the Son of Man ascending to where he was before? It is the Spirit that gives life, while the flesh is of no avail. The words I have spoken to you are Spirit and life. But there are some of you who do not believe." Jesus knew from the beginning the ones who would not believe and the one who would betray him. And he said, "For this reason I have told you that no one can come to me unless it is granted him by my Father."

As a result of this, many of his disciples returned to their former way of life and no longer walked with him. Jesus then said to the Twelve, "Do you also want to leave?" Simon Peter answered him, "Master, to whom shall we go? You have the words of eternal life. We have come to believe and are convinced that you are the Holy One of God."

Sunday, May 12

Fourth Sunday of Easter

First Reading
ACTS 13:14, 43-52

Paul and Barnabas continued on from Perga and reached Antioch in Pisidia. On the sabbath they entered the synagogue and took their seats. Many Jews and worshipers who were converts to Judaism followed Paul and Barnabas, who spoke to them and urged them to remain faithful to the grace of God.

On the following sabbath almost the whole city gathered to hear the word of the Lord. When the Jews saw the crowds, they were filled with jealousy and with violent abuse contradicted what Paul said. Both Paul and Barnabas spoke out boldly and said, "It was necessary that the word of God be spoken to you first, but since you reject it and condemn yourselves as unworthy of eternal life, we now turn to the Gentiles. For so the Lord has commanded us,

I have made you a light to the Gentiles,
that you may be an instrument of salvation
to the ends of the earth."

The Gentiles were delighted when they heard this and glorified the word of the Lord. All who were destined for eternal life came to believe, and the word of the Lord continued to spread through the whole region. The Jews, however, incited the women of prominence who were worshipers and the leading men of the city, stirred up a persecution against Paul and Barnabas, and expelled them from their territory. So they shook the dust from their feet in protest against them, and went to Iconium. The disciples were filled with joy and the Holy Spirit.

Responsorial Psalm
PSALM 100:1-2, 3, 5
R. We are his people, the sheep of his flock. (or R. Alleluia.)

Sing joyfully to the LORD, all you lands;
serve the LORD with gladness;
come before him with joyful song. **R.**
Know that the LORD is God;
he made us, his we are;
his people, the flock he tends. **R.**
The LORD is good:
his kindness endures forever,
and his faithfulness, to all generations. **R.**

Second Reading
REVELATION 7:9, 14b-17

I, John, had a vision of a great multitude, which no one could count, from every nation, race, people, and tongue. They stood before the throne and before the Lamb, wearing white robes and holding palm branches in their hands.

Then one of the elders said to me, "These are the ones who have survived the time of great distress; they have washed their robes and made them white in the blood of the Lamb.

"For this reason they stand before God's throne
and worship him day and night in his temple.
The one who sits on the throne will shelter them.
They will not hunger or thirst anymore,
nor will the sun or any heat strike them.
For the Lamb who is in the center of the throne
will shepherd them
and lead them to springs of life-giving water,
and God will wipe away every tear from their eyes."

Gospel
JOHN 10:27-30

Jesus said: "My sheep hear my voice; I know them, and they follow me. I give them eternal life, and they shall never perish. No one can take them out of my hand. My Father, who has given them to me, is greater than all, and no one can take them out of the Father's hand. The Father and I are one."

Monday, May 13

First Reading

ACTS 11:1-18

The Apostles and the brothers who were in Judea heard that the Gentiles too had accepted the word of God. So when Peter went up to Jerusalem the circumcised believers confronted him, saying, "You entered the house of uncircumcised people and ate with them." Peter began and explained it to them step by step, saying, "I was at prayer in the city of Joppa when in a trance I had a vision, something resembling a large sheet coming down, lowered from the sky by its four corners, and it came to me. Looking intently into it, I observed and saw the four-legged animals of the earth, the wild beasts, the reptiles, and the birds of the sky. I also heard a voice say to me, 'Get up, Peter. Slaughter and eat.' But I said, 'Certainly not, sir, because nothing profane or unclean has ever entered my mouth.' But a second time a voice from heaven answered, 'What God has made clean, you are not to call profane.' This happened three times, and then everything was drawn up again into the sky. Just then three men appeared at the house where we were, who had been sent to me from Caesarea. The Spirit told me to accompany them without discriminating. These six brothers also went with me, and we entered the man's house. He related to us how he had seen the angel standing in his house, saying, 'Send someone to Joppa and summon Simon, who is called Peter, who will speak words to you by which you and all your household will be saved.' As I began to speak, the Holy Spirit fell upon them as it had upon us at the beginning, and I remembered the word of the Lord, how he had said, 'John baptized with water but you will be baptized with the Holy Spirit.' If then God gave them the same gift he gave to us when we came to believe in the Lord Jesus Christ, who was I to be able to hinder God?" When they heard this, they stopped objecting and glorified God, saying, "God has then granted life-giving repentance to the Gentiles too."

Responsorial Psalm

PSALM 42:2-3; 43:3, 4

R. Athirst is my soul for the living God. (or R. Alleluia.)

As the hind longs for the running waters,
  so my soul longs for you, O God.
Athirst is my soul for God, the living God.
  When shall I go and behold the face of God? **R.**
Send forth your light and your fidelity;
  they shall lead me on
And bring me to your holy mountain,
  to your dwelling-place. **R.**

Then will I go in to the altar of God,
the God of my gladness and joy;
Then will I give you thanks upon the harp,
O God, my God! **R.**

Gospel

JOHN 10:1-10

Jesus said: "Amen, amen, I say to you, whoever does not enter a sheepfold through the gate but climbs over elsewhere is a thief and a robber. But whoever enters through the gate is the shepherd of the sheep. The gatekeeper opens it for him, and the sheep hear his voice, as he calls his own sheep by name and leads them out. When he has driven out all his own, he walks ahead of them, and the sheep follow him, because they recognize his voice. But they will not follow a stranger; they will run away from him, because they do not recognize the voice of strangers." Although Jesus used this figure of speech, they did not realize what he was trying to tell them.

So Jesus said again, "Amen, amen, I say to you, I am the gate for the sheep. All who came before me are thieves and robbers, but the sheep did not listen to them. I am the gate. Whoever enters through me will be saved, and will come in and go out and find pasture. A thief comes only to steal and slaughter and destroy; I came so that they might have life and have it more abundantly."

Tuesday, May 14

Saint Matthias, Apostle

First Reading

ACTS 1:15-17, 20-26

Peter stood up in the midst of the brothers and sisters (there was a group of about one hundred and twenty persons in the one place). He said, "My brothers and sisters, the Scripture had to be fulfilled which the Holy Spirit spoke beforehand through the mouth of David, concerning Judas, who was the guide for those who arrested Jesus. Judas was numbered among us and was allotted a share in this ministry. For it is written in the Book of Psalms:

Let his encampment become desolate,
and may no one dwell in it.

and:

May another take his office.

Therefore, it is necessary that one of the men who accompanied us the whole time the Lord Jesus came and went among us, beginning from the baptism of John until the day on which he was taken up from us, become with us a witness to his resurrection." So they proposed two, Joseph called Barsabbas, who was also known as Justus, and Matthias. Then they prayed, "You, Lord, who know the hearts of all, show which one of these two you have chosen to take the place in this apostolic ministry from which Judas turned away to go to his own place." Then they gave lots to them, and the lot fell upon Matthias, and he was counted with the Eleven Apostles.

Responsorial Psalm
PSALM 113:1-2, 3-4, 5-6, 7-8
R. The Lord will give him a seat with the leaders of his people.
(or R. Alleluia.)

Praise, you servants of the LORD,
praise the name of the LORD.
Blessed be the name of the LORD
both now and forever. **R.**
From the rising to the setting of the sun
is the name of the LORD to be praised.
High above all nations is the LORD;
above the heavens is his glory. **R.**
Who is like the LORD, our God, who is enthroned on high
and looks upon the heavens and the earth below? **R.**
He raises up the lowly from the dust;
from the dunghill he lifts up the poor
To seat them with princes,
with the princes of his own people. **R.**

Gospel
JOHN 15:9-17

Jesus said to his disciples: "As the Father loves me, so I also love you. Remain in my love. If you keep my commandments, you will remain in my love, just as I have kept my Father's commandments and remain in his love.

"I have told you this so that my joy might be in you and your joy might be complete. This is my commandment: love one another as I love you. No one has greater love than this, to lay down one's life for one's friends. You are my friends if you do what I command you. I no longer call you slaves, because a slave does not know what his master is doing. I have called you friends, because I have told you everything I have heard from my Father. It was not you who chose me, but I who chose you and appointed you to go and bear fruit that will remain, so that whatever you ask the Father in my name he may give you. This I command you: love one another."

Wednesday, May 15

First Reading

ACTS 12:24–13:5a

The word of God continued to spread and grow.

After Barnabas and Saul completed their relief mission, they returned to Jerusalem, taking with them John, who is called Mark.

Now there were in the Church at Antioch prophets and teachers: Barnabas, Symeon who was called Niger, Lucius of Cyrene, Manaen who was a close friend of Herod the tetrarch, and Saul. While they were worshiping the Lord and fasting, the Holy Spirit said, "Set apart for me Barnabas and Saul for the work to which I have called them." Then, completing their fasting and prayer, they laid hands on them and sent them off.

So they, sent forth by the Holy Spirit, went down to Seleucia and from there sailed to Cyprus. When they arrived in Salamis, they proclaimed the word of God in the Jewish synagogues.

Responsorial Psalm

PSALM 67:2-3, 5, 6 and 8

R. O God, let all the nations praise you! (or R. Alleluia.)

May God have pity on us and bless us;
  may he let his face shine upon us.
So may your way be known upon earth;
  among all nations, your salvation. **R.**
May the nations be glad and exult
  because you rule the peoples in equity;
  the nations on the earth you guide. **R.**
May the peoples praise you, O God;
  may all the peoples praise you!
May God bless us,
  and may all the ends of the earth fear him! **R.**

Gospel

JOHN 12:44-50

Jesus cried out and said, "Whoever believes in me believes not only in me but also in the one who sent me, and whoever sees me sees the one who sent me. I came into the world as light, so that everyone who believes in me might not remain in darkness. And if anyone hears my words and does not observe them, I do not condemn him, for I did not come to condemn the world but to save the world. Whoever rejects me and does not accept my words has something to judge him: the word that I spoke, it will condemn him on the last day, because I did not speak on my own, but the Father who sent me commanded me what to say and speak. And I know that his commandment is eternal life. So what I say, I say as the Father told me."

Thursday, May 16

First Reading

ACTS 13:13-25

From Paphos, Paul and his companions set sail and arrived at Perga in Pamphylia. But John left them and returned to Jerusalem. They continued on from Perga and reached Antioch in Pisidia. On the sabbath they entered into the synagogue and took their seats. After the reading of the law and the prophets, the synagogue officials sent word to them, "My brothers, if one of you has a word of exhortation for the people, please speak."

So Paul got up, motioned with his hand, and said, "Fellow children of Israel and you others who are God-fearing, listen. The God of this people Israel chose our ancestors and exalted the people during their sojourn in the land of Egypt. With uplifted arm he led them out, and for about forty years he put up with them in the desert. When he had destroyed seven nations in the land of Canaan, he gave them their land as an inheritance at the end of about four hundred and fifty years. After these things he provided judges up to Samuel the prophet. Then they asked for a king. God gave them Saul, son of Kish, a man from the tribe of Benjamin, for forty years. Then he removed him and raised up David as their king; of him he testified, *I have found David, son of Jesse, a man after my own heart; he will carry out my every wish.* From this man's descendants God, according to his promise, has brought to Israel a savior, Jesus. John heralded his coming by proclaiming a baptism of repentance to all the people of Israel; and as John was completing his course, he would say, 'What do you suppose that I am? I am not he. Behold, one is coming after me; I am not worthy to unfasten the sandals of his feet.'"

Responsorial Psalm

PSALM 89:2-3, 21-22, 25 and 27

R. For ever I will sing the goodness of the Lord.

(or R. Alleluia.)

The favors of the LORD I will sing forever;
through all generations my mouth shall proclaim your faithfulness.
For you have said, "My kindness is established forever";
in heaven you have confirmed your faithfulness. **R.**
"I have found David, my servant;
with my holy oil I have anointed him,
That my hand may be always with him,
and that my arm may make him strong." **R.**
"My faithfulness and my mercy shall be with him,
and through my name shall his horn be exalted.
He shall say of me, 'You are my father,
my God, the Rock, my savior.'" **R.**

Gospel

JOHN 13:16-20

When Jesus had washed the disciples' feet, he said to them: "Amen, amen, I say to you, no slave is greater than his master nor any messenger greater than the one who sent him. If you understand this, blessed are you if you do it. I am not speaking of all of you. I know those whom I have chosen. But so that the Scripture might be fulfilled, *The one who ate my food has raised his heel against me.* From now on I am telling you before it happens, so that when it happens you may believe that I AM. Amen, amen, I say to you, whoever receives the one I send receives me, and whoever receives me receives the one who sent me."

Friday, May 17

First Reading

ACTS 13:26-33

When Paul came to Antioch in Pisidia, he said in the synagogue: "My brothers, children of the family of Abraham, and those others among you who are God-fearing, to us this word of salvation has been sent. The inhabitants of Jerusalem and their leaders failed to recognize him, and by condemning him they fulfilled the oracles of the prophets that are read sabbath after sabbath. For even though they found no grounds for a death sentence, they asked Pilate to have him put to death, and when they had accomplished all that was written about him, they took him down from the tree and placed him in a tomb. But God raised him from the dead, and for many days he appeared to those who had come up with him from Galilee to Jerusalem. These are now his witnesses before the people. We ourselves are proclaiming this good news to you that what God promised our fathers he has brought to fulfillment for us, their children, by raising up Jesus, as it is written in the second psalm, *You are my Son; this day I have begotten you.*"

Responsorial Psalm
PSALM 2:6-7, 8-9, 10-11ab
R. You are my Son; this day I have begotten you.
(or R. Alleluia.)

"I myself have set up my king
 on Zion, my holy mountain."
I will proclaim the decree of the LORD:
 The LORD said to me, "You are my Son;
 this day I have begotten you." **R.**
"Ask of me and I will give you
 the nations for an inheritance
 and the ends of the earth for your possession.
You shall rule them with an iron rod;
 you shall shatter them like an earthen dish." **R.**
And now, O kings, give heed;
 take warning, you rulers of the earth.
Serve the LORD with fear, and rejoice before him;
 with trembling rejoice. **R.**

Gospel
JOHN 14:1-6

Jesus said to his disciples: "Do not let your hearts be troubled. You have faith in God; have faith also in me. In my Father's house there are many dwelling places. If there were not, would I have told you that I am going to prepare a place for you? And if I go and prepare a place for you, I will come back again and take you to myself, so that where I am you also may be. Where I am going you know the way." Thomas said to him, "Master, we do not know where you are going; how can we know the way?" Jesus said to him, "I am the way and the truth and the life. No one comes to the Father except through me."

Saturday, May 18

First Reading
ACTS 13:44-52

On the following sabbath almost the whole city gathered to hear the word of the Lord. When the Jews saw the crowds, they were filled with jealousy and with violent abuse contradicted what Paul said. Both Paul and Barnabas spoke out boldly and said, "It was necessary that the word of God be spoken to you first, but since you reject it and condemn yourselves as unworthy of eternal life, we now turn to the Gentiles. For so the Lord has commanded us, *I have made you a light to the Gentiles, that you may be an instrument of salvation to the ends of the earth.*"

The Gentiles were delighted when they heard this and glorified the word of the Lord. All who were destined for eternal life came to believe, and the word of the Lord continued to spread through the whole region. The Jews, however, incited the women of prominence who were worshipers and the leading men of the city, stirred up a persecution against Paul and Barnabas, and expelled them from their territory. So they shook the dust from their feet in protest against them and went to Iconium. The disciples were filled with joy and the Holy Spirit.

Responsorial Psalm
PSALM 98:1, 2-3ab, 3cd-4
R. All the ends of the earth have seen the saving power of God. (or R. Alleluia.)

Sing to the LORD a new song,
for he has done wondrous deeds;
His right hand has won victory for him,
his holy arm. **R.**
The LORD has made his salvation known:
in the sight of the nations he has revealed his justice.
He has remembered his kindness and his faithfulness
toward the house of Israel. **R.**
All the ends of the earth have seen
the salvation by our God.
Sing joyfully to the LORD, all you lands;
break into song; sing praise. **R.**

Gospel
JOHN 14:7-14

Jesus said to his disciples: "If you know me, then you will also know my Father. From now on you do know him and have seen him." Philip said to Jesus, "Master, show us the Father, and that will be enough for us." Jesus said to him, "Have I been with you for so long a time and you still do not know me, Philip? Whoever has seen me has seen the Father. How can you say, 'Show us the Father'? Do you not believe that I am in the Father and the Father is in me? The words that I speak to you I do not speak on my own. The Father who dwells in me is doing his works. Believe me that I am in the Father and the Father is in me, or else, believe because of the works themselves. Amen, amen, I say to you, whoever believes in me will do the works that I do, and will do greater ones than these, because I am going to the Father. And whatever you ask in my name, I will do, so that the Father may be glorified in the Son. If you ask anything of me in my name, I will do it."

Sunday, May 19

Fifth Sunday of Easter

First Reading

ACTS 14:21-27

After Paul and Barnabas had proclaimed the good news to that city and made a considerable number of disciples, they returned to Lystra and to Iconium and to Antioch. They strengthened the spirits of the disciples and exhorted them to persevere in the faith, saying, "It is necessary for us to undergo many hardships to enter the kingdom of God." They appointed elders for them in each church and, with prayer and fasting, commended them to the Lord in whom they had put their faith. Then they traveled through Pisidia and reached Pamphylia. After proclaiming the word at Perga they went down to Attalia. From there they sailed to Antioch, where they had been commended to the grace of God for the work they had now accomplished. And when they arrived, they called the church together and reported what God had done with them and how he had opened the door of faith to the Gentiles.

Responsorial Psalm

PSALM 145:8-9, 10-11, 12-13

R. I will praise your name for ever, my king and my God. (or R. Alleluia.)

The LORD is gracious and merciful,
 slow to anger and of great kindness.
The LORD is good to all
 and compassionate toward all his works. **R.**
Let all your works give you thanks, O LORD,
 and let your faithful ones bless you.
Let them discourse of the glory of your kingdom
 and speak of your might. **R.**
Let them make known your might to the children of Adam,
 and the glorious splendor of your kingdom.
Your kingdom is a kingdom for all ages,
 and your dominion endures through all generations. **R.**

Second Reading
REVELATION 21:1-5a

Then I, John, saw a new heaven and a new earth. The former heaven and the former earth had passed away, and the sea was no more. I also saw the holy city, a new Jerusalem, coming down out of heaven from God, prepared as a bride adorned for her husband. I heard a loud voice from the throne saying, “Behold, God’s dwelling is with the human race. He will dwell with them and they will be his people and God himself will always be with them as their God. He will wipe every tear from their eyes, and there shall be no more death or mourning, wailing or pain, for the old order has passed away.”

The One who sat on the throne said, “Behold, I make all things new.”

Gospel
JOHN 13:31-33a, 34-35

When Judas had left them, Jesus said, “Now is the Son of Man glorified, and God is glorified in him. If God is glorified in him, God will also glorify him in himself, and God will glorify him at once. My children, I will be with you only a little while longer. I give you a new commandment: love one another. As I have loved you, so you also should love one another. This is how all will know that you are my disciples, if you have love for one another.”

Monday, May 20

First Reading
ACTS 14:5-18

There was an attempt in Iconium by both the Gentiles and the Jews, together with their leaders, to attack and stone Paul and Barnabas. They realized it, and fled to the Lycaonian cities of Lystra and Derbe and to the surrounding countryside, where they continued to proclaim the Good News.

At Lystra there was a crippled man, lame from birth, who had never walked. He listened to Paul speaking, who looked intently at him, saw that he had the faith to be healed, and called out in a loud voice, “Stand up straight on your feet.” He jumped up and began to walk about. When the crowds saw what Paul had done, they cried out in Lycaonian, “The gods have come down to us in human form.” They called Barnabas “Zeus” and Paul “Hermes,” because he was the chief speaker. And the priest of Zeus, whose temple was at the entrance to the city, brought oxen and garlands to the gates, for he together with the people intended to offer sacrifice.

The Apostles Barnabas and Paul tore their garments when they heard this and rushed out into the crowd, shouting, "Men, why are you doing this? We are of the same nature as you, human beings. We proclaim to you good news that you should turn from these idols to the living God, *who made heaven and earth and sea and all that is in them.* In past generations he allowed all Gentiles to go their own ways; yet, in bestowing his goodness, he did not leave himself without witness, for he gave you rains from heaven and fruitful seasons, and filled you with nourishment and gladness for your hearts." Even with these words, they scarcely restrained the crowds from offering sacrifice to them.

Responsorial Psalm
PSALM 115:1-2, 3-4, 15-16
R. Not to us, O Lord, but to your name give the glory.
(or R. Alleluia.)

Not to us, O LORD, not to us
but to your name give glory
because of your mercy, because of your truth.
Why should the pagans say,
"Where is their God?" **R.**
Our God is in heaven;
whatever he wills, he does.
Their idols are silver and gold,
the handiwork of men. **R.**
May you be blessed by the LORD,
who made heaven and earth.
Heaven is the heaven of the LORD,
but the earth he has given to the children of men. **R.**

Gospel
JOHN 14:21-26

Jesus said to his disciples: "Whoever has my commandments and observes them is the one who loves me. Whoever loves me will be loved by my Father, and I will love him and reveal myself to him." Judas, not the Iscariot, said to him, "Master, then what happened that you will reveal yourself to us and not to the world?" Jesus answered and said to him, "Whoever loves me will keep my word, and my Father will love him, and we will come to him and make our dwelling with him. Whoever does not love me does not keep my words; yet the word you hear is not mine but that of the Father who sent me.

"I have told you this while I am with you. The Advocate, the Holy Spirit whom the Father will send in my name—he will teach you everything and remind you of all that I told you."

Tuesday, May 21

First Reading

ACTS 14:19-28

In those days, some Jews from Antioch and Iconium arrived and won over the crowds. They stoned Paul and dragged him out of the city, supposing that he was dead. But when the disciples gathered around him, he got up and entered the city. On the following day he left with Barnabas for Derbe.

After they had proclaimed the good news to that city and made a considerable number of disciples, they returned to Lystra and to Iconium and to Antioch. They strengthened the spirits of the disciples and exhorted them to persevere in the faith, saying, "It is necessary for us to undergo many hardships to enter the Kingdom of God." They appointed presbyters for them in each Church and, with prayer and fasting, commended them to the Lord in whom they had put their faith. Then they traveled through Pisidia and reached Pamphylia. After proclaiming the word at Perga they went down to Attalia. From there they sailed to Antioch, where they had been commended to the grace of God for the work they had now accomplished. And when they arrived, they called the Church together and reported what God had done with them and how he had opened the door of faith to the Gentiles. Then they spent no little time with the disciples.

Responsorial Psalm

PSALM 145:10-11, 12-13ab, 21

R. Your friends make known, O Lord, the glorious splendor of your kingdom. (or R. Alleluia.)

Let all your works give you thanks, O LORD,
  and let your faithful ones bless you.
Let them discourse of the glory of your kingdom
  and speak of your might. **R.**
Making known to men your might
  and the glorious splendor of your kingdom.
Your kingdom is a kingdom for all ages,
  and your dominion endures through all generations. **R.**
May my mouth speak the praise of the LORD,
  and may all flesh bless his holy name forever and ever. **R.**

Gospel

JOHN 14:27-31a

Jesus said to his disciples: "Peace I leave with you; my peace I give to you. Not as the world gives do I give it to you. Do not let your hearts be troubled or afraid. You heard me tell you, 'I am going away and I will come back to you.' If you loved me, you would rejoice that I am going to the Father; for the Father is greater than I. And now I have told you this before it happens, so that when it happens you may believe. I will no longer speak much with you, for the ruler of the world is coming. He has no power over me, but the world must know that I love the Father and that I do just as the Father has commanded me."

Wednesday, May 22

First Reading

ACTS 15:1-6

Some who had come down from Judea were instructing the brothers, "Unless you are circumcised according to the Mosaic practice, you cannot be saved." Because there arose no little dissension and debate by Paul and Barnabas with them, it was decided that Paul, Barnabas, and some of the others should go up to Jerusalem to the Apostles and presbyters about this question. They were sent on their journey by the Church, and passed through Phoenicia and Samaria telling of the conversion of the Gentiles, and brought great joy to all the brethren. When they arrived in Jerusalem, they were welcomed by the Church, as well as by the Apostles and the presbyters, and they reported what God had done with them. But some from the party of the Pharisees who had become believers stood up and said, "It is necessary to circumcise them and direct them to observe the Mosaic law."

The Apostles and the presbyters met together to see about this matter.

Responsorial Psalm

PSALM 122:1-2, 3-4ab, 4cd-5

R. Let us go rejoicing to the house of the Lord. (or R. Alleluia.)

I rejoiced because they said to me,
"We will go up to the house of the LORD."
And now we have set foot
within your gates, O Jerusalem. **R.**
Jerusalem, built as a city
with compact unity.
To it the tribes go up,
the tribes of the LORD. **R.**
According to the decree for Israel,
to give thanks to the name of the LORD.
In it are set up judgment seats,
seats for the house of David. **R.**

Gospel

JOHN 15:1-8

Jesus said to his disciples: "I am the true vine, and my Father is the vine grower. He takes away every branch in me that does not bear fruit, and everyone that does he prunes so that it bears more fruit. You are already pruned because of the word that I spoke to you. Remain in me, as I remain in you. Just as a branch cannot bear fruit on its own unless it remains on the vine, so neither can you unless you remain in me. I am the vine, you are the branches. Whoever remains in me and I in him will bear much fruit, because without me you can do nothing. Anyone who does not remain in me will be thrown out like a branch and wither; people will gather them and throw them into a fire and they will be burned. If you remain in me and my words remain in you, ask for whatever you want and it will be done for you. By this is my Father glorified, that you bear much fruit and become my disciples."

Thursday, May 23

First Reading

ACTS 15:7-21

After much debate had taken place, Peter got up and said to the Apostles and the presbyters, "My brothers, you are well aware that from early days God made his choice among you that through my mouth the Gentiles would hear the word of the Gospel and believe. And God, who knows the heart, bore witness by granting them the Holy Spirit just as he did us. He made no distinction between us and them, for by faith he purified their hearts. Why, then, are you now putting God to the test by placing on the shoulders of the disciples a yoke that neither our ancestors nor we have been able to bear? On the contrary, we believe that we are saved through the grace of the Lord Jesus, in the same way as they." The whole assembly fell silent, and they listened while Paul and Barnabas described the signs and wonders God had worked among the Gentiles through them.

After they had fallen silent, James responded, "My brothers, listen to me. Symeon has described how God first concerned himself with acquiring from among the Gentiles a people for his name. The words of the prophets agree with this, as is written:

After this I shall return
and rebuild the fallen hut of David;
from its ruins I shall rebuild it
and raise it up again,

so that the rest of humanity may seek out the Lord,
even all the Gentiles on whom my name is invoked.
Thus says the Lord who accomplishes these things,
known from of old.

It is my judgment, therefore, that we ought to stop troubling the Gentiles who turn to God, but tell them by letter to avoid pollution from idols, unlawful marriage, the meat of strangled animals, and blood. For Moses, for generations now, has had those who proclaim him in every town, as he has been read in the synagogues every sabbath."

Responsorial Psalm
PSALM 96:1-2a, 2b-3, 10
R. Proclaim God's marvelous deeds to all the nations.
(or R. Alleluia.)
Sing to the LORD a new song;
sing to the LORD, all you lands.
Sing to the LORD; bless his name. **R.**
Announce his salvation, day after day.
Tell his glory among the nations;
among all peoples, his wondrous deeds. **R.**
Say among the nations: The LORD is king.
He has made the world firm, not to be moved;
he governs the peoples with equity. **R.**

Gospel
JOHN 15:9-11
Jesus said to his disciples: "As the Father loves me, so I also love you. Remain in my love. If you keep my commandments, you will remain in my love, just as I have kept my Father's commandments and remain in his love.

"I have told you this so that my joy might be in you and your joy might be complete."

Friday, May 24

First Reading
ACTS 15:22-31
The Apostles and presbyters, in agreement with the whole Church, decided to choose representatives and to send them to Antioch with Paul and Barnabas. The ones chosen were Judas, who was called Barsabbas, and Silas, leaders among the brothers. This is the letter delivered by them: "The Apostles and the presbyters, your brothers, to the broth-

ers in Antioch, Syria, and Cilicia of Gentile origin: greetings. Since we have heard that some of our number who went out without any mandate from us have upset you with their teachings and disturbed your peace of mind, we have with one accord decided to choose representatives and to send them to you along with our beloved Barnabas and Paul, who have dedicated their lives to the name of our Lord Jesus Christ. So we are sending Judas and Silas who will also convey this same message by word of mouth: 'It is the decision of the Holy Spirit and of us not to place on you any burden beyond these necessities, namely, to abstain from meat sacrificed to idols, from blood, from meats of strangled animals, and from unlawful marriage. If you keep free of these, you will be doing what is right. Farewell.'"

And so they were sent on their journey. Upon their arrival in Antioch they called the assembly together and delivered the letter. When the people read it, they were delighted with the exhortation.

Responsorial Psalm

PSALM 57:8-9, 10 and 12

R. I will give you thanks among the peoples, O Lord. (or R. Alleluia.)

My heart is steadfast, O God; my heart is steadfast;
I will sing and chant praise.
Awake, O my soul; awake, lyre and harp!
I will wake the dawn. **R.**
I will give thanks to you among the peoples, O LORD,
I will chant your praise among the nations.
For your mercy towers to the heavens,
and your faithfulness to the skies.
Be exalted above the heavens, O God;
above all the earth be your glory! **R.**

Gospel

JOHN 15:12-17

Jesus said to his disciples: "This is my commandment: love one another as I love you. No one has greater love than this, to lay down one's life for one's friends. You are my friends if you do what I command you. I no longer call you slaves, because a slave does not know what his master is doing. I have called you friends, because I have told you everything I have heard from my Father. It was not you who chose me, but I who chose you and appointed you to go and bear fruit that will remain, so that whatever you ask the Father in my name he may give you. This I command you: love one another."

Saturday, May 25

First Reading

ACTS 16:1-10

Paul reached also Derbe and Lystra where there was a disciple named Timothy, the son of a Jewish woman who was a believer, but his father was a Greek. The brothers in Lystra and Iconium spoke highly of him, and Paul wanted him to come along with him. On account of the Jews of that region, Paul had him circumcised, for they all knew that his father was a Greek. As they traveled from city to city, they handed on to the people for observance the decisions reached by the Apostles and presbyters in Jerusalem. Day after day the churches grew stronger in faith and increased in number.

They traveled through the Phrygian and Galatian territory because they had been prevented by the Holy Spirit from preaching the message in the province of Asia. When they came to Mysia, they tried to go on into Bithynia, but the Spirit of Jesus did not allow them, so they crossed through Mysia and came down to Troas. During the night Paul had a vision. A Macedonian stood before him and implored him with these words, "Come over to Macedonia and help us." When he had seen the vision, we sought passage to Macedonia at once, concluding that God had called us to proclaim the Good News to them.

Responsorial Psalm

PSALM 100:1b-2, 3, 5

R. Let all the earth cry out to God with joy. (or R. Alleluia.)

Sing joyfully to the LORD, all you lands;
serve the LORD with gladness;
come before him with joyful song. **R.**
Know that the LORD is God;
he made us, his we are;
his people, the flock he tends. **R.**
The LORD is good:
his kindness endures forever,
and his faithfulness, to all generations. **R.**

Gospel

JOHN 15:18-21

Jesus said to his disciples: "If the world hates you, realize that it hated me first. If you belonged to the world, the world would love its own; but because you do not belong to the world, and I have chosen you out of the world, the world hates you. Remember the word I spoke to you, 'No slave is greater than his master.' If they persecuted me, they will also persecute you. If they kept my word, they will also keep yours. And they will do all these things to you on account of my name, because they do not know the one who sent me."

Sunday, May 26

[The second reading and Gospel from the Seventh Sunday of Easter may be used here if the Solemnity of the Ascension of the Lord is celebrated on the following Sunday, June 2.]

Sixth Sunday of Easter

First Reading
ACTS 15:1-2, 22-29

Some who had come down from Judea were instructing the brothers, "Unless you are circumcised according to the Mosaic practice, you cannot be saved." Because there arose no little dissension and debate by Paul and Barnabas with them, it was decided that Paul, Barnabas, and some of the others should go up to Jerusalem to the apostles and elders about this question.

The apostles and elders, in agreement with the whole church, decided to choose representatives and to send them to Antioch with Paul and Barnabas. The ones chosen were Judas, who was called Barsabbas, and Silas, leaders among the brothers. This is the letter delivered by them:

"The apostles and the elders, your brothers, to the brothers in Antioch, Syria, and Cilicia of Gentile origin: greetings. Since we have heard that some of our number who went out without any mandate from us have upset you with their teachings and disturbed your peace of mind, we have with one accord decided to choose representatives and to send them to you along with our beloved Barnabas and Paul, who have dedicated their lives to the name of our Lord Jesus Christ. So we are sending Judas and Silas who will also convey this same message by word of mouth: 'It is the decision of the Holy Spirit and of us not to place on you any burden beyond these necessities, namely, to abstain from meat sacrificed to idols, from blood, from meats of strangled animals, and from unlawful marriage. If you keep free of these, you will be doing what is right. Farewell.'"

Responsorial Psalm
PSALM 67:2-3, 5, 6, 8
R. O God, let all the nations praise you! (or R. Alleluia.)

May God have pity on us and bless us;
  may he let his face shine upon us.

So may your way be known upon earth;
among all nations, your salvation. **R.**
May the nations be glad and exult
because you rule the peoples in equity;
the nations on the earth you guide. **R.**
May the peoples praise you, O God;
may all the peoples praise you!
May God bless us,
and may all the ends of the earth fear him! **R.**

Second Reading
REVELATION 21:10-14, 22-23

The angel took me in spirit to a great, high mountain and showed me the holy city Jerusalem coming down out of heaven from God. It gleamed with the splendor of God. Its radiance was like that of a precious stone, like jasper, clear as crystal. It had a massive, high wall, with twelve gates where twelve angels were stationed and on which names were inscribed, the names of the twelve tribes of the Israelites. There were three gates facing east, three north, three south, and three west. The wall of the city had twelve courses of stones as its foundation, on which were inscribed the twelve names of the twelve apostles of the Lamb.

I saw no temple in the city for its temple is the Lord God almighty and the Lamb. The city had no need of sun or moon to shine on it, for the glory of God gave it light, and its lamp was the Lamb.

Gospel
JOHN 14:23-29

Jesus said to his disciples: "Whoever loves me will keep my word, and my Father will love him, and we will come to him and make our dwelling with him. Whoever does not love me does not keep my words; yet the word you hear is not mine but that of the Father who sent me.

"I have told you this while I am with you. The Advocate, the Holy Spirit, whom the Father will send in my name, will teach you everything and remind you of all that I told you. Peace I leave with you; my peace I give to you. Not as the world gives do I give it to you. Do not let your hearts be troubled or afraid. You heard me tell you, 'I am going away and I will come back to you.' If you loved me, you would rejoice that I am going to the Father; for the Father is greater than I. And now I have told you this before it happens, so that when it happens you may believe."

Monday, May 27

First Reading

ACTS 16:11-15

We set sail from Troas, making a straight run for Samothrace, and on the next day to Neapolis, and from there to Philippi, a leading city in that district of Macedonia and a Roman colony. We spent some time in that city. On the sabbath we went outside the city gate along the river where we thought there would be a place of prayer. We sat and spoke with the women who had gathered there. One of them, a woman named Lydia, a dealer in purple cloth, from the city of Thyatira, a worshiper of God, listened, and the Lord opened her heart to pay attention to what Paul was saying. After she and her household had been baptized, she offered us an invitation, "If you consider me a believer in the Lord, come and stay at my home," and she prevailed on us.

Responsorial Psalm

PSALM 149:1b-2, 3-4, 5-6a and 9b

R. The Lord takes delight in his people. (or R. Alleluia.)

Sing to the LORD a new song
  of praise in the assembly of the faithful.
Let Israel be glad in their maker,
  let the children of Zion rejoice in their king. **R.**
Let them praise his name in the festive dance,
  let them sing praise to him with timbrel and harp.
For the LORD loves his people,
  and he adorns the lowly with victory. **R.**
Let the faithful exult in glory;
  let them sing for joy upon their couches.
Let the high praises of God be in their throats.
  This is the glory of all his faithful. Alleluia. **R.**

Gospel

JOHN 15:26–16:4a

Jesus said to his disciples: "When the Advocate comes whom I will send you from the Father, the Spirit of truth who proceeds from the Father, he will testify to me. And you also testify, because you have been with me from the beginning.

"I have told you this so that you may not fall away. They will expel you from the synagogues; in fact, the hour is coming when everyone who kills you will think he is offering worship to God. They will do this because they have not known either the Father or me. I have told you this so that when their hour comes you may remember that I told you."

Tuesday, May 28

First Reading

ACTS 16:22-34

The crowd in Philippi joined in the attack on Paul and Silas, and the magistrates had them stripped and ordered them to be beaten with rods. After inflicting many blows on them, they threw them into prison and instructed the jailer to guard them securely. When he received these instructions, he put them in the innermost cell and secured their feet to a stake.

About midnight, while Paul and Silas were praying and singing hymns to God as the prisoners listened, there was suddenly such a severe earthquake that the foundations of the jail shook; all the doors flew open, and the chains of all were pulled loose. When the jailer woke up and saw the prison doors wide open, he drew his sword and was about to kill himself, thinking that the prisoners had escaped. But Paul shouted out in a loud voice, "Do no harm to yourself; we are all here." He asked for a light and rushed in and, trembling with fear, he fell down before Paul and Silas. Then he brought them out and said, "Sirs, what must I do to be saved?" And they said, "Believe in the Lord Jesus and you and your household will be saved." So they spoke the word of the Lord to him and to everyone in his house. He took them in at that hour of the night and bathed their wounds; then he and all his family were baptized at once. He brought them up into his house and provided a meal and with his household rejoiced at having come to faith in God.

Responsorial Psalm

PSALM 138:1-2ab, 2cde-3, 7c-8

R. Your right hand saves me, O Lord. (or R. Alleluia.)

I will give thanks to you, O LORD, with all my heart,
for you have heard the words of my mouth;
in the presence of the angels I will sing your praise;
I will worship at your holy temple,
and give thanks to your name. **R.**
Because of your kindness and your truth,
you have made great above all things
your name and your promise.
When I called, you answered me;
you built up strength within me. **R.**
Your right hand saves me.
The LORD will complete what he has done for me;
your kindness, O LORD, endures forever;
forsake not the work of your hands. **R.**

Gospel
JOHN 16:5-11

Jesus said to his disciples: "Now I am going to the one who sent me, and not one of you asks me, 'Where are you going?' But because I told you this, grief has filled your hearts. But I tell you the truth, it is better for you that I go. For if I do not go, the Advocate will not come to you. But if I go, I will send him to you. And when he comes he will convict the world in regard to sin and righteousness and condemnation: sin, because they do not believe in me; righteousness, because I am going to the Father and you will no longer see me; condemnation, because the ruler of this world has been condemned."

Wednesday, May 29

First Reading
ACTS 17:15, 22–18:1

After Paul's escorts had taken him to Athens, they came away with instructions for Silas and Timothy to join him as soon as possible.

Then Paul stood up at the Areopagus and said: "You Athenians, I see that in every respect you are very religious. For as I walked around looking carefully at your shrines, I even discovered an altar inscribed, 'To an Unknown God.' What therefore you unknowingly worship, I proclaim to you. The God who made the world and all that is in it, the Lord of heaven and earth, does not dwell in sanctuaries made by human hands, nor is he served by human hands because he needs anything. Rather it is he who gives to everyone life and breath and everything. He made from one the whole human race to dwell on the entire surface of the earth, and he fixed the ordered seasons and the boundaries of their regions, so that people might seek God, even perhaps grope for him and find him, though indeed he is not far from any one of us. For 'In him we live and move and have our being,' as even some of your poets have said, 'For we too are his offspring.' Since therefore we are the offspring of God, we ought not to think that the divinity is like an image fashioned from gold, silver, or stone by human art and imagination. God has overlooked the times of ignorance, but now he demands that all people everywhere repent because he has established a day on which he will 'judge the world with justice' through a man he has appointed, and he has provided confirmation for all by raising him from the dead."

When they heard about resurrection of the dead, some began to scoff, but others said, "We should like to hear you on this some other time." And so Paul left them. But some did join him, and became believers. Among them were Dionysius, a member of the Court of the Areopagus, a woman named Damaris, and others with them.

After this he left Athens and went to Corinth.

Responsorial Psalm

PSALM 148:1-2, 11-12, 13, 14

R. Heaven and earth are full of your glory. (or R. Alleluia.)

Praise the LORD from the heavens;
praise him in the heights.
Praise him, all you his angels;
praise him, all you his hosts. **R.**
Let the kings of the earth and all peoples,
the princes and all the judges of the earth,
Young men too, and maidens,
old men and boys. **R.**
Praise the name of the LORD,
for his name alone is exalted;
His majesty is above earth and heaven. **R.**
He has lifted up the horn of his people;
Be this his praise from all his faithful ones,
from the children of Israel, the people close to him.
Alleluia. **R.**

Gospel

JOHN 16:12-15

Jesus said to his disciples: "I have much more to tell you, but you cannot bear it now. But when he comes, the Spirit of truth, he will guide you to all truth. He will not speak on his own, but he will speak what he hears, and will declare to you the things that are coming. He will glorify me, because he will take from what is mine and declare it to you. Everything that the Father has is mine; for this reason I told you that he will take from what is mine and declare it to you."

Thursday, May 30

[Readings for ecclesiastical provinces that have *not* transferred the Solemnity of the Ascension of the Lord to the following Sunday, June 2:]

The Ascension of the Lord

First Reading

ACTS 1:1-11

In the first book, Theophilus, I dealt with all that Jesus did and taught until the day he was taken up, after giving instructions through the Holy Spirit to the apostles whom he had chosen. He presented himself alive to them by many proofs after he had suffered, appearing to them during forty days and speaking about the kingdom of God. While meeting with them, he enjoined them not to depart from Jerusalem, but to wait for "the promise of the Father about which you have heard me speak; for John baptized with water, but in a few days you will be baptized with the Holy Spirit."

When they had gathered together they asked him, "Lord, are you at this time going to restore the kingdom to Israel?" He answered them, "It is not for you to know the times or seasons that the Father has established by his own authority. But you will receive power when the Holy Spirit comes upon you, and you will be my witnesses in Jerusalem, throughout Judea and Samaria, and to the ends of the earth." When he had said this, as they were looking on, he was lifted up, and a cloud took him from their sight. While they were looking intently at the sky as he was going, suddenly two men dressed in white garments stood beside them. They said, "Men of Galilee, why are you standing there looking at the sky? This Jesus who has been taken up from you into heaven will return in the same way as you have seen him going into heaven."

Responsorial Psalm

PSALM 47:2-3, 6-7, 8-9

R. God mounts his throne to shouts of joy: a blare of trumpets for the Lord. (or R. Alleluia.)

All you peoples, clap your hands,
  shout to God with cries of gladness,
for the LORD, the Most High, the awesome,
  is the great king over all the earth. **R.**
God mounts his throne amid shouts of joy;
  the LORD, amid trumpet blasts.
Sing praise to God, sing praise;
  sing praise to our king, sing praise. **R.**
For king of all the earth is God;

sing hymns of praise.
God reigns over the nations,
God sits upon his holy throne. **R.**

Second Reading
EPHESIANS 1:17-23 (or HEBREWS 9:24-28; 10:19-23)

Brothers and sisters: May the God of our Lord Jesus Christ, the Father of glory, give you a Spirit of wisdom and revelation resulting in knowledge of him. May the eyes of your hearts be enlightened, that you may know what is the hope that belongs to his call, what are the riches of glory in his inheritance among the holy ones, and what is the surpassing greatness of his power for us who believe, in accord with the exercise of his great might, which he worked in Christ, raising him from the dead and seating him at his right hand in the heavens, far above every principality, authority, power, and dominion, and every name that is named not only in this age but also in the one to come. And he put all things beneath his feet and gave him as head over all things to the church, which is his body, the fullness of the one who fills all things in every way.

Gospel
LUKE 24:46-53

Jesus said to his disciples: "Thus it is written that the Christ would suffer and rise from the dead on the third day and that repentance, for the forgiveness of sins, would be preached in his name to all the nations, beginning from Jerusalem. You are witnesses of these things. And behold I am sending the promise of my Father upon you; but stay in the city until you are clothed with power from on high."

Then he led them out as far as Bethany, raised his hands, and blessed them. As he blessed them he parted from them and was taken up to heaven. They did him homage and then returned to Jerusalem with great joy, and they were continually in the temple praising God.

[Easter weekday Mass readings for the ecclesiastical provinces that have transferred the Solemnity of the Ascension of the Lord to the following Sunday, June 2:]

First Reading
ACTS 18:1-8

Paul left Athens and went to Corinth. There he met a Jew named Aquila, a native of Pontus, who had recently come from Italy with his wife Priscilla because Claudius had ordered all the Jews to leave Rome. He went to visit them and, because he practiced the same trade, stayed with them and worked, for they were tentmakers by trade. Every sabbath, he entered into discussions in the synagogue, attempting to convince both Jews and Greeks.

When Silas and Timothy came down from Macedonia, Paul began to occupy himself totally with preaching the word, testifying to the Jews that the Christ was Jesus. When they opposed him and reviled him, he shook out his garments and said to them, "Your blood be on your heads! I am clear of responsibility. From now on I will go to the Gentiles." So he left there and went to a house belonging to a man named Titus Justus, a worshiper of God; his house was next to a synagogue. Crispus, the synagogue official, came to believe in the Lord along with his entire household, and many of the Corinthians who heard believed and were baptized.

Responsorial Psalm
PSALM 98:1, 2-3ab, 3cd-4
R. The Lord has revealed to the nations his saving power.
(or R. Alleluia.)

Sing to the LORD a new song,
for he has done wondrous deeds;
His right hand has won victory for him,
his holy arm. **R.**
The LORD has made his salvation known:
in the sight of the nations he has revealed his justice.
He has remembered his kindness and his faithfulness
toward the house of Israel. **R.**
All the ends of the earth have seen
the salvation by our God.
Sing joyfully to the LORD, all you lands;
break into song; sing praise. **R.**

Gospel
JOHN 16:16-20

Jesus said to his disciples: "A little while and you will no longer see me, and again a little while later and you will see me." So some of his disciples said to one another, "What does this mean that he is saying to us, 'A little while and you will not see me, and again a little while and you will see me,' and 'Because I am going to the Father'?" So they said, "What is this 'little while' of which he speaks? We do not know what he means." Jesus knew that they wanted to ask him, so he said to them, "Are you discussing with one another what I said, 'A little while and you will not see me, and again a little while and you will see me'? Amen, amen, I say to you, you will weep and mourn, while the world rejoices; you will grieve, but your grief will become joy."

Friday, May 31

The Visitation of the Blessed Virgin Mary

First Reading

ZEPHANIAH 3:14-18a (or ROMANS 12:9-16)

Shout for joy, O daughter Zion!
 Sing joyfully, O Israel!
Be glad and exult with all your heart,
 O daughter Jerusalem!
The LORD has removed the judgment against you,
 he has turned away your enemies;
The King of Israel, the LORD, is in your midst,
 you have no further misfortune to fear.
On that day, it shall be said to Jerusalem:
 Fear not, O Zion, be not discouraged!
The LORD, your God, is in your midst,
 a mighty savior;
He will rejoice over you with gladness,
 and renew you in his love,
He will sing joyfully because of you,
 as one sings at festivals.

Responsorial Psalm

ISAIAH 12:2-3, 4bcd, 5-6

R. Among you is the great and Holy One of Israel.

God indeed is my savior;
 I am confident and unafraid.
My strength and my courage is the LORD,
 and he has been my savior.
With joy you will draw water
 at the fountain of salvation. **R.**
Give thanks to the LORD, acclaim his name;
 among the nations make known his deeds,
 proclaim how exalted is his name. **R.**
Sing praise to the LORD for his glorious achievement;
 let this be known throughout all the earth.
Shout with exultation, O city of Zion,
 for great in your midst
 is the Holy One of Israel! **R.**

Gospel
LUKE 1:39-56

Mary set out and traveled to the hill country in haste to a town of Judah, where she entered the house of Zechariah and greeted Elizabeth. When Elizabeth heard Mary's greeting, the infant leaped in her womb, and Elizabeth, filled with the Holy Spirit, cried out in a loud voice and said, "Most blessed are you among women, and blessed is the fruit of your womb. And how does this happen to me, that the mother of my Lord should come to me? For at the moment the sound of your greeting reached my ears, the infant in my womb leaped for joy. Blessed are you who believed that what was spoken to you by the Lord would be fulfilled."

And Mary said:

"My soul proclaims the greatness of the Lord;
my spirit rejoices in God my Savior,
for he has looked with favor on his lowly servant.
From this day all generations will call me blessed:
the Almighty has done great things for me,
and holy is his Name.

He has mercy on those who fear him
in every generation.
He has shown the strength of his arm,
he has scattered the proud in their conceit.
He has cast down the mighty from their thrones,
and has lifted up the lowly.
He has filled the hungry with good things,
and the rich he has sent away empty.
He has come to the help of his servant Israel
for he has remembered his promise of mercy,
the promise he made to our fathers,
to Abraham and his children for ever."

Mary remained with her about three months and then returned to her home.

JUNE

Saturday, June 1

First Reading
ACTS 18:23-28

After staying in Antioch some time, Paul left and traveled in orderly sequence through the Galatian country and Phrygia, bringing strength to all the disciples.

A Jew named Apollos, a native of Alexandria, an eloquent speaker, arrived in Ephesus. He was an authority on the Scriptures. He had been instructed in the Way of the Lord and, with ardent spirit, spoke and taught accurately about Jesus, although he knew only the baptism of John. He began to speak boldly in the synagogue; but when Priscilla and Aquila heard him, they took him aside and explained to him the Way of God more accurately. And when he wanted to cross to Achaia, the brothers encouraged him and wrote to the disciples there to welcome him. After his arrival he gave great assistance to those who had come to believe through grace. He vigorously refuted the Jews in public, establishing from the Scriptures that the Christ is Jesus.

Responsorial Psalm
PSALM 47:2-3, 8-9, 10
R. God is king of all the earth. (or R. Alleluia.)

All you peoples, clap your hands;
  shout to God with cries of gladness.
For the LORD, the Most High, the awesome,
  is the great king over all the earth. **R.**
For king of all the earth is God;
  sing hymns of praise.
God reigns over the nations,
  God sits upon his holy throne. **R.**
The princes of the peoples are gathered together
  with the people of the God of Abraham.
For God's are the guardians of the earth;
  he is supreme. **R.**

Gospel
JOHN 16:23b-28

Jesus said to his disciples: "Amen, amen, I say to you, whatever you ask the Father in my name he will give you. Until now you have not asked anything in my name; ask and you will receive, so that your joy may be complete.

"I have told you this in figures of speech. The hour is coming when I will no longer speak to you in figures but I will tell you clearly about the Father. On that day you will ask in my name, and I do not tell you that I will ask the Father for you. For the Father himself loves you, because you have loved me and have come to believe that I came from God. I came from the Father and have come into the world. Now I am leaving the world and going back to the Father."

Sunday, June 2

[Ecclesiastical provinces that have transferred the Solemnity of the Ascension of the Lord to the Seventh Sunday of Easter should use the Ascension readings for Thursday, May 30.

The following readings should be used in those provinces that have *not* transferred the Solemnity of the Ascension of the Lord to the Seventh Sunday of Easter:]

Seventh Sunday of Easter

First Reading
ACTS 7:55-60

Stephen, filled with the Holy Spirit, looked up intently to heaven and saw the glory of God and Jesus standing at the right hand of God, and Stephen said, "Behold, I see the heavens opened and the Son of Man standing at the right hand of God." But they cried out in a loud voice, covered their ears, and rushed upon him together. They threw him out of the city, and began to stone him. The witnesses laid down their cloaks at the feet of a young man named Saul. As they were stoning Stephen, he called out, "Lord Jesus, receive my spirit." Then he fell to his knees and cried out in a loud voice, "Lord, do not hold this sin against them"; and when he said this, he fell asleep.

Responsorial Psalm
PSALM 97:1-2, 6-7, 9
R. The Lord is king, the most high over all the earth.
(or R. Alleluia.)

The LORD is king; let the earth rejoice;
let the many islands be glad.
Justice and judgment are the foundation of his throne. **R.**
The heavens proclaim his justice,
and all peoples see his glory.

All gods are prostrate before him. **R.**
You, O LORD, are the Most High over all the earth,
exalted far above all gods. **R.**

Second Reading
REVELATION 22:12-14, 16-17, 20

I, John, heard a voice saying to me: "Behold, I am coming soon. I bring with me the recompense I will give to each according to his deeds. I am the Alpha and the Omega, the first and the last, the beginning and the end."

Blessed are they who wash their robes so as to have the right to the tree of life and enter the city through its gates.

"I, Jesus, sent my angel to give you this testimony for the churches. I am the root and offspring of David, the bright morning star."

The Spirit and the bride say, "Come." Let the hearer say, "Come." Let the one who thirsts come forward, and the one who wants it receive the gift of life-giving water.

The one who gives this testimony says, "Yes, I am coming soon." Amen! Come, Lord Jesus!

Gospel
JOHN 17:20-26

Lifting up his eyes to heaven, Jesus prayed saying: "Holy Father, I pray not only for them, but also for those who will believe in me through their word, so that they may all be one, as you, Father, are in me and I in you, that they also may be in us, that the world may believe that you sent me. And I have given them the glory you gave me, so that they may be one, as we are one, I in them and you in me, that they may be brought to perfection as one, that the world may know that you sent me, and that you loved them even as you loved me. Father, they are your gift to me. I wish that where I am they also may be with me, that they may see my glory that you gave me, because you loved me before the foundation of the world. Righteous Father, the world also does not know you, but I know you, and they know that you sent me. I made known to them your name and I will make it known, that the love with which you loved me may be in them and I in them."

Monday, June 3

First Reading
ACTS 19:1-8

While Apollos was in Corinth, Paul traveled through the interior of the country and down to Ephesus where he found some disciples. He said to them, "Did you receive the Holy Spirit when you became believers?" They answered him, "We have never even heard that there is a Holy Spirit." He said, "How were you baptized?" They replied, "With the baptism of John." Paul then said, "John baptized with a baptism of repentance, telling the people to believe in the one who was to come after him, that is, in Jesus." When they heard this, they were baptized in the name of the Lord Jesus. And when Paul laid his hands on them, the Holy Spirit came upon them, and they spoke in tongues and prophesied. Altogether there were about twelve men.

He entered the synagogue, and for three months debated boldly with persuasive arguments about the Kingdom of God.

Responsorial Psalm

PSALM 68:2-3ab, 4-5acd, 6-7ab

R. Sing to God, O kingdoms of the earth. (or R. Alleluia.)

God arises; his enemies are scattered,
 and those who hate him flee before him.
As smoke is driven away, so are they driven;
 as wax melts before the fire. **R.**
But the just rejoice and exult before God;
 they are glad and rejoice.
Sing to God, chant praise to his name;
 whose name is the LORD. **R.**
The father of orphans and the defender of widows
 is God in his holy dwelling.
God gives a home to the forsaken;
 he leads forth prisoners to prosperity. **R.**

Gospel

JOHN 16:29-33

The disciples said to Jesus, "Now you are talking plainly, and not in any figure of speech. Now we realize that you know everything and that you do not need to have anyone question you. Because of this we believe that you came from God." Jesus answered them, "Do you believe now? Behold, the hour is coming and has arrived when each of you will be scattered to his own home and you will leave me alone. But I am not alone, because the Father is with me. I have told you this so that you might have peace in me. In the world you will have trouble, but take courage, I have conquered the world."

Tuesday, June 4

First Reading

ACTS 20:17-27

From Miletus Paul had the presbyters of the Church at Ephesus summoned. When they came to him, he addressed them, "You know how I lived among you the whole time from the day I first came to the province of Asia. I served the Lord with all humility and with the tears and trials that came to me because of the plots of the Jews, and I did not at all shrink from telling you what was for your benefit, or from teaching you in public or in your homes. I earnestly bore witness for both Jews and Greeks to repentance before God and to faith in our Lord Jesus. But now, compelled by the Spirit, I am going to Jerusalem. What will happen to me there I do not know, except that in one city after another the Holy Spirit has been warning me that imprisonment and hardships await me. Yet I consider life of no importance to me, if only I may finish my course and the ministry that I received from the Lord Jesus, to bear witness to the Gospel of God's grace.

"But now I know that none of you to whom I preached the kingdom during my travels will ever see my face again. And so I solemnly declare to you this day that I am not responsible for the blood of any of you, for I did not shrink from proclaiming to you the entire plan of God."

Responsorial Psalm

PSALM 68:10-11, 20-21

R. Sing to God, O kingdoms of the earth. (or R. Alleluia.)

A bountiful rain you showered down, O God, upon your inheritance;
you restored the land when it languished;
Your flock settled in it;
in your goodness, O God, you provided it for the needy. **R.**
Blessed day by day be the Lord,
who bears our burdens; God, who is our salvation.
God is a saving God for us;
the LORD, my Lord, controls the passageways of death. **R.**

Gospel

JOHN 17:1-11a

Jesus raised his eyes to heaven and said, "Father, the hour has come. Give glory to your son, so that your son may glorify you, just as you gave him authority over all people, so that your son may give eternal life to all you gave him. Now this is eternal life, that they should know you, the only true God, and the one whom you sent, Jesus Christ. I glorified you on earth by accomplishing the work that you gave me to do. Now glorify me, Father, with you, with the glory that I had with you before the world began.

"I revealed your name to those whom you gave me out of the world. They belonged to you, and you gave them to me, and they have kept your word. Now they know that everything you gave me is from you, because the words you gave to me I have given to them, and they accepted them and truly understood that I came from you, and they have believed that you sent me. I pray for them. I do not pray for the world but for the ones you have given me, because they are yours, and everything of mine is yours and everything of yours is mine, and I have been glorified in them. And now I will no longer be in the world, but they are in the world, while I am coming to you."

Wednesday, June 5

First Reading

ACTS 20:28-38

At Miletus, Paul spoke to the presbyters of the Church of Ephesus: "Keep watch over yourselves and over the whole flock of which the Holy Spirit has appointed you overseers, in which you tend the Church of God that he acquired with his own Blood. I know that after my departure savage wolves will come among you, and they will not spare the flock. And from your own group, men will come forward perverting the truth to draw the disciples away after them. So be vigilant and remember that for three years, night and day, I unceasingly admonished each of you with tears. And now I commend you to God and to that gracious word of his that can build you up and give you the inheritance among all who are consecrated. I have never wanted anyone's silver or gold or clothing. You know well that these very hands have served my needs and my companions. In every way I have shown you that by hard work of that sort we must help the weak, and keep in mind the words of the Lord Jesus who himself said, 'It is more blessed to give than to receive.'"

When he had finished speaking he knelt down and prayed with them all. They were all weeping loudly as they threw their arms around Paul and kissed him, for they were deeply distressed that he had said that they would never see his face again. Then they escorted him to the ship.

Responsorial Psalm

PSALM 68:29-30, 33-35a, 35bc-36ab

R. Sing to God, O kingdoms of the earth. (or R. Alleluia.)

Show forth, O God, your power,
  the power, O God, with which you took our part;

For your temple in Jerusalem
  let the kings bring you gifts. **R.**
You kingdoms of the earth, sing to God,
  chant praise to the Lord
  who rides on the heights of the ancient heavens.
Behold, his voice resounds, the voice of power:
  "Confess the power of God!" **R.**
Over Israel is his majesty;
  his power is in the skies.
Awesome in his sanctuary is God, the God of Israel;
  he gives power and strength to his people. **R.**

Gospel
JOHN 17:11b-19

Lifting up his eyes to heaven, Jesus prayed, saying: "Holy Father, keep them in your name that you have given me, so that they may be one just as we are one. When I was with them I protected them in your name that you gave me, and I guarded them, and none of them was lost except the son of destruction, in order that the Scripture might be fulfilled. But now I am coming to you. I speak this in the world so that they may share my joy completely. I gave them your word, and the world hated them, because they do not belong to the world any more than I belong to the world. I do not ask that you take them out of the world but that you keep them from the Evil One. They do not belong to the world any more than I belong to the world. Consecrate them in the truth. Your word is truth. As you sent me into the world, so I sent them into the world. And I consecrate myself for them, so that they also may be consecrated in truth."

Thursday, June 6

First Reading
ACTS 22:30; 23:6-11

Wishing to determine the truth about why Paul was being accused by the Jews, the commander freed him and ordered the chief priests and the whole Sanhedrin to convene. Then he brought Paul down and made him stand before them.

Paul was aware that some were Sadducees and some Pharisees, so he called out before the Sanhedrin, "My brothers, I am a Pharisee, the son of Pharisees; I am on trial for hope in the resurrection of the dead." When he said this, a dispute broke out between the Pharisees and Sadducees, and the group became divided. For the Sadducees say that there is no resurrection or angels or spirits, while the Pharisees acknowledge all three. A great uproar occurred, and some scribes belonging to the Pharisee party stood up and sharply argued, "We find nothing wrong with this man. Suppose a spirit or an angel has spoken to him?" The dispute was so serious that the commander, afraid that Paul would be torn to pieces by them, ordered his troops to go down and rescue Paul from their midst and take him into the compound. The following night the Lord stood by him and said, "Take courage. For just as you have borne witness to my cause in Jerusalem, so you must also bear witness in Rome."

Responsorial Psalm
PSALM 16:1-2a and 5, 7-8, 9-10, 11
R. Keep me safe, O God; you are my hope. (or R. Alleluia.)

Keep me, O God, for in you I take refuge;
  I say to the LORD, "My Lord are you."
O LORD, my allotted portion and my cup,
  you it is who hold fast my lot. **R.**
I bless the LORD who counsels me;
  even in the night my heart exhorts me.
I set the LORD ever before me;
  with him at my right hand I shall not be disturbed. **R.**
Therefore my heart is glad and my soul rejoices,
  my body, too, abides in confidence;
Because you will not abandon my soul to the nether world,
  nor will you suffer your faithful one to undergo corruption. **R.**
You will show me the path to life,
  fullness of joys in your presence,
  the delights at your right hand forever. **R.**

Gospel
JOHN 17:20-26

Lifting up his eyes to heaven, Jesus prayed saying: "I pray not only for these, but also for those who will believe in me through their word, so that they may all be one, as you, Father, are in me and I in you, that they also may be in us, that the world may believe that you sent me. And I have given them the glory you gave me, so that they may be one, as we are one, I in them and you in me, that they may be brought to perfection as one, that the world may know that you sent me, and that you loved them even as you loved me. Father, they are your gift to me. I wish that where I am they also may be with me, that they may see my glory that you gave me, because you loved me before the foundation of the world. Righteous Father, the world also does not know you, but I know you, and they know that you sent me. I made known to them your name and I will make it known, that the love with which you loved me may be in them and I in them."

Friday, June 7

First Reading

ACTS 25:13b-21

King Agrippa and Bernice arrived in Caesarea on a visit to Festus. Since they spent several days there, Festus referred Paul's case to the king, saying, "There is a man here left in custody by Felix. When I was in Jerusalem the chief priests and the elders of the Jews brought charges against him and demanded his condemnation. I answered them that it was not Roman practice to hand over an accused person before he has faced his accusers and had the opportunity to defend himself against their charge. So when they came together here, I made no delay; the next day I took my seat on the tribunal and ordered the man to be brought in. His accusers stood around him, but did not charge him with any of the crimes I suspected. Instead they had some issues with him about their own religion and about a certain Jesus who had died but who Paul claimed was alive. Since I was at a loss how to investigate this controversy, I asked if he were willing to go to Jerusalem and there stand trial on these charges. And when Paul appealed that he be held in custody for the Emperor's decision, I ordered him held until I could send him to Caesar."

Responsorial Psalm

PSALM 103:1-2, 11-12, 19-20ab

R. The Lord has established his throne in heaven.
(or R. Alleluia.)

Bless the LORD, O my soul;
  and all my being, bless his holy name.
Bless the LORD, O my soul,
  and forget not all his benefits. **R.**
For as the heavens are high above the earth,
  so surpassing is his kindness toward those who fear him.
As far as the east is from the west,
  so far has he put our transgressions from us. **R.**
The LORD has established his throne in heaven,
  and his kingdom rules over all.
Bless the LORD, all you his angels,
  you mighty in strength, who do his bidding. **R.**

Gospel

JOHN 21:15-19

After Jesus had revealed himself to his disciples and eaten breakfast with them, he said to Simon Peter, "Simon, son of John, do you love me more than these?" Simon Peter answered him, "Yes, Lord, you know that I love you." Jesus said to him, "Feed my lambs." He then said to Simon Peter a second time, "Simon, son of John, do you love me?" Simon Peter answered him, "Yes, Lord, you know that I love you." He said to him, "Tend my sheep." He said to him the third time, "Simon, son of John, do you love me?" Peter was distressed that he had said to him a third time, "Do you love me?" and he said to him, "Lord, you know everything; you know that I love you." Jesus said to him, "Feed my sheep. Amen, amen, I say to you, when you were younger, you used to dress yourself and go where you wanted; but when you grow old, you will stretch out your hands, and someone else will dress you and lead you where you do not want to go." He said this signifying by what kind of death he would glorify God. And when he had said this, he said to him, "Follow me."

Saturday, June 8

First Reading
ACTS 28:16-20, 30-31

When he entered Rome, Paul was allowed to live by himself, with the soldier who was guarding him.

Three days later he called together the leaders of the Jews. When they had gathered he said to them, "My brothers, although I had done nothing against our people or our ancestral customs, I was handed over to the Romans as a prisoner from Jerusalem. After trying my case the Romans wanted to release me, because they found nothing against me deserving the death penalty. But when the Jews objected, I was obliged to appeal to Caesar, even though I had no accusation to make against my own nation. This is the reason, then, I have requested to see you and to speak with you, for it is on account of the hope of Israel that I wear these chains."

He remained for two full years in his lodgings. He received all who came to him, and with complete assurance and without hindrance he proclaimed the Kingdom of God and taught about the Lord Jesus Christ.

Responsorial Psalm
PSALM 11:4, 5 and 7

R. The just will gaze on your face, O Lord. (or R. Alleluia.)

The LORD is in his holy temple;
the LORD's throne is in heaven.
His eyes behold,
his searching glance is on mankind. **R.**
The LORD searches the just and the wicked;
the lover of violence he hates.
For the LORD is just, he loves just deeds;
the upright shall see his face. **R.**

Gospel
JOHN 21:20-25

Peter turned and saw the disciple following whom Jesus loved, the one who had also reclined upon his chest during the supper and had said, "Master, who is the one who will betray you?" When Peter saw him, he said to Jesus, "Lord, what about him?" Jesus said to him, "What if I want him to remain until I come? What concern is it of yours? You follow me." So the word spread among the brothers that that disciple would not die. But Jesus had not told him that he would not die, just "What if I want him to remain until I come? What concern is it of yours?"

It is this disciple who testifies to these things and has written them, and we know that his testimony is true. There are also many other things that Jesus did, but if these were to be described individually, I do not think the whole world would contain the books that would be written.

Sunday, June 9

Pentecost Vigil (Saturday Evening)

First Reading
GENESIS 11:1-9

The whole world spoke the same language, using the same words.
While the people were migrating in the east,
they came upon a valley in the land of Shinar and settled there. They said to one another, "Come, let us mold bricks and harden them with fire." They used bricks for stone, and bitumen for mortar. Then they said, "Come, let us build ourselves a city and a tower with its top in the sky, and so make a name for ourselves; otherwise we shall be scattered all over the earth."

The LORD came down to see the city and the tower that the people had built. Then the LORD said: "If now, while they are one people, all speaking the same language, they have started to do this, nothing will later stop them from doing whatever they presume to do. Let us then go down there and confuse their language, so that one will not understand what another says." Thus the LORD scattered them from there all over the earth, and they stopped building the city. That is why it was called Babel, because there the LORD confused the speech of all the world. It was from that place that he scattered them all over the earth.

Responsorial Psalm

PSALM 33:10-11, 12-13, 14-15

R. Blessed the people the Lord has chosen to be his own.

The LORD brings to nought the plans of nations;
he foils the designs of peoples.
But the plan of the LORD stands forever;
the design of his heart, through all generations. **R.**
Blessed the nation whose God is the LORD,
the people he has chosen for his own inheritance.
From heaven the LORD looks down;
he sees all mankind. **R.**
From his fixed throne he beholds
all who dwell on the earth,
He who fashioned the heart of each,
he who knows all their works. **R.**

Second Reading

EXODUS 19:3-8a, 16-20b

Moses went up the mountain to God. Then the LORD called to him and said, "Thus shall you say to the house of Jacob; tell the Israelites: You have seen for yourselves how I treated the Egyptians and how I bore you up on eagle wings and brought you here to myself. Therefore, if you hearken to my voice and keep my covenant, you shall be my special possession, dearer to me than all other people, though all the earth is mine. You shall be to me a kingdom of priests, a holy nation. That is what you must tell the Israelites." So Moses went and summoned the elders of the people. When he set before them all that the LORD had ordered him to tell them, the people all answered together, "Everything the LORD has said, we will do."

On the morning of the third day there were peals of thunder and lightning, and a heavy cloud over the mountain, and a very loud trumpet blast, so that all the people in the camp trembled. But Moses led the people out of the camp to meet God, and they stationed themselves at the foot of the mountain. Mount Sinai was all wrapped in smoke, for the LORD came down upon it in fire. The smoke rose from it as though from a furnace, and the whole mountain trembled violently. The trumpet blast grew louder and louder, while Moses was speaking, and God answering him with thunder.

When the LORD came down to the top of Mount Sinai, he summoned Moses to the top of the mountain.

Responsorial Psalm
DANIEL 3:52, 53, 54, 55, 56
R. Glory and praise forever!
"Blessed are you, O Lord, the God of our fathers,
praiseworthy and exalted above all forever;
And blessed is your holy and glorious name,
praiseworthy and exalted above all for all ages." **R.**
"Blessed are you in the temple of your holy glory,
praiseworthy and glorious above all forever." **R.**
"Blessed are you on the throne of your Kingdom,
praiseworthy and exalted above all forever." **R.**
"Blessed are you who look into the depths
from your throne upon the cherubim,
praiseworthy and exalted above all forever." **R.**
"Blessed are you in the firmament of heaven,
praiseworthy and glorious forever." **R.**

OR

Responsorial Psalm
PSALM 19:8, 9, 10, 11
R. Lord, you have the words of everlasting life.
The law of the LORD is perfect,
refreshing the soul;
The decree of the LORD is trustworthy,
giving wisdom to the simple. **R.**
The precepts of the LORD are right,
rejoicing the heart;
The command of the LORD is clear,
enlightening the eye. **R.**
The fear of the LORD is pure,
enduring forever;
The ordinances of the LORD are true,
all of them just. **R.**
They are more precious than gold,
than a heap of purest gold;
Sweeter also than syrup
or honey from the comb. **R.**

Third Reading
EZEKIEL 37:1-14
The hand of the LORD came upon me, and he led me out in the spirit of the LORD and set me in the center of the plain, which was now filled with bones. He made me walk among the bones in every direction so

that I saw how many they were on the surface of the plain. How dry they were! He asked me: Son of man, can these bones come to life? I answered, "Lord GOD, you alone know that." Then he said to me: Prophesy over these bones, and say to them: Dry bones, hear the word of the LORD! Thus says the Lord GOD to these bones: See! I will bring spirit into you, that you may come to life. I will put sinews upon you, make flesh grow over you, cover you with skin, and put spirit in you so that you may come to life and know that I am the LORD. I, Ezekiel, prophesied as I had been told, and even as I was prophesying I heard a noise; it was a rattling as the bones came together, bone joining bone. I saw the sinews and the flesh come upon them, and the skin cover them, but there was no spirit in them. Then the LORD said to me: Prophesy to the spirit, prophesy, son of man, and say to the spirit: Thus says the Lord GOD: From the four winds come, O spirit, and breathe into these slain that they may come to life. I prophesied as he told me, and the spirit came into them; they came alive and stood upright, a vast army. Then he said to me: Son of man, these bones are the whole house of Israel. They have been saying, "Our bones are dried up, our hope is lost, and we are cut off." Therefore, prophesy and say to them: Thus says the Lord GOD: O my people, I will open your graves and have you rise from them, and bring you back to the land of Israel. Then you shall know that I am the LORD, when I open your graves and have you rise from them, O my people! I will put my spirit in you that you may live, and I will settle you upon your land; thus you shall know that I am the LORD. I have promised, and I will do it, says the LORD.

Responsorial Psalm

PSALM 107:2-3, 4-5, 6-7, 8-9

R. Give thanks to the Lord; his love is everlasting. (or R. Alleluia.)

Let the redeemed of the LORD say,
those whom he has redeemed from the hand of the foe
And gathered from the lands,
from the east and the west, from the north and the south. **R.**
They went astray in the desert wilderness;
the way to an inhabited city they did not find.
Hungry and thirsty,
their life was wasting away within them. **R.**
They cried to the LORD in their distress;
from their straits he rescued them.
And he led them by a direct way
to reach an inhabited city. **R.**
Let them give thanks to the LORD for his mercy
and his wondrous deeds to the children of men,

Because he satisfied the longing soul
and filled the hungry soul with good things. **R.**

Fourth Reading

JOEL 3:1-5

Thus says the LORD:
I will pour out my spirit upon all flesh.
Your sons and daughters shall prophesy,
your old men shall dream dreams,
your young men shall see visions;
even upon the servants and the handmaids,
in those days, I will pour out my spirit.
And I will work wonders in the heavens and on the earth,
blood, fire, and columns of smoke;
the sun will be turned to darkness,
and the moon to blood,
at the coming of the day of the LORD,
the great and terrible day.
Then everyone shall be rescued
who calls on the name of the LORD;
for on Mount Zion there shall be a remnant,
as the LORD has said,
and in Jerusalem survivors
whom the LORD shall call.

Responsorial Psalm

PSALM 104:1-2, 24 and 35, 27-28, 29-30

R. Lord, send out your Spirit, and renew the face of the earth. (or R. Alleluia.)

Bless the LORD, O my soul!
O LORD, my God, you are great indeed!
You are clothed with majesty and glory,
robed in light as with a cloak. **R.**
How manifold are your works, O LORD!
In wisdom you have wrought them all—
the earth is full of your creatures;
bless the LORD, O my soul! Alleluia. **R.**
Creatures all look to you
to give them food in due time.
When you give it to them, they gather it;
when you open your hand, they are filled with good things. R.
If you take away their breath, they perish
and return to their dust.

When you send forth your spirit, they are created,
and you renew the face of the earth. **R.**

Epistle
ROMANS 8:22-27

Brothers and sisters: Are you unaware that we who were baptized into Christ Jesus were baptized into his death? We were indeed buried with him through baptism into death, so that, just as Christ was raised from the dead by the glory of the Father, we too might live in newness of life.

For if we have grown into union with him through a death like his, we shall also be united with him in the resurrection. We know that our old self was crucified with him, so that our sinful body might be done away with, that we might no longer be in slavery to sin. For a dead person has been absolved from sin. If, then, we have died with Christ, we believe that we shall also live with him. We know that Christ, raised from the dead, dies no more; death no longer has power over him. As to his death, he died to sin once and for all; as to his life, he lives for God. Consequently, you too must think of yourselves as being dead to sin and living for God in Christ Jesus.

Gospel
JOHN 7:37-39

On the last and greatest day of the feast, Jesus stood up and exclaimed, "Let anyone who thirsts come to me and drink.

As Scripture says:

Rivers of living water will flow from within him
who believes in me."

He said this in reference to the Spirit that those who came to believe in him were to receive. There was, of course, no Spirit yet, because Jesus had not yet been glorified.

Pentecost Sunday

First Reading
ACTS 2:1-11

When the time for Pentecost was fulfilled, they were all in one place together. And suddenly there came from the sky a noise like a strong driving wind, and it filled the entire house in which they were. Then there appeared to them tongues as of fire, which parted and came to rest on each one of them. And they were all filled with the

Holy Spirit and began to speak in different tongues, as the Spirit enabled them to proclaim.

Now there were devout Jews from every nation under heaven staying in Jerusalem. At this sound, they gathered in a large crowd, but they were confused because each one heard them speaking in his own language. They were astounded, and in amazement they asked, "Are not all these people who are speaking Galileans? Then how does each of us hear them in his native language? We are Parthians, Medes, and Elamites, inhabitants of Mesopotamia, Judea and Cappadocia, Pontus and Asia, Phrygia and Pamphylia, Egypt and the districts of Libya near Cyrene, as well as travelers from Rome, both Jews and converts to Judaism, Cretans and Arabs, yet we hear them speaking in our own tongues of the mighty acts of God."

Responsorial Psalm

PSALM 104:1, 24, 29-30, 31, 34

R. Lord, send out your Spirit, and renew the face of the earth. (or R. Alleluia.)

Bless the LORD, O my soul!
  O LORD, my God, you are great indeed!
How manifold are your works, O LORD!
  The earth is full of your creatures. **R.**
If you take away their breath, they perish
  and return to their dust.
When you send forth your spirit, they are created,
  and you renew the face of the earth. **R.**
May the glory of the LORD endure forever;
  may the LORD be glad in his works!
Pleasing to him be my theme;
  I will be glad in the LORD. **R.**

Second Reading

1 CORINTHIANS 12:3b-7, 12-13 (or ROMANS 8:8-17)

Brothers and sisters: No one can say, "Jesus is Lord," except by the Holy Spirit.

There are different kinds of spiritual gifts but the same Spirit; there are different forms of service but the same Lord; there are different workings but the same God who produces all of them in everyone. To each individual the manifestation of the Spirit is given for some benefit.

As a body is one though it has many parts, and all the parts of the body, though many, are one body, so also Christ. For in one Spirit we were all baptized into one body, whether Jews or Greeks, slaves or free persons, and we were all given to drink of one Spirit.

Gospel
JOHN 20:19-23 (or JOHN 14:15-16, 23b-26)

On the evening of that first day of the week, when the doors were locked, where the disciples were, for fear of the Jews, Jesus came and stood in their midst and said to them, "Peace be with you." When he had said this, he showed them his hands and his side. The disciples rejoiced when they saw the Lord. Jesus said to them again, "Peace be with you. As the Father has sent me, so I send you." And when he had said this, he breathed on them and said to them, "Receive the Holy Spirit. Whose sins you forgive are forgiven them, and whose sins you retain are retained."

Monday, June 10

Blessed Virgin Mary, Mother of the Church

First Reading
GENESIS 3:9-15, 20 (or ACTS 1:12-14)

After the man, Adam, had eaten of the tree, the LORD God called to the man and asked him, "Where are you?" He answered, "I heard you in the garden; but I was afraid, because I was naked, so I hid myself." Then he asked, "Who told you that you were naked? You have eaten, then, from the tree of which I had forbidden you to eat!" The man replied, "The woman whom you put here with me—she gave me fruit from the tree, and so I ate it." The LORD God then asked the woman, "Why did you do such a thing?" The woman answered, "The serpent tricked me into it, so I ate it."

Then the LORD God said to the serpent:
"Because you have done this, you shall be banned
from all the animals
and from all the wild creatures;
on your belly shall you crawl,
and dirt shall you eat
all the days of your life.
I will put enmity between you and the woman,
and between your offspring and hers;
he will strike at your head,
while you strike at his heel."

The man called his wife Eve, because she became the mother of all the living.

Responsorial Psalm
PSALM 87:1-2, 3 and 5, 6-7
R. Glorious things are told of you, O city of God.

His foundation upon the holy mountains
  the LORD loves:
The gates of Zion,
  more than any dwelling of Jacob. **R.**
Glorious things are said of you,
  O city of God!
And of Zion they shall say:
  "One and all were born in her;
And he who has established her
  is the Most High LORD." **R.**
They shall note, when the peoples are enrolled:
  "This man was born there."
And all shall sing, in their festive dance:
  "My home is within you." **R.**

Gospel
JOHN 19:25-34

Standing by the cross of Jesus were his mother and his mother's sister, Mary the wife of Clopas, and Mary Magdalene. When Jesus saw his mother and the disciple there whom he loved he said to his mother, "Woman, behold, your son." Then he said to the disciple, "Behold, your mother." And from that hour the disciple took her into his home.

After this, aware that everything was now finished, in order that the Scripture might be fulfilled, Jesus said, "I thirst." There was a vessel filled with common wine. So they put a sponge soaked in wine on a sprig of hyssop and put it up to his mouth. When Jesus had taken the wine, he said, "It is finished." And bowing his head, he handed over the spirit.

Now since it was preparation day, in order that the bodies might not remain on the cross on the sabbath, for the sabbath day of that week was a solemn one, the Jews asked Pilate that their legs be broken and they be taken down. So the soldiers came and broke the legs of the first and then of the other one who was crucified with Jesus. But when they came to Jesus and saw that he was already dead, they did not break his legs, but one soldier thrust his lance into his side, and immediately blood and water flowed out.

Tuesday, June 11

Saint Barnabas, Apostle

First Reading

ACTS 11:21b-26; 13:1-3

In those days a great number who believed turned to the Lord. The news about them reached the ears of the Church in Jerusalem, and they sent Barnabas to go to Antioch. When he arrived and saw the grace of God, he rejoiced and encouraged them all to remain faithful to the Lord in firmness of heart, for he was a good man, filled with the Holy Spirit and faith. And a large number of people was added to the Lord. Then he went to Tarsus to look for Saul, and when he had found him he brought him to Antioch. For a whole year they met with the Church and taught a large number of people, and it was in Antioch that the disciples were first called Christians.

Now there were in the Church at Antioch prophets and teachers: Barnabas, Symeon who was called Niger, Lucius of Cyrene, Manaen who was a close friend of Herod the tetrarch, and Saul. While they were worshiping the Lord and fasting, the Holy Spirit said, "Set apart for me Barnabas and Saul for the work to which I have called them." Then, completing their fasting and prayer, they laid hands on them and sent them off.

Responsorial Psalm

PSALM 98:1, 2-3ab, 3cd-4, 5-6

R. The Lord has revealed to the nations his saving power.

Sing to the LORD a new song,
for he has done wondrous deeds;
His right hand has won victory for him,
his holy arm. **R.**
The LORD has made his salvation known:
in the sight of the nations he has revealed his justice.
He has remembered his kindness and his faithfulness
toward the house of Israel. **R.**
All the ends of the earth have seen
the salvation by our God.
Sing joyfully to the LORD, all you lands;
break into song; sing praise. **R.**
Sing praise to the LORD with the harp,
with the harp and melodious song.
With trumpets and the sound of the horn
sing joyfully before the King, the LORD. **R.**

Gospel
MATTHEW 5:13-16

Jesus said to his disciples: "You are the salt of the earth. But if salt loses its taste, with what can it be seasoned? It is no longer good for anything but to be thrown out and trampled underfoot. You are the light of the world. A city set on a mountain cannot be hidden. Nor do they light a lamp and then put it under a bushel basket; it is set on a lampstand, where it gives light to all in the house. Just so, your light must shine before others, that they may see your good deeds and glorify your heavenly Father."

Wednesday, June 12

First Reading
2 CORINTHIANS 3:4-11

Brothers and sisters: Such confidence we have through Christ toward God. Not that of ourselves we are qualified to take credit for anything as coming from us; rather, our qualification comes from God, who has indeed qualified us as ministers of a new covenant, not of letter but of spirit; for the letter brings death, but the Spirit gives life.

Now if the ministry of death, carved in letters on stone, was so glorious that the children of Israel could not look intently at the face of Moses because of its glory that was going to fade, how much more will the ministry of the Spirit be glorious? For if the ministry of condemnation was glorious, the ministry of righteousness will abound much more in glory. Indeed, what was endowed with glory has come to have no glory in this respect because of the glory that surpasses it. For if what was going to fade was glorious, how much more will what endures be glorious.

Responsorial Psalm
PSALM 99:5, 6, 7, 8, 9
R. Holy is the Lord our God.

Extol the LORD, our God,
  and worship at his footstool;
  holy is he! **R.**
Moses and Aaron were among his priests,
  and Samuel, among those who called upon his name;
  they called upon the LORD, and he answered them. **R.**
From the pillar of cloud he spoke to them;
  they heard his decrees and the law he gave them. **R.**
O LORD, our God, you answered them;
  a forgiving God you were to them,
  though requiting their misdeeds. **R.**

Extol the LORD, our God,
and worship at his holy mountain;
for holy is the LORD, our God. **R.**

Gospel
MATTHEW 5:17-19

Jesus said to his disciples: "Do not think that I have come to abolish the law or the prophets. I have come not to abolish but to fulfill. Amen, I say to you, until heaven and earth pass away, not the smallest letter or the smallest part of a letter will pass from the law, until all things have taken place. Therefore, whoever breaks one of the least of these commandments and teaches others to do so will be called least in the Kingdom of heaven. But whoever obeys and teaches these commandments will be called greatest in the Kingdom of heaven."

Thursday, June 13

First Reading
2 CORINTHIANS 3:15–4:1, 3-6

Brothers and sisters: To this day, whenever Moses is read, a veil lies over the hearts of the children of Israel, but whenever a person turns to the Lord the veil is removed. Now the Lord is the Spirit and where the Spirit of the Lord is, there is freedom. All of us, gazing with unveiled face on the glory of the Lord, are being transformed into the same image from glory to glory, as from the Lord who is the Spirit.

Therefore, since we have this ministry through the mercy shown us, we are not discouraged. And even though our Gospel is veiled, it is veiled for those who are perishing, in whose case the god of this age has blinded the minds of the unbelievers, so that they may not see the light of the Gospel of the glory of Christ, who is the image of God. For we do not preach ourselves but Jesus Christ as Lord, and ourselves as your slaves for the sake of Jesus. For God who said, *Let light shine out of darkness*, has shone in our hearts to bring to light the knowledge of the glory of God on the face of Jesus Christ.

Responsorial Psalm
PSALM 85:9ab and 10, 11-12, 13-14
R. The glory of the Lord will dwell in our land.

I will hear what God proclaims;
the LORD—for he proclaims peace to his people.
Near indeed is his salvation to those who fear him,
glory dwelling in our land. **R.**

Kindness and truth shall meet;
  justice and peace shall kiss.
Truth shall spring out of the earth,
  and justice shall look down from heaven. **R.**
The LORD himself will give his benefits;
  our land shall yield its increase.
Justice shall walk before him,
  and salvation, along the way of his steps. **R.**

Gospel

MATTHEW 5:20-26

Jesus said to his disciples: "I tell you, unless your righteousness surpasses that of the scribes and Pharisees, you will not enter into the Kingdom of heaven.

"You have heard that it was said to your ancestors, *You shall not kill; and whoever kills will be liable to judgment.* But I say to you, whoever is angry with his brother will be liable to judgment, and whoever says to his brother, *Raqa,* will be answerable to the Sanhedrin, and whoever says, 'You fool,' will be liable to fiery Gehenna. Therefore, if you bring your gift to the altar, and there recall that your brother has anything against you, leave your gift there at the altar, go first and be reconciled with your brother, and then come and offer your gift. Settle with your opponent quickly while on the way to court with him. Otherwise your opponent will hand you over to the judge, and the judge will hand you over to the guard, and you will be thrown into prison. Amen, I say to you, you will not be released until you have paid the last penny."

Friday, June 14

First Reading

2 CORINTHIANS 4:7-15

Brothers and sisters: We hold this treasure in earthen vessels, that the surpassing power may be of God and not from us. We are afflicted in every way, but not constrained; perplexed, but not driven to despair; persecuted, but not abandoned; struck down, but not destroyed; always carrying about in the Body the dying of Jesus, so that the life of Jesus may also be manifested in our body. For we who live are constantly being given up to death for the sake of Jesus, so that the life of Jesus may be manifested in our mortal flesh.

So death is at work in us, but life in you. Since, then, we have the same spirit of faith, according to what is written, "I believed, therefore I spoke," we too believe and therefore speak, knowing that the one who raised the Lord Jesus will raise us also with Jesus and place us with you in his presence. Everything indeed is for you, so that the grace bestowed in abundance on more and more people may cause the thanksgiving to overflow for the glory of God.

Responsorial Psalm

PSALM 116:10-11, 15-16, 17-18

R. To you, Lord, I will offer a sacrifice of praise.

(or R. Alleluia.)

I believed, even when I said,
"I am greatly afflicted";
I said in my alarm,
"No man is dependable." **R.**
Precious in the eyes of the LORD
is the death of his faithful ones.
O LORD, I am your servant;
I am your servant, the son of your handmaid;
you have loosed my bonds. **R.**
To you will I offer sacrifice of thanksgiving,
and I will call upon the name of the LORD.
My vows to the LORD I will pay
in the presence of all his people. **R.**

Gospel

MATTHEW 5:27-32

Jesus said to his disciples: "You have heard that it was said, *You shall not commit adultery*. But I say to you, everyone who looks at a woman with lust has already committed adultery with her in his heart. If your right eye causes you to sin, tear it out and throw it away. It is better for you to lose one of your members than to have your whole body thrown into Gehenna. And if your right hand causes you to sin, cut it off and throw it away. It is better for you to lose one of your members than to have your whole body go into Gehenna.

"It was also said, *Whoever divorces his wife must give her a bill of divorce*. But I say to you, whoever divorces his wife (unless the marriage is unlawful) causes her to commit adultery, and whoever marries a divorced woman commits adultery."

Saturday, June 15

First Reading

2 CORINTHIANS 5:14-21

Brothers and sisters: The love of Christ impels us, once we have come to the conviction that one died for all; therefore, all have died. He indeed died for all, so that those who live might no longer live for themselves but for him who for their sake died and was raised.

Consequently, from now on we regard no one according to the flesh; even if we once knew Christ according to the flesh, yet now we know him so no longer. So whoever is in Christ is a new creation: the old things have passed away; behold, new things have come. And all this is from God, who has reconciled us to himself through Christ and given us the ministry of reconciliation, namely, God was reconciling the world to himself in Christ, not counting their trespasses against them and entrusting to us the message of reconciliation. So we are ambassadors for Christ, as if God were appealing through us. We implore you on behalf of Christ, be reconciled to God. For our sake he made him to be sin who did not know sin, so that we might become the righteousness of God in him.

Responsorial Psalm
PSALM 103:1-2, 3-4, 9-10, 11-12
R. The Lord is kind and merciful.

Bless the LORD, O my soul;
 and all my being, bless his holy name.
Bless the LORD, O my soul,
 and forget not all his benefits. **R.**
He pardons all your iniquities,
 he heals all your ills.
He redeems your life from destruction,
 he crowns you with kindness and compassion. **R.**
He will not always chide,
 nor does he keep his wrath forever.
Not according to our sins does he deal with us,
 nor does he requite us according to our crimes. **R.**
For as the heavens are high above the earth,
 so surpassing is his kindness toward those who fear him.
As far as the east is from the west,
 so far has he put our transgressions from us. **R.**

Gospel
MATTHEW 5:33-37

Jesus said to his disciples: "You have heard that it was said to your ancestors, *Do not take a false oath, but make good to the Lord all that you vow.* But I say to you, do not swear at all; not by heaven, for it is God's throne; nor by the earth, for it is his footstool; nor by Jerusalem, for it is the city of the great King. Do not swear by your head, for you cannot make a single hair white or black. Let your 'Yes' mean 'Yes,' and your 'No' mean 'No.' Anything more is from the Evil One."

Sunday, June 16

The Most Holy Trinity

First Reading
PROVERBS 8:22-31

Thus says the wisdom of God:
"The LORD possessed me, the beginning of his ways,
the forerunner of his prodigies of long ago;
from of old I was poured forth,
at the first, before the earth.
When there were no depths I was brought forth,
when there were no fountains or springs of water;
before the mountains were settled into place,
before the hills, I was brought forth;
while as yet the earth and fields were not made,
nor the first clods of the world.

"When the Lord established the heavens I was there,
when he marked out the vault over the face of the deep;
when he made firm the skies above,
when he fixed fast the foundations of the earth;
when he set for the sea its limit,
so that the waters should not transgress his command;
then was I beside him as his craftsman,
and I was his delight day by day,
playing before him all the while,
playing on the surface of his earth;
and I found delight in the human race."

Responsorial Psalm
PSALM 8:4-5, 6-7, 8-9
R. O Lord, our God, how wonderful your name in all the earth!
When I behold your heavens, the work of your fingers,
the moon and the stars which you set in place—
what is man that you should be mindful of him,
or the son of man that you should care for him? **R.**
You have made him little less than the angels,
and crowned him with glory and honor.
You have given him rule over the works of your hands,
putting all things under his feet: **R.**
All sheep and oxen,
yes, and the beasts of the field,

the birds of the air, the fishes of the sea,
    and whatever swims the paths of the seas. **R.**

Second Reading
ROMANS 5:1-5

Brothers and sisters: Therefore, since we have been justified by faith, we have peace with God through our Lord Jesus Christ, through whom we have gained access by faith to this grace in which we stand, and we boast in hope of the glory of God. Not only that, but we even boast of our afflictions, knowing that affliction produces endurance, and endurance, proven character, and proven character, hope, and hope does not disappoint, because the love of God has been poured out into our hearts through the Holy Spirit that has been given to us.

Gospel
JOHN 16:12-15

Jesus said to his disciples: "I have much more to tell you, but you cannot bear it now. But when he comes, the Spirit of truth, he will guide you to all truth. He will not speak on his own, but he will speak what he hears, and will declare to you the things that are coming. He will glorify me, because he will take from what is mine and declare it to you. Everything that the Father has is mine; for this reason I told you that he will take from what is mine and declare it to you."

Monday, June 17

(Eleventh Week in Ordinary Time)

First Reading
2 CORINTHIANS 6:1-10

Brothers and sisters: As your fellow workers, we appeal to you not to receive the grace of God in vain. For he says:

In an acceptable time I heard you,
    and on the day of salvation I helped you.

Behold, now is a very acceptable time; behold, now is the day of salvation. We cause no one to stumble in anything, in order that no fault may be found with our ministry; on the contrary, in everything we commend ourselves as ministers of God, through much endurance, in afflictions, hardships, constraints, beatings, imprisonments, riots, labors, vigils, fasts; by purity, knowledge, patience, kindness, in the Holy Spirit, in unfeigned love, in truthful speech, in the power of God; with weapons of righteousness at the right and at the left; through glory and dishonor, insult and praise. We are treated as deceivers and yet are truthful; as unrecognized and yet acknowledged; as dying and behold we live; as chastised and yet not put to death; as sorrowful yet always rejoicing; as poor yet enriching many; as having nothing and yet possessing all things.

Responsorial Psalm

PSALM 98:1, 2b, 3ab, 3cd-4

R. The Lord has made known his salvation.

Sing to the LORD a new song,
  for he has done wondrous deeds;
His right hand has won victory for him,
  his holy arm. **R.**
In the sight of the nations he has revealed his justice.
He has remembered his kindness and his faithfulness
  toward the house of Israel. **R.**
All the ends of the earth have seen
  the salvation by our God.
Sing joyfully to the LORD, all you lands;
  break into song; sing praise. **R.**

Gospel

MATTHEW 5:38-42

Jesus said to his disciples: "You have heard that it was said, *An eye for an eye and a tooth for a tooth*. But I say to you, offer no resistance to one who is evil. When someone strikes you on your right cheek, turn the other one to him as well. If anyone wants to go to law with you over your tunic, hand him your cloak as well. Should anyone press you into service for one mile, go with him for two miles. Give to the one who asks of you, and do not turn your back on one who wants to borrow."

Tuesday, June 18

First Reading

2 CORINTHIANS 8:1-9

We want you to know, brothers and sisters, of the grace of God that has been given to the churches of Macedonia, for in a severe test of affliction, the abundance of their joy and their profound poverty overflowed in a wealth of generosity on their part. For according to their means, I can testify, and beyond their means, spontaneously, they begged us insistently for the favor of taking part in the service to the holy ones, and this, not as we expected, but they gave themselves first to the Lord and to us through the will of God, so that we urged Titus that, as he had already begun, he should also complete for you this gracious act also. Now as you excel in every respect, in faith, discourse, knowledge, all earnestness, and in the love we have for you, may you excel in this gracious act also.

I say this not by way of command, but to test the genuineness of your love by your concern for others. For you know the gracious act of our Lord Jesus Christ, that for your sake he became poor although he was rich, so that by his poverty you might become rich.

Responsorial Psalm

PSALM 146:2, 5-6ab, 6c-7, 8-9a

R. Praise the Lord, my soul! (or R. Alleluia.)

Praise the LORD, my soul!
I will praise the LORD all my life;
I will sing praise to my God while I live. **R.**
Blessed he whose help is the God of Jacob,
whose hope is in the LORD, his God,
Who made heaven and earth,
the sea and all that is in them. **R.**
Who keeps faith forever,
secures justice for the oppressed,
gives food to the hungry.
The LORD sets captives free. **R.**
The LORD gives sight to the blind.
The LORD raises up those who were bowed down;
the LORD loves the just.
The LORD protects strangers. **R.**

Gospel

MATTHEW 5:43-48

Jesus said to his disciples: "You have heard that it was said, *You shall love your neighbor and hate your enemy.* But I say to you, love your enemies and pray for those who persecute you, that you may be children of your heavenly Father, for he makes his sun rise on the bad and the good, and causes rain to fall on the just and the unjust. For if you love those who love you, what recompense will you have? Do not the tax collectors do the same? And if you greet your brothers only, what is unusual about that? Do not the pagans do the same? So be perfect, just as your heavenly Father is perfect."

Wednesday, June 19

First Reading

2 CORINTHIANS 9:6-11

Brothers and sisters, consider this: whoever sows sparingly will also reap sparingly, and whoever sows bountifully will also reap bountifully. Each must do as already determined, without sadness or compulsion, for God loves a cheerful giver. Moreover, God is able to make every grace abundant for you, so that in all things, always having all you need, you may have an abundance for every good work. As it is written:

He scatters abroad, he gives to the poor;
his righteousness endures forever.

The one who supplies seed to the sower and bread for food will supply and multiply your seed and increase the harvest of your righteousness.

You are being enriched in every way for all generosity, which through us produces thanksgiving to God.

Responsorial Psalm

PSALM 112:1bc-2, 3-4, 9

R. Blessed the man who fears the Lord. (or R. Alleluia.)

Blessed the man who fears the LORD,
who greatly delights in his commands.
His posterity shall be mighty upon the earth;
the upright generation shall be blessed. **R.**
Wealth and riches shall be in his house;
his generosity shall endure forever.
Light shines through the darkness for the upright;
he is gracious and merciful and just. **R.**
Lavishly he gives to the poor;
his generosity shall endure forever;
his horn shall be exalted in glory. **R.**

Gospel

MATTHEW 6:1-6, 16-18

Jesus said to his disciples: "Take care not to perform righteous deeds in order that people may see them; otherwise, you will have no recompense from your heavenly Father. When you give alms, do not blow a trumpet before you, as the hypocrites do in the synagogues and in the streets to win the praise of others. Amen, I say to you, they have received their reward. But when you give alms, do not let your left hand know what your right is doing, so that your almsgiving may be secret. And your Father who sees in secret will repay you.

"When you pray, do not be like the hypocrites, who love to stand and pray in the synagogues and on street corners so that others may see them. Amen, I say to you, they have received their reward. But when you pray, go to your inner room, close the door, and pray to your Father in secret. And your Father who sees in secret will repay you.

"When you fast, do not look gloomy like the hypocrites. They neglect their appearance, so that they may appear to others to be fasting. Amen, I say to you, they have received their reward. But when you fast, anoint your head and wash your face, so that you may not appear to others to be fasting, except to your Father who is hidden. And your Father who sees what is hidden will repay you."

Thursday, June 20

First Reading

2 CORINTHIANS 11:1-11

Brothers and sisters: If only you would put up with a little foolishness from me! Please put up with me. For I am jealous of you with the jealousy of God, since I betrothed you to one husband to present you as a chaste virgin to Christ. But I am afraid that, as the serpent deceived Eve by his cunning, your thoughts may be corrupted from a sincere and pure commitment to Christ. For if someone comes and preaches another Jesus than the one we preached, or if you receive a different spirit from the one you received or a different gospel from the one you accepted, you put up with it well enough. For I think that I am not in any way inferior to these "superapostles." Even if I am untrained in speaking, I am not so in knowledge; in every way we have made this plain to you in all things.

Did I make a mistake when I humbled myself so that you might be exalted, because I preached the Gospel of God to you without charge? I plundered other churches by accepting from them in order to minister to you. And when I was with you and in need, I did not burden anyone, for the brothers who came from Macedonia supplied my needs. So I refrained and will refrain from burdening you in any way. By the truth of Christ in me, this boast of mine shall not be silenced in the regions of Achaia. And why? Because I do not love you? God knows I do!

Responsorial Psalm

PSALM 111:1b-2, 3-4, 7-8

R. Your works, O Lord, are justice and truth. (or R. Alleluia.)

I will give thanks to the LORD with all my heart
in the company and assembly of the just.

Great are the works of the LORD,
exquisite in all their delights. **R.**
Majesty and glory are his work,
and his justice endures forever.
He has won renown for his wondrous deeds;
gracious and merciful is the LORD. **R.**
The works of his hands are faithful and just;
sure are all his precepts,
Reliable forever and ever,
wrought in truth and equity. **R.**

Gospel
MATTHEW 6:7-15

Jesus said to his disciples: "In praying, do not babble like the pagans, who think that they will be heard because of their many words. Do not be like them. Your Father knows what you need before you ask him.

"This is how you are to pray:
'Our Father who art in heaven,
hallowed be thy name,
thy Kingdom come,
thy will be done,
on earth as it is in heaven.
Give us this day our daily bread;
and forgive us our trespasses,
as we forgive those who trespass against us;
and lead us not into temptation,
but deliver us from evil.'

"If you forgive others their transgressions, your heavenly Father will forgive you. But if you do not forgive others, neither will your Father forgive your transgressions."

Friday, June 21

First Reading
2 CORINTHIANS 11:18, 21-30

Brothers and sisters: Since many boast according to the flesh, I too will boast. To my shame I say that we were too weak!

But what anyone dares to boast of (I am speaking in foolishness) I also dare. Are they Hebrews? So am I. Are they children of Israel? So am I. Are they descendants of Abraham? So am I. Are they ministers of Christ? (I am talking like an insane person). I am still more, with far greater labors, far more imprisonments, far worse beatings, and numerous brushes with death. Five times at the hands of the Jews I received forty lashes minus one. Three times I was beaten with rods, once I was stoned, three times I was shipwrecked, I passed a night and a day on the deep; on frequent journeys, in dangers from rivers, dangers from robbers, dangers from my own race, dangers from Gentiles, dangers in the city, dangers in the wilderness, dangers at sea, dangers among false brothers; in toil and hardship, through many sleepless nights, through hunger and thirst, through frequent fastings, through cold and exposure. And apart from these things, there is the daily pressure upon me of my anxiety for all the churches. Who is weak, and I am not weak? Who is led to sin, and I am not indignant?

If I must boast, I will boast of the things that show my weakness.

Responsorial Psalm
PSALM 34:2-3, 4-5, 6-7
R. From all their distress God rescues the just.

I will bless the LORD at all times;
his praise shall be ever in my mouth.
Let my soul glory in the LORD;
the lowly will hear me and be glad. **R.**
Glorify the LORD with me,
let us together extol his name.
I sought the LORD, and he answered me
and delivered me from all my fears. **R.**
Look to him that you may be radiant with joy,
and your faces may not blush with shame.
When the poor one called out, the LORD heard,
and from all his distress he saved him. **R.**

Gospel
MATTHEW 6:19-23

Jesus said to his disciples: "Do not store up for yourselves treasures on earth, where moth and decay destroy, and thieves break in and steal. But store up treasures in heaven, where neither moth nor decay destroys, nor thieves break in and steal. For where your treasure is, there also will your heart be.

"The lamp of the body is the eye. If your eye is sound, your whole body will be filled with light; but if your eye is bad, your whole body will be in darkness. And if the light in you is darkness, how great will the darkness be."

Saturday, June 22

First Reading

2 CORINTHIANS 12:1-10

Brothers and sisters: I must boast; not that it is profitable, but I will go on to visions and revelations of the Lord. I know a man in Christ who, fourteen years ago (whether in the body or out of the body I do not know, God knows), was caught up to the third heaven. And I know that this man (whether in the body or out of the body I do not know, God knows) was caught up into Paradise and heard ineffable things, which no one may utter. About this man I will boast, but about myself I will not boast, except about my weaknesses. Although if I should wish to boast, I would not be foolish, for I would be telling the truth. But I refrain, so that no one may think more of me than what he sees in me or hears from me because of the abundance of the revelations. Therefore, that I might not become too elated, a thorn in the flesh was given to me, an angel of Satan, to beat me, to keep me from being too elated. Three times I begged the Lord about this, that it might leave me, but he said to me, "My grace is sufficient for you, for power is made perfect in weakness." I will rather boast most gladly of my weaknesses, in order that the power of Christ may dwell with me. Therefore, I am content with weaknesses, insults, hardships, persecutions, and constraints, for the sake of Christ; for when I am weak, then I am strong.

Responsorial Psalm

PSALM 34:8-9, 10-11, 12-13

R. Taste and see the goodness of the Lord.

The angel of the LORD encamps
  around those who fear him, and delivers them.
Taste and see how good the LORD is;
  blessed the man who takes refuge in him. **R.**
Fear the LORD, you his holy ones,
  for nought is lacking to those who fear him.
The great grow poor and hungry;
  but those who seek the LORD want for no good thing. **R.**
Come, children, hear me;
  I will teach you the fear of the LORD.
Which of you desires life,
  and takes delight in prosperous days? **R.**

Gospel
MATTHEW 6:24-34

Jesus said to his disciples: "No one can serve two masters. He will either hate one and love the other, or be devoted to one and despise the other. You cannot serve God and mammon.

"Therefore I tell you, do not worry about your life, what you will eat or drink, or about your body, what you will wear. Is not life more than food and the body more than clothing? Look at the birds in the sky; they do not sow or reap, they gather nothing into barns, yet your heavenly Father feeds them. Are not you more important than they? Can any of you by worrying add a single moment to your life-span? Why are you anxious about clothes? Learn from the way the wild flowers grow. They do not work or spin. But I tell you that not even Solomon in all his splendor was clothed like one of them. If God so clothes the grass of the field, which grows today and is thrown into the oven tomorrow, will he not much more provide for you, O you of little faith? So do not worry and say, 'What are we to eat?' or 'What are we to drink?' or 'What are we to wear?' All these things the pagans seek. Your heavenly Father knows that you need them all. But seek first the Kingdom of God and his righteousness, and all these things will be given you besides. Do not worry about tomorrow; tomorrow will take care of itself. Sufficient for a day is its own evil."

Sunday, June 23

The Most Holy Body and Blood of Christ (Corpus Christi)

First Reading
GENESIS 14:18-20

In those days, Melchizedek, king of Salem, brought out bread and wine, and being a priest of God Most High, he blessed Abram with these words:

"Blessed be Abram by God Most High,
    the creator of heaven and earth;
and blessed be God Most High,
    who delivered your foes into your hand."

Then Abram gave him a tenth of everything.

Responsorial Psalm

PSALM 110:1, 2, 3, 4

R. You are a priest for ever, in the line of Melchizedek.

The LORD said to my Lord: "Sit at my right hand
till I make your enemies your footstool." **R.**
The scepter of your power the LORD will stretch forth from Zion:
"Rule in the midst of your enemies." **R.**
"Yours is princely power in the day of your birth, in holy splendor;
before the daystar, like the dew, I have begotten you." **R.**
The LORD has sworn, and he will not repent:
"You are a priest forever, according to the order of Melchizedek." **R.**

Second Reading

1 CORINTHIANS 11:23-26

Brothers and sisters: I received from the Lord what I also handed on to you, that the Lord Jesus, on the night he was handed over, took bread, and, after he had given thanks, broke it and said, "This is my body that is for you. Do this in remembrance of me." In the same way also the cup, after supper, saying, "This cup is the new covenant in my blood. Do this, as often as you drink it, in remembrance of me." For as often as you eat this bread and drink the cup, you proclaim the death of the Lord until he comes.

Gospel

LUKE 9:11b-17

Jesus spoke to the crowds about the kingdom of God, and he healed those who needed to be cured. As the day was drawing to a close, the Twelve approached him and said, "Dismiss the crowd so that they can go to the surrounding villages and farms and find lodging and provisions; for we are in a deserted place here." He said to them, "Give them some food yourselves." They replied, "Five loaves and two fish are all we have, unless we ourselves go and buy food for all these people." Now the men there numbered about five thousand. Then he said to his disciples, "Have them sit down in groups of about fifty." They did so and made them all sit down. Then taking the five loaves and the two fish, and looking up to heaven, he said the blessing over them, broke them, and gave them to the disciples to set before the crowd. They all ate and were satisfied. And when the leftover fragments were picked up, they filled twelve wicker baskets.

Monday, June 24

The Nativity of Saint John the Baptist

First Reading

ISAIAH 49:1-6 (Vigil: JEREMIAH 1:4-10)

Hear me, O coastlands,
listen, O distant peoples.
The LORD called me from birth,
from my mother's womb he gave me my name.
He made of me a sharp-edged sword
and concealed me in the shadow of his arm.
He made me a polished arrow,
in his quiver he hid me.
You are my servant, he said to me,
Israel, through whom I show my glory.

Though I thought I had toiled in vain,
and for nothing, uselessly, spent my strength,
yet my reward is with the LORD,
my recompense is with my God.
For now the LORD has spoken
who formed me as his servant from the womb,
that Jacob may be brought back to him
and Israel gathered to him;
and I am made glorious in the sight of the LORD,
and my God is now my strength!
It is too little, he says, for you to be my servant,
to raise up the tribes of Jacob,
and restore the survivors of Israel;
I will make you a light to the nations,
that my salvation may reach to the ends of the earth.

Responsorial Psalm

PSALM 139:1b-3, 13-14ab, 14c-15 (Vigil: PSALM 71:1-2, 3-4a, 5-6ab, 15ab and 17)

R. I praise you, for I am wonderfully made.

O LORD, you have probed me, you know me:
you know when I sit and when I stand;
you understand my thoughts from afar.
My journeys and my rest you scrutinize,
with all my ways you are familiar. **R.**
Truly you have formed my inmost being;
you knit me in my mother's womb.

I give you thanks that I am fearfully, wonderfully made;
wonderful are your works. **R.**
My soul also you knew full well;
nor was my frame unknown to you
When I was made in secret,
when I was fashioned in the depths of the earth. **R.**

Second Reading

ACTS 13:22-26 (Vigil: 1 PETER 1:8-12)

In those days, Paul said: "God raised up David as king; of him God testified, *I have found David, son of Jesse, a man after my own heart; he will carry out my every wish.* From this man's descendants God, according to his promise, has brought to Israel a savior, Jesus. John heralded his coming by proclaiming a baptism of repentance to all the people of Israel; and as John was completing his course, he would say, 'What do you suppose that I am? I am not he. Behold, one is coming after me; I am not worthy to unfasten the sandals of his feet.'

"My brothers, sons of the family of Abraham, and those others among you who are God-fearing, to us this word of salvation has been sent."

Gospel

LUKE 1:57-66, 80 (Vigil: LUKE 1:5-17)

When the time arrived for Elizabeth to have her child she gave birth to a son. Her neighbors and relatives heard that the Lord had shown his great mercy toward her, and they rejoiced with her. When they came on the eighth day to circumcise the child, they were going to call him Zechariah after his father, but his mother said in reply, "No. He will be called John." But they answered her, "There is no one among your relatives who has this name." So they made signs, asking his father what he wished him to be called. He asked for a tablet and wrote, "John is his name," and all were amazed. Immediately his mouth was opened, his tongue freed, and he spoke blessing God. Then fear came upon all their neighbors, and all these matters were discussed throughout the hill country of Judea. All who heard these things took them to heart, saying, "What, then, will this child be?" For surely the hand of the Lord was with him.

The child grew and became strong in spirit, and he was in the desert until the day of his manifestation to Israel.

Tuesday, June 25

(Twelfth Week in Ordinary Time)

First Reading

GENESIS 13:2, 5-18

Abram was very rich in livestock, silver, and gold.

Lot, who went with Abram, also had flocks and herds and tents, so that the land could not support them if they stayed together; their possessions were so great that they could not dwell together. There were quarrels between the herdsmen of Abram's livestock and those of Lot's. (At this time the Canaanites and the Perizzites were occupying the land.)

So Abram said to Lot: "Let there be no strife between you and me, or between your herdsmen and mine, for we are kinsmen. Is not the whole land at your disposal? Please separate from me. If you prefer the left, I will go to the right; if you prefer the right, I will go to the left." Lot looked about and saw how well watered the whole Jordan Plain was as far as Zoar, like the LORD's own garden, or like Egypt. (This was before the LORD had destroyed Sodom and Gomorrah.) Lot, therefore, chose for himself the whole Jordan Plain and set out eastward. Thus they separated from each other; Abram stayed in the land of Canaan, while Lot settled among the cities of the Plain, pitching his tents near Sodom. Now the inhabitants of Sodom were very wicked in the sins they committed against the LORD.

After Lot had left, the LORD said to Abram: "Look about you, and from where you are, gaze to the north and south, east and west; all the land that you see I will give to you and your descendants forever. I will make your descendants like the dust of the earth; if anyone could count the dust of the earth, your descendants too might be counted. Set forth and walk about in the land, through its length and breadth, for to you I will give it." Abram moved his tents and went on to settle near the terebinth of Mamre, which is at Hebron. There he built an altar to the LORD.

Responsorial Psalm

PSALM 15:2-3a, 3bc-4ab, 5

R. He who does justice will live in the presence of the Lord.

He who walks blamelessly and does justice;
  who thinks the truth in his heart
  and slanders not with his tongue. **R.**

Who harms not his fellow man,
  nor takes up a reproach against his neighbor;
By whom the reprobate is despised,
  while he honors those who fear the LORD. **R.**

Who lends not his money at usury
  and accepts no bribe against the innocent.
He who does these things
  shall never be disturbed. **R.**

Gospel
MATTHEW 7:6, 12-14

Jesus said to his disciples: "Do not give what is holy to dogs, or throw your pearls before swine, lest they trample them underfoot, and turn and tear you to pieces.

"Do to others whatever you would have them do to you. This is the Law and the Prophets.

"Enter through the narrow gate; for the gate is wide and the road broad that leads to destruction, and those who enter through it are many. How narrow the gate and constricted the road that leads to life. And those who find it are few."

Wednesday, June 26

First Reading
GENESIS 15:1-12, 17-18

The word of the LORD came to Abram in a vision:

"Fear not, Abram!
  I am your shield;
  I will make your reward very great."

But Abram said, "O Lord GOD, what good will your gifts be, if I keep on being childless and have as my heir the steward of my house, Eliezer?" Abram continued, "See, you have given me no offspring, and so one of my servants will be my heir." Then the word of the LORD came to him: "No, that one shall not be your heir; your own issue shall be your heir." He took him outside and said: "Look up at the sky and count the stars, if you can. Just so," he added, "shall your descendants be." Abram put his faith in the LORD, who credited it to him as an act of righteousness.

He then said to him, "I am the LORD who brought you from Ur of the Chaldeans to give you this land as a possession." "O Lord GOD," he asked, "how am I to know that I shall possess it?" He answered him, "Bring me a three-year-old heifer, a three-year-old she-goat, a three-year-old ram, a turtledove, and a young pigeon." Abram brought him all these, split them in two, and placed each half opposite the other; but the birds he did not cut up. Birds of prey swooped down on the carcasses, but Abram stayed with them. As the sun was about to set, a trance fell upon Abram, and a deep, terrifying darkness enveloped him.

When the sun had set and it was dark, there appeared a smoking fire pot and a flaming torch, which passed between those pieces. It was on that occasion that the LORD made a covenant with Abram, saying: "To your descendants I give this land, from the Wadi of Egypt to the Great River the Euphrates."

Responsorial Psalm

PSALM 105:1-2, 3-4, 6-7, 8-9

R. The Lord remembers his covenant for ever. (or R. Alleluia.)

Give thanks to the LORD, invoke his name;
make known among the nations his deeds.
Sing to him, sing his praise,
proclaim all his wondrous deeds. **R.**
Glory in his holy name;
rejoice, O hearts that seek the LORD!
Look to the LORD in his strength;
seek to serve him constantly. **R.**
You descendants of Abraham, his servants,
sons of Jacob, his chosen ones!
He, the LORD, is our God;
throughout the earth his judgments prevail. **R.**
He remembers forever his covenant
which he made binding for a thousand generations—
Which he entered into with Abraham
and by his oath to Isaac. **R.**

Gospel

MATTHEW 7:15-20

Jesus said to his disciples: "Beware of false prophets, who come to you in sheep's clothing, but underneath are ravenous wolves. By their fruits you will know them. Do people pick grapes from thornbushes, or figs from thistles? Just so, every good tree bears good fruit, and a rotten tree bears bad fruit. A good tree cannot bear bad fruit, nor can a rotten tree bear good fruit. Every tree that does not bear good fruit will be cut down and thrown into the fire. So by their fruits you will know them."

Thursday, June 27

First Reading

GENESIS 16:1-12, 15-16 (or GENESIS 16:6b-12, 15-16)

Abram's wife Sarai had borne him no children. She had, however, an Egyptian maidservant named Hagar. Sarai said to Abram: "The LORD has kept me from bearing children. Have intercourse, then, with my maid; perhaps I shall have sons through her." Abram heeded Sarai's request. Thus, after Abram had lived ten years in the land of Canaan, his wife Sarai took her maid, Hagar the Egyptian, and gave her to her husband Abram to be his concubine. He had intercourse with her, and she became pregnant. When she became aware of her pregnancy, she looked on her mistress with disdain. So Sarai said to Abram: "You are responsible for this outrage against me. I myself gave my maid to your embrace; but ever since she became aware of her pregnancy, she has been looking on me with disdain. May the LORD decide between you and me!" Abram told Sarai: "Your maid is in your power. Do to her whatever you please." Sarai then abused her so much that Hagar ran away from her.

The LORD's messenger found her by a spring in the wilderness, the spring on the road to Shur, and he asked, "Hagar, maid of Sarai, where have you come from and where are you going?" She answered, "I am running away from my mistress, Sarai." But the LORD's messenger told her: "Go back to your mistress and submit to her abusive treatment. I will make your descendants so numerous," added the LORD's messenger, "that they will be too many to count. Besides," the LORD's messenger said to her:

"You are now pregnant and shall bear a son;
    you shall name him Ishmael,
For the LORD has heard you,
    God has answered you.

This one shall be a wild ass of a man,
    his hand against everyone,
    and everyone's hand against him;
In opposition to all his kin
    shall he encamp."

Hagar bore Abram a son, and Abram named the son whom Hagar bore him Ishmael. Abram was eighty-six years old when Hagar bore him Ishmael.

Responsorial Psalm

PSALM 106:1b-2, 3-4a, 4b-5

R. Give thanks to the Lord, for he is good. (or R. Alleluia.)

Give thanks to the LORD, for he is good,
for his mercy endures forever.
Who can tell the mighty deeds of the LORD,
or proclaim all his praises? **R.**
Blessed are they who observe what is right,
who do always what is just.
Remember us, O LORD, as you favor your people. **R.**
Visit me with your saving help,
that I may see the prosperity of your chosen ones,
rejoice in the joy of your people,
and glory with your inheritance. **R.**

Gospel

MATTHEW 7:21-29

Jesus said to his disciples: "Not everyone who says to me, 'Lord, Lord,' will enter the Kingdom of heaven, but only the one who does the will of my Father in heaven. Many will say to me on that day, 'Lord, Lord, did we not prophesy in your name? Did we not drive out demons in your name? Did we not do mighty deeds in your name?' Then I will declare to them solemnly, 'I never knew you. Depart from me, you evildoers.'

"Everyone who listens to these words of mine and acts on them will be like a wise man who built his house on rock. The rain fell, the floods came, and the winds blew and buffeted the house. But it did not collapse; it had been set solidly on rock. And everyone who listens to these words of mine but does not act on them will be like a fool who built his house on sand. The rain fell, the floods came, and the winds blew and buffeted the house. And it collapsed and was completely ruined."

When Jesus finished these words, the crowds were astonished at his teaching, for he taught them as one having authority, and not as their scribes.

Friday, June 28

The Most Sacred Heart of Jesus

First Reading

EZEKIEL 34:11-16

Thus says the Lord GOD: I myself will look after and tend my sheep. As a shepherd tends his flock when he finds himself among his scattered sheep, so will I tend my sheep. I will rescue them from every place where they were scattered when it was cloudy and dark. I will lead them out from among the peoples and gather them from the foreign lands; I will bring them back to their own country and pasture them upon the mountains of Israel in the land's ravines and all its inhabited places. In good pastures will I pasture them, and on the mountain heights of Israel shall be their grazing ground. There they shall lie down on good grazing ground, and in rich pastures shall they be pastured on the mountains of Israel. I myself will pasture my sheep; I myself will give them rest, says the Lord GOD. The lost I will seek out, the strayed I will bring back, the injured I will bind up, the sick I will heal, but the sleek and the strong I will destroy, shepherding them rightly.

Responsorial Psalm
PSALM 23:1-3a, 3b-4, 5, 6
R. The Lord is my shepherd; there is nothing I shall want.

The LORD is my shepherd; I shall not want.
In verdant pastures he gives me repose;
beside restful waters he leads me;
he refreshes my soul. **R.**
He guides me in right paths
for his name's sake.
Even though I walk in the dark valley
I fear no evil; for you are at my side
with your rod and your staff
that give me courage. **R.**
You spread the table before me
in the sight of my foes;
you anoint my head with oil;
my cup overflows. **R.**
Only goodness and kindness follow me
all the days of my life;
and I shall dwell in the house of the LORD
for years to come. **R.**

Second Reading
ROMANS 5:5b-11

Brothers and sisters: The love of God has been poured out into our hearts through the Holy Spirit that has been given to us. For Christ, while we were still helpless, died at the appointed time for the ungodly. Indeed, only with difficulty does one die for a just person, though perhaps for a good person one might even find courage to die. But God proves his love for us in that while we were still sinners Christ died for us. How much more then, since we are now justified by his blood, will we be saved through him from the wrath. Indeed, if, while we were enemies, we were reconciled to God through the death of his Son, how much more, once reconciled, will we be saved by his life. Not only that, but we also boast of God through our Lord Jesus Christ, through whom we have now received reconciliation.

Gospel
LUKE 15:3-7
Jesus addressed this parable to the Pharisees and scribes: "What man among you having a hundred sheep and losing one of them would not leave the ninety-nine in the desert and go after the lost one until he finds it? And when he does find it, he sets it on his shoulders with great joy and, upon his arrival home, he calls together his friends and neighbors and says to them, 'Rejoice with me because I have found my lost sheep.' I tell you, in just the same way there will be more joy in heaven over one sinner who repents than over ninety-nine righteous people who have no need of repentance."

Saturday, June 29

Saints Peter and Paul, Apostles

First Reading
ACTS 12:1-11 (Vigil: ACTS 3:1-10)
In those days, King Herod laid hands upon some members of the Church to harm them. He had James, the brother of John, killed by the sword, and when he saw that this was pleasing to the Jews he proceeded to arrest Peter also. —It was the feast of Unleavened Bread.— He had him taken into custody and put in prison under the guard of four squads of four soldiers each. He intended to bring him before the people after Passover. Peter thus was being kept in prison, but prayer by the Church was fervently being made to God on his behalf.

On the very night before Herod was to bring him to trial, Peter, secured by double chains, was sleeping between two soldiers, while outside the door guards kept watch on the prison. Suddenly the angel of the Lord stood by him and a light shone in the cell. He tapped Peter on the side and awakened him, saying, "Get up quickly." The chains fell from his wrists. The angel said to him, "Put on your belt and your sandals." He did so. Then he said to him, "Put on your cloak and follow me." So he followed him out, not realizing that what was happening through the angel was real; he thought he was seeing a vision. They passed the first guard, then the second, and came to the iron gate leading out to the city, which opened for them by itself. They emerged and made their way down an alley, and suddenly the angel left him. Then Peter recovered his senses and said, “Now I know for certain that the Lord sent his angel and rescued me from the hand of Herod and from all that the Jewish people had been expecting.”

Responsorial Psalm

PSALM 34:2-3, 4-5, 6-7, 8-9 (Vigil: PSALM 19:2-3, 4-5)

R. The angel of the Lord will rescue those who fear him.

I will bless the LORD at all times;
his praise shall be ever in my mouth.
Let my soul glory in the LORD;
the lowly will hear me and be glad. **R.**
Glorify the LORD with me,
let us together extol his name.
I sought the LORD, and he answered me
and delivered me from all my fears. **R.**
Look to him that you may be radiant with joy,
and your faces may not blush with shame.
When the poor one called out, the LORD heard,
and from all his distress he saved him. **R.**
The angel of the LORD encamps
around those who fear him, and delivers them.
Taste and see how good the LORD is;
blessed the man who takes refuge in him. **R.**

Second Reading

2 TIMOTHY 4:6-8, 17-18 (Vigil: GALATIANS 1:11-20)

I, Paul, am already being poured out like a libation, and the time of my departure is at hand. I have competed well; I have finished the race; I have kept the faith. From now on the crown of righteousness awaits me, which the Lord, the just judge, will award to me on that day, and not only to me, but to all who have longed for his appearance.

The Lord stood by me and gave me strength, so that through me the proclamation might be completed and all the Gentiles might hear it. And I was rescued from the lion’s mouth. The Lord will rescue me from every evil threat and will bring me safe to his heavenly Kingdom. To him be glory forever and ever. Amen.

Gospel

MATTHEW 16:13-19 (Vigil: JOHN 21:15-19)

When Jesus went into the region of Caesarea Philippi he asked his disciples, “Who do people say that the Son of Man is?” They replied, “Some say John the Baptist, others Elijah, still others Jeremiah or one of the prophets.” He said to them, “But who do you say that I am?” Simon Peter said in reply,

"You are the Christ, the Son of the living God." Jesus said to him in reply, "Blessed are you, Simon son of Jonah. For flesh and blood has not revealed this to you, but my heavenly Father. And so I say to you, you are Peter, and upon this rock I will build my Church, and the gates of the netherworld shall not prevail against it. I will give you the keys to the Kingdom of heaven. Whatever you bind on earth shall be bound in heaven; and whatever you loose on earth shall be loosed in heaven."

Sunday, June 30

Thirteenth Sunday in Ordinary Time

First Reading

1 KINGS 19:16b, 19-21

The LORD said to Elijah: "You shall anoint Elisha, son of Shaphat of Abel-meholah, as prophet to succeed you."

Elijah set out and came upon Elisha, son of Shaphat, as he was plowing with twelve yoke of oxen; he was following the twelfth. Elijah went over to him and threw his cloak over him. Elisha left the oxen, ran after Elijah, and said, "Please, let me kiss my father and mother goodbye, and I will follow you." Elijah answered, "Go back! Have I done anything to you?" Elisha left him, and taking the yoke of oxen, slaughtered them; he used the plowing equipment for fuel to boil their flesh, and gave it to his people to eat. Then Elisha left and followed Elijah as his attendant.

Responsorial Psalm

PSALM 16:1-2, 5, 7-8, 9-10, 11

R. You are my inheritance, O Lord.

Keep me, O God, for in you I take refuge;
 I say to the LORD, "My Lord are you.
O LORD, my allotted portion and my cup,
 you it is who hold fast my lot." **R.**
I bless the LORD who counsels me;
 even in the night my heart exhorts me.
I set the LORD ever before me;
 with him at my right hand I shall not be disturbed. **R.**
Therefore my heart is glad and my soul rejoices,
 my body, too, abides in confidence
because you will not abandon my soul to the netherworld,
 nor will you suffer your faithful one to undergo corruption. **R.**
You will show me the path to life,
 fullness of joys in your presence,
 the delights at your right hand forever. **R.**

Second Reading
GALATIANS 5:1, 13-18

Brothers and sisters: For freedom Christ set us free; so stand firm and do not submit again to the yoke of slavery.

For you were called for freedom, brothers and sisters. But do not use this freedom as an opportunity for the flesh; rather, serve one another through love. For the whole law is fulfilled in one statement, namely, *You shall love your neighbor as yourself.* But if you go on biting and devouring one another, beware that you are not consumed by one another.

I say, then: live by the Spirit and you will certainly not gratify the desire of the flesh. For the flesh has desires against the Spirit, and the Spirit against the flesh; these are opposed to each other, so that you may not do what you want. But if you are guided by the Spirit, you are not under the law.

Gospel
LUKE 9:51-62

When the days for Jesus' being taken up were fulfilled, he resolutely determined to journey to Jerusalem, and he sent messengers ahead of him. On the way they entered a Samaritan village to prepare for his reception there, but they would not welcome him because the destination of his journey was Jerusalem. When the disciples James and John saw this they asked, "Lord, do you want us to call down fire from heaven to consume them?" Jesus turned and rebuked them, and they journeyed to another village.

As they were proceeding on their journey someone said to him, "I will follow you wherever you go." Jesus answered him, "Foxes have dens and birds of the sky have nests, but the Son of Man has nowhere to rest his head."

And to another he said, "Follow me." But he replied, "Lord, let me go first and bury my father." But he answered him, "Let the dead bury their dead. But you, go and proclaim the kingdom of God." And another said, "I will follow you, Lord, but first let me say farewell to my family at home." To him Jesus said, "No one who sets a hand to the plow and looks to what was left behind is fit for the kingdom of God."

JULY

Monday, July 1

First Reading
GENESIS 18:16-33

Abraham and the men who had visited him by the Terebinth of Mamre set out from there and looked down toward Sodom; Abraham was walking with them, to see them on their way. The LORD reflected: "Shall I hide from Abraham what I am about to do, now that he is to become a great and populous nation, and all the nations of the earth are to find blessing in him? Indeed, I have singled him out that he may direct his children and his household after him to keep the way of the LORD by doing what is right and just, so that the LORD may carry into effect for Abraham the promises he made about him." Then the LORD said: "The outcry against Sodom and Gomorrah is so great, and their sin so grave, that I must go down and see whether or not their actions fully correspond to the cry against them that comes to me. I mean to find out."

While the two men walked on farther toward Sodom, the LORD remained standing before Abraham. Then Abraham drew nearer to him and said: "Will you sweep away the innocent with the guilty? Suppose there were fifty innocent people in the city; would you wipe out the place, rather than spare it for the sake of the fifty innocent people within it? Far be it from you to do such a thing, to make the innocent die with the guilty, so that the innocent and the guilty would be treated alike! Should not the judge of all the world act with justice?" The LORD replied, "If I find fifty innocent people in the city of Sodom, I will spare the whole place for their sake." Abraham spoke up again: "See how I am presuming to speak to my Lord, though I am but dust and ashes! What if there are five less than fifty innocent people? Will you destroy the whole city because of those five?" He answered, "I will not destroy it if I find forty-five there." But Abraham persisted, saying, "What if only forty are found there?" He replied, "I will forbear doing it for the sake of forty." Then Abraham said, "Let not my Lord grow impatient if I go on. What if only thirty are found there?" He replied, "I will forbear doing it if I can find but thirty there." Still Abraham went on, "Since I have thus dared to speak to my Lord, what if there are no more than twenty?" He answered, "I will not destroy it for the sake of the twenty." But he still persisted: "Please, let not my Lord grow angry if I speak up this last time. What if there are at least ten there?" He replied, "For the sake of those ten, I will not destroy it."

The LORD departed as soon as he had finished speaking with Abraham, and Abraham returned home.

Responsorial Psalm

PSALM 103:1b-2, 3-4, 8-9, 10-11

R. The Lord is kind and merciful.

Bless the LORD, O my soul;
and all my being, bless his holy name.
Bless the LORD, O my soul,
and forget not all his benefits. **R.**
He pardons all your iniquities,
he heals all your ills.
He redeems your life from destruction,
he crowns you with kindness and compassion. **R.**
Merciful and gracious is the LORD,
slow to anger and abounding in kindness.
He will not always chide,
nor does he keep his wrath forever. **R.**
Not according to our sins does he deal with us,
nor does he requite us according to our crimes.
For as the heavens are high above the earth,
so surpassing is his kindness toward those who fear him. **R.**

Gospel

MATTHEW 8:18-22

When Jesus saw a crowd around him, he gave orders to cross to the other shore. A scribe approached and said to him, "Teacher, I will follow you wherever you go." Jesus answered him, "Foxes have dens and birds of the sky have nests, but the Son of Man has nowhere to rest his head." Another of his disciples said to him, "Lord, let me go first and bury my father." But Jesus answered him, "Follow me, and let the dead bury their dead."

Tuesday, July 2

First Reading

GENESIS 19:15-29

As dawn was breaking, the angels urged Lot on, saying, "On your way! Take with you your wife and your two daughters who are here, or you will be swept away in the punishment of Sodom." When he hesitated, the men, by the LORD's mercy, seized his hand and the hands of his wife and his two daughters and led them to safety outside the city. As soon as they had been brought outside, he was told: "Flee for your life! Don't look back or stop anywhere on the Plain. Get off to the hills at once, or you will be swept away." "Oh, no, my lord!" Lot replied, "You have already thought enough of your servant to do me the great kindness of intervening to save my life. But I cannot flee to the hills to keep the disaster from overtaking me, and so I shall die. Look, this town ahead is near enough to escape to. It's only a small place. Let me flee there—it's a small place, is it not?—that my life may be saved." "Well, then," he replied, "I will also grant you the favor you now ask. I will not overthrow the town you speak of. Hurry, escape there! I cannot do anything until you arrive there." That is why the town is called Zoar.

The sun was just rising over the earth as Lot arrived in Zoar; at the same time the LORD rained down sulphurous fire upon Sodom and Gomorrah from the LORD out of heaven. He overthrew those cities and the whole Plain, together with the inhabitants of the cities and the produce of the soil. But Lot's wife looked back, and she was turned into a pillar of salt.

Early the next morning Abraham went to the place where he had stood in the LORD's presence. As he looked down toward Sodom and Gomorrah and the whole region of the Plain, he saw dense smoke over the land rising like fumes from a furnace.

Thus it came to pass: when God destroyed the Cities of the Plain, he was mindful of Abraham by sending Lot away from the upheaval by which God overthrew the cities where Lot had been living.

Responsorial Psalm

PSALM 26:2-3, 9-10, 11-12

R. O Lord, your mercy is before my eyes.

Search me, O LORD, and try me;
 test my soul and my heart.
For your mercy is before my eyes,
 and I walk in your truth. **R.**
Gather not my soul with those of sinners,
 nor with men of blood my life.
On their hands are crimes,
 and their right hands are full of bribes. **R.**
But I walk in integrity;
 redeem me, and have mercy on me.
My foot stands on level ground;
 in the assemblies I will bless the LORD. **R.**

Gospel

MATTHEW 8:23-27

As Jesus got into a boat, his disciples followed him. Suddenly a violent storm came up on the sea, so that the boat was being swamped by waves; but he was asleep. They came and woke him, saying, "Lord, save us! We are perishing!" He said to them, "Why are you terrified, O you of little faith?" Then he got up, rebuked the winds and the sea, and there was great calm. The men were amazed and said, "What sort of man is this, whom even the winds and the sea obey?"

Wednesday, July 3

Saint Thomas, Apostle

First Reading
EPHESIANS 2:19-22

Brothers and sisters: You are no longer strangers and sojourners, but you are fellow citizens with the holy ones and members of the household of God, built upon the foundation of the Apostles and prophets, with Christ Jesus himself as the capstone. Through him the whole structure is held together and grows into a temple sacred in the Lord; in him you also are being built together into a dwelling place of God in the Spirit.

Responsorial Psalm
PSALM 117:1bc, 2
R. Go out to all the world and tell the Good News.

Praise the LORD, all you nations;
glorify him, all you peoples! **R.**
For steadfast is his kindness for us,
and the fidelity of the LORD endures forever. **R.**

Gospel
JOHN 20:24-29

Thomas, called Didymus, one of the Twelve, was not with them when Jesus came. So the other disciples said to him, "We have seen the Lord." But Thomas said to them, "Unless I see the mark of the nails in his hands and put my finger into the nailmarks and put my hand into his side, I will not believe." Now a week later his disciples were again inside and Thomas was with them. Jesus came, although the doors were locked, and stood in their midst and said, "Peace be with you." Then he said to Thomas, "Put your finger here and see my hands, and bring your hand and put it into my side, and do not be unbelieving, but believe." Thomas answered and said to him, "My Lord and my God!" Jesus said to him, "Have you come to believe because you have seen me? Blessed are those who have not seen and have believed."

Thursday, July 4

[For Independence Day, readings from the *Lectionary for Mass,* vol. IV, the Mass "For the Country or a City," nos. 882-886, or "For Peace and Justice," nos. 887-891 may be substituted for those listed here.]

First Reading
GENESIS 22:1b-19

God put Abraham to the test. He called to him, "Abraham!" "Here I am," he replied. Then God said: "Take your son Isaac, your only one, whom you love, and go to the land of Moriah. There you shall offer him up as a burnt offering on a height that I will point out to you." Early the next morning Abraham saddled his donkey, took with him his son Isaac, and two of his servants as well, and with the wood that he had cut for the burnt offering, set out for the place of which God had told him.

On the third day Abraham got sight of the place from afar. Then he said to his servants: "Both of you stay here with the donkey, while the boy and I go on over yonder. We will worship and then come back to you." Thereupon Abraham took the wood for the burnt offering and laid it on his son Isaac's shoulders, while he himself carried the fire and the knife. As the two walked on together, Isaac spoke to his father Abraham: "Father!" he said. "Yes, son," he replied. Isaac continued, "Here are the fire and the wood, but where is the sheep for the burnt offering?" "Son," Abraham answered, "God himself will provide the sheep for the burnt offering." Then the two continued going forward.

When they came to the place of which God had told him, Abraham built an altar there and arranged the wood on it. Next he tied up his son Isaac, and put him on top of the wood on the altar. Then he reached out and took the knife to slaughter his son. But the LORD's messenger called to him from heaven, "Abraham, Abraham!" "Here I am," he answered. "Do not lay your hand on the boy," said the messenger. "Do not do the least thing to him. I know now how devoted you are to God, since you did not withhold from me your own beloved son." As Abraham looked about, he spied a ram caught by its horns in the thicket. So he went and took the ram and offered it up as a burnt offering in place of his son. Abraham named the site Yahweh-yireh; hence people now say, "On the mountain the LORD will see." Again the LORD's messenger called to Abraham from heaven and said: "I swear by myself, declares the LORD, that because you acted as you did in not withholding from me your beloved son, I will bless you abundantly and make your descendants as countless as the stars of the sky and the sands of the seashore; your descendants shall take possession of the gates of their enemies, and in your descendants all the nations of the earth shall find blessing—all this because you obeyed my command."

Abraham then returned to his servants, and they set out together for Beer-sheba, where Abraham made his home.

Responsorial Psalm

PSALM 115:1-2, 3-4, 5-6, 8-9

R. I will walk in the presence of the Lord, in the land of the living. (or R. Alleluia.)

Not to us, O LORD, not to us
but to your name give glory
because of your kindness, because of your truth.
Why should the pagans say,
"Where is their God?" **R.**
Our God is in heaven;
whatever he wills, he does.
Their idols are silver and gold,
the handiwork of men. **R.**
They have mouths but speak not;
they have eyes but see not;
They have ears but hear not;
they have noses but smell not. **R.**
Their makers shall be like them,
everyone who trusts in them.
The house of Israel trusts in the LORD;
he is their help and their shield. **R.**

Gospel

MATTHEW 9:1-8

After entering a boat, Jesus made the crossing, and came into his own town. And there people brought to him a paralytic lying on a stretcher. When Jesus saw their faith, he said to the paralytic, "Courage, child, your sins are forgiven." At that, some of the scribes said to themselves, "This man is blaspheming." Jesus knew what they were thinking, and said, "Why do you harbor evil thoughts? Which is easier, to say, 'Your sins are forgiven,' or to say, 'Rise and walk'? But that you may know that the Son of Man has authority on earth to forgive sins"—he then said to the paralytic, "Rise, pick up your stretcher, and go home." He rose and went home. When the crowds saw this they were struck with awe and glorified God who had given such authority to men.

Friday, July 5

First Reading

GENESIS 23:1-4, 19; 24:1-8, 62-67

The span of Sarah's life was one hundred and twenty-seven years. She died in Kiriatharba (that is, Hebron) in the land of Canaan, and Abraham performed the customary mourning rites for her. Then he left the side of his dead one and addressed the Hittites: "Although I am a resident alien among you, sell me from your holdings a piece of property for a burial ground, that I may bury my dead wife."

After the transaction, Abraham buried his wife Sarah in the cave of the field of Machpelah, facing Mamre (that is, Hebron) in the land of Canaan.

Abraham had now reached a ripe old age, and the LORD had blessed him in every way. Abraham said to the senior servant of his household, who had charge of all his possessions: "Put your hand under my thigh, and I will make you swear by the LORD, the God of heaven and the God of earth, that you will not procure a wife for my son from the daughters of the Canaanites among whom I live, but that you will go to my own land and to my kindred to get a wife for my son Isaac." The servant asked him: "What if the woman is unwilling to follow me to this land? Should I then take your son back to the land from which you migrated?" "Never take my son back there for any reason," Abraham told him. "The LORD, the God of heaven, who took me from my father's house and the land of my kin, and who confirmed by oath the promise he then made to me, 'I will give this land to your descendants'—he will send his messenger before you, and you will obtain a wife for my son there. If the woman is unwilling to follow you, you will be released from this oath. But never take my son back there!"

A long time later, Isaac went to live in the region of the Negeb. One day toward evening he went out . . . in the field, and as he looked around, he noticed that camels were approaching. Rebekah, too, was looking about, and when she saw him, she alighted from her camel and asked the servant, "Who is the man out there, walking through the fields toward us?" "That is my master," replied the servant. Then she covered herself with her veil.

The servant recounted to Isaac all the things he had done. Then Isaac took Rebekah into his tent; he married her, and thus she became his wife. In his love for her, Isaac found solace after the death of his mother Sarah.

Responsorial Psalm

PSALM 106:1b-2, 3-4a, 4b-5

R. Give thanks to the Lord, for he is good.

Give thanks to the LORD, for he is good,
for his mercy endures forever.
Who can tell the mighty deeds of the LORD,
or proclaim all his praises? **R.**
Blessed are they who observe what is right,
who do always what is just.
Remember us, O LORD, as you favor your people. **R.**
Visit me with your saving help,
that I may see the prosperity of your chosen ones,

rejoice in the joy of your people,
and glory with your inheritance. **R.**

Gospel
MATTHEW 9:9-13

As Jesus passed by, he saw a man named Matthew sitting at the customs post. He said to him, "Follow me." And he got up and followed him. While he was at table in his house, many tax collectors and sinners came and sat with Jesus and his disciples. The Pharisees saw this and said to his disciples, "Why does your teacher eat with tax collectors and sinners?" He heard this and said, "Those who are well do not need a physician, but the sick do. Go and learn the meaning of the words, *I desire mercy, not sacrifice.* I did not come to call the righteous but sinners."

Saturday, July 6

First Reading
GENESIS 27:1-5, 15-29

When Isaac was so old that his eyesight had failed him, he called his older son Esau and said to him, "Son!" "Yes father!" he replied. Isaac then said, "As you can see, I am so old that I may now die at any time. Take your gear, therefore—your quiver and bow—and go out into the country to hunt some game for me. With your catch prepare an appetizing dish for me, such as I like, and bring it to me to eat, so that I may give you my special blessing before I die."

Rebekah had been listening while Isaac was speaking to his son Esau. So, when Esau went out into the country to hunt some game for his father, Rebekah [then] took the best clothes of her older son Esau that she had in the house, and gave them to her younger son Jacob to wear; and with the skins of the kids she covered up his hands and the hairless parts of his neck. Then she handed her son Jacob the appetizing dish and the bread she had prepared.

Bringing them to his father, Jacob said, "Father!" "Yes?" replied Isaac. "Which of my sons are you?" Jacob answered his father: "I am Esau, your first-born. I did as you told me. Please sit up and eat some of my game, so that you may give me your special blessing." But Isaac asked, "How did you succeed so quickly, son?" He answered, "The LORD, your God, let things turn out well with me." Isaac then said to Jacob, "Come closer, son, that I may feel you, to learn whether you really are my son Esau or not." So Jacob moved up closer to his father. When Isaac felt him, he said, "Although the voice is Jacob's, the hands are Esau's." (He failed to identify him because his hands were hairy, like those of his brother Esau; so in the end he gave him his blessing.) Again he asked Jacob, "Are you really my son Esau?" "Certainly," Jacob replied. Then Isaac said, "Serve me your game, son, that I may eat of it and then give you my blessing." Jacob served it to him, and Isaac ate; he brought him wine, and he drank. Finally his father Isaac said to Jacob, "Come closer, son, and kiss me." As Jacob went up and kissed him, Isaac smelled the fragrance of his clothes. With that, he blessed him saying,

"Ah, the fragrance of my son
is like the fragrance of a field
that the LORD has blessed!

"May God give to you
of the dew of the heavens
And of the fertility of the earth
abundance of grain and wine.

"Let peoples serve you,
and nations pay you homage;
Be master of your brothers,
and may your mother's sons bow down to you.
Cursed be those who curse you,
and blessed be those who bless you."

Responsorial Psalm

PSALM 135:1b-2, 3-4, 5-6

R. Praise the Lord for the Lord is good! (or R. Alleluia.)

Praise the name of the LORD;
Praise, you servants of the LORD
Who stand in the house of the LORD,
in the courts of the house of our God. **R.**
Praise the LORD, for the LORD is good;
sing praise to his name, which we love;
For the LORD has chosen Jacob for himself,
Israel for his own possession. **R.**
For I know that the LORD is great;
our Lord is greater than all gods.
All that the LORD wills he does
in heaven and on earth,
in the seas and in all the deeps. **R.**

Gospel
MATTHEW 9:14-17

The disciples of John approached Jesus and said, "Why do we and the Pharisees fast much, but your disciples do not fast?" Jesus answered them, "Can the wedding guests mourn as long as the bridegroom is with them? The days will come when the bridegroom is taken away from them, and then they will fast. No one patches an old cloak with a piece of unshrunken cloth, for its fullness pulls away from the cloak and the tear gets worse. People do not put new wine into old wineskins. Otherwise the skins burst, the wine spills out, and the skins are ruined. Rather, they pour new wine into fresh wineskins, and both are preserved."

Sunday, July 7

Fourteenth Sunday in Ordinary Time

First Reading
ISAIAH 66:10-14c

Thus says the LORD:
Rejoice with Jerusalem and be glad because of her,
all you who love her;
exult, exult with her,
all you who were mourning over her!
Oh, that you may suck fully
of the milk of her comfort,
that you may nurse with delight
at her abundant breasts!
For thus says the LORD:
Lo, I will spread prosperity over Jerusalem like a river,
and the wealth of the nations like an overflowing torrent.
As nurslings, you shall be carried in her arms,
and fondled in her lap;
as a mother comforts her child,
so will I comfort you;
in Jerusalem you shall find your comfort.

When you see this, your heart shall rejoice
and your bodies flourish like the grass;
the LORD's power shall be known to his servants.

Responsorial Psalm

PSALM 66:1-3, 4-5, 6-7, 16, 20

R. Let all the earth cry out to God with joy.

Shout joyfully to God, all the earth,
sing praise to the glory of his name;
proclaim his glorious praise.
Say to God, "How tremendous are your deeds!" **R.**
"Let all on earth worship and sing praise to you,
sing praise to your name!"
Come and see the works of God,
his tremendous deeds among the children of Adam. **R.**
He has changed the sea into dry land;
through the river they passed on foot;
therefore let us rejoice in him.
He rules by his might forever. **R.**
Hear now, all you who fear God,
while I declare what he has done for me.
Blessed be God who refused me not
my prayer or his kindness! **R.**

Second Reading

GALATIANS 6:14-18

Brothers and sisters: May I never boast except in the cross of our Lord Jesus Christ, through which the world has been crucified to me, and I to the world. For neither does circumcision mean anything, nor does uncircumcision, but only a new creation. Peace and mercy be to all who follow this rule and to the Israel of God.

From now on, let no one make troubles for me; for I bear the marks of Jesus on my body.

The grace of our Lord Jesus Christ be with your spirit, brothers and sisters. Amen.

Gospel

LUKE 10:1-12, 17-20 (or LUKE 10:1-9)

At that time the Lord appointed seventy-two others whom he sent ahead of him in pairs to every town and place he intended to visit. He said to them, "The harvest is abundant but the laborers are few; so ask the master of the harvest to send out laborers for his harvest. Go on your way; behold, I am sending you like lambs among wolves. Carry no money bag, no sack, no sandals; and greet no one along the way. Into whatever house you enter, first say, 'Peace to this household.' If a peaceful person lives there, your peace will rest on him; but if not, it will return to you. Stay in the same house and eat and drink what is offered to you, for the laborer deserves his payment. Do not move about from one house to another. Whatever town you enter and they welcome you, eat what is set before you, cure the sick in it and say to them, 'The kingdom of God is at hand for you.' Whatever town you enter and they do not receive you, go out into the streets and say, 'The dust of your town that clings to our feet, even that we shake off against you.' Yet know this: the kingdom of God is at hand. I tell you, it will be more tolerable for Sodom on that day than for that town."

The seventy-two returned rejoicing, and said, "Lord, even the demons are subject to us because of your name." Jesus said, "I have observed Satan fall like lightning from the sky. Behold, I have given you the power to 'tread upon serpents' and scorpions and upon the full force of the enemy and nothing will harm you. Nevertheless, do not rejoice because the spirits are subject to you, but rejoice because your names are written in heaven."

Monday, July 8

First Reading

GENESIS 28:10-22a

Jacob departed from Beer-sheba and proceeded toward Haran. When he came upon a certain shrine, as the sun had already set, he stopped there for the night. Taking one of the stones at the shrine, he put it under his head and lay down to sleep at that spot. Then he had a dream: a stairway rested on the ground, with its top reaching to the heavens; and God's messengers were going up and down on it. And there was the LORD standing beside him and saying: "I, the LORD, am the God of your forefather Abraham and the God of Isaac; the land on which you are lying I will give to you and your descendants. These shall be as plentiful as the dust of the earth, and through them you shall spread out east and west, north and south. In you and your descendants all the nations of the earth shall find blessing. Know that I am with you; I will protect you wherever you go, and bring you back to this land. I will never leave you until I have done what I promised you."

When Jacob awoke from his sleep, he exclaimed, "Truly, the LORD is in this spot, although I did not know it!" In solemn wonder he cried out: "How awesome is this shrine! This is nothing else but an abode of God, and that is the gateway to heaven!" Early the next morning Jacob took the stone that he had put under his head, set it up as a memorial stone, and poured oil on top of it. He called the site Bethel, whereas the former name of the town had been Luz.

Jacob then made this vow: "If God remains with me, to protect me on this journey I am making and to give me enough bread to eat and clothing to wear, and I come back safe to my father's house, the LORD shall be my God. This stone that I have set up as a memorial stone shall be God's abode."

Responsorial Psalm
PSALM 91:1-2, 3-4, 14-15ab
R. In you, my God, I place my trust.
You who dwell in the shelter of the Most High,
 who abide in the shadow of the Almighty,
Say to the LORD, "My refuge and my fortress,
 my God, in whom I trust." **R.**
For he will rescue you from the snare of the fowler,
 from the destroying pestilence.
With his pinions he will cover you,
 and under his wings you shall take refuge. **R.**
Because he clings to me, I will deliver him;
 I will set him on high because he acknowledges my name.
He shall call upon me, and I will answer him;
 I will be with him in distress. **R.**

Gospel
MATTHEW 9:18-26
While Jesus was speaking, an official came forward, knelt down before him, and said, "My daughter has just died. But come, lay your hand on her, and she will live." Jesus rose and followed him, and so did his disciples. A woman suffering hemorrhages for twelve years came up behind him and touched the tassel on his cloak. She said to herself, "If only I can touch his cloak, I shall be cured." Jesus turned around and saw her, and said, "Courage, daughter! Your faith has saved you." And from that hour the woman was cured.

When Jesus arrived at the official's house and saw the flute players and the crowd who were making a commotion, he said, "Go away! The girl is not dead but sleeping." And they ridiculed him. When the crowd was put out, he came and took her by the hand, and the little girl arose. And news of this spread throughout all that land.

Tuesday, July 9

First Reading
GENESIS 32:23-33
In the course of the night, Jacob arose, took his two wives, with the two maidservants and his eleven children, and crossed the ford of the Jabbok. After he had taken them across the stream and had brought over all his possessions, Jacob was left there alone. Then some man wrestled with him until the break of dawn. When the man saw that he could not prevail over him, he struck Jacob's hip at its socket, so that the hip socket was wrenched as they wrestled. The man then said, "Let

me go, for it is daybreak." But Jacob said, "I will not let you go until you bless me." The man asked, "What is your name?" He answered, "Jacob." Then the man said, "You shall no longer be spoken of as Jacob, but as Israel, because you have contended with divine and human beings and have prevailed." Jacob then asked him, "Do tell me your name, please." He answered, "Why should you want to know my name?" With that, he bade him farewell. Jacob named the place Peniel, "Because I have seen God face to face," he said, "yet my life has been spared."

At sunrise, as he left Penuel, Jacob limped along because of his hip. That is why, to this day, the children of Israel do not eat the sciatic muscle that is on the hip socket, inasmuch as Jacob's hip socket was struck at the sciatic muscle.

Responsorial Psalm
PSALM 17:1b, 2-3, 6-7ab, 8b and 15
R. In justice, I shall behold your face, O Lord.

Hear, O LORD, a just suit;
attend to my outcry;
hearken to my prayer from lips without deceit. **R.**
From you let my judgment come;
your eyes behold what is right.
Though you test my heart, searching it in the night,
though you try me with fire, you shall find no malice in me. **R.**
I call upon you, for you will answer me, O God;
incline your ear to me; hear my word.
Show your wondrous mercies,
O savior of those who flee from their foes. **R.**
Hide me in the shadow of your wings.
I in justice shall behold your face;
on waking, I shall be content in your presence. **R.**

Gospel
MATTHEW 9:32-38

A demoniac who could not speak was brought to Jesus, and when the demon was driven out the mute man spoke. The crowds were amazed and said, "Nothing like this has ever been seen in Israel." But the Pharisees said, "He drives out demons by the prince of demons."

Jesus went around to all the towns and villages, teaching in their synagogues, proclaiming the Gospel of the Kingdom, and curing every disease and illness. At the sight of the crowds, his heart was moved with pity for them because they were troubled and abandoned, like sheep without a shepherd. Then he said to his disciples, "The harvest is abundant but the laborers are few; so ask the master of the harvest to send out laborers for his harvest."

Wednesday, July 10

First Reading

GENESIS 41:55-57; 42:5-7a, 17-24a

When hunger came to be felt throughout the land of Egypt and the people cried to Pharaoh for bread, Pharaoh directed all the Egyptians to go to Joseph and do whatever he told them. When the famine had spread throughout the land, Joseph opened all the cities that had grain and rationed it to the Egyptians, since the famine had gripped the land of Egypt. In fact, all the world came to Joseph to obtain rations of grain, for famine had gripped the whole world.

The sons of Israel were among those who came to procure rations.

It was Joseph, as governor of the country, who dispensed the rations to all the people. When Joseph's brothers came and knelt down before him with their faces to the ground, he recognized them as soon as he saw them. But Joseph concealed his own identity from them and spoke sternly to them.

With that, he locked them up in the guardhouse for three days.

On the third day Joseph said to his brothers: "Do this, and you shall live; for I am a God-fearing man. If you have been honest, only one of your brothers need be confined in this prison, while the rest of you may go and take home provisions for your starving families. But you must come back to me with your youngest brother. Your words will thus be verified, and you will not die." To this they agreed. To one another, however, they said: "Alas, we are being punished because of our brother. We saw the anguish of his heart when he pleaded with us, yet we paid no heed; that is why this anguish has now come upon us." Reuben broke in, "Did I not tell you not to do wrong to the boy? But you would not listen! Now comes the reckoning for his blood." The brothers did not know, of course, that Joseph understood what they said, since he spoke with them through an interpreter. But turning away from them, he wept.

Responsorial Psalm

PSALM 33:2-3, 10-11, 18-19

R. Lord, let your mercy be on us, as we place our trust in you.

Give thanks to the LORD on the harp;
with the ten-stringed lyre chant his praises.
Sing to him a new song;
pluck the strings skillfully, with shouts of gladness. **R.**
The LORD brings to nought the plans of nations;
he foils the designs of peoples.
But the plan of the LORD stands forever;
the design of his heart, through all generations. **R.**
But see, the eyes of the LORD are upon those who fear him,
upon those who hope for his kindness,

To deliver them from death
and preserve them in spite of famine. **R.**

Gospel
MATTHEW 10:1-7

Jesus summoned his Twelve disciples and gave them authority over unclean spirits to drive them out and to cure every disease and every illness. The names of the Twelve Apostles are these: first, Simon called Peter, and his brother Andrew; James, the son of Zebedee, and his brother John; Philip and Bartholomew, Thomas and Matthew the tax collector; James, the son of Alphaeus, and Thaddeus; Simon the Cananean, and Judas Iscariot who betrayed Jesus.

Jesus sent out these Twelve after instructing them thus, "Do not go into pagan territory or enter a Samaritan town. Go rather to the lost sheep of the house of Israel. As you go, make this proclamation: 'The Kingdom of heaven is at hand.'"

Thursday, July 11

First Reading
GENESIS 44:18-21, 23b-29; 45:1-5

Judah approached Joseph and said: "I beg you, my lord, let your servant speak earnestly to my lord, and do not become angry with your servant, for you are the equal of Pharaoh. My lord asked your servants, 'Have you a father, or another brother?' So we said to my lord, 'We have an aged father, and a young brother, the child of his old age. This one's full brother is dead, and since he is the only one by that mother who is left, his father dotes on him.' Then you told your servants, 'Bring him down to me that my eyes may look on him. Unless your youngest brother comes back with you, you shall not come into my presence again.' When we returned to your servant our father, we reported to him the words of my lord.

"Later, our father told us to come back and buy some food for the family. So we reminded him, 'We cannot go down there; only if our youngest brother is with us can we go, for we may not see the man if our youngest brother is not with us.' Then your servant our father said to us, 'As you know, my wife bore me two sons. One of them, however, disappeared, and I had to conclude that he must have been torn to pieces by wild beasts; I have not seen him since. If you now take this one away from me, too, and some disaster befalls him, you will send my white head down to the nether world in grief.'"

Joseph could no longer control himself in the presence of all his attendants, so he cried out, "Have everyone withdraw from me!" Thus no one else was about when he made himself known to his brothers. But his sobs were so loud that the Egyptians heard him, and so the news reached Pharaoh's palace. "I am Joseph," he said to his brothers. "Is my father still in good health?" But his brothers could give him no answer, so dumbfounded were they at him.

"Come closer to me," he told his brothers. When they had done so, he said: "I am your brother Joseph, whom you once sold into Egypt. But now do not be distressed, and do not reproach yourselves for having sold me here. It was really for the sake of saving lives that God sent me here ahead of you."

Responsorial Psalm

PSALM 105:16-17, 18-19, 20-21

R. Remember the marvels the Lord has done. (or R. Alleluia.)

When the LORD called down a famine on the land
  and ruined the crop that sustained them,
He sent a man before them,
  Joseph, sold as a slave. **R.**
They had weighed him down with fetters,
  and he was bound with chains,
Till his prediction came to pass
  and the word of the LORD proved him true. **R.**
The king sent and released him,
  the ruler of the peoples set him free.
He made him lord of his house
  and ruler of all his possessions. **R.**

Gospel

MATTHEW 10:7-15

Jesus said to his Apostles: "As you go, make this proclamation: 'The Kingdom of heaven is at hand.' Cure the sick, raise the dead, cleanse the lepers, drive out demons. Without cost you have received; without cost you are to give. Do not take gold or silver or copper for your belts; no sack for the journey, or a second tunic, or sandals, or walking stick. The laborer deserves his keep. Whatever town or village you enter, look for a worthy person in it, and stay there until you leave. As you enter a house, wish it peace. If the house is worthy, let your peace come upon it; if not, let your peace return to you. Whoever will not receive you or listen to your words—go outside that house or town and shake the dust from your feet. Amen, I say to you, it will be more tolerable for the land of Sodom and Gomorrah on the day of judgment than for that town."

Friday, July 12

First Reading

GENESIS 46:1-7, 28-30

Israel set out with all that was his. When he arrived at Beer-sheba, he offered sacrifices to the God of his father Isaac. There God, speaking to Israel in a vision by night, called, "Jacob! Jacob!" He answered, "Here I am." Then he said: "I am God, the God of your father. Do not be afraid to go down to Egypt, for there I will make you a great nation. Not only will I go down to Egypt with you; I will also bring you back here, after Joseph has closed your eyes."

So Jacob departed from Beer-sheba, and the sons of Israel put their father and their wives and children on the wagons that Pharaoh had sent for his transport. They took with them their livestock and the possessions they had acquired in the land of Canaan. Thus Jacob and all his descendants migrated to Egypt. His sons and his grandsons, his daughters and his granddaughters—all his descendants—he took with him to Egypt.

Israel had sent Judah ahead to Joseph, so that he might meet him in Goshen. On his arrival in the region of Goshen, Joseph hitched the horses to his chariot and rode to meet his father Israel in Goshen. As soon as Joseph saw him, he flung himself on his neck and wept a long time in his arms. And Israel said to Joseph, "At last I can die, now that I have seen for myself that Joseph is still alive."

Responsorial Psalm

PSALM 37:3-4, 18-19, 27-28, 39-40

R. The salvation of the just comes from the Lord.

Trust in the LORD and do good,
 that you may dwell in the land and be fed in security.
Take delight in the LORD,
 and he will grant you your heart's requests. **R.**
The LORD watches over the lives of the wholehearted;
 their inheritance lasts forever.
They are not put to shame in an evil time;
 in days of famine they have plenty. **R.**
Turn from evil and do good,
 that you may abide forever;
For the LORD loves what is right,
 and forsakes not his faithful ones. **R.**
The salvation of the just is from the LORD;
 he is their refuge in time of distress.
And the LORD helps them and delivers them;
 he delivers them from the wicked and saves them,
 because they take refuge in him. **R.**

Gospel
MATTHEW 10:16-23

Jesus said to his Apostles: "Behold, I am sending you like sheep in the midst of wolves; so be shrewd as serpents and simple as doves. But beware of men, for they will hand you over to courts and scourge you in their synagogues, and you will be led before governors and kings for my sake as a witness before them and the pagans. When they hand you over, do not worry about how you are to speak or what you are to say. You will be given at that moment what you are to say. For it will not be you who speak but the Spirit of your Father speaking through you. Brother will hand over brother to death, and the father his child; children will rise up against parents and have them put to death. You will be hated by all because of my name, but whoever endures to the end will be saved. When they persecute you in one town, flee to another. Amen, I say to you, you will not finish the towns of Israel before the Son of Man comes."

Saturday, July 13

First Reading
GENESIS 49:29-32; 50:15-26a

Jacob gave his sons this charge: "Since I am about to be taken to my people, bury me with my fathers in the cave that lies in the field of Ephron the Hittite, the cave in the field of Machpelah, facing on Mamre, in the land of Canaan, the field that Abraham bought from Ephron the Hittite for a burial ground. There Abraham and his wife Sarah are buried, and so are Isaac and his wife Rebekah, and there, too, I buried Leah—the field and the cave in it that had been purchased from the Hittites."

Now that their father was dead, Joseph's brothers became fearful and thought, "Suppose Joseph has been nursing a grudge against us and now plans to pay us back in full for all the wrong we did him!" So they approached Joseph and said: "Before your father died, he gave us these instructions: 'You shall say to Joseph, Jacob begs you to forgive the criminal wrongdoing of your brothers, who treated you so cruelly.' Please, therefore, forgive the crime that we, the servants of your father's God, committed." When they spoke these words to him, Joseph broke into tears. Then his brothers proceeded to fling themselves down before him and said, "Let us be your slaves!" But Joseph replied to them: "Have no fear. Can I take the place of God? Even though you meant harm to me, God meant it for good, to achieve his present end, the survival of many people. Therefore have no fear. I will provide for you and for your children." By thus speaking kindly to them, he reassured them.

Joseph remained in Egypt, together with his father's family. He lived a hundred and ten years. He saw Ephraim's children to the third generation, and the children of Manasseh's son Machir were also born on Joseph's knees.

Joseph said to his brothers: "I am about to die. God will surely take care of you and lead you out of this land to the land that he promised on oath to Abraham, Isaac and Jacob." Then, putting the sons of Israel under oath, he continued, "When God thus takes care of you, you must bring my bones up with you from this place." Joseph died at the age of a hundred and ten.

Responsorial Psalm

PSALM 105:1-2, 3-4, 6-7

R. Be glad you lowly ones; may your hearts be glad!

Give thanks to the LORD, invoke his name;
make known among the nations his deeds.
Sing to him, sing his praise,
proclaim all his wondrous deeds. **R.**

Glory in his holy name;
rejoice, O hearts that seek the LORD!
Look to the LORD in his strength;
seek to serve him constantly. **R.**

You descendants of Abraham, his servants,
sons of Jacob, his chosen ones!
He, the LORD, is our God;
throughout the earth his judgments prevail. **R.**

Gospel

MATTHEW 10:24-33

Jesus said to his Apostles: "No disciple is above his teacher, no slave above his master. It is enough for the disciple that he become like his teacher, for the slave that he become like his master. If they have called the master of the house Beelzebul, how much more those of his household!

"Therefore do not be afraid of them. Nothing is concealed that will not be revealed, nor secret that will not be known. What I say to you in the darkness, speak in the light; what you hear whispered, proclaim on the housetops. And do not be afraid of those who kill the body but cannot kill the soul; rather, be afraid of the one who can destroy both soul and body in Gehenna. Are not two sparrows sold for a small coin? Yet not one of them falls to the ground without your Father's knowledge. Even all the hairs of your head are counted. So do not be afraid; you are worth more than many sparrows. Everyone who acknowledges me before others I will acknowledge before my heavenly Father. But whoever denies me before others, I will deny before my heavenly Father."

Sunday, July 14

Fifteenth Sunday in Ordinary Time

First Reading
DEUTERONOMY 30:10-14

Moses said to the people: "If only you would heed the voice of the LORD, your God, and keep his commandments and statutes that are written in this book of the law, when you return to the LORD, your God, with all your heart and all your soul.

"For this command that I enjoin on you today is not too mysterious and remote for you. It is not up in the sky, that you should say, 'Who will go up in the sky to get it for us and tell us of it, that we may carry it out?' Nor is it across the sea, that you should say, 'Who will cross the sea to get it for us and tell us of it, that we may carry it out?' No, it is something very near to you, already in your mouths and in your hearts; you have only to carry it out."

Responsorial Psalm
PSALM 69:14, 17, 30-31, 33-34, 36, 37
(or PSALM 19:8, 9, 10, 11)
R. Turn to the Lord in your need, and you will live.

I pray to you, O LORD,
 for the time of your favor, O God!
In your great kindness answer me
 with your constant help.
Answer me, O LORD, for bounteous is your kindness:
 in your great mercy turn toward me. **R.**
I am afflicted and in pain;
 let your saving help, O God, protect me.
I will praise the name of God in song,
 and I will glorify him with thanksgiving. **R.**
"See, you lowly ones, and be glad;
 you who seek God, may your hearts revive!
For the LORD hears the poor,
 and his own who are in bonds he spurns not." **R.**
For God will save Zion
 and rebuild the cities of Judah.
The descendants of his servants shall inherit it,
 and those who love his name shall inhabit it. **R.**

Second Reading
COLOSSIANS 1:15-20

Christ Jesus is the image of the invisible God,
 the firstborn of all creation.

For in him were created all things in heaven and on earth,
the visible and the invisible,
whether thrones or dominions or principalities or powers;
all things were created through him and for him.
He is before all things,
and in him all things hold together.
He is the head of the body, the church.
He is the beginning, the firstborn from the dead,
that in all things he himself might be preeminent.
For in him all the fullness was pleased to dwell,
and through him to reconcile all things for him,
making peace by the blood of his cross
through him, whether those on earth or those in heaven.

Gospel
LUKE 10:25-37

There was a scholar of the law who stood up to test him and said, "Teacher, what must I do to inherit eternal life?" Jesus said to him, "What is written in the law? How do you read it?" He said in reply, "*You shall love the Lord, your God, with all your heart, with all your being, with all your strength, and with all your mind, and your neighbor as yourself.*" He replied to him, "You have answered correctly; do this and you will live."

But because he wished to justify himself, he said to Jesus, "And who is my neighbor?" Jesus replied, "A man fell victim to robbers as he went down from Jerusalem to Jericho. They stripped and beat him and went off leaving him half-dead. A priest happened to be going down that road, but when he saw him, he passed by on the opposite side. Likewise a Levite came to the place, and when he saw him, he passed by on the opposite side. But a Samaritan traveler who came upon him was moved with compassion at the sight. He approached the victim, poured oil and wine over his wounds and bandaged them. Then he lifted him up on his own animal, took him to an inn, and cared for him. The next day he took out two silver coins and gave them to the innkeeper with the instruction, 'Take care of him. If you spend more than what I have given you, I shall repay you on my way back.' Which of these three, in your opinion, was neighbor to the robbers' victim?" He answered, "The one who treated him with mercy." Jesus said to him, "Go and do likewise."

Monday, July 15

First Reading
EXODUS 1:8-14, 22

A new king, who knew nothing of Joseph, came to power in Egypt. He said to his subjects, "Look how numerous and powerful the people of the children of Israel are growing, more so than we ourselves! Come, let us deal shrewdly with them to stop their increase; otherwise, in time of war they too may join our enemies to fight against us, and so leave our country."

Accordingly, taskmasters were set over the children of Israel to oppress them with forced labor. Thus they had to build for Pharaoh the supply cities of Pithom and Raamses. Yet the more they were oppressed, the more they multiplied and spread. The Egyptians, then, dreaded the children of Israel and reduced them to cruel slavery, making life bitter for them with hard work in mortar and brick and all kinds of field work—the whole cruel fate of slaves.

Pharaoh then commanded all his subjects, "Throw into the river every boy that is born to the Hebrews, but you may let all the girls live."

Responsorial Psalm

PSALM 124:1b-3, 4-6, 7-8

R. Our help is in the name of the Lord.

Had not the LORD been with us—
let Israel say, had not the LORD been with us—
When men rose up against us,
then would they have swallowed us alive,
When their fury was inflamed against us. **R.**
Then would the waters have overwhelmed us;
The torrent would have swept over us;
over us then would have swept
the raging waters.
Blessed be the LORD, who did not leave us
a prey to their teeth. **R.**
We were rescued like a bird
from the fowlers' snare;
Broken was the snare,
and we were freed.
Our help is in the name of the LORD,
who made heaven and earth. **R.**

Gospel

MATTHEW 10:34–11:1

Jesus said to his Apostles: "Do not think that I have come to bring peace upon the earth. I have come to bring not peace but the sword. For I have come to set a man against his father, a daughter against her mother, and a daughter-in-law against her mother-in-law; and one's enemies will be those of his household.

"Whoever loves father or mother more than me is not worthy of me, and whoever loves son or daughter more than me is not worthy of me;

and whoever does not take up his cross and follow after me is not worthy of me. Whoever finds his life will lose it, and whoever loses his life for my sake will find it.

"Whoever receives you receives me, and whoever receives me receives the one who sent me. Whoever receives a prophet because he is a prophet will receive a prophet's reward, and whoever receives a righteous man because he is righteous will receive a righteous man's reward. And whoever gives only a cup of cold water to one of these little ones to drink because he is a disciple—amen, I say to you, he will surely not lose his reward."

When Jesus finished giving these commands to his Twelve disciples, he went away from that place to teach and to preach in their towns.

Tuesday, July 16

First Reading

EXODUS 2:1-15a

A certain man of the house of Levi married a Levite woman, who conceived and bore a son. Seeing that he was a goodly child, she hid him for three months. When she could hide him no longer, she took a papyrus basket, daubed it with bitumen and pitch, and putting the child in it, placed it among the reeds on the river bank. His sister stationed herself at a distance to find out what would happen to him.

Pharaoh's daughter came down to the river to bathe, while her maids walked along the river bank. Noticing the basket among the reeds, she sent her handmaid to fetch it. On opening it, she looked, and lo, there was a baby boy, crying! She was moved with pity for him and said, "It is one of the Hebrews' children." Then his sister asked Pharaoh's daughter, "Shall I go and call one of the Hebrew women to nurse the child for you?" "Yes, do so," she answered. So the maiden went and called the child's own mother. Pharaoh's daughter said to her, "Take this child and nurse it for me, and I will repay you." The woman therefore took the child and nursed it. When the child grew, she brought him to Pharaoh's daughter, who adopted him as her son and called him Moses; for she said, "I drew him out of the water."

On one occasion, after Moses had grown up, when he visited his kinsmen and witnessed their forced labor, he saw an Egyptian striking a Hebrew, one of his own kinsmen. Looking about and seeing no one, he slew the Egyptian and hid him in the sand. The next day he went out again, and now two Hebrews were fighting! So he asked the culprit, "Why are you striking your fellow Hebrew?" But the culprit replied, "Who has appointed you ruler and judge over us? Are you thinking of killing me as you killed the Egyptian?" Then Moses became afraid and thought, "The affair must certainly be known."

Pharaoh, too, heard of the affair and sought to put Moses to death. But Moses fled from him and stayed in the land of Midian.

Responsorial Psalm

PSALM 69:3, 14, 30-31, 33-34

R. Turn to the Lord in your need, and you will live.

I am sunk in the abysmal swamp
  where there is no foothold;
I have reached the watery depths;
  the flood overwhelms me. **R.**
But I pray to you, O LORD,
  for the time of your favor, O God!
In your great kindness answer me
  with your constant help. **R.**
But I am afflicted and in pain;
  let your saving help, O God, protect me;
I will praise the name of God in song,
  and I will glorify him with thanksgiving. **R.**
"See, you lowly ones, and be glad;
  you who seek God, may your hearts revive!
For the LORD hears the poor,
  and his own who are in bonds he spurns not." **R.**

Gospel

MATTHEW 11:20-24

Jesus began to reproach the towns where most of his mighty deeds had been done, since they had not repented. "Woe to you, Chorazin! Woe to you, Bethsaida! For if the mighty deeds done in your midst had been done in Tyre and Sidon, they would long ago have repented in sackcloth and ashes. But I tell you, it will be more tolerable for Tyre and Sidon on the day of judgment than for you. And as for you, Capernaum:

Will you be exalted to heaven?
  You will go down to the netherworld.

For if the mighty deeds done in your midst had been done in Sodom, it would have remained until this day. But I tell you, it will be more tolerable for the land of Sodom on the day of judgment than for you."

Wednesday, July 17

First Reading

EXODUS 3:1-6, 9-12

Moses was tending the flock of his father-in-law Jethro, the priest of Midian. Leading the flock across the desert, he came to Horeb, the mountain of God. There an angel of the LORD appeared to him in fire flaming out of a bush. As he looked on, he was surprised to see that the bush, though on fire, was not consumed. So Moses decided, "I must go over to look at this remarkable sight, and see why the bush is not burned."

When the LORD saw him coming over to look at it more closely, God called out to him from the bush, "Moses! Moses!" He answered, "Here I am." God said, "Come no nearer! Remove the sandals from your feet, for the place where you stand is holy ground. I am the God of your father," he continued, "the God of Abraham, the God of Isaac, the God of Jacob. The cry of the children of Israel has reached me, and I have truly noted that the Egyptians are oppressing them. Come, now! I will send you to Pharaoh to lead my people, the children of Israel, out of Egypt."

But Moses said to God, "Who am I that I should go to Pharaoh and lead the children of Israel out of Egypt?" He answered, "I will be with you; and this shall be your proof that it is I who have sent you: when you bring my people out of Egypt, you will worship God on this very mountain."

Responsorial Psalm

PSALM 103:1b-2, 3-4, 6-7

R. The Lord is kind and merciful.

Bless the LORD, O my soul;
  and all my being, bless his holy name.
Bless the LORD, O my soul,
  and forget not all his benefits. **R.**
He pardons all your iniquities,
  he heals all your ills.
He redeems your life from destruction,
  he crowns you with kindness and compassion. **R.**
The LORD secures justice
  and the rights of all the oppressed.
He has made known his ways to Moses,
  and his deeds to the children of Israel. **R.**

Gospel

MATTHEW 11:25-27

At that time Jesus exclaimed: "I give praise to you, Father, Lord of heaven and earth, for although you have hidden these things from the wise and the learned you have revealed them to the childlike. Yes, Father, such has been your gracious will. All things have been handed over to me by my Father. No one knows the Son except the Father, and no one knows the Father except the Son and anyone to whom the Son wishes to reveal him."

Thursday, July 18

First Reading

EXODUS 3:13-20

Moses, hearing the voice of the LORD from the burning bush, said to him, "When I go to the children of Israel and say to them, 'The God of your fathers has sent me to you,' if they ask me, 'What is his name?' what am I to tell them?" God replied, "I am who am." Then he added, "This is what you shall tell the children of Israel: I AM sent me to you."

God spoke further to Moses, "Thus shall you say to the children of Israel: The LORD, the God of your fathers, the God of Abraham, the God of Isaac, the God of Jacob, has sent me to you.

"This is my name forever;
 this my title for all generations.

"Go and assemble the elders of Israel, and tell them: The LORD, the God of your fathers, the God of Abraham, Isaac, and Jacob, has appeared to me and said: I am concerned about you and about the way you are being treated in Egypt; so I have decided to lead you up out of the misery of Egypt into the land of the Canaanites, Hittites, Amorites, Perizzites, Hivites, and Jebusites, a land flowing with milk and honey.

"Thus they will heed your message. Then you and the elders of Israel shall go to the king of Egypt and say to him: The LORD, the God of the Hebrews, has sent us word. Permit us, then, to go a three-days' journey in the desert, that we may offer sacrifice to the LORD, our God.

"Yet I know that the king of Egypt will not allow you to go unless he is forced. I will stretch out my hand, therefore, and smite Egypt by doing all kinds of wondrous deeds there. After that he will send you away."

Responsorial Psalm

PSALM 105:1 and 5, 8-9, 24-25, 26-27

R. The Lord remembers his covenant for ever. (or R. Alleluia.)

Give thanks to the LORD, invoke his name;
 make known among the nations his deeds.
Recall the wondrous deeds that he has wrought,
 his portents, and the judgments he has uttered. **R.**

He remembers forever his covenant
which he made binding for a thousand generations—
Which he entered into with Abraham
and by his oath to Isaac. **R.**
He greatly increased his people
and made them stronger than their foes,
Whose hearts he changed, so that they hated his people,
and dealt deceitfully with his servants. **R.**
He sent Moses his servant;
Aaron, whom he had chosen.
They wrought his signs among them,
and wonders in the land of Ham. **R.**

Gospel
MATTHEW 11:28-30

Jesus said: "Come to me, all you who labor and are burdened, and I will give you rest. Take my yoke upon you and learn from me, for I am meek and humble of heart; and you will find rest for yourselves. For my yoke is easy, and my burden light."

Friday, July 19

First Reading
EXODUS 11:10–12:14

Although Moses and Aaron performed various wonders in Pharaoh's presence, the LORD made Pharaoh obstinate, and he would not let the children of Israel leave his land.

The LORD said to Moses and Aaron in the land of Egypt, "This month shall stand at the head of your calendar; you shall reckon it the first month of the year. Tell the whole community of Israel: On the tenth of this month every one of your families must procure for itself a lamb, one apiece for each household. If a family is too small for a whole lamb, it shall join the nearest household in procuring one and shall share in the lamb in proportion to the number of persons who partake of it. The lamb must be a year-old male and without blemish. You may take it from either the sheep or the goats. You shall keep it until the fourteenth day of this month, and then, with the whole assembly of Israel present, it shall be slaughtered during the evening twilight. They shall take some of its blood and apply it to the two doorposts and the lintel of every house in which they partake of the lamb. That same night they shall eat its roasted flesh with unleavened bread and bitter herbs. It shall not be eaten raw or boiled, but roasted whole, with its head and shanks and inner organs. None of it must be kept beyond the next morning; whatever is left over in the morning shall be burned up.

"This is how you are to eat it: with your loins girt, sandals on your feet and your staff in hand, you shall eat like those who are in flight. It is the Passover of the LORD. For on this same night I will go through Egypt, striking down every first born of the land, both man and beast, and executing judgment on all the gods of Egypt—I, the LORD! But the blood will mark the houses where you are. Seeing the blood, I will pass over you; thus, when I strike the land of Egypt, no destructive blow will come upon you.

"This day shall be a memorial feast for you, which all your generations shall celebrate with pilgrimage to the LORD, as a perpetual institution."

Responsorial Psalm

PSALM 116:12-13, 15 and 16bc, 17-18

R. I will take the cup of salvation, and call on the name of the Lord.

How shall I make a return to the LORD
for all the good he has done for me?
The cup of salvation I will take up,
and I will call upon the name of the LORD. **R.**
Precious in the eyes of the LORD
is the death of his faithful ones.
I am your servant, the son of your handmaid;
you have loosed my bonds. **R.**
To you will I offer sacrifice of thanksgiving,
and I will call upon the name of the LORD.
My vows to the LORD I will pay
in the presence of all his people. **R.**

Gospel

MATTHEW 12:1-8

Jesus was going through a field of grain on the sabbath. His disciples were hungry and began to pick the heads of grain and eat them. When the Pharisees saw this, they said to him, "See, your disciples are doing what is unlawful to do on the sabbath." He said to them, "Have you not read what David did when he and his companions were hungry, how he went into the house of God and ate the bread of offering, which neither he nor his companions but only the priests could lawfully eat? Or have you not read in the law that on the sabbath the priests serving in the temple violate the sabbath and are innocent? I say to you, something greater than the temple is here. If you knew what this meant, *I desire mercy, not sacrifice*, you would not have condemned these innocent men. For the Son of Man is Lord of the sabbath."

Saturday, July 20

First Reading

EXODUS 12:37-42

The children of Israel set out from Rameses for Succoth, about six hundred thousand men on foot, not counting the little ones. A crowd of mixed ancestry also went up with them, besides their livestock, very numerous flocks and herds. Since the dough they had brought out of Egypt was not leavened, they baked it into unleavened loaves. They had rushed out of Egypt and had no opportunity even to prepare food for the journey.

The time the children of Israel had stayed in Egypt was four hundred and thirty years. At the end of four hundred and thirty years, all the hosts of the LORD left the land of Egypt on this very date. This was a night of vigil for the LORD, as he led them out of the land of Egypt; so on this same night all the children of Israel must keep a vigil for the LORD throughout their generations.

Responsorial Psalm

PSALM 136:1 and 23-24, 10-12, 13-15

R. His mercy endures forever. (or R. Alleluia.)

Give thanks to the LORD, for he is good,
for his mercy endures forever;
Who remembered us in our abjection,
for his mercy endures forever;
And freed us from our foes,
for his mercy endures forever. **R.**
Who smote the Egyptians in their first-born,
for his mercy endures forever;
And brought out Israel from their midst,
for his mercy endures forever;
With a mighty hand and an outstretched arm,
for his mercy endures forever. **R.**
Who split the Red Sea in twain,
for his mercy endures forever;
And led Israel through its midst,
for his mercy endures forever;
But swept Pharaoh and his army into the Red Sea,
for his mercy endures forever. **R.**

Gospel

MATTHEW 12:14-21

The Pharisees went out and took counsel against Jesus to put him to death.

When Jesus realized this, he withdrew from that place. Many people followed him, and he cured them all, but he warned them not to make him known. This was to fulfill what had been spoken through Isaiah the prophet:

Behold, my servant whom I have chosen,
my beloved in whom I delight;
I shall place my Spirit upon him,
and he will proclaim justice to the Gentiles.
He will not contend or cry out,
nor will anyone hear his voice in the streets.
A bruised reed he will not break,
a smoldering wick he will not quench,
until he brings justice to victory.
And in his name the Gentiles will hope.

Sunday, July 21

Sixteenth Sunday in Ordinary Time

First Reading
GENESIS 18:1-10a

The LORD appeared to Abraham by the terebinth of Mamre, as he sat in the entrance of his tent, while the day was growing hot. Looking up, Abraham saw three men standing nearby. When he saw them, he ran from the entrance of the tent to greet them; and bowing to the ground, he said: "Sir, if I may ask you this favor, please do not go on past your servant. Let some water be brought, that you may bathe your feet, and then rest yourselves under the tree. Now that you have come this close to your servant, let me bring you a little food, that you may refresh yourselves; and afterward you may go on your way." The men replied, "Very well, do as you have said."

Abraham hastened into the tent and told Sarah, "Quick, three measures of fine flour! Knead it and make rolls." He ran to the herd, picked out a tender, choice steer, and gave it to a servant, who quickly prepared it. Then Abraham got some curds and milk, as well as the steer that had been prepared, and set these before the three men; and he waited on them under the tree while they ate.

They asked Abraham, "Where is your wife Sarah?" He replied, "There in the tent." One of them said, "I will surely return to you about this time next year, and Sarah will then have a son."

Responsorial Psalm
PSALM 15:2-3, 3-4, 5
R. He who does justice will live in the presence of the Lord.
One who walks blamelessly and does justice;
who thinks the truth in his heart
and slanders not with his tongue. **R.**

Who harms not his fellow man,
   nor takes up a reproach against his neighbor;
by whom the reprobate is despised,
   while he honors those who fear the LORD. **R.**
Who lends not his money at usury
   and accepts no bribe against the innocent.
One who does these things
   shall never be disturbed. **R.**

Second Reading
COLOSSIANS 1:24-28

Brothers and sisters: Now I rejoice in my sufferings for your sake, and in my flesh I am filling up what is lacking in the afflictions of Christ on behalf of his body, which is the church, of which I am a minister in accordance with God's stewardship given to me to bring to completion for you the word of God, the mystery hidden from ages and from generations past. But now it has been manifested to his holy ones, to whom God chose to make known the riches of the glory of this mystery among the Gentiles; it is Christ in you, the hope for glory. It is he whom we proclaim, admonishing everyone and teaching everyone with all wisdom, that we may present everyone perfect in Christ.

Gospel
LUKE 10:38-42

Jesus entered a village where a woman whose name was Martha welcomed him. She had a sister named Mary who sat beside the Lord at his feet listening to him speak. Martha, burdened with much serving, came to him and said, "Lord, do you not care that my sister has left me by myself to do the serving? Tell her to help me." The Lord said to her in reply, "Martha, Martha, you are anxious and worried about many things. There is need of only one thing. Mary has chosen the better part and it will not be taken from her."

Monday, July 22

Saint Mary Magdalene

First Reading
SONG OF SONGS 3:1-4b (or 2 CORINTHIANS 5:14-17)

The Bride says:
On my bed at night I sought him
   whom my heart loves–
   I sought him but I did not find him.

I will rise then and go about the city;
  in the streets and crossings I will seek
Him whom my heart loves.
  I sought him but I did not find him.
The watchmen came upon me,
  as they made their rounds of the city:
  Have you seen him whom my heart loves?
I had hardly left them
  when I found him whom my heart loves.

Responsorial Psalm

PSALM 63: 2, 3-4, 5-6, 8-9

R. My soul is thirsting for you, O Lord my God.

O God, you are my God whom I seek;
  for you my flesh pines and my soul thirsts
  like the earth, parched, lifeless and without water. **R.**
Thus have I gazed toward you in the sanctuary
  to see your power and your glory,
For your kindness is a greater good than life;
  my lips shall glorify you. **R.**
Thus will I bless you while I live;
  lifting up my hands, I will call upon your name.
As with the riches of a banquet shall my soul be satisfied,
  and with exultant lips my mouth shall praise you. **R.**
You are my help,
  and in the shadow of your wings I shout for joy.
My soul clings fast to you;
  your right hand upholds me. **R.**

Gospel

JOHN 20:1-2, 11-18

On the first day of the week, Mary Magdalene came to the tomb early in the morning, while it was still dark, and saw the stone removed from the tomb. So she ran and went to Simon Peter and to the other disciple whom Jesus loved, and told them, "They have taken the Lord from the tomb, and we don't know where they put him."

Mary stayed outside the tomb weeping. And as she wept, she bent over into the tomb and saw two angels in white sitting there, one at the head and one at the feet where the Body of Jesus had been. And they said to her, "Woman, why are you weeping?" She said to them, "They have taken my Lord, and I don't know where they laid him." When she had said this, she turned around and saw Jesus there, but did not know it was Jesus. Jesus said to her, "Woman, why are you weeping? Whom are you looking for?" She thought it was the gardener and said to him,

"Sir, if you carried him away, tell me where you laid him, and I will take him." Jesus said to her, "Mary!" She turned and said to him in Hebrew, "Rabbouni," which means Teacher. Jesus said to her, "Stop holding on to me, for I have not yet ascended to the Father. But go to my brothers and tell them, 'I am going to my Father and your Father, to my God and your God.'" Mary Magdalene went and announced to the disciples, "I have seen the Lord," and then reported what he told her.

Tuesday, July 23

First Reading

EXODUS 14:21–15:1

Moses stretched out his hand over the sea, and the LORD swept the sea with a strong east wind throughout the night and so turned it into dry land. When the water was thus divided, the children of Israel marched into the midst of the sea on dry land, with the water like a wall to their right and to their left.

The Egyptians followed in pursuit; all Pharaoh's horses and chariots and charioteers went after them right into the midst of the sea. In the night watch just before dawn the LORD cast through the column of the fiery cloud upon the Egyptian force a glance that threw it into a panic; and he so clogged their chariot wheels that they could hardly drive. With that the Egyptians sounded the retreat before Israel, because the LORD was fighting for them against the Egyptians.

Then the LORD told Moses, "Stretch out your hand over the sea, that the water may flow back upon the Egyptians, upon their chariots and their charioteers." So Moses stretched out his hand over the sea, and at dawn the sea flowed back to its normal depth. The Egyptians were fleeing head on toward the sea, when the LORD hurled them into its midst. As the water flowed back, it covered the chariots and the charioteers of Pharaoh's whole army that had followed the children of Israel into the sea. Not a single one of them escaped. But the children of Israel had marched on dry land through the midst of the sea, with the water like a wall to their right and to their left. Thus the LORD saved Israel on that day from the power of the Egyptians. When Israel saw the Egyptians lying dead on the seashore and beheld the great power that the LORD had shown against the Egyptians, they feared the LORD and believed in him and in his servant Moses.

Then Moses and the children of Israel sang this song to the LORD:

I will sing to the LORD, for he is gloriously triumphant;
horse and chariot he has cast into the sea.

Responsorial Psalm
EXODUS 15:8-9, 10 and 12, 17
R. Let us sing to the Lord; he has covered himself in glory.
At the breath of your anger the waters piled up,
the flowing waters stood like a mound,
the flood waters congealed in the midst of the sea.
The enemy boasted, "I will pursue and overtake them;
I will divide the spoils and have my fill of them;
I will draw my sword; my hand shall despoil them!" **R.**
When your wind blew, the sea covered them;
like lead they sank in the mighty waters.
When you stretched out your right hand, the earth swallowed them! **R.**
And you brought them in and planted them on the mountain of your inheritance—
the place where you made your seat, O LORD,
the sanctuary, O LORD, which your hands established. **R.**

Gospel
MATTHEW 12:46-50
While Jesus was speaking to the crowds, his mother and his brothers appeared outside, wishing to speak with him. Someone told him, "Your mother and your brothers are standing outside, asking to speak with you." But he said in reply to the one who told him, "Who is my mother? Who are my brothers?" And stretching out his hand toward his disciples, he said, "Here are my mother and my brothers. For whoever does the will of my heavenly Father is my brother, and sister, and mother."

Wednesday, July 24

First Reading
EXODUS 16:1-5, 9-15
The children of Israel set out from Elim, and came into the desert of Sin, which is between Elim and Sinai, on the fifteenth day of the second month after their departure from the land of Egypt. Here in the desert the whole assembly of the children of Israel grumbled against Moses and Aaron. The children of Israel said to them, "Would that we had died at the LORD's hand in the land of Egypt, as we sat by our fleshpots and ate our fill of bread! But you had to lead us into this desert to make the whole community die of famine!"

Then the LORD said to Moses, "I will now rain down bread from heaven for you. Each day the people are to go out and gather their daily portion; thus will I test them, to see whether they follow my instructions or not. On the sixth day, however, when they prepare what they bring in, let it be twice as much as they gather on the other days."

Then Moses said to Aaron, "Tell the whole congregation of the children of Israel: Present yourselves before the LORD, for he has heard your grumbling." When Aaron announced this to the whole assembly of the children of Israel, they turned toward the desert, and lo, the glory of the LORD appeared in the cloud! The LORD spoke to Moses and said, "I have heard the grumbling of the children of Israel. Tell them: In the evening twilight you shall eat flesh, and in the morning you shall have your fill of bread, so that you may know that I, the LORD, am your God."

In the evening quail came up and covered the camp. In the morning a dew lay all about the camp, and when the dew evaporated, there on the surface of the desert were fine flakes like hoarfrost on the ground. On seeing it, the children of Israel asked one another, "What is this?" for they did not know what it was. But Moses told them, "This is the bread which the LORD has given you to eat."

Responsorial Psalm

PSALM 78:18-19, 23-24, 25-26, 27-28

R. The Lord gave them bread from heaven.

They tempted God in their hearts
 by demanding the food they craved.
Yes, they spoke against God, saying,
 "Can God spread a table in the desert?" **R.**
Yet he commanded the skies above
 and the doors of heaven he opened;
He rained manna upon them for food
 and gave them heavenly bread. **R.**
Man ate the bread of angels,
 food he sent them in abundance.
He stirred up the east wind in the heavens,
 and by his power brought on the south wind. **R.**
And he rained meat upon them like dust,
 and, like the sand of the sea, winged fowl,
Which fell in the midst of their camp
 round about their tents. **R.**

Gospel

MATTHEW 13:1-9

On that day, Jesus went out of the house and sat down by the sea. Such large crowds gathered around him that he got into a boat and sat down, and the whole crowd stood along the shore. And he spoke to them at length in parables, saying: "A sower went out to sow. And as he sowed, some seed fell on the path, and birds came and ate it up. Some fell on rocky ground, where it had little soil. It sprang up at once because the soil was not deep, and when the sun rose it was scorched, and it withered for lack of roots. Some seed fell among thorns, and the thorns grew up and choked it. But some seed fell on rich soil, and produced fruit, a hundred or sixty or thirtyfold. Whoever has ears ought to hear."

Thursday, July 25

Saint James, Apostle

First Reading
2 CORINTHIANS 4:7-15

Brothers and sisters: We hold this treasure in earthen vessels, that the surpassing power may be of God and not from us. We are afflicted in every way, but not constrained; perplexed, but not driven to despair; persecuted, but not abandoned; struck down, but not destroyed; always carrying about in the body the dying of Jesus, so that the life of Jesus may also be manifested in our body. For we who live are constantly being given up to death for the sake of Jesus, so that the life of Jesus may be manifested in our mortal flesh.

So death is at work in us, but life in you. Since, then, we have the same spirit of faith, according to what is written, *I believed, therefore I spoke*, we too believe and therefore speak, knowing that the one who raised the Lord Jesus will raise us also with Jesus and place us with you in his presence. Everything indeed is for you, so that the grace bestowed in abundance on more and more people may cause the thanksgiving to overflow for the glory of God.

Responsorial Psalm
PSALM 126:1bc-2ab, 2cd-3, 4-5, 6
R. Those who sow in tears shall reap rejoicing.

When the LORD brought back the captives of Zion,
we were like men dreaming.
Then our mouth was filled with laughter,
and our tongue with rejoicing. **R.**
Then they said among the nations,
"The LORD has done great things for them."
The LORD has done great things for us;
we are glad indeed. **R.**
Restore our fortunes, O LORD,
like the torrents in the southern desert.
Those that sow in tears
shall reap rejoicing. **R.**

Although they go forth weeping,
carrying the seed to be sown,
They shall come back rejoicing,
carrying their sheaves. **R.**

Gospel
MATTHEW 20:20-28

The mother of the sons of Zebedee approached Jesus with her sons and did him homage, wishing to ask him for something. He said to her, "What do you wish?" She answered him, "Command that these two sons of mine sit, one at your right and the other at your left, in your Kingdom." Jesus said in reply, "You do not know what you are asking. Can you drink the chalice that I am going to drink?" They said to him, "We can." He replied, "My chalice you will indeed drink, but to sit at my right and at my left, this is not mine to give but is for those for whom it has been prepared by my Father." When the ten heard this, they became indignant at the two brothers. But Jesus summoned them and said, "You know that the rulers of the Gentiles lord it over them, and the great ones make their authority over them felt. But it shall not be so among you. Rather, whoever wishes to be great among you shall be your servant; whoever wishes to be first among you shall be your slave. Just so, the Son of Man did not come to be served but to serve and to give his life as a ransom for many."

Friday, July 26

First Reading
EXODUS 20:1-17

In those days: God delivered all these commandments:

"I, the LORD, am your God, who brought you out of the land of Egypt, that place of slavery. You shall not have other gods besides me. You shall not carve idols for yourselves in the shape of anything in the sky above or on the earth below or in the waters beneath the earth; you shall not bow down before them or worship them. For I, the LORD, your God, am a jealous God, inflicting punishment for their fathers' wickedness on the children of those who hate me, down to the third and fourth generation; but bestowing mercy down to the thousandth generation on the children of those who love me and keep my commandments.

"You shall not take the name of the LORD, your God, in vain. For the LORD will not leave unpunished him who takes his name in vain.

"Remember to keep holy the sabbath day. Six days you may labor and do all your work, but the seventh day is the sabbath of the LORD, your God. No work may be done then either by you, or your son or daughter, or your male or female slave, or your beast, or by the alien who lives with you. In six days the LORD made the heavens and the earth, the sea and all that is in them; but on the seventh day he rested. That is why the LORD has blessed the sabbath day and made it holy.

"Honor your father and your mother, that you may have a long life in the land which the LORD, your God, is giving you.

"You shall not kill.

"You shall not commit adultery.

"You shall not steal.

"You shall not bear false witness against your neighbor.

"You shall not covet your neighbor's house.

You shall not covet your neighbor's wife, nor his male or female slave, nor his ox or ass, nor anything else that belongs to him."

Responsorial Psalm

PSALM 19:8, 9, 10, 11

R. Lord, you have the words of everlasting life.

The law of the LORD is perfect,
  refreshing the soul;
The decree of the LORD is trustworthy,
  giving wisdom to the simple. **R.**
The precepts of the LORD are right,
  rejoicing the heart;
The command of the LORD is clear,
  enlightening the eye. **R.**
The fear of the LORD is pure,
  enduring forever;
The ordinances of the LORD are true,
  all of them just. **R.**
They are more precious than gold,
  than a heap of purest gold;
Sweeter also than syrup
  or honey from the comb. **R.**

Gospel

MATTHEW 13:18-23

Jesus said to his disciples: "Hear the parable of the sower. The seed sown on the path is the one who hears the word of the Kingdom without understanding it, and the Evil One comes and steals away what was sown in his heart. The seed sown on rocky ground is the one who hears the word and receives it at once with joy. But he has no root and lasts only for a time. When some tribulation or persecution comes because of the word, he immediately falls away. The seed sown among thorns is the one who hears the word, but then worldly anxiety and the lure of riches choke the word and it bears no fruit. But the seed sown on rich soil is the one who hears the word and understands it, who indeed bears fruit and yields a hundred or sixty or thirtyfold."

Saturday, July 27

First Reading

EXODUS 24:3-8

When Moses came to the people and related all the words and ordinances of the LORD, they all answered with one voice, "We will do everything that the LORD has told us." Moses then wrote down all the words of the LORD and, rising early the next day, he erected at the foot of the mountain an altar and twelve pillars for the twelve tribes of Israel. Then, having sent certain young men of the children of Israel to offer burnt offerings and sacrifice young bulls as peace offerings to the LORD, Moses took half of the blood and put it in large bowls; the other half he splashed on the altar. Taking the book of the covenant, he read it aloud to the people, who answered, "All that the LORD has said, we will heed and do." Then he took the blood and sprinkled it on the people, saying, "This is the blood of the covenant that the LORD has made with you in accordance with all these words of his."

Responsorial Psalm

PSALM 50:1b-2, 5-6, 14-15

R. Offer to God a sacrifice of praise.

God the LORD has spoken and summoned the earth,
from the rising of the sun to its setting.
From Zion, perfect in beauty,
God shines forth. **R.**
"Gather my faithful ones before me,
those who have made a covenant with me by sacrifice."
And the heavens proclaim his justice;
for God himself is the judge. **R.**
"Offer to God praise as your sacrifice
and fulfill your vows to the Most High;
Then call upon me in time of distress;
I will rescue you, and you shall glorify me." **R.**

Gospel

MATTHEW 13:24-30

Jesus proposed a parable to the crowds. "The Kingdom of heaven may be likened to a man who sowed good seed in his field. While everyone was asleep his enemy came and sowed weeds all through the wheat, and then went off. When the crop grew and bore fruit, the weeds appeared as well. The slaves of the householder came to him and said, 'Master, did you not sow good seed in your field? Where have the weeds come from?' He answered, 'An enemy has done this.' His slaves said to him, 'Do you want us to go and pull them up?' He replied, 'No, if you pull up the weeds you might uproot the wheat along with them. Let them grow together until harvest; then at harvest time I will say to the harvesters, "First collect the weeds and tie them in bundles for burning; but gather the wheat into my barn."'"

Sunday, July 28

Seventeenth Sunday in Ordinary Time

First Reading

GENESIS 18:20-32

In those days, the LORD said: "The outcry against Sodom and Gomorrah is so great, and their sin so grave, that I must go down and see whether or not their actions fully correspond to the cry against them that comes to me. I mean to find out."

While Abraham's visitors walked on farther toward Sodom, the LORD remained standing before Abraham. Then Abraham drew nearer and said: "Will you sweep away the innocent with the guilty? Suppose there were fifty innocent people in the city; would you wipe out the place, rather than spare it for the sake of the fifty innocent people within it? Far be it from you to do such a thing, to make the innocent die with the guilty so that the innocent and the guilty would be treated alike! Should not the judge of all the world act with justice?" The LORD replied, "If I find fifty innocent people in the city of Sodom, I will spare the whole place for their sake." Abraham spoke up again: "See how I am presuming to speak to my Lord, though I am but dust and ashes! What if there are five less than fifty innocent people? Will you destroy the whole city because of those five?" He answered, "I will not destroy it, if I find forty-five there." But Abraham persisted, saying, "What if only forty are found there?" He replied, "I will forbear doing it for the sake of the forty." Then Abraham said, "Let not my Lord grow impatient if I go on. What if only thirty are found there?" He replied, "I will forbear doing it if I can find but thirty there." Still Abraham went on, "Since I have thus dared to speak to my Lord, what if there are no more than twenty?" The LORD answered, "I will not destroy it, for the sake of the twenty." But he still persisted: "Please, let not my Lord grow angry if I speak up this last time. What if there are at least ten there?" He replied, "For the sake of those ten, I will not destroy it."

Responsorial Psalm

PSALM 138:1-2, 2-3, 6-7, 7-8

R. Lord, on the day I called for help, you answered me.

I will give thanks to you, O LORD, with all my heart,
for you have heard the words of my mouth;
in the presence of the angels I will sing your praise;
I will worship at your holy temple
and give thanks to your name. **R.**
Because of your kindness and your truth;
for you have made great above all things
your name and your promise.
When I called you answered me;
you built up strength within me. **R.**
The LORD is exalted, yet the lowly he sees,
and the proud he knows from afar.
Though I walk amid distress, you preserve me;
against the anger of my enemies you raise your hand. **R.**
Your right hand saves me.
The LORD will complete what he has done for me;
your kindness, O LORD, endures forever;
forsake not the work of your hands. **R.**

Second Reading

COLOSSIANS 2:12-14

Brothers and sisters: You were buried with him in baptism, in which you were also raised with him through faith in the power of God, who raised him from the dead. And even when you were dead in transgressions and the uncircumcision of your flesh, he brought you to life along with him, having forgiven us all our transgressions; obliterating the bond against us, with its legal claims, which was opposed to us, he also removed it from our midst, nailing it to the cross.

Gospel

LUKE 11:1-13

Jesus was praying in a certain place, and when he had finished, one of his disciples said to him, "Lord, teach us to pray just as John taught his disciples." He said to them, "When you pray, say:

Father, hallowed be your name,
your kingdom come.
Give us each day our daily bread
and forgive us our sins
for we ourselves forgive everyone in debt to us,
and do not subject us to the final test."

And he said to them, "Suppose one of you has a friend to whom he goes at midnight and says, 'Friend, lend me three loaves of bread, for a friend of mine has arrived at my house from a journey and I have nothing to offer him,' and he says in reply from within, 'Do not bother me; the door has already been locked and my children and I are already in bed. I cannot get up to give you anything.' I tell you, if he does not get up to give the visitor the loaves because of their friendship, he will get up to give him whatever he needs because of his persistence.

"And I tell you, ask and you will receive; seek and you will find; knock and the door will be opened to you. For everyone who asks, receives; and the one who seeks, finds; and to the one who knocks, the door will be opened. What father among you would hand his son a snake when he asks for a fish? Or hand him a scorpion when he asks for an egg? If you then, who are wicked, know how to give good gifts to your children, how much more will the Father in heaven give the Holy Spirit to those who ask him?"

Monday, July 29

Saint Martha

First Reading
EXODUS 32:15-24, 30-34

Moses turned and came down the mountain with the two tablets of the commandments in his hands, tablets that were written on both sides, front and back; tablets that were made by God, having inscriptions on them that were engraved by God himself. Now, when Joshua heard the noise of the people shouting, he said to Moses, "That sounds like a battle in the camp." But Moses answered, "It does not sound like cries of victory, nor does it sound like cries of defeat; the sounds that I hear are cries of revelry." As he drew near the camp, he saw the calf and the dancing. With that, Moses' wrath flared up, so that he threw the tablets down and broke them on the base of the mountain. Taking the calf they had made, he fused it in the fire and then ground it down to powder, which he scattered on the water and made the children of Israel drink.

Moses asked Aaron, "What did this people ever do to you that you should lead them into so grave a sin?" Aaron replied, "Let not my lord be angry. You know well enough how prone the people are to evil. They said to me, 'Make us a god to be our leader; as for the man Moses who brought us out of the land of Egypt, we do not know what has happened to him.' So I told them, 'Let anyone who has gold jewelry take it off.' They gave it to me, and I threw it into the fire, and this calf came out."

On the next day Moses said to the people, "You have committed a grave sin. I will go up to the LORD, then; perhaps I may be able to make atonement for your sin." So Moses went back to the LORD and said, "Ah, this people has indeed committed a grave sin in making a god of gold for themselves! If you would only forgive their sin! If you will not, then strike me out of the book that you have written." The LORD answered, "Him only who has sinned against me will I strike out of my book. Now, go and lead the people to the place I have told you. My angel will go before you. When it is time for me to punish, I will punish them for their sin."

Responsorial Psalm

PSALM 106:19-20, 21-22, 23

R. Give thanks to the Lord, for he is good.

Our fathers made a calf in Horeb
  and adored a molten image;
They exchanged their glory
  for the image of a grass-eating bullock. **R.**
They forgot the God who had saved them,
  who had done great deeds in Egypt,
Wondrous deeds in the land of Ham,
  terrible things at the Red Sea. **R.**
Then he spoke of exterminating them,
  but Moses, his chosen one,
Withstood him in the breach
  to turn back his destructive wrath. **R.**

Gospel

JOHN 11:19-27 (or Luke 10:38-42)

Many of the Jews had come to Martha and Mary to comfort them about their brother [Lazarus, who had died]. When Martha heard that Jesus was coming, she went to meet him; but Mary sat at home. Martha said to Jesus, "Lord, if you had been here, my brother would not have died. But even now I know that whatever you ask of God, God will give you." Jesus said to her, "Your brother will rise." Martha said to him, "I know he will rise, in the resurrection on the last day." Jesus told her, "I am the resurrection and the life; whoever believes in me, even if he dies, will live, and anyone who lives and believes in me will never die. Do you believe this?" She said to him, "Yes, Lord. I have come to believe that you are the Christ, the Son of God, the one who is coming into the world."

Tuesday, July 30

First Reading

EXODUS 33:7-11; 34:5b-9, 28

The tent, which was called the meeting tent, Moses used to pitch at some distance away, outside the camp. Anyone who wished to consult the LORD would go to this meeting tent outside the camp. Whenever Moses went out to the tent, the people would all rise and stand at the entrance of their own tents, watching Moses until he entered the tent. As Moses entered the tent, the column of cloud would come down and stand at its entrance while the LORD spoke with Moses. On seeing the column of cloud stand at the entrance of the tent, all the people would rise and worship at the entrance of their own tents. The LORD used to speak to Moses face to face, as one man speaks to another. Moses would then return to the camp, but his young assistant, Joshua, son of Nun, would not move out of the tent.

Moses stood there with the LORD and proclaimed his name, "LORD." Thus the LORD passed before him and cried out, "The LORD, the LORD, a merciful and gracious God, slow to anger and rich in kindness and fidelity, continuing his kindness for a thousand generations, and forgiving wickedness and crime and sin; yet not declaring the guilty guiltless, but punishing children and grandchildren to the third and fourth generation for their fathers' wickedness!" Moses at once bowed down to the ground in worship. Then he said, "If I find favor with you, O LORD, do come along in our company. This is indeed a stiff-necked people; yet pardon our wickedness and sins, and receive us as your own."

So Moses stayed there with the LORD for forty days and forty nights, without eating any food or drinking any water, and he wrote on the tablets the words of the covenant, the ten commandments.

Responsorial Psalm

PSALM 103:6-7, 8-9, 10-11, 12-13

R. The Lord is kind and merciful.

The LORD secures justice
and the rights of all the oppressed.
He has made known his ways to Moses,
and his deeds to the children of Israel. **R.**
Merciful and gracious is the LORD,
slow to anger and abounding in kindness.
He will not always chide,
nor does he keep his wrath forever. **R.**
Not according to our sins does he deal with us,
nor does he requite us according to our crimes.

For as the heavens are high above the earth,
so surpassing is his kindness toward those who fear him. **R.**
As far as the east is from the west,
so far has he put our transgressions from us.
As a father has compassion on his children,
so the LORD has compassion on those who fear him. **R.**

Gospel
MATTHEW 13:36-43

Jesus dismissed the crowds and went into the house. His disciples approached him and said, "Explain to us the parable of the weeds in the field." He said in reply, "He who sows good seed is the Son of Man, the field is the world, the good seed the children of the Kingdom. The weeds are the children of the Evil One, and the enemy who sows them is the Devil. The harvest is the end of the age, and the harvesters are angels. Just as weeds are collected and burned up with fire, so will it be at the end of the age. The Son of Man will send his angels, and they will collect out of his Kingdom all who cause others to sin and all evildoers. They will throw them into the fiery furnace, where there will be wailing and grinding of teeth. Then the righteous will shine like the sun in the Kingdom of their Father. Whoever has ears ought to hear."

Wednesday, July 31

First Reading
EXODUS 34:29-35

As Moses came down from Mount Sinai with the two tablets of the commandments in his hands, he did not know that the skin of his face had become radiant while he conversed with the LORD. When Aaron, then, and the other children of Israel saw Moses and noticed how radiant the skin of his face had become, they were afraid to come near him. Only after Moses called to them did Aaron and all the rulers of the community come back to him. Moses then spoke to them. Later on, all the children of Israel came up to him, and he enjoined on them all that the LORD had told him on Mount Sinai. When he finished speaking with them, he put a veil over his face. Whenever Moses entered the presence of the LORD to converse with him, he removed the veil until he came out again. On coming out, he would tell the children of Israel all that had been commanded. Then the children of Israel would see that the skin of Moses' face was radiant; so he would again put the veil over his face until he went in to converse with the LORD.

Responsorial Psalm
PSALM 99:5, 6, 7, 9
R. Holy is the Lord our God.
Extol the LORD, our God,
and worship at his footstool;
holy is he! **R.**
Moses and Aaron were among his priests,
and Samuel, among those who called upon his name;
they called upon the LORD, and he answered them. **R.**
From the pillar of cloud he spoke to them;
they heard his decrees and the law he gave them. **R.**
Extol the LORD, our God,
and worship at his holy mountain;
for holy is the LORD, our God. **R.**

Gospel
MATTHEW 13:44-46
Jesus said to his disciples: "The Kingdom of heaven is like a treasure buried in a field, which a person finds and hides again, and out of joy goes and sells all that he has and buys that field. Again, the Kingdom of heaven is like a merchant searching for fine pearls. When he finds a pearl of great price, he goes and sells all that he has and buys it."

AUGUST

Thursday, August 1

First Reading

EXODUS 40:16-21, 34-38

Moses did exactly as the LORD had commanded him. On the first day of the first month of the second year the Dwelling was erected. It was Moses who erected the Dwelling. He placed its pedestals, set up its boards, put in its bars, and set up its columns. He spread the tent over the Dwelling and put the covering on top of the tent, as the LORD had commanded him. He took the commandments and put them in the ark; he placed poles alongside the ark and set the propitiatory upon it. He brought the ark into the Dwelling and hung the curtain veil, thus screening off the ark of the commandments, as the LORD had commanded him.

Then the cloud covered the meeting tent, and the glory of the LORD filled the Dwelling. Moses could not enter the meeting tent, because the cloud settled down upon it and the glory of the LORD filled the Dwelling. Whenever the cloud rose from the Dwelling, the children of Israel would set out on their journey. But if the cloud did not lift, they would not go forward; only when it lifted did they go forward. In the daytime the cloud of the LORD was seen over the Dwelling; whereas at night, fire was seen in the cloud by the whole house of Israel in all the stages of their journey.

Responsorial Psalm

PSALM 84:3, 4, 5-6a and 8a, 11

R. How lovely is your dwelling place, O Lord, mighty God!

My soul yearns and pines
for the courts of the LORD.
My heart and my flesh
cry out for the living God. **R.**
Even the sparrow finds a home,
and the swallow a nest
in which she puts her young—
Your altars, O LORD of hosts,
my king and my God! **R.**
Blessed they who dwell in your house!
continually they praise you.
Blessed the men whose strength you are!
They go from strength to strength. **R.**

I had rather one day in your courts
than a thousand elsewhere;
I had rather lie at the threshold of the house of my God
than dwell in the tents of the wicked. **R.**

Gospel
MATTHEW 13:47-53

Jesus said to the disciples: "The Kingdom of heaven is like a net thrown into the sea, which collects fish of every kind. When it is full they haul it ashore and sit down to put what is good into buckets. What is bad they throw away. Thus it will be at the end of the age. The angels will go out and separate the wicked from the righteous and throw them into the fiery furnace, where there will be wailing and grinding of teeth."

"Do you understand all these things?" They answered, "Yes." And he replied, "Then every scribe who has been instructed in the Kingdom of heaven is like the head of a household who brings from his storeroom both the new and the old." When Jesus finished these parables, he went away from there.

Friday, August 2

First Reading
LEVITICUS 23:1, 4-11, 15-16, 27, 34b-37

The LORD said to Moses, "These are the festivals of the LORD which you shall celebrate at their proper time with a sacred assembly. The Passover of the LORD falls on the fourteenth day of the first month, at the evening twilight. The fifteenth day of this month is the LORD's feast of Unleavened Bread. For seven days you shall eat unleavened bread. On the first of these days you shall hold a sacred assembly and do no sort of work. On each of the seven days you shall offer an oblation to the LORD. Then on the seventh day you shall again hold a sacred assembly and do no sort of work."

The LORD said to Moses, "Speak to the children of Israel and tell them: When you come into the land which I am giving you, and reap your harvest, you shall bring a sheaf of the first fruits of your harvest to the priest, who shall wave the sheaf before the LORD that it may be acceptable for you. On the day after the sabbath the priest shall do this.

"Beginning with the day after the sabbath, the day on which you bring the wave-offering sheaf, you shall count seven full weeks, and then on the day after the seventh week, the fiftieth day, you shall present the new cereal offering to the LORD.

"The tenth of this seventh month is the Day of Atonement, when you shall hold a sacred assembly and mortify yourselves and offer an oblation to the LORD.

"The fifteenth day of this seventh month is the LORD's feast of Booths, which shall continue for seven days. On the first day there shall be a sacred assembly, and you shall do no sort of work. For seven days you shall offer an oblation to the LORD, and on the eighth day you shall again hold a sacred assembly and offer an oblation to the LORD. On that solemn closing you shall do no sort of work.

"These, therefore, are the festivals of the LORD on which you shall proclaim a sacred assembly, and offer as an oblation to the LORD burnt offerings and cereal offerings, sacrifices and libations, as prescribed for each day."

Responsorial Psalm
PSALM 81:3-4, 5-6, 10-11ab
R. Sing with joy to God our help.

Take up a melody, and sound the timbrel,
the pleasant harp and the lyre.
Blow the trumpet at the new moon,
at the full moon, on our solemn feast. **R.**
For it is a statute in Israel,
an ordinance of the God of Jacob,
Who made it a decree for Joseph
when he came forth from the land of Egypt. **R.**
There shall be no strange god among you
nor shall you worship any alien god.
I, the LORD, am your God
who led you forth from the land of Egypt. **R.**

Gospel
MATTHEW 13:54-58

Jesus came to his native place and taught the people in their synagogue. They were astonished and said, "Where did this man get such wisdom and mighty deeds? Is he not the carpenter's son? Is not his mother named Mary and his brothers James, Joseph, Simon, and Judas? Are not his sisters all with us? Where did this man get all this?" And they took offense at him. But Jesus said to them, "A prophet is not without honor except in his native place and in his own house." And he did not work many mighty deeds there because of their lack of faith.

Saturday, August 3

First Reading

LEVITICUS 25:1, 8-17

The LORD said to Moses on Mount Sinai, "Seven weeks of years shall you count—seven times seven years—so that the seven cycles amount to forty-nine years. Then, on the tenth day of the seventh month, let the trumpet resound; on this, the Day of Atonement, the trumpet blast shall re-echo throughout your land. This fiftieth year you shall make sacred by proclaiming liberty in the land for all its inhabitants. It shall be a jubilee for you, when every one of you shall return to his own property, every one to his own family estate. In this fiftieth year, your year of jubilee, you shall not sow, nor shall you reap the aftergrowth or pick the grapes from the untrimmed vines. Since this is the jubilee, which shall be sacred for you, you may not eat of its produce, except as taken directly from the field.

"In this year of jubilee, then, every one of you shall return to his own property. Therefore, when you sell any land to your neighbor or buy any from him, do not deal unfairly. On the basis of the number of years since the last jubilee shall you purchase the land from your neighbor; and so also, on the basis of the number of years for crops, shall he sell it to you. When the years are many, the price shall be so much the more; when the years are few, the price shall be so much the less. For it is really the number of crops that he sells you. Do not deal unfairly, then; but stand in fear of your God. I, the LORD, am your God."

Responsorial Psalm

PSALM 67:2-3, 5, 7-8

R. O God, let all the nations praise you!

May God have pity on us and bless us;
may he let his face shine upon us.
So may your way be known upon earth;
among all nations, your salvation. **R.**
May the nations be glad and exult
because you rule the peoples in equity;
the nations on the earth you guide. **R.**
The earth has yielded its fruits;
God, our God, has blessed us.
May God bless us,
and may all the ends of the earth fear him! **R.**

Gospel

MATTHEW 14:1-12

Herod the tetrarch heard of the reputation of Jesus and said to his servants, "This man is John the Baptist. He has been raised from the dead; that is why mighty powers are at work in him."

Now Herod had arrested John, bound him, and put him in prison on account of Herodias, the wife of his brother Philip, for John had said to him, "It is not lawful for you to have her." Although he wanted to kill him, he feared the people, for they regarded him as a prophet. But at a birthday celebration for Herod, the daughter of Herodias performed a dance before the guests and delighted Herod so much that he swore to give her whatever she might ask for. Prompted by her mother, she said, "Give me here on a platter the head of John the Baptist." The king was distressed, but because of his oaths and the guests who were present, he ordered that it be given, and he had John beheaded in the prison. His head was brought in on a platter and given to the girl, who took it to her mother. His disciples came and took away the corpse and buried him; and they went and told Jesus.

Sunday, August 4

Eighteenth Sunday in Ordinary Time

First Reading

ECCLESIASTES 1:2; 2:21-23

Vanity of vanities, says Qoheleth,
vanity of vanities! All things are vanity!

Here is one who has labored with wisdom and knowledge and skill, and yet to another who has not labored over it, he must leave property. This also is vanity and a great misfortune. For what profit comes to man from all the toil and anxiety of heart with which he has labored under the sun? All his days sorrow and grief are his occupation; even at night his mind is not at rest. This also is vanity.

Responsorial Psalm

PSALM 90:3-4, 5-6, 12-13, 14, 17

R. If today you hear his voice, harden not your hearts.

You turn man back to dust,
saying, "Return, O children of men."
For a thousand years in your sight
are as yesterday, now that it is past,
or as a watch of the night. **R.**

You make an end of them in their sleep;
  the next morning they are like the changing grass,
which at dawn springs up anew,
  but by evening wilts and fades. **R.**
Teach us to number our days aright,
  that we may gain wisdom of heart.
Return, O LORD! How long?
  Have pity on your servants! **R.**
Fill us at daybreak with your kindness,
  that we may shout for joy and gladness all our days.
And may the gracious care of the LORD our God be ours;
  prosper the work of our hands for us!
  Prosper the work of our hands! **R.**

Second Reading
COLOSSIANS 3:1-5, 9-11

Brothers and sisters: If you were raised with Christ, seek what is above, where Christ is seated at the right hand of God. Think of what is above, not of what is on earth. For you have died, and your life is hidden with Christ in God. When Christ your life appears, then you too will appear with him in glory.

Put to death, then, the parts of you that are earthly: immorality, impurity, passion, evil desire, and the greed that is idolatry. Stop lying to one another, since you have taken off the old self with its practices and have put on the new self, which is being renewed, for knowledge, in the image of its creator. Here there is not Greek and Jew, circumcision and uncircumcision, barbarian, Scythian, slave, free; but Christ is all and in all.

Gospel
LUKE 12:13-21

Someone in the crowd said to Jesus, "Teacher, tell my brother to share the inheritance with me." He replied to him, "Friend, who appointed me as your judge and arbitrator?" Then he said to the crowd, "Take care to guard against all greed, for though one may be rich, one's life does not consist of possessions."

Then he told them a parable. "There was a rich man whose land produced a bountiful harvest. He asked himself, 'What shall I do, for I do not have space to store my harvest?' And he said, 'This is what I shall do: I shall tear down my barns and build larger ones. There I shall store all my grain and other goods and I shall say to myself, "Now as for you, you have so many good things stored up for many years, rest, eat, drink, be merry!"' But God said to him, 'You fool, this night your life will be demanded of you; and the things you have prepared, to whom will they belong?' Thus will it be for all who store up treasure for themselves but are not rich in what matters to God."

Monday, August 5

First Reading

NUMBERS 11:4b-15

The children of Israel lamented, "Would that we had meat for food! We remember the fish we used to eat without cost in Egypt, and the cucumbers, the melons, the leeks, the onions, and the garlic. But now we are famished; we see nothing before us but this manna."

Manna was like coriander seed and had the color of resin. When they had gone about and gathered it up, the people would grind it between millstones or pound it in a mortar, then cook it in a pot and make it into loaves, which tasted like cakes made with oil. At night, when the dew fell upon the camp, the manna also fell.

When Moses heard the people, family after family, crying at the entrance of their tents, so that the LORD became very angry, he was grieved. "Why do you treat your servant so badly?" Moses asked the LORD. "Why are you so displeased with me that you burden me with all this people? Was it I who conceived all this people? Or was it I who gave them birth, that you tell me to carry them at my bosom, like a foster father carrying an infant, to the land you have promised under oath to their fathers? Where can I get meat to give to all this people? For they are crying to me, 'Give us meat for our food.' I cannot carry all this people by myself, for they are too heavy for me. If this is the way you will deal with me, then please do me the favor of killing me at once, so that I need no longer face this distress."

Responsorial Psalm

PSALM 81:12-13, 14-15, 16-17

R. Sing with joy to God our help.

"My people heard not my voice,
  and Israel obeyed me not;
So I gave them up to the hardness of their hearts;
  they walked according to their own counsels." **R.**
"If only my people would hear me,
  and Israel walk in my ways,
Quickly would I humble their enemies;
  against their foes I would turn my hand." **R.**
"Those who hated the LORD would seek to flatter me,
  but their fate would endure forever,

While Israel I would feed with the best of wheat,
  and with honey from the rock I would fill them." **R.**

Gospel
MATTHEW 14:13-21

When Jesus heard of the death of John the Baptist, he withdrew in a boat to a deserted place by himself. The crowds heard of this and followed him on foot from their towns. When he disembarked and saw the vast crowd, his heart was moved with pity for them, and he cured their sick. When it was evening, the disciples approached him and said, "This is a deserted place and it is already late; dismiss the crowds so that they can go to the villages and buy food for themselves." He said to them, "There is no need for them to go away; give them some food yourselves." But they said to him, "Five loaves and two fish are all we have here." Then he said, "Bring them here to me," and he ordered the crowds to sit down on the grass. Taking the five loaves and the two fish, and looking up to heaven, he said the blessing, broke the loaves, and gave them to the disciples, who in turn gave them to the crowds. They all ate and were satisfied, and they picked up the fragments left over—twelve wicker baskets full. Those who ate were about five thousand men, not counting women and children.

Tuesday, August 6

The Transfiguration of the Lord

First Reading
DANIEL 7:9-10, 13-14

As I watched:

Thrones were set up
  and the Ancient One took his throne.
His clothing was bright as snow,
  and the hair on his head as white as wool;
his throne was flames of fire,
  with wheels of burning fire.
A surging stream of fire
  flowed out from where he sat;
Thousands upon thousands were ministering to him,
  and myriads upon myriads attended him.
The court was convened and the books were opened.

As the visions during the night continued, I saw:

One like a Son of man coming,
on the clouds of heaven;
When he reached the Ancient One
and was presented before him,
The one like a Son of man received dominion, glory, and kingship;
all peoples, nations, and languages serve him.
His dominion is an everlasting dominion
that shall not be taken away,
his kingship shall not be destroyed.

Responsorial Psalm
PSALM 97:1-2, 5-6, 9
R. The Lord is king, the Most High over all the earth.

The LORD is king; let the earth rejoice;
let the many islands be glad.
Clouds and darkness are round about him,
justice and judgment are the foundation of his throne. **R.**
The mountains melt like wax before the LORD,
before the LORD of all the earth.
The heavens proclaim his justice,
and all peoples see his glory. **R.**
Because you, O LORD, are the Most High over all the earth,
exalted far above all gods. **R.**

Second Reading
2 PETER 1:16-19

Beloved: We did not follow cleverly devised myths when we made known to you the power and coming of our Lord Jesus Christ, but we had been eyewitnesses of his majesty. For he received honor and glory from God the Father when that unique declaration came to him from the majestic glory, "This is my Son, my beloved, with whom I am well pleased." We ourselves heard this voice come from heaven while we were with him on the holy mountain. Moreover, we possess the prophetic message that is altogether reliable. You will do well to be attentive to it, as to a lamp shining in a dark place, until day dawns and the morning star rises in your hearts.

Gospel
LUKE 9:28b-36

Jesus took Peter, John, and James and went up a mountain to pray. While he was praying his face changed in appearance and his clothing became dazzling white. And behold, two men were conversing with him, Moses and Elijah, who appeared in glory and spoke of his exodus that he was going to accomplish in Jerusalem. Peter and his companions had been overcome by sleep, but becoming fully awake, they saw his glory and the two men standing with him. As they were about to part from him, Peter said to Jesus, "Master, it is good that we are here; let us make three tents, one for you, one for Moses, and one for Elijah." But he did not know what he was saying. While he was still speaking, a cloud came and cast a shadow over them, and they became frightened when they entered the cloud. Then from the cloud came a voice that said, "This is my chosen Son; listen to him." After the voice had spoken, Jesus was found alone. They fell silent and did not at that time tell anyone what they had seen.

Wednesday, August 7

First Reading

NUMBERS 13:1-2, 25–14:1, 26-29a, 34-35

The LORD said to Moses [in the desert of Paran,] "Send men to reconnoiter the land of Canaan, which I am giving the children of Israel. You shall send one man from each ancestral tribe, all of them princes."

After reconnoitering the land for forty days they returned, met Moses and Aaron and the whole congregation of the children of Israel in the desert of Paran at Kadesh, made a report to them all, and showed the fruit of the country to the whole congregation. They told Moses: "We went into the land to which you sent us. It does indeed flow with milk and honey, and here is its fruit. However, the people who are living in the land are fierce, and the towns are fortified and very strong. Besides, we saw descendants of the Anakim there. Amalekites live in the region of the Negeb; Hittites, Jebusites, and Amorites dwell in the highlands, and Canaanites along the seacoast and the banks of the Jordan."

Caleb, however, to quiet the people toward Moses, said, "We ought to go up and seize the land, for we can certainly do so." But the men who had gone up with him said, "We cannot attack these people; they are too strong for us." So they spread discouraging reports among the children of Israel about the land they had scouted, saying, "The land that we explored is a country that consumes its inhabitants. And all the people we saw there are huge, veritable giants (the Anakim were a race of giants); we felt like mere grasshoppers, and so we must have seemed to them."

At this, the whole community broke out with loud cries, and even in the night the people wailed.

The LORD said to Moses and Aaron: "How long will this wicked assembly grumble against me? I have heard the grumblings of the children of Israel against me. Tell them: By my life, says the LORD, I will do to you just what I have heard you say. Here in the desert shall your dead bodies fall. Forty days you spent in scouting the land; forty years shall you suffer for your crimes: one year for each day. Thus you will realize what it means to oppose me. I, the LORD, have sworn to do this to all this wicked assembly that conspired against me: here in the desert they shall die to the last man."

Responsorial Psalm

PSALM 106:6-7ab, 13-14, 21-22, 23

R. Remember us, O Lord, as you favor your people.

We have sinned, we and our fathers;
we have committed crimes; we have done wrong.
Our fathers in Egypt
considered not your wonders. **R.**
But soon they forgot his works;
they waited not for his counsel.
They gave way to craving in the desert
and tempted God in the wilderness. **R.**
They forgot the God who had saved them,
who had done great deeds in Egypt,
Wondrous deeds in the land of Ham,
terrible things at the Red Sea. **R.**
Then he spoke of exterminating them,
but Moses, his chosen one,
Withstood him in the breach
to turn back his destructive wrath. **R.**

Gospel

MATTHEW 15:21-28

At that time Jesus withdrew to the region of Tyre and Sidon. And behold, a Canaanite woman of that district came and called out, "Have pity on me, Lord, Son of David! My daughter is tormented by a demon." But he did not say a word in answer to her. His disciples came and asked him, "Send her away, for she keeps calling out after us." He said in reply, "I was sent only to the lost sheep of the house of Israel." But the woman came and did him homage, saying, "Lord, help me." He said in reply, "It is not right to take the food of the children and throw it to the dogs." She said, "Please, Lord, for even the dogs eat the scraps that fall from the table of their masters." Then Jesus said to her in reply, "O woman, great is your faith! Let it be done for you as you wish." And her daughter was healed from that hour.

Thursday, August 8

First Reading

NUMBERS 20:1-13

The whole congregation of the children of Israel arrived in the desert of Zin in the first month, and the people settled at Kadesh. It was here that Miriam died, and here that she was buried.

As the community had no water, they held a council against Moses and Aaron. The people contended with Moses, exclaiming, "Would that we too had perished with our kinsmen in the LORD's presence! Why have you brought the LORD's assembly into this desert where we and our livestock are dying? Why did you lead us out of Egypt, only to bring us to this wretched place which has neither grain nor figs nor vines nor pomegranates? Here there is not even water to drink!" But Moses and Aaron went away from the assembly to the entrance of the meeting tent, where they fell prostrate.

Then the glory of the LORD appeared to them, and the LORD said to Moses, "Take your staff and assemble the community, you and your brother Aaron, and in their presence order the rock to yield its waters. From the rock you shall bring forth water for the congregation and their livestock to drink." So Moses took his staff from its place before the LORD, as he was ordered. He and Aaron assembled the community in front of the rock, where he said to them, "Listen to me, you rebels! Are we to bring water for you out of this rock?" Then, raising his hand, Moses struck the rock twice with his staff, and water gushed out in abundance for the people and their livestock to drink. But the LORD said to Moses and Aaron, "Because you were not faithful to me in showing forth my sanctity before the children of Israel, you shall not lead this community into the land I will give them."

These are the waters of Meribah, where the children of Israel contended against the LORD, and where the LORD revealed his sanctity among them.

Responsorial Psalm

PSALM 95:1-2, 6-7, 8-9

R. If today you hear his voice, harden not your hearts.

Come, let us sing joyfully to the LORD;
  let us acclaim the Rock of our salvation.
Let us come into his presence with thanksgiving;
  let us joyfully sing psalms to him. **R.**
Come, let us bow down in worship;
  let us kneel before the LORD who made us.
For he is our God,
  and we are the people he shepherds, the flock he guides. **R.**

Oh, that today you would hear his voice:
"Harden not your hearts as at Meribah,
as in the day of Massah in the desert,
Where your fathers tested me;
they tested me though they had seen my works." **R.**

Gospel

MATTHEW 16:13-23

Jesus went into the region of Caesarea Philippi and he asked his disciples, "Who do people say that the Son of Man is?" They replied, "Some say John the Baptist, others Elijah, still others Jeremiah or one of the prophets." He said to them, "But who do you say that I am?" Simon Peter said in reply, "You are the Christ, the Son of the living God." Jesus said to him in reply, "Blessed are you, Simon son of Jonah. For flesh and blood has not revealed this to you, but my heavenly Father. And so I say to you, you are Peter, and upon this rock I will build my Church, and the gates of the netherworld shall not prevail against it. I will give you the keys to the Kingdom of heaven. Whatever you bind on earth shall be bound in heaven; and whatever you loose on earth shall be loosed in heaven." Then he strictly ordered his disciples to tell no one that he was the Christ.

From that time on, Jesus began to show his disciples that he must go to Jerusalem and suffer greatly from the elders, the chief priests, and the scribes, and be killed and on the third day be raised. Then Peter took Jesus aside and began to rebuke him, "God forbid, Lord! No such thing shall ever happen to you." He turned and said to Peter, "Get behind me, Satan! You are an obstacle to me. You are thinking not as God does, but as human beings do."

Friday, August 9

First Reading

DEUTERONOMY 4:32-40

Moses said to the people: "Ask now of the days of old, before your time, ever since God created man upon the earth; ask from one end of the sky to the other: Did anything so great ever happen before? Was it ever heard of? Did a people ever hear the voice of God speaking from the midst of fire, as you did, and live? Or did any god venture to go and take a nation for himself from the midst of another nation, by testings, by signs and wonders, by war, with his strong hand and outstretched arm, and by great terrors, all of which the LORD, your God, did for you in Egypt before your very eyes? All this you were allowed to see that you might know the LORD is God and there is no other. Out of the heavens he let you hear his voice to discipline you; on earth he let you see his great fire, and you heard him speaking out of the fire. For love of your fathers he chose their descendants and personally led you out of Egypt by his great power, driving out of your way nations greater and mightier than you, so as to bring you in and to make their land your heritage, as it is today. This is why you must now know, and fix in your heart, that the LORD is God in the heavens above and on earth below, and that there is no other. You must keep his statutes and commandments which I enjoin on you today, that you and your children after you may prosper, and that you may have long life on the land which the LORD, your God, is giving you forever."

Responsorial Psalm
PSALM 77:12-13, 14-15, 16 and 21
R. I remember the deeds of the Lord.

I remember the deeds of the LORD;
yes, I remember your wonders of old.
And I meditate on your works;
your exploits I ponder. **R.**
O God, your way is holy;
what great god is there like our God?
You are the God who works wonders;
among the peoples you have made known your power. **R.**
With your strong arm you redeemed your people,
the sons of Jacob and Joseph.
You led your people like a flock
under the care of Moses and Aaron. **R.**

Gospel
MATTHEW 16:24-28

Jesus said to his disciples, "Whoever wishes to come after me must deny himself, take up his cross, and follow me. For whoever wishes to save his life will lose it, but whoever loses his life for my sake will find it. What profit would there be for one to gain the whole world and forfeit his life? Or what can one give in exchange for his life? For the Son of Man will come with his angels in his Father's glory, and then he will repay each according to his conduct. Amen, I say to you, there are some standing here who will not taste death until they see the Son of Man coming in his Kingdom."

Saturday, August 10

Saint Lawrence, Deacon and Martyr

First Reading
2 CORINTHIANS 9:6-10

Brothers and sisters: Whoever sows sparingly will also reap sparingly, and whoever sows bountifully will also reap bountifully. Each must do as already determined, without sadness or compulsion, for God loves a cheerful giver. Moreover, God is able to make every grace abundant for you, so that in all things, always having all you need, you may have an abundance for every good work. As it is written:

He scatters abroad, he gives to the poor;
his righteousness endures forever.

The one who supplies seed to the sower and bread for food will supply and multiply your seed and increase the harvest of your righteousness.

Responsorial Psalm
PSALM 112:1-2, 5-6, 7-8, 9
R. Blessed the man who is gracious and lends to those in need.
Blessed the man who fears the LORD,
who greatly delights in his commands.
His posterity shall be mighty upon the earth;
the upright generation shall be blessed. **R.**
Well for the man who is gracious and lends,
who conducts his affairs with justice;
He shall never be moved;
the just one shall be in everlasting remembrance. **R.**
An evil report he shall not fear;
his heart is firm, trusting in the LORD.
His heart is steadfast; he shall not fear
till he looks down upon his foes. **R.**
Lavishly he gives to the poor,
his generosity shall endure forever;
his horn shall be exalted in glory. **R.**

Gospel
JOHN 12:24-26

Jesus said to his disciples: "Amen, amen, I say to you, unless a grain of wheat falls to the ground and dies, it remains just a grain of wheat; but if it dies, it produces much fruit. Whoever loves his life loses it, and whoever hates his life in this world will preserve it for eternal life. Whoever serves me must follow me, and where I am, there also will my servant be. The Father will honor whoever serves me."

Sunday, August 11

Nineteenth Sunday in Ordinary Time

First Reading
WISDOM 18:6-9

The night of the passover was known beforehand to our fathers,
that, with sure knowledge of the oaths in which they put their faith,
they might have courage.
Your people awaited the salvation of the just
and the destruction of their foes.
For when you punished our adversaries,
in this you glorified us whom you had summoned.
For in secret the holy children of the good were offering sacrifice
and putting into effect with one accord the divine institution.

Responsorial Psalm
PSALM 33:1, 12, 18-19, 20-22
R. Blessed the people the Lord has chosen to be his own.
Exult, you just, in the LORD;
praise from the upright is fitting.
Blessed the nation whose God is the LORD,
the people he has chosen for his own inheritance. **R.**
See, the eyes of the LORD are upon those who fear him,
upon those who hope for his kindness,
to deliver them from death
and preserve them in spite of famine. **R.**
Our soul waits for the LORD,
who is our help and our shield.
May your kindness, O LORD, be upon us
who have put our hope in you. **R.**

Second Reading
HEBREWS 11:1-2, 8-19 (or HEBREWS 11:1-2, 8-12)

Brothers and sisters: Faith is the realization of what is hoped for and evidence of things not seen. Because of it the ancients were well attested.

By faith Abraham obeyed when he was called to go out to a place that he was to receive as an inheritance; he went out, not knowing where he was to go. By faith he sojourned in the promised land as in a foreign country, dwelling in tents with Isaac and Jacob, heirs of the same promise; for he was looking forward to the city with foundations, whose architect and maker is God. By faith he received power to generate, even though he was past the normal age—and Sarah herself was sterile—for he thought that the one who had made the promise was trustworthy. So it was that there came forth from one man, himself as good as dead, descendants as numerous as the stars in the sky and as countless as the sands on the seashore.

All these died in faith. They did not receive what had been promised but saw it and greeted it from afar and acknowledged themselves to be strangers and aliens on earth, for those who speak thus show that they are seeking a homeland. If they had been thinking of the land from which they had come, they would have had opportunity to return. But now they desire a better homeland, a heavenly one. Therefore, God is not ashamed to be called their God, for he has prepared a city for them.

By faith Abraham, when put to the test, offered up Isaac, and he who had received the promises was ready to offer his only son, of whom it was said, "Through Isaac descendants shall bear your name." He reasoned that God was able to raise even from the dead, and he received Isaac back as a symbol.

Gospel
LUKE 12:32-48 (or LUKE 12:35-40)

Jesus said to his disciples: "Do not be afraid any longer, little flock, for your Father is pleased to give you the kingdom. Sell your belongings and give alms. Provide money bags for yourselves that do not wear out, an inexhaustible treasure in heaven that no thief can reach nor moth destroy. For where your treasure is, there also will your heart be.

"Gird your loins and light your lamps and be like servants who await their master's return from a wedding, ready to open immediately when he comes and knocks. Blessed are those servants whom the master finds vigilant on his arrival. Amen, I say to you, he will gird himself, have them recline at table, and proceed to wait on them. And should he come in the second or third watch and find them prepared in this way, blessed are those servants. Be sure of this: if the master of the house had known the hour when the thief was coming, he would not have let his house be broken into. You also must be prepared, for at an hour you do not expect, the Son of Man will come."

Then Peter said, "Lord, is this parable meant for us or for everyone?" And the Lord replied, "Who, then, is the faithful and prudent steward whom the master will put in charge of his servants to distribute the food allowance at the proper time? Blessed is that servant whom his master on arrival finds doing so. Truly, I say to you, the master will put the servant in charge of all his property. But if that servant says to himself, 'My master is delayed in coming,' and begins to beat the menservants and the maidservants, to eat and drink and get drunk, then that servant's master will come on an unexpected day and at an unknown hour and will punish the servant severely and assign him a place with the unfaithful. That servant who knew his master's will but did not make preparations nor act in accord with his will shall be beaten severely; and the servant who was ignorant of his master's will but acted in a way deserving of a severe beating shall be beaten only lightly. Much will be required of the person entrusted with much, and still more will be demanded of the person entrusted with more."

Monday, August 12

First Reading

DEUTERONOMY 10:12-22

Moses said to the people: "And now, Israel, what does the LORD, your God, ask of you but to fear the LORD, your God, and follow his ways exactly, to love and serve the LORD, your God, with all your heart and all your soul, to keep the commandments and statutes of the LORD which I enjoin on you today for your own good? Think! The heavens, even the highest heavens, belong to the LORD, your God, as well as the earth and everything on it. Yet in his love for your fathers the LORD was so attached to them as to choose you, their descendants, in preference to all other peoples, as indeed he has now done. Circumcise your hearts, therefore, and be no longer stiff-necked. For the LORD, your God, is the God of gods, the LORD of lords, the great God, mighty and awesome, who has no favorites, accepts no bribes; who executes justice for the orphan and the widow, and befriends the alien, feeding and clothing him. So you too must befriend the alien, for you were once aliens yourselves in the land of Egypt. The LORD, your God, shall you fear, and him shall you serve; hold fast to him and swear by his name. He is your glory, he, your God, who has done for you those great and terrible things which your own eyes have seen. Your ancestors went down to Egypt seventy strong, and now the LORD, your God, has made you as numerous as the stars of the sky."

Responsorial Psalm

PSALM 147:12-13, 14-15, 19-20

R. Praise the Lord, Jerusalem.

Glorify the LORD, O Jerusalem;
praise your God, O Zion.
For he has strengthened the bars of your gates;

he has blessed your children within you. **R.**
He has granted peace in your borders;
with the best of wheat he fills you.
He sends forth his command to the earth;
swiftly runs his word! **R.**
He has proclaimed his word to Jacob,
his statutes and his ordinances to Israel.
He has not done thus for any other nation;
his ordinances he has not made known to them. Alleluia. **R.**

Gospel
MATTHEW 17:22-27

As Jesus and his disciples were gathering in Galilee, Jesus said to them, "The Son of Man is to be handed over to men, and they will kill him, and he will be raised on the third day." And they were overwhelmed with grief.

When they came to Capernaum, the collectors of the temple tax approached Peter and said, "Does not your teacher pay the temple tax?" "Yes," he said. When he came into the house, before he had time to speak, Jesus asked him, "What is your opinion, Simon? From whom do the kings of the earth take tolls or census tax? From their subjects or from foreigners?" When he said, "From foreigners," Jesus said to him, "Then the subjects are exempt. But that we may not offend them, go to the sea, drop in a hook, and take the first fish that comes up. Open its mouth and you will find a coin worth twice the temple tax. Give that to them for me and for you."

Tuesday, August 13

First Reading
DEUTERONOMY 31:1-8

When Moses had finished speaking to all Israel, he said to them, "I am now one hundred and twenty years old and am no longer able to move about freely; besides, the LORD has told me that I shall not cross this Jordan. It is the LORD, your God, who will cross before you; he will destroy these nations before you, that you may supplant them. It is Joshua who will cross before you, as the LORD promised. The LORD will deal with them just as he dealt with Sihon and Og, the kings of the Amorites whom he destroyed, and with their country. When, therefore, the LORD delivers them up to you, you must deal with them exactly as I have ordered you. Be brave and steadfast; have no fear or dread of them, for it is the LORD, your God, who marches with you; he will never fail you or forsake you."

Then Moses summoned Joshua and in the presence of all Israel said to him, "Be brave and steadfast, for you must bring this people into the land which the LORD swore to their fathers he would give them; you must put them in possession of their heritage. It is the LORD who marches before you; he will be with you and will never fail you or forsake you. So do not fear or be dismayed."

Responsorial Psalm
DEUTERONOMY 32:3-4ab, 7, 8, 9 and 12
R. The portion of the Lord is his people.

For I will sing the LORD's renown.
Oh, proclaim the greatness of our God!
The Rock—how faultless are his deeds,
how right all his ways! **R.**
Think back on the days of old,
reflect on the years of age upon age.
Ask your father and he will inform you,
ask your elders and they will tell you. **R.**
When the Most High assigned the nations their heritage,
when he parceled out the descendants of Adam,
He set up the boundaries of the peoples
after the number of the sons of Israel. **R.**
While the LORD's own portion was Jacob,
his hereditary share was Israel.
The LORD alone was their leader,
no strange god was with him. **R.**

Gospel
MATTHEW 18:1-5, 10, 12-14

The disciples approached Jesus and said, "Who is the greatest in the Kingdom of heaven?" He called a child over, placed it in their midst, and said, "Amen, I say to you, unless you turn and become like children, you will not enter the Kingdom of heaven. Whoever becomes humble like this child is the greatest in the Kingdom of heaven. And whoever receives one child such as this in my name receives me.

"See that you do not despise one of these little ones, for I say to you that their angels in heaven always look upon the face of my heavenly Father. What is your opinion? If a man has a hundred sheep and one of them goes astray, will he not leave the ninety-nine in the hills and go in search of the stray? And if he finds it, amen, I say to you, he rejoices more over it than over the ninety-nine that did not stray. In just the same way, it is not the will of your heavenly Father that one of these little ones be lost."

Wednesday, August 14

First Reading

DEUTERONOMY 34:1-12

Moses went up from the plains of Moab to Mount Nebo, the headland of Pisgah which faces Jericho, and the LORD showed him all the land—Gilead, and as far as Dan, all Naphtali, the land of Ephraim and Manasseh, all the land of Judah as far as the Western Sea, the Negeb, the circuit of the Jordan with the lowlands at Jericho, city of palms, and as far as Zoar. The LORD then said to him, "This is the land which I swore to Abraham, Isaac, and Jacob that I would give to their descendants. I have let you feast your eyes upon it, but you shall not cross over." So there, in the land of Moab, Moses, the servant of the LORD, died as the LORD had said; and he was buried in the ravine opposite Beth-peor in the land of Moab, but to this day no one knows the place of his burial. Moses was one hundred and twenty years old when he died, yet his eyes were undimmed and his vigor unabated. For thirty days the children of Israel wept for Moses in the plains of Moab, till they had completed the period of grief and mourning for Moses.

Now Joshua, son of Nun, was filled with the spirit of wisdom, since Moses had laid his hands upon him; and so the children of Israel gave him their obedience, thus carrying out the LORD's command to Moses.

Since then no prophet has arisen in Israel like Moses, whom the LORD knew face to face. He had no equal in all the signs and wonders the LORD sent him to perform in the land of Egypt against Pharaoh and all his servants and against all his land, and for the might and the terrifying power that Moses exhibited in the sight of all Israel.

Responsorial Psalm

PSALM 66:1-3a, 5 and 8, 16-17

R. Blessed be God who filled my soul with fire!

Shout joyfully to God, all the earth;
sing praise to the glory of his name;
proclaim his glorious praise.
Say to God: "How tremendous are your deeds!" **R.**

Come and see the works of God,
his tremendous deeds among the children of Adam.
Bless our God, you peoples;
loudly sound his praise. **R.**

Hear now, all you who fear God, while I declare
what he has done for me.
When I appealed to him in words,
praise was on the tip of my tongue. **R.**

Gospel
MATTHEW 18:15-20

Jesus said to his disciples: "If your brother sins against you, go and tell him his fault between you and him alone. If he listens to you, you have won over your brother. If he does not listen, take one or two others along with you, so that every fact may be established on the testimony of two or three witnesses. If he refuses to listen to them, tell the Church. If he refuses to listen even to the Church, then treat him as you would a Gentile or a tax collector. Amen, I say to you, whatever you bind on earth shall be bound in heaven, and whatever you loose on earth shall be loosed in heaven. Again, amen, I say to you, if two of you agree on earth about anything for which they are to pray, it shall be granted to them by my heavenly Father. For where two or three are gathered together in my name, there am I in the midst of them."

Thursday, August 15

The Assumption of the Blessed Virgin Mary

First Reading
REVELATION 11:19a; 12:1-6a, 10ab (Vigil: 1 CHRONICLES 15:3-4, 15-16; 16:1-2)

God's temple in heaven was opened, and the ark of his covenant could be seen in the temple.

A great sign appeared in the sky, a woman clothed with the sun, with the moon under her feet, and on her head a crown of twelve stars. She was with child and wailed aloud in pain as she labored to give birth. Then another sign appeared in the sky; it was a huge red dragon, with seven heads and ten horns, and on its heads were seven diadems. Its tail swept away a third of the stars in the sky and hurled them down to the earth. Then the dragon stood before the woman about to give birth, to devour her child when she gave birth. She gave birth to a son, a male child, destined to rule all the nations with an iron rod. Her child was caught up to God and his throne. The woman herself fled into the desert where she had a place prepared by God.

Then I heard a loud voice in heaven say:

"Now have salvation and power come,
and the Kingdom of our God
and the authority of his Anointed One."

Responsorial Psalm
PSALM 45:10, 11, 12, 16 (Vigil: PSALM 132:6-7, 9-10, 13-14)
R. The queen stands at your right hand, arrayed in gold.
The queen takes her place at your right hand in gold of Ophir. **R.**
Hear, O daughter, and see; turn your ear,
forget your people and your father's house. **R.**
So shall the king desire your beauty;
for he is your lord. **R.**
They are borne in with gladness and joy;
they enter the palace of the king. **R.**

Second Reading
1 CORINTHIANS 15:20-27 (Vigil: 1 CORINTHIANS 15:54b-57)

Brothers and sisters: Christ has been raised from the dead, the firstfruits of those who have fallen asleep. For since death came through man, the resurrection of the dead came also through man. For just as in Adam all die, so too in Christ shall all be brought to life, but each one in proper order: Christ the firstfruits; then, at his coming, those who belong to Christ; then comes the end, when he hands over the Kingdom to his God and Father, when he has destroyed every sovereignty and every authority and power. For he must reign until he has put all his enemies under his feet. The last enemy to be destroyed is death, for "he subjected everything under his feet."

Gospel
LUKE 1:39-56 (Vigil: LUKE 11:27-28)

Mary set out and traveled to the hill country in haste to a town of Judah, where she entered the house of Zechariah and greeted Elizabeth. When Elizabeth heard Mary's greeting, the infant leaped in her womb, and Elizabeth, filled with the Holy Spirit, cried out in a loud voice and said, "Blessed are you among women, and blessed is the fruit of your womb. And how does this happen to me, that the mother of my Lord should come to me? For at the moment the sound of your greeting reached my ears, the infant in my womb leaped for joy. Blessed are you who believed that what was spoken to you by the Lord would be fulfilled."

And Mary said:

"My soul proclaims the greatness of the Lord;
my spirit rejoices in God my Savior
for he has looked with favor on his lowly servant.
From this day all generations will call me blessed:
the Almighty has done great things for me
and holy is his Name.

He has mercy on those who fear him
in every generation.
He has shown the strength of his arm,
and has scattered the proud in their conceit.
He has cast down the mighty from their thrones,
and has lifted up the lowly.
He has filled the hungry with good things,
and the rich he has sent away empty.
He has come to the help of his servant Israel
for he has remembered his promise of mercy,
the promise he made to our fathers,
to Abraham and his children forever."

Mary remained with her about three months and then returned to her home.

Friday, August 16

First Reading

JOSHUA 24:1-13

Joshua gathered together all the tribes of Israel at Shechem, summoning their elders, their leaders, their judges and their officers. When they stood in ranks before God, Joshua addressed all the people: "Thus says the LORD, the God of Israel: In times past your fathers, down to Terah, father of Abraham and Nahor, dwelt beyond the River and served other gods. But I brought your father Abraham from the region beyond the River and led him through the entire land of Canaan. I made his descendants numerous, and gave him Isaac. To Isaac I gave Jacob and Esau. To Esau I assigned the mountain region of Seir in which to settle, while Jacob and his children went down to Egypt.

"Then I sent Moses and Aaron, and smote Egypt with the prodigies which I wrought in her midst. Afterward I led you out of Egypt, and when you reached the sea, the Egyptians pursued your fathers to the Red Sea with chariots and horsemen. Because they cried out to the LORD, he put darkness between your people and the Egyptians, upon whom he brought the sea so that it engulfed them. After you witnessed what I did to Egypt, and dwelt a long time in the desert, I brought you into the land of the Amorites who lived east of the Jordan. They fought against you, but I delivered them into your power. You took possession of their land, and I destroyed them, the two kings of the Amorites, before you. Then Balak, son of Zippor, king of Moab, prepared to war against Israel. He summoned Balaam, son of Beor, to curse you; but I would not listen to Balaam. On the contrary, he had to bless you, and I saved you from him. Once you crossed the Jordan and came to Jericho, the men of Jericho fought against you, but I delivered them also into your power. And I sent the hornets ahead of you that drove them (the Amorites, Perizzites, Canaanites, Hittites, Girgashites, Hivites and Jebusites) out of your way; it was not your sword or your bow.

"I gave you a land that you had not tilled and cities that you had not built, to dwell in; you have eaten of vineyards and olive groves which you did not plant."

Responsorial Psalm

PSALM 136:1-3, 16-18, 21-22 and 24

R. His mercy endures forever.

Give thanks to the LORD, for he is good,
for his mercy endures forever;
Give thanks to the God of gods,
for his mercy endures forever;
Give thanks to the LORD of lords,
for his mercy endures forever. **R.**
Who led his people through the wilderness,
for his mercy endures forever;
Who smote great kings,
for his mercy endures forever;
And slew powerful kings,
for his mercy endures forever. **R.**
And made their land a heritage,
for his mercy endures forever;
The heritage of Israel his servant,
for his mercy endures forever;
And freed us from our foes,
for his mercy endures forever. **R.**

Gospel

MATTHEW 19:3-12

Some Pharisees approached Jesus, and tested him, saying, "Is it lawful for a man to divorce his wife for any cause whatever?" He said in reply, "Have you not read that from the beginning the Creator *made them male and female* and said, *For this reason a man shall leave his father and mother and be joined to his wife, and the two shall become one flesh*? So they are no longer two, but one flesh. Therefore, what God has joined together, man must not separate." They said to him, "Then why did Moses command that the man give the woman a bill of divorce and dismiss her?" He said to them, "Because of the hardness of your hearts Moses allowed you to divorce your wives, but from the beginning it was not so. I say to you, whoever divorces his wife (unless the marriage is unlawful) and marries another commits adultery." His disciples said to him, "If that is the case of a man with his wife, it is better not to marry." He answered, "Not all can accept this word, but only those to whom that is granted. Some are incapable of marriage because they were born so; some, because they were made so by others; some, because they have renounced marriage for the sake of the Kingdom of heaven. Whoever can accept this ought to accept it."

Saturday, August 17

First Reading

JOSHUA 24:14-29

Joshua gathered together all the tribes of Israel at Shechem, and addressed them, saying: "Fear the LORD and serve him completely and sincerely. Cast out the gods your fathers served beyond the River and in Egypt, and serve the LORD. If it does not please you to serve the LORD, decide today whom you will serve, the gods your fathers served beyond the River or the gods of the Amorites in whose country you are dwelling. As for me and my household, we will serve the LORD."

But the people answered, "Far be it from us to forsake the LORD for the service of other gods. For it was the LORD, our God, who brought us and our fathers up out of the land of Egypt, out of a state of slavery. He performed those great miracles before our very eyes and protected us along our entire journey and among all the peoples through whom we passed. At our approach the LORD drove out all the peoples, including the Amorites who dwelt in the land. Therefore we also will serve the LORD, for he is our God."

Joshua in turn said to the people, "You may not be able to serve the LORD, for he is a holy God; he is a jealous God who will not forgive your transgressions or your sins. If, after the good he has done for you, you forsake the LORD and serve strange gods, he will do evil to you and destroy you."

But the people answered Joshua, "We will still serve the LORD." Joshua therefore said to the people, "You are your own witnesses that you have chosen to serve the LORD." They replied, "We are, indeed!" Joshua continued: "Now, therefore, put away the strange gods that are among you and turn your hearts to the LORD the God of Israel." Then the people promised Joshua, "We will serve the LORD, our God, and obey his voice."

So Joshua made a covenant with the people that day and made statutes and ordinances for them at Shechem, which he recorded in the book of the law of God. Then he took a large stone and set it up there under the oak that was in the sanctuary of the LORD. And Joshua said to all the people, "This stone shall be our witness, for it has heard all the words which the LORD spoke to us. It shall be a witness against you, should you wish to deny your God." Then Joshua dismissed the people, each to his own heritage.

After these events, Joshua, son of Nun, servant of the LORD, died at the age of a hundred and ten.

Responsorial Psalm

PSALM 16:1-2a and 5, 7-8, 11

R. You are my inheritance, O Lord.

Keep me, O God, for in you I take refuge;
  I say to the LORD, "My Lord are you."
O LORD, my allotted portion and my cup,
  you it is who hold fast my lot. **R.**
I bless the LORD who counsels me;
  even in the night my heart exhorts me.
I set the LORD ever before me;
  with him at my right hand I shall not be disturbed. **R.**
You will show me the path to life,
  fullness of joys in your presence,
  the delights at your right hand forever. **R.**

Gospel

MATTHEW 19:13-15

Children were brought to Jesus that he might lay his hands on them and pray. The disciples rebuked them, but Jesus said, "Let the children come to me, and do not prevent them; for the Kingdom of heaven belongs to such as these." After he placed his hands on them, he went away.

Sunday, August 18

Twentieth Sunday in Ordinary Time

First Reading

JEREMIAH 38:4-6, 8-10

In those days, the princes said to the king: "Jeremiah ought to be put to death; he is demoralizing the soldiers who are left in this city, and all the people, by speaking such things to them; he is not interested in the welfare of our people, but in their ruin." King Zedekiah answered: "He is in your power"; for the king could do nothing with them. And so they took Jeremiah and threw him into the cistern of Prince Malchiah, which was in the quarters of the guard, letting him down with ropes. There was no water in the cistern, only mud, and Jeremiah sank into the mud.

Ebed-melech, a court official, went there from the palace and said to him: "My lord king, these men have been at fault in all they have done to the prophet Jeremiah, casting him into the cistern. He will die of famine on the spot, for there is no more food in the city." Then the king ordered Ebed-melech the Cushite to take three men along with him, and draw the prophet Jeremiah out of the cistern before he should die.

Responsorial Psalm

PSALM 40:2, 3, 4, 18

R. Lord, come to my aid!

I have waited, waited for the LORD,
 and he stooped toward me. **R.**
The LORD heard my cry.
He drew me out of the pit of destruction,
 out of the mud of the swamp;
he set my feet upon a crag;
 he made firm my steps. **R.**
And he put a new song into my mouth,
 a hymn to our God.
Many shall look on in awe
 and trust in the LORD. **R.**
Though I am afflicted and poor,
 yet the LORD thinks of me.
You are my help and my deliverer;
 O my God, hold not back! **R.**

Second Reading

HEBREWS 12:1-4

Brothers and sisters: Since we are surrounded by so great a cloud of witnesses, let us rid ourselves of every burden and sin that clings to us and persevere in running the race that lies before us while keeping our eyes fixed on Jesus, the leader and perfecter of faith. For the sake of the joy that lay before him he endured the cross, despising its shame, and has taken his seat at the right of the throne of God. Consider how he endured such opposition from sinners, in order that you may not grow weary and lose heart. In your struggle against sin you have not yet resisted to the point of shedding blood.

Gospel

LUKE 12:49-53

Jesus said to his disciples: "I have come to set the earth on fire, and how I wish it were already blazing! There is a baptism with which I must be baptized, and how great is my anguish until it is accomplished! Do you think that I have come to establish peace on the earth? No, I tell you, but rather division. From now on a household of five will be divided, three against two and two against three; a father will be divided against his son and a son against his father, a mother against her daughter and a daughter against her mother, a mother-in-law against her daughter-in-law and a daughter-in-law against her mother-in-law."

Monday, August 19

First Reading

JUDGES 2:11-19

The children of Israel offended the LORD by serving the Baals. Abandoning the LORD, the God of their fathers, who led them out of the land of Egypt, they followed the other gods of the various nations around them, and by their worship of these gods provoked the LORD.

Because they had thus abandoned him and served Baal and the Ashtaroth, the anger of the LORD flared up against Israel, and he delivered them over to plunderers who despoiled them. He allowed them to fall into the power of their enemies round about whom they were no longer able to withstand. Whatever they undertook, the LORD turned into disaster for them, as in his warning he had sworn he would do, till they were in great distress. Even when the LORD raised up judges to deliver them from the power of their despoilers, they did not listen to their judges, but abandoned themselves to the worship of other gods. They were quick to stray from the way their fathers had taken, and did not follow their example of obedience to the commandments of the LORD. Whenever the LORD raised up judges for them, he would be with the judge and save them from the power of their enemies as long as the judge lived; it was thus the LORD took pity on their distressful cries of affliction under their oppressors. But when the judge died, they would relapse and do worse than their ancestors, following other gods in service and worship, relinquishing none of their evil practices or stubborn conduct.

Responsorial Psalm

PSALM 106:34-35, 36-37, 39-40, 43ab and 44

R. Remember us, O Lord, as you favor your people.

They did not exterminate the peoples,
    as the LORD had commanded them,
But mingled with the nations
    and learned their works. **R.**
They served their idols,
    which became a snare for them.

They sacrificed their sons
and their daughters to demons. **R.**
They became defiled by their works,
and wanton in their crimes.
And the LORD grew angry with his people,
and abhorred his inheritance. **R.**
Many times did he rescue them,
but they embittered him with their counsels.
Yet he had regard for their affliction
when he heard their cry. **R.**

Gospel
MATTHEW 19:16-22

A young man approached Jesus and said, "Teacher, what good must I do to gain eternal life?" He answered him, "Why do you ask me about the good? There is only One who is good. If you wish to enter into life, keep the commandments." He asked him, "Which ones?" And Jesus replied, "*You shall not kill; you shall not commit adultery; you shall not steal; you shall not bear false witness; honor your father and your mother*; and *you shall love your neighbor as yourself.*" The young man said to him, "All of these I have observed. What do I still lack?" Jesus said to him, "If you wish to be perfect, go, sell what you have and give to the poor, and you will have treasure in heaven. Then come, follow me." When the young man heard this statement, he went away sad, for he had many possessions.

Tuesday, August 20

First Reading
JUDGES 6:11-24a

The angel of the LORD came and sat under the terebinth in Ophrah that belonged to Joash the Abiezrite. While his son Gideon was beating out wheat in the wine press to save it from the Midianites, the angel of the LORD appeared to him and said, "The LORD is with you, O champion!" Gideon said to him, "My Lord, if the LORD is with us, why has all this happened to us? Where are his wondrous deeds of which our fathers told us when they said, 'Did not the LORD bring us up from Egypt?' For now the LORD has abandoned us and has delivered us into the power of Midian." The LORD turned to him and said, "Go with the strength you have and save Israel from the power of Midian. It is I who send you." But Gideon answered him, "Please, my lord, how can I save Israel? My family is the lowliest in Manasseh, and I am the most insignificant in my father's house." "I shall be with you," the LORD said to him, "and you will cut down Midian to the last man." Gideon answered him, "If I find favor with you, give me a sign that you are speaking with me. Do not depart from here, I pray you, until I come back to you and bring out my offering and set it before you." He answered, "I will await your return."

So Gideon went off and prepared a kid and a measure of flour in the form of unleavened cakes. Putting the meat in a basket and the broth in a pot, he brought them out to him under the terebinth and presented them. The angel of God said to him, "Take the meat and unleavened cakes and lay them on this rock; then pour out the broth." When he had done so, the angel of the LORD stretched out the tip of the staff he held, and touched the meat and unleavened cakes. Thereupon a fire came up from the rock that consumed the meat and unleavened cakes, and the angel of the LORD disappeared from sight. Gideon, now aware that it had been the angel of the LORD, said, "Alas, Lord GOD, that I have seen the angel of the LORD face to face!" The LORD answered him, "Be calm, do not fear. You shall not die." So Gideon built there an altar to the LORD and called it Yahweh-shalom.

Responsorial Psalm

PSALM 85:9, 11-12, 13-14

R. The Lord speaks of peace to his people.

I will hear what God proclaims;
  the LORD—for he proclaims peace
To his people, and to his faithful ones,
  and to those who put in him their hope. **R.**
Kindness and truth shall meet;
  justice and peace shall kiss.
Truth shall spring out of the earth,
  and justice shall look down from heaven. **R.**
The LORD himself will give his benefits;
  our land shall yield its increase.
Justice shall walk before him,
  and salvation, along the way of his steps. **R.**

Gospel

MATTHEW 19:23-30

Jesus said to his disciples: "Amen, I say to you, it will be hard for one who is rich to enter the Kingdom of heaven. Again I say to you, it is easier for a camel to pass through the eye of a needle than for one who is rich to enter the Kingdom of God." When the disciples heard this, they were greatly astonished and said, "Who then can be saved?" Jesus looked at them and said, "For men this is impossible, but for God all things are possible." Then Peter said to him in reply, "We have given up everything and followed you. What will there be for us?" Jesus said to them, "Amen, I say to you that you who have followed me, in the new age, when the Son of Man is seated on his throne of glory, will yourselves sit on twelve thrones, judging the twelve tribes of Israel. And everyone who has given up houses or brothers or sisters or father or mother or children or lands for the sake of my name will receive a hundred times more, and will inherit eternal life. But many who are first will be last, and the last will be first."

Wednesday, August 21

First Reading

JUDGES 9:6-15

All the citizens of Shechem and all Beth-millo came together and proceeded to make Abimelech king by the terebinth at the memorial pillar in Shechem.

When this was reported to him, Jotham went to the top of Mount Gerizim and, standing there, cried out to them in a loud voice: "Hear me, citizens of Shechem, that God may then hear you! Once the trees went to anoint a king over themselves. So they said to the olive tree, 'Reign over us.' But the olive tree answered them, 'Must I give up my rich oil, whereby men and gods are honored, and go to wave over the trees?' Then the trees said to the fig tree, 'Come; you reign over us!' But the fig tree answered them, 'Must I give up my sweetness and my good fruit, and go to wave over the trees?' Then the trees said to the vine, 'Come you, and reign over us.' But the vine answered them, 'Must I give up my wine that cheers gods and men, and go to wave over the trees?' Then all the trees said to the buckthorn, 'Come; you reign over us!' But the buckthorn replied to the trees, 'If you wish to anoint me king over you in good faith, come and take refuge in my shadow. Otherwise, let fire come from the buckthorn and devour the cedars of Lebanon.'"

Responsorial Psalm

PSALM 21:2-3, 4-5, 6-7

R. Lord, in your strength the king is glad.

O LORD, in your strength the king is glad;
in your victory how greatly he rejoices!
You have granted him his heart's desire;
you refused not the wish of his lips. **R.**
For you welcomed him with goodly blessings,
you placed on his head a crown of pure gold.
He asked life of you: you gave him
length of days forever and ever. **R.**

Great is his glory in your victory;
majesty and splendor you conferred upon him.
You made him a blessing forever,
you gladdened him with the joy of your face. **R.**

Gospel
MATTHEW 20:1-16

Jesus told his disciples this parable: "The Kingdom of heaven is like a landowner who went out at dawn to hire laborers for his vineyard. After agreeing with them for the usual daily wage, he sent them into his vineyard. Going out about nine o'clock, he saw others standing idle in the marketplace, and he said to them, 'You too go into my vineyard, and I will give you what is just.' So they went off. And he went out again around noon, and around three o'clock, and did likewise. Going out about five o'clock, he found others standing around, and said to them, 'Why do you stand here idle all day?' They answered, 'Because no one has hired us.' He said to them, 'You too go into my vineyard.' When it was evening the owner of the vineyard said to his foreman, 'Summon the laborers and give them their pay, beginning with the last and ending with the first.' When those who had started about five o'clock came, each received the usual daily wage. So when the first came, they thought that they would receive more, but each of them also got the usual wage. And on receiving it they grumbled against the landowner, saying, 'These last ones worked only one hour, and you have made them equal to us, who bore the day's burden and the heat.' He said to one of them in reply, 'My friend, I am not cheating you. Did you not agree with me for the usual daily wage? Take what is yours and go. What if I wish to give this last one the same as you? Or am I not free to do as I wish with my own money? Are you envious because I am generous?' Thus, the last will be first, and the first will be last."

Thursday, August 22

First Reading
JUDGES 11:29-39a

The Spirit of the LORD came upon Jephthah. He passed through Gilead and Manasseh, and through Mizpah-Gilead as well, and from there he went on to the Ammonites. Jephthah made a vow to the LORD. "If you deliver the Ammonites into my power," he said, "whoever comes out of the doors of my house to meet me when I return in triumph from the Ammonites shall belong to the LORD. I shall offer him up as a burnt offering."

Jephthah then went on to the Ammonites to fight against them, and the LORD delivered them into his power, so that he inflicted a severe defeat on them, from Aroer to the approach of Minnith (twenty cities in all) and as far as Abel-keramim. Thus were the Ammonites brought into subjection by the children of Israel. When Jephthah returned to his house in Mizpah, it was his daughter who came forth, playing the tambourines and dancing. She was an only child: he had neither son nor daughter besides her. When he saw her, he rent his garments and said, "Alas, daughter, you have struck me down and brought calamity upon me. For I have made a vow to the LORD and I cannot retract." She replied, "Father, you have made a vow to the LORD. Do with me as you have vowed, because the LORD has wrought vengeance for you on your enemies the Ammonites." Then she said to her father, "Let me have this favor. Spare me for two months, that I may go off down the mountains to mourn my virginity with my companions." "Go," he replied, and sent her away for two months. So she departed with her companions and mourned her virginity on the mountains. At the end of the two months she returned to her father, who did to her as he had vowed.

Responsorial Psalm

PSALM 40:5, 7-8a, 8b-9, 10

R. Here I am, Lord; I come to do your will.

Blessed the man who makes the LORD his trust;
who turns not to idolatry
or to those who stray after falsehood. **R.**
Sacrifice or oblation you wished not,
but ears open to obedience you gave me.
Burnt offerings or sin-offerings you sought not;
then said I, "Behold I come." **R.**
"In the written scroll it is prescribed for me.
To do your will, O my God, is my delight,
and your law is within my heart!" **R.**
I announced your justice in the vast assembly;
I did not restrain my lips, as you, O LORD, know. **R.**

Gospel

MATTHEW 22:1-14

Jesus again in reply spoke to the chief priests and the elders of the people in parables saying, "The Kingdom of heaven may be likened to a king who gave a wedding feast for his son. He dispatched his servants to summon the invited guests to the feast, but they refused to come. A second time he sent other servants, saying, 'Tell those invited: "Behold, I have prepared my banquet, my calves and fattened cattle are killed, and everything is ready; come to the feast."' Some ignored the invitation and went away, one to his farm, another to his business. The rest laid hold of his servants, mistreated them, and killed them. The king was enraged and sent his troops, destroyed those murderers, and burned their city. Then the king said to his servants, 'The feast is ready, but those who were invited were not worthy to come. Go out, therefore, into the main roads and invite to the feast whomever you find.' The servants went out into the streets and gathered all they found, bad and good alike, and the hall was filled with guests. But when the king came in to meet the guests he saw a man there not dressed in a wedding garment. He said to him, 'My friend, how is it that you came in here without a wedding garment?' But he was reduced to silence. Then the king said to his attendants, 'Bind his hands and feet, and cast him into the darkness outside, where there will be wailing and grinding of teeth.' Many are invited, but few are chosen."

Friday, August 23

First Reading

RUTH 1:1, 3-6, 14b-16, 22

Once in the time of the judges there was a famine in the land; so a man from Bethlehem of Judah departed with his wife and two sons to reside on the plateau of Moab. Elimelech, the husband of Naomi, died, and she was left with her two sons, who married Moabite women, one named Orpah, the other Ruth. When they had lived there about ten years, both Mahlon and Chilion died also, and the woman was left with neither her two sons nor her husband. She then made ready to go back from the plateau of Moab because word reached her there that the LORD had visited his people and given them food.

Orpah kissed her mother-in-law good-bye, but Ruth stayed with her.

Naomi said, "See now! Your sister-in-law has gone back to her people and her god. Go back after your sister-in-law!" But Ruth said, "Do not ask me to abandon or forsake you! For wherever you go, I will go, wherever you lodge I will lodge, your people shall be my people, and your God my God."

Thus it was that Naomi returned with the Moabite daughter-in-law, Ruth, who accompanied her back from the plateau of Moab. They arrived in Bethlehem at the beginning of the barley harvest.

Responsorial Psalm

PSALM 146:5-6ab, 6c-7, 8-9a, 9bc-10

R. Praise the Lord, my soul!

Blessed is he whose help is the God of Jacob,
whose hope is in the LORD, his God,

Who made heaven and earth,
the sea and all that is in them. **R.**
The LORD keeps faith forever,
secures justice for the oppressed,
gives food to the hungry.
The LORD sets captives free. **R.**
The LORD gives sight to the blind.
The LORD raises up those who were bowed down;
The LORD loves the just.
The LORD protects strangers. **R.**
The fatherless and the widow he sustains,
but the way of the wicked he thwarts.
The LORD shall reign forever;
your God, O Zion, through all generations. Alleluia. **R.**

Gospel
MATTHEW 22:34-40

When the Pharisees heard that Jesus had silenced the Sadducees, they gathered together, and one of them, a scholar of the law, tested him by asking, "Teacher, which commandment in the law is the greatest?" He said to him, "You shall love the Lord, your God, with all your heart, with all your soul, and with all your mind. This is the greatest and the first commandment. The second is like it: You shall love your neighbor as yourself. The whole law and the prophets depend on these two commandments."

Saturday, August 24

Saint Bartholomew, Apostle

First Reading
REVELATION 21:9b-14

The angel spoke to me, saying, "Come here. I will show you the bride, the wife of the Lamb." He took me in spirit to a great, high mountain and showed me the holy city Jerusalem coming down out of heaven from God. It gleamed with the splendor of God. Its radiance was like that of a precious stone, like jasper, clear as crystal. It had a massive, high wall, with twelve gates where twelve angels were stationed and on which names were inscribed, the names of the twelve tribes of the children of Israel. There were three gates facing east, three north, three south, and three west. The wall of the city had twelve courses of stones as its foundation, on which were inscribed the twelve names of the twelve Apostles of the Lamb.

Responsorial Psalm
PSALM 145:10-11, 12-13, 17-18
R. Your friends make known, O Lord, the glorious splendor of your Kingdom.

Let all your works give you thanks, O LORD,
 and let your faithful ones bless you.
Let them discourse of the glory of your Kingdom
 and speak of your might. **R.**
Making known to men your might
 and the glorious splendor of your Kingdom.
Your Kingdom is a Kingdom for all ages,
 and your dominion endures through all generations. **R.**
The LORD is just in all his ways
 and holy in all his works.
The LORD is near to all who call upon him,
 to all who call upon him in truth. **R.**

Gospel
JOHN 1:45-51

Philip found Nathanael and told him, "We have found the one about whom Moses wrote in the law, and also the prophets, Jesus son of Joseph, from Nazareth." But Nathanael said to him, "Can anything good come from Nazareth?" Philip said to him, "Come and see." Jesus saw Nathanael coming toward him and said of him, "Here is a true child of Israel. There is no duplicity in him." Nathanael said to him, "How do you know me?" Jesus answered and said to him, "Before Philip called you, I saw you under the fig tree." Nathanael answered him, "Rabbi, you are the Son of God; you are the King of Israel." Jesus answered and said to him, "Do you believe because I told you that I saw you under the fig tree? You will see greater things than this." And he said to him, "Amen, amen, I say to you, you will see heaven opened and the angels of God ascending and descending on the Son of Man."

Sunday, August 25

Twenty-first Sunday in Ordinary Time

First Reading
ISAIAH 66:18-21

Thus says the LORD: I know their works and their thoughts, and I come to gather nations of every language; they shall come and see my glory. I will set a sign among them; from them I will send fugitives to the nations: to Tarshish, Put and Lud, Mosoch, Tubal and Javan, to the distant coastlands that have never heard of my fame, or seen my glory; and they shall proclaim my glory among the nations. They shall bring all your brothers and sisters from all the nations as an offering to the LORD, on horses and in chariots, in carts, upon mules and dromedaries, to Jerusalem, my holy mountain, says the LORD, just as the Israelites bring their offering to the house of the LORD in clean vessels. Some of these I will take as priests and Levites, says the LORD.

Responsorial Psalm
PSALM 117:1, 2
R. Go out to all the world and tell the Good News.
(or R. Alleluia.)
Praise the LORD all you nations;
  glorify him, all you peoples! **R.**
For steadfast is his kindness toward us,
  and the fidelity of the LORD endures forever. **R.**

Second Reading
HEBREWS 12:5-7, 11-13

Brothers and sisters: You have forgotten the exhortation addressed to you as children: "My son, do not disdain the discipline of the Lord or lose heart when reproved by him; for whom the Lord loves, he disciplines; he scourges every son he acknowledges." Endure your trials as "discipline"; God treats you as sons. For what "son" is there whom his father does not discipline? At the time, all discipline seems a cause not for joy but for pain, yet later it brings the peaceful fruit of righteousness to those who are trained by it.

So strengthen your drooping hands and your weak knees. Make straight paths for your feet, that what is lame may not be disjointed but healed.

Gospel
LUKE 13:22-30

Jesus passed through towns and villages, teaching as he went and making his way to Jerusalem. Someone asked him, "Lord, will only a few people be saved?" He answered them, "Strive to enter through the narrow gate, for many, I tell you, will attempt to enter but will not be strong enough. After the master of the house has arisen and locked the door, then will you stand outside knocking and saying, 'Lord, open the door for us.' He will say to you in reply, 'I do not know where you are from.' And you will say, 'We ate and drank in your company and you taught in our streets.' Then he will say to you, 'I do not know where you are from. Depart from me, all you evildoers!' And there will be wailing and grinding of teeth when you see Abraham, Isaac, and Jacob and all the prophets in the kingdom of God and you yourselves cast out. And people will come from the east and the west and from the north and the south and will recline at table in the kingdom of God. For behold, some are last who will be first, and some are first who will be last."

Monday, August 26

First Reading

1 THESSALONIANS 1:1-5, 8b-10

Paul, Silvanus, and Timothy to the Church of the Thessalonians in God the Father and the Lord Jesus Christ: grace to you and peace.

We give thanks to God always for all of you, remembering you in our prayers, unceasingly calling to mind your work of faith and labor of love and endurance in hope of our Lord Jesus Christ, before our God and Father, knowing, brothers and sisters loved by God, how you were chosen. For our Gospel did not come to you in word alone, but also in power and in the Holy Spirit and with much conviction. You know what sort of people we were among you for your sake. In every place your faith in God has gone forth, so that we have no need to say anything. For they themselves openly declare about us what sort of reception we had among you, and how you turned to God from idols to serve the living and true God and to await his Son from heaven, whom he raised from the dead, Jesus, who delivers us from the coming wrath.

Responsorial Psalm

PSALM 149:1b-2, 3-4, 5-6a and 9b

R. The Lord takes delight in his people. (or R. Alleluia.)

Sing to the LORD a new song
 of praise in the assembly of the faithful.
Let Israel be glad in their maker,
 let the children of Zion rejoice in their king. **R.**
Let them praise his name in the festive dance,
 let them sing praise to him with timbrel and harp.
For the LORD loves his people,
 and he adorns the lowly with victory. **R.**
Let the faithful exult in glory;
 let them sing for joy upon their couches;
Let the high praises of God be in their throats.
 This is the glory of all his faithful. Alleluia. **R.**

Gospel

MATTHEW 23:13-22

Jesus said to the crowds and to his disciples: "Woe to you, scribes and Pharisees, you hypocrites. You lock the Kingdom of heaven before men. You do not enter yourselves, nor do you allow entrance to those trying to enter.

"Woe to you, scribes and Pharisees, you hypocrites. You traverse sea and land to make one convert, and when that happens you make him a child of Gehenna twice as much as yourselves.

"Woe to you, blind guides, who say, 'If one swears by the temple, it means nothing, but if one swears by the gold of the temple, one is obligated.' Blind fools, which is greater, the gold, or the temple that made the gold sacred? And you say, 'If one swears by the altar, it means nothing, but if one swears by the gift on the altar, one is obligated.' You blind ones, which is greater, the gift, or the altar that makes the gift sacred? One who swears by the altar swears by it and all that is upon it; one who swears by the temple swears by it and by him who dwells in it; one who swears by heaven swears by the throne of God and by him who is seated on it."

Tuesday, August 27

First Reading

1 THESSALONIANS 2:1-8

You yourselves know, brothers and sisters, that our reception among you was not without effect. Rather, after we had suffered and been insolently treated, as you know, in Philippi, we drew courage through our God to speak to you the Gospel of God with much struggle. Our exhortation was not from delusion or impure motives, nor did it work through deception. But as we were judged worthy by God to be entrusted with the Gospel, that is how we speak, not as trying to please men, but rather God, who judges our hearts. Nor, indeed, did we ever appear with flattering speech, as you know, or with a pretext for greed—God is witness—nor did we seek praise from men, either from you or from others, although we were able to impose our weight as Apostles of Christ. Rather, we were gentle among you, as a nursing mother cares for her children. With such affection for you, we were determined to share with you not only the Gospel of God, but our very selves as well, so dearly beloved had you become to us.

Responsorial Psalm

PSALM 139:1-3, 4-6

R. You have searched me and you know me, Lord.

O LORD, you have probed me and you know me;
  you know when I sit and when I stand;
  you understand my thoughts from afar.
My journeys and my rest you scrutinize,
  with all my ways you are familiar. **R.**

Even before a word is on my tongue,
  behold, O LORD, you know the whole of it.
Behind me and before, you hem me in
  and rest your hand upon me.
Such knowledge is too wonderful for me;
  too lofty for me to attain. **R.**

Gospel

MATTHEW 23:23-26

Jesus said: "Woe to you, scribes and Pharisees, you hypocrites. You pay tithes of mint and dill and cummin, and have neglected the weightier things of the law: judgment and mercy and fidelity. But these you should have done, without neglecting the others. Blind guides, who strain out the gnat and swallow the camel!

"Woe to you, scribes and Pharisees, you hypocrites. You cleanse the outside of cup and dish, but inside they are full of plunder and self-indulgence. Blind Pharisee, cleanse first the inside of the cup, so that the outside also may be clean."

Wednesday, August 28

First Reading

1 THESSALONIANS 2:9-13

You recall, brothers and sisters, our toil and drudgery. Working night and day in order not to burden any of you, we proclaimed to you the Gospel of God. You are witnesses, and so is God, how devoutly and justly and blamelessly we behaved toward you believers. As you know, we treated each one of you as a father treats his children, exhorting and encouraging you and insisting that you walk in a manner worthy of the God who calls you into his Kingdom and glory.

And for this reason we too give thanks to God unceasingly, that, in receiving the word of God from hearing us, you received it not as the word of men, but as it truly is, the word of God, which is now at work in you who believe.

Responsorial Psalm

PSALM 139:7-8, 9-10, 11-12ab

R. You have searched me and you know me, Lord.

Where can I go from your spirit?
  From your presence where can I flee?
If I go up to the heavens, you are there;
  if I sink to the nether world, you are present there. **R.**

If I take the wings of the dawn,
if I settle at the farthest limits of the sea,
Even there your hand shall guide me,
and your right hand hold me fast. **R.**
If I say, "Surely the darkness shall hide me,
and night shall be my light"—
For you darkness itself is not dark,
and night shines as the day. **R.**

Gospel
MATTHEW 23:27-32

Jesus said, "Woe to you, scribes and Pharisees, you hypocrites. You are like whitewashed tombs, which appear beautiful on the outside, but inside are full of dead men's bones and every kind of filth. Even so, on the outside you appear righteous, but inside you are filled with hypocrisy and evildoing.

"Woe to you, scribes and Pharisees, you hypocrites. You build the tombs of the prophets and adorn the memorials of the righteous, and you say, 'If we had lived in the days of our ancestors, we would not have joined them in shedding the prophets' blood.' Thus you bear witness against yourselves that you are the children of those who murdered the prophets; now fill up what your ancestors measured out!"

Thursday, August 29

First Reading
1 THESSALONIANS 3:7-13

We have been reassured about you, brothers and sisters, in our every distress and affliction, through your faith. For we now live, if you stand firm in the Lord.

What thanksgiving, then, can we render to God for you, for all the joy we feel on your account before our God? Night and day we pray beyond measure to see you in person and to remedy the deficiencies of your faith. Now may God himself, our Father, and our Lord Jesus direct our way to you, and may the Lord make you increase and abound in love for one another and for all, just as we have for you, so as to strengthen your hearts, to be blameless in holiness before our God and Father at the coming of our Lord Jesus with all his holy ones. Amen.

Responsorial Psalm
PSALM 90:3-5a, 12-13, 14 and 17
R. Fill us with your love, O Lord, and we will sing for joy!

You turn man back to dust,
saying, "Return, O children of men."
For a thousand years in your sight
are as yesterday, now that it is past,
or as a watch of the night. **R.**
Teach us to number our days aright,
that we may gain wisdom of heart.
Return, O LORD! How long?
Have pity on your servants! **R.**
Fill us at daybreak with your kindness,
that we may shout for joy and gladness all our days.
And may the gracious care of the LORD our God be ours;
prosper the work of our hands for us!
Prosper the work of our hands! **R.**

Gospel
MARK 6:17-29

Herod was the one who had John the Baptist arrested and bound in prison on account of Herodias, the wife of his brother Philip, whom he had married. John had said to Herod, "It is not lawful for you to have your brother's wife." Herodias harbored a grudge against him and wanted to kill him but was unable to do so. Herod feared John, knowing him to be a righteous and holy man, and kept him in custody. When he heard him speak he was very much perplexed, yet he liked to listen to him. She had an opportunity one day when Herod, on his birthday, gave a banquet for his courtiers, his military officers, and the leading men of Galilee. Herodias' own daughter came in and performed a dance that delighted Herod and his guests. The king said to the girl, "Ask of me whatever you wish and I will grant it to you." He even swore many things to her, "I will grant you whatever you ask of me, even to half of my kingdom." She went out and said to her mother, "What shall I ask for?" She replied, "The head of John the Baptist." The girl hurried back to the king's presence and made her request, "I want you to give me at once on a platter the head of John the Baptist." The king was deeply distressed, but because of his oaths and the guests he did not wish to break his word to her. So he promptly dispatched an executioner with orders to bring back his head. He went off and beheaded him in the prison. He brought in the head on a platter and gave it to the girl. The girl in turn gave it to her mother. When his disciples heard about it, they came and took his body and laid it in a tomb.

Friday, August 30

First Reading

1 THESSALONIANS 4:1-8

Brothers and sisters, we earnestly ask and exhort you in the Lord Jesus that, as you received from us how you should conduct yourselves to please God—and as you are conducting yourselves—you do so even more. For you know what instructions we gave you through the Lord Jesus.

This is the will of God, your holiness: that you refrain from immorality, that each of you know how to acquire a wife for himself in holiness and honor, not in lustful passion as do the Gentiles who do not know God; not to take advantage of or exploit a brother or sister in this matter, for the Lord is an avenger in all these things, as we told you before and solemnly affirmed. For God did not call us to impurity but to holiness. Therefore, whoever disregards this, disregards not a human being but God, who also gives his Holy Spirit to you.

Responsorial Psalm

PSALM 97:1 and 2b, 5-6, 10, 11-12

R. Rejoice in the Lord, you just!

The LORD is king; let the earth rejoice;
let the many isles be glad.
Justice and judgment are the foundation of his throne. **R.**
The mountains melt like wax before the LORD,
before the LORD of all the earth.
The heavens proclaim his justice,
and all peoples see his glory. **R.**
The LORD loves those who hate evil;
he guards the lives of his faithful ones;
from the hand of the wicked he delivers them. **R.**
Light dawns for the just;
and gladness, for the upright of heart.
Be glad in the LORD, you just,
and give thanks to his holy name. **R.**

Gospel

MATTHEW 25:1-13

Jesus told his disciples this parable: "The Kingdom of heaven will be like ten virgins who took their lamps and went out to meet the bridegroom. Five of them were foolish and five were wise. The foolish ones, when taking their lamps, brought no oil with them, but the wise brought flasks of oil with their lamps. Since the bridegroom was long delayed, they all became drowsy and fell asleep. At midnight, there was a cry,

'Behold, the bridegroom! Come out to meet him!' Then all those virgins got up and trimmed their lamps. The foolish ones said to the wise, 'Give us some of your oil, for our lamps are going out.' But the wise ones replied, 'No, for there may not be enough for us and you. Go instead to the merchants and buy some for yourselves.' While they went off to buy it, the bridegroom came and those who were ready went into the wedding feast with him. Then the door was locked. Afterwards the other virgins came and said, 'Lord, Lord, open the door for us!' But he said in reply, 'Amen, I say to you, I do not know you.' Therefore, stay awake, for you know neither the day nor the hour."

Saturday, August 31

First Reading

1 THESSALONIANS 4:9-11

Brothers and sisters: On the subject of fraternal charity you have no need for anyone to write you, for you yourselves have been taught by God to love one another. Indeed, you do this for all the brothers throughout Macedonia. Nevertheless we urge you, brothers and sisters, to progress even more, and to aspire to live a tranquil life, to mind your own affairs, and to work with your own hands, as we instructed you.

Responsorial Psalm

PSALM 98:1, 7-8, 9

R. The Lord comes to rule the earth with justice.

Sing to the LORD a new song,
for he has done wondrous deeds;
His right hand has won victory for him,
his holy arm. **R.**
Let the sea and what fills it resound,
the world and those who dwell in it;
Let the rivers clap their hands,
the mountains shout with them for joy. **R.**
Before the LORD, for he comes,
for he comes to rule the earth;
He will rule the world with justice
and the peoples with equity. **R.**

Gospel

MATTHEW 25:14-30

Jesus told his disciples this parable: "A man going on a journey called in his servants and entrusted his possessions to them. To one he gave five talents; to another, two; to a third, one—to each according to his ability. Then he went away. Immediately the one who received five talents went and traded with them, and made another five. Likewise, the one who received two made another two. But the man who received one went off and dug a hole in the ground and buried his master's money. After a long time the master of those servants came back and settled accounts with them. The one who had received five talents came forward bringing the additional five. He said, 'Master, you gave me five talents. See, I have made five more.' His master said to him, 'Well done, my good and faithful servant. Since you were faithful in small matters, I will give you great responsibilities. Come, share your master's joy.' Then the one who had received two talents also came forward and said, 'Master, you gave me two talents. See, I have made two more.' His master said to him, 'Well done, my good and faithful servant. Since you were faithful in small matters, I will give you great responsibilities. Come, share your master's joy.' Then the one who had received the one talent came forward and said, 'Master, I knew you were a demanding person, harvesting where you did not plant and gathering where you did not scatter; so out of fear I went off and buried your talent in the ground. Here it is back.' His master said to him in reply, 'You wicked, lazy servant! So you knew that I harvest where I did not plant and gather where I did not scatter? Should you not then have put my money in the bank so that I could have got it back with interest on my return? Now then! Take the talent from him and give it to the one with ten. For to everyone who has, more will be given and he will grow rich; but from the one who has not, even what he has will be taken away. And throw this useless servant into the darkness outside, where there will be wailing and grinding of teeth.'"

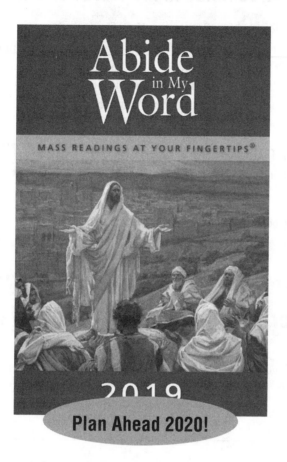

SEPTEMBER

Sunday, September 1

Twenty-second Sunday in Ordinary Time

First Reading
SIRACH 3:17-18, 20, 28-29

My child, conduct your affairs with humility,
 and you will be loved more than a giver of gifts.
Humble yourself the more, the greater you are,
 and you will find favor with God.
What is too sublime for you, seek not,
 into things beyond your strength search not.
The mind of a sage appreciates proverbs,
 and an attentive ear is the joy of the wise.
Water quenches a flaming fire,
 and alms atone for sins.

Responsorial Psalm
PSALM 68:4-5, 6-7, 10-11
R. God, in your goodness, you have made a home for the poor.

The just rejoice and exult before God;
 they are glad and rejoice.
Sing to God, chant praise to his name;
 whose name is the LORD. **R.**
The father of orphans and the defender of widows
 is God in his holy dwelling.
God gives a home to the forsaken;
 he leads forth prisoners to prosperity. **R.**
A bountiful rain you showered down, O God, upon your inheritance;
 you restored the land when it languished;
your flock settled in it;
 in your goodness, O God, you provided it for the needy. **R.**

Second Reading
HEBREWS 12:18-19, 22-24a

Brothers and sisters: You have not approached that which could be touched and a blazing fire and gloomy darkness and storm and a trumpet blast and a voice speaking words such that those who heard begged that no message be further addressed to them. No, you have approached Mount Zion and the city of the living God, the heavenly Jerusalem, and countless angels in festal gathering, and the assembly of the firstborn enrolled in heaven, and God the judge of all, and the spirits of the just made perfect, and Jesus, the mediator of a new covenant, and the sprinkled blood that speaks more eloquently than that of Abel.

Gospel
LUKE 14:1, 7-14

On a sabbath Jesus went to dine at the home of one of the leading Pharisees, and the people there were observing him carefully.

He told a parable to those who had been invited, noticing how they were choosing the places of honor at the table. "When you are invited by someone to a wedding banquet, do not recline at table in the place of honor. A more distinguished guest than you may have been invited by him, and the host who invited both of you may approach you and say, 'Give your place to this man,' and then you would proceed with embarrassment to take the lowest place. Rather, when you are invited, go and take the lowest place so that when the host comes to you he may say, 'My friend, move up to a higher position.' Then you will enjoy the esteem of your companions at the table. For every one who exalts himself will be humbled, but the one who humbles himself will be exalted." Then he said to the host who invited him, "When you hold a lunch or a dinner, do not invite your friends or your brothers or your relatives or your wealthy neighbors, in case they may invite you back and you have repayment. Rather, when you hold a banquet, invite the poor, the crippled, the lame, the blind; blessed indeed will you be because of their inability to repay you. For you will be repaid at the resurrection of the righteous."

Monday, September 2

First Reading
1 THESSALONIANS 4:13-18

We do not want you to be unaware, brothers and sisters, about those who have fallen asleep, so that you may not grieve like the rest, who have no hope. For if we believe that Jesus died and rose, so too will God, through Jesus, bring with him those who have fallen asleep. Indeed, we tell you this, on the word of the Lord, that we who are alive, who are left until the coming of the Lord, will surely not precede those who have fallen asleep. For the Lord himself, with a word of command, with the voice of an archangel and with the trumpet of God, will come down from heaven, and the dead in Christ will rise first. Then we who are alive, who are left, will be caught up together with them in the clouds to meet the

Lord in the air. Thus we shall always be with the Lord. Therefore, console one another with these words.

Responsorial Psalm

PSALM 96:1 and 3, 4-5, 11-12, 13

R. The Lord comes to judge the earth.

Sing to the LORD a new song;
  sing to the LORD, all you lands.
Tell his glory among the nations;
  among all peoples, his wondrous deeds. **R.**
For great is the LORD and highly to be praised;
  awesome is he, beyond all gods.
For all the gods of the nations are things of nought,
  but the LORD made the heavens. **R.**
Let the heavens be glad and the earth rejoice;
  let the sea and what fills it resound;
  let the plains be joyful and all that is in them!
Then shall all the trees of the forest exult. **R.**
Before the LORD, for he comes;
  for he comes to rule the earth.
He shall rule the world with justice
  and the peoples with his constancy. **R.**

Gospel

LUKE 4:16-30

Jesus came to Nazareth, where he had grown up, and went according to his custom into the synagogue on the sabbath day. He stood up to read and was handed a scroll of the prophet Isaiah. He unrolled the scroll and found the passage where it was written:

The Spirit of the Lord is upon me,
  because he has anointed me
    to bring glad tidings to the poor.
He has sent me to proclaim liberty to captives
  and recovery of sight to the blind,
    to let the oppressed go free,
and to proclaim a year acceptable to the Lord.

Rolling up the scroll, he handed it back to the attendant and sat down, and the eyes of all in the synagogue looked intently at him. He said to them, "Today this Scripture passage is fulfilled in your hearing." And all spoke highly of him and were amazed at the gracious words that came from his mouth. They also asked, "Is this not the son of Joseph?" He said to them, "Surely you will quote me this proverb, 'Physician, cure yourself,' and say, 'Do here in your native place the things that we heard were done in Capernaum.'" And he said, "Amen, I say to you, no prophet is accepted in his own native place. Indeed, I tell you, there were many widows in Israel in the days of Elijah when the sky was closed for three and a half years and a severe famine spread over the entire land. It was to none of these that Elijah was sent, but only to a widow in Zarephath in the land of Sidon. Again, there were many lepers in Israel during the time of Elisha the prophet; yet not one of them was cleansed, but only Naaman the Syrian." When the people in the synagogue heard this, they were all filled with fury. They rose up, drove him out of the town, and led him to the brow of the hill on which their town had been built, to hurl him down headlong. But he passed through the midst of them and went away.

Tuesday, September 3

First Reading

1 THESSALONIANS 5:1-6, 9-11

Concerning times and seasons, brothers and sisters, you have no need for anything to be written to you. For you yourselves know very well that the day of the Lord will come like a thief at night. When people are saying, "Peace and security," then sudden disaster comes upon them, like labor pains upon a pregnant woman, and they will not escape.

But you, brothers and sisters, are not in darkness, for that day to overtake you like a thief. For all of you are children of the light and children of the day. We are not of the night or of darkness. Therefore, let us not sleep as the rest do, but let us stay alert and sober. For God did not destine us for wrath, but to gain salvation through our Lord Jesus Christ, who died for us, so that whether we are awake or asleep we may live together with him. Therefore, encourage one another and build one another up, as indeed you do.

Responsorial Psalm

PSALM 27:1, 4, 13-14

R. I believe that I shall see the good things of the Lord in the land of the living.

The LORD is my light and my salvation;
whom should I fear?
The LORD is my life's refuge;
of whom should I be afraid? **R.**
One thing I ask of the LORD;
this I seek:

To dwell in the house of the LORD
all the days of my life,
That I may gaze on the loveliness of the LORD
and contemplate his temple. **R.**
I believe that I shall see the bounty of the LORD
in the land of the living.
Wait for the LORD with courage;
be stouthearted, and wait for the LORD. **R.**

Gospel
LUKE 4:31-37

Jesus went down to Capernaum, a town of Galilee. He taught them on the sabbath, and they were astonished at his teaching because he spoke with authority. In the synagogue there was a man with the spirit of an unclean demon, and he cried out in a loud voice, "What have you to do with us, Jesus of Nazareth? Have you come to destroy us? I know who you are—the Holy One of God!" Jesus rebuked him and said, "Be quiet! Come out of him!" Then the demon threw the man down in front of them and came out of him without doing him any harm. They were all amazed and said to one another, "What is there about his word? For with authority and power he commands the unclean spirits, and they come out." And news of him spread everywhere in the surrounding region.

Wednesday, September 4

First Reading
COLOSSIANS 1:1-8

Paul, an Apostle of Christ Jesus by the will of God, and Timothy our brother, to the holy ones and faithful brothers and sisters in Christ in Colossae: grace to you and peace from God our Father.

We always give thanks to God, the Father of our Lord Jesus Christ, when we pray for you, for we have heard of your faith in Christ Jesus and the love that you have for all the holy ones because of the hope reserved for you in heaven. Of this you have already heard through the word of truth, the Gospel, that has come to you. Just as in the whole world it is bearing fruit and growing, so also among you, from the day you heard it and came to know the grace of God in truth, as you learned it from Epaphras our beloved fellow slave, who is a trustworthy minister of Christ on your behalf and who also told us of your love in the Spirit.

Responsorial Psalm
PSALM 52:10, 11
R. I trust in the mercy of God for ever.
I, like a green olive tree
in the house of God,
Trust in the mercy of God
forever and ever. **R.**
I will thank you always for what you have done,
and proclaim the goodness of your name
before your faithful ones. **R.**

Gospel
Luke 4:38-44
After Jesus left the synagogue, he entered the house of Simon. Simon's mother-in-law was afflicted with a severe fever, and they interceded with him about her. He stood over her, rebuked the fever, and it left her. She got up immediately and waited on them.

At sunset, all who had people sick with various diseases brought them to him. He laid his hands on each of them and cured them. And demons also came out from many, shouting, "You are the Son of God." But he rebuked them and did not allow them to speak because they knew that he was the Christ.

At daybreak, Jesus left and went to a deserted place. The crowds went looking for him, and when they came to him, they tried to prevent him from leaving them. But he said to them, "To the other towns also I must proclaim the good news of the Kingdom of God, because for this purpose I have been sent." And he was preaching in the synagogues of Judea.

Thursday, September 5

First Reading
COLOSSIANS 1:9-14
Brothers and sisters: From the day we heard about you, we do not cease praying for you and asking that you may be filled with the knowledge of God's will through all spiritual wisdom and understanding to walk in a manner worthy of the Lord, so as to be fully pleasing, in every good work bearing fruit and growing in the knowledge of God, strengthened with every power, in accord with his glorious might, for all endurance and patience, with joy giving thanks to the Father, who has made you fit to share in the inheritance of the holy ones in light. He delivered us from the power of darkness and transferred us to the Kingdom of his beloved Son, in whom we have redemption, the forgiveness of sins.

Responsorial Psalm
PSALM 98:2-3ab, 3cd-4, 5-6
R. The Lord has made known his salvation.
The LORD has made his salvation known:
in the sight of the nations he has revealed his justice.
He has remembered his kindness and his faithfulness
toward the house of Israel. **R.**
All the ends of the earth have seen
the salvation by our God.
Sing joyfully to the LORD, all you lands;
break into song; sing praise. **R.**
Sing praise to the LORD with the harp,
with the harp and melodious song.
With trumpets and the sound of the horn
sing joyfully before the King, the LORD. **R.**

Gospel
LUKE 5:1-11
While the crowd was pressing in on Jesus and listening to the word of God, he was standing by the Lake of Gennesaret. He saw two boats there alongside the lake; the fishermen had disembarked and were washing their nets. Getting into one of the boats, the one belonging to Simon, he asked him to put out a short distance from the shore. Then he sat down and taught the crowds from the boat. After he had finished speaking, he said to Simon, "Put out into deep water and lower your nets for a catch." Simon said in reply, "Master, we have worked hard all night and have caught nothing, but at your command I will lower the nets." When they had done this, they caught a great number of fish and their nets were tearing. They signaled to their partners in the other boat to come to help them. They came and filled both boats so that the boats were in danger of sinking. When Simon Peter saw this, he fell at the knees of Jesus and said, "Depart from me, Lord, for I am a sinful man." For astonishment at the catch of fish they had made seized him and all those with him, and likewise James and John, the sons of Zebedee, who were partners of Simon. Jesus said to Simon, "Do not be afraid; from now on you will be catching men." When they brought their boats to the shore, they left everything and followed him.

Friday, September 6

First Reading
COLOSSIANS 1:15-20
Brothers and sisters:

Christ Jesus is the image of the invisible God,
the firstborn of all creation.
For in him were created all things in heaven and on earth,
the visible and the invisible,
whether thrones or dominions or principalities or powers;
all things were created through him and for him.
He is before all things,
and in him all things hold together.
He is the head of the Body, the Church.
He is the beginning, the firstborn from the dead,
that in all things he himself might be preeminent.
For in him all the fullness was pleased to dwell,
and through him to reconcile all things for him,
making peace by the Blood of his cross
through him, whether those on earth or those in heaven.

Responsorial Psalm

PSALM 100:1b-2, 3, 4, 5

R. Come with joy into the presence of the Lord.

Sing joyfully to the LORD, all you lands;
serve the LORD with gladness;
come before him with joyful song. **R.**
Know that the LORD is God;
he made us, his we are;
his people, the flock he tends. **R.**
Enter his gates with thanksgiving,
his courts with praise;
Give thanks to him; bless his name. **R.**
The LORD is good,
the LORD, whose kindness endures forever,
and his faithfulness, to all generations. **R.**

Gospel

LUKE 5:33-39

The scribes and Pharisees said to Jesus, "The disciples of John the Baptist fast often and offer prayers, and the disciples of the Pharisees do the same; but yours eat and drink." Jesus answered them, "Can you make the wedding guests fast while the bridegroom is with them? But the days will come, and when the bridegroom is taken away from them, then they will fast in those days." And he also told them a parable. "No one tears a piece from a new cloak to patch an old one. Otherwise, he will tear the new and the piece from it will not match the old cloak. Likewise, no one pours new wine into old wineskins. Otherwise, the new wine will burst the skins, and it will be spilled, and the skins will be ruined. Rather, new wine must be poured into fresh wineskins. And no one who has been drinking old wine desires new, for he says, 'The old is good.'"

Saturday, September 7

First Reading
COLOSSIANS 1:21-23

Brothers and sisters: You once were alienated and hostile in mind because of evil deeds; God has now reconciled you in the fleshly Body of Christ through his death, to present you holy, without blemish, and irreproachable before him, provided that you persevere in the faith, firmly grounded, stable, and not shifting from the hope of the Gospel that you heard, which has been preached to every creature under heaven, of which I, Paul, am a minister.

Responsorial Psalm
PSALM 54:3-4, 6 and 8
R. God himself is my help.

O God, by your name save me,
  and by your might defend my cause.
O God, hear my prayer;
  hearken to the words of my mouth. **R.**
Behold, God is my helper;
  the Lord sustains my life.
Freely will I offer you sacrifice;
  I will praise your name, O LORD, for its goodness. **R.**

Gospel
LUKE 6:1-5

While Jesus was going through a field of grain on a sabbath, his disciples were picking the heads of grain, rubbing them in their hands, and eating them. Some Pharisees said, "Why are you doing what is unlawful on the sabbath?" Jesus said to them in reply, "Have you not read what David did when he and those who were with him were hungry? How he went into the house of God, took the bread of offering, which only the priests could lawfully eat, ate of it, and shared it with his companions?" Then he said to them, "The Son of Man is lord of the sabbath."

Sunday, September 8

Twenty-third Sunday in Ordinary Time

First Reading
WISDOM 9:13-18b

Who can know God's counsel,
or who can conceive what the LORD intends?
For the deliberations of mortals are timid,
and unsure are our plans.
For the corruptible body burdens the soul
and the earthen shelter weighs down the mind
that has many concerns.
And scarce do we guess the things on earth,
and what is within our grasp we find with difficulty;
but when things are in heaven, who can search them out?
Or who ever knew your counsel, except you had given wisdom
and sent your holy spirit from on high?
And thus were the paths of those on earth made straight.

Responsorial Psalm
PSALM 90:3-4, 5-6, 12-13, 14 and 17
R. In every age, O Lord, you have been our refuge.

You turn man back to dust,
saying, "Return, O children of men."
For a thousand years in your sight
are as yesterday, now that it is past,
or as a watch of the night. **R.**
You make an end of them in their sleep;
the next morning they are like the changing grass,
which at dawn springs up anew,
but by evening wilts and fades. **R.**
Teach us to number our days aright,
that we may gain wisdom of heart.
Return, O LORD! How long?
Have pity on your servants! **R.**
Fill us at daybreak with your kindness,
that we may shout for joy and gladness all our days.
And may the gracious care of the LORD our God be ours;
prosper the work of our hands for us!
Prosper the work of our hands! **R.**

Second Reading
PHILEMON 9-10, 12-17

I, Paul, an old man, and now also a prisoner for Christ Jesus, urge you on behalf of my child Onesimus, whose father I have become in my imprisonment; I am sending him, that is, my own heart, back to you. I should have liked to retain him for myself, so that he might serve me on your behalf in my imprisonment for the gospel, but I did not want to do anything without your consent, so that the good you do might not be forced but voluntary. Perhaps this is why he was away from you for a while, that you might have him back forever, no longer as a slave but more than a slave, a brother, beloved especially to me, but even more so to you, as a man and in the Lord. So if you regard me as a partner, welcome him as you would me.

Gospel
LUKE 14:25-33

Great crowds were traveling with Jesus, and he turned and addressed them, "If anyone comes to me without hating his father and mother, wife and children, brothers and sisters, and even his own life, he cannot be my disciple. Whoever does not carry his own cross and come after me cannot be my disciple. Which of you wishing to construct a tower does not first sit down and calculate the cost to see if there is enough for its completion? Otherwise, after laying the foundation and finding himself unable to finish the work the onlookers should laugh at him and say, 'This one began to build but did not have the resources to finish.' Or what king marching into battle would not first sit down and decide whether with ten thousand troops he can successfully oppose another king advancing upon him with twenty thousand troops? But if not, while he is still far away, he will send a delegation to ask for peace terms. In the same way, anyone of you who does not renounce all his possessions cannot be my disciple."

Monday, September 9

First Reading
COLOSSIANS 1:24–2:3

Brothers and sisters: I rejoice in my sufferings for your sake, and in my flesh I am filling up what is lacking in the afflictions of Christ on behalf of his Body, which is the Church, of which I am a minister in accordance with God's stewardship given to me to bring to completion for you the word of God, the mystery hidden from ages and from generations past. But now it has been manifested to his holy ones, to whom God chose to make known the riches of the glory of this mystery among the Gentiles; it is Christ in you, the hope for glory. It is he whom we proclaim, admonishing everyone and teaching everyone with all wisdom, that we may present everyone perfect in Christ. For this I labor and struggle, in accord with the exercise of his power working within me.

For I want you to know how great a struggle I am having for you and for those in Laodicea and all who have not seen me face to face, that their hearts may be encouraged as they are brought together in love, to have all the richness of assured understanding, for the knowledge of the mystery of God, Christ, in whom are hidden all the treasures of wisdom and knowledge.

Responsorial Psalm

PSALM 62:6-7, 9

R. In God is my safety and my glory.

Only in God be at rest, my soul,
  for from him comes my hope.
He only is my rock and my salvation,
  my stronghold; I shall not be disturbed. **R.**
Trust in him at all times, O my people!
  Pour out your hearts before him;
  God is our refuge! **R.**

Gospel

LUKE 6:6-11

On a certain sabbath Jesus went into the synagogue and taught, and there was a man there whose right hand was withered. The scribes and the Pharisees watched him closely to see if he would cure on the sabbath so that they might discover a reason to accuse him. But he realized their intentions and said to the man with the withered hand, "Come up and stand before us." And he rose and stood there. Then Jesus said to them, "I ask you, is it lawful to do good on the sabbath rather than to do evil, to save life rather than to destroy it?" Looking around at them all, he then said to him, "Stretch out your hand." He did so and his hand was restored. But they became enraged and discussed together what they might do to Jesus.

Tuesday, September 10

First Reading

COLOSSIANS 2:6-15

Brothers and sisters: As you received Christ Jesus the Lord, walk in him, rooted in him and built upon him and established in the faith as you were taught, abounding in thanksgiving. See to it that no one captivate you with an empty, seductive philosophy according to the tradition of men, according to the elemental powers of the world and not according to Christ.

For in him dwells the whole fullness of the deity bodily, and you share in this fullness in him, who is the head of every principality and power. In him you were also circumcised with a circumcision not administered by hand, by stripping off the carnal body, with the circumcision of Christ. You were buried with him in baptism, in which you were also raised with him through faith in the power of God, who raised him from the dead. And even when you were dead in transgressions and the uncircumcision of your flesh, he brought you to life along with him, having forgiven us all our transgressions; obliterating the bond against us, with its legal claims, which was opposed to us, he also removed it from our midst, nailing it to the cross; despoiling the principalities and the powers, he made a public spectacle of them, leading them away in triumph by it.

Responsorial Psalm

PSALM 145:1b-2, 8-9, 10-11

R. The Lord is compassionate toward all his works.

I will extol you, O my God and King,
  and I will bless your name forever and ever.
Every day will I bless you,
  and I will praise your name forever and ever. **R.**
The LORD is gracious and merciful,
  slow to anger and of great kindness.
The LORD is good to all
  and compassionate toward all his works. **R.**
Let all your works give you thanks, O LORD,
  and let your faithful ones bless you.
Let them discourse of the glory of your Kingdom
  and speak of your might. **R.**

Gospel

LUKE 6:12-19

Jesus departed to the mountain to pray, and he spent the night in prayer to God. When day came, he called his disciples to himself, and from them he chose Twelve, whom he also named Apostles: Simon, whom he named Peter, and his brother Andrew, James, John, Philip, Bartholomew, Matthew, Thomas, James the son of Alphaeus, Simon who was called a Zealot, and Judas the son of James, and Judas Iscariot, who became a traitor.

And he came down with them and stood on a stretch of level ground. A great crowd of his disciples and a large number of the people from all Judea and Jerusalem and the coastal region of Tyre and Sidon came to hear him and to be healed of their diseases; and even those who were tormented by unclean spirits were cured. Everyone in the crowd sought to touch him because power came forth from him and healed them all.

Wednesday, September 11

First Reading
COLOSSIANS 3:1-11

Brothers and sisters: If you were raised with Christ, seek what is above, where Christ is seated at the right hand of God. Think of what is above, not of what is on earth. For you have died, and your life is hidden with Christ in God. When Christ your life appears, then you too will appear with him in glory.

Put to death, then, the parts of you that are earthly: immorality, impurity, passion, evil desire, and the greed that is idolatry. Because of these the wrath of God is coming upon the disobedient. By these you too once conducted yourselves, when you lived in that way. But now you must put them all away: anger, fury, malice, slander, and obscene language out of your mouths. Stop lying to one another, since you have taken off the old self with its practices and have put on the new self, which is being renewed, for knowledge, in the image of its creator. Here there is not Greek and Jew, circumcision and uncircumcision, barbarian, Scythian, slave, free; but Christ is all and in all.

Responsorial Psalm
PSALM 145:2-3, 10-11, 12-13ab
R. The Lord is compassionate toward all his works.

Every day will I bless you,
  and I will praise your name forever and ever.
Great is the LORD and highly to be praised;
  his greatness is unsearchable. **R.**
Let all your works give you thanks, O LORD,
  and let your faithful ones bless you.
Let them discourse of the glory of your Kingdom
  and speak of your might. **R.**
Making known to men your might
  and the glorious splendor of your Kingdom.
Your Kingdom is a Kingdom for all ages,
  and your dominion endures through all generations. **R.**

Gospel
LUKE 6:20-26

Raising his eyes toward his disciples Jesus said:

"Blessed are you who are poor,
for the Kingdom of God is yours.
Blessed are you who are now hungry,
for you will be satisfied.
Blessed are you who are now weeping,
for you will laugh.
Blessed are you when people hate you,
and when they exclude and insult you,
and denounce your name as evil
on account of the Son of Man.

"Rejoice and leap for joy on that day! Behold, your reward will be great in heaven. For their ancestors treated the prophets in the same way.

But woe to you who are rich,
for you have received your consolation.
But woe to you who are filled now,
for you will be hungry.
Woe to you who laugh now,
for you will grieve and weep.
Woe to you when all speak well of you,
for their ancestors treated the false prophets in this way."

Thursday, September 12

First Reading
COLOSSIANS 3:12-17

Brothers and sisters: Put on, as God's chosen ones, holy and beloved, heartfelt compassion, kindness, humility, gentleness, and patience, bearing with one another and forgiving one another, if one has a grievance against another; as the Lord has forgiven you, so must you also do. And over all these put on love, that is, the bond of perfection. And let the peace of Christ control your hearts, the peace into which you were also called in one Body. And be thankful. Let the word of Christ dwell in you richly, as in all wisdom you teach and admonish one another, singing psalms, hymns, and spiritual songs with gratitude in your hearts to God. And whatever you do, in word or in deed, do everything in the name of the Lord Jesus, giving thanks to God the Father through him.

Responsorial Psalm
PSALM 150:1b-2, 3-4, 5-6
R. Let everything that breathes praise the Lord!
Praise the LORD in his sanctuary,
praise him in the firmament of his strength.

Praise him for his mighty deeds,
praise him for his sovereign majesty. **R.**
Praise him with the blast of the trumpet,
praise him with lyre and harp,
Praise him with timbrel and dance,
praise him with strings and pipe. **R.**
Praise him with sounding cymbals,
praise him with clanging cymbals.
Let everything that has breath
praise the LORD! Alleluia. **R.**

Gospel
LUKE 6:27-38

Jesus said to his disciples: "To you who hear I say, love your enemies, do good to those who hate you, bless those who curse you, pray for those who mistreat you. To the person who strikes you on one cheek, offer the other one as well, and from the person who takes your cloak, do not withhold even your tunic. Give to everyone who asks of you, and from the one who takes what is yours do not demand it back. Do to others as you would have them do to you. For if you love those who love you, what credit is that to you? Even sinners love those who love them. And if you do good to those who do good to you, what credit is that to you? Even sinners do the same. If you lend money to those from whom you expect repayment, what credit is that to you? Even sinners lend to sinners, and get back the same amount. But rather, love your enemies and do good to them, and lend expecting nothing back; then your reward will be great and you will be children of the Most High, for he himself is kind to the ungrateful and the wicked. Be merciful, just as also your Father is merciful.

"Stop judging and you will not be judged. Stop condemning and you will not be condemned. Forgive and you will be forgiven. Give and gifts will be given to you; a good measure, packed together, shaken down, and overflowing, will be poured into your lap. For the measure with which you measure will in return be measured out to you."

Friday, September 13

First Reading
1 TIMOTHY 1:1-2, 12-14

Paul, an Apostle of Christ Jesus by command of God our savior and of Christ Jesus our hope, to Timothy, my true child in faith: grace, mercy, and peace from God the Father and Christ Jesus our Lord.

I am grateful to him who has strengthened me, Christ Jesus our Lord, because he considered me trustworthy in appointing me to the ministry. I was once a blasphemer and a persecutor and an arrogant man, but I have been mercifully treated because I acted out of ignorance in my unbelief. Indeed, the grace of our Lord has been abundant, along with the faith and love that are in Christ Jesus.

Responsorial Psalm

PSALM 16:1b-2a and 5, 7-8, 11

R. You are my inheritance, O Lord.

Keep me, O God, for in you I take refuge;
  I say to the LORD, "My Lord are you."
O LORD, my allotted portion and my cup,
  you it is who hold fast my lot. **R.**
I bless the LORD who counsels me;
  even in the night my heart exhorts me.
I set the LORD ever before me;
  with him at my right hand I shall not be disturbed. **R.**
You will show me the path to life,
  fullness of joys in your presence,
  the delights at your right hand forever. **R.**

Gospel

LUKE 6:39-42

Jesus told his disciples a parable: "Can a blind person guide a blind person? Will not both fall into a pit? No disciple is superior to the teacher; but when fully trained, every disciple will be like his teacher. Why do you notice the splinter in your brother's eye, but do not perceive the wooden beam in your own? How can you say to your brother, 'Brother, let me remove that splinter in your eye,' when you do not even notice the wooden beam in your own eye? You hypocrite! Remove the wooden beam from your eye first; then you will see clearly to remove the splinter in your brother's eye."

Saturday, September 14

The Exaltation of the Holy Cross

First Reading

NUMBERS 21:4b-9

With their patience worn out by the journey, the people complained against God and Moses, "Why have you brought us up from Egypt to die in this desert, where there is no food or water? We are disgusted with this wretched food!"

In punishment the LORD sent among the people saraph serpents, which bit the people so that many of them died. Then the people came to Moses and said, "We have sinned in complaining against the LORD and you. Pray the LORD to take the serpents from us." So Moses prayed for the people, and the LORD said to Moses, "Make a saraph and mount it on a pole, and if any who have been bitten look at it, they will live." Moses accordingly made a bronze serpent and mounted it on a pole, and whenever anyone who had been bitten by a serpent looked at the bronze serpent, he lived.

Responsorial Psalm
PSALM 78:1bc-2, 34-35, 36-37, 38
R. Do not forget the works of the Lord!
Hearken, my people, to my teaching;
incline your ears to the words of my mouth.
I will open my mouth in a parable,
I will utter mysteries from of old. **R.**
While he slew them they sought him
and inquired after God again,
Remembering that God was their rock
and the Most High God, their redeemer. **R.**
But they flattered him with their mouths
and lied to him with their tongues,
Though their hearts were not steadfast toward him,
nor were they faithful to his covenant. **R.**
But he, being merciful, forgave their sin
and destroyed them not;
Often he turned back his anger
and let none of his wrath be roused. **R.**

Second Reading
PHILIPPIANS 2:6-11
Brothers and sisters:
Christ Jesus, though he was in the form of God,
did not regard equality with God something to be grasped.
Rather, he emptied himself,
taking the form of a slave,
coming in human likeness;
and found human in appearance,
he humbled himself,
becoming obedient to death,
even death on a cross.

Because of this, God greatly exalted him
and bestowed on him the name
that is above every name,
that at the name of Jesus
every knee should bend,
of those in heaven and on earth and under the earth,
and every tongue confess that
Jesus Christ is Lord,
to the glory of God the Father.

Gospel

JOHN 3:13-17

Jesus said to Nicodemus: "No one has gone up to heaven except the one who has come down from heaven, the Son of Man. And just as Moses lifted up the serpent in the desert, so must the Son of Man be lifted up, so that everyone who believes in him may have eternal life."

For God so loved the world that he gave his only Son, so that everyone who believes in him might not perish but might have eternal life. For God did not send his Son into the world to condemn the world, but that the world might be saved through him.

Sunday, September 15

Twenty-fourth Sunday in Ordinary Time

First Reading

EXODUS 32:7-11, 13-14

The LORD said to Moses, "Go down at once to your people, whom you brought out of the land of Egypt, for they have become depraved. They have soon turned aside from the way I pointed out to them, making for themselves a molten calf and worshiping it, sacrificing to it and crying out, 'This is your God, O Israel, who brought you out of the land of Egypt!' I see how stiff-necked this people is," continued the LORD to Moses. "Let me alone, then, that my wrath may blaze up against them to consume them. Then I will make of you a great nation."

But Moses implored the LORD, his God, saying, "Why, O LORD, should your wrath blaze up against your own people, whom you brought out of the land of Egypt with such great power and with so strong a hand? Remember your servants Abraham, Isaac, and Israel, and how you swore to them by your own self, saying, 'I will make your descendants as numerous as the stars in the sky; and all this land that I promised, I will give your descendants as their perpetual heritage.'" So the LORD relented in the punishment he had threatened to inflict on his people.

Responsorial Psalm
PSALM 51:3-4, 12-13, 17, 19
R. I will rise and go to my father.

Have mercy on me, O God, in your goodness;
in the greatness of your compassion wipe out my offense.
Thoroughly wash me from my guilt
and of my sin cleanse me. **R.**
A clean heart create for me, O God,
and a steadfast spirit renew within me.
Cast me not out from your presence,
and your Holy Spirit take not from me. **R.**
O Lord, open my lips,
and my mouth shall proclaim your praise.
My sacrifice, O God, is a contrite spirit;
a heart contrite and humbled, O God, you will not spurn. **R.**

Second Reading
1 TIMOTHY 1:12-17

Beloved: I am grateful to him who has strengthened me, Christ Jesus our Lord, because he considered me trustworthy in appointing me to the ministry. I was once a blasphemer and a persecutor and arrogant, but I have been mercifully treated because I acted out of ignorance in my unbelief. Indeed, the grace of our Lord has been abundant, along with the faith and love that are in Christ Jesus. This saying is trustworthy and deserves full acceptance: Christ Jesus came into the world to save sinners. Of these I am the foremost. But for that reason I was mercifully treated, so that in me, as the foremost, Christ Jesus might display all his patience as an example for those who would come to believe in him for everlasting life. To the king of ages, incorruptible, invisible, the only God, honor and glory forever and ever. Amen.

Gospel
LUKE 15:1-32 (or LUKE 15:1-10)

Tax collectors and sinners were all drawing near to listen to Jesus, but the Pharisees and scribes began to complain, saying, "This man welcomes sinners and eats with them." So to them he addressed this parable. "What man among you having a hundred sheep and losing one of them would not leave the ninety-nine in the desert and go after the lost one until he finds it? And when he does find it, he sets it on his shoulders with great joy and, upon his arrival home, he calls together his friends and neighbors and says to them, 'Rejoice with me because I have found my lost sheep.' I tell you, in just the same way there will be more joy in heaven over one sinner who repents than over ninety-nine righteous people who have no need of repentance.

"Or what woman having ten coins and losing one would not light a lamp and sweep the house, searching carefully until she finds it? And when she does find it, she calls together her friends and neighbors and says to them, 'Rejoice with me because I have found the coin that I lost.' In just the same way, I tell you, there will be rejoicing among the angels of God over one sinner who repents."

Then he said, "A man had two sons, and the younger son said to his father, 'Father give me the share of your estate that should come to me.' So the father divided the property between them. After a few days, the younger son collected all his belongings and set off to a distant country where he squandered his inheritance on a life of dissipation. When he had freely spent everything, a severe famine struck that country, and he found himself in dire need. So he hired himself out to one of the local citizens who sent him to his farm to tend the swine. And he longed to eat his fill of the pods on which the swine fed, but nobody gave him any. Coming to his senses he thought, 'How many of my father's hired workers have more than enough food to eat, but here am I, dying from hunger. I shall get up and go to my father and I shall say to him, "Father, I have sinned against heaven and against you. I no longer deserve to be called your son; treat me as you would treat one of your hired workers."' So he got up and went back to his father. While he was still a long way off, his father caught sight of him, and was filled with compassion. He ran to his son, embraced him and kissed him. His son said to him, 'Father, I have sinned against heaven and against you; I no longer deserve to be called your son.' But his father ordered his servants, 'Quickly bring the finest robe and put it on him; put a ring on his finger and sandals on his feet. Take the fattened calf and slaughter it. Then let us celebrate with a feast, because this son of mine was dead, and has come to life again; he was lost, and has been found.' Then the celebration began. Now the older son had been out in the field and, on his way back, as he neared the house, he heard the sound of music and dancing. He called one of the servants and asked what this might mean. The servant said to him, 'Your brother has returned and your father has slaughtered the fattened calf because he has him back safe and sound.' He became angry, and when he refused to enter the house, his father came out and pleaded with him. He said to his father in reply, 'Look, all these years I served you and not once did I disobey your orders; yet you never gave me even a young goat to feast on with my friends. But when your son returns, who swallowed up your property with prostitutes, for him you slaughter the fattened calf.' He said to him, 'My son, you are here with me always; everything I have is yours. But now we must celebrate and rejoice, because your brother was dead and has come to life again; he was lost and has been found.'"

Monday, September 16

First Reading
1 TIMOTHY 2:1-8

Beloved: First of all, I ask that supplications, prayers, petitions, and thanksgivings be offered for everyone, for kings and for all in authority, that we may lead a quiet and tranquil life in all devotion and dignity. This is good and pleasing to God our savior, who wills everyone to be saved and to come to knowledge of the truth.

For there is one God.
There is also one mediator between God and men,
the man Christ Jesus,
who gave himself as ransom for all.

This was the testimony at the proper time. For this I was appointed preacher and Apostle (I am speaking the truth, I am not lying), teacher of the Gentiles in faith and truth.

It is my wish, then, that in every place the men should pray, lifting up holy hands, without anger or argument.

Responsorial Psalm
PSALM 28:2, 7, 8-9
R. Blessed be the Lord, for he has heard my prayer.
Hear the sound of my pleading, when I cry to you,
lifting up my hands toward your holy shrine. **R.**
The LORD is my strength and my shield.
In him my heart trusts, and I find help;
then my heart exults, and with my song I give him thanks. **R.**
The LORD is the strength of his people,
the saving refuge of his anointed.
Save your people, and bless your inheritance;
feed them, and carry them forever! **R.**

Gospel
LUKE 7:1-10

When Jesus had finished all his words to the people, he entered Capernaum. A centurion there had a slave who was ill and about to die, and he was valuable to him. When he heard about Jesus, he sent elders of the Jews to him, asking him to come and save the life of his slave. They approached Jesus and strongly urged him to come, saying, "He deserves to have you do this for him, for he loves our nation and he built the synagogue for us." And Jesus went with them, but when he was only a short distance from the house, the centurion sent friends to tell him,

"Lord, do not trouble yourself, for I am not worthy to have you enter under my roof. Therefore, I did not consider myself worthy to come to you; but say the word and let my servant be healed. For I too am a person subject to authority, with soldiers subject to me. And I say to one, 'Go,' and he goes; and to another, 'Come here,' and he comes; and to my slave, 'Do this,' and he does it." When Jesus heard this he was amazed at him and, turning, said to the crowd following him, "I tell you, not even in Israel have I found such faith." When the messengers returned to the house, they found the slave in good health.

Tuesday, September 17

First Reading

1 TIMOTHY 3:1-13

Beloved, this saying is trustworthy: whoever aspires to the office of bishop desires a noble task. Therefore, a bishop must be irreproachable, married only once, temperate, self-controlled, decent, hospitable, able to teach, not a drunkard, not aggressive, but gentle, not contentious, not a lover of money. He must manage his own household well, keeping his children under control with perfect dignity; for if a man does not know how to manage his own household, how can he take care of the Church of God? He should not be a recent convert, so that he may not become conceited and thus incur the Devil's punishment. He must also have a good reputation among outsiders, so that he may not fall into disgrace, the Devil's trap.

Similarly, deacons must be dignified, not deceitful, not addicted to drink, not greedy for sordid gain, holding fast to the mystery of the faith with a clear conscience. Moreover, they should be tested first; then, if there is nothing against them, let them serve as deacons. Women, similarly, should be dignified, not slanderers, but temperate and faithful in everything. Deacons may be married only once and must manage their children and their households well. Thus those who serve well as deacons gain good standing and much confidence in their faith in Christ Jesus.

Responsorial Psalm

PSALM 101:1b-2ab, 2cd-3ab, 5, 6

R. I will walk with blameless heart.

Of mercy and judgment I will sing;
  to you, O LORD, I will sing praise.
I will persevere in the way of integrity;
  when will you come to me? **R.**
I will walk with blameless heart,
  within my house;

I will not set before my eyes
any base thing. **R.**
Whoever slanders his neighbor in secret,
him will I destroy.
The man of haughty eyes and puffed-up heart
I will not endure. **R.**
My eyes are upon the faithful of the land,
that they may dwell with me.
He who walks in the way of integrity
shall be in my service. **R.**

Gospel
LUKE 7:11-17

Jesus journeyed to a city called Nain, and his disciples and a large crowd accompanied him. As he drew near to the gate of the city, a man who had died was being carried out, the only son of his mother, and she was a widow. A large crowd from the city was with her. When the Lord saw her, he was moved with pity for her and said to her, "Do not weep." He stepped forward and touched the coffin; at this the bearers halted, and he said, "Young man, I tell you, arise!" The dead man sat up and began to speak, and Jesus gave him to his mother. Fear seized them all, and they glorified God, exclaiming, "A great prophet has arisen in our midst," and "God has visited his people." This report about him spread through the whole of Judea and in all the surrounding region.

Wednesday, September 18

First Reading
1 TIMOTHY 3:14-16

Beloved: I am writing you, although I hope to visit you soon. But if I should be delayed, you should know how to behave in the household of God, which is the Church of the living God, the pillar and foundation of truth. Undeniably great is the mystery of devotion,

Who was manifested in the flesh,
vindicated in the spirit,
seen by angels,
proclaimed to the Gentiles,
believed in throughout the world,
taken up in glory.

Responsorial Psalm
PSALM 111:1-2, 3-4, 5-6
R. How great are the works of the Lord!

I will give thanks to the LORD with all my heart
in the company and assembly of the just.
Great are the works of the LORD,
exquisite in all their delights. **R.**
Majesty and glory are his work,
and his justice endures forever.
He has won renown for his wondrous deeds;
gracious and merciful is the LORD. **R.**
He has given food to those who fear him;
he will forever be mindful of his covenant.
He has made known to his people the power of his works,
giving them the inheritance of the nations. **R.**

Gospel
LUKE 7:31-35

Jesus said to the crowds: "To what shall I compare the people of this generation? What are they like? They are like children who sit in the marketplace and call to one another,

'We played the flute for you, but you did not dance.
We sang a dirge, but you did not weep.'

For John the Baptist came neither eating food nor drinking wine, and you said, 'He is possessed by a demon.' The Son of Man came eating and drinking and you said, 'Look, he is a glutton and a drunkard, a friend of tax collectors and sinners.' But wisdom is vindicated by all her children."

Thursday, September 19

First Reading
1 TIMOTHY 4:12-16

Beloved: Let no one have contempt for your youth, but set an example for those who believe, in speech, conduct, love, faith, and purity. Until I arrive, attend to the reading, exhortation, and teaching. Do not neglect the gift you have, which was conferred on you through the prophetic word with the imposition of hands by the presbyterate. Be diligent in these matters, be absorbed in them, so that your progress may be evident to everyone. Attend to yourself and to your teaching; persevere in both tasks, for by doing so you will save both yourself and those who listen to you.

Responsorial Psalm

PSALM 111:7-8, 9, 10

R. How great are the works of the Lord!

The works of his hands are faithful and just;
sure are all his precepts,
Reliable forever and ever,
wrought in truth and equity. **R.**
He has sent deliverance to his people;
he has ratified his covenant forever;
holy and awesome is his name. **R.**
The fear of the LORD is the beginning of wisdom;
prudent are all who live by it.
His praise endures forever. **R.**

Gospel

LUKE 7:36-50

A certain Pharisee invited Jesus to dine with him, and he entered the Pharisee's house and reclined at table. Now there was a sinful woman in the city who learned that he was at table in the house of the Pharisee. Bringing an alabaster flask of ointment, she stood behind him at his feet weeping and began to bathe his feet with her tears. Then she wiped them with her hair, kissed them, and anointed them with the ointment. When the Pharisee who had invited him saw this he said to himself, "If this man were a prophet, he would know who and what sort of woman this is who is touching him, that she is a sinner." Jesus said to him in reply, "Simon, I have something to say to you." "Tell me, teacher," he said. "Two people were in debt to a certain creditor; one owed five hundred days' wages and the other owed fifty. Since they were unable to repay the debt, he forgave it for both. Which of them will love him more?" Simon said in reply, "The one, I suppose, whose larger debt was forgiven." He said to him, "You have judged rightly." Then he turned to the woman and said to Simon, "Do you see this woman? When I entered your house, you did not give me water for my feet, but she has bathed them with her tears and wiped them with her hair. You did not give me a kiss, but she has not ceased kissing my feet since the time I entered. You did not anoint my head with oil, but she anointed my feet with ointment. So I tell you, her many sins have been forgiven; hence, she has shown great love. But the one to whom little is forgiven, loves little." He said to her, "Your sins are forgiven." The others at table said to themselves, "Who is this who even forgives sins?" But he said to the woman, "Your faith has saved you; go in peace."

Friday, September 20

First Reading

1 TIMOTHY 6:2c-12

Beloved: Teach and urge these things. Whoever teaches something different and does not agree with the sound words of our Lord Jesus Christ and the religious teaching is conceited, understanding nothing, and has a morbid disposition for arguments and verbal disputes. From these come envy, rivalry, insults, evil suspicions, and mutual friction among people with corrupted minds, who are deprived of the truth, supposing religion to be a means of gain. Indeed, religion with contentment is a great gain. For we brought nothing into the world, just as we shall not be able to take anything out of it. If we have food and clothing, we shall be content with that. Those who want to be rich are falling into temptation and into a trap and into many foolish and harmful desires, which plunge them into ruin and destruction. For the love of money is the root of all evils, and some people in their desire for it have strayed from the faith and have pierced themselves with many pains.

But you, man of God, avoid all this. Instead, pursue righteousness, devotion, faith, love, patience, and gentleness. Compete well for the faith. Lay hold of eternal life, to which you were called when you made the noble confession in the presence of many witnesses.

Responsorial Psalm

PSALM 49:6-7, 8-10, 17-18, 19-20

R. Blessed the poor in spirit; the Kingdom of heaven is theirs!

Why should I fear in evil days
when my wicked ensnarers ring me round?
They trust in their wealth;
the abundance of their riches is their boast. **R.**

Yet in no way can a man redeem himself,
or pay his own ransom to God;
Too high is the price to redeem one's life; he would never have enough
to remain alive always and not see destruction. **R.**

Fear not when a man grows rich,
when the wealth of his house becomes great,
For when he dies, he shall take none of it;
his wealth shall not follow him down. **R.**

Though in his lifetime he counted himself blessed,
"They will praise you for doing well for yourself,"
He shall join the circle of his forebears
who shall never more see light. **R.**

Gospel
LUKE 8:1-3

Jesus journeyed from one town and village to another, preaching and proclaiming the good news of the Kingdom of God. Accompanying him were the Twelve and some women who had been cured of evil spirits and infirmities, Mary, called Magdalene, from whom seven demons had gone out, Joanna, the wife of Herod's steward Chuza, Susanna, and many others who provided for them out of their resources.

Saturday, September 21

Saint Matthew, Apostle and Evangelist

First Reading
EPHESIANS 4:1-7, 11-13

Brothers and sisters: I, a prisoner for the Lord, urge you to live in a manner worthy of the call you have received, with all humility and gentleness, with patience, bearing with one another through love, striving to preserve the unity of the Spirit through the bond of peace: one Body and one Spirit, as you were also called to the one hope of your call; one Lord, one faith, one baptism; one God and Father of all, who is over all and through all and in all.

But grace was given to each of us according to the measure of Christ's gift.

And he gave some as Apostles, others as prophets, others as evangelists, others as pastors and teachers, to equip the holy ones for the work of ministry, for building up the Body of Christ, until we all attain to the unity of faith and knowledge of the Son of God, to mature manhood, to the extent of the full stature of Christ.

Responsorial Psalm
PSALM 19:2-3, 4-5
R. Their message goes out through all the earth.

The heavens declare the glory of God;
   and the firmament proclaims his handiwork.
Day pours out the word to day,
   and night to night imparts knowledge. **R.**
Not a word nor a discourse
   whose voice is not heard;
Through all the earth their voice resounds,
   and to the ends of the world, their message. **R.**

Gospel
MATTHEW 9:9-13

As Jesus passed by, he saw a man named Matthew sitting at the customs post. He said to him, "Follow me." And he got up and followed him. While he was at table in his house, many tax collectors and sinners came and sat with Jesus and his disciples. The Pharisees saw this and said to his disciples, "Why does your teacher eat with tax collectors and sinners?" He heard this and said, "Those who are well do not need a physician, but the sick do. Go and learn the meaning of the words, *I desire mercy, not sacrifice*. I did not come to call the righteous but sinners."

Sunday, September 22

Twenty-fifth Sunday in Ordinary Time

First Reading
AMOS 8:4-7

Hear this, you who trample upon the needy
  and destroy the poor of the land!
"When will the new moon be over," you ask,
  "that we may sell our grain,
  and the sabbath, that we may display the wheat?
We will diminish the ephah,
  add to the shekel,
  and fix our scales for cheating!
We will buy the lowly for silver,
  and the poor for a pair of sandals;
  even the refuse of the wheat we will sell!"
The LORD has sworn by the pride of Jacob:
  Never will I forget a thing they have done!

Responsorial Psalm
PSALM 113:1-2, 4-6, 7-8
R. Praise the Lord, who lifts up the poor. (or R. Alleluia.)

Praise, you servants of the LORD,
  praise the name of the LORD.
Blessed be the name of the LORD
  both now and forever. **R.**
High above all nations is the LORD;
  above the heavens is his glory.
Who is like the LORD, our God, who is enthroned on high
  and looks upon the heavens and the earth below? **R.**

He raises up the lowly from the dust;
 from the dunghill he lifts up the poor
to seat them with princes,
 with the princes of his own people. **R.**

Second Reading
1 TIMOTHY 2:1-8

Beloved: First of all, I ask that supplications, prayers, petitions, and thanksgivings be offered for everyone, for kings and for all in authority, that we may lead a quiet and tranquil life in all devotion and dignity. This is good and pleasing to God our savior, who wills everyone to be saved and to come to knowledge of the truth.

For there is one God.
There is also one mediator between God and men,
the man Christ Jesus,
who gave himself as ransom for all.

This was the testimony at the proper time. For this I was appointed preacher and apostle—I am speaking the truth, I am not lying—, teacher of the Gentiles in faith and truth.

It is my wish, then, that in every place the men should pray, lifting up holy hands, without anger or argument.

Gospel
LUKE 16:1-13 (or LUKE 16:10-13)

Jesus said to his disciples, "A rich man had a steward who was reported to him for squandering his property. He summoned him and said, 'What is this I hear about you? Prepare a full account of your stewardship, because you can no longer be my steward.' The steward said to himself, 'What shall I do, now that my master is taking the position of steward away from me? I am not strong enough to dig and I am ashamed to beg. I know what I shall do so that, when I am removed from the stewardship, they may welcome me into their homes.' He called in his master's debtors one by one. To the first he said, 'How much do you owe my master?' He replied, 'One hundred measures of olive oil.' He said to him, 'Here is your promissory note. Sit down and quickly write one for fifty.' Then to another the steward said, 'And you, how much do you owe?' He replied, 'One hundred kors of wheat.' The steward said to him, 'Here is your promissory note; write one for eighty.' And the master commended that dishonest steward for acting prudently.

"For the children of this world are more prudent in dealing with their own generation than are the children of light. I tell you, make friends for yourselves with dishonest wealth, so that when it fails, you will be welcomed into eternal dwellings. The person who is trustworthy in very small matters is also trustworthy in great ones; and the person who is dishonest in very small matters is also dishonest in great ones. If, therefore, you are not trustworthy with dishonest wealth, who will trust you with true wealth? If you are not trustworthy with what belongs to another, who will give you what is yours? No servant can serve two masters. He will either hate one and love the other, or be devoted to one and despise the other. You cannot serve both God and mammon."

Monday, September 23

First Reading

EZRA 1:1-6

In the first year of Cyrus, king of Persia, in order to fulfill the word of the LORD spoken by Jeremiah, the LORD inspired King Cyrus of Persia to issue this proclamation throughout his kingdom, both by word of mouth and in writing: "Thus says Cyrus, king of Persia: 'All the kingdoms of the earth the LORD, the God of heaven, has given to me, and he has also charged me to build him a house in Jerusalem, which is in Judah. Therefore, whoever among you belongs to any part of his people, let him go up, and may his God be with him! Let everyone who has survived, in whatever place he may have dwelt, be assisted by the people of that place with silver, gold, goods, and cattle, together with free-will offerings for the house of God in Jerusalem.'"

Then the family heads of Judah and Benjamin and the priests and Levites—everyone, that is, whom God had inspired to do so—prepared to go up to build the house of the LORD in Jerusalem. All their neighbors gave them help in every way, with silver, gold, goods, and cattle, and with many precious gifts besides all their free-will offerings.

Responsorial Psalm

PSALM 126:1b-2ab, 2cd-3, 4-5, 6

R. The Lord has done marvels for us.

When the LORD brought back the captives of Zion,
we were like men dreaming.
Then our mouth was filled with laughter,
and our tongue with rejoicing. **R.**
Then they said among the nations,
"The LORD has done great things for them."
The LORD has done great things for us;
we are glad indeed. **R.**

Restore our fortunes, O LORD,
  like the torrents in the southern desert.
Those that sow in tears
  shall reap rejoicing. **R.**
Although they go forth weeping,
  carrying the seed to be sown,
They shall come back rejoicing,
  carrying their sheaves. **R.**

Gospel
LUKE 8:16-18

Jesus said to the crowd: "No one who lights a lamp conceals it with a vessel or sets it under a bed; rather, he places it on a lampstand so that those who enter may see the light. For there is nothing hidden that will not become visible, and nothing secret that will not be known and come to light. Take care, then, how you hear. To anyone who has, more will be given, and from the one who has not, even what he seems to have will be taken away."

Tuesday, September 24

First Reading
EZRA 6:7-8, 12b, 14-20

King Darius issued an order to the officials of West-of-Euphrates: "Let the governor and the elders of the Jews continue the work on that house of God; they are to rebuild it on its former site. I also issue this decree concerning your dealing with these elders of the Jews in the rebuilding of that house of God: From the royal revenue, the taxes of West-of-Euphrates, let these men be repaid for their expenses, in full and without delay. I, Darius, have issued this decree; let it be carefully executed."

The elders of the Jews continued to make progress in the building, supported by the message of the prophets, Haggai and Zechariah, son of Iddo. They finished the building according to the command of the God of Israel and the decrees of Cyrus and Darius and of Artaxerxes, king of Persia. They completed this house on the third day of the month Adar, in the sixth year of the reign of King Darius. The children of Israel—priests, Levites, and the other returned exiles—celebrated the dedication of this house of God with joy. For the dedication of this house of God, they offered one hundred bulls, two hundred rams, and four hundred lambs, together with twelve he-goats as a sin-offering for all Israel, in keeping with the number of the tribes of Israel. Finally, they set up the priests in their classes and the Levites in their divisions for the service of God in Jerusalem, as is prescribed in the book of Moses.

The exiles kept the Passover on the fourteenth day of the first month. The Levites, every one of whom had purified himself for the occasion, sacrificed the Passover for the rest of the exiles, for their brethren the priests, and for themselves.

Responsorial Psalm
PSALM 122:1-2, 3-4ab, 4cd-5
R. Let us go rejoicing to the house of the Lord.
I rejoiced because they said to me,
"We will go up to the house of the LORD."
And now we have set foot
within your gates, O Jerusalem. **R.**
Jerusalem, built as a city
with compact unity.
To it the tribes go up,
the tribes of the LORD. **R.**
According to the decree for Israel,
to give thanks to the name of the LORD.
In it are set up judgment seats,
seats for the house of David. **R.**

Gospel
LUKE 8:19-21

The mother of Jesus and his brothers came to him but were unable to join him because of the crowd. He was told, "Your mother and your brothers are standing outside and they wish to see you." He said to them in reply, "My mother and my brothers are those who hear the word of God and act on it."

Wednesday, September 25

First Reading
EZRA 9:5-9

At the time of the evening sacrifice, I, Ezra, rose in my wretchedness, and with cloak and mantle torn I fell on my knees, stretching out my hands to the LORD, my God.

I said: "My God, I am too ashamed and confounded to raise my face to you, O my God, for our wicked deeds are heaped up above our heads and our guilt reaches up to heaven. From the time of our fathers even to this day great has been our guilt, and for our wicked deeds we have been delivered up, we and our kings and our priests, to the will of the kings of foreign lands, to the sword, to captivity, to pillage, and to disgrace, as is the case today.

"And now, but a short time ago, mercy came to us from the LORD, our God, who left us a remnant and gave us a stake in his holy place; thus our God has brightened our eyes and given us relief in our servitude. For slaves we are, but in our servitude our God has not abandoned us; rather, he has turned the good will of the kings of Persia toward us. Thus he has given us new life to raise again the house of our God and restore its ruins, and has granted us a fence in Judah and Jerusalem."

Responsorial Psalm

TOBIT 13:2, 3-4a, 4befghn, 7-8

R. Blessed be God, who lives for ever.

He scourges and then has mercy;
he casts down to the depths of the nether world,
and he brings up from the great abyss.
No one can escape his hand. **R.**
Praise him, you children of Israel, before the Gentiles,
for though he has scattered you among them,
he has shown you his greatness even there. **R.**
So now consider what he has done for you,
and praise him with full voice.
Bless the Lord of righteousness,
and exalt the King of ages. **R.**
In the land of my exile I praise him
and show his power and majesty to a sinful nation. **R.**
Bless the Lord, all you his chosen ones,
and may all of you praise his majesty.
Celebrate days of gladness, and give him praise. **R.**

Gospel

LUKE 9:1-6

Jesus summoned the Twelve and gave them power and authority over all demons and to cure diseases, and he sent them to proclaim the Kingdom of God and to heal the sick. He said to them, "Take nothing for the journey, neither walking stick, nor sack, nor food, nor money, and let no one take a second tunic. Whatever house you enter, stay there and leave from there. And as for those who do not welcome you, when you leave that town, shake the dust from your feet in testimony against them." Then they set out and went from village to village proclaiming the good news and curing diseases everywhere.

Thursday, September 26

First Reading

HAGGAI 1:1-8

On the first day of the sixth month in the second year of King Darius, the word of the LORD came through the prophet Haggai to the governor of Judah, Zerubbabel, son of Shealtiel, and to the high priest Joshua, son of Jehozadak:

Thus says the LORD of hosts: This people says: "The time has not yet come to rebuild the house of the LORD." (Then this word of the LORD came through Haggai, the prophet:) Is it time for you to dwell in your own paneled houses, while this house lies in ruins?

Now thus says the LORD of hosts:
Consider your ways!
You have sown much, but have brought in little;
you have eaten, but have not been satisfied;
You have drunk, but have not been exhilarated;
have clothed yourselves, but not been warmed;
And whoever earned wages
earned them for a bag with holes in it.

Thus says the LORD of hosts:
Consider your ways!
Go up into the hill country;
bring timber, and build the house
That I may take pleasure in it
and receive my glory, says the LORD.

Responsorial Psalm

PSALM 149:1b-2, 3-4, 5-6a and 9b

R. The Lord takes delight in his people.

Sing to the LORD a new song
of praise in the assembly of the faithful.
Let Israel be glad in their maker,
let the children of Zion rejoice in their king. **R.**
Let them praise his name in the festive dance,
let them sing praise to him with timbrel and harp.
For the LORD loves his people,
and he adorns the lowly with victory. **R.**
Let the faithful exult in glory;
let them sing for joy upon their couches;
Let the high praises of God be in their throats.
This is the glory of all his faithful. Alleluia. **R.**

Gospel
LUKE 9:7-9

Herod the tetrarch heard about all that was happening, and he was greatly perplexed because some were saying, "John has been raised from the dead"; others were saying, "Elijah has appeared"; still others, "One of the ancient prophets has arisen." But Herod said, "John I beheaded. Who then is this about whom I hear such things?" And he kept trying to see him.

Friday, September 27

First Reading
HAGGAI 2:1-9

In the second year of King Darius, on the twenty-first day of the seventh month, the word of the LORD came through the prophet Haggai: Tell this to the governor of Judah, Zerubbabel, son of Shealtiel, and to the high priest Joshua, son of Jehozadak, and to the remnant of the people:

Who is left among you
  that saw this house in its former glory?
And how do you see it now?
  Does it not seem like nothing in your eyes?
But now take courage, Zerubbabel, says the LORD,
  and take courage, Joshua, high priest, son of Jehozadak,
And take courage, all you people of the land,
  says the LORD, and work!
  For I am with you, says the LORD of hosts.
This is the pact that I made with you
  when you came out of Egypt,
And my spirit continues in your midst;
  do not fear!
  For thus says the LORD of hosts:
One moment yet, a little while,
  and I will shake the heavens and the earth,
  the sea and the dry land.
I will shake all the nations,
  and the treasures of all the nations will come in,
And I will fill this house with glory,
  says the LORD of hosts.
Mine is the silver and mine the gold,
  says the LORD of hosts.
Greater will be the future glory of this house

than the former, says the LORD of hosts;
And in this place I will give you peace,
says the LORD of hosts!

Responsorial Psalm

PSALM 43:1, 2, 3, 4

R. Hope in God; I will praise him, my savior and my God.

Do me justice, O God, and fight my fight
against a faithless people;
from the deceitful and impious man rescue me. **R.**
For you, O God, are my strength.
Why do you keep me so far away?
Why must I go about in mourning,
with the enemy oppressing me? **R.**
Send forth your light and your fidelity;
they shall lead me on
And bring me to your holy mountain,
to your dwelling-place. **R.**
Then will I go in to the altar of God,
the God of my gladness and joy;
Then will I give you thanks upon the harp,
O God, my God! **R.**

Gospel

LUKE 9:18-22

Once when Jesus was praying in solitude, and the disciples were with him, he asked them, "Who do the crowds say that I am?" They said in reply, "John the Baptist; others, Elijah; still others, 'One of the ancient prophets has arisen.'" Then he said to them, "But who do you say that I am?" Peter said in reply, "The Christ of God." He rebuked them and directed them not to tell this to anyone.

He said, "The Son of Man must suffer greatly and be rejected by the elders, the chief priests, and the scribes, and be killed and on the third day be raised."

Saturday, September 28

First Reading

ZECHARIAH 2:5-9, 14-15a

I, Zechariah, raised my eyes and looked: there was a man with a measuring line in his hand. I asked, "Where are you going?" He answered, "To measure Jerusalem, to see how great is its width and how great its length."

Then the angel who spoke with me advanced, and another angel came out to meet him and said to him, "Run, tell this to that young man: People will live in Jerusalem as though in open country, because of the multitude of men and beasts in her midst. But I will be for her an encircling wall of fire, says the LORD, and I will be the glory in her midst."

Sing and rejoice, O daughter Zion! See, I am coming to dwell among you, says the LORD. Many nations shall join themselves to the LORD on that day, and they shall be his people and he will dwell among you.

Responsorial Psalm

JEREMIAH 31:10, 11-12ab, 13

R. The Lord will guard us as a shepherd guards his flock.

Hear the word of the LORD, O nations,
proclaim it on distant isles, and say:
He who scattered Israel, now gathers them together,
he guards them as a shepherd guards his flock. **R.**
The LORD shall ransom Jacob,
he shall redeem him from the hand of his conqueror.
Shouting, they shall mount the heights of Zion,
they shall come streaming to the LORD's blessings. **R.**
Then the virgins shall make merry and dance,
and young men and old as well.
I will turn their mourning into joy,
I will console and gladden them after their sorrows. **R.**

Gospel

LUKE 9:43b-45

While they were all amazed at his every deed, Jesus said to his disciples, "Pay attention to what I am telling you. The Son of Man is to be handed over to men." But they did not understand this saying; its meaning was hidden from them so that they should not understand it, and they were afraid to ask him about this saying.

Sunday, September 29

Twenty-sixth Sunday in Ordinary Time

First Reading

AMOS 6:1a, 4-7

Thus says the LORD the God of hosts:
Woe to the complacent in Zion!
Lying upon beds of ivory,
stretched comfortably on their couches,

they eat lambs taken from the flock,
and calves from the stall!
Improvising to the music of the harp,
like David, they devise their own accompaniment.
They drink wine from bowls
and anoint themselves with the best oils;
yet they are not made ill by the collapse of Joseph!
Therefore, now they shall be the first to go into exile,
and their wanton revelry shall be done away with.

Responsorial Psalm
PSALM 146:7, 8-9, 9-10
R. Praise the Lord, my soul! (or R. Alleluia.)

Blessed he who keeps faith forever,
secures justice for the oppressed,
gives food to the hungry.
The LORD sets captives free. **R.**
The LORD gives sight to the blind;
the LORD raises up those who were bowed down.
The LORD loves the just.
The LORD protects strangers. **R.**
The fatherless and the widow he sustains,
but the way of the wicked he thwarts.
The LORD shall reign forever;
your God, O Zion, through all generations. Alleluia. **R.**

Second Reading
1 TIMOTHY 6:11-16

But you, man of God, pursue righteousness, devotion, faith, love, patience, and gentleness. Compete well for the faith. Lay hold of eternal life, to which you were called when you made the noble confession in the presence of many witnesses. I charge you before God, who gives life to all things, and before Christ Jesus, who gave testimony under Pontius Pilate for the noble confession, to keep the commandment without stain or reproach until the appearance of our Lord Jesus Christ that the blessed and only ruler will make manifest at the proper time, the King of kings and Lord of lords, who alone has immortality, who dwells in unapproachable light, and whom no human being has seen or can see. To him be honor and eternal power. Amen.

Gospel
LUKE 16:19-31

Jesus said to the Pharisees: "There was a rich man who dressed in purple garments and fine linen and dined sumptuously each day. And lying at his door was a poor man named Lazarus, covered with sores, who would gladly have eaten his fill of the scraps that fell from the rich man's table. Dogs even used to come and lick his sores. When the poor man died, he was carried away by angels to the bosom of Abraham. The rich man also died and was buried, and from the netherworld, where he was in torment, he raised his eyes and saw Abraham far off and Lazarus at his side. And he cried out, 'Father Abraham, have pity on me. Send Lazarus to dip the tip of his finger in water and cool my tongue, for I am suffering torment in these flames.' Abraham replied, 'My child, remember that you received what was good during your lifetime while Lazarus likewise received what was bad; but now he is comforted here, whereas you are tormented. Moreover, between us and you a great chasm is established to prevent anyone from crossing who might wish to go from our side to yours or from your side to ours.' He said, 'Then I beg you, father, send him to my father's house, for I have five brothers, so that he may warn them, lest they too come to this place of torment.' But Abraham replied, 'They have Moses and the prophets. Let them listen to them.' He said, 'Oh no, father Abraham, but if someone from the dead goes to them, they will repent.' Then Abraham said, 'If they will not listen to Moses and the prophets, neither will they be persuaded if someone should rise from the dead.'"

Monday, September 30

First Reading
ZECHARIAH 8:1-8

This word of the LORD of hosts came:

Thus says the LORD of hosts:

I am intensely jealous for Zion,
stirred to jealous wrath for her.
Thus says the LORD:
I will return to Zion,
and I will dwell within Jerusalem;
Jerusalem shall be called the faithful city,
and the mountain of the LORD of hosts,
the holy mountain.

Thus says the LORD of hosts: Old men and old women, each with staff in hand because of old age, shall again sit in the streets of Jerusalem. The city shall be filled with boys and girls playing in its streets. Thus says the LORD of hosts: Even if this should seem impossible in the eyes of the remnant of this people, shall it in those days be impossible in my eyes also, says the LORD of hosts? Thus says the LORD of hosts: Lo, I will rescue my people from the land of the rising sun, and from the land of the setting sun. I will bring them back to dwell within Jerusalem. They shall be my people, and I will be their God, with faithfulness and justice.

Responsorial Psalm

PSALM 102:16-18, 19-21, 29 and 22-23

R. The Lord will build up Zion again, and appear in all his glory.

The nations shall revere your name, O LORD,
  and all the kings of the earth your glory,
When the LORD has rebuilt Zion
  and appeared in his glory;
When he has regarded the prayer of the destitute,
  and not despised their prayer. **R.**

Let this be written for the generation to come,
  and let his future creatures praise the LORD:
"The LORD looked down from his holy height,
  from heaven he beheld the earth,
To hear the groaning of the prisoners,
  to release those doomed to die." **R.**

The children of your servants shall abide,
  and their posterity shall continue in your presence.
That the name of the LORD may be declared in Zion;
  and his praise, in Jerusalem,
When the peoples gather together,
  and the kingdoms, to serve the LORD. **R.**

Gospel

LUKE 9:46-50

An argument arose among the disciples about which of them was the greatest. Jesus realized the intention of their hearts and took a child and placed it by his side and said to them, "Whoever receives this child in my name receives me, and whoever receives me receives the one who sent me. For the one who is least among all of you is the one who is the greatest."

Then John said in reply, "Master, we saw someone casting out demons in your name and we tried to prevent him because he does not follow in our company." Jesus said to him, "Do not prevent him, for whoever is not against you is for you."

OCTOBER

Tuesday, October 1

First Reading
ZECHARIAH 8:20-23

Thus says the LORD of hosts: There shall yet come peoples, the inhabitants of many cities; and the inhabitants of one city shall approach those of another, and say, "Come! let us go to implore the favor of the LORD"; and, "I too will go to seek the LORD." Many peoples and strong nations shall come to seek the LORD of hosts in Jerusalem and to implore the favor of the LORD. Thus says the LORD of hosts: In those days ten men of every nationality, speaking different tongues, shall take hold, yes, take hold of every Jew by the edge of his garment and say,

"Let us go with you, for we have heard that God is with you."

Responsorial Psalm
PSALM 87:1b-3, 4-5, 6-7
R. God is with us.

His foundation upon the holy mountains
the LORD loves:
The gates of Zion,
more than any dwelling of Jacob.
Glorious things are said of you,
O city of God! **R.**
I tell of Egypt and Babylon
among those that know the LORD;
Of Philistia, Tyre, Ethiopia:
"This man was born there."
And of Zion they shall say:
"One and all were born in her;
And he who has established her
is the Most High LORD." **R.**
They shall note, when the peoples are enrolled:
"This man was born there."
And all shall sing, in their festive dance:
"My home is within you." **R.**

Gospel
Luke 9:51-56

When the days for Jesus to be taken up were fulfilled, he resolutely determined to journey to Jerusalem, and he sent messengers ahead of him. On the way they entered a Samaritan village to prepare for his reception there, but they would not welcome him because the destination of his journey was Jerusalem. When the disciples James and John saw this they asked, "Lord, do you want us to call down fire from heaven to consume them?" Jesus turned and rebuked them, and they journeyed to another village.

Wednesday, October 2

The Holy Guardian Angels

First Reading

NEHEMIAH 2:1-8

In the month Nisan of the twentieth year of King Artaxerxes, when the wine was in my charge, I took some and offered it to the king. As I had never before been sad in his presence, the king asked me, "Why do you look sad? If you are not sick, you must be sad at heart." Though I was seized with great fear, I answered the king: "May the king live forever! How could I not look sad when the city where my ancestors are buried lies in ruins, and its gates have been eaten out by fire?" The king asked me, "What is it, then, that you wish?" I prayed to the God of heaven and then answered the king: "If it please the king, and if your servant is deserving of your favor, send me to Judah, to the city of my ancestors' graves, to rebuild it." Then the king, and the queen seated beside him, asked me how long my journey would take and when I would return. I set a date that was acceptable to him, and the king agreed that I might go.

I asked the king further: "If it please the king, let letters be given to me for the governors of West-of-Euphrates, that they may afford me safe-conduct until I arrive in Judah; also a letter for Asaph, the keeper of the royal park, that he may give me wood for timbering the gates of the temple-citadel and for the city wall and the house that I shall occupy." The king granted my requests, for the favoring hand of my God was upon me.

Responsorial Psalm

PSALM 137:1-2, 3, 4-5, 6

R. Let my tongue be silenced if I ever forget you!

By the streams of Babylon
  we sat and wept
  when we remembered Zion.
On the aspens of that land
  we hung up our harps. **R.**

Though there our captors asked of us
the lyrics of our songs,
And our despoilers urged us to be joyous:
"Sing for us the songs of Zion!" **R.**
How could we sing a song of the LORD
in a foreign land?
If I forget you, Jerusalem,
may my right hand be forgotten! **R.**
May my tongue cleave to my palate
if I remember you not,
If I place not Jerusalem
ahead of my joy. **R.**

Gospel
MATTHEW 18:1-5, 10

The disciples approached Jesus and said, "Who is the greatest in the Kingdom of heaven?" He called a child over, placed it in their midst, and said, "Amen, I say to you, unless you turn and become like children, you will not enter the Kingdom of heaven. Whoever humbles himself like this child is the greatest in the Kingdom of heaven. And whoever receives one child such as this in my name receives me.

"See that you do not despise one of these little ones, for I say to you that their angels in heaven always look upon the face of my heavenly Father."

Thursday, October 3

First Reading
NEHEMIAH 8:1-4a, 5-6, 7b-12

The whole people gathered as one in the open space before the Water Gate, and they called upon Ezra the scribe to bring forth the book of the law of Moses which the LORD prescribed for Israel. On the first day of the seventh month, therefore, Ezra the priest brought the law before the assembly, which consisted of men, women, and those children old enough to understand. Standing at one end of the open place that was before the Water Gate, he read out of the book from daybreak until midday, in the presence of the men, the women, and those children old enough to understand; and all the people listened attentively to the book of the law. Ezra the scribe stood on a wooden platform that had been made for the occasion. He opened the scroll so that all the people might see it (for he was standing higher up than any of the people); and, as he opened it, all the people rose. Ezra blessed the LORD, the great God, and all the people, their hands raised high, answered, "Amen,

amen!" Then they bowed down and prostrated themselves before the LORD, their faces to the ground. As the people remained in their places, Ezra read plainly from the book of the law of God, interpreting it so that all could understand what was read. Then Nehemiah, that is, His Excellency, and Ezra the priest-scribe and the Levites who were instructing the people said to all the people: "Today is holy to the LORD your God. Do not be sad, and do not weep"—for all the people were weeping as they heard the words of the law. He said further: "Go, eat rich foods and drink sweet drinks, and allot portions to those who had nothing prepared; for today is holy to our LORD. Do not be saddened this day, for rejoicing in the LORD must be your strength!" And the Levites quieted all the people, saying, "Hush, for today is holy, and you must not be saddened." Then all the people went to eat and drink, to distribute portions, and to celebrate with great joy, for they understood the words that had been expounded to them.

Responsorial Psalm

PSALM 19:8, 9, 10, 11

R. The precepts of the Lord give joy to the heart.

The law of the LORD is perfect,
  refreshing the soul;
The decree of the LORD is trustworthy,
  giving wisdom to the simple. **R.**
The precepts of the LORD are right,
  rejoicing the heart;
The command of the LORD is clear,
  enlightening the eye. **R.**
The fear of the LORD is pure,
  enduring forever;
The ordinances of the LORD are true,
  all of them just. **R.**
They are more precious than gold,
  than a heap of purest gold;
Sweeter also than syrup
  or honey from the comb. **R.**

Gospel

LUKE 10:1-12

Jesus appointed seventy-two other disciples whom he sent ahead of him in pairs to every town and place he intended to visit. He said to them, "The harvest is abundant but the laborers are few; so ask the master of the harvest to send out laborers for his harvest. Go on your way; behold, I am sending you like lambs among wolves. Carry no money bag, no sack, no sandals; and greet no one along the way. Into whatever house you enter, first say, 'Peace to this household.' If a peaceful person lives there, your peace will rest on him; but if not, it will return to you. Stay in the same house and eat and drink what is offered to you, for the laborer deserves his payment. Do not move about from one house to another. Whatever town you enter and they welcome you, eat what is set before you, cure the sick in it and say to them, 'The Kingdom of God is at hand for you.' Whatever town you enter and they do not receive you, go out into the streets and say, 'The dust of your town that clings to our feet, even that we shake off against you.' Yet know this: the Kingdom of God is at hand. I tell you, it will be more tolerable for Sodom on that day than for that town."

Friday, October 4

First Reading

BARUCH 1:15-22

During the Babylonian captivity, the exiles prayed: "Justice is with the Lord, our God; and we today are flushed with shame, we men of Judah and citizens of Jerusalem, that we, with our kings and rulers and priests and prophets, and with our ancestors, have sinned in the Lord's sight and disobeyed him. We have neither heeded the voice of the Lord, our God, nor followed the precepts which the Lord set before us. From the time the Lord led our ancestors out of the land of Egypt until the present day, we have been disobedient to the Lord, our God, and only too ready to disregard his voice. And the evils and the curse that the Lord enjoined upon Moses, his servant, at the time he led our ancestors forth from the land of Egypt to give us the land flowing with milk and honey, cling to us even today. For we did not heed the voice of the Lord, our God, in all the words of the prophets whom he sent us, but each one of us went off after the devices of his own wicked heart, served other gods, and did evil in the sight of the Lord, our God."

Responsorial Psalm

PSALM 79:1b-2, 3-5, 8, 9

R. For the glory of your name, O Lord, deliver us.

O God, the nations have come into your inheritance;
they have defiled your holy temple,
they have laid Jerusalem in ruins.
They have given the corpses of your servants
as food to the birds of heaven,
the flesh of your faithful ones to the beasts of the earth. **R.**

They have poured out their blood like water
round about Jerusalem,
and there is no one to bury them.
We have become the reproach of our neighbors,
the scorn and derision of those around us.
O LORD, how long? Will you be angry forever?
Will your jealousy burn like fire? **R.**
Remember not against us the iniquities of the past;
may your compassion quickly come to us,
for we are brought very low. **R.**
Help us, O God our savior,
because of the glory of your name;
Deliver us and pardon our sins
for your name's sake. **R.**

Gospel
LUKE 10:13-16

Jesus said to them, "Woe to you, Chorazin! Woe to you, Bethsaida! For if the mighty deeds done in your midst had been done in Tyre and Sidon, they would long ago have repented, sitting in sackcloth and ashes. But it will be more tolerable for Tyre and Sidon at the judgment than for you. And as for you, Capernaum, 'Will you be exalted to heaven? You will go down to the netherworld.' Whoever listens to you listens to me. Whoever rejects you rejects me. And whoever rejects me rejects the one who sent me."

Saturday, October 5

First Reading
BARUCH 4:5-12, 27-29

Fear not, my people!
Remember, Israel,
You were sold to the nations
not for your destruction;
It was because you angered God
that you were handed over to your foes.
For you provoked your Maker
with sacrifices to demons, to no-gods;
You forsook the Eternal God who nourished you,
and you grieved Jerusalem who fostered you.
She indeed saw coming upon you
the anger of God; and she said:

"Hear, you neighbors of Zion!
God has brought great mourning upon me,
For I have seen the captivity
that the Eternal God has brought
upon my sons and daughters.
With joy I fostered them;
but with mourning and lament I let them go.
Let no one gloat over me, a widow,
bereft of many:
For the sins of my children I am left desolate,
because they turned from the law of God.

"Fear not, my children; call out to God!
He who brought this upon you will remember you.
As your hearts have been disposed to stray from God,
turn now ten times the more to seek him;
For he who has brought disaster upon you
will, in saving you, bring you back enduring joy."

Responsorial Psalm
PSALM 69:33-35, 36-37
R. The Lord listens to the poor.
"See, you lowly ones, and be glad;
you who seek God, may your hearts revive!
For the LORD hears the poor,
and his own who are in bonds he spurns not.
Let the heavens and the earth praise him,
the seas and whatever moves in them!" **R.**
For God will save Zion
and rebuild the cities of Judah.
They shall dwell in the land and own it,
and the descendants of his servants shall inherit it,
and those who love his name shall inhabit it. **R.**

Gospel
LUKE 10:17-24

The seventy-two disciples returned rejoicing and said to Jesus, "Lord, even the demons are subject to us because of your name." Jesus said, "I have observed Satan fall like lightning from the sky. Behold, I have given you the power 'to tread upon serpents' and scorpions and upon the full force of the enemy and nothing will harm you. Nevertheless, do not rejoice because the spirits are subject to you, but rejoice because your names are written in heaven."

At that very moment he rejoiced in the Holy Spirit and said, "I give you praise, Father, Lord of heaven and earth, for although you have hidden these things from the wise and the learned you have revealed them to the childlike. Yes, Father, such has been your gracious will. All things have been handed over to me by my Father. No one knows who the Son is except the Father, and who the Father is except the Son and anyone to whom the Son wishes to reveal him."

Turning to the disciples in private he said, "Blessed are the eyes that see what you see. For I say to you, many prophets and kings desired to see what you see, but did not see it, and to hear what you hear, but did not hear it."

Sunday, October 6

Twenty-seventh Sunday in Ordinary Time

First Reading
HABAKKUK 1:2-3; 2:2-4

How long, O LORD? I cry for help
  but you do not listen!
I cry out to you, "Violence!"
  but you do not intervene.
Why do you let me see ruin;
  why must I look at misery?
Destruction and violence are before me;
  there is strife, and clamorous discord.
Then the LORD answered me and said:
  Write down the vision clearly upon the tablets,
  so that one can read it readily.
For the vision still has its time,
  presses on to fulfillment, and will not disappoint;
if it delays, wait for it,
  it will surely come, it will not be late.
The rash one has no integrity;
  but the just one, because of his faith, shall live.

Responsorial Psalm
PSALM 95:1-2, 6-7, 8-9
R. If today you hear his voice, harden not your hearts.
Come, let us sing joyfully to the LORD;
  let us acclaim the Rock of our salvation.
Let us come into his presence with thanksgiving;
  let us joyfully sing psalms to him. **R.**

Come, let us bow down in worship;
  let us kneel before the LORD who made us.
For he is our God,
  and we are the people he shepherds, the flock he guides. **R.**
Oh, that today you would hear his voice:
  "Harden not your hearts as at Meribah,
  as in the day of Massah in the desert,
where your fathers tempted me;
  they tested me though they had seen my works." **R.**

Second Reading
2 TIMOTHY 1:6-8, 13-14

Beloved: I remind you, to stir into flame the gift of God that you have through the imposition of my hands. For God did not give us a spirit of cowardice but rather of power and love and self-control. So do not be ashamed of your testimony to our Lord, nor of me, a prisoner for his sake; but bear your share of hardship for the gospel with the strength that comes from God.

Take as your norm the sound words that you heard from me, in the faith and love that are in Christ Jesus. Guard this rich trust with the help of the Holy Spirit that dwells within us.

Gospel
LUKE 17:5-10

The apostles said to the Lord, "Increase our faith." The Lord replied, "If you have faith the size of a mustard seed, you would say to this mulberry tree, 'Be uprooted and planted in the sea,' and it would obey you.

"Who among you would say to your servant who has just come in from plowing or tending sheep in the field, 'Come here immediately and take your place at table'? Would he not rather say to him, 'Prepare something for me to eat. Put on your apron and wait on me while I eat and drink. You may eat and drink when I am finished'? Is he grateful to that servant because he did what was commanded? So should it be with you. When you have done all you have been commanded, say, 'We are unprofitable servants; we have done what we were obliged to do.'"

Monday, October 7

First Reading
JONAH 1:1–2:2, 11

This is the word of the LORD that came to Jonah, son of Amittai:

"Set out for the great city of Nineveh, and preach against it; their wickedness has come up before me." But Jonah made ready to flee to

Tarshish away from the LORD. He went down to Joppa, found a ship going to Tarshish, paid the fare, and went aboard to journey with them to Tarshish, away from the LORD.

The LORD, however, hurled a violent wind upon the sea, and in the furious tempest that arose the ship was on the point of breaking up. Then the mariners became frightened and each one cried to his god. To lighten the ship for themselves, they threw its cargo into the sea. Meanwhile, Jonah had gone down into the hold of the ship, and lay there fast asleep. The captain came to him and said, "What are you doing asleep? Rise up, call upon your God! Perhaps God will be mindful of us so that we may not perish."

Then they said to one another, "Come, let us cast lots to find out on whose account we have met with this misfortune." So they cast lots, and thus singled out Jonah. "Tell us," they said, "what is your business? Where do you come from? What is your country, and to what people do you belong?" Jonah answered them, "I am a Hebrew, I worship the LORD, the God of heaven, who made the sea and the dry land."

Now the men were seized with great fear and said to him, "How could you do such a thing!"—They knew that he was fleeing from the LORD, because he had told them.—They asked, "What shall we do with you, that the sea may quiet down for us?" For the sea was growing more and more turbulent. Jonah said to them, "Pick me up and throw me into the sea, that it may quiet down for you; since I know it is because of me that this violent storm has come upon you."

Still the men rowed hard to regain the land, but they could not, for the sea grew ever more turbulent. Then they cried to the LORD: "We beseech you, O LORD, let us not perish for taking this man's life; do not charge us with shedding innocent blood, for you, LORD, have done as you saw fit." Then they took Jonah and threw him into the sea, and the sea's raging abated. Struck with great fear of the LORD, the men offered sacrifice and made vows to him.

But the LORD sent a large fish, that swallowed Jonah; and Jonah remained in the belly of the fish three days and three nights. From the belly of the fish Jonah prayed to the LORD, his God. Then the LORD commanded the fish to spew Jonah upon the shore.

Responsorial Psalm

JONAH 2:3, 4, 5, 8

R. You will rescue my life from the pit, O Lord.

Out of my distress I called to the LORD,
  and he answered me;
From the midst of the nether world I cried for help,
  and you heard my voice. **R.**

For you cast me into the deep, into the heart of the sea,
and the flood enveloped me;
All your breakers and your billows
passed over me. **R.**
Then I said, "I am banished from your sight!
yet would I again look upon your holy temple." **R.**
When my soul fainted within me,
I remembered the LORD;
My prayer reached you
in your holy temple. **R.**

Gospel
LUKE 10:25-37

There was a scholar of the law who stood up to test Jesus and said, "Teacher, what must I do to inherit eternal life?" Jesus said to him, "What is written in the law? How do you read it?" He said in reply, "You shall love the Lord, your God, with all your heart, with all your being, with all your strength, and with all your mind, and your neighbor as yourself." He replied to him, "You have answered correctly; do this and you will live."

But because he wished to justify himself, he said to Jesus, "And who is my neighbor?" Jesus replied, "A man fell victim to robbers as he went down from Jerusalem to Jericho. They stripped and beat him and went off leaving him half-dead. A priest happened to be going down that road, but when he saw him, he passed by on the opposite side. Likewise a Levite came to the place, and when he saw him, he passed by on the opposite side. But a Samaritan traveler who came upon him was moved with compassion at the sight. He approached the victim, poured oil and wine over his wounds and bandaged them. Then he lifted him up on his own animal, took him to an inn, and cared for him. The next day he took out two silver coins and gave them to the innkeeper with the instruction, 'Take care of him. If you spend more than what I have given you, I shall repay you on my way back.' Which of these three, in your opinion, was neighbor to the robbers' victim?" He answered, "The one who treated him with mercy." Jesus said to him, "Go and do likewise."

Tuesday, October 8

First Reading
JONAH 3:1-10

The word of the LORD came to Jonah a second time: "Set out for the great city of Nineveh, and announce to it the message that I will tell you." So Jonah made ready and went to Nineveh, according to the LORD's bidding. Now Nineveh was an enormously large city; it took three days to go through it. Jonah began his journey through the city, and had gone but a single day's walk announcing, "Forty days more and Nineveh shall be destroyed," when the people of Nineveh believed God; they proclaimed a fast and all of them, great and small, put on sackcloth.

When the news reached the king of Nineveh, he rose from his throne, laid aside his robe, covered himself with sackcloth, and sat in the ashes. Then he had this proclaimed throughout Nineveh, by decree of the king and his nobles: "Neither man nor beast, neither cattle nor sheep, shall taste anything; they shall not eat, nor shall they drink water. Man and beast shall be covered with sackcloth and call loudly to God; every man shall turn from his evil way and from the violence he has in hand. Who knows, God may relent and forgive, and withhold his blazing wrath, so that we shall not perish." When God saw by their actions how they turned from their evil way, he repented of the evil that he had threatened to do to them; he did not carry it out.

Responsorial Psalm

PSALM 130:1b-2, 3-4ab, 7-8

R. If you, O Lord, mark iniquities, who can stand?

Out of the depths I cry to you, O LORD;
LORD, hear my voice!
Let your ears be attentive
to my voice in supplication. **R.**

If you, O LORD, mark iniquities,
LORD, who can stand?
But with you is forgiveness,
that you may be revered. **R.**

Let Israel wait for the LORD,
For with the LORD is kindness
and with him is plenteous redemption;
And he will redeem Israel
from all their iniquities. **R.**

Gospel

LUKE 10:38-42

Jesus entered a village where a woman whose name was Martha welcomed him. She had a sister named Mary who sat beside the Lord at his feet listening to him speak. Martha, burdened with much serving, came to him and said, "Lord, do you not care that my sister has left me by myself to do the serving? Tell her to help me." The Lord said to her in reply, "Martha, Martha, you are anxious and worried about many things. There is need of only one thing. Mary has chosen the better part and it will not be taken from her."

Wednesday, October 9

First Reading

JONAH 4:1-11

Jonah was greatly displeased and became angry that God did not carry out the evil he threatened against Nineveh. He prayed, "I beseech you, LORD, is not this what I said while I was still in my own country? This is why I fled at first to Tarshish. I knew that you are a gracious and merciful God, slow to anger, rich in clemency, loathe to punish. And now, LORD, please take my life from me; for it is better for me to die than to live." But the LORD asked, "Have you reason to be angry?"

Jonah then left the city for a place to the east of it, where he built himself a hut and waited under it in the shade, to see what would happen to the city. And when the LORD God provided a gourd plant that grew up over Jonah's head, giving shade that relieved him of any discomfort, Jonah was very happy over the plant. But the next morning at dawn God sent a worm that attacked the plant, so that it withered. And when the sun arose, God sent a burning east wind; and the sun beat upon Jonah's head till he became faint. Then Jonah asked for death, saying, "I would be better off dead than alive."

But God said to Jonah, "Have you reason to be angry over the plant?" "I have reason to be angry," Jonah answered, "angry enough to die." Then the LORD said, "You are concerned over the plant which cost you no labor and which you did not raise; it came up in one night and in one night it perished. And should I not be concerned over Nineveh, the great city, in which there are more than a hundred and twenty thousand persons who cannot distinguish their right hand from their left, not to mention the many cattle?"

Responsorial Psalm

PSALM 86:3-4, 5-6, 9-10

R. Lord, you are merciful and gracious.

Have mercy on me, O Lord,
for to you I call all the day.
Gladden the soul of your servant,
for to you, O Lord, I lift up my soul. **R.**
For you, O Lord, are good and forgiving,
abounding in kindness to all who call upon you.
Hearken, O LORD, to my prayer
and attend to the sound of my pleading. **R.**
All the nations you have made shall come
and worship you, O Lord,
and glorify your name.

For you are great, and you do wondrous deeds;
you alone are God. **R.**

Gospel
LUKE 11:1-4

Jesus was praying in a certain place, and when he had finished, one of his disciples said to him, "Lord, teach us to pray just as John taught his disciples." He said to them, "When you pray, say:

Father, hallowed be your name,
your Kingdom come.
Give us each day our daily bread
and forgive us our sins
for we ourselves forgive everyone in debt to us,
and do not subject us to the final test."

Thursday, October 10

First Reading
MALACHI 3:13-20b

You have defied me in word, says the LORD,
yet you ask, "What have we spoken against you?"
You have said, "It is vain to serve God,
and what do we profit by keeping his command,
And going about in penitential dress
in awe of the LORD of hosts?
Rather must we call the proud blessed;
for indeed evildoers prosper,
and even tempt God with impunity."
Then they who fear the LORD spoke with one another,
and the LORD listened attentively;
And a record book was written before him
of those who fear the LORD and trust in his name.
And they shall be mine, says the LORD of hosts,
my own special possession, on the day I take action.
And I will have compassion on them,
as a man has compassion on his son who serves him.
Then you will again see the distinction
between the just and the wicked;
Between the one who serves God,
and the one who does not serve him.
For lo, the day is coming, blazing like an oven,
when all the proud and all evildoers will be stubble,

And the day that is coming will set them on fire,
leaving them neither root nor branch,
says the LORD of hosts.
But for you who fear my name, there will arise
the sun of justice with its healing rays.

Responsorial Psalm
PSALM 1:1-2, 3, 4 and 6
R. Blessed are they who hope in the Lord.

Blessed the man who follows not
the counsel of the wicked
Nor walks in the way of sinners,
nor sits in the company of the insolent,
But delights in the law of the LORD
and meditates on his law day and night. **R.**
He is like a tree
planted near running water,
That yields its fruit in due season,
and whose leaves never fade.
Whatever he does, prospers. **R.**
Not so the wicked, not so;
they are like chaff which the wind drives away.
For the LORD watches over the way of the just,
but the way of the wicked vanishes. **R.**

Gospel
LUKE 11:5-13

Jesus said to his disciples: "Suppose one of you has a friend to whom he goes at midnight and says, 'Friend, lend me three loaves of bread, for a friend of mine has arrived at my house from a journey and I have nothing to offer him,' and he says in reply from within, 'Do not bother me; the door has already been locked and my children and I are already in bed. I cannot get up to give you anything.' I tell you, if he does not get up to give him the loaves because of their friendship, he will get up to give him whatever he needs because of his persistence.

"And I tell you, ask and you will receive; seek and you will find; knock and the door will be opened to you. For everyone who asks, receives; and the one who seeks, finds; and to the one who knocks, the door will be opened. What father among you would hand his son a snake when he asks for a fish? Or hand him a scorpion when he asks for an egg? If you then, who are wicked, know how to give good gifts to your children, how much more will the Father in heaven give the Holy Spirit to those who ask him?"

Friday, October 11

First Reading

JOEL 1:13-15; 2:1-2

Gird yourselves and weep, O priests!
wail, O ministers of the altar!
Come, spend the night in sackcloth,
O ministers of my God!
The house of your God is deprived
of offering and libation.
Proclaim a fast,
call an assembly;
Gather the elders,
all who dwell in the land,
Into the house of the LORD, your God,
and cry to the LORD!

Alas, the day!
for near is the day of the LORD,
and it comes as ruin from the Almighty.

Blow the trumpet in Zion,
sound the alarm on my holy mountain!
Let all who dwell in the land tremble,
for the day of the LORD is coming;
Yes, it is near, a day of darkness and of gloom,
a day of clouds and somberness!
Like dawn spreading over the mountains,
a people numerous and mighty!
Their like has not been from of old,
nor will it be after them,
even to the years of distant generations.

Responsorial Psalm

PSALM 9:2-3, 6 and 16, 8-9

R. The Lord will judge the world with justice.

I will give thanks to you, O LORD, with all my heart;
I will declare all your wondrous deeds.
I will be glad and exult in you;
I will sing praise to your name, Most High. **R.**
You rebuked the nations and destroyed the wicked;
their name you blotted out forever and ever.
The nations are sunk in the pit they have made;
in the snare they set, their foot is caught. **R.**

But the LORD sits enthroned forever;
he has set up his throne for judgment.
He judges the world with justice;
he governs the peoples with equity. **R.**

Gospel
LUKE 11:15-26

When Jesus had driven out a demon, some of the crowd said: "By the power of Beelzebul, the prince of demons, he drives out demons." Others, to test him, asked him for a sign from heaven. But he knew their thoughts and said to them, "Every kingdom divided against itself will be laid waste and house will fall against house. And if Satan is divided against himself, how will his kingdom stand? For you say that it is by Beelzebul that I drive out demons. If I, then, drive out demons by Beelzebul, by whom do your own people drive them out? Therefore they will be your judges. But if it is by the finger of God that I drive out demons, then the Kingdom of God has come upon you. When a strong man fully armed guards his palace, his possessions are safe. But when one stronger than he attacks and overcomes him, he takes away the armor on which he relied and distributes the spoils. Whoever is not with me is against me, and whoever does not gather with me scatters.

"When an unclean spirit goes out of someone, it roams through arid regions searching for rest but, finding none, it says, 'I shall return to my home from which I came.' But upon returning, it finds it swept clean and put in order. Then it goes and brings back seven other spirits more wicked than itself who move in and dwell there, and the last condition of that man is worse than the first."

Saturday, October 12

First Reading
JOEL 4:12-21

Thus says the LORD:
Let the nations bestir themselves and come up
to the Valley of Jehoshaphat;
For there will I sit in judgment
upon all the neighboring nations.

Apply the sickle,
for the harvest is ripe;
Come and tread,
for the wine press is full;

The vats overflow,
for great is their malice.
Crowd upon crowd
in the valley of decision;
For near is the day of the LORD
in the valley of decision.
Sun and moon are darkened,
and the stars withhold their brightness.
The LORD roars from Zion,
and from Jerusalem raises his voice;
The heavens and the earth quake,
but the LORD is a refuge to his people,
a stronghold to the children of Israel.

Then shall you know that I, the LORD, am your God,
dwelling on Zion, my holy mountain;
Jerusalem shall be holy,
and strangers shall pass through her no more.
And then, on that day,
the mountains shall drip new wine,
and the hills shall flow with milk;
And the channels of Judah
shall flow with water:
A fountain shall issue from the house of the LORD,
to water the Valley of Shittim.
Egypt shall be a waste,
and Edom a desert waste,
Because of violence done to the people of Judah,
because they shed innocent blood in their land.
But Judah shall abide forever,
and Jerusalem for all generations.
I will avenge their blood,
and not leave it unpunished.
The LORD dwells in Zion.

Responsorial Psalm
PSALM 97:1-2, 5-6, 11-12
R. Rejoice in the Lord, you just!
The LORD is king; let the earth rejoice;
let the many isles be glad.
Clouds and darkness are round about him,
justice and judgment are the foundation of his throne. **R.**
The mountains melt like wax before the LORD,
before the LORD of all the earth.

The heavens proclaim his justice,
 and all peoples see his glory. **R.**
Light dawns for the just;
 and gladness, for the upright of heart.
Be glad in the LORD, you just,
 and give thanks to his holy name. **R.**

Gospel
LUKE 11:27-28

While Jesus was speaking, a woman from the crowd called out and said to him, "Blessed is the womb that carried you and the breasts at which you nursed." He replied, "Rather, blessed are those who hear the word of God and observe it."

Sunday, October 13

Twenty-eighth Sunday in Ordinary Time

First Reading
2 KINGS 5:14-17

Naaman went down and plunged into the Jordan seven times at the word of Elisha, the man of God. His flesh became again like the flesh of a little child, and he was clean of his leprosy.

Naaman returned with his whole retinue to the man of God. On his arrival he stood before Elisha and said, "Now I know that there is no God in all the earth, except in Israel. Please accept a gift from your servant."

Elisha replied, "As the LORD lives whom I serve, I will not take it"; and despite Naaman's urging, he still refused. Naaman said: "If you will not accept, please let me, your servant, have two mule-loads of earth, for I will no longer offer holocaust or sacrifice to any other god except to the LORD."

Responsorial Psalm
PSALM 98:1, 2-3, 3-4
R. The Lord has revealed to the nations his saving power.

Sing to the LORD a new song,
 for he has done wondrous deeds;
his right hand has won victory for him,
 his holy arm. **R.**
The LORD has made his salvation known:
 in the sight of the nations he has revealed his justice.

He has remembered his kindness and his faithfulness
toward the house of Israel. **R.**
All the ends of the earth have seen
the salvation by our God.
Sing joyfully to the LORD, all you lands:
break into song; sing praise. **R.**

Second Reading
2 TIMOTHY 2:8-13

Beloved: Remember Jesus Christ, raised from the dead, a descendant of David: such is my gospel, for which I am suffering, even to the point of chains, like a criminal. But the word of God is not chained. Therefore, I bear with everything for the sake of those who are chosen, so that they too may obtain the salvation that is in Christ Jesus, together with eternal glory. This saying is trustworthy:

If we have died with him
we shall also live with him;
if we persevere
we shall also reign with him.
But if we deny him
he will deny us.
If we are unfaithful
he remains faithful,
for he cannot deny himself.

Gospel
LUKE 17:11-19

As Jesus continued his journey to Jerusalem, he traveled through Samaria and Galilee. As he was entering a village, ten lepers met him. They stood at a distance from him and raised their voices, saying, "Jesus, Master! Have pity on us!" And when he saw them, he said, "Go show yourselves to the priests." As they were going they were cleansed. And one of them, realizing he had been healed, returned, glorifying God in a loud voice; and he fell at the feet of Jesus and thanked him. He was a Samaritan. Jesus said in reply, "Ten were cleansed, were they not? Where are the other nine? Has none but this foreigner returned to give thanks to God?" Then he said to him, "Stand up and go; your faith has saved you."

Monday, October 14

First Reading
ROMANS 1:1-7

Paul, a slave of Christ Jesus, called to be an Apostle and set apart for the Gospel of God, which he promised previously through his prophets in the holy Scriptures, the Gospel about his Son, descended from David according to the flesh, but established as Son of God in power according to the Spirit of holiness through resurrection from the dead, Jesus Christ our Lord. Through him we have received the grace of apostleship, to bring about the obedience of faith, for the sake of his name, among all the Gentiles, among whom are you also, who are called to belong to Jesus Christ; to all the beloved of God in Rome, called to be holy. Grace to you and peace from God our Father and the Lord Jesus Christ.

Responsorial Psalm
PSALM 98:1bcde, 2-3ab, 3cd-4
R. The Lord has made known his salvation.

Sing to the LORD a new song,
for he has done wondrous deeds;
His right hand has won victory for him,
his holy arm. **R.**
The LORD has made his salvation known:
in the sight of the nations he has revealed his justice.
He has remembered his kindness and his faithfulness
toward the house of Israel. **R.**
All the ends of the earth have seen
the salvation by our God.
Sing joyfully to the LORD, all you lands;
break into song; sing praise. **R.**

Gospel
LUKE 11:29-32

While still more people gathered in the crowd, Jesus said to them, "This generation is an evil generation; it seeks a sign, but no sign will be given it, except the sign of Jonah. Just as Jonah became a sign to the Ninevites, so will the Son of Man be to this generation. At the judgment the queen of the south will rise with the men of this generation and she will condemn them, because she came from the ends of the earth to hear the wisdom of Solomon, and there is something greater than Solomon here. At the judgment the men of Nineveh will arise with this generation and condemn it, because at the preaching of Jonah they repented, and there is something greater than Jonah here."

Tuesday, October 15

First Reading
ROMANS 1:16-25

Brothers and sisters: I am not ashamed of the Gospel. It is the power of God for the salvation of everyone who believes: for Jew first, and then Greek. For in it is revealed the righteousness of God from faith to faith; as it is written, "The one who is righteous by faith will live."

The wrath of God is indeed being revealed from heaven against every impiety and wickedness of those who suppress the truth by their wickedness. For what can be known about God is evident to them, because God made it evident to them. Ever since the creation of the world, his invisible attributes of eternal power and divinity have been able to be understood and perceived in what he has made. As a result, they have no excuse; for although they knew God they did not accord him glory as God or give him thanks. Instead, they became vain in their reasoning, and their senseless minds were darkened. While claiming to be wise, they became fools and exchanged the glory of the immortal God for the likeness of an image of mortal man or of birds or of four-legged animals or of snakes.

Therefore, God handed them over to impurity through the lusts of their hearts for the mutual degradation of their bodies. They exchanged the truth of God for a lie and revered and worshiped the creature rather than the creator, who is blessed forever. Amen.

Responsorial Psalm
PSALM 19:2-3, 4-5
R. The heavens proclaim the glory of God.

The heavens declare the glory of God,
and the firmament proclaims his handiwork.
Day pours out the word to day,
and night to night imparts knowledge. **R.**
Not a word nor a discourse
whose voice is not heard;
Through all the earth their voice resounds,
and to the ends of the world, their message. **R.**

Gospel
LUKE 11:37-41

After Jesus had spoken, a Pharisee invited him to dine at his home. He entered and reclined at table to eat. The Pharisee was amazed to see that he did not observe the prescribed washing before the meal. The Lord said to him, "Oh you Pharisees! Although you cleanse the outside of the cup and the dish, inside you are filled with plunder and evil. You fools! Did not the maker of the outside also make the inside? But as to what is within, give alms, and behold, everything will be clean for you."

Wednesday, October 16

First Reading

ROMANS 2:1-11

You, O man, are without excuse, every one of you who passes judgment. For by the standard by which you judge another you condemn yourself, since you, the judge, do the very same things. We know that the judgment of God on those who do such things is true. Do you suppose, then, you who judge those who engage in such things and yet do them yourself, that you will escape the judgment of God? Or do you hold his priceless kindness, forbearance, and patience in low esteem, unaware that the kindness of God would lead you to repentance? By your stubbornness and impenitent heart, you are storing up wrath for yourself for the day of wrath and revelation of the just judgment of God, who will repay everyone according to his works, eternal life to those who seek glory, honor, and immortality through perseverance in good works, but wrath and fury to those who selfishly disobey the truth and obey wickedness. Yes, affliction and distress will come upon everyone who does evil, Jew first and then Greek. But there will be glory, honor, and peace for everyone who does good, Jew first and then Greek. There is no partiality with God.

Responsorial Psalm

PSALM 62:2-3, 6-7, 9

R. Lord, you give back to everyone according to his works.

Only in God is my soul at rest;
  from him comes my salvation.
He only is my rock and my salvation,
  my stronghold; I shall not be disturbed at all. **R.**
Only in God be at rest, my soul,
  for from him comes my hope.
He only is my rock and my salvation,
  my stronghold; I shall not be disturbed. **R.**
Trust in him at all times, O my people!
  Pour out your hearts before him;
  God is our refuge! **R.**

Gospel
LUKE 11:42-46

The Lord said: "Woe to you Pharisees! You pay tithes of mint and of rue and of every garden herb, but you pay no attention to judgment and to love for God. These you should have done, without overlooking the others. Woe to you Pharisees! You love the seat of honor in synagogues and greetings in marketplaces. Woe to you! You are like unseen graves over which people unknowingly walk."

Then one of the scholars of the law said to him in reply, "Teacher, by saying this you are insulting us too." And he said, "Woe also to you scholars of the law! You impose on people burdens hard to carry, but you yourselves do not lift one finger to touch them."

Thursday, October 17

First Reading
ROMANS 3:21-30

Brothers and sisters: Now the righteousness of God has been manifested apart from the law, though testified to by the law and the prophets, the righteousness of God through faith in Jesus Christ for all who believe. For there is no distinction; all have sinned and are deprived of the glory of God. They are justified freely by his grace through the redemption in Christ Jesus, whom God set forth as an expiation, through faith, by his Blood, to prove his righteousness because of the forgiveness of sins previously committed, through the forbearance of God—to prove his righteousness in the present time, that he might be righteous and justify the one who has faith in Jesus.

What occasion is there then for boasting? It is ruled out. On what principle, that of works? No, rather on the principle of faith. For we consider that a person is justified by faith apart from works of the law. Does God belong to Jews alone? Does he not belong to Gentiles, too? Yes, also to Gentiles, for God is one and will justify the circumcised on the basis of faith and the uncircumcised through faith.

Responsorial Psalm
PSALM 130:1b-2, 3-4, 5-6ab
R. With the Lord there is mercy, and fullness of redemption.
Out of the depths I cry to you, O LORD;
  LORD, hear my voice!
Let your ears be attentive
  to my voice in supplication. **R.**
If you, O LORD, mark iniquities,
  LORD, who can stand?

But with you is forgiveness,
  that you may be revered. **R.**
I trust in the LORD;
  my soul trusts in his word.
My soul waits for the LORD
  more than sentinels wait for the dawn. **R.**

Gospel
LUKE 11:47-54
The Lord said: "Woe to you who build the memorials of the prophets whom your fathers killed. Consequently, you bear witness and give consent to the deeds of your ancestors, for they killed them and you do the building. Therefore, the wisdom of God said, 'I will send to them prophets and Apostles; some of them they will kill and persecute' in order that this generation might be charged with the blood of all the prophets shed since the foundation of the world, from the blood of Abel to the blood of Zechariah who died between the altar and the temple building. Yes, I tell you, this generation will be charged with their blood! Woe to you, scholars of the law! You have taken away the key of knowledge. You yourselves did not enter and you stopped those trying to enter." When Jesus left, the scribes and Pharisees began to act with hostility toward him and to interrogate him about many things, for they were plotting to catch him at something he might say.

Friday, October 18

Saint Luke, Evangelist

First Reading
2 TIMOTHY 4:10-17b
Beloved: Demas, enamored of the present world, deserted me and went to Thessalonica, Crescens to Galatia, and Titus to Dalmatia. Luke is the only one with me. Get Mark and bring him with you, for he is helpful to me in the ministry. I have sent Tychicus to Ephesus. When you come, bring the cloak I left with Carpus in Troas, the papyrus rolls, and especially the parchments.

Alexander the coppersmith did me a great deal of harm; the Lord will repay him according to his deeds. You too be on guard against him, for he has strongly resisted our preaching.

At my first defense no one appeared on my behalf, but everyone deserted me. May it not be held against them! But the Lord stood by me and gave me strength, so that through me the proclamation might be completed and all the Gentiles might hear it.

Responsorial Psalm
PSALM 145:10-11, 12-13, 17-18
R. Your friends make known, O Lord, the glorious splendor of your Kingdom.

Let all your works give you thanks, O LORD,
and let your faithful ones bless you.
Let them discourse of the glory of your Kingdom
and speak of your might. **R.**
Making known to men your might
and the glorious splendor of your Kingdom.
Your Kingdom is a Kingdom for all ages,
and your dominion endures through all generations. **R.**
The LORD is just in all his ways
and holy in all his works.
The LORD is near to all who call upon him,
to all who call upon him in truth **R.**

Gospel
LUKE 10:1-9

The Lord Jesus appointed seventy-two disciples whom he sent ahead of him in pairs to every town and place he intended to visit. He said to them, "The harvest is abundant but the laborers are few; so ask the master of the harvest to send out laborers for his harvest. Go on your way; behold, I am sending you like lambs among wolves. Carry no money bag, no sack, no sandals; and greet no one along the way. Into whatever house you enter, first say, 'Peace to this household.' If a peaceful person lives there, your peace will rest on him; but if not, it will return to you. Stay in the same house and eat and drink what is offered to you, for the laborer deserves payment. Do not move about from one house to another. Whatever town you enter and they welcome you, eat what is set before you, cure the sick in it and say to them, 'The Kingdom of God is at hand for you.'"

Saturday, October 19

First Reading
ROMANS 4:13, 16-18

Brothers and sisters: It was not through the law that the promise was made to Abraham and his descendants that he would inherit the world, but through the righteousness that comes from faith. For this reason, it depends on faith, so that it may be a gift, and the promise may be guaranteed to all his descendants, not to those who only adhere to the law but to those who follow the faith of Abraham, who is the father of all of us, as it is written, *I have made you father of many nations*. He is our father in the sight of God, in whom he believed, who gives life to the dead and calls into being what does not exist. He believed, hoping against hope, that he would become *the father of many nations*, according to what was said, *Thus shall your descendants be*.

Responsorial Psalm

PSALM 105:6-7, 8-9, 42-43

R. The Lord remembers his covenant for ever.

You descendants of Abraham, his servants,
sons of Jacob, his chosen ones!
He, the LORD, is our God;
throughout the earth his judgments prevail. **R.**
He remembers forever his covenant
which he made binding for a thousand generations—
Which he entered into with Abraham
and by his oath to Isaac. **R.**
For he remembered his holy word
to his servant Abraham.
And he led forth his people with joy;
with shouts of joy, his chosen ones. **R.**

Gospel

LUKE 12:8-12

Jesus said to his disciples: "I tell you, everyone who acknowledges me before others the Son of Man will acknowledge before the angels of God. But whoever denies me before others will be denied before the angels of God.

"Everyone who speaks a word against the Son of Man will be forgiven, but the one who blasphemes against the Holy Spirit will not be forgiven. When they take you before synagogues and before rulers and authorities, do not worry about how or what your defense will be or about what you are to say. For the Holy Spirit will teach you at that moment what you should say."

Sunday, October 20

Twenty-ninth Sunday in Ordinary Time

First Reading

EXODUS 17:8-13

In those days, Amalek came and waged war against Israel. Moses, therefore, said to Joshua, "Pick out certain men, and tomorrow go out and engage Amalek in battle. I will be standing on top of the hill with the staff of God in my hand." So Joshua did as Moses told him: he engaged Amalek in battle after Moses had climbed to the top of the hill with Aaron and Hur. As long as Moses kept his hands raised up, Israel had the better of the fight, but when he let his hands rest, Amalek had the better of the fight. Moses' hands, however, grew tired; so they put a rock in place for him to sit on. Meanwhile Aaron and Hur supported his hands, one on one side and one on the other, so that his hands remained steady till sunset. And Joshua mowed down Amalek and his people with the edge of the sword.

Responsorial Psalm

PSALM 121:1-2, 3-4, 5-6, 7-8

R. Our help is from the Lord, who made heaven and earth.

I lift up my eyes toward the mountains;
 whence shall help come to me?
My help is from the LORD,
 who made heaven and earth. **R.**
May he not suffer your foot to slip;
 may he slumber not who guards you:
indeed he neither slumbers nor sleeps,
 the guardian of Israel. **R.**
The LORD is your guardian; the LORD is your shade;
 he is beside you at your right hand.
The sun shall not harm you by day,
 nor the moon by night. **R.**
The LORD will guard you from all evil;
 he will guard your life.
The LORD will guard your coming and your going,
 both now and forever. **R.**

Second Reading

2 TIMOTHY 3:14–4:2

Beloved: Remain faithful to what you have learned and believed, because you know from whom you learned it, and that from infancy you have known the sacred Scriptures, which are capable of giving you wisdom for salvation through faith in Christ Jesus. All Scripture is inspired by God and is useful for teaching, for refutation, for correction, and for training in righteousness, so that one who belongs to God may be competent, equipped for every good work.

I charge you in the presence of God and of Christ Jesus, who will judge the living and the dead, and by his appearing and his kingly power: proclaim the word; be persistent whether it is convenient or inconvenient; convince, reprimand, encourage through all patience and teaching.

Gospel
LUKE 18:1-8

Jesus told his disciples a parable about the necessity for them to pray always without becoming weary. He said, "There was a judge in a certain town who neither feared God nor respected any human being. And a widow in that town used to come to him and say, 'Render a just decision for me against my adversary.' For a long time the judge was unwilling, but eventually he thought, 'While it is true that I neither fear God nor respect any human being, because this widow keeps bothering me I shall deliver a just decision for her lest she finally come and strike me.'" The Lord said, "Pay attention to what the dishonest judge says. Will not God then secure the rights of his chosen ones who call out to him day and night? Will he be slow to answer them? I tell you, he will see to it that justice is done for them speedily. But when the Son of Man comes, will he find faith on earth?"

Monday, October 21

First Reading
ROMANS 4:20-25

Brothers and sisters: Abraham did not doubt God's promise in unbelief; rather, he was empowered by faith and gave glory to God and was fully convinced that what God had promised he was also able to do. That is why *it was credited to him as righteousness*. But it was not for him alone that it was written that *it was credited to him*; it was also for us, to whom it will be credited, who believe in the one who raised Jesus our Lord from the dead, who was handed over for our transgressions and was raised for our justification.

Responsorial Psalm
LUKE 1:69-70, 71-72, 73-75
R. Blessed be the Lord, the God of Israel; he has come to his people.

He has come to his people and set them free.
He has raised up for us a mighty savior,
  born of the house of his servant David. **R.**
Through his holy prophets he promised of old
  that he would save us from our enemies,
  from the hands of all who hate us.
He promised to show mercy to our fathers
  and to remember his holy covenant. **R.**
This was the oath he swore to our father Abraham:
  to set us free from the hands of our enemies,

free to worship him without fear,
holy and righteous in his sight
all the days of our life. **R.**

Gospel
LUKE 12:13-21

Someone in the crowd said to Jesus, "Teacher, tell my brother to share the inheritance with me." He replied to him, "Friend, who appointed me as your judge and arbitrator?" Then he said to the crowd, "Take care to guard against all greed, for though one may be rich, one's life does not consist of possessions."

Then he told them a parable. "There was a rich man whose land produced a bountiful harvest. He asked himself, 'What shall I do, for I do not have space to store my harvest?' And he said, 'This is what I shall do: I shall tear down my barns and build larger ones. There I shall store all my grain and other goods and I shall say to myself, "Now as for you, you have so many good things stored up for many years, rest, eat, drink, be merry!"' But God said to him, 'You fool, this night your life will be demanded of you; and the things you have prepared, to whom will they belong?' Thus will it be for the one who stores up treasure for himself but is not rich in what matters to God."

Tuesday, October 22

First Reading
ROMANS 5:12, 15b, 17-19, 20b-21

Brothers and sisters: Through one man sin entered the world, and through sin, death, and thus death came to all men, inasmuch as all sinned.

If by that one person's transgression the many died, how much more did the grace of God and the gracious gift of the one man Jesus Christ overflow for the many. For if, by the transgression of the one, death came to reign through that one, how much more will those who receive the abundance of grace and the gift of justification come to reign in life through the one Jesus Christ. In conclusion, just as through one transgression condemnation came upon all, so, through one righteous act acquittal and life came to all. For just as through the disobedience of one man the many were made sinners, so, through the obedience of the one the many will be made righteous. Where sin increased, grace overflowed all the more, so that, as sin reigned in death, grace also might reign through justification for eternal life through Jesus Christ our Lord.

Responsorial Psalm
PSALM 40:7-8a, 8b-9, 10, 17

R. Here I am, Lord; I come to do your will.

Sacrifice or oblation you wished not,
 but ears open to obedience you gave me.
Burnt offerings or sin-offerings you sought not;
 then said I, "Behold I come." **R.**
"In the written scroll it is prescribed for me,
To do your will, O my God, is my delight,
 and your law is within my heart!" **R.**
I announced your justice in the vast assembly;
 I did not restrain my lips, as you, O LORD, know. **R.**
May all who seek you
 exult and be glad in you,
And may those who love your salvation
 say ever, "The LORD be glorified." **R.**

Gospel
LUKE 12:35-38

Jesus said to his disciples: "Gird your loins and light your lamps and be like servants who await their master's return from a wedding, ready to open immediately when he comes and knocks. Blessed are those servants whom the master finds vigilant on his arrival. Amen, I say to you, he will gird himself, have them recline at table, and proceed to wait on them. And should he come in the second or third watch and find them prepared in this way, blessed are those servants."

Wednesday, October 23

First Reading
ROMANS 6:12-18

Brothers and sisters: Sin must not reign over your mortal bodies so that you obey their desires. And do not present the parts of your bodies to sin as weapons for wickedness, but present yourselves to God as raised from the dead to life and the parts of your bodies to God as weapons for righteousness. For sin is not to have any power over you, since you are not under the law but under grace.

What then? Shall we sin because we are not under the law but under grace? Of course not! Do you not know that if you present yourselves to someone as obedient slaves, you are slaves of the one you obey, either of sin, which leads to death, or of obedience, which leads to righteousness? But thanks be to God that, although you were once slaves of sin, you have become obedient from the heart to the pattern of teaching to which you were entrusted. Freed from sin, you have become slaves of righteousness.

Responsorial Psalm
PSALM 124:1b-3, 4-6, 7-8
R. Our help is in the name of the Lord.

Had not the LORD been with us,
let Israel say, had not the LORD been with us—
When men rose up against us,
then would they have swallowed us alive;
When their fury was inflamed against us. **R.**
Then would the waters have overwhelmed us;
The torrent would have swept over us;
over us then would have swept the
raging waters.
Blessed be the LORD, who did not leave us
a prey to their teeth. **R.**
We were rescued like a bird
from the fowlers' snare;
Broken was the snare,
and we were freed.
Our help is in the name of the LORD,
who made heaven and earth. **R.**

Gospel
LUKE 12:39-48

Jesus said to his disciples: "Be sure of this: if the master of the house had known the hour when the thief was coming, he would not have let his house be broken into. You also must be prepared, for at an hour you do not expect, the Son of Man will come."

Then Peter said, "Lord, is this parable meant for us or for everyone?" And the Lord replied, "Who, then, is the faithful and prudent steward whom the master will put in charge of his servants to distribute the food allowance at the proper time? Blessed is that servant whom his master on arrival finds doing so. Truly, I say to you, he will put him in charge of all his property. But if that servant says to himself, 'My master is delayed in coming,' and begins to beat the menservants and the maidservants, to eat and drink and get drunk, then that servant's master will come on an unexpected day and at an unknown hour and will punish the servant severely and assign him a place with the unfaithful. That servant who knew his master's will but did not make preparations nor act in accord with his will shall be beaten severely; and the servant who was ignorant of his master's will but acted in a way deserving of a severe beating shall be beaten only lightly.

Much will be required of the person entrusted with much, and still more will be demanded of the person entrusted with more."

Thursday, October 24

First Reading
ROMANS 6:19-23

Brothers and sisters: I am speaking in human terms because of the weakness of your nature. For just as you presented the parts of your bodies as slaves to impurity and to lawlessness for lawlessness, so now present them as slaves to righteousness for sanctification. For when you were slaves of sin, you were free from righteousness. But what profit did you get then from the things of which you are now ashamed? For the end of those things is death. But now that you have been freed from sin and have become slaves of God, the benefit that you have leads to sanctification, and its end is eternal life. For the wages of sin is death, but the gift of God is eternal life in Christ Jesus our Lord.

Responsorial Psalm
PSALM 1:1-2, 3, 4 and 6
R. Blessed are they who hope in the Lord.

Blessed the man who follows not
the counsel of the wicked
Nor walks in the way of sinners,
nor sits in the company of the insolent,
But delights in the law of the LORD
and meditates on his law day and night. **R.**
He is like a tree
planted near running water,
That yields its fruit in due season,
and whose leaves never fade.
Whatever he does, prospers. **R.**
Not so the wicked, not so;
they are like chaff which the wind drives away.
For the LORD watches over the way of the just,
but the way of the wicked vanishes. **R.**

Gospel
LUKE 12:49-53

Jesus said to his disciples: "I have come to set the earth on fire, and how I wish it were already blazing! There is a baptism with which I must be baptized, and how great is my anguish until it is accomplished! Do you think that I have come to establish peace on the earth? No, I tell you, but rather division. From now on a household of five will be divided, three against two and two against three; a father will be divided against his son and a son against his father, a mother against her daughter and a daughter against her mother, a mother-in-law against her daughter-in-law and a daughter-in-law against her mother-in-law."

Friday, October 25

First Reading
ROMANS 7:18-25a

Brothers and sisters: I know that good does not dwell in me, that is, in my flesh. The willing is ready at hand, but doing the good is not. For I do not do the good I want, but I do the evil I do not want. Now if I do what I do not want, it is no longer I who do it, but sin that dwells in me. So, then, I discover the principle that when I want to do right, evil is at hand. For I take delight in the law of God, in my inner self, but I see in my members another principle at war with the law of my mind, taking me captive to the law of sin that dwells in my members. Miserable one that I am! Who will deliver me from this mortal body? Thanks be to God through Jesus Christ our Lord.

Responsorial Psalm
PSALM 119:66, 68, 76, 77, 93, 94
R. Lord, teach me your statutes.

Teach me wisdom and knowledge,
for in your commands I trust. **R.**
You are good and bountiful;
teach me your statutes. **R.**
Let your kindness comfort me
according to your promise to your servants. **R.**
Let your compassion come to me that I may live,
for your law is my delight. **R.**
Never will I forget your precepts,
for through them you give me life. **R.**
I am yours; save me,
for I have sought your precepts. **R.**

Gospel
LUKE 12:54-59

Jesus said to the crowds, "When you see a cloud rising in the west you say immediately that it is going to rain—and so it does; and when you notice that the wind is blowing from the south you say that it is going to be hot—and so it is. You hypocrites! You know how to interpret the appearance of the earth and the sky; why do you not know how to interpret the present time?

"Why do you not judge for yourselves what is right? If you are to go with your opponent before a magistrate, make an effort to settle the matter on the way; otherwise your opponent will turn you over to the judge, and the judge hand you over to the constable, and the constable throw you into prison. I say to you, you will not be released until you have paid the last penny."

Saturday, October 26

First Reading

ROMANS 8:1-11

Brothers and sisters: Now there is no condemnation for those who are in Christ Jesus. For the law of the spirit of life in Christ Jesus has freed you from the law of sin and death. For what the law, weakened by the flesh, was powerless to do, this God has done: by sending his own Son in the likeness of sinful flesh and for the sake of sin, he condemned sin in the flesh, so that the righteous decree of the law might be fulfilled in us, who live not according to the flesh but according to the spirit. For those who live according to the flesh are concerned with the things of the flesh, but those who live according to the spirit with the things of the spirit. The concern of the flesh is death, but the concern of the spirit is life and peace. For the concern of the flesh is hostility toward God; it does not submit to the law of God, nor can it; and those who are in the flesh cannot please God. But you are not in the flesh; on the contrary, you are in the spirit, if only the Spirit of God dwells in you. Whoever does not have the Spirit of Christ does not belong to him. But if Christ is in you, although the body is dead because of sin, the spirit is alive because of righteousness. If the Spirit of the one who raised Jesus from the dead dwells in you, the one who raised Christ from the dead will give life to your mortal bodies also, through his Spirit that dwells in you.

Responsorial Psalm

PSALM 24:1b-2, 3-4ab, 5-6

R. Lord, this is the people that longs to see your face.

The LORD's are the earth and its fullness;
 the world and those who dwell in it.
For he founded it upon the seas
 and established it upon the rivers. **R.**
Who can ascend the mountain of the LORD?
 or who may stand in his holy place?

He whose hands are sinless, whose heart is clean,
who desires not what is vain. **R.**
He shall receive a blessing from the LORD,
a reward from God his savior.
Such is the race that seeks for him,
that seeks the face of the God of Jacob. **R.**

Gospel
LUKE 13:1-9

Some people told Jesus about the Galileans whose blood Pilate had mingled with the blood of their sacrifices. He said to them in reply, "Do you think that because these Galileans suffered in this way they were greater sinners than all other Galileans? By no means! But I tell you, if you do not repent, you will all perish as they did! Or those eighteen people who were killed when the tower at Siloam fell on them—do you think they were more guilty than everyone else who lived in Jerusalem? By no means! But I tell you, if you do not repent, you will all perish as they did!"

And he told them this parable: "There once was a person who had a fig tree planted in his orchard, and when he came in search of fruit on it but found none, he said to the gardener, 'For three years now I have come in search of fruit on this fig tree but have found none. So cut it down. Why should it exhaust the soil?' He said to him in reply, 'Sir, leave it for this year also, and I shall cultivate the ground around it and fertilize it; it may bear fruit in the future. If not you can cut it down.'"

Sunday, October 27

Thirtieth Sunday in Ordinary Time

First Reading
SIRACH 35:12-14, 16-18

The LORD is a God of justice,
who knows no favorites.
Though not unduly partial toward the weak,
yet he hears the cry of the oppressed.
The Lord is not deaf to the wail of the orphan,
nor to the widow when she pours out her complaint.
The one who serves God willingly is heard;
his petition reaches the heavens.
The prayer of the lowly pierces the clouds;
it does not rest till it reaches its goal,

nor will it withdraw till the Most High responds,
judges justly and affirms the right,
and the Lord will not delay.

Responsorial Psalm
PSALM 34:2-3, 17-18, 19, 23
R. The Lord hears the cry of the poor.
I will bless the LORD at all times;
his praise shall be ever in my mouth.
Let my soul glory in the LORD;
the lowly will hear me and be glad. **R.**
The LORD confronts the evildoers,
to destroy remembrance of them from the earth.
When the just cry out, the LORD hears them,
and from all their distress he rescues them. **R.**
The LORD is close to the brokenhearted;
and those who are crushed in spirit he saves.
The LORD redeems the lives of his servants;
no one incurs guilt who takes refuge in him. **R.**

Second Reading
2 TIMOTHY 4:6-8, 16-18
Beloved: I am already being poured out like a libation, and the time of my departure is at hand. I have competed well; I have finished the race; I have kept the faith. From now on the crown of righteousness awaits me, which the Lord, the just judge, will award to me on that day, and not only to me, but to all who have longed for his appearance.

At my first defense no one appeared on my behalf, but everyone deserted me. May it not be held against them! But the Lord stood by me and gave me strength, so that through me the proclamation might be completed and all the Gentiles might hear it. And I was rescued from the lion's mouth. The Lord will rescue me from every evil threat and will bring me safe to his heavenly kingdom. To him be glory forever and ever. Amen.

Gospel
LUKE 18:9-14
Jesus addressed this parable to those who were convinced of their own righteousness and despised everyone else. "Two people went up to the temple area to pray; one was a Pharisee and the other was a tax collector. The Pharisee took up his position and spoke this prayer to himself, 'O God, I thank you that I am not like the rest of humanity—greedy, dishonest, adulterous—or even like this tax collector. I fast twice a week, and I pay tithes on my whole income.' But the tax collector stood off at a

distance and would not even raise his eyes to heaven but beat his breast and prayed, 'O God, be merciful to me a sinner.' I tell you, the latter went home justified, not the former; for whoever exalts himself will be humbled, and the one who humbles himself will be exalted."

Monday, October 28

Saints Simon and Jude, Apostles

First Reading
EPHESIANS 2:19-22

Brothers and sisters: You are no longer strangers and sojourners, but you are fellow citizens with the holy ones and members of the household of God, built upon the foundation of the Apostles and prophets, with Christ Jesus himself as the capstone. Through him the whole structure is held together and grows into a temple sacred in the Lord; in him you also are being built together into a dwelling place of God in the Spirit.

Responsorial Psalm
PSALM 19:2-3, 4-5
R. Their message goes out through all the earth.

The heavens declare the glory of God,
  and the firmament proclaims his handiwork.
Day pours out the word to day,
  and night to night imparts knowledge. **R.**
Not a word nor a discourse
  whose voice is not heard;
Through all the earth their voice resounds,
  and to the ends of the world, their message. **R.**

Gospel
LUKE 6:12-16

Jesus went up to the mountain to pray, and he spent the night in prayer to God. When day came, he called his disciples to himself, and from them he chose Twelve, whom he also named Apostles: Simon, whom he named Peter, and his brother Andrew, James, John, Philip, Bartholomew, Matthew, Thomas, James the son of Alphaeus, Simon who was called a Zealot, and Judas the son of James, and Judas Iscariot, who became a traitor.

Tuesday, October 29

First Reading
ROMANS 8:18-25

Brothers and sisters: I consider that the sufferings of this present time are as nothing compared with the glory to be revealed for us. For creation awaits with eager expectation the revelation of the children of God; for creation was made subject to futility, not of its own accord but because of the one who subjected it, in hope that creation itself would be set free from slavery to corruption and share in the glorious freedom of the children of God. We know that all creation is groaning in labor pains even until now; and not only that, but we ourselves, who have the firstfruits of the Spirit, we also groan within ourselves as we wait for adoption, the redemption of our bodies. For in hope we were saved. Now hope that sees for itself is not hope. For who hopes for what one sees? But if we hope for what we do not see, we wait with endurance.

Responsorial Psalm
PSALM 126:1b-2ab, 2cd-3, 4-5, 6
R. The Lord has done marvels for us.

When the LORD brought back the captives of Zion,
  we were like men dreaming.
Then our mouth was filled with laughter,
  and our tongue with rejoicing. **R.**
Then they said among the nations,
  "The LORD has done great things for them."
The LORD has done great things for us;
  we are glad indeed. **R.**
Restore our fortunes, O LORD,
  like the torrents in the southern desert.
Those that sow in tears
  shall reap rejoicing. **R.**
Although they go forth weeping,
  carrying the seed to be sown,
They shall come back rejoicing,
  carrying their sheaves. **R.**

Gospel
LUKE 13:18-21

Jesus said, "What is the Kingdom of God like? To what can I compare it? It is like a mustard seed that a man took and planted in the garden. When it was fully grown, it became a large bush and 'the birds of the sky dwelt in its branches.'"

Again he said, "To what shall I compare the Kingdom of God? It is like yeast that a woman took and mixed in with three measures of wheat flour until the whole batch of dough was leavened."

Wednesday, October 30

First Reading

ROMANS 8:26-30

Brothers and sisters: The Spirit comes to the aid of our weakness; for we do not know how to pray as we ought, but the Spirit himself intercedes with inexpressible groanings. And the one who searches hearts knows what is the intention of the Spirit, because he intercedes for the holy ones according to God's will.

We know that all things work for good for those who love God, who are called according to his purpose. For those he foreknew he also predestined to be conformed to the image of his Son, so that he might be the firstborn among many brothers. And those he predestined he also called; and those he called he also justified; and those he justified he also glorified.

Responsorial Psalm

PSALM 13:4-5, 6

R. My hope, O Lord, is in your mercy.

Look, answer me, O LORD, my God!
Give light to my eyes that I may not sleep in death
lest my enemy say, "I have overcome him";
lest my foes rejoice at my downfall. **R.**
Though I trusted in your mercy,
Let my heart rejoice in your salvation;
let me sing of the LORD, "He has been good to me." **R.**

Gospel

LUKE 13:22-30

Jesus passed through towns and villages, teaching as he went and making his way to Jerusalem. Someone asked him, "Lord, will only a few people be saved?" He answered them, "Strive to enter through the narrow gate, for many, I tell you, will attempt to enter but will not be strong enough. After the master of the house has arisen and locked the door, then will you stand outside knocking and saying, 'Lord, open the door for us.' He will say to you in reply, 'I do not know where you are from.' And you will say, 'We ate and drank in your company and you taught in our streets.' Then he will say to you, 'I do not know where you are from. Depart from me, all you evildoers!' And there will be wailing and grinding of teeth when you see Abraham, Isaac, and Jacob and all the prophets in the Kingdom of God and you yourselves cast out. And people will come from the east and the west and from the north and the south and will recline at table in the Kingdom of God. For behold, some are last who will be first, and some are first who will be last."

Thursday, October 31

First Reading

ROMANS 8:31b-39

Brothers and sisters: If God is for us, who can be against us? He did not spare his own Son but handed him over for us all, how will he not also give us everything else along with him? Who will bring a charge against God's chosen ones? It is God who acquits us. Who will condemn? It is Christ Jesus who died, rather, was raised, who also is at the right hand of God, who indeed intercedes for us. What will separate us from the love of Christ? Will anguish, or distress, or persecution, or famine, or nakedness, or peril, or the sword? As it is written:

For your sake we are being slain all the day;
we are looked upon as sheep to be slaughtered.

No, in all these things we conquer overwhelmingly through him who loved us. For I am convinced that neither death, nor life, nor angels, nor principalities, nor present things, nor future things, nor powers, nor height, nor depth, nor any other creature will be able to separate us from the love of God in Christ Jesus our Lord.

Responsorial Psalm

PSALM 109:21-22, 26-27, 30-31

R. Save me, O Lord, in your mercy.

Do you, O GOD, my Lord, deal kindly with me for your name's sake;
in your generous mercy rescue me;
For I am wretched and poor,
and my heart is pierced within me. **R.**
Help me, O LORD, my God;
save me, in your mercy,
And let them know that this is your hand;
that you, O LORD, have done this. **R.**
I will speak my thanks earnestly to the LORD,
and in the midst of the throng I will praise him,
For he stood at the right hand of the poor man,
to save him from those who would condemn his soul. **R.**

Gospel
LUKE 13:31-35

Some Pharisees came to Jesus and said, “Go away, leave this area because Herod wants to kill you.” He replied, “Go and tell that fox, ‘Behold, I cast out demons and I perform healings today and tomorrow, and on the third day I accomplish my purpose. Yet I must continue on my way today, tomorrow, and the following day, for it is impossible that a prophet should die outside of Jerusalem.’

“Jerusalem, Jerusalem, you who kill the prophets and stone those sent to you, how many times I yearned to gather your children together as a hen gathers her brood under her wings, but you were unwilling! Behold, your house will be abandoned. But I tell you, you will not see me until the time comes when you say,

Blessed is he who comes in the name of the Lord.”

NOVEMBER

Friday, November 1

All Saints

First Reading
REVELATION 7:2-4, 9-14

I, John, saw another angel come up from the East, holding the seal of the living God. He cried out in a loud voice to the four angels who were given power to damage the land and the sea, "Do not damage the land or the sea or the trees until we put the seal on the foreheads of the servants of our God." I heard the number of those who had been marked with the seal, one hundred and forty-four thousand marked from every tribe of the children of Israel.

After this I had a vision of a great multitude, which no one could count, from every nation, race, people, and tongue. They stood before the throne and before the Lamb, wearing white robes and holding palm branches in their hands. They cried out in a loud voice:

> "Salvation comes from our God, who is seated on the throne,
> and from the Lamb."

All the angels stood around the throne and around the elders and the four living creatures. They prostrated themselves before the throne, worshiped God, and exclaimed:

> "Amen. Blessing and glory, wisdom and thanksgiving,
> honor, power, and might
> be to our God forever and ever. Amen."

Then one of the elders spoke up and said to me, "Who are these wearing white robes, and where did they come from?" I said to him, "My lord, you are the one who knows." He said to me, "These are the ones who have survived the time of great distress; they have washed their robes and made them white in the Blood of the Lamb."

Responsorial Psalm
PSALM 24:1bc-2, 3-4ab, 5-6
R. Lord, this is the people that longs to see your face.

The LORD's are the earth and its fullness;
the world and those who dwell in it.

For he founded it upon the seas
and established it upon the rivers. **R.**
Who can ascend the mountain of the LORD?
or who may stand in his holy place?
One whose hands are sinless, whose heart is clean,
who desires not what is vain. **R.**
He shall receive a blessing from the LORD,
a reward from God his savior.
Such is the race that seeks him,
that seeks the face of the God of Jacob. **R.**

Second Reading
1 JOHN 3:1-3

Beloved: See what love the Father has bestowed on us that we may be called the children of God. Yet so we are. The reason the world does not know us is that it did not know him. Beloved, we are God's children now; what we shall be has not yet been revealed. We do know that when it is revealed we shall be like him, for we shall see him as he is. Everyone who has this hope based on him makes himself pure, as he is pure.

Gospel
MATTHEW 5:1-12a

When Jesus saw the crowds, he went up the mountain, and after he had sat down, his disciples came to him. He began to teach them, saying:

"Blessed are the poor in spirit,
for theirs is the Kingdom of heaven.
Blessed are they who mourn,
for they will be comforted.
Blessed are the meek,
for they will inherit the land.
Blessed are they who hunger and thirst for righteousness,
for they will be satisfied.
Blessed are the merciful,
for they will be shown mercy.
Blessed are the clean of heart,
for they will see God.
Blessed are the peacemakers,
for they will be called children of God.
Blessed are they who are persecuted for the sake of righteousness,
for theirs is the Kingdom of heaven.
Blessed are you when they insult you and persecute you
and utter every kind of evil against you falsely because of me.

Rejoice and be glad,
for your reward will be great in heaven."

Saturday, November 2

The Commemoration of All the Faithful Departed (All Souls' Day)

[Any readings from no. 668 or from the *Lectionary for Masses* (vol. IV), the Masses for the Dead, nos. 1011-1016, may be substituted for those listed here.]

First Reading

WISDOM 3:1-9

The souls of the just are in the hand of God,
and no torment shall touch them.
They seemed, in the view of the foolish, to be dead;
and their passing away was thought an affliction
and their going forth from us, utter destruction.
But they are in peace.
For if before men, indeed, they be punished,
yet is their hope full of immortality;
chastised a little, they shall be greatly blessed,
because God tried them
and found them worthy of himself.
As gold in the furnace, he proved them,
and as sacrificial offerings he took them to himself.
In the time of their visitation they shall shine,
and shall dart about as sparks through stubble;
they shall judge nations and rule over peoples,
and the LORD shall be their King forever.
Those who trust in him shall understand truth,
and the faithful shall abide with him in love:
because grace and mercy are with his holy ones,
and his care is with his elect.

Responsorial Psalm

PSALM 23:1-3a, 3b-4, 5, 6

R. The Lord is my shepherd; there is nothing I shall want. (or R. Though I walk in the valley of darkness, I fear no evil, for you are with me.)

The LORD is my shepherd; I shall not want.
In verdant pastures he gives me repose;

beside restful waters he leads me;
 he refreshes my soul. **R.**
He guides me in right paths
 for his name's sake.
Even though I walk in the dark valley
 I fear no evil; for you are at my side
with your rod and your staff
 that give me courage. **R.**
You spread the table before me
 in the sight of my foes;
You anoint my head with oil;
 my cup overflows. **R.**
Only goodness and kindness follow me
 all the days of my life;
and I shall dwell in the house of the LORD
 for years to come. **R.**

Second Reading
ROMANS 5:5-11 (or ROMANS 6:3-9)

Brothers and sisters: Hope does not disappoint, because the love of God has been poured out into our hearts through the Holy Spirit that has been given to us. For Christ, while we were still helpless, died at the appointed time for the ungodly. Indeed, only with difficulty does one die for a just person, though perhaps for a good person one might even find courage to die. But God proves his love for us in that while we were still sinners Christ died for us. How much more then, since we are now justified by his Blood, will we be saved through him from the wrath. Indeed, if, while we were enemies, we were reconciled to God through the death of his Son, how much more, once reconciled, will we be saved by his life. Not only that, but we also boast of God through our Lord Jesus Christ, through whom we have now received reconciliation.

Gospel
JOHN 6:37-40

Jesus said to the crowds: "Everything that the Father gives me will come to me, and I will not reject anyone who comes to me, because I came down from heaven not to do my own will but the will of the one who sent me. And this is the will of the one who sent me, that I should not lose anything of what he gave me, but that I should raise it on the last day. For this is the will of my Father, that everyone who sees the Son and believes in him may have eternal life, and I shall raise him on the last day."

Sunday, November 3

Thirty-first Sunday in Ordinary Time

First Reading
WISDOM 11:22–12:2

Before the LORD the whole universe is as a grain from a balance
or a drop of morning dew come down upon the earth.
But you have mercy on all, because you can do all things;
and you overlook people's sins that they may repent.
For you love all things that are
and loathe nothing that you have made;
for what you hated, you would not have fashioned.
And how could a thing remain, unless you willed it;
or be preserved, had it not been called forth by you?
But you spare all things, because they are yours,
O LORD and lover of souls,
for your imperishable spirit is in all things!
Therefore you rebuke offenders little by little,
warn them and remind them of the sins they are committing,
that they may abandon their wickedness and believe in you, O LORD!

Responsorial Psalm
PSALM 145:1-2, 8-9, 10-11, 13, 14
R. I will praise your name for ever, my king and my God.

I will extol you, O my God and King,
and I will bless your name forever and ever.
Every day will I bless you,
and I will praise your name forever and ever. **R.**
The LORD is gracious and merciful,
slow to anger and of great kindness.
The LORD is good to all
and compassionate toward all his works. **R.**
Let all your works give you thanks, O LORD,
and let your faithful ones bless you.
Let them discourse of the glory of your kingdom
and speak of your might. **R.**
The LORD is faithful in all his words
and holy in all his works.
The LORD lifts up all who are falling
and raises up all who are bowed down. **R.**

Second Reading
2 THESSALONIANS 1:11–2:2

Brothers and sisters: We always pray for you, that our God may make you worthy of his calling and powerfully bring to fulfillment every good purpose and every effort of faith, that the name of our Lord Jesus may be glorified in you, and you in him, in accord with the grace of our God and Lord Jesus Christ.

We ask you, brothers and sisters, with regard to the coming of our Lord Jesus Christ and our assembling with him, not to be shaken out of your minds suddenly, or to be alarmed either by a "spirit," or by an oral statement, or by a letter allegedly from us to the effect that the day of the Lord is at hand.

Gospel
LUKE 19:1-10

At that time, Jesus came to Jericho and intended to pass through the town. Now a man there named Zacchaeus, who was a chief tax collector and also a wealthy man, was seeking to see who Jesus was; but he could not see him because of the crowd, for he was short in stature. So he ran ahead and climbed a sycamore tree in order to see Jesus, who was about to pass that way. When he reached the place, Jesus looked up and said, "Zacchaeus, come down quickly, for today I must stay at your house." And he came down quickly and received him with joy. When they all saw this, they began to grumble, saying, "He has gone to stay at the house of a sinner." But Zacchaeus stood there and said to the Lord, "Behold, half of my possessions, Lord, I shall give to the poor, and if I have extorted anything from anyone I shall repay it four times over." And Jesus said to him, "Today salvation has come to this house because this man too is a descendant of Abraham. For the Son of Man has come to seek and to save what was lost."

Monday, November 4

First Reading
ROMANS 11:29-36

Brothers and sisters: The gifts and the call of God are irrevocable.

Just as you once disobeyed God but have now received mercy because of their disobedience, so they have now disobeyed in order that, by virtue of the mercy shown to you, they too may now receive mercy. For God delivered all to disobedience, that he might have mercy upon all.

Oh, the depth of the riches and wisdom and knowledge of God! How inscrutable are his judgments and how unsearchable his ways!

For who has known the mind of the Lord
or who has been his counselor?
Or who has given him anything
that he may be repaid?

For from him and through him and for him are all things. To God be glory forever. Amen.

Responsorial Psalm
PSALM 69:30-31, 33-34, 36
R. Lord, in your great love, answer me.
But I am afflicted and in pain;
let your saving help, O God, protect me.
I will praise the name of God in song,
and I will glorify him with thanksgiving. **R.**
"See, you lowly ones, and be glad;
you who seek God, may your hearts revive!
For the LORD hears the poor,
and his own who are in bonds he spurns not." **R.**
For God will save Zion
and rebuild the cities of Judah.
They shall dwell in the land and own it,
and the descendants of his servants shall inherit it,
and those who love his name shall inhabit it. **R.**

Gospel
LUKE 14:12-14
On a sabbath Jesus went to dine at the home of one of the leading Pharisees. He said to the host who invited him, "When you hold a lunch or a dinner, do not invite your friends or your brothers or sisters or your relatives or your wealthy neighbors, in case they may invite you back and you have repayment. Rather, when you hold a banquet, invite the poor, the crippled, the lame, the blind; blessed indeed will you be because of their inability to repay you. For you will be repaid at the resurrection of the righteous."

Tuesday, November 5

First Reading
ROMANS 12:5-16b
Brothers and sisters: We, though many, are one Body in Christ and individually parts of one another. Since we have gifts that differ according to the grace given to us, let us exercise them: if prophecy, in

proportion to the faith; if ministry, in ministering; if one is a teacher, in teaching; if one exhorts, in exhortation; if one contributes, in generosity; if one is over others, with diligence; if one does acts of mercy, with cheerfulness.

Let love be sincere; hate what is evil, hold on to what is good; love one another with mutual affection; anticipate one another in showing honor. Do not grow slack in zeal, be fervent in spirit, serve the Lord. Rejoice in hope, endure in affliction, persevere in prayer. Contribute to the needs of the holy ones, exercise hospitality. Bless those who persecute you, bless and do not curse them. Rejoice with those who rejoice, weep with those who weep. Have the same regard for one another; do not be haughty but associate with the lowly.

Responsorial Psalm

PSALM 131:1bcde, 2, 3

R. In you, O Lord, I have found my peace.

O LORD, my heart is not proud,
nor are my eyes haughty;
I busy not myself with great things,
nor with things too sublime for me. **R.**

Nay rather, I have stilled and quieted
my soul like a weaned child.
Like a weaned child on its mother's lap,
so is my soul within me. **R.**

O Israel, hope in the LORD,
both now and forever. **R.**

Gospel

LUKE 14:15-24

One of those at table with Jesus said to him, "Blessed is the one who will dine in the Kingdom of God." He replied to him, "A man gave a great dinner to which he invited many. When the time for the dinner came, he dispatched his servant to say to those invited, 'Come, everything is now ready.' But one by one, they all began to excuse themselves. The first said to him, 'I have purchased a field and must go to examine it; I ask you, consider me excused.' And another said, 'I have purchased five yoke of oxen and am on my way to evaluate them; I ask you, consider me excused.' And another said, 'I have just married a woman, and therefore I cannot come.' The servant went and reported this to his master. Then the master of the house in a rage commanded his servant, 'Go out quickly into the streets and alleys of the town and bring in here the poor and the crippled, the blind and the lame.' The servant reported, 'Sir, your orders have been carried out and still there is room.' The master then ordered the servant, 'Go out to the highways and hedgerows and make people come in that my home may be filled. For, I tell you, none of those men who were invited will taste my dinner.'"

Wednesday, November 6

First Reading
ROMANS 13:8-10

Brothers and sisters: Owe nothing to anyone, except to love one another; for the one who loves another has fulfilled the law. The commandments, *You shall not commit adultery; you shall not kill; you shall not steal; you shall not covet*, and whatever other commandment there may be, are summed up in this saying, namely, *You shall love your neighbor as yourself.* Love does no evil to the neighbor; hence, love is the fulfillment of the law.

Responsorial Psalm
PSALM 112:1b-2, 4-5, 9
R. Blessed the man who is gracious and lends to those in need. (or R. Alleluia.)

Blessed the man who fears the LORD,
  who greatly delights in his commands.
His posterity shall be mighty upon the earth;
  the upright generation shall be blessed. **R.**
He dawns through the darkness, a light for the upright;
  he is gracious and merciful and just.
Well for the man who is gracious and lends,
  who conducts his affairs with justice. **R.**
Lavishly he gives to the poor;
  his generosity shall endure forever;
  his horn shall be exalted in glory. **R.**

Gospel
LUKE 14:25-33

Great crowds were traveling with Jesus, and he turned and addressed them, "If anyone comes to me without hating his father and mother, wife and children, brothers and sisters, and even his own life, he cannot be my disciple. Whoever does not carry his own cross and come after me cannot be my disciple. Which of you wishing to construct a tower does not first sit down and calculate the cost to see if there is enough for its completion? Otherwise, after laying the foundation and finding himself unable to finish the work the onlookers should laugh at him and say, 'This one began to build but did not have the resources to finish.' Or what king marching into battle would not first sit down and decide whether with ten thousand troops he can successfully oppose another king advancing upon him with twenty thousand troops? But if not, while he is still far away, he will send a delegation to ask for peace terms. In the same way, everyone of you who does not renounce all his possessions cannot be my disciple."

Thursday, November 7

First Reading

ROMANS 14:7-12

Brothers and sisters: None of us lives for oneself, and no one dies for oneself. For if we live, we live for the Lord, and if we die, we die for the Lord; so then, whether we live or die, we are the Lord's. For this is why Christ died and came to life, that he might be Lord of both the dead and the living. Why then do you judge your brother or sister? Or you, why do you look down on your brother or sister? For we shall all stand before the judgment seat of God; for it is written:

As I live, says the Lord, every knee shall bend before me,
and every tongue shall give praise to God.

So then each of us shall give an account of himself to God.

Responsorial Psalm

PSALM 27:1bcde, 4, 13-14

R. I believe that I shall see the good things of the Lord in the land of the living.

The LORD is my light and my salvation;
whom should I fear?
The LORD is my life's refuge;
of whom should I be afraid? **R.**
One thing I ask of the LORD;
this I seek:
To dwell in the house of the LORD
all the days of my life,
That I may gaze on the loveliness of the LORD
and contemplate his temple. **R.**
I believe that I shall see the bounty of the LORD
in the land of the living.
Wait for the LORD with courage;
be stouthearted, and wait for the LORD. **R.**

Gospel
LUKE 15:1-10

The tax collectors and sinners were all drawing near to listen to Jesus, but the Pharisees and scribes began to complain, saying, "This man welcomes sinners and eats with them." So Jesus addressed this parable to them. "What man among you having a hundred sheep and losing one of them would not leave the ninety-nine in the desert and go after the lost one until he finds it? And when he does find it, he sets it on his shoulders with great joy and, upon his arrival home, he calls together his friends and neighbors and says to them, 'Rejoice with me because I have found my lost sheep.' I tell you, in just the same way there will be more joy in heaven over one sinner who repents than over ninety-nine righteous people who have no need of repentance.

"Or what woman having ten coins and losing one would not light a lamp and sweep the house, searching carefully until she finds it? And when she does find it, she calls together her friends and neighbors and says to them, 'Rejoice with me because I have found the coin that I lost.' In just the same way, I tell you, there will be rejoicing among the angels of God over one sinner who repents."

Friday, November 8

First Reading
ROMANS 15:14-21

I myself am convinced about you, my brothers and sisters, that you yourselves are full of goodness, filled with all knowledge, and able to admonish one another. But I have written to you rather boldly in some respects to remind you, because of the grace given me by God to be a minister of Christ Jesus to the Gentiles in performing the priestly service of the Gospel of God, so that the offering up of the Gentiles may be acceptable, sanctified by the Holy Spirit. In Christ Jesus, then, I have reason to boast in what pertains to God. For I will not dare to speak of anything except what Christ has accomplished through me to lead the Gentiles to obedience by word and deed, by the power of signs and wonders, by the power of the Spirit of God, so that from Jerusalem all the way around to Illyricum I have finished preaching the Gospel of Christ. Thus I aspire to proclaim the Gospel not where Christ has already been named, so that I do not build on another's foundation, but as it is written:

Those who have never been told of him shall see,
and those who have never heard of him shall understand.

Responsorial Psalm

PSALM 98:1, 2-3ab, 3cd-4

R. The Lord has revealed to the nations his saving power.

Sing to the LORD a new song,
  for he has done wondrous deeds;
His right hand has won victory for him,
  his holy arm. **R.**

The LORD has made his salvation known:
  in the sight of the nations he has revealed his justice.
He has remembered his kindness and his faithfulness
  toward the house of Israel. **R.**

All the ends of the earth have seen
  the salvation by our God.
Sing joyfully to the LORD, all you lands;
  break into song; sing praise. **R.**

Gospel

LUKE 16:1-8

Jesus said to his disciples, "A rich man had a steward who was reported to him for squandering his property. He summoned him and said, 'What is this I hear about you? Prepare a full account of your stewardship, because you can no longer be my steward.' The steward said to himself, 'What shall I do, now that my master is taking the position of steward away from me? I am not strong enough to dig and I am ashamed to beg. I know what I shall do so that, when I am removed from the stewardship, they may welcome me into their homes.' He called in his master's debtors one by one. To the first he said, 'How much do you owe my master?' He replied, 'One hundred measures of olive oil.' He said to him, 'Here is your promissory note. Sit down and quickly write one for fifty.' Then to another he said, 'And you, how much do you owe?' He replied, 'One hundred measures of wheat.' He said to him, 'Here is your promissory note; write one for eighty.' And the master commended that dishonest steward for acting prudently. For the children of this world are more prudent in dealing with their own generation than the children of light."

Saturday, November 9

The Dedication of the Lateran Basilica

First Reading

EZEKIEL 47:1-2, 8-9, 12

The angel brought me back to the entrance of the temple, and I saw water flowing out from beneath the threshold of the temple toward the east, for the façade of the temple was toward the east; the water flowed down from the southern side of the temple, south of the altar. He led me outside by the north gate, and around to the outer gate facing the east, where I saw water trickling from the southern side. He said to me, "This water flows into the eastern district down upon the Arabah, and empties into the sea, the salt waters, which it makes fresh. Wherever the river flows, every sort of living creature that can multiply shall live, and there shall be abundant fish, for wherever this water comes the sea shall be made fresh. Along both banks of the river, fruit trees of every kind shall grow; their leaves shall not fade, nor their fruit fail. Every month they shall bear fresh fruit, for they shall be watered by the flow from the sanctuary. Their fruit shall serve for food, and their leaves for medicine."

Responsorial Psalm
PSALM 46:2-3, 5-6, 8-9

R. The waters of the river gladden the city of God, the holy dwelling of the Most High!

God is our refuge and our strength,
  an ever-present help in distress.
Therefore, we fear not, though the earth be shaken
  and mountains plunge into the depths of the sea. **R.**
There is a stream whose runlets gladden the city of God,
  the holy dwelling of the Most High.
God is in its midst; it shall not be disturbed;
  God will help it at the break of dawn. **R.**
The LORD of hosts is with us;
  our stronghold is the God of Jacob.
Come! behold the deeds of the LORD,
  the astounding things he has wrought on earth. **R.**

Second Reading
1 CORINTHIANS 3:9c-11, 16-17

Brothers and sisters: You are God's building. According to the grace of God given to me, like a wise master builder I laid a foundation, and another is building upon it. But each one must be careful how he builds upon it, for no one can lay a foundation other than the one that is there, namely, Jesus Christ.

Do you not know that you are the temple of God, and that the Spirit of God dwells in you? If anyone destroys God's temple, God will destroy that person; for the temple of God, which you are, is holy.

Gospel
JOHN 2:13-22

Since the Passover of the Jews was near, Jesus went up to Jerusalem. He found in the temple area those who sold oxen, sheep, and doves, as well as the money-changers seated there. He made a whip out of cords and drove them all out of the temple area, with the sheep and oxen, and spilled the coins of the money-changers and overturned their tables, and to those who sold doves he said, "Take these out of here, and stop making my Father's house a marketplace." His disciples recalled the words of Scripture, *Zeal for your house will consume me.* At this the Jews answered and said to him, "What sign can you show us for doing this?" Jesus answered and said to them, "Destroy this temple and in three days I will raise it up." The Jews said, "This temple has been under construction for forty-six years, and you will raise it up in three days?" But he was speaking about the temple of his Body. Therefore, when he was raised from the dead, his disciples remembered that he had said this, and they came to believe the Scripture and the word Jesus had spoken.

Sunday, November 10

Thirty-second Sunday in Ordinary Time

First Reading
2 MACCABEES 7:1-2, 9-14

It happened that seven brothers with their mother were arrested and tortured with whips and scourges by the king, to force them to eat pork in violation of God's law. One of the brothers, speaking for the others, said: "What do you expect to achieve by questioning us? We are ready to die rather than transgress the laws of our ancestors."

At the point of death he said: "You accursed fiend, you are depriving us of this present life, but the King of the world will raise us up to live again forever. It is for his laws that we are dying."

After him the third suffered their cruel sport. He put out his tongue at once when told to do so, and bravely held out his hands, as he spoke these noble words: "It was from Heaven that I received these; for the sake of his laws I disdain them; from him I hope to receive them again." Even the king and his attendants marveled at the young man's courage, because he regarded his sufferings as nothing.

After he had died, they tortured and maltreated the fourth brother in the same way. When he was near death, he said, "It is my choice to die at the hands of men with the hope God gives of being raised up by him; but for you, there will be no resurrection to life."

Responsorial Psalm
PSALM 17:1, 5-6, 8, 15
R. Lord, when your glory appears, my joy will be full.

Hear, O LORD, a just suit;
attend to my outcry;
hearken to my prayer from lips without deceit. **R.**
My steps have been steadfast in your paths,
my feet have not faltered.
I call upon you, for you will answer me, O God;
incline your ear to me; hear my word. **R.**
Keep me as the apple of your eye,
hide me in the shadow of your wings.
But I in justice shall behold your face;
on waking I shall be content in your presence. **R.**

Second Reading
2 THESSALONIANS 2:16–3:5

Brothers and sisters: May our Lord Jesus Christ himself and God our Father, who has loved us and given us everlasting encouragement and good hope through his grace, encourage your hearts and strengthen them in every good deed and word.

Finally, brothers and sisters, pray for us, so that the word of the Lord may speed forward and be glorified, as it did among you, and that we may be delivered from perverse and wicked people, for not all have faith. But the Lord is faithful; he will strengthen you and guard you from the evil one. We are confident of you in the Lord that what we instruct you, you are doing and will continue to do. May the Lord direct your hearts to the love of God and to the endurance of Christ.

Gospel
LUKE 20:27-38 (or LUKE 20:27, 34-38)

Some Sadducees, those who deny that there is a resurrection, came forward and put this question to Jesus, saying, "Teacher, Moses wrote for us, *If someone's brother dies leaving a wife but no child, his brother must take the wife and raise up descendants for his brother*. Now there were seven brothers; the first married a woman but died childless. Then the second and the third married her, and likewise all the seven died childless. Finally the woman also died. Now at the resurrection whose wife will that woman be? For all seven had been married to her." Jesus said to them, "The children of this age marry and remarry; but those who are deemed worthy to attain to the coming age and to the resurrection of the dead neither marry nor are given in marriage. They can no longer die, for they are like angels; and they are the children of God because they are the ones who will rise. That the dead will rise even Moses made known in the passage about the bush, when he called out 'Lord,' the God of Abraham, the God of Isaac, and the God of Jacob; and he is not God of the dead, but of the living, for to him all are alive."

Monday, November 11

First Reading
WISDOM 1:1-7

Love justice, you who judge the earth;
think of the Lord in goodness,
and seek him in integrity of heart;
Because he is found by those who test him not,
and he manifests himself to those who do not disbelieve him.
For perverse counsels separate a man from God,
and his power, put to the proof, rebukes the foolhardy;
Because into a soul that plots evil, wisdom enters not,
nor dwells she in a body under debt of sin.
For the holy Spirit of discipline flees deceit
and withdraws from senseless counsels;
and when injustice occurs it is rebuked.
For wisdom is a kindly spirit,
yet she acquits not the blasphemer of his guilty lips;
Because God is the witness of his inmost self
and the sure observer of his heart
and the listener to his tongue.
For the Spirit of the Lord fills the world,
is all-embracing, and knows what man says.

Responsorial Psalm
PSALM 139:1b-3, 4-6, 7-8, 9-10
R. Guide me, Lord, along the everlasting way.

O LORD, you have probed me and you know me;
you know when I sit and when I stand;
you understand my thoughts from afar.
My journeys and my rest you scrutinize,
with all my ways you are familiar. **R.**
Even before a word is on my tongue,
behold, O LORD, you know the whole of it.
Behind me and before, you hem me in
and rest your hand upon me.
Such knowledge is too wonderful for me;
too lofty for me to attain. **R.**

Where can I go from your spirit?
From your presence where can I flee?
If I go up to the heavens, you are there;
if I sink to the nether world, you are present there. **R.**
If I take the wings of the dawn,
if I settle at the farthest limits of the sea,
Even there your hand shall guide me,
and your right hand hold me fast. **R.**

Gospel
LUKE 17:1-6

Jesus said to his disciples, "Things that cause sin will inevitably occur, but woe to the one through whom they occur. It would be better for him if a millstone were put around his neck and he be thrown into the sea than for him to cause one of these little ones to sin. Be on your guard! If your brother sins, rebuke him; and if he repents, forgive him. And if he wrongs you seven times in one day and returns to you seven times saying, 'I am sorry,' you should forgive him."

And the Apostles said to the Lord, "Increase our faith." The Lord replied, "If you have faith the size of a mustard seed, you would say to this mulberry tree, 'Be uprooted and planted in the sea,' and it would obey you."

Tuesday, November 12

First Reading
WISDOM 2:23–3:9

God formed man to be imperishable;
the image of his own nature he made him.
But by the envy of the Devil, death entered the world,
and they who are in his possession experience it.

But the souls of the just are in the hand of God,
and no torment shall touch them.
They seemed, in the view of the foolish, to be dead;
and their passing away was thought an affliction
and their going forth from us, utter destruction.
But they are in peace.
For if before men, indeed, they be punished,
yet is their hope full of immortality;
Chastised a little, they shall be greatly blessed,
because God tried them
and found them worthy of himself.

As gold in the furnace, he proved them,
 and as sacrificial offerings he took them to himself.
In the time of their visitation they shall shine,
 and shall dart about as sparks through stubble;
They shall judge nations and rule over peoples,
 and the Lord shall be their King forever.
Those who trust in him shall understand truth,
 and the faithful shall abide with him in love:
Because grace and mercy are with his holy ones,
 and his care is with his elect.

Responsorial Psalm

PSALM 34:2-3, 16-17, 18-19

R. I will bless the Lord at all times.

I will bless the LORD at all times;
 his praise shall be ever in my mouth.
Let my soul glory in the LORD;
 the lowly will hear me and be glad. **R.**
The LORD has eyes for the just,
 and ears for their cry.
The LORD confronts the evildoers,
 to destroy remembrance of them from the earth. **R.**
When the just cry out, the LORD hears them,
 and from all their distress he rescues them.
The LORD is close to the brokenhearted;
 and those who are crushed in spirit he saves. **R.**

Gospel

LUKE 17:7-10

Jesus said to the Apostles: "Who among you would say to your servant who has just come in from plowing or tending sheep in the field, 'Come here immediately and take your place at table'? Would he not rather say to him, 'Prepare something for me to eat. Put on your apron and wait on me while I eat and drink. You may eat and drink when I am finished'? Is he grateful to that servant because he did what was commanded? So should it be with you. When you have done all you have been commanded, say, 'We are unprofitable servants; we have done what we were obliged to do.'"

Wednesday, November 13

First Reading

WISDOM 6:1-11

Hear, O kings, and understand;
learn, you magistrates of the earth's expanse!
Hearken, you who are in power over the multitude
and lord it over throngs of peoples!
Because authority was given you by the LORD
and sovereignty by the Most High,
who shall probe your works and scrutinize your counsels.
Because, though you were ministers of his kingdom, you judged
not rightly,
and did not keep the law,
nor walk according to the will of God,
Terribly and swiftly shall he come against you,
because judgment is stern for the exalted—
For the lowly may be pardoned out of mercy
but the mighty shall be mightily put to the test.
For the Lord of all shows no partiality,
nor does he fear greatness,
Because he himself made the great as well as the small,
and he provides for all alike;
but for those in power a rigorous scrutiny impends.
To you, therefore, O princes, are my words addressed
that you may learn wisdom and that you may not sin.
For those who keep the holy precepts hallowed shall be found holy,
and those learned in them will have ready a response.
Desire therefore my words;
long for them and you shall be instructed.

Responsorial Psalm

PSALM 82:3-4, 6-7

R. Rise up, O God, bring judgment to the earth.

Defend the lowly and the fatherless;
render justice to the afflicted and the destitute.
Rescue the lowly and the poor;
from the hand of the wicked deliver them. **R.**

I said: "You are gods,
all of you sons of the Most High;
yet like men you shall die,
and fall like any prince." **R.**

Gospel
LUKE 17:11-19

As Jesus continued his journey to Jerusalem, he traveled through Samaria and Galilee. As he was entering a village, ten lepers met him. They stood at a distance from him and raised their voice, saying, "Jesus, Master! Have pity on us!" And when he saw them, he said, "Go show yourselves to the priests." As they were going they were cleansed. And one of them, realizing he had been healed, returned, glorifying God in a loud voice; and he fell at the feet of Jesus and thanked him. He was a Samaritan. Jesus said in reply, "Ten were cleansed, were they not? Where are the other nine? Has none but this foreigner returned to give thanks to God?" Then he said to him, "Stand up and go; your faith has saved you."

Thursday, November 14

First Reading
WISDOM 7:22b–8:1

In Wisdom is a spirit
  intelligent, holy, unique,
Manifold, subtle, agile,
  clear, unstained, certain,
Not baneful, loving the good, keen,
  unhampered, beneficent, kindly,
Firm, secure, tranquil,
  all-powerful, all-seeing,
And pervading all spirits,
  though they be intelligent, pure and very subtle.
For Wisdom is mobile beyond all motion,
  and she penetrates and pervades all things by reason of her purity.
For she is an aura of the might of God
  and a pure effusion of the glory of the Almighty;
  therefore nought that is sullied enters into her.
For she is the refulgence of eternal light,
  the spotless mirror of the power of God,
  the image of his goodness.
And she, who is one, can do all things,
  and renews everything while herself perduring;
And passing into holy souls from age to age,
  she produces friends of God and prophets.
For there is nought God loves, be it not one who dwells with Wisdom.
For she is fairer than the sun
  and surpasses every constellation of the stars.

Compared to light, she takes precedence;
for that, indeed, night supplants,
but wickedness prevails not over Wisdom.

Indeed, she reaches from end to end mightily
and governs all things well.

Responsorial Psalm

PSALM 119:89, 90, 91, 130, 135, 175

R. Your word is for ever, O Lord.

Your word, O LORD, endures forever;
it is firm as the heavens. **R.**
Through all generations your truth endures;
you have established the earth, and it stands firm. **R.**
According to your ordinances they still stand firm:
all things serve you. **R.**
The revelation of your words sheds light,
giving understanding to the simple. **R.**
Let your countenance shine upon your servant,
and teach me your statutes. **R.**
Let my soul live to praise you,
and may your ordinances help me. **R.**

Gospel

LUKE 17:20-25

Asked by the Pharisees when the Kingdom of God would come, Jesus said in reply, "The coming of the Kingdom of God cannot be observed, and no one will announce, 'Look, here it is,' or, 'There it is.' For behold, the Kingdom of God is among you."

Then he said to his disciples, "The days will come when you will long to see one of the days of the Son of Man, but you will not see it. There will be those who will say to you, 'Look, there he is,' or 'Look, here he is.' Do not go off, do not run in pursuit. For just as lightning flashes and lights up the sky from one side to the other, so will the Son of Man be in his day. But first he must suffer greatly and be rejected by this generation."

Friday, November 15

First Reading

WISDOM 13:1-9

All men were by nature foolish who were in ignorance of God,
and who from the good things seen did not succeed in
knowing him who is,

and from studying the works did not discern the artisan;
But either fire, or wind, or the swift air,
or the circuit of the stars, or the mighty water,
or the luminaries of heaven, the governors of the world,
they considered gods.
Now if out of joy in their beauty they thought them gods,
let them know how far more excellent is the Lord than these;
for the original source of beauty fashioned them.
Or if they were struck by their might and energy,
let them from these things realize how much more powerful is
he who made them.
For from the greatness and the beauty of created things
their original author, by analogy, is seen.
But yet, for these the blame is less;
For they indeed have gone astray perhaps,
though they seek God and wish to find him.
For they search busily among his works,
but are distracted by what they see, because the things seen
are fair.
But again, not even these are pardonable.
For if they so far succeeded in knowledge
that they could speculate about the world,
how did they not more quickly find its Lord?

Responsorial Psalm
PSALM 19:2-3, 4-5ab
R. The heavens proclaim the glory of God.
The heavens declare the glory of God,
and the firmament proclaims his handiwork.
Day pours out the word to day,
and night to night imparts knowledge. **R.**
Not a word nor a discourse
whose voice is not heard;
Through all the earth their voice resounds,
and to the ends of the world, their message. **R.**

Gospel
LUKE 17:26-37

Jesus said to his disciples: "As it was in the days of Noah, so it will be in the days of the Son of Man; they were eating and drinking, marrying and giving in marriage up to the day that Noah entered the ark, and the flood came and destroyed them all. Similarly, as it was in the days of Lot: they were eating, drinking, buying, selling, planting, building; on the day when Lot left Sodom, fire and brimstone rained from the sky to destroy them all.

So it will be on the day the Son of Man is revealed. On that day, someone who is on the housetop and whose belongings are in the house must not go down to get them, and likewise one in the field must not return to what was left behind. Remember the wife of Lot. Whoever seeks to preserve his life will lose it, but whoever loses it will save it. I tell you, on that night there will be two people in one bed; one will be taken, the other left. And there will be two women grinding meal together; one will be taken, the other left." They said to him in reply, "Where, Lord?" He said to them, "Where the body is, there also the vultures will gather."

Saturday, November 16

First Reading

WISDOM 18:14-16; 19:6-9

When peaceful stillness compassed everything
and the night in its swift course was half spent,
Your all-powerful word, from heaven's royal throne
bounded, a fierce warrior, into the doomed land,
bearing the sharp sword of your inexorable decree.
And as he alighted, he filled every place with death;
he still reached to heaven, while he stood upon the earth.

For all creation, in its several kinds, was being made over anew,
serving its natural laws,
that your children might be preserved unharmed.
The cloud overshadowed their camp;
and out of what had before been water, dry land was
seen emerging:
Out of the Red Sea an unimpeded road,
and a grassy plain out of the mighty flood.
Over this crossed the whole nation sheltered by your hand,
after they beheld stupendous wonders.
For they ranged about like horses,
and bounded about like lambs,
praising you, O Lord! their deliverer.

Responsorial Psalm

PSALM 105:2-3, 36-37, 42-43

R. Remember the marvels the Lord has done! (or R. Alleluia.)

Sing to him, sing his praise,
proclaim all his wondrous deeds.
Glory in his holy name;
rejoice, O hearts that seek the LORD! **R.**

Then he struck every first-born throughout their land,
 the firstfruits of all their manhood.
And he led them forth laden with silver and gold,
 with not a weakling among their tribes. **R.**
For he remembered his holy word
 to his servant Abraham.
And he led forth his people with joy;
 with shouts of joy, his chosen ones. **R.**

Gospel

LUKE 18:1-8

Jesus told his disciples a parable about the necessity for them to pray always without becoming weary. He said, "There was a judge in a certain town who neither feared God nor respected any human being. And a widow in that town used to come to him and say, 'Render a just decision for me against my adversary.' For a long time the judge was unwilling, but eventually he thought, 'While it is true that I neither fear God nor respect any human being, because this widow keeps bothering me I shall deliver a just decision for her lest she finally come and strike me.'" The Lord said, "Pay attention to what the dishonest judge says. Will not God then secure the rights of his chosen ones who call out to him day and night? Will he be slow to answer them? I tell you, he will see to it that justice is done for them speedily. But when the Son of Man comes, will he find faith on earth?"

Sunday, November 17

Thirty-third Sunday in Ordinary Time

First Reading

MALACHI 3:19-20a

Lo, the day is coming, blazing like an oven,
 when all the proud and all evildoers will be stubble,
and the day that is coming will set them on fire,
 leaving them neither root nor branch,
 says the LORD of hosts.
But for you who fear my name, there will arise
 the sun of justice with its healing rays.

Responsorial Psalm

PSALM 98:5-6, 7-8, 9

R. The Lord comes to rule the earth with justice.

Sing praise to the LORD with the harp,
 with the harp and melodious song.

With trumpets and the sound of the horn
sing joyfully before the King, the LORD. **R.**
Let the sea and what fills it resound,
the world and those who dwell in it;
let the rivers clap their hands,
the mountains shout with them for joy. **R.**
Before the LORD, for he comes,
for he comes to rule the earth,
he will rule the world with justice
and the peoples with equity. **R.**

Second Reading
2 THESSALONIANS 3:7-12

Brothers and sisters: You know how one must imitate us. For we did not act in a disorderly way among you, nor did we eat food received free from anyone. On the contrary, in toil and drudgery, night and day we worked, so as not to burden any of you. Not that we do not have the right. Rather, we wanted to present ourselves as a model for you, so that you might imitate us. In fact, when we were with you, we instructed you that if anyone was unwilling to work, neither should that one eat. We hear that some are conducting themselves among you in a disorderly way, by not keeping busy but minding the business of others. Such people we instruct and urge in the Lord Jesus Christ to work quietly and to eat their own food.

Gospel
LUKE 21:5-19

While some people were speaking about how the temple was adorned with costly stones and votive offerings, Jesus said, "All that you see here—the days will come when there will not be left a stone upon another stone that will not be thrown down."

Then they asked him, "Teacher, when will this happen? And what sign will there be when all these things are about to happen?" He answered, "See that you not be deceived, for many will come in my name, saying, 'I am he,' and 'The time has come.' Do not follow them! When you hear of wars and insurrections, do not be terrified; for such things must happen first, but it will not immediately be the end." Then he said to them, "Nation will rise against nation, and kingdom against kingdom. There will be powerful earthquakes, famines, and plagues from place to place; and awesome sights and mighty signs will come from the sky.

"Before all this happens, however, they will seize and persecute you, they will hand you over to the synagogues and to prisons, and they will have you led before kings and governors because of my name. It will lead to your giving testimony. Remember, you are not to prepare your defense beforehand, for I myself shall give you a wisdom in speaking that all your adversaries will be powerless to resist or refute. You will even be handed over by parents, brothers, relatives, and friends, and they will put some of you to death. You will be hated by all because of my name, but not a hair on your head will be destroyed. By your perseverance you will secure your lives."

Monday, November 18

First Reading

1 MACCABEES 1:10-15, 41-43, 54-57, 62-63

[From the descendants of Alexander's officers] there sprang a sinful offshoot, Antiochus Epiphanes, son of King Antiochus, once a hostage at Rome. He became king in the year one hundred and thirty-seven of the kingdom of the Greeks.

In those days there appeared in Israel men who were breakers of the law, and they seduced many people, saying: "Let us go and make an alliance with the Gentiles all around us; since we separated from them, many evils have come upon us." The proposal was agreeable; some from among the people promptly went to the king, and he authorized them to introduce the way of living of the Gentiles. Thereupon they built a gymnasium in Jerusalem according to the Gentile custom. They covered over the mark of their circumcision and abandoned the holy covenant; they allied themselves with the Gentiles and sold themselves to wrongdoing.

Then the king wrote to his whole kingdom that all should be one people, each abandoning his particular customs. All the Gentiles conformed to the command of the king, and many children of Israel were in favor of his religion; they sacrificed to idols and profaned the sabbath.

On the fifteenth day of the month Chislev, in the year one hundred and forty-five, the king erected the horrible abomination upon the altar of burnt offerings and in the surrounding cities of Judah they built pagan altars. They also burned incense at the doors of the houses and in the streets. Any scrolls of the law which they found they tore up and burnt. Whoever was found with a scroll of the covenant, and whoever observed the law, was condemned to death by royal decree. But many in Israel were determined and resolved in their hearts not to eat anything unclean; they preferred to die rather than to be defiled with unclean food or to profane the holy covenant; and they did die. Terrible affliction was upon Israel.

Responsorial Psalm

PSALM 119:53, 61, 134, 150, 155, 158

R. Give me life, O Lord, and I will do your commands.

Indignation seizes me because of the wicked
who forsake your law. **R.**
Though the snares of the wicked are twined about me,
your law I have not forgotten. **R.**
Redeem me from the oppression of men,
that I may keep your precepts. **R.**
I am attacked by malicious persecutors
who are far from your law. **R.**
Far from sinners is salvation,
because they seek not your statutes. **R.**
I beheld the apostates with loathing,
because they kept not to your promise. **R.**

Gospel

LUKE 18:35-43

As Jesus approached Jericho a blind man was sitting by the roadside begging, and hearing a crowd going by, he inquired what was happening. They told him, "Jesus of Nazareth is passing by." He shouted, "Jesus, Son of David, have pity on me!" The people walking in front rebuked him, telling him to be silent, but he kept calling out all the more, "Son of David, have pity on me!" Then Jesus stopped and ordered that he be brought to him; and when he came near, Jesus asked him, "What do you want me to do for you?" He replied, "Lord, please let me see." Jesus told him, "Have sight; your faith has saved you." He immediately received his sight and followed him, giving glory to God. When they saw this, all the people gave praise to God.

Tuesday, November 19

First Reading

2 MACCABEES 6:18-31

Eleazar, one of the foremost scribes, a man of advanced age and noble appearance, was being forced to open his mouth to eat pork. But preferring a glorious death to a life of defilement, he spat out the meat, and went forward of his own accord to the instrument of torture, as people ought to do who have the courage to reject the food which it is unlawful to taste even for love of life. Those in charge of that unlawful ritual meal took the man aside privately, because of their long acquaintance with him, and urged him to bring meat of his own providing, such as he could legitimately eat, and to pretend to be eating some of the meat of the sacrifice prescribed by the king; in this way he would escape the death penalty, and be treated kindly because of their old friendship with him. But Eleazar made up his mind in a noble manner, worthy of his years, the dignity of his advanced age, the merited distinction of his gray hair, and of the admirable life he had lived from childhood; and so he declared that above all he would be loyal to the holy laws given by God.

He told them to send him at once to the abode of the dead, explaining: "At our age it would be unbecoming to make such a pretense; many young people would think the ninety-year-old Eleazar had gone over to an alien religion. Should I thus pretend for the sake of a brief moment of life, they would be led astray by me, while I would bring shame and dishonor on my old age. Even if, for the time being, I avoid the punishment of men, I shall never, whether alive or dead, escape the hands of the Almighty. Therefore, by manfully giving up my life now, I will prove myself worthy of my old age, and I will leave to the young a noble example of how to die willingly and generously for the revered and holy laws."

Eleazar spoke thus, and went immediately to the instrument of torture. Those who shortly before had been kindly disposed, now became hostile toward him because what he had said seemed to them utter madness. When he was about to die under the blows, he groaned and said: "The Lord in his holy knowledge knows full well that, although I could have escaped death, I am not only enduring terrible pain in my body from this scourging, but also suffering it with joy in my soul because of my devotion to him." This is how he died, leaving in his death a model of courage and an unforgettable example of virtue not only for the young but for the whole nation.

Responsorial Psalm
PSALM 3:2-3, 4-5, 6-7
R. The Lord upholds me.

O LORD, how many are my adversaries!
Many rise up against me!
Many are saying of me,
"There is no salvation for him in God." **R.**

But you, O LORD, are my shield;
my glory, you lift up my head!
When I call out to the LORD,
he answers me from his holy mountain. **R.**

When I lie down in sleep,
I wake again, for the LORD sustains me.
I fear not the myriads of people
arrayed against me on every side. **R.**

Gospel
LUKE 19:1-10

At that time Jesus came to Jericho and intended to pass through the town. Now a man there named Zacchaeus, who was a chief tax collector and also a wealthy man, was seeking to see who Jesus was; but he could not see him because of the crowd, for he was short in stature. So he ran ahead and climbed a sycamore tree in order to see Jesus, who was about to pass that way. When he reached the place, Jesus looked up and said, "Zacchaeus, come down quickly, for today I must stay at your house." And he came down quickly and received him with joy. When they saw this, they began to grumble, saying, "He has gone to stay at the house of a sinner." But Zacchaeus stood there and said to the Lord, "Behold, half of my possessions, Lord, I shall give to the poor, and if I have extorted anything from anyone I shall repay it four times over." And Jesus said to him, "Today salvation has come to this house because this man too is a descendant of Abraham. For the Son of Man has come to seek and to save what was lost."

Wednesday, November 20

First Reading
2 MACCABEES 7:1, 20-31

It happened that seven brothers with their mother were arrested and tortured with whips and scourges by the king, to force them to eat pork in violation of God's law.

Most admirable and worthy of everlasting remembrance was the mother, who saw her seven sons perish in a single day, yet bore it courageously because of her hope in the Lord. Filled with a noble spirit that stirred her womanly heart with manly courage, she exhorted each of them in the language of their ancestors with these words: "I do not know how you came into existence in my womb; it was not I who gave you the breath of life, nor was it I who set in order the elements of which each of you is composed. Therefore, since it is the Creator of the universe who shapes each man's beginning, as he brings about the origin of everything, he, in his mercy, will give you back both breath and life, because you now disregard yourselves for the sake of his law."

Antiochus, suspecting insult in her words, thought he was being ridiculed. As the youngest brother was still alive, the king appealed to him, not with mere words, but with promises on oath, to make him rich and happy if he would abandon his ancestral customs: he would make him his Friend and entrust him with high office. When the youth paid no attention to him at all, the king appealed to the mother, urging her to advise her boy to save his life. After he had urged her for a long time, she went through the motions of persuading her son. In derision of the cruel tyrant, she leaned over close to her son and said in their native language: "Son, have pity on me, who carried you in my womb for nine months, nursed you for three years, brought you up, educated and supported you to your present age. I beg you, child, to look at the heavens and the earth and see all that is in them; then you will know that God did not make them out of existing things; and in the same way the human race came into existence. Do not be afraid of this executioner, but be worthy of your brothers and accept death, so that in the time of mercy I may receive you again with them."

She had scarcely finished speaking when the youth said: "What are you waiting for? I will not obey the king's command. I obey the command of the law given to our fathers through Moses. But you, who have contrived every kind of affliction for the Hebrews, will not escape the hands of God."

Responsorial Psalm

PSALM 17:1bcd, 5-6, 8b and 15

R. Lord, when your glory appears, my joy will be full.

Hear, O LORD, a just suit;
attend to my outcry;
hearken to my prayer from lips without deceit. **R.**
My steps have been steadfast in your paths,
my feet have not faltered.
I call upon you, for you will answer me, O God;
incline your ear to me; hear my word. **R.**
Keep me as the apple of your eye;
hide me in the shadow of your wings.
But I in justice shall behold your face;
on waking, I shall be content in your presence. **R.**

Gospel

LUKE 19:11-28

While people were listening to Jesus speak, he proceeded to tell a parable because he was near Jerusalem and they thought that the Kingdom of God would appear there immediately. So he said, "A nobleman went off to a distant country to obtain the kingship for himself and then to return. He called ten of his servants and gave them ten gold coins and told them, 'Engage in trade with these until I return.' His fellow citizens, however, despised him and sent a delegation after him to announce, 'We do not want this man to be our king.' But when he returned after obtaining the kingship, he had the servants called, to whom he had given the money, to learn what they had gained by trading. The first came forward and said, 'Sir, your gold coin has earned ten additional ones.' He replied, 'Well done, good servant! You have been faithful in this very small matter; take charge of ten cities.' Then the second came and reported, 'Your gold coin, sir, has earned five more.' And to this servant too he said, 'You, take charge of five cities.' Then the other servant came and said, 'Sir, here is your gold coin; I kept it stored away in a handkerchief, for I was afraid of you, because you are a demanding man; you take up what you did not lay down and you harvest what you did not plant.' He said to him, 'With your own words I shall condemn you, you wicked servant. You knew I was a demanding man, taking up what I did not lay down and harvesting what I did not plant; why did you not put my money in a bank? Then on my return I would have collected it with interest.' And to those standing by he said, 'Take the gold coin from him and give it to the servant who has ten.' But they said to him, 'Sir, he has ten gold coins.' He replied, 'I tell you, to everyone who has, more will be given, but from the one who has not, even what he has will be taken away. Now as for those enemies of mine who did not want me as their king, bring them here and slay them before me.'"

After he had said this, he proceeded on his journey up to Jerusalem.

Thursday, November 21

First Reading

1 MACCABEES 2:15-29

The officers of the king in charge of enforcing the apostasy came to the city of Modein to organize the sacrifices. Many of Israel joined them, but Mattathias and his sons gathered in a group apart. Then the officers of the king addressed Mattathias: "You are a leader, an honorable and great man in this city, supported by sons and kin. Come now, be the first to obey the king's command, as all the Gentiles and the men of Judah and those who are left in Jerusalem have done. Then you and your sons shall be numbered among the King's Friends, and shall be enriched with silver and gold and many gifts." But Mattathias answered in a loud voice: "Although all the Gentiles in the king's realm obey him, so that each forsakes the religion of his fathers and consents to the king's orders, yet I and my sons and my kin will keep to the covenant of our fathers. God forbid that we should forsake the law and the commandments. We will not obey the words of the king nor depart from our religion in the slightest degree."

As he finished saying these words, a certain Jew came forward in the sight of all to offer sacrifice on the altar in Modein according to the king's order. When Mattathias saw him, he was filled with zeal; his heart was moved and his just fury was aroused; he sprang forward and killed him upon the altar. At the same time, he also killed the messenger of the king who was forcing them to sacrifice, and he tore down the altar. Thus he showed his zeal for the law, just as Phinehas did with Zimri, son of Salu.

Then Mattathias went through the city shouting, "Let everyone who is zealous for the law and who stands by the covenant follow after me!" Thereupon he fled to the mountains with his sons, leaving behind in the city all their possessions. Many who sought to live according to righteousness and religious custom went out into the desert to settle there.

Responsorial Psalm

PSALM 50:1b-2, 5-6, 14-15

R. To the upright I will show the saving power of God.

God the LORD has spoken and summoned the earth,
 from the rising of the sun to its setting.
From Zion, perfect in beauty,
 God shines forth. **R.**
"Gather my faithful ones before me,
 those who have made a covenant with me by sacrifice."
And the heavens proclaim his justice;
 for God himself is the judge. **R.**
"Offer to God praise as your sacrifice
 and fulfill your vows to the Most High;
Then call upon me in time of distress;
 I will rescue you, and you shall glorify me." **R.**

Gospel

LUKE 19:41-44

As Jesus drew near Jerusalem, he saw the city and wept over it, saying, "If this day you only knew what makes for peace—but now it is hidden from your eyes. For the days are coming upon you when your enemies will raise a palisade against you; they will encircle you and hem you in on all sides. They will smash you to the ground and your children within you, and they will not leave one stone upon another within you because you did not recognize the time of your visitation."

Friday, November 22

First Reading

1 MACCABEES 4:36-37, 52-59

Judas and his brothers said, "Now that our enemies have been crushed, let us go up to purify the sanctuary and rededicate it." So the whole army assembled, and went up to Mount Zion.

Early in the morning on the twenty-fifth day of the ninth month, that is, the month of Chislev, in the year one hundred and forty-eight, they arose and offered sacrifice according to the law on the new altar of burnt offerings that they had made. On the anniversary of the day on which the Gentiles had defiled it, on that very day it was reconsecrated with songs, harps, flutes, and cymbals. All the people prostrated themselves and adored and praised Heaven, who had given them success.

For eight days they celebrated the dedication of the altar and joyfully offered burnt offerings and sacrifices of deliverance and praise. They ornamented the façade of the temple with gold crowns and shields; they repaired the gates and the priests' chambers and furnished them with doors. There was great joy among the people now that the disgrace of the Gentiles was removed. Then Judas and his brothers and the entire congregation of Israel decreed that the days of the dedication of the altar should be observed with joy and gladness on the anniversary every year for eight days, from the twenty-fifth day of the month Chislev.

Responsorial Psalm
1 CHRONICLES 29:10bcd, 11abc, 11d-12a, 12bcd
R. We praise your glorious name, O mighty God.

"Blessed may you be, O LORD,
God of Israel our father,
from eternity to eternity." **R.**
"Yours, O LORD, are grandeur and power,
majesty, splendor, and glory.
For all in heaven and on earth is yours." **R.**
"Yours, O LORD, is the sovereignty;
you are exalted as head over all.
Riches and honor are from you." **R.**
"You have dominion over all,
In your hand are power and might;
it is yours to give grandeur and strength to all." **R.**

Gospel
LUKE 19:45-48

Jesus entered the temple area and proceeded to drive out those who were selling things, saying to them, "It is written, *My house shall be a house of prayer, but you have made it a den of thieves.*" And every day he was teaching in the temple area. The chief priests, the scribes, and the leaders of the people, meanwhile, were seeking to put him to death, but they could find no way to accomplish their purpose because all the people were hanging on his words.

Saturday, November 23

First Reading

1 MACCABEES 6:1-13

As King Antiochus was traversing the inland provinces, he heard that in Persia there was a city called Elymais, famous for its wealth in silver and gold, and that its temple was very rich, containing gold helmets, breastplates, and weapons left there by Alexander, son of Philip, king of Macedon, the first king of the Greeks. He went therefore and tried to capture and pillage the city. But he could not do so, because his plan became known to the people of the city who rose up in battle against him. So he retreated and in great dismay withdrew from there to return to Babylon.

While he was in Persia, a messenger brought him news that the armies sent into the land of Judah had been put to flight; that Lysias had gone at first with a strong army and been driven back by the children of Israel; that they had grown strong by reason of the arms, men, and abundant possessions taken from the armies they had destroyed; that they had pulled down the Abomination which he had built upon the altar in Jerusalem; and that they had surrounded with high walls both the sanctuary, as it had been before, and his city of Beth-zur.

When the king heard this news, he was struck with fear and very much shaken. Sick with grief because his designs had failed, he took to his bed. There he remained many days, overwhelmed with sorrow, for he knew he was going to die.

So he called in all his Friends and said to them: "Sleep has departed from my eyes, for my heart is sinking with anxiety. I said to myself: 'Into what tribulation have I come, and in what floods of sorrow am I now! Yet I was kindly and beloved in my rule.' But I now recall the evils I did in Jerusalem, when I carried away all the vessels of gold and silver that were in it, and for no cause gave orders that the inhabitants of Judah be destroyed. I know that this is why these evils have overtaken me; and now I am dying, in bitter grief, in a foreign land."

Responsorial Psalm

PSALM 9:2-3, 4 and 6, 16 and 19

R. I will rejoice in your salvation, O Lord.

I will give thanks to you, O LORD, with all my heart;
  I will declare all your wondrous deeds.
I will be glad and exult in you;
  I will sing praise to your name, Most High. **R.**
Because my enemies are turned back,
  overthrown and destroyed before you.

You rebuked the nations and destroyed the wicked;
their name you blotted out forever and ever. **R.**
The nations are sunk in the pit they have made;
in the snare they set, their foot is caught.
For the needy shall not always be forgotten,
nor shall the hope of the afflicted forever perish. **R.**

Gospel
LUKE 20:27-40

Some Sadducees, those who deny that there is a resurrection, came forward and put this question to Jesus, saying, "Teacher, Moses wrote for us, *If someone's brother dies leaving a wife but no child, his brother must take the wife and raise up descendants for his brother*. Now there were seven brothers; the first married a woman but died childless. Then the second and the third married her, and likewise all the seven died childless. Finally the woman also died. Now at the resurrection whose wife will that woman be? For all seven had been married to her." Jesus said to them, "The children of this age marry and remarry; but those who are deemed worthy to attain to the coming age and to the resurrection of the dead neither marry nor are given in marriage. They can no longer die, for they are like angels; and they are the children of God because they are the ones who will rise. That the dead will rise even Moses made known in the passage about the bush, when he called 'Lord' the God of Abraham, the God of Isaac, and the God of Jacob; and he is not God of the dead, but of the living, for to him all are alive." Some of the scribes said in reply, "Teacher, you have answered well." And they no longer dared to ask him anything.

Sunday, November 24

Our Lord Jesus Christ, King of the Universe

First Reading
2 SAMUEL 5:1-3

In those days, all the tribes of Israel came to David in Hebron and said: "Here we are, your bone and your flesh. In days past, when Saul was our king, it was you who led the Israelites out and brought them back. And the LORD said to you, 'You shall shepherd my people Israel and shall be commander of Israel.'" When all the elders of Israel came to David in Hebron, King David made an agreement with them there before the LORD, and they anointed him king of Israel.

Responsorial Psalm
PSALM 122:1-2, 3-4, 4-5
R. Let us go rejoicing to the house of the Lord.

I rejoiced because they said to me,
"We will go up to the house of the LORD."
And now we have set foot
within your gates, O Jerusalem. **R.**

Jerusalem, built as a city
with compact unity.
To it the tribes go up,
the tribes of the LORD. **R.**

According to the decree for Israel,
to give thanks to the name of the LORD.
In it are set up judgment seats,
seats for the house of David. **R.**

Second Reading
COLOSSIANS 1:12-20

Brothers and sisters: Let us give thanks to the Father, who has made you fit to share in the inheritance of the holy ones in light. He delivered us from the power of darkness and transferred us to the kingdom of his beloved Son, in whom we have redemption, the forgiveness of sins.

He is the image of the invisible God,
the firstborn of all creation.
For in him were created all things in heaven and on earth,
the visible and the invisible,
whether thrones or dominions or principalities or powers;
all things were created through him and for him.
He is before all things,
and in him all things hold together.
He is the head of the body, the church.
He is the beginning, the firstborn from the dead,
that in all things he himself might be preeminent.
For in him all the fullness was pleased to dwell,
and through him to reconcile all things for him,
making peace by the blood of his cross
through him, whether those on earth or those in heaven.

Gospel
LUKE 23:35-43

The rulers sneered at Jesus and said, "He saved others, let him save himself if he is the chosen one, the Christ of God." Even the soldiers jeered at him. As they approached to offer him wine they called out, "If you are King of the Jews, save yourself." Above him there was an inscription that read, "This is the King of the Jews."

Now one of the criminals hanging there reviled Jesus, saying, "Are you not the Christ? Save yourself and us." The other, however, rebuking him, said in reply, "Have you no fear of God, for you are subject to the same condemnation? And indeed, we have been condemned justly, for the sentence we received corresponds to our crimes, but this man has done nothing criminal." Then he said, "Jesus, remember me when you come into your kingdom." He replied to him, "Amen, I say to you, today you will be with me in Paradise."

Monday, November 25

(Thirty-fourth or Last Week in Ordinary Time)

First Reading

DANIEL 1:1-6, 8-20

In the third year of the reign of Jehoiakim, king of Judah, King Nebuchadnezzar of Babylon came and laid siege to Jerusalem. The Lord handed over to him Jehoiakim, king of Judah, and some of the vessels of the temple of God; he carried them off to the land of Shinar, and placed the vessels in the temple treasury of his god.

The king told Ashpenaz, his chief chamberlain, to bring in some of the children of Israel of royal blood and of the nobility, young men without any defect, handsome, intelligent and wise, quick to learn, and prudent in judgment, such as could take their place in the king's palace; they were to be taught the language and literature of the Chaldeans; after three years' training they were to enter the king's service. The king allotted them a daily portion of food and wine from the royal table. Among these were men of Judah: Daniel, Hananiah, Mishael, and Azariah.

But Daniel was resolved not to defile himself with the king's food or wine; so he begged the chief chamberlain to spare him this defilement. Though God had given Daniel the favor and sympathy of the chief chamberlain, he nevertheless said to Daniel, "I am afraid of my lord the king; it is he who allotted your food and drink. If he sees that you look wretched by comparison with the other young men of your age, you will endanger my life with the king." Then Daniel said to the steward whom the chief chamberlain had put in charge of Daniel, Hananiah, Mishael, and Azariah, "Please test your servants for ten days. Give us vegetables to eat and water to drink. Then see how we look in comparison with the other young men who eat from the royal table, and treat your servants according to what you see." He acceded to this request, and tested them for ten days; after ten days they looked healthier and better fed than any of the young men who ate from the royal table. So the steward continued to take away the food and wine they were to receive, and gave them vegetables.

To these four young men God gave knowledge and proficiency in all literature and science, and to Daniel the understanding of all visions and dreams. At the end of the time the king had specified for their preparation, the chief chamberlain brought them before Nebuchadnezzar. When the king had spoken with all of them, none was found equal to Daniel, Hananiah, Mishael, and Azariah; and so they entered the king's service. In any question of wisdom or prudence which the king put to them, he found them ten times better than all the magicians and enchanters in his kingdom.

Responsorial Psalm

DANIEL 3:52, 53, 54, 55, 56

R. Glory and praise for ever!

"Blessed are you, O Lord, the God of our fathers,
praiseworthy and exalted above all forever;
And blessed is your holy and glorious name,
praiseworthy and exalted above all for all ages." **R.**
"Blessed are you in the temple of your holy glory,
praiseworthy and glorious above all forever." **R.**
"Blessed are you on the throne of your Kingdom,
praiseworthy and exalted above all forever." **R.**
"Blessed are you who look into the depths
from your throne upon the cherubim,
praiseworthy and exalted above all forever." **R.**
"Blessed are you in the firmament of heaven,
praiseworthy and glorious forever." **R.**

Gospel

LUKE 21:1-4

When Jesus looked up he saw some wealthy people putting their offerings into the treasury and he noticed a poor widow putting in two small coins. He said, "I tell you truly, this poor widow put in more than all the rest; for those others have all made offerings from their surplus wealth, but she, from her poverty, has offered her whole livelihood."

Tuesday, November 26

First Reading

DANIEL 2:31-45

Daniel said to Nebuchadnezzar: "In your vision, O king, you saw a statue, very large and exceedingly bright, terrifying in appearance as it stood before you. The head of the statue was pure gold, its chest and arms were silver, its belly and thighs bronze, the legs iron, its feet partly iron and partly tile. While you looked at the statue, a stone which was hewn from a mountain without a hand being put to it, struck its iron and tile feet, breaking them in pieces. The iron, tile, bronze, silver, and gold all crumbled at once, fine as the chaff on the threshing floor in summer, and the wind blew them away without leaving a trace. But the stone that struck the statue became a great mountain and filled the whole earth.

"This was the dream; the interpretation we shall also give in the king's presence. You, O king, are the king of kings; to you the God of heaven has given dominion and strength, power and glory; men, wild beasts, and birds of the air, wherever they may dwell, he has handed over to you, making you ruler over them all; you are the head of gold. Another kingdom shall take your place, inferior to yours, then a third kingdom, of bronze, which shall rule over the whole earth. There shall be a fourth kingdom, strong as iron; it shall break in pieces and subdue all these others, just as iron breaks in pieces and crushes everything else. The feet and toes you saw, partly of potter's tile and partly of iron, mean that it shall be a divided kingdom, but yet have some of the hardness of iron. As you saw the iron mixed with clay tile, and the toes partly iron and partly tile, the kingdom shall be partly strong and partly fragile. The iron mixed with clay tile means that they shall seal their alliances by intermarriage, but they shall not stay united, any more than iron mixes with clay. In the lifetime of those kings the God of heaven will set up a kingdom that shall never be destroyed or delivered up to another people; rather, it shall break in pieces all these kingdoms and put an end to them, and it shall stand forever. That is the meaning of the stone you saw hewn from the mountain without a hand being put to it, which broke in pieces the tile, iron, bronze, silver, and gold. The great God has revealed to the king what shall be in the future; this is exactly what you dreamed, and its meaning is sure."

Responsorial Psalm

DANIEL 3:57, 58, 59, 60, 61

R. Give glory and eternal praise to him.

"Bless the Lord, all you works of the Lord,
praise and exalt him above all forever." **R.**

"Angels of the Lord, bless the Lord,
praise and exalt him above all forever." **R.**
"You heavens, bless the Lord,
praise and exalt him above all forever." **R.**
"All you waters above the heavens, bless the Lord,
praise and exalt him above all forever." **R.**
"All you hosts of the Lord, bless the Lord;
praise and exalt him above all forever." **R.**

Gospel
LUKE 21:5-11

While some people were speaking about how the temple was adorned with costly stones and votive offerings, Jesus said, "All that you see here—the days will come when there will not be left a stone upon another stone that will not be thrown down."

Then they asked him, "Teacher, when will this happen? And what sign will there be when all these things are about to happen?" He answered, "See that you not be deceived, for many will come in my name, saying, 'I am he,' and 'The time has come.' Do not follow them! When you hear of wars and insurrections, do not be terrified; for such things must happen first, but it will not immediately be the end." Then he said to them, "Nation will rise against nation, and kingdom against kingdom. There will be powerful earthquakes, famines, and plagues from place to place; and awesome sights and mighty signs will come from the sky."

Wednesday, November 27

First Reading
DANIEL 5:1-6, 13-14, 16-17, 23-28

King Belshazzar gave a great banquet for a thousand of his lords, with whom he drank. Under the influence of the wine, he ordered the gold and silver vessels which Nebuchadnezzar, his father, had taken from the temple in Jerusalem, to be brought in so that the king, his lords, his wives and his entertainers might drink from them. When the gold and silver vessels taken from the house of God in Jerusalem had been brought in, and while the king, his lords, his wives and his entertainers were drinking wine from them, they praised their gods of gold and silver, bronze and iron, wood and stone.

Suddenly, opposite the lampstand, the fingers of a human hand appeared, writing on the plaster of the wall in the king's palace. When the king saw the wrist and hand that wrote, his face blanched; his thoughts terrified him, his hip joints shook, and his knees knocked.

Then Daniel was brought into the presence of the king. The king asked him, "Are you the Daniel, the Jewish exile, whom my father, the king, brought from Judah? I have heard that the Spirit of God is in you, that you possess brilliant knowledge and extraordinary wisdom. I have heard that you can interpret dreams and solve difficulties; if you are able to read the writing and tell me what it means, you shall be clothed in purple, wear a gold collar about your neck, and be third in the government of the kingdom."

Daniel answered the king: "You may keep your gifts, or give your presents to someone else; but the writing I will read for you, O king, and tell you what it means. You have rebelled against the Lord of heaven. You had the vessels of his temple brought before you, so that you and your nobles, your wives and your entertainers, might drink wine from them; and you praised the gods of silver and gold, bronze and iron, wood and stone, that neither see nor hear nor have intelligence. But the God in whose hand is your life breath and the whole course of your life, you did not glorify. By him were the wrist and hand sent, and the writing set down.

"This is the writing that was inscribed: MENE, TEKEL, and PERES. These words mean: MENE, God has numbered your kingdom and put an end to it; TEKEL, you have been weighed on the scales and found wanting; PERES, your kingdom has been divided and given to the Medes and Persians."

Responsorial Psalm

DANIEL 3:62, 63, 64, 65, 66, 67

R. Give glory and eternal praise to him.

"Sun and moon, bless the Lord;
praise and exalt him above all forever." **R.**
"Stars of heaven, bless the Lord;
praise and exalt him above all forever." **R.**
"Every shower and dew, bless the Lord;
praise and exalt him above all forever." **R.**
"All you winds, bless the Lord;
praise and exalt him above all forever." **R.**
"Fire and heat, bless the Lord;
praise and exalt him above all forever." **R.**
"Cold and chill, bless the Lord;
praise and exalt him above all forever." **R.**

Gospel

LUKE 21:12-19

Jesus said to the crowd: "They will seize and persecute you, they will hand you over to the synagogues and to prisons, and they will have you led before kings and governors because of my name. It will lead to your giving testimony. Remember, you are not to prepare your defense beforehand, for I myself shall give you a wisdom in speaking that all your adversaries will be powerless to resist or refute. You will even be handed over by parents, brothers, relatives, and friends, and they will put some of you to death. You will be hated by all because of my name, but not a hair on your head will be destroyed. By your perseverance you will secure your lives."

Thursday, November 28

[For Thanksgiving Day, any readings from the *Lectionary for Masses* (vol. IV), the Mass "In Thanksgiving to God," nos. 943-947, may be substituted for those listed here.]

First Reading
DANIEL 6:12-28

Some men rushed into the upper chamber of Daniel's home and found him praying and pleading before his God. Then they went to remind the king about the prohibition: "Did you not decree, O king, that no one is to address a petition to god or man for thirty days, except to you, O king; otherwise he shall be cast into a den of lions?" The king answered them, "The decree is absolute, irrevocable under the Mede and Persian law." To this they replied, "Daniel, the Jewish exile, has paid no attention to you, O king, or to the decree you issued; three times a day he offers his prayer." The king was deeply grieved at this news and he made up his mind to save Daniel; he worked till sunset to rescue him. But these men insisted. They said, "Keep in mind, O king, that under the Mede and Persian law every royal prohibition or decree is irrevocable." So the king ordered Daniel to be brought and cast into the lions' den. To Daniel he said, "May your God, whom you serve so constantly, save you." To forestall any tampering, the king sealed with his own ring and the rings of the lords the stone that had been brought to block the opening of the den.

Then the king returned to his palace for the night; he refused to eat and he dismissed the entertainers. Since sleep was impossible for him, the king rose very early the next morning and hastened to the lions' den. As he drew near, he cried out to Daniel sorrowfully, "O Daniel, servant of the living God, has the God whom you serve so constantly been able to save you from the lions?" Daniel answered the king: "O king, live forever! My God has sent his angel and closed the lions' mouths so that they have not hurt me. For I have been found innocent before him; neither to you have I done any harm, O king!" This gave the king great joy. At his order Daniel was removed from the den, unhurt because he trusted in his God. The king then ordered the men who had accused Daniel, along with their children and their wives, to be cast into the lions' den. Before they reached the bottom of the den, the lions overpowered them and crushed all their bones.

Then King Darius wrote to the nations and peoples of every language, wherever they dwell on the earth: "All peace to you! I decree that throughout my royal domain the God of Daniel is to be reverenced and feared:

"For he is the living God, enduring forever;
his Kingdom shall not be destroyed,
and his dominion shall be without end.
He is a deliverer and savior,
working signs and wonders in heaven and on earth,
and he delivered Daniel from the lions' power."

Responsorial Psalm
DANIEL 3:68, 69, 70, 71, 72, 73, 74
R. Give glory and eternal praise to him.
"Dew and rain, bless the Lord;
praise and exalt him above all forever." **R.**
"Frost and chill, bless the Lord;
praise and exalt him above all forever." **R.**
"Ice and snow, bless the Lord;
praise and exalt him above all forever." **R.**
"Nights and days, bless the Lord;
praise and exalt him above all forever." **R.**
"Light and darkness, bless the Lord;
praise and exalt him above all forever." **R.**
"Lightnings and clouds, bless the Lord;
praise and exalt him above all forever." **R.**
"Let the earth bless the Lord,
praise and exalt him above all forever." **R.**

Gospel
LUKE 21:20-28

Jesus said to his disciples: "When you see Jerusalem surrounded by armies, know that its desolation is at hand. Then those in Judea must flee to the mountains. Let those within the city escape from it, and let those in the countryside not enter the city, for these days are the time of punishment when all the Scriptures are fulfilled. Woe to pregnant women and nursing mothers in those days, for a terrible calamity will come upon the earth and a wrathful judgment upon this people. They will fall by the edge of the sword and be taken as captives to all the Gentiles; and

Jerusalem will be trampled underfoot by the Gentiles until the times of the Gentiles are fulfilled.

"There will be signs in the sun, the moon, and the stars, and on earth nations will be in dismay, perplexed by the roaring of the sea and the waves. People will die of fright in anticipation of what is coming upon the world, for the powers of the heavens will be shaken. And then they will see the Son of Man coming in a cloud with power and great glory. But when these signs begin to happen, stand erect and raise your heads because your redemption is at hand."

Friday, November 29

First Reading

DANIEL 7:2-14

In a vision I, Daniel, saw during the night, the four winds of heaven stirred up the great sea, from which emerged four immense beasts, each different from the others. The first was like a lion, but with eagle's wings. While I watched, the wings were plucked; it was raised from the ground to stand on two feet like a man, and given a human mind. The second was like a bear; it was raised up on one side, and among the teeth in its mouth were three tusks. It was given the order, "Up, devour much flesh." After this I looked and saw another beast, like a leopard; on its back were four wings like those of a bird, and it had four heads. To this beast dominion was given. After this, in the visions of the night I saw the fourth beast, different from all the others, terrifying, horrible, and of extraordinary strength; it had great iron teeth with which it devoured and crushed, and what was left it trampled with its feet. I was considering the ten horns it had, when suddenly another, a little horn, sprang out of their midst, and three of the previous horns were torn away to make room for it. This horn had eyes like a man, and a mouth that spoke arrogantly. As I watched,

Thrones were set up
 and the Ancient One took his throne.
His clothing was snow bright,
 and the hair on his head as white as wool;
His throne was flames of fire,
 with wheels of burning fire.
A surging stream of fire
 flowed out from where he sat;
Thousands upon thousands were ministering to him,
 and myriads upon myriads attended him.

The court was convened, and the books were opened. I watched, then, from the first of the arrogant words which the horn spoke, until the beast was slain and its body thrown into the fire to be burnt up. The other beasts, which also lost their dominion, were granted a prolongation of life for a time and a season. As the visions during the night continued, I saw

One like a son of man coming,
    on the clouds of heaven;
When he reached the Ancient One
    and was presented before him,
He received dominion, glory, and kingship;
    nations and peoples of every language serve him.
His dominion is an everlasting dominion
    that shall not be taken away,
    his kingship shall not be destroyed.

Responsorial Psalm
DANIEL 3:75, 76, 77, 78, 79, 80, 81
R. Give glory and eternal praise to him!
"Mountains and hills, bless the Lord;
    praise and exalt him above all forever." **R.**
"Everything growing from the earth, bless the Lord;
    praise and exalt him above all forever." **R.**
"You springs, bless the Lord;
    praise and exalt him above all forever." **R.**
"Seas and rivers, bless the Lord;
    praise and exalt him above all forever." **R.**
"You dolphins and all water creatures, bless the Lord;
    praise and exalt him above all forever." **R.**
"All you birds of the air, bless the Lord;
    praise and exalt him above all forever." **R.**
"All you beasts, wild and tame, bless the Lord;
    praise and exalt him above all forever." **R.**

Gospel
LUKE 21:29-33
Jesus told his disciples a parable. "Consider the fig tree and all the other trees. When their buds burst open, you see for yourselves and know that summer is now near; in the same way, when you see these things happening, know that the Kingdom of God is near. Amen, I say to you, this generation will not pass away until all these things have taken place. Heaven and earth will pass away, but my words will not pass away."

Saturday, November 30

Saint Andrew, Apostle

First Reading
ROMANS 10:9-18

Brothers and sisters: If you confess with your mouth that Jesus is Lord and believe in your heart that God raised him from the dead, you will be saved. For one believes with the heart and so is justified, and one confesses with the mouth and so is saved. The Scripture says, *No one who believes in him will be put to shame.* There is no distinction between Jew and Greek; the same Lord is Lord of all, enriching all who call upon him. *For everyone who calls on the name of the Lord will be saved.*

But how can they call on him in whom they have not believed? And how can they believe in him of whom they have not heard? And how can they hear without someone to preach? And how can people preach unless they are sent? As it is written, *How beautiful are the feet of those who bring the good news*! But not everyone has heeded the good news; for Isaiah says, *Lord, who has believed what was heard from us*? Thus faith comes from what is heard, and what is heard comes through the word of Christ. But I ask, did they not hear? Certainly they did; for

Their voice has gone forth to all the earth,
and their words to the ends of the world.

Responsorial Psalm
PSALM 19:8, 9, 10, 11
R. The judgments of the Lord are true, and all of them are just. (or R. Your words, Lord, are Spirit and life.)

The law of the LORD is perfect,
refreshing the soul;
The decree of the LORD is trustworthy,
giving wisdom to the simple. **R.**
The precepts of the LORD are right,
rejoicing the heart;
The command of the LORD is clear,
enlightening the eye. **R.**
The fear of the LORD is pure,
enduring forever;
The ordinances of the LORD are true,
all of them just. **R.**
They are more precious than gold,
than a heap of purest gold;

Sweeter also than syrup
  or honey from the comb. **R.**

Gospel

MATTHEW 4:18-22

As Jesus was walking by the Sea of Galilee, he saw two brothers, Simon who is called Peter, and his brother Andrew, casting a net into the sea; they were fishermen. He said to them, "Come after me, and I will make you fishers of men." At once they left their nets and followed him. He walked along from there and saw two other brothers, James, the son of Zebedee, and his brother John. They were in a boat, with their father Zebedee, mending their nets. He called them, and immediately they left their boat and their father and followed him.

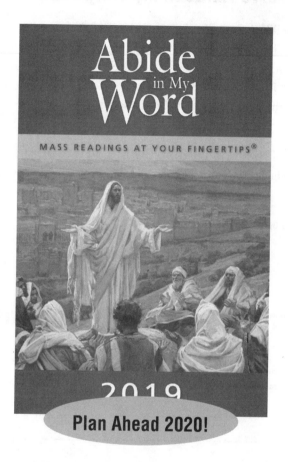

DECEMBER

Sunday, December 1

First Sunday of Advent

First Reading
ISAIAH 2:1-5

This is what Isaiah, son of Amoz, saw concerning Judah and Jerusalem.

In days to come,
the mountain of the LORD's house
shall be established as the highest mountain
and raised above the hills.
All nations shall stream toward it;
many peoples shall come and say:
"Come, let us climb the LORD's mountain,
to the house of the God of Jacob,
that he may instruct us in his ways,
and we may walk in his paths."
For from Zion shall go forth instruction,
and the word of the LORD from Jerusalem.
He shall judge between the nations,
and impose terms on many peoples.
They shall beat their swords into plowshares
and their spears into pruning hooks;
one nation shall not raise the sword against another,
nor shall they train for war again.
O house of Jacob, come,
let us walk in the light of the LORD!

Responsorial Psalm
PSALM 122:1-2, 3-4, 4-5, 6-7, 8-9
R. Let us go rejoicing to the house of the Lord.
I rejoiced because they said to me,
"We will go up to the house of the LORD."
And now we have set foot
within your gates, O Jerusalem. **R.**
Jerusalem, built as a city
with compact unity.
To it the tribes go up,
the tribes of the LORD. **R.**

According to the decree for Israel,
to give thanks to the name of the LORD.
In it are set up judgment seats,
seats for the house of David. **R.**
Pray for the peace of Jerusalem!
May those who love you prosper!
May peace be within your walls,
prosperity in your buildings. **R.**
Because of my brothers and friends
I will say, "Peace be within you!"
Because of the house of the LORD, our God,
I will pray for your good. **R.**

Second Reading
ROMANS 13:11-14

Brothers and sisters: You know the time; it is the hour now for you to awake from sleep. For our salvation is nearer now than when we first believed; the night is advanced, the day is at hand. Let us then throw off the works of darkness and put on the armor of light; let us conduct ourselves properly as in the day, not in orgies and drunkenness, not in promiscuity and lust, not in rivalry and jealousy. But put on the Lord Jesus Christ, and make no provision for the desires of the flesh.

Gospel
MATTHEW 24:37-44

Jesus said to his disciples: "As it was in the days of Noah, so it will be at the coming of the Son of Man. In those days before the flood, they were eating and drinking, marrying and giving in marriage, up to the day that Noah entered the ark. They did not know until the flood came and carried them all away. So will it be also at the coming of the Son of Man. Two men will be out in the field; one will be taken, and one will be left. Two women will be grinding at the mill; one will be taken, and one will be left. Therefore, stay awake! For you do not know on which day your Lord will come. Be sure of this: if the master of the house had known the hour of night when the thief was coming, he would have stayed awake and not let his house be broken into. So too, you also must be prepared, for at an hour you do not expect, the Son of Man will come."

Monday, December 2

First Reading
ISAIAH 4:2-6

On that day,
The branch of the LORD will be luster and glory,
and the fruit of the earth will be honor and splendor
for the survivors of Israel.
He who remains in Zion
and he who is left in Jerusalem
Will be called holy:
every one marked down for life in Jerusalem.
When the LORD washes away
the filth of the daughters of Zion,
And purges Jerusalem's blood from her midst
with a blast of searing judgment,
Then will the LORD create,
over the whole site of Mount Zion
and over her place of assembly,
A smoking cloud by day
and a light of flaming fire by night.
For over all, the LORD's glory will be shelter and protection:
shade from the parching heat of day,
refuge and cover from storm and rain.

Responsorial Psalm
PSALM 122:1-2, 3-4b, 4cd-5, 6-7, 8-9
R. Let us go rejoicing to the house of the Lord.

I rejoiced because they said to me,
"We will go up to the house of the LORD."
And now we have set foot
within your gates, O Jerusalem. **R.**
Jerusalem, built as a city
with compact unity.
To it the tribes go up,
the tribes of the LORD. **R.**
According to the decree for Israel,
to give thanks to the name of the LORD.
In it are set up judgment seats,
seats for the house of David. **R.**
Pray for the peace of Jerusalem!
May those who love you prosper!
May peace be within your walls,
prosperity in your buildings. **R.**

Because of my relatives and friends
 I will say, "Peace be within you!"
Because of the house of the LORD, our God,
 I will pray for your good. **R.**

Gospel
MATTHEW 8:5-11

When Jesus entered Capernaum, a centurion approached him and appealed to him, saying, "Lord, my servant is lying at home paralyzed, suffering dreadfully." He said to him, "I will come and cure him." The centurion said in reply, "Lord, I am not worthy to have you enter under my roof; only say the word and my servant will be healed. For I too am a man subject to authority, with soldiers subject to me. And I say to one, 'Go,' and he goes; and to another, 'Come here,' and he comes; and to my slave, 'Do this,' and he does it." When Jesus heard this, he was amazed and said to those following him, "Amen, I say to you, in no one in Israel have I found such faith. I say to you, many will come from the east and the west, and will recline with Abraham, Isaac, and Jacob at the banquet in the Kingdom of heaven."

Tuesday, December 3

First Reading
ISAIAH 11:1-10

  On that day,
A shoot shall sprout from the stump of Jesse,
 and from his roots a bud shall blossom.
The Spirit of the LORD shall rest upon him:
 a Spirit of wisdom and of understanding,
A Spirit of counsel and of strength,
 a Spirit of knowledge and of fear of the LORD,
 and his delight shall be the fear of the LORD.
Not by appearance shall he judge,
 nor by hearsay shall he decide,
But he shall judge the poor with justice,
 and decide aright for the land's afflicted.
He shall strike the ruthless with the rod of his mouth,
 and with the breath of his lips he shall slay the wicked.
Justice shall be the band around his waist,
 and faithfulness a belt upon his hips.

Then the wolf shall be a guest of the lamb,
 and the leopard shall lie down with the kid;

The calf and the young lion shall browse together,
with a little child to guide them.
The cow and the bear shall be neighbors,
together their young shall rest;
the lion shall eat hay like the ox.
The baby shall play by the cobra's den,
and the child lay his hand on the adder's lair.
There shall be no harm or ruin on all my holy mountain;
for the earth shall be filled with knowledge of the LORD,
as water covers the sea.

On that day,
The root of Jesse,
set up as a signal for the nations,
The Gentiles shall seek out,
for his dwelling shall be glorious.

Responsorial Psalm

PSALM 72:1-2, 7-8, 12-13, 17

R. Justice shall flourish in his time, and fullness of peace for ever.

O God, with your judgment endow the king,
and with your justice, the king's son;
He shall govern your people with justice
and your afflicted ones with judgment. **R.**
Justice shall flower in his days,
and profound peace, till the moon be no more.
May he rule from sea to sea,
and from the River to the ends of the earth. **R.**
He shall rescue the poor when he cries out,
and the afflicted when he has no one to help him.
He shall have pity for the lowly and the poor;
the lives of the poor he shall save. **R.**
May his name be blessed forever;
as long as the sun his name shall remain.
In him shall all the tribes of the earth be blessed;
all the nations shall proclaim his happiness. **R.**

Gospel

LUKE 10:21-24

Jesus rejoiced in the Holy Spirit and said, "I give you praise, Father, Lord of heaven and earth, for although you have hidden these things from the wise and the learned you have revealed them to the childlike. Yes, Father, such has been your gracious will. All things have been handed over to me by my Father. No one knows who the Son is except the Father, and who the Father is except the Son and anyone to whom the Son wishes to reveal him."

Turning to the disciples in private he said, "Blessed are the eyes that see what you see. For I say to you, many prophets and kings desired to see what you see, but did not see it, and to hear what you hear, but did not hear it."

Wednesday, December 4

First Reading

ISAIAH 25:6-10a

On this mountain the LORD of hosts
will provide for all peoples
A feast of rich food and choice wines,
juicy, rich food and pure, choice wines.
On this mountain he will destroy
the veil that veils all peoples,
The web that is woven over all nations;
he will destroy death forever.
The Lord GOD will wipe away
the tears from all faces;
The reproach of his people he will remove
from the whole earth; for the LORD has spoken.

On that day it will be said:
"Behold our God, to whom we looked to save us!
This is the LORD for whom we looked;
let us rejoice and be glad that he has saved us!"
For the hand of the LORD will rest on this mountain.

Responsorial Psalm

PSALM 23:1-3a, 3b-4, 5, 6

R. I shall live in the house of the Lord all the days of my life.

The LORD is my shepherd; I shall not want.
In verdant pastures he gives me repose;
Beside restful waters he leads me;
he refreshes my soul. **R.**
He guides me in right paths
for his name's sake.
Even though I walk in the dark valley
I fear no evil; for you are at my side

With your rod and your staff
 that give me courage. **R.**
You spread the table before me
 in the sight of my foes;
You anoint my head with oil;
 my cup overflows. **R.**
Only goodness and kindness follow me
 all the days of my life;
And I shall dwell in the house of the LORD
 for years to come. **R.**

Gospel
MATTHEW 15:29-37

At that time: Jesus walked by the Sea of Galilee, went up on the mountain, and sat down there. Great crowds came to him, having with them the lame, the blind, the deformed, the mute, and many others. They placed them at his feet, and he cured them. The crowds were amazed when they saw the mute speaking, the deformed made whole, the lame walking, and the blind able to see, and they glorified the God of Israel.

Jesus summoned his disciples and said, "My heart is moved with pity for the crowd, for they have been with me now for three days and have nothing to eat. I do not want to send them away hungry, for fear they may collapse on the way." The disciples said to him, "Where could we ever get enough bread in this deserted place to satisfy such a crowd?" Jesus said to them, "How many loaves do you have?" "Seven," they replied, "and a few fish." He ordered the crowd to sit down on the ground. Then he took the seven loaves and the fish, gave thanks, broke the loaves, and gave them to the disciples, who in turn gave them to the crowds. They all ate and were satisfied. They picked up the fragments left over—seven baskets full.

Thursday, December 5

First Reading
ISAIAH 26:1-6

On that day they will sing this song in the land of Judah:

"A strong city have we;
 he sets up walls and ramparts to protect us.
Open up the gates
 to let in a nation that is just,
 one that keeps faith.
A nation of firm purpose you keep in peace;
 in peace, for its trust in you."

Trust in the LORD forever!
For the LORD is an eternal Rock.
He humbles those in high places,
and the lofty city he brings down;
He tumbles it to the ground,
levels it with the dust.
It is trampled underfoot by the needy,
by the footsteps of the poor.

Responsorial Psalm
PSALM 118:1 and 8-9, 19-21, 25-27a
R. Blessed is he who comes in the name of the Lord.
(or R. Alleluia.)
Give thanks to the LORD, for he is good,
for his mercy endures forever.
It is better to take refuge in the LORD
than to trust in man.
It is better to take refuge in the LORD
than to trust in princes. **R.**
Open to me the gates of justice;
I will enter them and give thanks to the LORD.
This gate is the LORD's;
the just shall enter it.
I will give thanks to you, for you have answered me
and have been my savior. **R.**
O LORD, grant salvation!
O LORD, grant prosperity!
Blessed is he who comes in the name of the LORD;
we bless you from the house of the LORD.
The LORD is God, and he has given us light. **R.**

Gospel
MATTHEW 7:21, 24-27
Jesus said to his disciples: "Not everyone who says to me, 'Lord, Lord,' will enter the Kingdom of heaven, but only the one who does the will of my Father in heaven.

"Everyone who listens to these words of mine and acts on them will be like a wise man who built his house on rock. The rain fell, the floods came, and the winds blew and buffeted the house. But it did not collapse; it had been set solidly on rock. And everyone who listens to these words of mine but does not act on them will be like a fool who built his house on sand. The rain fell, the floods came, and the winds blew and buffeted the house. And it collapsed and was completely ruined."

Friday, December 6

First Reading

ISAIAH 29:17-24

Thus says the Lord GOD:
But a very little while,
and Lebanon shall be changed into an orchard,
and the orchard be regarded as a forest!
On that day the deaf shall hear
the words of a book;
And out of gloom and darkness,
the eyes of the blind shall see.
The lowly will ever find joy in the LORD,
and the poor rejoice in the Holy One of Israel.
For the tyrant will be no more
and the arrogant will have gone;
All who are alert to do evil will be cut off,
those whose mere word condemns a man,
Who ensnare his defender at the gate,
and leave the just man with an empty claim.
Therefore thus says the LORD,
the God of the house of Jacob,
who redeemed Abraham:
Now Jacob shall have nothing to be ashamed of,
nor shall his face grow pale.
When his children see
the work of my hands in his midst,
They shall keep my name holy;
they shall reverence the Holy One of Jacob,
and be in awe of the God of Israel.
Those who err in spirit shall acquire understanding,
and those who find fault shall receive instruction.

Responsorial Psalm

PSALM 27:1, 4, 13-14

R. The Lord is my light and my salvation.

The LORD is my light and my salvation;
whom should I fear?
The LORD is my life's refuge;
of whom should I be afraid? **R.**
One thing I ask of the LORD;
this I seek:
To dwell in the house of the LORD
all the days of my life,

That I may gaze on the loveliness of the LORD
and contemplate his temple. **R.**
I believe that I shall see the bounty of the LORD
in the land of the living.
Wait for the LORD with courage;
be stouthearted, and wait for the LORD. **R.**

Gospel

MATTHEW 9:27-31

As Jesus passed by, two blind men followed him, crying out, "Son of David, have pity on us!" When he entered the house, the blind men approached him and Jesus said to them, "Do you believe that I can do this?" "Yes, Lord," they said to him. Then he touched their eyes and said, "Let it be done for you according to your faith." And their eyes were opened. Jesus warned them sternly, "See that no one knows about this." But they went out and spread word of him through all that land.

Saturday, December 7

First Reading

ISAIAH 30:19-21, 23-26

Thus says the Lord GOD,
the Holy One of Israel:
O people of Zion, who dwell in Jerusalem,
no more will you weep;
He will be gracious to you when you cry out,
as soon as he hears he will answer you.
The Lord will give you the bread you need
and the water for which you thirst.
No longer will your Teacher hide himself,
but with your own eyes you shall see your Teacher,
While from behind, a voice shall sound in your ears:
"This is the way; walk in it,"
when you would turn to the right or to the left.

He will give rain for the seed
that you sow in the ground,
And the wheat that the soil produces
will be rich and abundant.
On that day your flock will be given pasture
and the lamb will graze in spacious meadows;
The oxen and the asses that till the ground
will eat silage tossed to them

with shovel and pitchfork.
Upon every high mountain and lofty hill
there will be streams of running water.
On the day of the great slaughter,
when the towers fall,
The light of the moon will be like that of the sun
and the light of the sun will be seven times greater
like the light of seven days.
On the day the LORD binds up the wounds of his people,
he will heal the bruises left by his blows.

Responsorial Psalm

PSALM 147:1-2, 3-4, 5-6

R. Blessed are all who wait for the Lord.

Praise the LORD, for he is good;
sing praise to our God, for he is gracious;
it is fitting to praise him.
The LORD rebuilds Jerusalem;
the dispersed of Israel he gathers. **R.**
He heals the brokenhearted
and binds up their wounds.
He tells the number of the stars;
he calls each by name. **R.**
Great is our LORD and mighty in power:
to his wisdom there is no limit.
The LORD sustains the lowly;
the wicked he casts to the ground. **R.**

Gospel

MATTHEW 9:35–10:1, 5a, 6-8

Jesus went around to all the towns and villages, teaching in their synagogues, proclaiming the Gospel of the Kingdom, and curing every disease and illness. At the sight of the crowds, his heart was moved with pity for them because they were troubled and abandoned, like sheep without a shepherd. Then he said to his disciples, "The harvest is abundant but the laborers are few; so ask the master of the harvest to send out laborers for his harvest."

Then he summoned his Twelve disciples and gave them authority over unclean spirits to drive them out and to cure every disease and every illness.

Jesus sent out these twelve after instructing them thus, "Go to the lost sheep of the house of Israel. As you go, make this proclamation: 'The Kingdom of heaven is at hand.' Cure the sick, raise the dead, cleanse lepers, drive out demons. Without cost you have received; without cost you are to give."

Sunday, December 8

Second Sunday of Advent

First Reading
ISAIAH 11:1-10

On that day, a shoot shall sprout from the stump of Jesse,
and from his roots a bud shall blossom.
The spirit of the LORD shall rest upon him:
a spirit of wisdom and of understanding,
a spirit of counsel and of strength,
a spirit of knowledge and of fear of the LORD,
and his delight shall be the fear of the LORD.
Not by appearance shall he judge,
nor by hearsay shall he decide,
but he shall judge the poor with justice,
and decide aright for the land's afflicted.
He shall strike the ruthless with the rod of his mouth,
and with the breath of his lips he shall slay the wicked.
Justice shall be the band around his waist,
and faithfulness a belt upon his hips.
Then the wolf shall be a guest of the lamb,
and the leopard shall lie down with the kid;
the calf and the young lion shall browse together,
with a little child to guide them.
The cow and the bear shall be neighbors,
together their young shall rest;
the lion shall eat hay like the ox.
The baby shall play by the cobra's den,
and the child lay his hand on the adder's lair.
There shall be no harm or ruin on all my holy mountain;
for the earth shall be filled with knowledge of the LORD,
as water covers the sea.
On that day, the root of Jesse,
set up as a signal for the nations,
the Gentiles shall seek out,
for his dwelling shall be glorious.

Responsorial Psalm
PSALM 72:1-2, 7-8, 12-13, 17
R. Justice shall flourish in his time, and fullness of peace for ever.

O God, with your judgment endow the king,
and with your justice, the king's son;
he shall govern your people with justice
and your afflicted ones with judgment. **R.**
Justice shall flower in his days,
and profound peace, till the moon be no more.
May he rule from sea to sea,
and from the River to the ends of the earth. **R.**
For he shall rescue the poor when he cries out,
and the afflicted when he has no one to help him.
He shall have pity for the lowly and the poor;
the lives of the poor he shall save. **R.**
May his name be blessed forever;
as long as the sun his name shall remain.
In him shall all the tribes of the earth be blessed;
all the nations shall proclaim his happiness. **R.**

Second Reading
ROMANS 15:4-9

Brothers and sisters: Whatever was written previously was written for our instruction, that by endurance and by the encouragement of the Scriptures we might have hope. May the God of endurance and encouragement grant you to think in harmony with one another, in keeping with Christ Jesus, that with one accord you may with one voice glorify the God and Father of our Lord Jesus Christ.

Welcome one another, then, as Christ welcomed you, for the glory of God. For I say that Christ became a minister of the circumcised to show God's truthfulness, to confirm the promises to the patriarchs, but so that the Gentiles might glorify God for his mercy. As it is written:

Therefore, I will praise you among the Gentiles
and sing praises to your name.

Gospel
MATTHEW 3:1-12

John the Baptist appeared, preaching in the desert of Judea and saying, "Repent, for the kingdom of heaven is at hand!" It was of him that the prophet Isaiah had spoken when he said:

A voice of one crying out in the desert,
Prepare the way of the Lord,
make straight his paths.

John wore clothing made of camel's hair and had a leather belt around his waist. His food was locusts and wild honey. At that time Jerusalem, all Judea, and the whole region around the Jordan were going out to him and were being baptized by him in the Jordan River as they acknowledged their sins.

When he saw many of the Pharisees and Sadducees coming to his baptism, he said to them, "You brood of vipers! Who warned you to flee from the coming wrath? Produce good fruit as evidence of your repentance. And do not presume to say to yourselves, 'We have Abraham as our father.' For I tell you, God can raise up children to Abraham from these stones. Even now the ax lies at the root of the trees. Therefore every tree that does not bear good fruit will be cut down and thrown into the fire. I am baptizing you with water, for repentance, but the one who is coming after me is mightier than I. I am not worthy to carry his sandals. He will baptize you with the Holy Spirit and fire. His winnowing fan is in his hand. He will clear his threshing floor and gather his wheat into his barn, but the chaff he will burn with unquenchable fire."

Monday, December 9

The Immaculate Conception of the Blessed Virgin Mary

First Reading
GENESIS 3:9-15, 20

After the man, Adam, had eaten of the tree, the LORD God called to the man and asked him, "Where are you?" He answered, "I heard you in the garden; but I was afraid, because I was naked, so I hid myself." Then he asked, "Who told you that you were naked? You have eaten, then, from the tree of which I had forbidden you to eat!" The man replied, "The woman whom you put here with me—she gave me fruit from the tree, and so I ate it." The LORD God then asked the woman, "Why did you do such a thing?" The woman answered, "The serpent tricked me into it, so I ate it."

Then the LORD God said to the serpent:
"Because you have done this, you shall be banned
from all the animals
and from all the wild creatures;
on your belly shall you crawl,
and dirt shall you eat

all the days of your life.
I will put enmity between you and the woman,
and between your offspring and hers;
he will strike at your head,
while you strike at his heel."

The man called his wife Eve, because she became the mother of all the living.

Responsorial Psalm
PSALM 98:1, 2-3ab, 3cd-4
R. Sing to the Lord a new song, for he has done marvelous deeds.

Sing to the LORD a new song,
for he has done wondrous deeds;
His right hand has won victory for him,
his holy arm. **R.**
The LORD has made his salvation known:
in the sight of the nations he has revealed his justice.
He has remembered his kindness and his faithfulness
toward the house of Israel. **R.**
All the ends of the earth have seen
the salvation by our God.
Sing joyfully to the LORD, all you lands;
break into song; sing praise. **R.**

Second Reading
EPHESIANS 1:3-6, 11-12

Brothers and sisters: Blessed be the God and Father of our Lord Jesus Christ, who has blessed us in Christ with every spiritual blessing in the heavens, as he chose us in him, before the foundation of the world, to be holy and without blemish before him. In love he destined us for adoption to himself through Jesus Christ, in accord with the favor of his will, for the praise of the glory of his grace that he granted us in the beloved.

In him we were also chosen, destined in accord with the purpose of the One who accomplishes all things according to the intention of his will, so that we might exist for the praise of his glory, we who first hoped in Christ.

Gospel
LUKE 1:26-38

The angel Gabriel was sent from God to a town of Galilee called Nazareth, to a virgin betrothed to a man named Joseph, of the house of David, and the virgin's name was Mary. And coming to her, he said, "Hail, full of grace! The Lord is with you." But she was greatly troubled at what was said and pondered what sort of greeting this might be. Then the angel said to her, "Do not be afraid, Mary, for you have found favor with God. Behold, you will conceive in your womb and bear a son, and you shall name him Jesus. He will be great and will be called Son of the Most High, and the Lord God will give him the throne of David his father, and he will rule over the house of Jacob forever, and of his Kingdom there will be no end." But Mary said to the angel, "How can this be, since I have no relations with a man?" And the angel said to her in reply, "The Holy Spirit will come upon you, and the power of the Most High will overshadow you. Therefore the child to be born will be called holy, the Son of God. And behold, Elizabeth, your relative, has also conceived a son in her old age, and this is the sixth month for her who was called barren; for nothing will be impossible for God." Mary said, "Behold, I am the handmaid of the Lord. May it be done to me according to your word." Then the angel departed from her.

Tuesday, December 10

First Reading

ISAIAH 40:1-11

Comfort, give comfort to my people,
  says your God.
Speak tenderly to Jerusalem, and proclaim to her
  that her service is at an end,
  her guilt is expiated;
Indeed, she has received from the hand of the LORD
  double for all her sins.

A voice cries out:
In the desert prepare the way of the LORD!
  Make straight in the wasteland a highway for our God!
Every valley shall be filled in,
  every mountain and hill shall be made low;
The rugged land shall be made a plain,
  the rough country, a broad valley.
Then the glory of the LORD shall be revealed,
  and all people shall see it together;
  for the mouth of the LORD has spoken.

A voice says, "Cry out!"
  I answer, "What shall I cry out?"

"All flesh is grass,
and all their glory like the flower of the field.
The grass withers, the flower wilts,
when the breath of the LORD blows upon it.
So then, the people is the grass.
Though the grass withers and the flower wilts,
the word of our God stands forever."

Go up onto a high mountain,
Zion, herald of glad tidings;
Cry out at the top of your voice,
Jerusalem, herald of good news!
Fear not to cry out
and say to the cities of Judah:
Here is your God!
Here comes with power
the Lord GOD,
who rules by his strong arm;
Here is his reward with him,
his recompense before him.
Like a shepherd he feeds his flock;
in his arms he gathers the lambs,
Carrying them in his bosom,
and leading the ewes with care.

Responsorial Psalm
PSALM 96:1-2, 3 and 10ac, 11-12, 13
R. The Lord our God comes with power.
Sing to the LORD a new song;
sing to the LORD, all you lands.
Sing to the LORD; bless his name;
announce his salvation, day after day. **R.**
Tell his glory among the nations;
among all peoples, his wondrous deeds.
Say among the nations: The LORD is king;
he governs the peoples with equity. **R.**
Let the heavens be glad and the earth rejoice;
let the sea and what fills it resound;
let the plains be joyful and all that is in them!
Then let all the trees of the forest rejoice. **R.**
They shall exult before the LORD, for he comes;
for he comes to rule the earth.
He shall rule the world with justice
and the peoples with his constancy. **R.**

Gospel
MATTHEW 18:12-14

Jesus said to his disciples: "What is your opinion? If a man has a hundred sheep and one of them goes astray, will he not leave the ninety-nine in the hills and go in search of the stray? And if he finds it, amen, I say to you, he rejoices more over it than over the ninety-nine that did not stray. In just the same way, it is not the will of your heavenly Father that one of these little ones be lost."

Wednesday, December 11

First Reading
ISAIAH 40:25-31

To whom can you liken me as an equal?
  says the Holy One.
Lift up your eyes on high
  and see who has created these things:
He leads out their army and numbers them,
  calling them all by name.
By his great might and the strength of his power
  not one of them is missing!
Why, O Jacob, do you say,
  and declare, O Israel,
"My way is hidden from the LORD,
  and my right is disregarded by my God"?

Do you not know
  or have you not heard?
The LORD is the eternal God,
  creator of the ends of the earth.
He does not faint nor grow weary,
  and his knowledge is beyond scrutiny.
He gives strength to the fainting;
  for the weak he makes vigor abound.
Though young men faint and grow weary,
  and youths stagger and fall,
They that hope in the LORD will renew their strength,
  they will soar as with eagles' wings;
They will run and not grow weary,
  walk and not grow faint.

Responsorial Psalm
PSALM 103:1-2, 3-4, 8 and 10
R. O bless the Lord, my soul!
Bless the LORD, O my soul;
and all my being, bless his holy name.
Bless the LORD, O my soul,
and forget not all his benefits. **R.**
He pardons all your iniquities,
he heals all your ills.
He redeems your life from destruction,
he crowns you with kindness and compassion. **R.**
Merciful and gracious is the LORD,
slow to anger and abounding in kindness.
Not according to our sins does he deal with us,
nor does he requite us according to our crimes. **R.**

Gospel
MATTHEW 11:28-30
Jesus said to the crowds: "Come to me, all you who labor and are burdened, and I will give you rest. Take my yoke upon you and learn from me, for I am meek and humble of heart; and you will find rest for yourselves. For my yoke is easy, and my burden light."

Thursday, December 12

Our Lady of Guadalupe

[Readings from the *Lectionary for Mass,* vol. IV, the Common of the Blessed Virgin Mary, nos. 707–712, may be substituted for those listed here.]

First Reading
ZECHARIAH 2:14-17 (or REVELATION 11:19a; 12:1-6a, 10ab)
Sing and rejoice, O daughter Zion! See, I am coming to dwell among you, says the LORD. Many nations shall join themselves to the LORD on that day, and they shall be his people, and he will dwell among you, and you shall know that the LORD of hosts has sent me to you. The LORD will possess Judah as his portion in the holy land, and he will again choose Jerusalem. Silence, all mankind, in the presence of the LORD! For he stirs forth from his holy dwelling.

Responsorial Psalm
JUDITH 13:18bcde, 19
R. You are the highest honor of our race.
Blessed are you, daughter, by the Most High God,
above all the women on earth;
and blessed be the LORD God,
the creator of heaven and earth. **R.**
Your deed of hope will never be forgotten
by those who tell of the might of God. **R.**

Gospel
LUKE 1:26-38 (or LUKE 1:39-47)
The angel Gabriel was sent from God to a town of Galilee called Nazareth, to a virgin betrothed to a man named Joseph, of the house of David, and the virgin's name was Mary. And coming to her, he said, "Hail, full of grace! The Lord is with you." But she was greatly troubled at what was said and pondered what sort of greeting this might be. Then the angel said to her, "Do not be afraid, Mary, for you have found favor with God. Behold, you will conceive in your womb and bear a son, and you shall name him Jesus. He will be great and will be called Son of the Most High, and the Lord God will give him the throne of David his father, and he will rule over the house of Jacob forever, and of his Kingdom there will be no end." But Mary said to the angel, "How can this be, since I have no relations with a man?" And the angel said to her in reply, "The Holy Spirit will come upon you, and the power of the Most High will overshadow you. Therefore the child to be born will be called holy, the Son of God. And behold, Elizabeth, your relative, has also conceived a son in her old age, and this is the sixth month for her who was called barren; for nothing will be impossible for God." Mary said, "Behold, I am the handmaid of the Lord. May it be done to me according to your word." Then the angel departed from her.

Friday, December 13

First Reading
ISAIAH 48:17-19
Thus says the LORD, your redeemer,
the Holy One of Israel:
I, the LORD, your God,
teach you what is for your good,
and lead you on the way you should go.
If you would hearken to my commandments,

your prosperity would be like a river,
and your vindication like the waves of the sea;
Your descendants would be like the sand,
and those born of your stock like its grains,
Their name never cut off
or blotted out from my presence.

Responsorial Psalm

PSALM 1:1-2, 3, 4 and 6

R. Those who follow you, Lord, will have the light of life.

Blessed the man who follows not
the counsel of the wicked
Nor walks in the way of sinners,
nor sits in the company of the insolent,
But delights in the law of the LORD
and meditates on his law day and night. **R.**
He is like a tree
planted near running water,
That yields its fruit in due season,
and whose leaves never fade.
Whatever he does, prospers. **R.**
Not so the wicked, not so;
they are like chaff which the wind drives away.
For the LORD watches over the way of the just,
but the way of the wicked vanishes. **R.**

Gospel

MATTHEW 11:16-19

Jesus said to the crowds: "To what shall I compare this generation? It is like children who sit in marketplaces and call to one another, 'We played the flute for you, but you did not dance, we sang a dirge but you did not mourn.' For John came neither eating nor drinking, and they said, 'He is possessed by a demon.' The Son of Man came eating and drinking and they said, 'Look, he is a glutton and a drunkard, a friend of tax collectors and sinners.' But wisdom is vindicated by her works."

Saturday, December 14

First Reading

SIRACH 48:1-4, 9-11

In those days,
like a fire there appeared the prophet Elijah
whose words were as a flaming furnace.

Their staff of bread he shattered,
in his zeal he reduced them to straits;
By the Lord's word he shut up the heavens
and three times brought down fire.
How awesome are you, Elijah, in your wondrous deeds!
Whose glory is equal to yours?
You were taken aloft in a whirlwind of fire,
in a chariot with fiery horses.
You were destined, it is written, in time to come
to put an end to wrath before the day of the LORD,
To turn back the hearts of fathers toward their sons,
and to re-establish the tribes of Jacob.
Blessed is he who shall have seen you
and who falls asleep in your friendship.

Responsorial Psalm
PSALM 80:2ac and 3b, 15-16, 18-19
R. Lord, make us turn to you; let us see your face and we shall be saved.
O shepherd of Israel, hearken,
From your throne upon the cherubim, shine forth.
Rouse your power. **R.**
Once again, O LORD of hosts,
look down from heaven, and see;
Take care of this vine,
and protect what your right hand has planted,
the son of man whom you yourself made strong. **R.**
May your help be with the man of your right hand,
with the son of man whom you yourself made strong.
Then we will no more withdraw from you;
give us new life, and we will call upon your name. **R.**

Gospel
MATTHEW 17:9a, 10-13
As they were coming down from the mountain, the disciples asked Jesus, "Why do the scribes say that Elijah must come first?" He said in reply, "Elijah will indeed come and restore all things; but I tell you that Elijah has already come, and they did not recognize him but did to him whatever they pleased. So also will the Son of Man suffer at their hands." Then the disciples understood that he was speaking to them of John the Baptist.

Sunday, December 15

Third Sunday of Advent

First Reading

ISAIAH 35:1-6a, 10

The desert and the parched land will exult;
the steppe will rejoice and bloom.
They will bloom with abundant flowers,
and rejoice with joyful song.
The glory of Lebanon will be given to them,
the splendor of Carmel and Sharon;
they will see the glory of the LORD,
the splendor of our God.
Strengthen the hands that are feeble,
make firm the knees that are weak,
say to those whose hearts are frightened:
Be strong, fear not!
Here is your God,
he comes with vindication;
with divine recompense
he comes to save you.
Then will the eyes of the blind be opened,
the ears of the deaf be cleared;
then will the lame leap like a stag,
then the tongue of the mute will sing.

Those whom the LORD has ransomed will return
and enter Zion singing,
crowned with everlasting joy;
they will meet with joy and gladness,
sorrow and mourning will flee.

Responsorial Psalm

PSALM 146:6-7, 8-9, 9-10

R. Lord, come and save us. (or R. Alleluia.)

The LORD God keeps faith forever,
secures justice for the oppressed,
gives food to the hungry.
The LORD sets captives free. **R.**
The LORD gives sight to the blind;
the LORD raises up those who were bowed down.
The LORD loves the just;
the LORD protects strangers. **R.**

The fatherless and the widow he sustains,
but the way of the wicked he thwarts.
The LORD shall reign forever;
your God, O Zion, through all generations. **R.**

Second Reading
JAMES 5:7-10

Be patient, brothers and sisters, until the coming of the Lord. See how the farmer waits for the precious fruit of the earth, being patient with it until it receives the early and the late rains. You too must be patient. Make your hearts firm, because the coming of the Lord is at hand. Do not complain, brothers and sisters, about one another, that you may not be judged. Behold, the Judge is standing before the gates. Take as an example of hardship and patience, brothers and sisters, the prophets who spoke in the name of the Lord.

Gospel
MATTHEW 11:2-11

When John the Baptist heard in prison of the works of the Christ, he sent his disciples to Jesus with this question, "Are you the one who is to come, or should we look for another?" Jesus said to them in reply, "Go and tell John what you hear and see: the blind regain their sight, the lame walk, lepers are cleansed, the deaf hear, the dead are raised, and the poor have the good news proclaimed to them. And blessed is the one who takes no offense at me."

As they were going off, Jesus began to speak to the crowds about John, "What did you go out to the desert to see? A reed swayed by the wind? Then what did you go out to see? Someone dressed in fine clothing? Those who wear fine clothing are in royal palaces. Then why did you go out? To see a prophet? Yes, I tell you, and more than a prophet. This is the one about whom it is written:

Behold, I am sending my messenger ahead of you;
he will prepare your way before you.

Amen, I say to you, among those born of women there has been none greater than John the Baptist; yet the least in the kingdom of heaven is greater than he."

Monday, December 16

First Reading

NUMBERS 24:2-7, 15-17a

When Balaam raised his eyes and saw Israel encamped, tribe by tribe, the spirit of God came upon him, and he gave voice to his oracle:

The utterance of Balaam, son of Beor,
  the utterance of a man whose eye is true,
The utterance of one who hears what God says,
  and knows what the Most High knows,
Of one who sees what the Almighty sees,
  enraptured, and with eyes unveiled:
How goodly are your tents, O Jacob;
  your encampments, O Israel!
They are like gardens beside a stream,
  like the cedars planted by the LORD.
His wells shall yield free-flowing waters,
  he shall have the sea within reach;
His king shall rise higher,
  and his royalty shall be exalted.

Then Balaam gave voice to his oracle:

The utterance of Balaam, son of Beor,
  the utterance of the man whose eye is true,
The utterance of one who hears what God says,
  and knows what the Most High knows,
Of one who sees what the Almighty sees,
  enraptured, and with eyes unveiled.
I see him, though not now;
  I behold him, though not near:
A star shall advance from Jacob,
  and a staff shall rise from Israel.

Responsorial Psalm

PSALM 25:4-5ab, 6 and 7bc, 8-9

R. Teach me your ways, O Lord.

Your ways, O LORD, make known to me;
  teach me your paths,
Guide me in your truth and teach me,
  for you are God my savior. **R.**
Remember that your compassion, O LORD,
  and your kindness are from of old.

In your kindness remember me,
  because of your goodness, O LORD. **R.**
Good and upright is the LORD;
  thus he shows sinners the way.
He guides the humble to justice,
  he teaches the humble his way. **R.**

Gospel
MATTHEW 21:23-27

When Jesus had come into the temple area, the chief priests and the elders of the people approached him as he was teaching and said, "By what authority are you doing these things? And who gave you this authority?" Jesus said to them in reply, "I shall ask you one question, and if you answer it for me, then I shall tell you by what authority I do these things. Where was John's baptism from? Was it of heavenly or of human origin?" They discussed this among themselves and said, "If we say 'Of heavenly origin,' he will say to us, 'Then why did you not believe him?' But if we say, 'Of human origin,' we fear the crowd, for they all regard John as a prophet." So they said to Jesus in reply, "We do not know." He himself said to them, "Neither shall I tell you by what authority I do these things."

Tuesday, December 17

First Reading
GENESIS 49:2, 8-10

Jacob called his sons and said to them:
"Assemble and listen, sons of Jacob,
  listen to Israel, your father.

"You, Judah, shall your brothers praise
  —your hand on the neck of your enemies;
  the sons of your father shall bow down to you.
Judah, like a lion's whelp,
  you have grown up on prey, my son.
He crouches like a lion recumbent,
  the king of beasts—who would dare rouse him?
The scepter shall never depart from Judah,
  or the mace from between his legs,
While tribute is brought to him,
  and he receives the people's homage."

Responsorial Psalm

PSALM 72:1-2, 3-4ab, 7-8, 17

R. Justice shall flourish in his time, and fullness of peace for ever.

O God, with your judgment endow the king,
and with your justice, the king's son;
He shall govern your people with justice
and your afflicted ones with judgment. **R.**

The mountains shall yield peace for the people,
and the hills justice.
He shall defend the afflicted among the people,
save the children of the poor. **R.**

Justice shall flower in his days,
and profound peace, till the moon be no more.
May he rule from sea to sea,
and from the River to the ends of the earth. **R.**

May his name be blessed forever;
as long as the sun his name shall remain.
In him shall all the tribes of the earth be blessed;
all the nations shall proclaim his happiness. **R.**

Gospel

MATTHEW 1:1-17

The book of the genealogy of Jesus Christ, the son of David, the son of Abraham.

Abraham became the father of Isaac, Isaac the father of Jacob, Jacob the father of Judah and his brothers. Judah became the father of Perez and Zerah, whose mother was Tamar. Perez became the father of Hezron, Hezron the father of Ram, Ram the father of Amminadab. Amminadab became the father of Nahshon, Nahshon the father of Salmon, Salmon the father of Boaz, whose mother was Rahab. Boaz became the father of Obed, whose mother was Ruth. Obed became the father of Jesse, Jesse the father of David the king.

David became the father of Solomon, whose mother had been the wife of Uriah. Solomon became the father of Rehoboam, Rehoboam the father of Abijah, Abijah the father of Asaph. Asaph became the father of Jehoshaphat, Jehoshaphat the father of Joram, Joram the father of Uzziah. Uzziah became the father of Jotham, Jotham the father of Ahaz, Ahaz the father of Hezekiah. Hezekiah became the father of Manasseh, Manasseh the father of Amos, Amos the father of Josiah. Josiah became the father of Jechoniah and his brothers at the time of the Babylonian exile.

After the Babylonian exile, Jechoniah became the father of Shealtiel, Shealtiel the father of Zerubbabel, Zerubbabel the father of Abiud.

Abiud became the father of Eliakim, Eliakim the father of Azor, Azor the father of Zadok. Zadok became the father of Achim, Achim the father of Eliud, Eliud the father of Eleazar. Eleazar became the father of Matthan, Matthan the father of Jacob, Jacob the father of Joseph, the husband of Mary. Of her was born Jesus who is called the Christ.

Thus the total number of generations from Abraham to David is fourteen generations; from David to the Babylonian exile, fourteen generations; from the Babylonian exile to the Christ, fourteen generations.

Wednesday, December 18

First Reading

JEREMIAH 23:5-8

Behold, the days are coming, says the LORD,
  when I will raise up a righteous shoot to David;
As king he shall reign and govern wisely,
  he shall do what is just and right in the land.
In his days Judah shall be saved,
  Israel shall dwell in security.
This is the name they give him:
  "The LORD our justice."

Therefore, the days will come, says the LORD, when they shall no longer say, "As the LORD lives, who brought the children of Israel out of the land of Egypt"; but rather, "As the LORD lives, who brought the descendants of the house of Israel up from the land of the north"—and from all the lands to which I banished them; they shall again live on their own land.

Responsorial Psalm

PSALM 72:1-2, 12-13, 18-19

R. Justice shall flourish in his time, and fullness of peace for ever.

O God, with your judgment endow the king,
  and with your justice, the king's son;
He shall govern your people with justice
  and your afflicted ones with judgment. **R.**
For he shall rescue the poor when he cries out,
  and the afflicted when he has no one to help him.
He shall have pity for the lowly and the poor;
  the lives of the poor he shall save. **R.**
Blessed be the LORD, the God of Israel,
  who alone does wondrous deeds.
And blessed forever be his glorious name;
  may the whole earth be filled with his glory. **R.**

Gospel
MATTHEW 1:18-25

This is how the birth of Jesus Christ came about. When his mother Mary was betrothed to Joseph, but before they lived together, she was found with child through the Holy Spirit. Joseph her husband, since he was a righteous man, yet unwilling to expose her to shame, decided to divorce her quietly. Such was his intention when, behold, the angel of the Lord appeared to him in a dream and said, "Joseph, son of David, do not be afraid to take Mary your wife into your home. For it is through the Holy Spirit that this child has been conceived in her. She will bear a son and you are to name him Jesus, because he will save his people from their sins." All this took place to fulfill what the Lord had said through the prophet:

Behold, the virgin shall be with child and bear a son,
and they shall name him Emmanuel,

which means "God is with us." When Joseph awoke, he did as the angel of the Lord had commanded him and took his wife into his home. He had no relations with her until she bore a son, and he named him Jesus.

Thursday, December 19

First Reading
JUDGES 13:2-7, 24-25a

There was a certain man from Zorah, of the clan of the Danites, whose name was Manoah. His wife was barren and had borne no children. An angel of the LORD appeared to the woman and said to her, "Though you are barren and have had no children, yet you will conceive and bear a son. Now, then, be careful to take no wine or strong drink and to eat nothing unclean. As for the son you will conceive and bear, no razor shall touch his head, for this boy is to be consecrated to God from the womb. It is he who will begin the deliverance of Israel from the power of the Philistines."

The woman went and told her husband, "A man of God came to me; he had the appearance of an angel of God, terrible indeed. I did not ask him where he came from, nor did he tell me his name. But he said to me, 'You will be with child and will bear a son. So take neither wine nor strong drink, and eat nothing unclean. For the boy shall be consecrated to God from the womb, until the day of his death.'"

The woman bore a son and named him Samson. The boy grew up and the LORD blessed him; the Spirit of the LORD stirred him.

Responsorial Psalm

PSALM 71:3-4a, 5-6ab, 16-17

R. My mouth shall be filled with your praise, and I will sing your glory!

Be my rock of refuge,
  a stronghold to give me safety,
  for you are my rock and my fortress.
O my God, rescue me from the hand of the wicked. **R.**
For you are my hope, O LORD;
  my trust, O God, from my youth.
On you I depend from birth;
  from my mother's womb you are my strength. **R.**
I will treat of the mighty works of the LORD;
  O God, I will tell of your singular justice.
O God, you have taught me from my youth,
  and till the present I proclaim your wondrous deeds. **R.**

Gospel

LUKE 1:5-25

In the days of Herod, King of Judea, there was a priest named Zechariah of the priestly division of Abijah; his wife was from the daughters of Aaron, and her name was Elizabeth. Both were righteous in the eyes of God, observing all the commandments and ordinances of the Lord blamelessly. But they had no child, because Elizabeth was barren and both were advanced in years.

Once when he was serving as priest in his division's turn before God, according to the practice of the priestly service, he was chosen by lot to enter the sanctuary of the Lord to burn incense. Then, when the whole assembly of the people was praying outside at the hour of the incense offering, the angel of the Lord appeared to him, standing at the right of the altar of incense. Zechariah was troubled by what he saw, and fear came upon him.

But the angel said to him, "Do not be afraid, Zechariah, because your prayer has been heard. Your wife Elizabeth will bear you a son, and you shall name him John. And you will have joy and gladness, and many will rejoice at his birth, for he will be great in the sight of the Lord. He will drink neither wine nor strong drink. He will be filled with the Holy Spirit even from his mother's womb, and he will turn many of the children of Israel to the Lord their God. He will go before him in the spirit and power of Elijah to turn the hearts of fathers toward children and the disobedient to the understanding of the righteous, to prepare a people fit for the Lord."

Then Zechariah said to the angel, "How shall I know this? For I am an old man, and my wife is advanced in years." And the angel said to him in reply, "I am Gabriel, who stand before God. I was sent to speak to you and to announce to you this good news. But now you will be speechless and unable to talk until the day these things take place, because you did not believe my words, which will be fulfilled at their proper time."

Meanwhile the people were waiting for Zechariah and were amazed that he stayed so long in the sanctuary. But when he came out, he was unable to speak to them, and they realized that he had seen a vision in the sanctuary. He was gesturing to them but remained mute.

Then, when his days of ministry were completed, he went home.

After this time his wife Elizabeth conceived, and she went into seclusion for five months, saying, "So has the Lord done for me at a time when he has seen fit to take away my disgrace before others."

Friday, December 20

First Reading

ISAIAH 7:10-14

The LORD spoke to Ahaz: Ask for a sign from the LORD, your God; let it be deep as the nether world, or high as the sky! But Ahaz answered, "I will not ask! I will not tempt the LORD!" Then Isaiah said: Listen, O house of David! Is it not enough for you to weary men, must you also weary my God? Therefore the Lord himself will give you this sign: the virgin shall conceive and bear a son, and shall name him Emmanuel.

Responsorial Psalm

PSALM 24:1-2, 3-4ab, 5-6

R. Let the Lord enter; he is the king of glory.

The LORD's are the earth and its fullness;
the world and those who dwell in it.
For he founded it upon the seas
and established it upon the rivers. **R.**
Who can ascend the mountain of the LORD?
or who may stand in his holy place?
He whose hands are sinless, whose heart is clean,
who desires not what is vain. **R.**
He shall receive a blessing from the LORD,
a reward from God his savior.
Such is the race that seeks for him,
that seeks the face of the God of Jacob. **R.**

Gospel
LUKE 1:26-38

In the sixth month, the angel Gabriel was sent from God to a town of Galilee called Nazareth, to a virgin betrothed to a man named Joseph, of the house of David, and the virgin's name was Mary. And coming to her, he said, "Hail, full of grace! The Lord is with you." But she was greatly troubled at what was said and pondered what sort of greeting this might be. Then the angel said to her, "Do not be afraid, Mary, for you have found favor with God. Behold, you will conceive in your womb and bear a son, and you shall name him Jesus. He will be great and will be called Son of the Most High, and the Lord God will give him the throne of David his father, and he will rule over the house of Jacob forever, and of his Kingdom there will be no end."

But Mary said to the angel, "How can this be, since I have no relations with a man?" And the angel said to her in reply, "The Holy Spirit will come upon you, and the power of the Most High will overshadow you. Therefore the child to be born will be called holy, the Son of God. And behold, Elizabeth, your relative, has also conceived a son in her old age, and this is the sixth month for her who was called barren; for nothing will be impossible for God."

Mary said, "Behold, I am the handmaid of the Lord. May it be done to me according to your word." Then the angel departed from her.

Saturday, December 21

First Reading
SONG OF SONGS 2:8-14 (or ZEPHANIAH 3:14-18a)

Hark! my lover—here he comes
springing across the mountains,
leaping across the hills.
My lover is like a gazelle
or a young stag.
Here he stands behind our wall,
gazing through the windows,
peering through the lattices.
My lover speaks; he says to me,
"Arise, my beloved, my dove, my beautiful one,
and come!
"For see, the winter is past,
the rains are over and gone.
The flowers appear on the earth,
the time of pruning the vines has come,
and the song of the dove is heard in our land.

The fig tree puts forth its figs,
and the vines, in bloom, give forth fragrance.
Arise, my beloved, my beautiful one,
and come!

"O my dove in the clefts of the rock,
in the secret recesses of the cliff,
Let me see you,
let me hear your voice,
For your voice is sweet,
and you are lovely."

Responsorial Psalm

PSALM 33:2-3, 11-12, 20-21

R. Exult, you just, in the Lord! Sing to him a new song.

Give thanks to the LORD on the harp;
with the ten-stringed lyre chant his praises.
Sing to him a new song;
pluck the strings skillfully, with shouts of gladness. **R.**
But the plan of the LORD stands forever;
the design of his heart, through all generations.
Blessed the nation whose God is the LORD,
the people he has chosen for his own inheritance. **R.**
Our soul waits for the LORD,
who is our help and our shield,
For in him our hearts rejoice;
in his holy name we trust. **R.**

Gospel

LUKE 1:39-45

Mary set out in those days and traveled to the hill country in haste to a town of Judah, where she entered the house of Zechariah and greeted Elizabeth. When Elizabeth heard Mary's greeting, the infant leaped in her womb, and Elizabeth, filled with the Holy Spirit, cried out in a loud voice and said, "Most blessed are you among women, and blessed is the fruit of your womb. And how does this happen to me, that the mother of my Lord should come to me? For at the moment the sound of your greeting reached my ears, the infant in my womb leaped for joy. Blessed are you who believed that what was spoken to you by the Lord would be fulfilled."

Sunday, December 22

Fourth Sunday of Advent

First Reading
ISAIAH 7:10-14

The LORD spoke to Ahaz, saying: Ask for a sign from the LORD, your God; let it be deep as the netherworld, or high as the sky! But Ahaz answered, "I will not ask! I will not tempt the LORD!" Then Isaiah said: Listen, O house of David! Is it not enough for you to weary people, must you also weary my God? Therefore the Lord himself will give you this sign: the virgin shall conceive, and bear a son, and shall name him Emmanuel.

Responsorial Psalm
PSALM 24:1-2, 3-4, 5-6
R. Let the Lord enter; he is king of glory.

The LORD's are the earth and its fullness;
 the world and those who dwell in it.
For he founded it upon the seas
 and established it upon the rivers. **R.**
Who can ascend the mountain of the LORD?
 or who may stand in his holy place?
One whose hands are sinless, whose heart is clean,
 who desires not what is vain. **R.**
He shall receive a blessing from the LORD,
 a reward from God his savior.
Such is the race that seeks for him,
 that seeks the face of the God of Jacob. **R.**

Second Reading
ROMANS 1:1-7

Paul, a slave of Christ Jesus, called to be an apostle and set apart for the gospel of God, which he promised previously through his prophets in the holy Scriptures, the gospel about his Son, descended from David according to the flesh, but established as Son of God in power according to the Spirit of holiness through resurrection from the dead, Jesus Christ our Lord. Through him we have received the grace of apostleship, to bring about the obedience of faith, for the sake of his name, among all the Gentiles, among whom are you also, who are called to belong to Jesus Christ; to all the beloved of God in Rome, called to be holy. Grace to you and peace from God our Father and the Lord Jesus Christ.

Gospel
MATTHEW 1:18-24

This is how the birth of Jesus Christ came about. When his mother Mary was betrothed to Joseph, but before they lived together, she was found with child through the Holy Spirit. Joseph her husband, since he was a righteous man, yet unwilling to expose her to shame, decided to divorce her quietly. Such was his intention when, behold, the angel of the Lord appeared to him in a dream and said, "Joseph, son of David, do not be afraid to take Mary your wife into your home. For it is through the Holy Spirit that this child has been conceived in her. She will bear a son and you are to name him Jesus, because he will save his people from their sins." All this took place to fulfill what the Lord had said through the prophet:

Behold, the virgin shall conceive and bear a son,
and they shall name him Emmanuel,

which means "God is with us." When Joseph awoke, he did as the angel of the Lord had commanded him and took his wife into his home.

Monday, December 23

First Reading
MALACHI 3:1-4, 23-24

Thus says the Lord GOD:
Lo, I am sending my messenger
to prepare the way before me;
And suddenly there will come to the temple
the LORD whom you seek,
And the messenger of the covenant whom you desire.
Yes, he is coming, says the LORD of hosts.
But who will endure the day of his coming?
And who can stand when he appears?
For he is like the refiner's fire,
or like the fuller's lye.
He will sit refining and purifying silver,
and he will purify the sons of Levi,
Refining them like gold or like silver
that they may offer due sacrifice to the LORD.
Then the sacrifice of Judah and Jerusalem
will please the LORD,
as in the days of old, as in years gone by.

Lo, I will send you
  Elijah, the prophet,
Before the day of the LORD comes,
  the great and terrible day,
To turn the hearts of the fathers to their children,
  and the hearts of the children to their fathers,
Lest I come and strike
  the land with doom.

Responsorial Psalm

PSALM 25:4-5ab, 8-9, 10 and 14

R. Lift up your heads and see; your redemption is near at hand.

Your ways, O LORD, make known to me;
  teach me your paths,
Guide me in your truth and teach me,
  for you are God my savior. **R.**
Good and upright is the LORD;
  thus he shows sinners the way.
He guides the humble to justice,
  he teaches the humble his way. **R.**
All the paths of the LORD are kindness and constancy
  toward those who keep his covenant and his decrees.
The friendship of the LORD is with those who fear him,
  and his covenant, for their instruction. **R.**

Gospel

LUKE 1:57-66

When the time arrived for Elizabeth to have her child she gave birth to a son. Her neighbors and relatives heard that the Lord had shown his great mercy toward her, and they rejoiced with her. When they came on the eighth day to circumcise the child, they were going to call him Zechariah after his father, but his mother said in reply, "No. He will be called John." But they answered her, "There is no one among your relatives who has this name." So they made signs, asking his father what he wished him to be called. He asked for a tablet and wrote, "John is his name," and all were amazed. Immediately his mouth was opened, his tongue freed, and he spoke blessing God. Then fear came upon all their neighbors, and all these matters were discussed throughout the hill country of Judea. All who heard these things took them to heart, saying, "What, then, will this child be?" For surely the hand of the Lord was with him.

Tuesday, December 24

Mass in the morning:

First Reading

2 SAMUEL 7:1-5, 8b-12, 14a, 16

When King David was settled in his palace, and the LORD had given him rest from his enemies on every side, he said to Nathan the prophet, "Here I am living in a house of cedar, while the ark of God dwells in a tent!" Nathan answered the king, "Go, do whatever you have in mind, for the LORD is with you." But that night the LORD spoke to Nathan and said: "Go, tell my servant David, 'Thus says the LORD: Should you build me a house to dwell in?

"'It was I who took you from the pasture and from the care of the flock to be commander of my people Israel. I have been with you wherever you went, and I have destroyed all your enemies before you. And I will make you famous like the great ones of the earth. I will fix a place for my people Israel; I will plant them so that they may dwell in their place without further disturbance. Neither shall the wicked continue to afflict them as they did of old, since the time I first appointed judges over my people Israel. I will give you rest from all your enemies. The LORD also reveals to you that he will establish a house for you. And when your time comes and you rest with your ancestors, I will raise up your heir after you, sprung from your loins, and I will make his Kingdom firm. I will be a father to him, and he shall be a son to me. Your house and your Kingdom shall endure forever before me; your throne shall stand firm forever.'"

Responsorial Psalm

PSALM 89:2-3, 4-5, 27 and 29

R. For ever I will sing the goodness of the Lord.

The favors of the LORD I will sing forever;
 through all generations my mouth shall proclaim your faithfulness.
For you have said, "My kindness is established forever";
 in heaven you have confirmed your faithfulness. **R.**
"I have made a covenant with my chosen one,
 I have sworn to David my servant:
Forever will I confirm your posterity
 and establish your throne for all generations." **R.**
"He shall say of me, 'You are my father,
 my God, the rock, my savior.'
Forever I will maintain my kindness toward him,
 and my covenant with him stands firm." **R.**

Gospel
LUKE 1:67-79
Zechariah his father, filled with the Holy Spirit, prophesied, saying:

"Blessed be the Lord, the God of Israel;
for he has come to his people and set them free.
He has raised up for us a mighty Savior,
born of the house of his servant David.
Through his prophets he promised of old
that he would save us from our enemies,
from the hands of all who hate us.
He promised to show mercy to our fathers
and to remember his holy covenant.
This was the oath he swore to our father Abraham:
to set us free from the hand of our enemies,
free to worship him without fear,
holy and righteous in his sight
all the days of our life.
You, my child, shall be called the prophet of the Most High,
for you will go before the Lord to prepare his way,
to give his people knowledge of salvation
by the forgiveness of their sins.
In the tender compassion of our God
the dawn from on high shall break upon us,
to shine on those who dwell in darkness and the shadow of death,
and to guide our feet into the way of peace."

Wednesday, December 25

The Nativity of the Lord (Christmas)

First Reading
ISAIAH 52:7-10 (Vigil: ISAIAH 62:1-5; Midnight: ISAIAH 9:1-6; Dawn: ISAIAH 62:11-12)
How beautiful upon the mountains
are the feet of him who brings glad tidings,
announcing peace, bearing good news,
announcing salvation, and saying to Zion,
"Your God is King!"

Hark! Your sentinels raise a cry,
together they shout for joy,

for they see directly, before their eyes,
the LORD restoring Zion.
Break out together in song,
O ruins of Jerusalem!
For the LORD comforts his people,
he redeems Jerusalem.
The LORD has bared his holy arm
in the sight of all the nations;
all the ends of the earth will behold
the salvation of our God.

Responsorial Psalm

PSALM 98:1, 2-3, 3-4, 5-6 (Vigil: PSALM 89:4-5, 16-17, 27, 29; Midnight: PSALM 96:1-2,2-3,11-12, 13; Dawn: PSALM 97:1, 6, 11-12)

R. All the ends of the earth have seen the saving power of God.

Sing to the LORD a new song,
for he has done wondrous deeds;
his right hand has won victory for him,
his holy arm. **R.**
The LORD has made his salvation known:
in the sight of the nations he has revealed his justice.
He has remembered his kindness and his faithfulness
toward the house of Israel. **R.**
All the ends of the earth have seen
the salvation by our God.
Sing joyfully to the LORD, all you lands;
break into song; sing praise. **R.**
Sing praise to the LORD with the harp,
with the harp and melodious song.
With trumpets and the sound of the horn
sing joyfully before the King, the LORD. **R.**

Second Reading

HEBREWS 1:1-6 (Vigil: ACTS 13:16-17, 22-25; Midnight: TITUS 2:11-14; Dawn: TITUS 3:4-7)

Brothers and sisters: In times past, God spoke in partial and various ways to our ancestors through the prophets; in these last days, he has spoken to us through the Son, whom he made heir of all things and through whom he created the universe,

who is the refulgence of his glory, the very imprint of his being,
and who sustains all things by his mighty word.
When he had accomplished purification from sins,
he took his seat at the right hand of the Majesty on high,

as far superior to the angels
as the name he has inherited is more excellent than theirs.
For to which of the angels did God ever say:

You are my son; this day I have begotten you?

Or again:

I will be a father to him, and he shall be a son to me?

And again, when he leads the firstborn into the world, he says:

Let all the angels of God worship him.

Gospel
JOHN 1:1-18 (or JOHN 1:1-5, 9-14) (Vigil: MATTHEW 1:1-25 or MATTHEW 1:18-25; Midnight: LUKE 2:1-14; Dawn: LUKE 2:15-20)

In the beginning was the Word,
and the Word was with God,
and the Word was God.
He was in the beginning with God.
All things came to be through him,
and without him nothing came to be.
What came to be through him was life,
and this life was the light of the human race;
the light shines in the darkness,
and the darkness has not overcome it.

A man named John was sent from God. He came for testimony, to testify to the light, so that all might believe through him. He was not the light, but came to testify to the light. The true light, which enlightens everyone, was coming into the world.

He was in the world,
and the world came to be through him,
but the world did not know him.
He came to what was his own,
but his own people did not accept him.

But to those who did accept him he gave power to become children of God, to those who believe in his name, who were born not by natural generation nor by human choice nor by a man's decision but of God.

And the Word became flesh
and made his dwelling among us,
and we saw his glory,

the glory as of the Father's only Son,
full of grace and truth.

John testified to him and cried out, saying, "This was he of whom I said, 'The one who is coming after me ranks ahead of me because he existed before me.'" From his fullness we have all received, grace in place of grace, because while the law was given through Moses, grace and truth came through Jesus Christ. No one has ever seen God. The only Son, God, who is at the Father's side, has revealed him.

Thursday, December 26

Saint Stephen, The First Martyr

First Reading

ACTS 6:8-10; 7:54-59

Stephen, filled with grace and power, was working great wonders and signs among the people. Certain members of the so-called Synagogue of Freedmen, Cyrenians, and Alexandrians, and people from Cilicia and Asia, came forward and debated with Stephen, but they could not withstand the wisdom and the spirit with which he spoke.

When they heard this, they were infuriated, and they ground their teeth at him. But he, filled with the Holy Spirit, looked up intently to heaven and saw the glory of God and Jesus standing at the right hand of God, and he said, "Behold, I see the heavens opened and the Son of Man standing at the right hand of God." But they cried out in a loud voice, covered their ears, and rushed upon him together. They threw him out of the city, and began to stone him. The witnesses laid down their cloaks at the feet of a young man named Saul. As they were stoning Stephen, he called out "Lord Jesus, receive my spirit."

Responsorial Psalm

PSALM 31:3cd-4, 6 and 8ab, 16bc and 17

R. Into your hands, O Lord, I commend my spirit.

Be my rock of refuge,
a stronghold to give me safety.
You are my rock and my fortress;
for your name's sake you will lead and guide me. **R.**
Into your hands I commend my spirit;
you will redeem me, O LORD, O faithful God.
I will rejoice and be glad because of your mercy. **R.**
Rescue me from the clutches of my enemies and my persecutors.
Let your face shine upon your servant;
save me in your kindness. **R.**

Gospel
MATTHEW 10:17-22
Jesus said to his disciples: "Beware of men, for they will hand you over to courts and scourge you in their synagogues, and you will be led before governors and kings for my sake as a witness before them and the pagans. When they hand you over, do not worry about how you are to speak or what you are to say. You will be given at that moment what you are to say. For it will not be you who speak but the Spirit of your Father speaking through you. Brother will hand over brother to death, and the father his child; children will rise up against parents and have them put to death. You will be hated by all because of my name, but whoever endures to the end will be saved."

Friday, December 27

Saint John, Apostle and Evangelist

First Reading
1 JOHN 1:1-4
Beloved:
What was from the beginning,
what we have heard,
what we have seen with our eyes,
what we looked upon
and touched with our hands
concerns the Word of life—
for the life was made visible;
we have seen it and testify to it
and proclaim to you the eternal life
that was with the Father and was made visible to us—
what we have seen and heard
we proclaim now to you,
so that you too may have fellowship with us;
for our fellowship is with the Father
and with his Son, Jesus Christ.
We are writing this so that our joy may be complete.

Responsorial Psalm
PSALM 97:1-2, 5-6, 11-12
R. Rejoice in the Lord, you just!
The LORD is king; let the earth rejoice;
let the many isles be glad.

Clouds and darkness are around him,
justice and judgment are the foundation of his throne. **R.**
The mountains melt like wax before the LORD,
before the LORD of all the earth.
The heavens proclaim his justice,
and all peoples see his glory. **R.**
Light dawns for the just;
and gladness, for the upright of heart.
Be glad in the LORD, you just,
and give thanks to his holy name. **R.**

Gospel

JOHN 20:1a, 2-8

On the first day of the week, Mary Magdalene ran and went to Simon Peter and to the other disciple whom Jesus loved, and told them, "They have taken the Lord from the tomb, and we do not know where they put him." So Peter and the other disciple went out and came to the tomb. They both ran, but the other disciple ran faster than Peter and arrived at the tomb first; he bent down and saw the burial cloths there, but did not go in. When Simon Peter arrived after him, he went into the tomb and saw the burial cloths there, and the cloth that had covered his head, not with the burial cloths but rolled up in a separate place. Then the other disciple also went in, the one who had arrived at the tomb first, and he saw and believed.

Saturday, December 28

The Holy Innocents, Martyrs

First Reading

1 JOHN 1:5–2:2

Beloved: This is the message that we have heard from Jesus Christ and proclaim to you: God is light, and in him there is no darkness at all. If we say, "We have fellowship with him," while we continue to walk in darkness, we lie and do not act in truth. But if we walk in the light as he is in the light, then we have fellowship with one another, and the Blood of his Son Jesus cleanses us from all sin. If we say, "We are without sin," we deceive ourselves, and the truth is not in us. If we acknowledge our sins, he is faithful and just and will forgive our sins and cleanse us from every wrongdoing. If we say, "We have not sinned," we make him a liar, and his word is not in us.

My children, I am writing this to you so that you may not commit sin. But if anyone does sin, we have an Advocate with the Father, Jesus

Christ the righteous one. He is expiation for our sins, and not for our sins only but for those of the whole world.

Responsorial Psalm
PSALM 124:2-3, 4-5, 7cd-8
R. Our soul has been rescued like a bird from the fowler's snare.

Had not the LORD been with us—
When men rose up against us,
  then would they have swallowed us alive,
When their fury was inflamed against us. **R.**
Then would the waters have overwhelmed us;
The torrent would have swept over us;
  over us then would have swept the raging waters. **R.**
Broken was the snare,
  and we were freed.
Our help is in the name of the LORD,
  who made heaven and earth. **R.**

Gospel
MATTHEW 2:13-18

When the magi had departed, behold, the angel of the Lord appeared to Joseph in a dream and said, "Rise, take the child and his mother, flee to Egypt, and stay there until I tell you. Herod is going to search for the child to destroy him." Joseph rose and took the child and his mother by night and departed for Egypt. He stayed there until the death of Herod, that what the Lord had said through the prophet might be fulfilled,

Out of Egypt I called my son.

When Herod realized that he had been deceived by the magi, he became furious. He ordered the massacre of all the boys in Bethlehem and its vicinity two years old and under, in accordance with the time he had ascertained from the magi. Then was fulfilled what had been said through Jeremiah the prophet:

A voice was heard in Ramah,
  sobbing and loud lamentation;
Rachel weeping for her children,
  and she would not be consoled,
  since they were no more.

Sunday, December 29

The Holy Family of Jesus, Mary, and Joseph

First Reading

SIRACH 3:2-6, 12-14

God sets a father in honor over his children;
 a mother's authority he confirms over her sons.
Whoever honors his father atones for sins,
 and preserves himself from them.
When he prays, he is heard;
 he stores up riches who reveres his mother.
Whoever honors his father is gladdened by children,
 and, when he prays, is heard.
Whoever reveres his father will live a long life;
 he who obeys his father brings comfort to his mother.

My son, take care of your father when he is old;
 grieve him not as long as he lives.
Even if his mind fail, be considerate of him;
 revile him not all the days of his life;
kindness to a father will not be forgotten,
 firmly planted against the debt of your sins
 —a house raised in justice to you.

Responsorial Psalm

PSALM 128:1-2, 3, 4-5

R. Blessed are those who fear the Lord and walk in his ways.

Blessed is everyone who fears the LORD,
 who walks in his ways!
For you shall eat the fruit of your handiwork;
 blessed shall you be, and favored. **R.**
Your wife shall be like a fruitful vine
 in the recesses of your home;
your children like olive plants
 around your table. **R.**
Behold, thus is the man blessed
 who fears the LORD.
The LORD bless you from Zion:
 may you see the prosperity of Jerusalem
 all the days of your life. **R.**

Second Reading
COLOSSIANS 3:12-21 (or COLOSSIANS 3:12-17)

Brothers and sisters: Put on, as God's chosen ones, holy and beloved, heartfelt compassion, kindness, humility, gentleness, and patience, bearing with one another and forgiving one another, if one has a grievance against another; as the Lord has forgiven you, so must you also do. And over all these put on love, that is, the bond of perfection. And let the peace of Christ control your hearts, the peace into which you were also called in one body. And be thankful. Let the word of Christ dwell in you richly, as in all wisdom you teach and admonish one another, singing psalms, hymns, and spiritual songs with gratitude in your hearts to God. And whatever you do, in word or in deed, do everything in the name of the Lord Jesus, giving thanks to God the Father through him.

Wives, be subordinate to your husbands, as is proper in the Lord. Husbands, love your wives, and avoid any bitterness toward them. Children, obey your parents in everything, for this is pleasing to the Lord. Fathers, do not provoke your children, so they may not become discouraged.

Gospel
MATTHEW 2:13-15, 19-23

When the magi had departed, behold, the angel of the Lord appeared to Joseph in a dream and said, "Rise, take the child and his mother, flee to Egypt, and stay there until I tell you. Herod is going to search for the child to destroy him." Joseph rose and took the child and his mother by night and departed for Egypt. He stayed there until the death of Herod, that what the Lord had said through the prophet might be fulfilled,

Out of Egypt I called my son.

When Herod had died, behold, the angel of the Lord appeared in a dream to Joseph in Egypt and said, "Rise, take the child and his mother and go to the land of Israel, for those who sought the child's life are dead." He rose, took the child and his mother, and went to the land of Israel. But when he heard that Archelaus was ruling over Judea in place of his father Herod, he was afraid to go back there. And because he had been warned in a dream, he departed for the region of Galilee. He went and dwelt in a town called Nazareth, so that what had been spoken through the prophets might be fulfilled,

He shall be called a Nazorean.

Monday, December 30

First Reading

1 JOHN 2:12-17

I am writing to you, children, because your sins have been forgiven for his name's sake.

I am writing to you, fathers, because you know him who is from the beginning.

I am writing to you, young men, because you have conquered the Evil One.

I write to you, children, because you know the Father.

I write to you, fathers, because you know him who is from the beginning.

I write to you, young men, because you are strong and the word of God remains in you, and you have conquered the Evil One.

Do not love the world or the things of the world. If anyone loves the world, the love of the Father is not in him. For all that is in the world, sensual lust, enticement for the eyes, and a pretentious life, is not from the Father but is from the world. Yet the world and its enticement are passing away. But whoever does the will of God remains forever.

Responsorial Psalm

PSALM 96:7-8a, 8b-9, 10

R. Let the heavens be glad and the earth rejoice!

Give to the LORD, you families of nations,
  give to the LORD glory and praise;
  give to the LORD the glory due his name! **R.**
Bring gifts, and enter his courts;
  worship the LORD in holy attire.
Tremble before him, all the earth. **R.**
Say among the nations: The LORD is king.
He has made the world firm, not to be moved;
  he governs the peoples with equity. **R.**

Gospel

LUKE 2:36-40

There was a prophetess, Anna, the daughter of Phanuel, of the tribe of Asher. She was advanced in years, having lived seven years with her husband after her marriage, and then as a widow until she was eighty-four. She never left the temple, but worshiped night and day with fasting and prayer. And coming forward at that very time, she gave thanks to God and spoke about the child to all who were awaiting the redemption of Jerusalem.

When they had fulfilled all the prescriptions of the law of the Lord, they returned to Galilee, to their own town of Nazareth. The child grew and became strong, filled with wisdom; and the favor of God was upon him.

Tuesday, December 31

First Reading

1 JOHN 2:18-21

Children, it is the last hour; and just as you heard that the antichrist was coming, so now many antichrists have appeared. Thus we know this is the last hour. They went out from us, but they were not really of our number; if they had been, they would have remained with us. Their desertion shows that none of them was of our number. But you have the anointing that comes from the Holy One, and you all have knowledge. I write to you not because you do not know the truth but because you do, and because every lie is alien to the truth.

Responsorial Psalm

PSALM 96:1-2, 11-12, 13

R. Let the heavens be glad and the earth rejoice!

Sing to the LORD a new song;
    sing to the LORD, all you lands.
Sing to the LORD; bless his name;
    announce his salvation, day after day. **R.**
Let the heavens be glad and the earth rejoice;
    let the sea and what fills it resound;
    let the plains be joyful and all that is in them!
Then shall all the trees of the forest exult before the LORD. **R.**
The LORD comes,
    he comes to rule the earth.
He shall rule the world with justice
    and the peoples with his constancy. **R.**

Gospel

JOHN 1:1-18

In the beginning was the Word,
    and the Word was with God,
    and the Word was God.
He was in the beginning with God.
All things came to be through him,
    and without him nothing came to be.

What came to be through him was life,
    and this life was the light of the human race;
    the light shines in the darkness,
    and the darkness has not overcome it.

A man named John was sent from God. He came for testimony, to testify to the light, so that all might believe through him. He was not the light, but came to testify to the light. The true light, which enlightens everyone, was coming into the world.

He was in the world,
    and the world came to be through him,
    but the world did not know him.
He came to what was his own,
    but his own people did not accept him.

But to those who did accept him he gave power to become children of God, to those who believe in his name, who were born not by natural generation nor by human choice nor by a man's decision but of God.

And the Word became flesh
    and made his dwelling among us,
    and we saw his glory,
    the glory as of the Father's only-begotten Son,
    full of grace and truth.

John testified to him and cried out, saying, "This was he of whom I said, 'The one who is coming after me ranks ahead of me because he existed before me.'" From his fullness we have all received, grace in place of grace, because while the law was given through Moses, grace and truth came through Jesus Christ. No one has ever seen God. The only-begotten Son, God, who is at the Father's side, has revealed him.

theWORD among us®

The Spirit of Catholic Living

This book was published by The Word Among Us. Since 1981, The Word Among Us has been answering the call of the Second Vatican Council to help Catholic laypeople encounter Christ in the Scriptures.

The name of our company comes from the prologue to the Gospel of John and reflects the vision and purpose of all of our publications: to be an instrument of the Spirit, whose desire is to manifest Jesus' presence in and to the children of God. In this way, we hope to contribute to the Church's ongoing mission of proclaiming the gospel to the world so that all people would know the love and mercy of our Lord and grow more deeply in their faith as missionary disciples.

Our monthly devotional magazine, *The Word Among Us*, features meditations on the daily and Sunday Mass readings, and currently reaches more than one million Catholics in North America and another half million Catholics in one hundred countries around the world. Our book division, The Word Among Us Press, publishes numerous books, Bible studies, and pamphlets that help Catholics grow in their faith.

To learn more about who we are and what we publish, visit us at www.wau.org. There you will find a variety of Catholic resources that will help you grow in your faith.

Embrace His Word, Listen to God . . .

www.wau.org

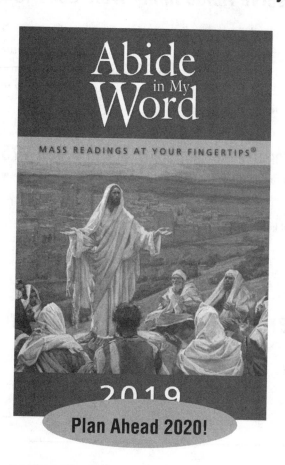

Reserve *Abide in My Word 2020* Today!

Abide in My Word: Mass Readings at Your Fingertips ®
Keep abreast of the daily Mass readings and make personal Scripture reading easier! *Abide in My Word* provides each day's Scripture readings in an easy-to-locate format. Each day is clearly listed so that it only takes a few minutes to draw near to the Lord through the Mass readings.

To order, use the card below or call **1-800-775-9673**

You'll find up-to-date product information on our website www.wau.org

Fill in the card below and mail in an envelope to:

The Word Among Us
7115 Guilford Drive, Suite 100
Frederick, MD 21704

Order 2 or more copies and save 20%!

☐ **YES!** Send me _____ copies of *2020 Abide in My Word*. AB2020
(1 *Abide in My Word* @ $15.95; 2 or more @ $12.76 each plus shipping & handling)

Name ______________________________

Address ______________________________

City ______________________________

State ______________ Zip ______________

Phone ( ) ______________________________

Email (optional) ______________________________

Send no money now. We will bill you.

SHIPPING & HANDLING (Add to total product order):				
Order amount:	**$0-$15**	**$16-$35**	**$36-$50**	**$51-$75**
Shipping & handling:	**$5**	**$7**	**$9**	**$11**

CPAB19Z

Pricing in U.S. dollars only.